THE CHRIS LABINJO
LIVING DOLLS
ORIGIN

Matador
9 Priory Business Park,
Wistow Road, Kibworth Beauchamp,
Leicestershire. LE8 0RX
Tel: 0116 279 2299
Email: books@troubador.co.uk
Web: www.troubador.co.uk/matador
Twitter: @matadorbooks

ISBN 978 1784624 514

British Library Cataloguing in Publication Data.
A catalogue record for this book is available from the British Library.

Printed and bound by CPI Group (UK) Ltd, Croydon, CR0 4YY
Typeset in 11pt Aldine401 BT Roman by Troubador Publishing Ltd, Leicester, UK

Matador is an imprint of Troubador Publishing Ltd

To the students of 11Bi-U (Emanuel School, London, 2012), who convinced me that the dream would make a good story... your inspiration has changed my life. Thank you.

THE LIVING DOLLS TRILOGY

WWW.THELIVINGDOLLSBOOKS.CO.UK

WWW.THELIVINGDOLLSBOOKS.COM

PART I

THE LIVING DOLLS MEET THE WORLD

JACK AND JILL

Jack and Jill went up the hill
To fetch a pail of water
Jack fell down and broke his crown,
And Jill came tumbling after.

Up Jack got, and home did trot,
As fast as he could caper,
He went to bed to mend his head,
With vinegar and brown paper.

I B C - USA

Icilda Biotech Company – United States of America
Inspiring future hope

CHRONOS

THE INTRODUCTION

Karl took a step forward.

He turned to his right and struck the agreed pose, presenting his best angle to the media circus. Digital flashes flickered all around him – miniature explosions of white light.

He stood perfectly still, his confidence well rehearsed. He was being watched; scrutinised by viewers all across the globe. A thrill raced down his spine. The eyes and ears of the world were on him; he felt like a Caesar.

Karl knew he looked good. He had checked his image several times as he passed into the auditorium.

Designer suit. Diamond cuff links. Black shoes, Italian leather. Thick quartz hair. Sculpted cheekbones. Strong jaw. Straight nose. Not a hair out of place. Perfect.

Today he was the orator, commanding and transcendent. The audience were a sea of enthusiastic followers – *my citizens.* Their applause had quietened now, their voices low and full of anticipation. He surveyed the ocean of faces, drawn from different nations, assembled to listen to his wisdom.

Karl inhaled deeply, slowly; closing his eyes as he entered his zone. *I can't afford to be overwhelmed by the occasion. There is work to do here.*

He exhaled. His eyelids snapped open as he felt the chi force riding on his outgoing breath.

I'm ready.

He spoke.

'Good afternoon ladies and gentlemen. Thank you for attending. My name is Dr Karl Winwood, some of you already know me.' He adjusted his IQt tablet. It rested atop a glass podium, engraved with the emblem: IBC-USA.

15.01. Right on schedule.

'For those who do not know me, I am the Director of Natural Sciences at IBC-Korea.' He scanned the crowd. Some faces he recognised, others he did not. 'This is a portentous occasion and we are glad to have you here to share in its gravity. Today is in every sense historical. Indeed, today represents a breakthrough, the culmination of a great deal of hard work by my colleagues and our industry as a whole. So on behalf of the Icilda Biotech Company, it is with the greatest of pleasures that I now present to you, the first human chimeras,' he paused, holding their gaze, 'Ladies and gentlemen, we give you the Living Dolls!'

As he spoke, a holographic sequence materialised above the stage. The room was filled with the sound of Grieg's *Morning Mood*.

A swirling spectrum of photons began to take shape before the audience: two incandescent, infantile forms appeared as the movement reached its crescendo. They looked to be around five or six years of age. Light beams pulsed and condensed, lasers sculpting features onto the two holographic bodies. Individual atoms dictated the photons' positions, creating a precise image: a replica of the real live children.

Both children had large, limpid blue eyes with long sweeping lashes. They were holding hands. Karl felt another shiver run through him.

You two represent a new chapter in the evolution of the human race. Do you even know that?

A susurrus passed through the audience. Karl thought he detected a plurality amongst them; a mixture of immediate parental instinct with an undercurrent of intense, tenuous curiosity.

Jill was cute in her floral dress and white shoes. Someone had managed to convince her to put those shoes on. Jack's suit matched his own. *He really is like me – a miniature version.* He felt suddenly warm. The children seemed taller than he remembered – or was that the lighting? Both had raven hair; Jill's restrained in a gold clasp, Jack's neat but free. All of their clothing matched, perfectly coordinated. *They really are splendid. PR will be pleased.*

After spending so much time with them Karl was surprised, then amused by the realisation that he actually liked them; somewhere along the line they had formed a genuine bond. The feelings were identical to those he had felt as a boy, for Momo.

Good old Momo.

Karl smiled, exposing his perfectly bleached teeth. He scanned the room.

The Miranda Ferrell Auditorium was known to insiders as the Crystal Thought Temple. Whichever name he used, it remained an ideal venue for the event. It was perhaps a little large, given the calibre of the audience. Even so, the seats were all full. There were at least five hundred guests. *Someone must have relaxed the fire safety regulations; we're well over the seating capacity.* Karl licked his lower lip, before biting it gently.

Having to stand… Some of these celebs aren't used to. It's good to be back. So many memories…

He knew the auditorium inside out. His first world-wide broadcast had come from this stage. As part of the preparation for his job interview he'd studied every aspect of the company's history; right down to the construction of this building. These days he considered himself to be an expert, a walking encyclopaedia, full of knowledge about IBC.

In the press briefing he was sure he'd impressed the reporters by knowing more about the place than they did. Right down to the intricacies of the architect's goal. She'd aimed to capture the movement of light in association with thought. The auditorium was hexagonal with huge, panoramic windows beneath a spiralling crystal ceiling. It all carried the eye upwards.

For Karl, it symbolised the ascension of mankind. A species heading towards perfection. The exquisite, hand blown chandeliers were each comprised of five thousand individual units, suspended by vibrant glassy threads that sent light scattering in all directions; pure white beams splitting into restless, spectral colours.

The twins hovered in the spiral, anticipant.

Karl spotted Stella Apfelbaum. She sat on the second row; an interesting woman and a reported for Intersky. He'd noticed her lingering glances in the past; the giggles and frequent touching of his arm whenever she got close to him. He thought her both attractive and witty.

Obviously she's into me.

The audience seemed enthralled, drinking in the overwhelming atmosphere.

It was awesome. Karl trembled with excitement. Still, it was only a show, designed to capture its audience. The twins were not going to walk out onto that stage. Their physical location remained a closely guarded secret: a necessary precaution. The ethics and welfare committee had agreed unanimously that the children were not to be exposed to the health risks associated with physical, public scrutiny; let alone even the remotest possibility of their abduction. Karl hoped that their significance would be understood by the media contingent and sympathetically reported, despite their absence. Karl recognised other faces in the audience; fellow members of the think tank organisation known as *The Light*.

And there's the bauble lady. Back again. She'd become quite a regular at events hosted by IBC. *She's like a display cabinet at Tiffany's. Money to burn.* Pangs of jealously stirred in his stomach. *So much money!*

You're married to some wealthy dude or your family is loaded. Her mouth and eyes were wide open, staring at the holograms. *If you bid the right price, one of them could be yours… Keep breathing honey.*

His mind threw up image of Melissa. Her surgically modified features loomed before him; that calm, smug smile on her enhanced lips.

You two-timing drama queen.

The very thought of her made his blood simmer.

The silence hung, but the audience's anticipation was boiling over. He had left it just long enough. He continued, 'For more in depth information about the Living Dolls, I would like to introduce you to our Head of Human Technology. She has been caring for them since their birth. Ladies and Gentlemen, Dr Louise Dalton.'

Another wave of thunderous applause erupted from the crowd as Louise stepped onto the platform to one side of Karl.

Digital flashes followed her progress from the left wing, tracking her to the podium. Her pace was considered, steady. She smiled confidently, acknowledging Karl.

For a brief moment the audience's attention shifted. Karl was impressed. She'd managed to pull off her first PR catwalk. Whoever's decision the outfit had been, he was thankful for it.

Her light grey Chanel jacket and a knee-length skirt were classically cut, matching her stiletto heels. Louise crossed the stage in business-like fashion, carrying a quiet air of authority and dignity. She had been well briefed on coping with press conferences; she had even insisted on receiving professional coaching before the event.

Karl's jaw slackened as Louise stepped fully into the light. He had a clear view.

Those eyes: deep chestnut brown. And that figure… But you'd never wear any of this in the lab… For me… Would you? The false lashes created a bewitching, wide-eyed expression. *And what have you done to your hair? Is this really the plain, boring Louise; the "I don't wear make–up" Louise; the "Don't touch me, I'm a feminist" Louise?*

She was about to speak… Karl couldn't help but think of Agent Hart, emerging from the plane hangar in *Miss Congeniality*. He stepped backwards, feeling for the chair before sitting down in case he missed it. This sudden deep desire, the burning craving for his colleague; it was a unique emotional response, totally unusual, sensual and smouldering.

Breathe Karl. Down, boy.

Still, he noticed the frequent smoothing down of her skirt with her left hand. It was the only indication of her nervousness.

So she is afraid.

Nonetheless, Louise spoke.

'The UN Treaty of 2026 finally gave our industry and the sciences in general, official permission to consider the ways in which we might change the very substance that defines us as human beings. DNA, Deoxyribonucleic Acid, is the macromolecule that defines life.' She paused to take a breath.

Karl winced as he realised that Louise had forgotten to read the first line of the speech – *It's meant to read, "Welcome, ladies, gentlemen and members of the press…"* They had practised the sequence so many times he knew her lines. Perhaps she was more nervous than he had thought?

Come on Louise, you can do it.

'What you inherit genetically determines what you become.' A holographic representation appeared above the heads of the Living Dolls; a helix, slowly rotating in all its complexity and intrinsic beauty. 'Fundamental changes to this complex macromolecule enable us to adapt to challenges in our environment, it's that or encounter the threat of extinction. DNA determines the proteins that become the foundation of life, and our proteins define us as bacteria or, for instance, humans.'

Karl noticed two people in the front row having a private conversation. The content of the speech had been carefully chosen to make it accessible to its non-industry audience. Now he wondered whether it was coming across as too technical. Part of him wanted to march off the stage and reprimand them. Instead, he fired a menacing glare in their direction.

It failed, their conversation continued.

'Proteins determine the functions that cells can fulfil. They make up the scaffolding that builds cellular structure and are involved in important chemical reactions.' Louise gestured to the accompanying holographics. 'Change the DNA and you change the organism.'

A short visual presentation followed, skilfully edited and cut to the rhythm of *Spring* from Vivaldi's *Four Seasons*. The pause allowed Louise to drink a little water.

She seemed to have composed herself. *Good,* thought Karl. He watched her replace the glass, gently pushing the stray lock of auburn hair from her face. Once again, she used her left hand to smooth her skirt. She turned her head, making eye contact with him.

Karl tilted his head. *Get ready for the next sequence, you know what to do.*

Pictures of a range of human proteins and different organisms replaced the image of the DNA molecule. The visual sequence traced the evolutionary pathway of man from the simplest organisms to its present state.

Bauble lady had lost it. She was definitely crying, clutching her handkerchief. Karl refrained from vocalising his delight.

'But it's time to break the mould and explore the sort of possibilities that our predecessors only dreamed of,' Louise turned the page. As she did, she met his eyes again, then launched into the final section of her speech.

'At IBC, we have spent four years designing scientific techniques and procedures that have enabled us to change the human genome forever. In 2000, the world started to map the secret code that makes us unique; today, we redefine it. These children represent a new understanding of what it means to be human.'

Karl followed the script in his memory, line by line. Thick silence filled the room, right on cue. *So far so good, aside from that missed line at the beginning.* Louise shifted her gaze back to Karl. *Why does she keep eyeing me?*

He smiled back. He felt suave, but only on the outside. *Get on with it Louise.*

This was the part that had worried her the most in rehearsal. She was so scared by the thought of public speaking that she'd panicked when they had read the lines together. *But the professional coaching should have paid off by now.*

The skin on his neck itched. *What material had they used in this shirt? I told the image consultant that I only wear Egyptian cotton.*

He had not checked the label, the excitement of the event curtailing his normally meticulous routine. Karl possessed an incredible attention for detail when it came to clothing. Today, the colour had been selected to complement his suit and emphasise his authority. At least, that was the way it had been sold.

Karl felt uncomfortable. If there were even a few strands of polyester, he would break out in a rash; the itching continued..

'I am ready for your questions.' Louise stood straight and tall.

Good, she's following the coach's instructions. Karl leaned forward. He checked the pre-prepared list discretely: first up, Stella Apfelbaum. Her media outlet must have made a generous contribution to the IBC charity fund.

A moment of hesitation, then hands shot up all over the room. IBC had invited over two hundred representatives of the world wide press; but all of this had been carefully choreographed by the PR department.

Louise pointed to the Intersky representative on her left.

'Under the binomial system of classification, how will they be grouped? What will you call them?' Stella was pristinely dressed.

Obviously she's done her homework.

Karl knew that the woman had an ulterior motive. To be classified by the binomial system, the children would have to be able to reproduce; that was what she really wanted to know.

Well Louise, how about that?

Louise smiled, 'They have already been named, Jack and Jill. Like the nursery rhyme.'

A smart move, Karl thought: deliberately ignoring the initial question and responding to the second. *Very… political.* Coaching had paid off. He tried to catch Louise's attention. *That was good, if you keep this up you'll have nothing to worry about.*

Polite laughter filled the auditorium. Stella balked, then seemed to regrouped swiftly. She glanced at Karl, then spoke again.

'Hardly appropriate names for such a breakthrough in science.' Stella shook her head several times. 'I'm surprised that you didn't select more fitting terminology to mark this historical, dare I say, sacred moment.' An awkward unwelcome silence hung in the room. The reproof had taken Louise by surprise, her hand slipping down to her skirt again.

That had unnerved her. Karl could see it in her body language: the dropped jaw and hunched shoulders; the material of her jacket was swaying gently with her breath and deep furrows appeared on her forehead; her hands trembling trembled slightly.

It might not have been obvious on the television, and probably wasn't all that noticeable from the auditorium's floor, but from where he was sitting, it was all too clear. She had better regain her sense of authority or the flight emotions would take over.

He moved even closer to the edge of his seat, ready to get up if she needed his help, his tablet secure in his sweaty hands. Something about the gesture seemed to enliven Louise. She reclaimed the floor.

'Jack and Jill are children first. Their role in scientific experiments is secondary,' the tone reminded Karl of an old high school teacher of his, Mr Griffin; he had always used that nasal tone when he was irritated. 'We treat them with dignity and respect. By naming them, we are giving them a sense of being, of belonging.'

Stella squirmed, more than a little embarrassed. Karl smiled again and allowed himself to slide back onto the seat a little. *How does it feel, now, Stella; being put down on television?*

Louise was the focus of the cameras again. Karl relished her moment of triumph. *That's the way it should be. We are in control here, not you.*

He eased further back into his seat. Louise pointed, nodding at a reporter to her right. Karl checked his list. *Neil Yeung.*

'What species have you incorporated into the human gene pool?' They had been prepared for this. It was by far the most obvious question.

'That remains a confidential matter and one which IBC is not prepared to discuss at this moment.'

Company policy. No detailed disclosure of genetic contributions at this stage. Good.

'Then how do we know that these *Dolls* are not just a couple of children?' He pointed at the holograms. 'They might have been produced using IVF. You might have picked them up from an orphanage.'

For some reason this response troubled Louise. The shaking in her hand returned with new intensity, all semblances of confidence and authority had evaporated. She coughed lightly, struggling to maintain her formality.

Louise's left hand passed across her body defensively, her right gripped the podium, exposing the whites of her knuckles. He noticed her right foot buckle twice, revealing the red bottoms of her stiletto shoes; only the podium had stopped her from taking a tumble.

This is not the time to fall flat on your face. These are natural questions. You know that! Remember the techniques, breathe Louise!

'A DNA analysis of the children will reveal that 33% of their genes are from the human genome; the remaining genetic contributions are identifiable as non-human in origin.'

Karl offered her his undivided attention. The maths should have presented no problem for their guests. He grinned. Louise seemed to regain her composure; her left arm dropped back to her side, palm open.

She's back.

Karl breathed out, the air made a gushing sound.

Louise smoothed her skirt, this time leaving a faint damp patch. Karl saw the marks, almost wanting to bite his knuckles. This was not going as well as he had hoped. The unrestrained murmuring amongst the guests – that was plain rude. So what, if some of the guests were unhappy with the revelation. *Carry on Louise. Stick with my philosophy – SWSWSW next; some will, some won't, so what next!*

Another voice from the floor, 'Why are you being so secretive? What do you have to hide?'

More stupid questions. This time from the BBC. Really? Karl crossed his legs, folding and unfolding his arms, unable to get comfortable. He hoped that his foot tapping had been out of the cameras' line of sight.

He knew that IBC had a long way to go before they could convince people of the legitimacy of their work. The PR department had rightly anticipated that they would be openly scrutinised. *They just don't get it though – they're like dinosaurs with no imaginations.*

The image consultant had told him to stay calm. It was harder than he had expected. The tight sensation around his mouth now spread to his jaw – he was on edge; and his was a dangerous edge.

'Nothing is being hidden; this is typical industrial practice.' A few more strands of hair were slipping out of place, but Louise focused on her challenger. 'Our competitors would not disclose their programmes during a press release; you would not share a scoop with your contemporaries, would you?' Her chin jutted forward. 'The information will be released into the public domain in due course. For now, I can disclose that the twins are tri-genomic organisms.'

Suddenly, two people stood up further back in the room; they began waving placards and calling for genetic purity. Immediately, the cameras shifted from Louise. Ripples of sound began to break out all over the auditorium; security officers began moving from their positions but were met with a confusion of people, all trying to get a look at the demonstrators.

How did they get in, what happened to the entrance screenings? How did they get those placards in? Security checks, body scans, how has this happened? Karl's head moved rapidly from left to right. Louise was standing there, saying and doing nothing. *The baton is in your hands woman! Respond to them! Put them down!*

His twitching neck muscles were annoying, and he itched like crazy. Karl shifted, as if to get up and, suddenly, the children shifted. Jack hid behind his sister, moving with a sense of trepidation.

They've only just realised that Jack and Jill were not entirely static! Of course both of them were present in real time! Idiots! The itching would not go away; the camera's were not on him and he scratched, but to no effect.

A camera swung back towards him, focusing on the twins. Jill seemed unsure but stood firm. She was taller than her brother, her dainty, white patent leather shoes added a few centimetres to her stature; she was protecting him.

Karl felt something stirring deep within his gut. It was not pleasant. He only got that feeling just before something really bad happened. He detected a change in the atmosphere; the crowd were on the side of the twins, the children's innocence playing on their emotions.

That's good at least – very good.

One elderly gentleman stood up, two rows behind the booing delegates, reprimanding them; his voice was commanding – *possibly military* – Karl thought. The pair were shocked into silence, and security had finally arrived. The cameras swung to and fro, capturing everything.

Maybe we can get back to the planned proceedings!

Jack and Jill still looked scared. *Are Jack's lips trembling?* Karl squinted, scanning the details of Jack's face. So difficult to see from his seat, the camera angles concealed the vital information with their wide angle perspective.

Karl watched as two of the burly security officers reached the troublemakers, wrenching them roughly from their seats before escorting them out of the auditorium. He nodded approvingly, the voice of opposition silenced. The cameras followed every move of the drama played out before the world – through tight close ups, head and shoulder shots and sweeping wide angled views.

Serves them right, they will be punished for that display.

He stabbed at the screen of his tablet, typing a short comment. Then he glanced up, suddenly aware of who was standing there, apparently paralysed. *That woman is totally unbelievable, why did I fight to get her on the team?*

All eyes returned to the living breathing twins, capturing their terrified expressions while Louise seemed forgotten, silent. A static hologram.

She should have anticipated the possibility of opposition, the PR department should have seen this coming. Louise should have asked them to be quiet; she was striking, she should have used that to commanded the cameras. *If it had been me on stage…* Karl's thoughts rattled along the tracks of his troubled mind, circling.

Besides, who let them in?

Guests were supposed to have been screened – only active supporters of the work. Louise had totally lost it, looking scared herself. This required action on his part, he started to stand up. *A man's got to—*

And then out of the air, a child's voice.

'What are… the people doing? Why are they being so… mean?'

Jill's voice was like any other three-year-old girl's. The sound emanated from the same speakers used by everyone else on the podium, loud and crystal clear.

Jack finally plucked up courage to speak his own thoughts. 'I can see lots and lots of people, and they look mad!'

Karl's annoyance increased as he noticed a close-up on one of the camera monitors, showing Jill holding onto Jack's hand, tightening her grip.

She whispered in his ear, 'Maybe that's why they are so mean.' How embarrassing. Karl glanced down.

I wonder if anyone else feels this, it's like I'm eavesdropping. Not good, this is not good!

He bit his lip, his fists still clenched, observing his knuckles becoming paler and paler. As far as he knew, this interruption had not been scripted. The twins were connected to microphones so that they could deliver a formal greeting and a short introduction. That was down on the programme.

Someone's meant to be there to make sure they're not having a stubborn moment. Louise often told him how difficult they were when they worked together. This was not on. It was meant to be charming… For the guests.

An audience member stood up. Not a reporter, this time. Cameras and heads alike turned to look.

'And how much do they cost, what would be a sensible starting bid?' The shareholder's booming voice ricocheted off the walls of the auditorium.

Louise balked. Colour appearing on her face, spreading from her cheeks. Karl rolled his eyes, watching her take a long, slow deep breath.

Wait a minute. She might even talk again.

'They are not for sale… they are children,' Louise pointed to the holograms for the first time in the presentation, 'Children who may open the way for a new direction in what it means to be human. Profit has nothing to do with it. We will profit from what we *learn*, and what that *leads to*; not from the sale of the children themselves. They are children. Real children.'

He wanted to stand and applaud Louise… *sarcastically*. Sure, she had managed to find her voice, only to give out incorrect information. This would create confusion among the shareholders. She'd gone off script and well outside of her remit as a spokesperson for the scientific core of the project. That had not been a question for her to answer. Nor was it her job to decide the outcomes and objectives of the work. It wasn't even his.

Of course the twins are for sale. Not exactly, but it's open to negotiation. You idiot woman – you were told not to respond to financial questions – private bidding has already started!

He sighed in exasperation, tapping the stage with his right foot. Both arms were folded across his chest and he was scowling, sensing all his facial muscles contract; a rigid and frozen mask instead of happy smiling Karl. Somewhere inside an old voice nagged… *This whole thing is my fault.*

Louise's lower lip trembled. From where he sat she seemed close to tears. Perhaps she was aware that she had just lied to the auditorium; to the very people whose money would go towards the actualisations of all of her theories. Karl watched Louise take another breath, as if to speak.

These people hold the keys to our dreams, and you are not going to ruin both of our careers live on stage. Karl struggled to contain himself; this was not scripted. None of this was scripted. *But you can put it right, Karl. Like you always do.*

He stood up, shoving Louise to one side – deftly, for the cameras' benefit, but not without force – and took over the central position on the podium.

Louise wobbled on her heels, now on the edge of the podium. Karl studied her for a second.

She looks awful all of a sudden. It was as if her face had been distorted, a band of tight muscles across her eyes and nose creating a squint and shortening her large nose. Karl was not sure whether it was physical or emotional pain.

At any rate, he didn't care.

Karl carried on, 'Ladies and gentlemen, this is only an introduction to our work. As you have been made aware, further, exciting and more detailed information about the financial situation of the children will be available to shareholders at a later date.'

He glanced and smiled reassuringly at Louise. Her shaking unnerved him. Karl knew that the smile was not genuine. He just didn't want her to fall apart on stage.

Not on his shift, not in front of the world.

Back to the audience… He drew another breath and was cut off.

'I don't like those people… they are nasty people. I don't like them,' Jack declared.

Now Karl felt himself shaking. *I've been betrayed by Jack?*

The twins had been meant to deliver the little speeches they had been practising. That was on the programme. Not this mess. *What is happening with them? This whole thing is chaotic, it's out of control!*

Suddenly, Karl hated being in this place. Order needed to be restored. The heat from the overhead lights irritated him. He wanted to scratch himself badly, but the cameras were on him. All over him. Someone would have hell to pay. They'd have to navigate forward through the agenda. Nothing else could be done.

Jack was still hiding behind Jill. He continued to frown. Karl watched as Jill spun around, giving her brother a big hug. They saw the audience. The cameras refocused on the twins.

This was a troubling situation. The growing sense of frustration was nibbling away at his confidence. Crowds were not part of their normal lives. They lived in a protected environment. A room full of adults was new to them.

Karl glanced at the script; the words were becoming blurred. The audio link was still running. His thigh muscles jumped in alternating fashion, the tightness in his chest, along with the hopping throbs, added to his discomfort.

Why the hell haven't they followed the script? Why is no one overseeing the procedure at their end? Shut it down. Please, someone; and let me regain the crowd. I can do it. I can tell them what they want to hear!

He wondered if he had been set up. *Does someone have it in for me? Was this some form of payback?* His mind raced. *Am I the fall guy?*

Nothing changed. Just that image of the embarrassed hug. Karl knew that he had to take control. He spoke.

'I'm sorry, we're going to wrap up questions and answers now,' the improvisation from Karl seemed to aggravate the audience. During the ensuing susurrus of complaint, he whispered to Louise, she scuttled off into the wings. But it had to be done. He knew it had to be done.

A stabbing pain hit the middle of his head. It twisted into his brain, diminished and then intensified. Nausea spread through him. *I think I'm going to be sick.*

Seconds later, a sharp click indicated that the audio link between the auditorium and the children's location had been severed. He hoped the twins' voices would not be heard again that day.

Louise was back on stage, resuming her position, brushing the creases out of her skirt. Karl nodded in gratitude. *At least you've done something right.*

The twins hugged each other, their lips moving. A half-private conversation.

Ignoring the holograms, Karl continued.

'Apologies for the technical difficulties. Please contact our investor representative, Tanya English, for further financial information. Biofact sheets on the twins can be hyper-mailed to you if you have not already received them. Details about personal visits to see Jack and Jill are in the grey section near the back of the main booklet.' As he spoke, the auditorium lost its rigid structure becoming fluid, swaying from side to side. He rushed through the comments, pointing to Tanya, who stood nervously on the right hand side of the stage.

'History has been made and IBC will continue to pursue cutting edge technologies in science.' Karl surveyed Louise's script, deciding to recite the words before him, 'Thank you for your time.'

In the light of the fiasco, he was not convinced of his own future, let alone that of the PR team. Even Louise had been caught off guard, despite the services of an expensive vocal coach.

A public disaster – intense heat was building up in his cheeks and the prickling sensation at his collar was still there, nagging at his self control.

Karl decided not to wait for the audience's response, leaving the stage behind Louise. Her hands were shaking, her shoulders low. She seemed to stumble every third step.

You'll break an ankle if you're not careful.

He directed one final, piercing stare at Tanya.

Karl gripped the table and locked eyes with one of the people he held responsible for this mess; he felt the screen splinter beneath his fingers. He wished they'd kept it all private. Words would have to be had back at IBC. Things would not be easy for him.

I need fresh air… and a bottle of Southern Comfort. Make that two bottles. Let them write.

+ + +

After their departure, the room erupted into chaos. Reporters from several news outlets shouted for Karl and Louise. On the whole, the media representatives were delighted – the day had evolved into a public farce and the game was on to compete for the eye catching and witty headline.

Stella continued to type into her quantum tablet, eaves dropping on the conversations happening all over the stadium.

Louise's final, unconfirmed comments had been noted by shareholders present at the press release. Their interest in IBC rested on a solid history of good yields on investments. The promise of future dividends, generated as the company spearheaded its way along the path of new technology, kept their money in the IBC account. Now they had heard for themselves that the Living Dolls would not be for sale.

Dr Louise Dalton was an upcoming and already influential figure in the scientific community but not an executive. If her comments proved to be true, it would indicate an extremely poor business decision and a betrayal of their trust.

Eager investors had submitted early bids, anticipating the gravity of the event. Suddenly, the deal had died in front of them. The management team had disappeared from stage and within moments, the holographic image of the now fearful twins popped out of existence. A number of quantum smartphones bleeped and vibrated. Loud and angry conversations commenced, alongside the stirring sounds of *Summer*, from the *Four Seasons*.

There would be plenty to write about.

DR DALTON AND THE BIGGER PICTURE

A blood sacrifice. Now the gods would be appeased. Louise understood the concept – being the chosen one, the pure and innocent virgin, slain on the altar.

In her case, it had been a public execution by the media. The IBC conference room felt like the loneliest place on the earth.

Several pieces of modern art adorned the walls. Louise did not recognise any of the artists. Fresh orchids sat at the centre of the table; there were bottles of spring water and bowls of exquisite sweets. Even so, the room lacked any real warmth. A purely functional space.

That press conference had changed everything. The appointment schedule was now abandoned and her more intimate meeting with the press had been cancelled. She'd had to wait for an hour before the debrief from Karl. It would be more appropriate to call it a sadistic autopsy. The time was 16.30.

Her first speech to the world…

I'm a complete idiot; sounded like a cavewoman on Prozac. A drooling mess, my jaw opening and closing and no sound coming out – who on earth would believe that I have a First from Oxford?

All of her old lecturers, classmates, students and yes, now her colleagues at IBC would see it. How embarrassing. All her thoughts seemed to mesh together inside her head. *Why am I so incredibly useless?*

Fresh blood. Louise wanted to run away and never come back. Public crucifixion – a slow and tortuous death. Two of her worst fears rolled into one – being naked in public and being assaulted. The terror of being exposed and vulnerable, of not having a way out; even the thought filled her with cold dread.

Why did I allow Karl to talk me into doing this?

The media reminded her of piranhas or starving wolves – *one drop and you generate a feeding frenzy.*

And those ridiculous shoes! The instruments of torture lay on their sides, exposing their soles, bright red. *Christian Louboutins. Who cares? Now for the face. This stupid make–up!*

The image in the compact seemed like that of a stranger. The eyes, shaped like almonds, with long lashes. Louise thought back to the giraffes she had seen at the London zoo as a child. Somehow, her nose seemed less prominent. *Is that a trick?* In proportion to her eyes and mouth. She checked the side view: still the same, yet, from the front, totally different. Her hair though; she had to admit that it looked great. The extensions added volume, the dye intensified her natural colour. Louise liked the difference. But still, it tugged at her angrily.

… Because I'm not worth it.

Straight auburn hair, with a generous fringe, hiding her forehead – *thankfully*. Yes, they had done a super job; it had been a lovely hair day. Her natural curls had been removed by the heat of the tongs. That heat had broken the hydrogen bonds of the keratin – *oh yes* – she thought – *I know all about protein structure*. Under the right conditions, it would return back to normal. Like Cinderella after the ball.

Her lips, normally thin and dry, were now luscious, full and coated with nude lipstick. *I really do not know who you are. Are you me?* She scrubbed them, pulling at them viciously, dropping the wet wipes onto the floor. Not caring.

The image in the compact was unfamiliar, unnatural. Even that had been given to her by the consultant – *all part of the service, honey.*

What would Mum and Dad think? Mum was probably worrying about Louise's damaged image; about the dwindling numbers of prospective suitors and how to handle the sympathetic comments of the tight friendship circle that made up her gossip-hungry Thursday morning coffee group. Dad, well he would be more reflective, wondering about his Louise, how she would make a comeback from this life lesson. Good old Dad.

And Adrian? He would have made a cruel joke out of the matter. He knew how to keep Louise in her place, the rights of the elder sibling. Adrian had never taken life all that seriously.

All gone – her lips were normal again.

It would not go away, bouncing around in the back of her mind, the phrase 'the personal is political' used by a number of women back in 2013.

As a teenager she had attended a rally, protesting about the way women were portrayed in the media. She has even bunked off school and would have got away with it, but media exposure revealed her deceit. A camera had singled her out, shouting and raising her fist – and *that* clip had been included on an evening news feature, on national TV.

Mum went wild, screaming and accusing her of 'sabotaging her future'. Dad seemed alarmed, even shocked. After her mother had scuttled off, he had reassured Louise, whispering that he totally understood; that standing up for the truth was not always easy. Admittedly, his big hug had helped, that and being told that he was proud of her.

Now in her moment of trial, Louise had failed – she had lost her voice. Her courage had evaporated like early morning mist. She had remained silent. *I should have spoken up.* Worst of all, Karl had stepped in to rescue her. He, the bright shining knight; she, the damsel in distress. The world had witnessed his gallant and thoroughly false act of chivalry.

She'd even submitted to the fake world of beauty treatment, spending more hours getting ready for *this* event than she had in preparation for all the major events she had *ever* attended in her life – put together. *I might as well lay aside any claims to be part of the fifth wave of feminism. Pathetic, Louise.*

Smug, professional Karl; even he had lost his cool out there. So persuasive, with his careful choice of words and seductive smile. She had never seen him quite so rattled. There was no denying that he was gorgeous, even good enough for the catwalk. His thick black hair, those green and hazel eyes, his broad angular jaw and dimples; and the generous smile that revealed his perfect teeth.

The illusion shattered when he opened his mouth, releasing the stream of typically sarcastic words. So disappointing. *How did he talk me into doing this?* Louise's head rested in her hands, her face clamped between the palms.

Another wave of confusion swept through her. *Overwhelmed. I am drowning.*

She looked, seeing nothing. All she wanted to do was curl up into a tight ball, sink into a duvet and not surface for a few decades. *I need you Marco.* Admitting it took away the edge of loneliness, but it made it seem as if they had a real relationship. He usually knew what to say; his words soothed, charmed and encouraged Louise, but she had no idea where he was. *It would be weak to call him just because I need him, but we haven't spoken for at least four weeks... Has it really been four weeks?* Things had been so busy with the conference, the paperwork, the committee meetings and the preparation for the adoption process.

Louise promised herself that she would make it up to Marco somehow. Then again, she wondered what had stopped him from contacting her?

There was a scratchy feeling in her throat. Her body felt cold despite the room's warmth.. A sheet of tiredness descended, a cold wave of numbness – *draining, this thing is draining me*. She closed her eyes. The weight on her shoulders, her yoke.

For the first time in her life she seriously considered memory augmentation therapy – "wipe away the blues and start again."

Just as long as they don't suggest that Karl and I are an item. Her eyes flipped open. *That would be worse than death… I need to gather myself… To regain my centre. If only… my cello was here.*

She closed her eyes again. The tender hands of sleep cradled her, offering a moment of comfort. She accepted its embrace.

+++

The temple – an ancient Roman temple set in the midst of a barren landscape, complete with a stone altar, dressed with wood.

Wood for burning.

Louise lay bound on the altar; her flowing white gown caught passing gusts of wind, rippling. The smell of cinnamon and frankincense drifted in and out, carried on the wings of an invisible vector.

The terror was silenced by the gag in her mouth. She was struggling, achieving nothing; the bindings were too tight, cutting her skin as she struggled. She drew rapid, shallow breaths of stale yet pungent air.

Small rivulets of blood leaked from the grooves on her wrists… And Karl, standing over her; the high priest with a flaming torch in his left hand, grinning. In the other hand, a sharpened, ornamental knife poised over her heart – she heard its sound echoing in her ears.

One movement and it would be over.

'Like a Virgin' was blasting from some unknown source; turned to full volume. The gag was wet with her spit. Karl moved.

The scream died in her throat.

+++

The sound grew in volume, bringing Louise back from her nightmare. Panic lingered momentarily, then evaporated.

Louise fumbled for the origin of the noise – *my phone.*

A message – she blinked, squinting down at the screen: 'Sorry Louise, major delay. See you at 17.50.' The phone's clock read 17.20.

Where am I? A conference room; not the biotech lab. Philadelphia; not Pohang – and did I just give the worst speech of my life in front of the entire world?

Memories of the fiasco came flooding back to her. She cringed.

Yes, I did.

Louise toyed with the idea of tidying herself up but concluded against it.

It's only Karl.

Oh, heroic, noble Karl.

That dream. So vivid. Detailed.

She checked herself over in her compact: there were crease-lines on her forehead and slight indentations on her cheeks, where she'd slept on her knuckles. The beauty technician had told her off for moving at least four times. She laugh without much mirth, then sighed quietly. *If only she could see me now.*

Chloe would have loved this. Louise pictured her countenance – the smile revealing paired pearls of perfection, the full lips and sparkling child-like delight on her radiant face. *Lovely Chloe. Great for her, but not for me.* She checked the compact again. Her hair… *Might as well forget it.* The sweat from her roots was undoing all the technician's hard work. Frizz was on its way back. Louise used her fingers to comb through what was left of her style.

Well… I don't have a hairbrush or comb, so he will just have to take me as he finds me. My wonderful boss; this man who cares so much about my welfare.

She yawned as she poured a herself a glass of water, selecting one of the ornate bottles at random. He hand began to shake then, jerking water across the table. Normally she would have wiped it up. Someone else needed to clean up after her today.

Did I make the right decision when I joined IBC-Korea?

Louise wrestled with some serious doubts. The list of doubts grew daily. The department's use of S-Tetrin v4 without clinical trials had worried her first, then the surrogate mother selection process, the fight to secure tight regulations around the adoption procedure… Now money would be the final factor in deciding which home the children ended up in. As if that wasn't bad enough, it didn't even feel like the end of the list.

Something terrible was looming on the horizon. Not tangible, but perceived – *call it intuition.* She could sense its ominous approach. She felt weak.

The empty glass demanded to be filled. She broke the seal on the next bottle. *This whole enterprise might end badly. Selling the twinnes! Selling a prototype! Selling children!*

Louise recalled sitting in on numerous ethics and welfare committee meetings, producing several reports on the *twinnes* for the members of the group. The minutes had stated that strict adoption procedures would be adhered to, including personality profiles and financial checks on prospective applicants; but no one had mentioned an auction. *When did the money become so important? Who came up with the idea of bidding?* Someone had clearly made decisions without informing the worker ants. She had double checked all the minutes in detail, but not a word of this had been mentioned in any meeting she had attended.

Did Karl know? For all their differences, he of all people understood that true scientific development should not be restrained; too much control would invariably choke any life out of the process. Independence lay at the heart of a real pioneer in this discipline – she'd thought they both stood by that.

A bowl of luxury sweets sat at the centre of the table – they seemed to call to her. She peeled three of them, dropping their gold-leaf wrappers on the floor, then tossed them in the air one by one, catching them in her mouth. It felt good. Simple. Adrian had never been able to compete; he had once chipped one of his incisors during an attempt. Mum had gone ballistic.

The attraction of IBC? They were pioneers in the area of genetic engineering, and the fact that they were at the top of the nanotechnology industry added to their allure. *They recruited the best mind, harboured the best resources.* But on reflection, the business focus curbed all sense of liberty. Genuine breakthroughs were typically shrouded in secrecy – great care and thought had to go into every conversation with the 'enemy': fellow scientists and those working in the same field. It was tiring. And her freedom had been allowed to die, slowly. At first it had been mildly irritating. Now, in the light of recent events, the irritation loomed much larger, taking on gigantic proportions.

It felt like a boa constrictor's death grip.

Her thoughts wandered back to Jack and Jill. She missed them, her *twinnes.* Their daily schedule, their amazing senses of humour, their naughtiness and genuine thirst for knowledge. Warmth flowed over her weary mind. They were fast learners, their vocabulary matched the average for a child of five.

That scene in the auditorium was so like them. Louise pitied whoever was in charge of them at that moment. Someone was in serious trouble with Karl. She pictured him, accusing one of the nannies, yelling at them, questioning… *'They're only kids, why couldn't you control them?'* He had no idea. She could tell the world a thing or two about those children.

Jack and Jill reminded her of her early years with Adrian. His death at sixteen had been followed by the lowest point in Louise's life. Thinking about it made her shudder. A dark cloud of intense sadness shrouded the memory of his passing – they had been very dark days. The sugar rush kicked in and a surge of energy erupted behind her eyes.

Adrian and Louise had known the meaning of fun during their childhood. Their parents had tried so hard to shield them from the impending sadness accompanying Adrian's gradual loss of mobility – his condition. Mum and Dad had lived with the threat of his death from the first diagnosis, but they had never really discussed it as a family. Life had been about making each moment count Louise had decided that the *twinnes* would enjoy their lives to the full. Being poked, prodded and stabbed was all part of the daily routine for Jack and Jill but Louise had built in play time, every day, regardless of other necessities. Laughter was guaranteed for at least an hour, whether it arose from cartoons, puppets, artwork or good old face painting.

Speech development had been interesting; Jill had formed words first. She was braver in public, the more outgoing of the two. Jack remained quiet, but he had already developed a reputation for thinking things through. In private, he became the braver one. Jill had helped Jack to create coherent speech but she was concerned that they needed more conversational opportunities with outsiders. She placed the tumbler on a coaster, embossed with the IBC logo.

I need to book a meeting with their speech therapist.

Louise registered his footsteps in the corridor before Karl burst into the room, visibly flustered. The surprise brought her back to reality. She ignored the shivers swimming down her legs.

'Sorry about the delay. I've just been on the phone to head office. That press release was a disaster! Our esteemed PR officer might no longer be working for IBC.' Karl scanned the screen of his quantum tablet. *That officer is called Laura Ingram; she has two kids. Typical Karl. All facts – no emotion.* Her eyes narrowed as she glared at Karl. He remained oblivious.

She watched him slide his attaché case onto the conference table before collapsing into the leather chair. He tossed the tablet down. *Not like him –* he was normally obsessively careful with his toys. Louise noted its cracked screen. Karl reached into the inner pocket of his jacket, extracting a Biomedi-pod before self-medicating, pressing the device against his right temple. The furrows on his forehead melted away; his countenance became softer. *I might as well be invisible.* She thought of waving her hands in front of him and saying something rude and loud. His eyes opened suddenly, the pupils dilating before finally locking onto her.

'How are you feeling Louise?'

She paused for a moment, then spoke. 'I am furious, Karl. Absolutely furious.' Louise jumped up, suddenly unable to sit down. Waves of heat coursed through her body. 'Money, money, money – is that all people think about?' She clamped both arms by her sides, ready for the first punch, fists tightly clenched, the sound of her rapid, shallow breathing magnified in her ears as she paced beside the conference table .

'Why are you so upset?'

'Do you really want to know?' Her nostrils flared. *You are part of the problem. You coward.* She moved towards him, pushing into his personal space.

'Yes Louise, I do.'

'Not everything is for sale in this world.' Louise mimicked the tone of the shareholder who had asked *the question*,. 'But how much are they?'

She retreated back to her seat, dropping into it. The chair sighed and rocked. The shooting pain in her neck made her wince and she rubbed the area just below the base of her skull. Her calf muscles ached – the left one twitched jerkily.

'They're shareholders; they expect profit.' Karl shrugged. 'IBC is an enterprise, not a charity.'

Everything about Karl irritated Louise. His vocabulary, his clothes, his cologne. 'I know that,' she snapped. 'Do not lecture me.'

Karl's mouth fell open.

He's never seen me like this. Louise found it difficult to recognise it in herself; she was normally the epitome of controlled politeness.

'Ok Louise, take it easy. I—'

'You don't have to answer for IBC, Karl. I do have a First class degree from Oxford. I am not stupid.' Her right fist slammed onto the desk. 'But I should have been briefed by someone in your position. I should have been given a chance to argue.'

Karl pushed his chair away from the table and stood up slowly. He seemed to hesitate before taking two steps in her direction. A single seat separated them His expression showed a mixture of surprise and annoyance. Louise didn't really care. He had left her out to dry in front of the world. *Dr Karl Winwood deserves everything he'll get.*

Karl continued, 'I was saying… That science is what IBC does to make money, and we're each of us part of the process.' He moved even closer to Louise leaning forward now; the heat from him made her feel uncomfortable. She bit her lower lip.

'That does not mean I have to –'

'Jack and Jill will be adopted by the highest bidder who also fulfils the adoption criteria. We set out a protocol to which we all agreed.' He paused, his cologne forcing itself into her nostrils. Louise felt a moment of nausea pass. 'Our shareholders have a unique opportunity to be the first to care for either Jack or Jill, or maybe even both of them.'

Louise's body temperature was changing rapidly, from hot to cold, then back to hot again. The skin on her cheeks burned. Louise slumped deeper in the chair, silent. Her fists were gone now. Blood rushed to her brain, even her eyes burned. 'Did I hear you correctly?' Louise attempted to control the volume of her voice but lost it. 'So the highest *bidder* will just be *allowed* to *adopt*?'

'This has always been the plan. You did sit in on the committee meetings when we talked about this?' Karl pivoted, his back towards her, slowly returning to his seat.

He's trying to annoy me, playing his silly little game. This had never been discussed at any meeting she had been privy to. She had known about the vetting; the adoption process, but never the financial circumstances. 'Who's plan was this?' The words exploded from Louise's lips. 'How could you—'

'Why are you making this personal? IBC is—'

'I know it's a business decision, Karl! But what about their futures?' She heard herself yelling. 'They're children, not accessories to be sold to the highest bidder!' Louise sensed his discomfort at her emotional display. Inside, she was screaming, *don't call me naïve!* Yet the truth was that she had been so focused on her own work that she had lost sight of the bigger picture. *Another cog in the machine. I'm a naïve fool!*

Karl shook his head, both eyes darting from side to side. 'They're not *your* children, Louise. They belong to IBC.' The comment, slammed into her like a punch. She reeled, then staggered. Two sentences circled her mind, dragging slowly, painfully. She sensed the weight of each syllable. *The twins belong to IBC. My twinnes belong to IBC.*

'Karl, I cannot believe this. How did this happen? Why is money the most important part of this process?' Louise reached out with her heart, but its voice seemed foreign. There was strength there though, enabling her to respond to the horrible idea of her loss. Her mouth slackened as she took a small breath.

'Louise, I'm not seeking your approval. This will happen regardless of what either of us says – soon at that. You've got to get used to it.'

'I... I... I just don't know what to say. Karl, has anyone thought about Jack and Jill's long term welfare?'

'Louise, that's why the ethics and welfare committee exists; you knew they would be passed on to other homes. You were part of that decision. It makes no difference now that there is money involved. You've been on this team long enough; known IBC long enough, so what did you honestly expect?'

'We know so little about them... This is not like adopting a normal child, Karl. You know that.' her eyes met his, he glanced away. 'We all know that! We were supposed to monitor their development as children, not as playthings or bargaining chips!' Sadness clung to Louise, squeezing her anger out. 'And as for splitting them up, to get your money's worth, it's ridiculous, Karl! This has not been thought through! – How will they cope with separation, with new environments?' She knew that her words were only delay tactics..

The tension at the base of her skull increased. She arched her back, attempting to loosen the stress – nothing changed. 'How long do I have?'

'About three to four weeks, then the ten day orientation programme and... they will be off.'

'You will still be able to keep in touch with Jack and Jill. Their development will need to be monitored; you should be able to visit them. Or they could visit you,' he paused.

Louise shrugged her shoulders. Karl sat down again, He studied her for a second, before continuing, 'Besides, you will be needed; as you know, the others will require just as much attention.' Images raced through her mind like a nightmare on wheels. A huge factory with two long conveyor belts; one belt carrying multiple Jacks, frightened, crying; the other belt was toting defiant Jills. One by one, they reached the ends of the belts and, as they did, each child fell quickly, into separate, large and doll-like boxes. *How enterprising... Get the latest model. Show all your friends. Step right up! Science sold out to business!*

This is not the way it is supposed to be. Instinctively she reached for her chain. *I'm not wearing it.* The PR consultant had told her not to put it on, she had obeyed. This would be one of the rare times when Adrian's signet ring had not been close to her heart. She felt suddenly guilty. *Changing the quality of human life – that was what I wanted.* Adrian had been her catalyst, his memory fuelling her pursuit. It had never been about money. The conclusion energised her. But an unfamiliar, authoritative voice boomed inside her – *you chose this job because of the salary!*

Karl was still staring her down, challenging her integrity. Louise looked away, focusing instead on the water in her glass; she stayed still for a moment before speaking quietly.

'I'm not totally innocent.'

THURSDAY 9TH MAY 2030

Karl perched on the edge of a leather sofa. He rubbed, anxiously, at a minute crease in his designer jeans before returning his attention to the tablet in his hands. The room was still, calm – and he felt out of place. He hated the irony; these rooms were 'relaxation zones'.

The interior had been designed by a top designer. Its layout even reflected his personal taste, a combination of luxury comfort and utilitarian design; precise, neat, clean and progressively decorated.

Both hands trembled as he repeatedly rolled his teeth over his taut lips. A fluttery, empty sensation filled his stomach – he'd decided to skip the complimentary breakfast tray. It lay on the table, untouched. Sleep evaded him and his eyelids felt grainy on the inside. He scratched at his stubble; for once, he had chosen to skip shaving. The adrenaline from the day before was still circulating somewhere in his system. He would have time to be tired later. Right now he was on another up, reading from his tablet.

Stella had focused on his appearance, describing him as:

"… a stunningly handsome academic who chose to replace the lab coat with an Akira Isogawa suit… spearheading the creation of mixed species, designer children – along with the beautiful, but seemingly shy, Dr Louise Dalton…"

The title of the article could only be described as blatantly provocative: *Designer Clothes, Designer Babies – A Marriage Made in Heaven (or Hell)?*

Stella played me; toyed with me. I fell for it, for her fake charms. He tightened his grip on the news tablet, feeling it resist his touch. *I could break this.*

The tone of the article was far too cynical for his liking, almost accusing him of manipulation. He read on:

"A slick presentation to educate the masses – subtle if a little preachy – rich with symbolism that made what should have felt like a secular experience into an irritatingly religious one; all housed within the confines of what certain staff at IBC refer to as the Crystal Thought Temple."

How dare she, she stole that phrase from me. Who does she think she is? The little thief. Journalists are meant to be objective! Bitch. Karl's heart raced. A dry sensation lingered in his mouth while hot pinpricks jabbed at him, under his arms.

If I could get my hands on her now…

He read on, scrolling quickly through the writing, "… this blatant marriage of convenience… the partnership between business and science… a covenant sealed with a secret hand shake… IBC has taken a sacred moment and trivialised the proceedings… naming the new species after characters from an ancient nursery rhyme… casually referred to as Jack and Jill. Such contempt towards—"

That's enough!

Karl hurled the news tablet at the opposite wall, watching it shatter, showering the floor with shards of glass.. Karl sighed and stood, glaring at a stack of newspapers and industry magazines, accusing him from the polished glass table. His Rolex had been strategically placed between two Jim Beam bottles, both standing like sentries; one empty, the other containing an inch of whisky.

Part of him wanted to hurt her. He had given Stella extra information, an inside eye; and she dared to criticise him in public. Everyone would know; everyone would be talking about him. *This should be about the science, the breakthrough and the very existence of Jack and Jill. And I was good out there. I tried to save it all. And now this. This is my reward?*

Four years, four gruelling years of baths filled with sweat, buckets of tears and bloodshed, reduced to this? This... This character assassination by a group of ignorant plebs. It's not fair!

First Louise... He had fought to have her on the team and now she was a major liability. *Just like her predecessor. Louise, freezing in front of the camera...* He blamed himself. He'd insisted that she be the one to stand with him. *I should have done it all myself.*

And the debrief... Had she wanted to attack him? *All venom and false eyelashes.* The image had been broken, her magic dispelled – she had been her normal, dull self again. *No, not her normal self.* She was one angry Brit. Karl disliked the stereotype, but Louise reminded him of a pitted bulldog; hungry and salivating, teeth exposed, poised on its hunches, ready to pounce at any moment. *Practically growling over her litter – they're mine – over her "twinnes". Disgusting.*

If she thought she had managed to disguise her fists, she was wrong. She was so much smaller without her heels, stomping around the room in her tights. He giggled uncontrollably, then smiled at his own spontaneity. She had been annoying at the time but, admittedly, it was hilarious now. *What a nerve.* She'd allowed herself to become emotionally attached to them. Perhaps he should have done more to stop it. Her job involved working with them on a daily basis and he had assumed that it was inevitable; but he was a scientist not a psychologist and he had expected the rest of the team to support him in getting her to letting them go. He supervised her lab work. Her personal life was her business; *her psychological state should have been dealt with by HR. By the staff medical team. Someone should have been on this from the start.*

He scratched his chin and winced at the sound it made; he knew the signs, another migraine was on the way. A deep, throbbing sensation was building in the middle of his head. Yes, the familiar routine. It would bring with it the blinding pain and shining needles of light.

As for Laura... Another useless woman. She had apologised profusely, weeping and mumbling about her family, about the implications. *What does that have to do with me, with IBC?* She had cried on him; telling him that her team had been fully briefed, that she didn't understand how they had failed to handle the children. He had been cold. *She was supposed to do her job and she didn't do it well enough. She should have recruited better, trained them better; made sure they were capable babysitters for heaven's sake; made sure that Louise didn't falter.* Karl was ashamed to work with such people. Indeed, he had already made a strong recommendation that Laura be let go. *Waterworks just don't work with me. Tears mean nothing. Everyone sees me as the junior zookeeper, cleaning up after all the animals. Shovel load after shovel load of crap.* Stella, Laura and Louise. *A fine menagerie.*

Flashes of red light danced across his vision, his heart growing in his chest, ready to explode. *Why does everyone let me down? Why are all of these women such disappointments? All except Glenda – Glenda is different.*

It took almost ten seconds for Karl to realise that he was grinding his teeth. *I've not done that in years; see what they've done to me.* The inner cobra thrashed, rippling coils and deadly eyes, emerging from its lair. Stella, Laura and Louise had broken its dormancy. Hunger – raw, naked, instinct driven, a beast with an insatiable need. Karl instantly recognised the feelings, frightening feelings, indicators that he was close to the imaginary line between reality and fantasy.

In this case a violent fantasy.

It took five long minutes before the relaxation technique kicked in and the grinding stopped. The cobra slunk back to its hibernation, disappointed. The throbbing dulled, present but not as intense. He appreciated his anger management counsellor and her advice, that stuff still worked after all these years.

He leaned back on the sofa, sighing. *Ignore the personal assessments by the media.* He wished he could. He had to know, yet did not want to. He reached out for the pile of magazines.

What have the other journalists said about me? What do they think? Am I a failure?

+++

The views of the journalists had ranged from the comic to the absurdly gothic, including a number of variations to the tune of Shelley's *Frankenstein*.

Karl's hatred for the media continued to grow. The second bottle was now empty, lying on the floor next to his chair. However, other pressing matters rose to the top of his agenda. His anxiety levels spiked at the thought of the flight back to Korea. There, Max would want to discuss this mess in person.

Karl let himself slide, his focus blurring.

Images of destruction flashed through his mind, one after the other and in rapid succession. Speeding up in frequency; a carousel of catastrophe with Karl on the red horse with its flaming tail and eyes of supernova white, whilst eerie and discordant fairground music wailed on in the background.

He watched himself became a blur as his control slipped away, the terror in his eyes multiplying with each revolution. Faster and faster, whirling and spinning.

Max was standing there, growing larger, his arms folded, his expression displaying his disgust; his disappointment in his useless protégé. The face morphed and he saw his father's pan replace the angry distorted features. The smell of booze – that familiar odour, stale and rancid – and his heavy, laboured breathing.

'You're useless. Worthless… I'm going to show ya… show ya what I do to failures.' His knarled and blistered hands, reaching out to grab hold of Karl. The mask was contorted by hate and an appetite for violence.

Now he swallowed it all: the stench that heralded approaching doom and pain. Tears made no difference, before or after. Karl knew what would happen next. A simpering sound escaped from his lips, unexpected and unwelcome.

Deep within his brain stem a primeval response circuit triggered.

Wetness.

PART II

THE INVESTIGATION

'Inside every acorn there is a mighty oak tree.'
(Luellen Mayhew; October 2013)

What follows is a series of incidents, eye-witness accounts (EWA), recollections (R), medical records (MR), written documentation (WD), electronic evidence (EE), published articles (PA) and brain mapping (BM) associated with those involved in the creation of IBC and the development of the Living Doll Project.

I have focused on the following subjects:

Charles Ferrell, Karthik Kothaka, Karl Winwood, Max Augustine, Louise Dalton and Chloe Bartell.

There were many more who could have been investigated.

C.

KAIROS

1998 – 2001

MONDAY 14TH NOVEMBER 1988 (WD)

Chelsea Place,
Dehli

14th November 1988
My Dear Son,
How are you? We all miss you very much. All of your brothers and sisters send their love and lots of kisses. It has been such a long time that we have seen you. Thank you for sending the latest picture from your school. You look very smart in your uniform. I have put it on my dressing table. I kiss your photograph every time I see it.

Ajay from next door, wishes me to remember him to you. It would be wonderful if you could write him a letter. I will read if for him, he is still struggling with his English language. You used to be such a help to him. His mummy also sends her love to you.

Your Father will be in the USA next year. What would you like him to bring for you? He is very busy at the moment. We hardly see him. There is a lot of new development taking place, a new shopping complex is being planned for the centre of Dehli.

I do miss you. Your last poem seemed very short. Write more words next time. Were you in a hurry? I read them many times and always think of you. Have your re-arranged your room?

It is still winter for us, yesterday the temperature reached 24°C. That will seem very hot to you. I saw on the weather report that you had snow. You must tell me all about your winter adventures.

Chitral, the driver, is not well. He hurt his back lifting some crates. I have told him to stay at home until he is better. His wife is expecting their third child. I may go and visit him if I have time this afternoon.

In response to your question, we will be going to see your Uncle and his wife. I will let them know that you are thinking of them. They miss you too. I may ask your Father to order some more copies of your school photograph. I will send them a copy.

No birthdays this month. Next month there will be two. I have already started planning the surprises. I will have to send you something special when your birthday comes around next year.

Tell me about your studies at Parkton. How is your friend, Matthew? Did you make up after the fight that you had? I have always taught you to be kind and generous even if other people are horrible.

I will have to go now. I am having a tea party, and will be serving your favourite dish. I wish I could send you a very big portion.

I miss you so much my dear. I often think of you alone in New York. We know that you will be okay but it must be very lonely at times. I will ask your Father if he can arrange for you to be taken to the international call centre more often. I want to hear your lovely voice.

I am putting many kisses on the bottom of the page. They will jump off the page and into your heart.

With all of my love,
Mummy

PS. I am sending you some posters. One of your uncles will be in New York next month. That should help brighten up your room. I may send the rug as well if it is finished. The weaver has been working very hard, your colour choices make it very difficult - red, yellow and white!

10th December 1988

Dear Mummy,

Thank you for your letter. I will answer all of your questions.

My bed is right underneath the very large window. I always keep it neat the way you taught me. My writing desk is underneath my notice board, I write notes and pin them up. If I have important things to remember. I stick them there as well. My bookcase is hungry, send me more books! Please ask Father to take me book shopping the next time he is in New York.

It is very very cold – I do not like snow. The driver takes me right up to the building so I do not have to step on too much ice. I fell over last week and bruised my knee. It hurt a lot.

Please send my love to Uncle Raju. I hope his back will be better soon. Has Auntie Seeta had her baby yet?'

In the States I find people so rude. I call all the servants Uncle and Auntie. We are like one big family.

Karthik chewed on his fountain pen. He had a music lesson in twenty minutes, leaving him just enough time to get the letter finished. *Perhaps it could be sent in the afternoon post?* He wrote:

My studies are going very well. I have been upgraded in my lessons. I am on the accelerated learning scheme. I find them more difficult, they used to be very easy. I do not like the homework. I must study every evening and at the weekend. I have no time for being lazy. Even though it is not easy. I do enjoy it some time.

My teacher, Mr Morris, tells me I am one of the best students he has ever seen. My head became like balloon. You have always told me not to be big headed but I could not help it.

I am not talking to Matthew. I will make up as you have asked me to. I will speak to him tomorrow and say sorry.

Only because you ask me to. Karthik stopped. *Matthew. He is too snobby. And he always takes the mickey out of my accent.* He decided that he could not tell

Mummy that Matthew had said something rude about her. That was how he earned Karthik's punches.

Thank you for the rug. I have put in in the middle of the room. It is just the way I asked it to be made. My friends think the colours are very strange but I love them.

Thank you also for the posters. I am looking forward to seeing Qayamat Se Qayamat Tak. I can then show off my new posters. No one here knows who Juhi Chawla is or Aamir Khan. I have a lot of educating to do. How did you get hold of the other posters of Anil Kapoor and Madhuri Dixit? They will brighten up my boring room.

Thank you Mummy.

I too am sending you many kisses.
I love you Mummy.
Your son,
Karthik

PS I did not forget the poem. I am having too much work so I will write a very long one and include it my next letter.

Karthik started on the airmail envelope. *I miss India, I miss my brothers, even Aahlaad, and sisters. I miss my Mummy.*

He kissed the bottom of the letter ten times, carefully placing it in the envelope. After licking the edge, he trapped his letter inside. Two more kisses on the back.

Five minutes to spare. He stood up, then grasped his clarinet which was propped against his bed. *Do I have any spares reeds?* He should have checked.

Armed with letter and instrument he slammed the door. This week he had practised, Mr Soloviev would be pleased.

As he ran down the empty corridor, the letter flapped in his hand.

WEDNESDAY 18TH JANUARY 1989 (BM, R)

'Kothaka.'

'Yes sir.' He stopped writing. Karthik's forehead furrowed from concentration, pen poised mid-sentence.

'Can you stay behind and see me at the end of the lesson?' A few heads turned. Karthik's concern showed on his face, mild alarm.

'Don't worry. You are not in trouble.' Mr Morris smiled causing the edges of his mouth to crinkle ad he walked past Karthik's desk. Five minutes passed quickly – the school-bell rang.

'Okay everyone, you know the text I want you to read for tomorrow. Do not come with excuses or you will find yourselves in homework detention.' Mr Morris's voice was low but menacing.

Scraping sounds filled the room as students dragged their chairs on the wooden floor, grateful that the lesson had come to an end. He watched them wearily packing their bags. *That was a tough lesson.* Mr Morris knew he stretched them, but they were able, so he was willing. 'Hargreaves, pick up that piece of paper on the floor.'

'But sir, I didn't—'

'Call it social service. Bin!' He gestured to the hungry basket near his desk. Hargreaves moved slowly then dropped in his offering, failing to disguise his displeasure.

'Are you in pain?' Mr Morris stuck out his chin.

'No sir.'

'Then fix your face.' An instruction, not an option. *Attitude determines altitude, young man.*

Hargreaves replaced the frown with a forced smile. He sauntered back to his bag, slung it across his back and escaped.

'You wanted to see me sir.' Karthik seemed exhausted. His eyes were half-open, both shoulders sloped downwards, his arms dangling loosely.

'I just wanted to remind you that the debating finals are next week. I want you to pulverise the team, the way you took on Silverhurst.' Karthik had been ruthless, publically thrashing the opposition, showing them no mercy. There had been a complaint from one of the parents that he had made her son cry with his aggressive manner.

'Yes sir, I did remember.'

'Look at me when I am talking to you.' He still retained that reserved cultural manner that prevented him fully engaging adults. Two deep brown eyes focused on him. 'That's better. You are a smart young man and I am proud of you.' The resultant smile stretched from one end of the room to the other.

'Thank... thank you sir.'

'Did you finish the essay?' Karthik nodded. 'Did you give an alternative point of view and balance your conclusion?'

'Yes sir, just as you taught us.' Somehow he seemed to gather energy from somewhere. His eyes seemed to sparkle.

'Good. I'm looking forward to reading your response. Did you get hold of that book I told you about?' Mr Morris headed towards his desk, dreading the meeting with a difficult parent straight after school.

'I've reserved a copy at the library.' Karthik took the cue and finished packing his rucksack, talking as he piled in his books. 'I am going to pick it up on my way home tonight.'

'Not many people do what I ask them to do when it is not about homework or classwork. You seem genuinely keen.' He stared down his nose, lifting one eyebrow.

'I always do what you ask sir.' That was true. He always followed advice, going beyond the norm. When he had first arrived at the school his handwriting had been awful, uncontrolled sprawling. At his suggestion, Karthik had gone along to voluntary after-school handwriting classes. The transformation had become clear after only a few weeks. Now his writing was almost a work of art. Yes, he did do as he was told. 'I read your draft essay entry for this year's School Essay Competition, it's really very good. Some argument flaws but still very good.'

'Will you help me, sir?' The intensity of the voice and the straight upright posture. *He means business.*

'Yes, see me… on Friday after school. Come to my office. I should be there.' He watched with amusement as Karthik struggled to fit the third textbook into his rucksack, then gave up.

'I will be there sir. May I go please?'

'Yes Karthik. Sort out your tie first, then you may leave.' Mr Morris checked as Karthik wiggled the tie, eagerly seeking his approval. He nodded, Karthik spun around and skipped out of the room, rucksack over one shoulder, textbook tucked under arm.

That boy…

+++

'Hello Miss Geraldine.'

'Hello Karthik,' she turned around at the sound of his excited voice, 'It's

Geraldine, not Miss Geraldine.' She gently scolded him for the umpteenth time.

'Sorry, I forgot many times.'

'Sorry, sometimes I forget,' she offered an alternative response.

'Yes, very sorry.'

The boy seemed to lose his grasp of English whenever he became too excited. 'What can I do for you?' She put down the three books and leaned on the desk. At this time in the afternoon the library appeared bleak, devoid of human life. She often felt lonely. It was good to see a cheery face.

'Is it in?' His eyes were pleading, imploring her, his grin exaggerated.

'Is what in?'

'My order,' he almost jumped on the spot, his rucksack swinging from side to side.

'Let me check.' Geraldine tapped a few buttons on the keyboard. 'Yes… It is in. Came in yesterday.'

'Wonderful, wonderful.' He clapped his hands together and ran on the spot, she had never seen anyone so joyful over a book of philosophy.

'You can have it on long loan.' She scoured the reservation section, searching for the title. 'That *is* heavy.' She almost dropped it. The computer bleeped as she scanned the spine. Managing the book required both hands; she slid it over the deactivator pad and amended the date in the entry column. 'Have you got room in your bag for this?' The bulging sides and straining drawstrings indicated that he did not.

'I will carry it home.'

A moment of surprise… Then she remembered. Of course, he lived in the exclusive residence on the Manhattan corridor, literally on the doorstop of the library.

Their eyes were level when she spoke to him, 'Why,' she pointed at him, 'do you need that book?' Geraldine jabbed at the heavy tome. Her eyes playful but interested.

'I… I…' her intensity seemed to unnerve him, so she drew back, standing upright. 'I'm entering a essay competition and I think I will find some killer facts in this book.'

'Okay then,' Geraldine nodded. 'Well, do let me know how things go. If you need—'

Suddenly he was moving, his excitement palpable.

'Bye!' He cut her off, turning for the door at record speed. 'Got to go!'

He disappeared, armed with his new weapon.

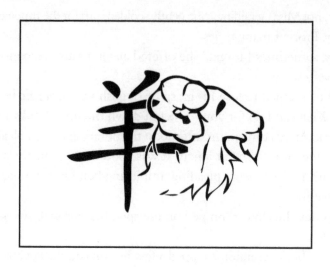

WEDNESDAY 20TH NOVEMBER 1991 (BM, EE, R)

My first chance to impress the deputy principal.

Daphne pushed two desks towards the front of her classroom, making the teacher's desk central. She nodded, happy with the arrangement. She couldn't quite get a grip on her feelings; there was raw relief at the fact that the day was over and then slight anxiety about the meeting.

As Max Augustine's Year Head, she would be expected to lead the meeting – hopefully gaining the approval of Mrs Duman… *That will be another tick in the box. Another step towards promotion.*

It's all well and good being good at your job, but the secret is to be seen to be good at your job.

Room 12 was situated on the ground floor of the main building at Silverhurst Middle School. It was close to one of the main entry points and – between lessons; and before and after school – the noise levels would rise in huge increments. During those crucial times, the long and narrow corridor outside Room 12 would be filled with noisy students, keen to meet their friends for a brief chat, excited about their next lesson or dragging their heels to avoid another boring lecture; all of them chaperoned by busy and stressed teachers, each with a list of ten things that needed doing yesterday.

Today, the exodus had taken place. Daphne checked the wall clock: 4.00pm. The school day ended at 3.45pm and, today, her Spanish class had cheered when the bell rang. The sound had been like a starting gun and she had exhaled gratefully as the students departed, savouring the promise of impending calm.

The place was usually full of living noise: shouts, occasional screams, cutting comments about staff and students, promises of commitment to call later that evening and discussions about homework. Now the corridor was quiet, interrupted only by the hushed whispers of passing students or the strangely loud conversations staff members.

Everything was ready, notes were prepared and she held three copies of all the relevant documents. Daphne wanted to justify her promotion to the position of Year Head. After all, she had only been a relatively short time in teaching. It had been a hectic few years – *from the world of banking to that of the Spanish teacher.* Many of her former colleagues had thought she was suffering from some form of mental health issue – stemming, perhaps, from abject stupidity. But money was not everything to Daphne. Teaching was hard, but it also gave her something that she had never been able to find working in finance.

She had ordered some drinks from the cafeteria and had managed to procure a few of their popular homemade biscuits. Daphne knew that Sheila, Mrs Duman, liked a latte with no sugar, whilst Paul went for a cappuccino with vanilla flavouring and two sugars. Her contact in catering knew all the personal preferences of the other staff. It was quite a feat considering that there were more than forty of them.

She sat back down in her chair and looked around calmly. The main yard outside was empty now, aside from a small and distant group of children practicing softball catches. The place seemed void of life. She had a lesson with her 8th grade class tomorrow, they could be tricky. She loved her room, but the wall displays needed refreshing. They had been there for more than a year. Inspirational posters – bright and colourful images, active people, dancing, singing, eating, enjoying life – with all the quotes and comments in Spanish. The large poster of the bullfighter seemed to capture the essence of the eminent meeting.

Working with Max and his father felt like taking part in a bullfight. She would take on the role of the matador – they, the angry bull. The red cape, known to infuriate the beast, yet used to draw the it to the matador. *Where's the skill? Why that's in managing not to get horned – the thrill of being so close to death and yet not dying.*

An art or insanity? Depends on your view of bullfighting.

She heard a distant door slam; any students still on site last were involved in the busy after-school programme, attending extra study sessions or using the library to get started on their heavy homework schedule – it was a relentless marathon.

They would be here in the next few minutes.

There were two major challenges for Paul Simpson, she thought: getting through his first year in teaching and having Max in his tutor group. It would make for a time he would never forget. She smiled wryly, knowing how difficult it must have been for him to cope with being Max's tutor, having to be in the front line dealing with his parents and the many teachers who were baying for Augustine blood. As an 8th Grade tutor, he faced the puberty madness that went along with the students' first years as teenagers – they were all trying to be themselves yet not knowing who they were.

It was his job to keep that difficult balance: being there for the students but also having to discipline them. In her view he was doing a pretty good job, and today would be her chance to reinforce that. Yet another positive point… *Daphne is able to encourage members of her team…* Mrs Duman would see that; another a good statement to have included in her annual staff appraisal.

I want a glowing reference when I am ready to apply for a deputy principal's position.

The door opened. Sheila walked in, Paul trailing behind.

'Hello Sheila, Hello Paul,' Daphne stood, gesturing to the two chairs behind the trio of desks, 'make yourself comfortable. Drinks and snacks are ready.'

Sheila was about forty, stocky build, wearing a purple twin set with a long black skirt. Her short brown hair was always immaculate, as were her nails. Other staff described her as tough but caring. Paul still carried the marks of youth but they had been tempered with maturity, sharp clothes and scuffed brown brogues.

'You have no idea what kind of day I have had… Must be something in the water.' Sheila spotted the latte. 'Is that for me?' Her eyes glowed, the smile exposing her bottom teeth.

'Just the way you like it,' Daphne congratulated herself – *Well done!*

She studied the look on Sheila's face as she sipped the drink – it was close to ecstasy.

'I so needed that… And biscuits too. You *are* thoughtful.'

Paul looked nervous, fidgeting with the files in his hands. He put them on a neighbouring desk.

'Paul, the cappuccino is for you... Two sugars... And a dash of vanilla flavouring?'

'Daphne, how did you know?'

She tapped her nose and winked. A mug of green tea did it for her. They drank together.

'Shall we get things going?' Sheila's voice had taken on an authoritarian tone. Daphne watched her extract a hardback book from her handbag, along with a silver fountain pen. "Daphne, you *are* leading?"

She nodded, handing out the prepared booklets. 'I thought we'd start—'

A piercing scream filled the room. Daphne rushed towards the door. As she pulled it open, two 7th Graders ran past, laughing as they almost made it through the exit.

"Just a moment, you two."

They stood like statures, looking sheepish. Only one of them was vaguely familiar to Daphne.

'Firstly, why are you making such a noise?'

They looked at each other, the taller of the two girls spoke, 'Sorry miss, we were just being silly.'

'You disturbed my meeting.' Daphne put on her best teacher-in-control voice, conscious of her audience in room 12. 'Supposing I was talking to a parent, they would think we are running a school for badly behaved children. If they were a prospective parent, they might not send their child here.'

Both of them had their heads down. One glanced at the other, who spoke.

'Sorry Miss...'

Daphne folded her arms, 'I hope I do not have to talk to either of you about this type of behaviour ever again. It will not be repeated.'

'No Miss,' they said together.

'Off you go,' she waved them away. Watching them leave quietly.

Good – now back to the meeting.

'You handled that really well. You seem to have mastered the art of knowing when to and when not to engage.'

The affirmation felt good. She resumed her seat. This was going well already. *Promotion, here I come.* There was no sign of her biscuits – only crumbs on the desk .

Daphne continued, 'I thought we could start by going over the history of Max's behavioural issues and then deal with the most recent incident.' The words were directed at Sheila, who nodded, showing her approval.

Daphne turned to her other companion, 'Paul, perhaps you could start... What about the Economics incident?'

Paul cleared his throat while nervously thumbing through the sheets in front of him. Daphne knew he was on edge; tiny beads of sweat were forming just below his hairline.

'Okay,' he said as Sheila opened her book and began to write. 'Max disagreed with Mr Songt's view on the state of the national finance, particularly his assessment of the GDP in respect to cultivating ways forward.'

He paused, licked his lips then continued. 'He confronted the teacher, Mr Songt, and stated his opinion.' Paul wiped his forehead. 'Max wanted to debate the issues there and then. Mr Songt refused—'

Daphne realised that the flight instinct was taking over; Paul's words were gaining speed.

'Paul,' her interruption resulted in a hurt look, his mouth half open. 'You are rushing... take your time.'

'Oh, sorry,' larger beads were forming, a few coalesced before making the journey down his forehead. He breathed in, then continued, 'Max refused to back down, he refused to be quiet, he refused to leave the classroom.'

He gulped from the mug. 'Eventually, Mr Songt called for outside assistance and Max was escorted out of the lesson.'

As he finished, Daphne watched his fleeting look at Sheila, busily writing. His raised eyebrows, silently asking whether his performance was okay.

'Thank you Paul,' said Daphne, winking at him.

'What action did we take?' Sheila looked up, her pen centralised on the page.

'We wrote to his parents, informing them of his behaviour,' Daphne took over. 'Mr Songt received a very aggressive phone call from Max's father backing his son's behaviour. I phoned the home number and spoke to his mother. She was shocked and most apologetic; she had not been informed about the letter. Mrs Augustine managed to get Max to write a letter of apology. Bear in mind that he had already stated that he was not going to write one, and that his father approved of this.'

Sheila continued with her note taking. Daphne nodded reassuringly at Paul.

'So, two different parental styles within the same home,' Sheila spoke without looking up. Her next comment seemed like a loud aside, 'No wonder we end up with so many problems at school.'

Daphne decided to speed things up. Paul seemed particularly stressed out by his involvement. She coughed and said, 'After all of this, Max targeted a student who had disagreed with his views on the economy. When the student was interviewed the whole story came to light.'

Daphne saw the look of horror on Sheila's face as she stopped writing.

'This should have come to my attention, this is the first I have heard about this matter. All cases of bullying should be passed on immediately.' Sheila's pen pointed in Daphne's direction.

Daphne felt the anxiety return; a sudden tightness at the top of her shoulders. She knew the policy on bullying by heart.

'Ah…' Her right hand moved towards her mouth. *Help – brain fog!*

'Please carry on Miss Purser, we can discuss this when Mr Simpson has left,' Sheila's eyes flashed – a danger placard danced across the screen of Daphne's brain. Shelia flipped through the documents, stopping at regular intervals, then continued to write, muttering as she did so.

She called me Miss Purser – that was a bad sign.

'There had been a gradual progression in his campaign of… terror,' Daphne stopped. Sheila looked ready to explode. She said nothing, stabbed her pen at Daphne again and continued to scribble, mumbling little comments to herself.

Daphne felt tearful, her plans to impress seemed to be going wrong.

'He managed to convince others to join him in intimidating the victim, who was then excluded from the group,' her voice had begun to warble. Paul did nothing to help.

She turned away and cleared her throat. The pen continued to write.

'This was followed by a planned physical assault. Max wanted to escalate the verbal abuse, calling him an idiot for his views to something more… trivial. The——'

Sheila slapped down her book shut. 'Miss Purser, you should have notified me of this matter.' Saliva flew out of her mouth as she spoke. 'Why did you think you had the authority to handle this yourself? We have policies on this type of behaviour and you are supposed to follow them.'

Paul looked as if he wanted to disappear. Daphne placed one hand on the desk, supporting herself.

'Max is a bully,' Paul's voice sounded surprisingly strong, confident, 'He did not do anything physical. He didn't even get as far as intimidation. But he did begin to plan for others to do it for him.' He looked straight at Sheila. 'One of my tutor group overheard him discussing his ideas for a campaign and came and told me. Nobody got... pulverised... which was what he had planned to have them do.'

Sheila stopped staring at Daphne and turned to Paul. 'Why was I not informed, when did this happen?'

'You were on bereavement leave so this went straight to the principal.' Daphne found her voice.

Sheila's hand dropped onto the cover of her notebook, 'Oh, so he never told me.' She opened it and continued her writing.

Daphne mimed a thank you in Paul's direction.

'Is there anything else I need to be updated on?' asked Sheila, one eyebrow raised.

Daphne told her about the call from father and the subsequent meeting between the patriarch, Mrs Augustine, Paul and Daphne. During that meeting Mr Augustine had displayed his displeasure at being called from work, stating that he was a busy man.

Paul took over, giving his recollection of events. He explained that Daphne had remained calm and composed in what was a tense situation. His glowing account, mentioned her display of courage coupled with fortitude, and how that had really impressed him.

Paul had sipped and listened while Daphne was talking. To his mind, Lukas Augustine had racist views and he did not like Daphne's having authority over Max. When she introduced herself, his facial expression had suggested that he had not been expecting an Afro-Caribbean woman to teach his son. It was something about the way he looked at her; something about his condescending tone throughout the whole episode. Still, Paul explained, she had coped well with the situation.

Daphne took over then, explaining that the boy's mother was the more responsive of the two: she seemed worried about Max's future. Daphne also mentioned that Mr Augustine had threatened the school with legal action

– something they both felt was more of an act of intimidation than a genuine threat.

Legal action – that man had a nerve. Paul stirred his cappuccino. *Does money give you the right to do just as you please and to use the legal system to support your stance? That seems like a misuse of justice.* Sheila seemed to appreciate the information, her scribbling increased, as did her frequent nods.

Daphne summed up the events. Max had been suspended for three days and had been booked in to see the school counsellor. The principal had authorised and signed all the relevant paperwork. All of the material was now in his school file. She concluded by lifting up her copy of the booklet she had handed out at the start of the meeting, a summary of all the documentation.

Sheila admitted that she had not looked at his file, nor had she spoken to the principal about this. She clicked the lid back onto her pen and spoke.

'I'm sorry I snapped. It's just that… well it's quite shocking really. And it's the sort of thing that should worry us all. So… thank you, both of you, Daphne, Paul. You've actually done a sterling job.'

Daphne's face betrayed her relief.

Even from his short time in teaching Paul knew that paperwork was the lifeblood of the profession. Too busy to do the basics – that's how teaching felt at times. He got that point. So even deputies could fall down on key areas. That made them seem more human.

They then dealt with the matter of the bus driver and talked about Max's possible expulsion should his behavioural record fail to improve.

Daphne had told Paul that Max had called the driver an idiot and told him to get an education. *What nerve. Just like his father.* Yet there was something about Max… The boy was nonetheless intelligent and Paul felt that he could not give up on him.

'So we finally get to the most recent incident. One of which I am *aware*. But only scarcely. Would you two care to elaborate?' Sheila's voice lacked energy, her words almost slurred. It was now 4.40pm.

'Yes… So this took place yesterday, during a biology lesson. He refused to do the work. The teacher told him to attend a detention session scheduled for tonight and he refused that too. He even wrote an email,' Daphne checked her booklet, 'It's the second page from the end.'

To: dap@silverhurstmiddleschool.com
From: max1augustine@hotmail.com
Date: 20/11/1991

Dear Ms Purser,

I am writing to you to clarify why I believe that the detention I have been issued is grossly unfair and serves no purpose other than to satisfy some unexplainable need to punish me for something I haven't done.

It was not a 'refusal to complete work'. I will not attend the detention because I have already handed in the biology work – if the teacher had checked they would have found it.

Due to the arguments I have stated above I will not be attending the detention tomorrow.

Yours sincerely,
Max Augustine

'What do you think?' Daphne waited for Sheila to finish reading the email.

'What do you think you should do?' Sheila turned the question back on Daphne.

She responded, 'Personally I would like to see him expelled. He needs to do the detention. I would really like to take on the parents, especially the father.' Secretly, she was still smarting from the last incident with Lucas Augustine. The one regarding the bus driver. He had called her incompetent, saying that she did not understand the boy's needs.

Sheila mused over her thoughts, then spoke: 'Compared to other incidents this one is on a smaller scale. Why use a cannon when a fly swat will do? What is at stake here is our image, and that is likely to be damaged by the poor publicity that would arise from a court case with high profile attendees. Sadly, his father is very influential.'

With military precision, Sheila laid out her own plan of action, which included following the school's policy to the letter, showing up areas of violation and pointing out the written sanction for those violations.

'When parents join Silverhurst, they sign an agreement to uphold our policies. Talk to the mother and show her the specific sections of the code of conduct that Max has violated. If you have any further problems, send them in my direction. I am ready to handle Mr

Augustine and you two don't need to be involved in that personally. I will take that on myself.'

Daphne saw fire in her eyes. She was not joking.

'Furthermore, he will attend that detention. That is his sanction for failing to adhere to our policy. If they refuse the sanction, then we will be suspending him until he carries out the punishment. Ask them to support us by upholding the terms of our agreement and the standards of the school, and by helping Max to grow up and get ready for the real world.' Sheila closed her book, looked over at the clock and sighed loudly. 'Well, I hope I can catch the end of *Home and Away*.'

Daphne hoped she had hidden her shock well enough, over that last little revelation. 'Thank you for your time Mrs Duman.'

Sheila smiled generously, 'Any time, my dear. Do come and talk to me. You have real potential.' She turned to Paul, 'You understand that boy. He will come to appreciate you in years to come. You know, you have probably kept him in this school.'

Paul stood up, allowing her to pass by. She placed her mug on Daphne's desk. 'Have a good evening, both of you. And get home safely.'

The door closed. It was just her and Paul now. Daphne was quiet. She thanked him for his support, he seemed embarrassed almost wanting to brush it off as nothing. She watched him leave. *What will I do now? How do I handle this?*.

In truth, she didn't really know.

As Paul walked down the corridor, he wondered how Sheila had sussed him out with so little evidence.

FRIDAY 22ND NOVEMBER 1991 (BM, EWA)

As Daphne and Sheila walked past the detention room, they spotted Max, sitting at the second desk from the front, writing with determination and focus, the tip of his tongue protruding.

'What kind of person do you think he will be in the future?' Daphne asked.

They continued to walk. Sheila frowned, thoughtfully. 'I can't say, but would hate to be on the wrong side of him. He has a real dark side.'

'Do you think he'll make it through High School?'

'Well that's largely up to us isn't it.' It was not a question. 'I think he will, Daphne. As long as we have Mr Simpson.'

THURSDAY 26TH AUGUST 1993 (EE)

To: pbs@silverhurstmiddleschool.com
From: max1augustine@hotmail.com
Date: 26/08/1993

Dear Sir,
This is Max Augustine. I am enjoying High School. I miss your teaching and your words of inspiration. Your assemblies were the best.

Can I put you down as a referee? It has to be someone who has known me for at least three years. I think that you know me very well.

My current tutor, Mr Clarke, is very strict and not even half as good as you are.

I miss you,
Max

FRIDAY 18TH NOVEMBER 1994 (EE)

To: pbs@silverhurstmiddleschool.com
From: max1augustine@hotmail.com
Date: 18/11/1994

Dear Sir,

Thank your email and thank you for yet another reference.

I am choosing between Colleges at the moment. I know you went to Harvard. I am thinking about studying something to do with government? Do you think I would be good enough? Any advice you can offer would be very helpful. This is a very confusing time for me.

You'll be pleased to know I have not had many detentions since I have been at High School. Your chats has clearly rubbed off on me!

Can I come and visit you after school sometime? I have a few family issues that are annoying me. I know that I can trust you. If you are too busy that is okay. I would talk to the school counsellor but to be honest I think she is easily lead astray. Sorry if that sounds horrible but it is the truth.

Thank you.
Max

MONDAY 4TH SEPTEMBER 1995 (EE)

To: pbs@silverhurstmiddleschool.com
From: max1augustine@hotmail.com
Date: 04/09/1995

Dear Mr Simpson,

How are you? Congratulations on your marriage. Do you recommend married life?

I'm loving Harvard. Fresher's week was insane, I did not go crazy but the others around me did. I am not a great fan of alcohol so I was spared some unpleasant experiences. Your prep talk just before I left was timely and apt.

The Government course is very intense – nothing at Harvard is easy. The reading list is so long and again, I'd like to thank you for your wisdom about using the library instead of rushing out and buying books. It's not really a money thing, though I appreciate the sentiment. It's just a whole lot easier than having to find all these books in a shop and have them delivered to my room! I did get some of the major texts second hand. My first essay is due next Friday.

I have not made up my mind about extra-curricular things. I hope to never pick up another football in my life unless I am playing with my own kids. So I thought I might try out some of the societies – thinking about the Harvard Secular Society (HSS) and possibly the Harvard Society for Transhumanist

Theory (HSTT). What do you think? I am mindful that I need to develop my curricular vitae while gaining a degree.

Can I take this moment to say how much I appreciate you? I think back to my ways in Middle school. I think you believed in me, I put you through a lot of stress. Somehow I knew you were on my side, even when you had to tell me off – which was quite often. I am glad you stayed in touch. I still keep the little encouragement notes you gave to all the members of our tutor group. I hope you still do that.

Will have to run. How is Ms Purser? I heard that she is pregnant?

Bye sir,
Max

Saturday 20th January 1996 (BM)

I need inspiration.

He needed to get this college reference completed tonight but everything seemed so crucial. *How can I best portray Karthik's ability?*

Aha! I know… The essay competition!

Karthik's first entry to the APN Essay Competition, back in 1992 – it had been judged to be the best piece of prose ever submitted by a student of his age. He had just turned fifteen – *that's right, he was in the 9th grade*. It had been hard to pin point a beginning… The boy's progress during his time at Parkton was nothing short of legendary. And now, Mr Morris found it hard to accept that this was Karthik's final year.

As his students approached the age of eighteen, the university selection process was in full swing. College applications were raining down on the school. As Karthik's tutor, he'd been assigned the task of writing his reference – not a task he particularly enjoyed. There were many sections, too much wonderful history, too little space; a tutor's nightmare.

Mr Morris recalled his using the contents of that essay for his staff room conversations for months after. His colleagues were so impressed.

He'd observed the ferocious hunger in his student; the boy was constantly adding to his already extensive canon of academic knowledge. They were given a lesson on rapid retrieval techniques, he recalled, and

Karthik had employed the methods immediately, producing good results. In twenty-seven years of teaching, he had never seen such a feat.

Of course, the boy's photographic memory was a useful addition. It only added to the growing array of skills and talents he possessed, allowing him to engage with a range of increasingly complex discourses without the need for deep revision.

Mr Morris was a little surprised to realise that he, himself, envied Karthik. He rolled the pen in between his thumb and forefinger.

He had spent many of his free evenings watching Karthik in action, as he skilfully out manoeuvred hugely talented students in interschool competitions. He possessed the ideal nature for debates and academic challenges – and he had played a major role in securing many of the debating trophies that now sat in the school's decorated foyer. Nobody wanted to be pitted against him, and these days, that included the staff. *Especially me.* Mr Morris laughed dryly.

His impending departure from Parkton saddened him and his colleagues, but it was a cause of great celebration amongst the students. *Perhaps a sign of things to come? After all, he is outstanding.* Mr Morris had told his colleagues that Harvard were obliged to open their doors to such a phenomenal young man.

He had enough material for a good opening paragraph, now. Smiling, he began to draft. Mr Morris wrote for an hour. The reference took on a life of its own.

+++

Nobody expressed surprise at Karthik's full scholarship award.

Mr Morris rejoiced though, crying in front of the assembly hall when he announced the news. Staff and students were openly shocked at his emotional display; some of his colleagues knew too well though, that Mr Morris' developing career had gained everything for his tutelage of Karthik. After all, all those awards reflected on the teaching.

Even so, Karthik struggled not believing it himself. Tears… from his tutor?

Mortified and concerned in equal measure, Karthik went to check on Mr Morris immediately after the assembly.

On seeing Karthik Mr Morris' emotions took over. He hugged him, though this was strictly against the school's policies on appropriate relationships between staff and pupils.

In the fall of 1995 Karthik left Parkton High School. He was heading for Harvard.

A bright star vanished from the school. Nothing seemed to fill its place.

Mr Morris opted for early retirement the following year. Life was not the same after Karthik left.

FRIDAY 2ND FEBRUARY 1996 (EE)

To: pbs@silverhurstmiddleschool.com
From: max1augustine@hotmail.com
Date: 02/02/1996

Dear Paul,

Thanks for getting back to me. Calling you Paul seems a bit weird.

I got a really good mark for my first essay. The professor said that I showed promise. Silverhurst gave me a good grounding for life. I have a tutorial tomorrow as part of the preparation for my next essay. We've been given a choice of three – I am thinking of doing the option on the history of money.

I have a couple of business ideas that I might try out. I have spotted a couple of potential ideas. You used to say that 'opportunity is always knocking but we are often too busy to answer the door.' Will let you know when I make my first million (joke).

I had a bit of an argument with my dad over my plans for the future. He seems to think that I will go straight into the family business (he works in the pharmaceutical industry). I am not sure that is right for me. What do you think?

I hope that Ms Purser's last semester goes well. She was very tough on me. Still I respected her. Is your wife staying in the police?

Loving the HSTT. Initially I thought it was on a par to Star Trek. After the first lecture I would have described myself as curiously apathetic. I have kept attending and taking part in the debates I think the ideology is creeping up on me. I am starting to see their side of things. Quite exciting. Who knows perhaps one day I will be a spokesman for transhumanism (joke)? I am seeing the connection between the hopes of society and the role of science in fulfilling them. It seems there is a great potential for growth for us as human beings – evolution is never static.

Have you heard of Max More? He may be coming to speak near the end of this semester. He is quite a prominent voice on transhumanism. Not sure if I will be able to attend, it clashes with a performance of Bizet's *Carman*.

I have applied for a Summer school course at the Harvard Business School – it will involve a week of my summer vacation. It is a management training course – sounds so interesting. Only a few places on offer so I will have to wait and see.

If you do come into the area, let me know. I know all the coffee shops and even some bars! How are the twins? They must be about five now?

Max

SUNDAY 20TH OCTOBER 1996 (WD)

20th October 1996

Dearest Mummy,
I apologise for the delay in replying to your latest letter. The workload at Harvard has been overwhelming since day one. The reading list is impossible to complete, you would have to give up sleep, life and eating. You know how fond I am of all of these, especially sleep.

I am so excited about Jayagi's forthcoming marriage. I have checked my schedule and I am going to be in the middle of exams. I would have asked Father to send me a ticket, however I must complete these papers. Ask my sister why she has not replied to my last letter. She has no excuse, even being in love. Give my love to my other brothers and sisters. I miss them.

Everyone else seems to have kept up with their letter writing, I do appreciate the calls when you can get into town.

How did your appointment at the hospital go? Was it your yearly check-up?

I have found the move to Harvard very difficult. I feel so lost and alone. The debating society has been a breath of life for me. My reputation preceded me. They were waiting for me when I arrived. I have met some interesting characters, I am no longer at the top of the tree. Others are brighter and sharper than me. Humbling but true, I tell you the truth.

I have been given a special honour on account of my debating ability. I have gained guest places at a number of events organised by the Postgraduate Society for debate. I am, of course, the society's youngest member and its only undergraduate representative – a genuine honour.

Some of my team members have suggested that I tone down my approach. Describing me as overly aggressive. What do you think? You know how much I value your balanced and gentle approach to life.

When is Father next due to visit the States? He was unable to see me last time because of his busy schedule.

I have renewed my joy of reading for pleasure. One new discovery has been the work of Helena Blavatsky. Have you heard of her? She has impacted me more deeply than many of the philosophers on my course.

Her ideas are distinctive and fresh. I find myself identifying with her perspective and reasoning – it resonates with me.

Here is a quote from her:

"Do not be afraid of your difficulties. Do not wish you could be in other circumstances than you are. For when you have made the best of an adversity, it becomes a stepping stone to a splendid opportunity."

What do you think? I think this will become one of my life values.

I have been invited to a meeting about Transhumansim. I have read about this topic but only to a limited extent. They have a top speaker on the subject –

Max More. I am debating whether to go or not (hope you appreciated the joke!). It will depend on how much work I have to do.

How is Badal? He must be nearly seven. Are there any more children on the way? Give my fondest love to Uncle Raju and Auntie Seeta.

Writing to you means the world to me. I can be myself and let all my inner thoughts flood out. You are my best friend and my therapist all rolled into one. I do not know what I would do without you.

Would Father let you come to the States? Please ask him again. If you could work on him … You would love it here. I would like to come back to India next summer. Please ask for me. Hearing your voice only makes me feel partially complete.

I love you Mummy. I always will.
Write soon or phone!
Your ever loving son,

Karthik

Thursday 14th November 1996 (BM, EWA, R)

'Hi Karthik, got a minute?' Craig, stood in the doorway blocking the entrance to the cafeteria.

'Craig, I am hungry and I have a lecture after lunch. Need I quote to you 'Man shall not—'

'Enough, Karthik,' he sounded irritated.

'Sorry, just being me.' Karthik normally managed to coax a smile out of Craig. Their friendship had become deeper and more relaxed over time, this seemed strange, out of character.

'I'm so tired, I was up most of the night getting my essay finished and making sure I got this completed.' He held out a series of typed sheets.

'What's that?' Karthik took them.

'It's my article on the first meeting you attended. Looking to build up the CV by getting some of my work published in the society newsletter.' Craig scratched his head and allowed a young female student to pass by, much to Karthik's annoyance.

'What do you want me to do with this?'

'Read it, you'll see why. Remember POV – point of view.'

'POV?'

'You are in it. If you want me to remove anything, you have twenty four hours.' Craig grinned suddenly., then sped off, merging with the stream of hungry students trying to get into the cafeteria.

It took an age for to pay for his food and, by the time that he was ready to eat it, the sheets of writing were splattered with oily blobs from Karthik's lunch. He sat down in one of the corner seats, reviewing them all the same.

"Initially reluctant, Karthik accepted the invitation to attend a meeting of the Harvard Society for Transhumanist Theory (HSTT) by the persistence of Craig, his best friend and academic equal.

Max More, the guest speaker…"

That needs editing – a lot of editing.

"… was responsible for having created a great deal of the language now in use when discussing transhumanism. Max pioneered a specific vocabulary; one which has allowed clear communication of the philosophy and its underlying ideology. His work has helped to transform an abstract philosophy into an active doctrine."

Karthik nodded, engrossed.

"After the talk Karthik cornered Max. He congratulated the esteemed speaker on his ideas but wanted to point out a few flaws in his overall argument. The monopoly of Max's valuable time caused Aatif Bashim, secretary of the society, to physically pull Karthik away."

That is not going into print. It makes me look bad. You wait 'til I catch up with you Craig. No wonder you ran off.

"… Max appreciated the respite, saying that it had been quite a while since he had experienced such an ferocious attack on his ideas. He asked Aatif for the name of his opponent.

Max commented: 'Something about that young man reminds me of my own early days – when I was passionate and stubborn.' He continued: 'That young man will go far!'

The meeting was a resounding success – Karthik enjoyed himself and left feeling inspired. His only disappointment: not getting to the bottom of where Max stood on the role of consciousness in evolution. Karthik concluded that Max still has a long way to go before his arguments are watertight."

I sound like a pompous, conceited academic. This whole thing focuses on me. Craig is not a journalist. Yet something about the piece made Karthik smile.

Returning to his food, he considered his editing duties.

WEDNESDAY 15TH JANUARY 1997 (BM, EWA, R)

Meticulous planning; every detail matters; a significant occasion. Kelly looked at her work and smiled confidently.

The table was almost ready, one more plate needed organising.

Each place setting was marked by one small drinking glass with exactly an inch of clear liquid in it. In front of each glass lay a heap of coloured shapes, the size and colours of M&M's – blue, green, red and yellow. The same number in each pile, Kelly neatly arranged them in the shape of a smiley face on the white paper plates.

Seven places in all, each plate representing a three-year period.

The photo albums were neatly laid out in the centre of the cheap glass coffee table. In chronological order, ready for viewing – to reminisce over good times and bad times.

Her life story in still images. Kelly recognised that she'd inherited the habit from her mother, who had taken pictures at any time and for any reason. The early years of her life were extensively documented – events, with names and dates on the back of the photos. Kelly continued the tradition.

She had never imagined that love would kill her. Today, Kelly would reflect on her life, as she put an end to her life.

It had just got too much. She'd had enough of the beatings – too many black eyes. *No one can help you now*; those words kept circling her, like vultures waiting for a meal.

Her abuse covered a five-year period; never reported, never included on any police statistics, a silent number. Only a few friends knew the truth, begging her to leave him. She said she could not, each time, that he needed her, that Karl needed her; poor little Karl, forever cursed with his father's last name. *The Winwoods. We could have been such a happy family.*

But everything is lost now, Kelly. And everything is going to be better soon. No more pain. And just look at all these pictures…

The third album, the one where her life suddenly began to change.

It started at the New Year's party – 1991 going into 1992, he was her first love. Back then she'd been coy and shy, wondering what he could possibly see in her. He'd seemed older, mature, even mysterious, back then. The photograph showed her in the middle of a group of friends, looking happy and very drunk, her dress was so, so pretty; this was life before Carlton. She touched the image, stoking it. Slim, dark haired, pretty bordering on beautiful. Life was good. She smiled in those days.

She had already downed the third bottle of pills, along with the shot of vodka. Oddly, she still felt okay.

Carlton, he'd been so unlike the other boys that she had known back then. She, only eighteen at the time. He'd had a job as a trained welder and, at twenty five, he was a real man. Her friends dared her to go out with him. She resisted him three times before she finally caved in, accepting his offer of a date.

What was the attraction of an older man? He was on his way somewhere, she'd guessed. He'd had a place of his own, even though it was rented – Jefferson Avenue, the low income apartments. Carlton listened to her dreams; even approved of them. He'd paid attention to her, in a way no one else had. He'd had no fixed plans of his own, instead he'd toyed with a number of possible ideas of things he wanted to do. Yes, a man with good ideas. On top of that he'd had a car; she'd been so very excited about that. So excited to ride with him in that Ford Taurus. Which boy would be able to compete with that? He'd had a history of jobs before the welding position came up, but that held his attention in a way that the other jobs had not. He was working hard. Learning how to run the shop. Going places. That's what he'd told her.

The way he'd looked at her, it got her every time. He'd been such a gentleman. She told her friends that she was happy, really, finally happy; and back then she had been. He'd paid attention to her. She'd fallen in love.

He'd started to check on her because he cared; anxious to know who she was talking to and why she was talking to other men. He'd questioned her a lot. She understood that – after all he was protecting her, watching over her.

Her parents had told her that going out with him would end badly. She'd hoped that they had been wrong – but as time passed she had come to the shocking realisation that they were right.

And she'd wept bitterly when she had found out that she was pregnant.

Friday, 13th March 1992. There was an earthquake that same day registering 6.8 on the Richter scale, leaving five hundred Turks dead. Part of her wondered if her life was over.

The thought of carrying a child filled her with fear. Instinct had told her to have an abortion. Her friends had told her that too; even her mother said it was for the best. But the rest of her family were event-Catholics, going to church at Christmas and Easter. All that had made it hard for her to cope with the thought of ending a new life. After a few months of anxiety, nature had made its decision for her. The child had kicked. There had been no turning back.

The fifth album: a record of her pregnancy. Her eyes blurred then returned to normal. Perspiration dripped down the back of her neck.

The polaroid of her sixth month knocked up; Carlton had been taken that one and it was out of focus, showing her looking strained and tired, having just come back from an ante-natal class. Carlton had refused to go, saying that he found hospitals claustrophobic and nauseating. The polaroid camera had been sitting on the table; he had picked it up spontaneously, quite unlike him.

Carlton had been uninterested in the whole affair, telling her to get rid of it right from the start. Later on, he suggested that she move in with him; to ease the stress of the situation.

1024 Jefferson place, Jefferson Avenue, Washington, Pennsylvania. A first floor apartment in a wood framed house. *Home bitter home.*

That was when she'd started to see another side of him, violent and cruel. By then, she was showing; but he persisted in telling her to get it out. During a drunken rage he'd tried to do it himself, punching her hard in the stomach. It was the first time that he'd hit her.

She blamed it on the booze – he'd lost control, that was all. He was so ashamed afterwards; so repentant that he'd cried like a baby, clinging to her legs, on his knees. 'Sorry,' he just kept saying that he was sorry. And she could tell it, from his eyes, his body language, his shaking hands – she'd thought.

Apology accepted.

Looking back she thought that this moment, this one instance of acceptance, was her biggest mistake; she'd believed him. No harm had come to the baby; there just an enormous bruise on her back from where she'd gone sailing into edge of the couch. It was just above her waist, the size of a small dinner plate. She studied it for three weeks, watching its transition through various shades of purple and green, then yellow, before it faded.

Did I think of leaving him then? No, she could not leave him because of an odd moment or two; based on what evidence? He loved her, he told her she was beautiful, he cried like a child at the very thought of her leaving. Relationships had to be worked on, and so she convinced herself that she had to you have to give it a go.

Things had seemed to slip down the rubbish chute when he'd gotten himself laid off from work. At the time Kelly had worked as a seamstress, which had taken up her day times. She'd got that job straight out of High School. In the evenings she'd worked the late shift, stacking shelves in the local five and dime. The two jobs had helped them to stay afloat. So she had coped with being pregnant and working two jobs.

She'd grown larger – it had become a struggle, coping with the hours she was expected to spend on her feet, so the stacking job went first. There was one photograph of her surrounded by the other folk from the store, they had given her such a wonderful baby shower, with touching gifts and a good wad of cash. She looked as if she was about to explode back then, her face full and pensive.

Carlton had seemed unable or unwilling to look for a new job, spending more and more time on the sofa at home, drinking away his frustration and watching soap operas. He loved telling her about the latest story lines, who was sleeping with who, and who was planning to kill who. She listened out of a sense of duty, often falling asleep as he spoke. He would wake her up by throwing water on her face, he thought it was a joke. She could still hear his deep, hysterical laughter.

Finances became tighter. Reluctant loans from her Mom and Dad had kept them afloat. Karl's imminent arrival had meant it was becoming awkward, trying to cope with the uncomfortable positions needed to work the sewing machine for long periods of time. The backache was beyond the reach of any pain medication that she was allowed to take; her productivity went downhill.

She got the sack and the little savings she did have soon dried up: rent had to be paid, as did the car payments. He could have sold the car and eventually he did, holding out to the last possible moment. He had loved that car. And as much as she hated it, they were forced to sign up for welfare.

She sat there now, amongst the albums. She'd kept Karl out of a sort of religious duty, but she had no love for him. He was an accident, unwanted, an inconvenience. She felt unable to love him, even now. And, she thought, that made her a bad person.

I'm weak. I'm pathetic. I'm inhuman. What sort of mother am I?

With her out of the picture, he would have a chance in life. They would all find out what his homelife was like. He would be free of this family. She just couldn't find it in herself to stay there and see it through, to be his mother; there was no trace there of that maternal love that she felt that she should have had for Karl. And this was was how she rationalised her suicide, glorifying its consequences.

The sixth album – the beginning of Karl's life, from day one. He'd changed so much during those first sixth months. Thankfully he'd slept well and feeding him was easy; he just guzzled everything that came his way.

The world moved in slow motion, a video on slow mode. Turning the pages took effort now and she wanted to sleep, fighting to beat the drowsiness. Determined to finish, going through the albums that recorded her increasing sense of shame.

The labour had lasted three days. In the end, forceps had pulled Karl into the world. He was born on Friday 5th February 1993 at 20.46 at the Washington D.C. Memorial hospital. Carlton did not make it to the birth. She found out later on that he had been chatting up a local bar's hostess; and the woman had allowed him to at that, because, when it came to repeat bar custom, Carlton was a loyal as loyal could be. One of Kelly's closet friends knew the woman, filling Kelly in over a pot of coffee and a lukewarm diner breakfast, some months later.

By the time that Carlton made it to the hospital, Karl had been fast asleep. Carlton glanced at him, said he looked wrinkly, then asked Kelly when she was coming home. He was hungry and – *you know it* – 'A man hasta eat!'

Selfish bastard.

Kelly still found herself cooking and cleaning with no help from Carlton. And of course he still wanted *the business*. He'd come to her one evening – cloying. She had declined.

A foolish move. Indeed, he had hit her twice. The second time that she declined, he hit her two more times and punched her in the chest. She'd hardly been able to breathe for a full minute.

Each refusal summoned up more force and increased the number of times he would punch her, all in proportion to his growing rage. Finally, she agreed, and the stitches did not hold; she'd ended up having to go to the hospital – *to be repaired*.

This had marked, for her, the unofficial beginning of the end of their relationship.

Carlton could not look after him. Kelly dreamed of a loving family that would take Karl in and lavish him with love in a way she could not. That was why she had planned it so carefully. Karl was asleep, taking his afternoon nap; her neighbour would come round and find her dead around the time that she had scheduled, just Karl would just be waking up.

Carlton's struggle with liquor plagued much of their son's early years. The frequent shouting, the violence, the insults and the screaming rows had become a normal part of life. He experienced the world through innocent eyes, but he was not exempt from the violence. On some occasions she'd stepped in to take punches that were meant for him.

Kelly dreaded to think about what might happen to Karl in her absence; she could only picture the fruit of Carlton's annoyance. But all these things she had seen before: the fresh bruise, the grazed elbow or knee, marks determined by whether Karl had fallen down with the blows or had been thrown into a cupboard or door; the frequent bed wetting. She'd hid that in particular from Carlton. He would have been furious, punishing Karl cruelly. She had been unable to prevent the rest though.

She'll find him. They'll all look into it. They'll take him off Carlton. Karl will be better off in care… away from me – away from his daddy.

She'd thought about every possible angle. Mrs Stevens – Doreen – was as reliable as clockwork, she often helped out when Kelly got part time work covering last minute absences at the *Five and Dime*. Doreen had four grown up children; they'd left home, leaving her with her miserable husband, Jeffrey. Still, he allowed her to look after Karl without too much fuss. Doreen knew how to quieten her husband. Her visits always brought with them a bag of goodies. She was a kind woman. Today, she should still be able to make the journey, despite the appalling weather.

Carlton checked Kelly's purse on a regular basis, scrutinising her receipts, checking the numbers on her phone, looking for any evidence of a threat from outside. He would not tolerate other men; anyone who looked at her while they were out together was apt to be sworn at or worse. There had been fist fights over things as simple as a glance. Kelly had to be smart then, she had another phone that she kept in her hiding place, at the bottom of the linen basket. She would charge it up whenever Carlton fell asleep. She had saved for that phone; the lies had hurt but it had made other things possible. It had made her something more than a prisoner, outside communication became possible.

By this stage, Carlton's getting a job seemed about as likely as her appointment to the position of *Five and Dime* CEO. He had simply lost the will to look for work. Life had become a cyclical journey for him, a passage from the apartment to the liquor store and back, or, on adventurous days, to the nearest bar, depending on how far he was prepared to walk. Today was such a day. He was out – on a bar crawl. She knew that he would stick to his routine, despite the weather's being nineteen below freezing. In his a way, she thought, he was as trapped as she was.

She imagined him making the daily trip up its three steps, into the narrow green felt porch, leading to the creaking screen door that opened to reveal the peeling wooden door – a standard fit on all the properties in the low-income apartment. Clothed in his winter gear but imperious to the cold, booze coursing through his body.

Part of her knew that he was a victim of his own self-destruction. There had been good times too. Times when she had gone out with Karl and Carlton, when he had been at least a little sober. There had been fun-fairs – God knew, Carlton loved the opportunity to become a child again. He had grown up too fast, she thought. They both had. And there had been times when they had embraced that, smiled and feasted on candy floss. They had felt like a family on those occasions. The photo of them at the fairground had been taken for them by a passing stranger. They were all in it. Karl was in the middle; he would have been three at that time. Both Carlton and Karl stood there with pink floss on a stick. All of them beaming.

As long as he was sober…

If he was happy, Kelly was happy. It was funny how her happiness became bound up in his. And she knew that she was a coward. She enjoyed being with someone, anyone, and yes he was violent and aggressive, but the thought of living with an alternative was too much for her.

He often blamed her, told Kelly it was her fault, that she provoked him, pushing him to his limits. She'd believed him for so long, spending her time by trying to be the perfect partner. If she wound him up, then it was her fault. *My behaviour is my fault, so I need to change* – that thought had passed through her mind often, circling like a scratched record. She had fallen for the same trick so many times.

I'm a fool.

A fool.

It was getting harder to breathe, the air seemed globular, each movement taking longer.

Today she could afford to face the brutal truth.

Everyone else had seen it coming – except her.

When they had a fight or row it was horrible. He would sulk and not talk, leaving her to do the making up. Sometimes he would buy her gifts – flowers or chocolates – as little tokens of his affection; then he would claim that he did everything for her, when in fact he did next to nothing.

And he told her that he loved her – after every punch.

He told her that he loved her – as every bruise went through its rainbow spectrum.

He told her that he loved her – she'd heard the words so many times and she still believed.

But today she'd stopped caring to. What did it matter? Today was not really about her life. It was about leaving it all behind. About freeing her son.

Kelly closed the seventh album. On this occasion she broke the pattern, deciding to take the pills after looking through it; leaving the images in her mind as she faded out of consciousness. She was feeling weak now – and so sleepy. Her sight stayed blurred, her thoughts became less coherent. It was pleasant. *I'm doing good.*

She swallowed her last set of pills, swigging them down with the final inch of vodka.

Gulping.

It felt right. *I'm doing good.*

+++

Six rings, then the answer machine switched on.

'Hello this is Kelly and Carlton's place. Sorry we can't take your call at the moment. If you would like to leave your name and number and a short message after the bleep then one of us will get back to you. Have a nice day!'

The bleep lasted two seconds.

'Oh, hello Kelly, this is Mrs Stevens. I am sorry but I am not going to be able to look after Karl this evening. Jeffrey's had an accident at work, so I am going straight to the hospital. I hope you can find someone else. Sorry to let you down at such short notice. Give me a call later.'

The answer machine clicked several times, the tape whirled as the message was saved. Waiting for retrieval.

+++

Karl found the body.

He was three, but his fourth birthday was only a few weeks away. He thought mommy was playing a game. He'd woken up to a quiet house and had gone looking for her. Karl kept asking her to get up yet she lay there on the sofa. Now he was getting angry. He was hungry and his daddy often talked about being hungry when mommy was making food, so he copied his voice. Karl mimicking his daddy, it was all part of the game. He thought that mommy would laugh with him, the way she often did when daddy was not around.

She did not get up.

He kept shaking her body and calling her name. She did not answer.

He promised to stop wetting the bed and to be a very good boy all the time. Still no response. Karl began to cry, sobbing gently at first before wailing at the top of his voice.

+++

Carlton found him asleep clinging to the body in an exhausted and distressed state when he returned home, drunk, around 9.30pm. Kelly had been dead for nearly four hours.

He prised Karl from the cooling dead body; it was already stiffening with early rigor mortis. In panic, he rang the police and in the most coherent manner he could manage informed the operator that his partner was unconscious.

When questioned about her breathing, he told the operator he did not know; he was unable to follow the instructions he was being given over the phone. The operator immediately dispatched an ambulance, before trying to talk him through mouth-to-mouth resuscitation.

Charlton was far too drunk to cope with such a complex procedure.

+++

Everyone saw the end of the relationship coming but no one pictured it like this. The community was left shaking. There were guilty conversations, people wishing that they had done more or that they had called the local patrol unit when they first heard the shouting or the screaming instead of ignoring it, pacifying themselves, telling themselves that the two were nothing more than a young couple, working things out in their relationship.

Officer MaCahon had heard it all before. This area one of the many on the red list at the precinct. Murders too frequent, rapes off the scale. A place where poverty and violence met and cohabited. Hidden dark resentments became eruptions of senseless violence, unresolved issues that seemed to pass from one generation to the next, like a genetic virus. Folk dwelling with perceived slights, imagined or otherwise alongside the river of deprivation.

He hated his job, hated the area. The drudgery of the door-to-door relationship post-mortem in the freezing cold, during of one of the worst winters on record. His leaky shoes added to his woes, he ordered new ones but his shoe size meant it would take at least two weeks to have them custom made – *big feet, who needs them?*

Part of him wished he listened to his wife and moved back to Connecticut. At least they were partially civilised there… Or they were when he was a boy. Why did he have to deal with second rate citizens? Retirement was still another fifteen years away.

Despite the stresses of her family life, Kelly smiled a lot and she seemed to be coping well. The same information kept coming up. He and two other rookie officers were selected to carry out the information gathering exercise – dialogue on the doorstep.

Murder on the block – it could have been pulp fiction or a bad B movie. Shocked, strained expressions, tears and horror-etched lines on faces along with deep remorse. The community discovering the truth behind the smile. Shame turned Kelly into an exceptional actress, successfully hiding her pain behind a mask of joy. It grieved him to think of her suffering.

Seated back at the Washington precinct he and the investigation team worked under a heavy atmosphere. It lingered over their busy office as they typed out the pages of endless notes. Officer MaCahon's shift finished at 7pm, it was only 5.20pm.

He could speak on behalf of the whole team, for all of them this was another statistic, another case. Everyone suspected but no one did anything. No one wanted to get involved.

If she was the only case that would be bad enough, but there were many Kellys. They knew that. Everyone did. A check through the records would confirm this. She was simply the latest, and no doubt, would not be the last.

He hoped his wife had gone for dinner beef stew as her chilli… Well, it could take the lining off a cow's stomach.

7pm, the end of his shift, seemed a long way off.

THURSDAY 16TH JANUARY 1997 (BM, EWA, R, WD)

Philomena hated interviewing suspects. Despite her training in psychology, she often found that gut instinct worked just fine. After three years on the job, working with cases of domestic violence, the pain did not go away. Instead, it seemed to accumulate over time as she heard the intimate details of tragedy after tragedy. Her husband had become her sounding board, helping her to cope with the continuous stress. He seemed to exist in stark contrast to the brutes that sat in front of her daily.

Carlton was a brute.

He stood around six feet tall, and had short brown hair and a thin face with deep set eyes. His pale skin stretched over a thin frame. Maybe he had been attractive once, but now just looked tired and worried. According to his file he was thirty. He had committed a few minor offences as a teenager but they were limited to petty theft and the use of soft drugs.

She watched him through the glass panel in the door; he was waiting, his head down, wiping his forehead every few minutes, his sweaty brow glistening. She checked her watch – it was time. Steeling herself, she pushed open the door.

He looked up as she entered the interview room.

'Hello Carlton, I am Philomena, chief investigation officer on this case.'

She did not offer him any pleasantries as she sat down in the chair opposite him. The recording devices were set up.

'Let's start with the part when you got home. What happened?' He made her skin itch, she wanted to slap him across his face.

'When I came in she was on the floor. The kid ah, Karl... Well, he was all over her. Like a limpet,' his voice seemed to be trailing away as he relived the scene.

'What happened next Carlton?'

'I think I walked over and told him to get up. He was fast asleep, looking really tired. I pulled him off her... He looked scared. I guess he woke up at the same time.' He acted out the scene with his hands, his voice was a little sinister, accompanied by intense, jerky movements.

'Then what did you do next?' She felt a growing sense of irritation creep through her as she looked at this pathetic specimen of manhood. She'd seen the pictures of the body covered in marks, the evidence of past beatings and frequent assaults.

'I tried shaking her, calling her... she didn't get up. Other times...' he stopped. His eyes looked scared. He stumbled with is words, 'I mean when I have found her like...' confused hand movements matched the words.

'You mean that you have found her unconscious before?' Philomena had no intention of making this easy for him.

'Yes.'

'Why was this?' She moved in closer, her face observing every detail.

'She sometimes... fell over.' He looked down at the desk, drumming his fingers on the surface.

The eruption inside her chest told her that he'd caused the falls. Still, she needed to focus on the specifics of this event.

'What did you do next?

'I called 911 and spoke to the operator.'

'Did you check her body, to see if she was unconscious or breathing?' He looked confused, his blinking indicated that he'd had no clue as to what was going on.

'I tried shaking her and calling her name. Nothing. The operator told me to do mouth to mouth resuscitation. It was difficult, I couldn't do much. I was shaking. Kelly was gone. My Kelly was gone.' Several tears rolled out of his eyes and his words became choked. His whole frame trembled.

I wonder if that is out of compassion or self-pity. *You pathetic lump of mankind.*

'Carlton,' he looked up at her, still crying. 'Do you have any idea why Kelly would take her own life?' *This would be interesting, did he know the truth or would he try and hide it, conceal it.*

'I have… no idea. We were very happy and Karl… The kid made us complete.' The twitch in his right eye gave his game away. A complete lie. She decided to push deeper.

'Have you ever,' she hesitated, 'hurt Kelly in anyway?'

His lower lip wobbled, he tugged on his right ear. 'No, never would, never could. I love Kelly.' His right hand waved a little as he spoke. His expression was one of utter sincerity but she had seen this too often not to know exactly what was going on.

'There were a number of marks and bruises on her body, some old,' she took in a deep breathe, 'some more recent. Did you,' she moved in even closer, pointing in his face, 'hit Kelly, Carlton?'

Now he was scared. Almost convulsing, his shoulders shook like a plate of jello. 'I… No… No! I said it… I said I would never hit Kelly.'

Philomena leaned back and sighed deeply. No, he may not have rammed the pills down her throat, and that was what some of her colleagues had feared, but he most certainly had pushed this young woman to the brink of despair. She knew it in her gut. She'd known it all along. This was no murder. No, it was far sadder than that.

No clear evidence pointed to his having an active role in the death; but there was a whole history written across her body like a map, traces of his cruelty and violence. She was exactly as Philomena had thought, another victim of domestic violence; another suicide.

She suddenly wondered how long she could cope in this unit. Perhaps a transfer might be in order?

He was pathetic. How she despised him – and all the others like him. Weak men who preyed on women. It was a power game.

Her mind and thoughts turned to Karl.

I wonder how Tony is getting on with the little one?

+++

'Hello Karl. My name is Tony and I am a police officer.' Tony held out his hand to the terrified youngster.

They had offered him a happy meal and he shocked them by boldly insisting that a strawberry milkshake be included in the order. The food disappeared in a few moments. Now the serious work would begin.

This was the special place; the children's investigation unit. It was colourful and bright and full of secrets – a child's paradise, hidden in a police station.

Tony stood next to Karl, watching him as he sat crossed legged on the large, central rug; his tiny arms wrapped around his chest. Tony crouched down to complete the gesture.

Karl's large, sad eyes were fixed on him. The boy looked pale and he was so thin. His little hand reached up. Tony shook it and smiled warmly.

'You are a very brave boy, Karl.' His words seemed to have an instant impact on the youngster. He grinned briefly, then the lost expression returned.

'I have a very special place for you to come and see. But... it's a secret. Would you like to know a secret, Karl?' Tony widened his eyes, their eyes were level.

Karl nodded his head, his curiosity aroused.

'Come with me,' Tony crawled over to the green door with a brass handle embedded into the yellow wall. The door was only slightly taller than Karl. It was designed to work as a portal, a hidden path into a new world. It had its own sort of power, sparking the imagination of kids. It was a key to working with traumatised children.

Tony sat next to the green door, cross-legged. Karl followed him.

'Only brave children can look inside the green door.' He smiled broadly as he pointed at Karl. 'And you... a brave boy?'

'What's inside the cupboard?' Karl studied the door, looking at it from various angles.

'Would you like to see inside it?'

'Yes,' said Karl as he moved even closer to the mysterious door.

Tony grabbed the brass handle. 'When you look inside, you can choose one item and that will be yours... to keep.'

Karl stood on his tiptoes, holding his breath.

Tony pulled the door open and stood back. Karl rushed forward and gasped.

'Wow!'

Tony knew that for a three year old the contents were like an Aladdin's cave of wonder. All of the toys had been carefully picked to engage children, to enable them to act out their worst horrors – through play. Classical cuddly toys sat alongside the current favourites – Gigapets, Star Wars figures, Tamagotchi virtual pets and a Tickle Me Elmo.

'Which one would you like Karl?' Tony watched the transformation as Karl became a curious hunter, lifting and checking his prizes. To Tony's surprise Karl choose the medium sized teddy bear instead of one of the more exciting toys. Karl clutched the teddy bear to his chest, rocking it and smiling intensely.

Tony crawled over to the sitting corner where the recording equipment was concealed, hidden behind a two-way mirror. The speakers were disguised, located inside smiling flowers with giant petals. He switched the devices on.

'Come over here Karl,' the toddler ran over, his face beaming as he became acquainted with his new friend. He sat down, the teddy trapped in his arms; he was stroking the bear.

'You can even think of a name for him later.' This was the hard part – getting him to go back to that horrible memory.

'Karl, can you tell me what happened to your mommy today?'

Karl's eyes glazed over, he buried his face in teddy's head.

'Your mommy fell over, didn't she Karl? Did you find her?' Tony's heart raced. His successful work with toddlers was well known in the local police community; he had a way with children. Yet he still felt the weight of it every time. It took him back to his childhood, back to his own terror. To his abuse.

Karl spoke through the top of teddy's head, 'Mommy didn't play the statue game today. Mommy stayed still.'

Tony wondered if he knew, if he understood the gravity of the situation. *Does he know that she won't be back?*

'Did mommy always play the statue game?'

'Only when daddy's not home.' His face seemed serious, tense.

'Does daddy not like the statue game?' He had to get information out of this child.

Karl shook his head before hugging the teddy again.

'How does daddy treat mommy, could you show me using teddy.'

Karl nodded, then hugged teddy twisting his body from side to side. He then punched Teddy on the back and threw him down. Then Karl picked him up and hugged him again. He looked up at Tony.

Tony sighed heavily. As they had suspected mommy had been the reluctant victim of many of daddy's games.

Wednesday 22nd January 1997 (BM, EWA, WD, R)

It seemed to be a clear-cut case. Karl Winwood would need to be put up for adoption. He would remain in emergency foster care but in his best interest, he needed stability, care and lots of love. The police force provided sufficient evidence for social services to decide this was the best course of action.

Margaret Curzon, was responsible for compiling the final adoption request and overseeing the adoption process. She had gathered all the pieces of information, like putting together a living puzzle. It was her job; also her passion.

Children mattered, every child was unique. Life had gone wrong some and social services provided the opportunity to give them a second chance. She readily acknowledged that they did not always get it right, that they tried their best, under difficult circumstances, struggling with cuts, squabbles between the different departments and staff shortages.

Her office was a mess; she knew it, promising herself that she would do something about it when she had the time. She was thirty five and, lately, it seemed that her life was moving rapidly enough already. Her fiancé seemed determined to end her career once they were married. It was a point of vigorous discussion.

Getting married – at one time that had seemed like a faint hope. Then along came Barry Foreman. Intelligent, handsome, in a great job, everything going for him… except his race. Her parents were shocked, feeling she had strayed outside the lines of decency. After all they were middle class, decent folk; so what was she doing with a man of colour? That still needed working on.

The police wanted to press charges against the father, for neglect and child abuse. Little Karl was the only witness. He held onto the memories of his own suffering – and that of his mother. The suicide had sent the husband into a deep alcoholic spiral, according to the latest report. Now he had been diagnosed as having middling stages of liver disease. Apparently certain members of the police force felt that this was karma, that he had sown and now that it was time for him to reap. Certainly, nobody she spoke to felt sorry for him. Karl was their concern. The case officers were adamant that Karl should be given every consideration. They still paid him visits, well outside their professional remit.

You only had to spend half an hour with him, to feel the strings of your heart being plucked. He was so cute, with his angelic smile and huge eyes. Quiet yet sparky, if you managed to capture his attention. He lived in a dream world, often retreating into his own private refuge. It was not unusual for children such as he; escaping from reality. He was, however, a stickler for rules; very tidy to the point of being obsessive.

Karl's traumatic past made it difficult for some couples to feel that they could provide for him a secure and stable home. Thankfully, the Kuhlmans were on the adoption list, their personal philosophy was very impressive indeed – they were adamant about it, insisting that love could always make a difference. They lived in Oak Lawn, Dallas. That meant that Karl faced a big move. Their five unit complex would have plenty of room for him though. The photograph made the place look spacious and bright, with a generous back yard full of greenery and packed with places to play – ideal for the children. According to the application form, Brenda said the large kitchen served as a meeting point. She called it her "sanity room". Margaret smiled to herself.

Of course they had their doubts. Any adopting family would. Taking on a child was tough… an abused child, well that took a lot of guts. As Margaret read their file for the third time, she felt that they were the right couple for Karl. Of course she could offer them advice and support on the challenge that Karl would face. With the right kind of help maybe they could make a difference in his fractured life.

The initial steps were in place, the steam roller of adoption had its engine revved up. Margaret hoped this one would work out.

WEDNESDAY 12TH MARCH 1997 (BM, EWA, R)

'Being part of HSTT has changed my life.'

Charles Ferrell nodded, nudging Karthik. 'Well you've certainly changed.' He scratched his beard before continuing, 'Do you think that this is just a phase, or is this a serious discussion for the future? What about society – are we ready for the issues and ethics that go along with the transition?

The campus was busy with students, the academic year in full swing.. Conversations flowed back and forth, half overheard, half ignored. Both of them stood in the forecourt, leaning against a marble statue of one of the founders.

Loneliness had been less of a companion lately and Karthik, enjoyed the company of his fellow society members. Getting involved had forced him into the public arena and, to his great surprise, he actually enjoyed it. Shyness had held him back without him being aware of its restricting effect. The twins of loneliness and shyness cooperating and assisting each other in keeping him confined. Charles had helped change all of this. Karthik felt and maintained a deep sense of gratitude towards him, realising his first assessment had been wrong, now he really liked Charles.

Indeed, his insistent presence and rapid progress within the organisation concluded in his election to its presidency. He still remembered how he had met and debated with Charles at one of the early meetings, he being a freshman at the time. Charles seemed to be struggling in his sophomore year.

Although they had attended some common classes, Karthik had found Charles to be aloof at first and, in his opinion, the man displayed a lack of academic ability as well as being more than a little wealth minded. The combination of the three had seemed particularly limiting when they first met.

Karthik used the term *wealth minded* to describe what he thought to be a distinctly American illness; a mental condition delivered to those born into affluent families, people with personal fortunes responsible for the creation of false senses of entitlement.

But their shared interest in transhumanism soon changed his first impression. Charles openly displayed kindness and a genuine care towards others, always trying to bring out the best in people. Karthik had personal experience of this positive emotional atmosphere. He boldly evangelised countless people clearly stating that Charles helped him to open up to others; becoming his social mentor.

Totally ignoring his questions Karthik continued, 'So what will you do after Harvard?' He looked into the man's eyes, unusually comfortable with the intimacy.

'I'm thinking of going… well, going into business,' Charles pondered.

Karthik thought Charles' dark brown locks needed a cut. As a student he could get away with that. Once he entered the business world his whole appearance would need grooming. By the looks of things he had not shaved for at least four months, the beard and moustache were still a little pubescent, but at least they were the same shade as the rest of his hair.

All the same, it was a very uncouth look. One adopted by so many of the wealth minded on campus. *You would never see me looking so scruffy. People in the West so rarely consider their formal appearance.*

'Your own, or one of your father's companies?'

'Not sure, still early days.' Charles was distracted; a young lady had walked by them, turning around to smile at him. In contrast, the look she gave Karthik was menacing and accusing. She continued walking; her long brown hair was tied in a braid, swaying gently.

'How do you do that?' Karthik asked, envious of Charles, but worried by the strange way that the woman had responded to him. *Does she think I'm competition?*

'Do what?' Charles seemed genuinely unaware of his magnetism when it came to women.

'Never mind. Anyway, look, I am expecting a call from home so I'll have to go, but I will also have to catch up with you sometime soon. You owe me for helping you with that English assignment.'

Charles blushed, 'Oh yeah. Maybe a meal…'

'I'll let you know.' Karthik shook his hand and moved off towards the bus stop, still mystified by the evil eye that young woman had given him.

WEDNESDAY 27TH MAY 1998 (BM, EWA, R)

The news.

Karthik's sense of security and confidence had been brutally torn from his grasp. Numb, cold and exhausted; he was struggling to hold on to any purpose, fighting with a desire to die.

His beloved Mummy had died.

Karthik wondered why the counsellor had told him, rather than his father; otherwise, his mind remained blank as he walked back to his room. With the door firmly, closed the first wave of sobbing hit. Followed by another and another. Breathing became difficult, his vision blurred by a film of tears that would not stop. The pull on his abdomen, the cramps in his legs; they all weakened him further.

He collapsed on the floor, tasting the saltiness of his tears, his mouth closed yet wanting to scream. He sobbed in intense, gut-wrenching moans.

Somehow, he summoned enough strength to make the call. His father answered after three rings. They spoke for fifteen minutes. Prior to the call he believed his capacity for sorrow had been reached, but the blip that marked the end of the call opened up another level of agony.

Desperately, he tried to piece together all that he had just heard. Only parts of it and made any sense.

Sweeti, Mummy, had been buried three weeks ago. She'd died on Friday 15th May, in the middle of his exam period. He had been hit once by the counsellor, and now his father had taken up a sledge hammer and continued the act of violence.

Praveen, his protector and provider, must have taken the executive decision not to inform Karthik of his mother's illness and death.

Totally unforgiveable.

As his breathing became regular, more of the information made sense. His mother's illness had not been sudden. *Why did no one tell me?* For a brief moment he felt hatred towards his mother: *Why did she not tell me? Why did Mummy go along with this act of betrayal? If she had phoned me… I would have been there.*

None of this made any sense. His right temple throbbed at the pace of his pulse.

Ovarian cancer. The illness had remained a secret, concealed by Sweeti until she could no longer cope with the pain. His father had sounded apologetic as he disclosed the devastating, hidden history. The diagnosis had proved to be a death sentence; to her hope no longer existed.

More tears erupted from his eyes. *Why was my love not enough Mummy?* The spasmodic throbbing sensation, his right eye twitched.

Mummy, dear Mummy. She stood, powerless, as the disease ravaged through her body, like a raging inferno consuming a tinder-dry twig.

From diagnosis to death in less than six weeks. Images swirled around Karthik's mind, skeletal forms appearing in different rooms in the family house while the rest of the tormented family watched helplessly. Karthik shuddered: a large grey skeletal form stepped forward from his subconscious, gloating.

Go away!

The image dissolved.

Father's voice sounded as if he were choking as he disclosed the final blow: the disease had spread to her brain.

Karthik wished his hearing had been switched off at that precise point. The malevolent invader triumphed over her desire to live. A parasitic form celebrating the devastation of the human body – the image imprinted itself in his memory; now he would have to live with his own personal haunting.

Getting through the last few days of term became an obsession, Karthik's mind and body functioned in automatic mode. The counsellor called round and offered bereavement therapy but Karthik refused his gestures of sympathy, vigorously asking him to leave as he wanted to be alone.

The struggle with intense feelings of guilt and regret drained him mentally and physically. Whenever he stopped being busy, accusing thoughts bombarded him, accompanied by haunting images of her emaciation.

Such torment was further intensified by the worst shame of all: he had been the only family member absent at her death, the only child missing at her funeral.

Bitterness.

I feel so betrayed.

He knew he was unable to do nothing about it. That truth pierced Karthik, twisting into his intestines like a corkscrew.

A decision had been made: to hide the impending death from Karthik, as his final exams were so close.

This rationale kept replaying in front of his eyes like a BBC news bulletin; the taste of bitter lemon filled his mouth each time he thought about it, he had to resist the nausea it induced.

How can my own father do this to me?

Logically, it made sense.

Praveen desired the best for his son.

Karthik knew this, but it was not a good enough excuse.

+++

Subsequent calls led to more information. Justification made his father sound cold, calculating – as if he were on trial and needed to give clear evidence to the jury as he sat as the accused. Karthik found it difficult not to mock his father's feeble attempt to explain the decision.

He was recognised as one of the best students in the history of the Philosophy department. Such news would have distracted him; he could not have helped his mother.

Seeing his father so openly exposed made Karthik question: *why did Mummy stay with you?* He suspected the answer without being told: the children, for the sake of the children. Tied into the cultural norm for women, she made a choice to continue to suffer, in silence – for a long time, emotionally, but now he knew of the physical side of her agony.

Every time he went over the situation he came to the same conclusion. His father lacked emotional intelligence. A brilliant business mind without a doubt, yet failing as the head of the a family, abdicating his role as defender and encourager.

Heaviness cloaked Karthik. He had no appetite and found it difficult be around those of his friends who remained on campus. It was summer recess. Families were assembling, getting ready for holidays, looking forward to being together.

I have been forsaken.

FRIDAY 29TH MAY 1998 (BM)

Not a particularly inspiring book, but it gave him something to think about.

Karthik sat, relaxed, his right ankle resting on his left knee. He turned the page, deciding that he did not agree with the arguments; there were too many flaws in the underlying assumptions. He had already read the first fifty pages.

Foucault had clear ideas about authority, institution, and power structures. Strong leadership and ruling from a position of knowledge and understanding. That was so obvious. How had the author missed, even denied, the influence of Nietzsche, Wittgenstein, Hume, Schopenhauer? Had their philosophies not formed the foundation of contemporary thinking?

He slammed it shut and threw it onto the bed. *Rubbish, weak academic work. Pathetic! A child of ten might have made a better effort.* 'Call yourself an academic!' The book stayed silent.

The cup of coffee grew cold. The lights were dimming; early evening in Manhattan. Today, the traffic seemed quiet; those who were able had already left the city had. He would be joining the departure in a matter of days.

The holiday would mean meeting with his father. The thought of that stirred up the simmering hatred that always lay just below the surface. He lost all sense of focus, yielding to the sensation of heat and destruction. How bitter it tasted, yet how energising it felt. *My father and his issues…*

The accelerated heart rate seemed strange, he had never experienced that effect when meditating on his father. The change in air pressure… also strange. The two combined phenomena distracted him from his negative and consuming contemplation.

Then the air crackled, charged with static electricity. Energy, unfamiliar energy.

Karthik detected the precise moment at which the presence came into the room. The hairs on the back of his neck stood up, a cool breeze passed by his face. Immediately his racing heart beat increased second by second till it had doubled its normal rate. A sense of heaviness came along with an energy surge. It felt unnerving, strange and internal. He had been thinking about his father – *had that caused this?* That possible link brought no comfort to him; the familiar hate fuelled fire was alive in his stomach. Now it raced up his gullet and singed his throat. Yet this was something else…

The wave approached him, centimetre by centimetre. It stood close by, perhaps a hand's reach away. It shifted and loomed over his head, a cloud of shimmering power, a raincloud of energy. Then it descended and rested upon his head, like a crown, then passed through his skull. At that precise moment he saw a spiral of colour, purple and blue spinning round and round inside his head. It seemed to be confined to his skull, then broke free diffusing through bone, muscle and skin.

The colours awakened all of his senses; his hearing, sight, smell, taste and touch heightened, and he became aware of another dimension to his existence. Something different, not normally tangible. And now, here and today, it opened up in front of him. He gasped with wonder as the membranes of reality parted, opening like the petals of a lotus flower. A strange beauty.

Spiritual, this was spiritual.

He had no point of reference, nothing with which to compare this experience. Like a map without a compass; he had no idea to how to navigate it, nor how to interpret all the sensations that he was struggling with. Karthik was bewildered and afraid. The creeping sense of dread began somewhere below him. It rose up from around his knees and moved through his body in waves, peaking at his neck bursting into his brain before dissipating. It was as if he were being covered with waters that threatened to take his very life.

He could feel the rippling of muscles beneath his skin while goose bumps covering his entire body. A sheet of movement, back and forth, up and down, repeatedly.

The first sound – *metallic*. A slow clanging tone. Rhythmic and slow: sonorous. The sound you would make if you took two hollow metal tubes and hit them against another – echoing and dull. His normal vision now overlaid by a strange mist – a thick, grey condensation that shimmered. As if it was being blown by some invisible wind; thick then thin, shifting. He could not make out any details. The musty damp smell. It sat in his nostrils – dense and static. Overexciting his olfactory system till he no longer registered the odour. His tongue detected an acidic taste, something combined with metal – sharp, citric and stomach churning.

After a few minutes the sensations subsided. The intensity diminishing, the goose bumps remained. As if a cloak of dread lifted. The energy cloud seemed to hesitate. He had a sense of being watched, even assessed. Like when you are making your mind up between a latte or a cappuccino.

A decision was made, the cloud began to dissipate, then passed through the walls.

It departed… the first visitation.

Monday 1st June 1998 (BM)

Less nerve-wracking than the first time, more visually detailed than the second; the third meeting changed everything.

He heard the voice. It spoke his name, slowly, letter by letter, spelling it out.

K… a… r… t… h… i… k…

Intelligence, this energy source possessed intelligence. The idea shocked and excited Karthik. He had never experienced anything like this. It repeated his name.

'Karthik.' Glancing down, he noticed that his fingers were clenching and unclenching of their own accord. He gulped dryly.

So do I reply?

He sat on the edge of his neatly made bed; it was mid-afternoon, in his own room, in his own home. An informal meeting then. He decided to remain silent, waiting. A digit flitted past his open eyes, slid into his peripheral view, passed from right to left and then vanished.

The number three – clear and in three dimensions, bright red; blood red.

The dry sensation in his mouth, the ripples on the back of his hands, the throb of the veins in his neck; the increasingly familiar sensations that accompanied these encounters. The shaking had stopped now, so had the desire to empty his bladder. He closed both eyes, concentrating, blotting out the visual input, trying to focus on the voice.

'Karthik.' The sound emanated from inside his head. He opened his eyes and then shut them again.

Nothing. The sense of frustration grew and replaced his excitement.

Somehow he enjoyed the meetings, but he could not predict when they would happen. So far they had been confined to times when he was alone in his room. *What vocabulary could be used to describe this?* As part of his studies he had investigated the role of the supernatural in inspiration. You could not call him a novice. The problem – it was happening to him, not to somebody else. *But why?*

Some spiritual encounters were inspired by drugs, others had guides, others ecstatic utterances. He knew all of the methods of engagement. But he didn't have to do anything except sit in his room, alone.

Why me? Why now? A chance to access the consciousness of the universe? Perhaps a chance to experience, even to hold, the hidden wisdom that waited for those who were brave enough to take the leap of faith? His lifelong hunger for knowledge had been served hor d'euovres and now he wanted more – much more. Blavatsky had given credit to her guide, acknowledging that he had allowed her access to unknown realms of wisdom. Her whole being had blossomed. What would he give for an opportunity like that?

Emotionally drained, the toil of grief and the rage against his father had taken its toll. Yet after each experience he felt energised, alive. Now nothing. He was alone again.

He was meant to be flying home tomorrow; a first-class seat was already booked. He did not relish his first face to face meeting with his father and the rest of the family since her departure. The only positive angle was his return to the States to complete his course. It would only be for a short time.

Charles had called to express his sympathy. He departed for Europe in a few days – off on a family holiday. Karthik received his words, grateful for the fact that he had stayed in touch, glad to have someone with whom to share his heavy load.

Charles was a genuinely good man. Suddenly, Karthik experienced a rush of sentiment. He gulped it back and refined it, refocusing. *I'm glad he is my friend.* He lay down on the bed, staring at the cream ceiling. Something here was beyond his control. He needed to be in control. He closed his eyes – the digit appeared again.

But no voice.

Wednesday 3rd June 1998 (BM, EWA, R)

Jayagi rubbed her hand across her abdomen. The baby was kicking again.

It would be good to see Karthik again. She loved all of her brothers but he was her favourite. His loving nature and kind words were always encouraging.

Her mother's touch could be seen in every part of this place – it had been their playroom. The colourful fabrics, the silk cushions, the embroidered table cloths, the hand-woven cream rug and the ornaments; all items bought by Father as he travelled all over the world. He had invited Mother many times.

Her home, her palace.

Nothing had changed since her death. Father had insisted that everything remain the same. A living memorial of his wife. Her touch, her style and her spirit kept alive – a constant reminder of his wife. He hardly spoke of her, yet his eyes poured out his pain and deep sadness. Business as usual.

Karthik's heart would be heavy. Father had told her that he had responded badly to the news of mother's death and the fact that he had not been told. *He should have been told.* It was complicated but she had followed his instructions, even though her heart disagreed with them.

Her husband told her that she had done the right thing. She knew how much mother loved Karthik and how he loved her back. They were close, so close. In some ways she felt jealous of that bond. Mother and daughter should naturally be intimate, but somehow he had managed to gain a special place in her heart; one that no other member of the family had been able to access.

Not even me.

She dreaded the questions that would be asked. If she told the truth, she would be considered part of the conspiracy. If she lied, her brother would be left without key pieces of the puzzle.

I will speak to Father and ask him for advice. She glanced at the clock. *16.00...* Karthik would be at the house within the next two hours, depending on the traffic.

She rose up slowly, holding her back. The ache was deep and persistent. She paused. Her swollen abdomen hid her feet from view. *This one will be a cricketer, not like his sister.* She rested her hand on the bulge, rubbing it in small circles. The coolness of the room was kind to her. It was a welcome distraction from the local weather, at least. Here, the temperature was always under control. Even during power cuts, there were generators. *Control.* Father insisted on it.

+++

'Sister!'

Jayagi could hear him from the steps of the house, even before he came into view.

'Karthik, dear Karthik.' Jayagi wanted to run to him, hug him, to kiss him. She held back, waiting for him to leap up the steps and embrace her.

'My dear, dear sister.' His tears fell on her neck. She sensed his whole body tense, then relax.

'Karthik, Karthik, I've missed you. We all have.' They remained entwined. He wept. She held him, feeling her own tears rolling down her cheeks.

Jayagi watched as the driver removed the luggage from the back of the Mercedes. 'Madam, where would you have me to take the luggage?'

'Take his bags to his room.' She held onto her brother, gently swaying with him. Rocking him like a child, the way she comforted her daughter. The way their mother had rocked them as them as children. She stepped sideways to allow the laden servant to pass by, still embracing Karthik. The driver lumbered through the doorway, into the hall, a suitcase in each hand.

'Shall we go inside?' She did not want to hurry the moment, but being in that position made her back ache. He needed time. This meeting would not be easy. Heaviness crept all over her heart.

He let go first, then stepped back. His eyes were bloodshot, pained and dim. His face seemed much thinner than she had remembered. His beard and moustache were still trimmed though, and in full colour. 'How are you, my brother?' She took his hands, still inspecting him.

'Better, now that I've have seen you, thank you.' The gentle tone of his voice was normal – *but the slow rhythm of his words; it's not like him.* His hands were trembling. He wiped his eyes, forcing a smile. 'I'm tired and hungry.'

'Let's sort that out immediately. We can chat later.' She patted his hand, and led him through the expansive doorway, into the foyer-hall. 'Dalaja,' she shouted. No response. 'Dalaja!'

'Yes Ma.' The female voice proceeded from one of the rooms followed by the appearance of a thin young girl. She wiped her hands on her apron, her face flustered. She curtseyed.

'My brother would like something to eat. What will you have Karthik? Your favourite? Or have your tastes changed since the days of peanut butter and salad cream?' She narrowed her eyes. He blushed, she laughed. 'I still remember.'

'Do you have any cottage cheese?' The girl looked mystified, shaking her head. 'What about chick peas and pitta bread, with some salad?'

'Yes sir. And to drink?' She did not look up as she spoke to his shoes.

'Water, sparkling water; thank you Dalaja.'

Jayagi noted how he looked right into the servant's face. She did not return the gaze. Dalaja curtseyed again and scurried away.

'Peanut butter and salad cream?' Karthik leaned his head to one side, squinting with one eye.

'Yes Karthik. And that,' she pointed at him, 'is the way you used to position your head as a boy.'

He straightened his head as if to deny the accusation. 'I don't—'

'Well I do. Big sisters always remember.' She grabbed his hand, pulling him towards the living room.

+++

'Why should I ask Father?'

She shuddered, alarmed by his loud voice. The words were sharp, piercing. 'You need to talk to him.'

'What on earth is going on in this family, eh?'

He stood up from the sofa, and turned to look at her. She squirmed on the cushions that were supposed to make her comfortable. 'You sound as if you are not part of it.' Jayagi glanced at him then turned away.

'Sometimes… Sometimes I wonder if I am a part of it.'

Jayagi grasped. *He's trying to wound me with his words.* She shook her head as if she was attempting to dislodge the offensive words. 'Karthik, that was horrible.'

Karthik knelt, tenderly taking her hand in his, his voice becoming calm again. 'I cannot tell you the pain I have suffered over this matter.'

'We have all suffered.' She closed her eyes, 'You were not here when she died, you did not see the suffering that Mother went through.'

He remained silent. His grip tightened. 'Karthik, you're hurting me.'

Karthik dropped her hand then stood up. He paused, then strode towards the door. 'Where are you going? We have—'

'I have nothing more to say to you.'

'Karthi—' She saw his expression and the plea remained in her throat.

'I'll be in my room.' Karthik's voice trailed behind him.

He could hear her wrenching sobs as he walked up the stairs. So could the rest of the house. Father would have a lot of explaining to do.

+++

Three gentle raps on the door.

'Yes,' Karthik raised himself resting on his elbows, the cotton sheets cool against his skin.

'May I come in?' Jayagi's voice unsure, hesitant.

'Yes,' Karthik softened his tone, 'Come in.' The door creaked as it opened, Jayagi's face appeared.

'Father is downstairs and he wants to see you.' Their eyes met.

'Jayagi, wait.' Her head remained in view. He sat up, 'I'm sorry for the way I spoke to you earlier. You did not deserve to be spoken to like that.' Karthik swivelled his legs off the bed, placing them on the cold, tiled floor.

'I know that you are upset—'

'Not with you. With *him*.' He spat the words out. Jayagi just stared, her mouth closed. He saw her fear. 'Look... I will be down shortly.' He pushed his feet into the leather slippers, stretched his back and yawned.

'Yes Karthik,' Jayagi whispered. The door closed quietly.

Karthik adopted the correct posture; he became formal and emotionless. This was the moment he had been thinking about since the day he had spoken to his father. The confrontation. The opening of closed books. The resolution. Part of him struggled. He was scared. As a child he had always followed the rules, fulfilled cultural expectations. Knowing his place, he had stayed within the boundaries of normality. Watching his friends with their fathers had filled him with simmering envy, though he had ever told anyone as much. He had avoided the truth all these year , denying that his sense of personal worth vanished every time he spoke to his father.

Their roles were founded on a deep sense of inequality. He felt like a slave boy before his master, his father cruel and jaded. What he wanted and desired relied on open communication – to be himself and share life with his father. *But no. He would only think me westernised if I were to express my real feelings.* All his life he had longed to hear his father say that he was proud of him. Never. Not even once had such words emanated from his father's lips. Karthik breathed deeply, exhaling slowly. *His time has come.*

+++

He knocked on the living room door.

'Enter.' The voice was stern, commanding. He breathed in then grasped the gilt door handle. The dull thudding in his chest increased.

Father sat on the sofa. Just a few hours ago it had been the battlefield between Karthik and Jayagi. Slouched shoulders, the shiny bald crown exposed – so sad. On seeing Karthik he stood, extending his hands.

'My son, my brilliant son.'

A sheet of ice descended in front of Karthik. He noted the tired eyes, extra lines etched into his skin – a look of defeat. Truthfully, he had aged.

Badly. He counted every step as he moved towards his father. The ice sheet thickened and he felt its coldness in his hands, it spread up both arms, towards his heart. He extended his right hand, a human automaton.

'Hello Father.' The words were mechanical. Hands met and interlocked. As soon as his father let go, Karthik pulled his hand away. He remained standing.

'Sit down son.' He gestured to the adjacent easy chair. 'You look tired, how was your journey?'

You look tired as well. Praveen Kothaka, business man and part-time father.

Karthik rested his hands on either side of the chair as he sat down, resting his eyes on his father's feet.

'My flight was fine, sir. Everything was very precise, on time,' he licked his lips, glancing into his father's face. That bald head was furrowed, weary. It was a gift from their ancestors; one that Karthik felt destined to inherit. The greyish tone beneath the man's skin was further evidence of his decline. He seemed to slump a little. Karthik thought he recognised the early stages of kyphosis.

Poor Praveen.

'Good, glad to hear that. And your studies? How were the exams?' As he brought up the subject both eyes twinkled, then the dullness returned. 'I am expecting top grades from you, top grades.' He rubbed his hands, dryly. A thin smile rested on is lips, as it if had been conjured up by the static.

He didn't even ask how I am doing. The ice wall thickened.

'Studies are going well, I will get my results in a few weeks.' Karthik shifted his body weight.

'Excellent, you will do well. You always do well. Your mot——'

A wave of liquid coldness washed over him, slowing down his body, like falling into icy water. Praveen stopped, seeming to notice. Karthik watched his father shrink in front of him, dwarfed by the chesterfield.

'Your mother would have been proud.' Praveen turned away from Karthik.

Is he crying?

Words formed in his mouth but Karthik could not allow himself the luxury of their release. *Why didn't you tell me? Why did you let my Mummy die without me?*

'Sweeti loved you very much. She would often tell me that I had made a mistake in sending you to America.' He coughed gently. 'I loved your mother. She was my sweetheart, my sanity and the mother of all of you.'

The voice in Karthik's mind demanded to be heard. It travelled towards his lips with sleek precision, ignoring his silent protest.

'Father… I want…' his voice trailed off, nerves fired, sending warning messages. *Don't upset the situation. Be the good, faithful son, who follows all the rules and stays on the rails.* Another voice demanded to be heard, to be allowed expression – *Say what you feel, what you have wanted to say for years. Let it go.* Jerkily, he gripped the arms of the chair.

'Why did…' Karthik struggled to control the words, to regulate their flow and to manage the emotions that flew with them. 'Why did no one tell me?'

Praveen's eyebrows furrowed and twitched, meeting and then parting. His mouth sagged. 'Karthik.'

That is the first time today you've used my name.

'We wanted to allow you to concentrate on your studies; to be free, never distracted by something that you could not have changed.' Praveen looked down, his eyes closed.

Karthik felt tears forming in his eyes. A painful stabbing sensation jabbed at his stomach. 'Being with Mother was…' His breathe came in gulps, '… It was more important than my studies.' He had said it, it was out in the open. *What will he say?*

'Your mother did not want you to know.'

It was like an explosion. It shook him, as if something inside his mind had detonated, uprooting him, sending earth, trees and water into orbit. The whole world was racing upwards; and then there came the slow descent. He felt his stomach drop, his hands go limp.

'What did you say?' Karthik's words were measured. His insides were spinning as he tried to comprehend his father's words.

'Your mothe—'

'I thought you said it was your decision.'

'No, Karthik. Your mother did not want you to be distracted from your studies.'

Karthik shook his head. *Can this be the case; was she protecting me? Did he play along with it for her, or for me, not for him? Did he want me here really? Did he know how I would feel; that we would be here now?* All this time he had blamed his father, hating him.

A voice spoke calmly inside of his head. *How could she do this to me; placing my studies above my love for her?*

He reached out to grab something, anything that he could hold onto. For security. The hole opened up to welcome him, to engulf him, to swallow him.

She wanted to protect me. Alone in her torment – without his love.

Praveen sighed. Opening his eyes again. All that rage and hate only to discover he was not responsible for the decision. Karthik stumbled off the chair, falling at his father's feet.

'Father, I am sorry… So sorry.'

He reached down and caressed his son's head, 'Sorry? My son, why are you sorry? We are happy that you are our son. Your mother was so proud of you.'

Karthik clung onto his father's legs, repentant and humbled. Things were not as he had thought. Everything was so confusing. Father was innocent, *she* was guilty.

The world had changed again.

+++

Contentment, deep serenity and warmth. Fullness. Karthik sat in his mother's favourite room, surrounded by the familiar décor.

The evening meal had been a wonderful occasion full of laughter, even a few tears. They had feasted and celebrated. A family meal.

Father and Rahul were off early in the morning and they had decided to retire early. His sister's husband, Rahul's business sense fell in line with the Kothaka way of thinking. Praveen had been deeply impressed, welcoming him not only into the family but also into the enterprise. They were both on a steering committee, planning a new development in Mumbai.

Jayagi had endured a difficult day with her persistent back pain, relief fleeting. She wanted to lie as flat as possible for as long as possible. Personal comfort would have to be set aside until the birth of the little one. Besides, she faced the long car journey back home. Rahul joining her after his trip to Mumbai.

Karthik contemplated his new emotional equilibrium. Things had shifted, the balance tipping in favour of his father, leaving him with a number of unanswered questions about Mummy. He decided to be close to her that evening, spending time in her sitting room.

The ornaments – memories of trips to different part of the world including London, Paris, Switzerland and New York. Every visit marked by a gift from father.

He sat, comfortable in his mother's favourite seat. Her colourful and welcoming happy space. The mahogany bookcase was still under the window. Books from his childhood were still on the shelves. He used to love those stories. Mummy used to read to him and in time he read to her. Something drew him to the bookcase.

The bookcase was polished with beeswax at least once every two months. Mummy had been strict about her routines. 'Discipline is needed for greatness,' she'd often told Karthik. Her finger pointing at him, her eyes serious despite her laughter.

He enjoyed scoured the titles with his finger, the familiar touch stirred so many memories. One title made him stop – "The Kothaka Lineage – A View of History" by Jayagi Kothaka. After extracting the leather bound book he thumbed through it, deciding this would be his reading assignment for the evening.

Jayagi had given up a promising career in journalism after she had her first child. Her ability in English was immense. She had travelled to Europe and America on a few occasions and her spoken language was articulate and free from any discernible accent. Jayagi also held the title of being the first Kothaka to become a published author. Sales had, however, amounted to less than thirty copies; enough for the family and little else. *Is it fair to call them sales when they were given away?* Father would not have been pleased with this from a business perspective; , had it been a work of fiction, he would have sent her away to re-think her proposal. But it was not, it was a history book, and she written it to commemorate their parents' Silver Wedding Anniversary.

His sister had secretly researched and interviewed hundreds of people, scouring the public records extracting every last bit of information. Quite an achievement for a nineteen year old woman. Karthik remembered how busy she had been, however the book had not made his reading list – he'd been eleven at the time. Just the thought made him smile.

Jayagi possessed sharpness and perception as well as a wicked sense of humour. Its construction had been a mammoth task, requiring whole weeks spent interviewing people and travelling to libraries and archives around the country. The book represented her love, sweat and dedication.

He drank from his glass of chilled beer. Setting it on the coffee table, he turned to the index. It fell open on a section regarding the families properties, starting with his present location. He began to read:

Chelsea Place, Delhi

The Kothaka ancestors refused to take part in the rebellion of the Sepoys. They had worked too hard and for too long to risk losing all they had achieved; their decision paid off. In 1858, the establishment of the British Raj, their lands were secured as a family inheritance. The creation of property deeds in 1860 confirmed their position, it was now in writing. Their loyalty publically acknowledged.

Under the Lieutenant-Governor of the Punjab Province, Lord Hamillin, their favoured status created many new opportunities, gave them a comfortable life in comparison with the many who suffered poverty and inequality, and an invitation to the tea party attended by the Empress of India, Queen Victoria – their loyalty publically acknowledged.

Changing domestic situations resulted in the British decision to leave the management of the nation to the indigenous people. The imminent departure of the Governor-Lieutenant raised questions as to what would happen to the residence, known affectionately as Chelsea Place, a reminder of the life left behind in England.

Situated close to the local river Kamruddin Nagar, Delhi, an idyllic setting, The Kothaka's had their eye on the property and began preparations to purchase the property well before the rest of the competition.

Success followed this venture and subsequent business transactions, from landowners to business creators, part of the new developing middle class; not everyone grieved over the decline of the British Empire.

Her satirical touch was sabre-like sharp and poignant. Only she could get away with such outrageous comments. Humorous and critical, he heard his Mummy's philosophy concealed behind those sentiments. Jayagi's awareness of political issues, the plight of those who suffered, the inequality – all concepts she had opinions on but for which she lacked a platform. This book gave her that missing plinth.

'The one and a half story house known in India as a bungalow occupies a central position in the plantation that once provided employment to hundreds of the local people, with its peaked roof, standing out from the other houses in the area. The building served as both home and administration centre as the Lieutenant-Governor used to conducted much of the paperwork from the dual purpose accommodation.

Approaching from the ornamental steel gate, the house sits comfortably in the centre of a well maintained lawn, beautified by green bushes bearing fragrant flowers all the same shape and height. The lush green in contrast with other parts of the city which took on a yellow brown colouration as sufficient water could not be provided for all residents, even for drinking purposes.

The bright white sandstone was the bane of the groundskeepers as they faced the weekly task of washing the stones in order to maintain their brilliant look. The white colour reflected the heat, allowing some solace from the relentless and punishing sun. However the dry climate and the clay soil always regained the upper hand whenever strong winds blew.

Seven magnificent bays in total; three on each side of the central bay, housing the solid mahogany door. Each of the supporting bays perforated by a large sash window, forming a semi-circle at the top. The windows divided into eight partitions by wooden dividers, the top two sections rounded to fit within the frame.

A pair of while wooden shutters on either side of the window, which could be closed should storms approach, protecting the eyes of the building. Each window possessing its own eyelids, now wide open staring and observing life as it passed by their close scrutiny.'

Karthik paused, he had never thought of the house being alive. Watching and observing all those who passed by and those who entered. A living history stored within its walls, hidden information waiting to be revealed. *Interesting.*

'The piece de resistance, the porch. The colonnade made up of four Corinthian columns topped by a horizontal entablature of Dholpur white sandstone. Each Corinthian column cut from solid India onyx marble which sparkled in the daylight, topped with curving acanthus leaves. The supporting pedestals completed the grand statement, Kashmir gold granite. Regal and somewhat out of place.

The Governor-Lieutenant developed a passion for Greek architecture while at boarding school. When shown the architecture plans of the building he decided this was his final opportunity to keep his childhood dream alive. In England he would never be able to afford such grandeur.

The overall effect was stunning.'

True, they did live in a palace compared to their neighbours – 'Regal and somewhat out of place' – Mummy would have picked up on that statement. She enjoyed a privileged life but never forgot her own, humble background. She refused to forget that her education had given her a chance to move up the social ladder in large, striding steps. Her heart for the poor stayed with her, invigorated by having the means to help others.

His heart softened – *Mummy loved everyone, not just me. She always thought about others. Self-sacrificing even to the very end.* He sniffed, before wiping away a tear.

'Through the porch entrance, the mahogany door prevented entry into the main heat of the building. Divided into eight panes, it represented security and opulence; ten local carpenters spent four weeks turning it from trees into an entry. The multi-paned transom light allowed light to stream into the foyer, the opaque door prevented the path of light.

With such a mixture of styles, it would have seen strange in another part of the world. However in India the combination of style and cultures allowed plenty of room for personal expression. The merging of British and Indian culture was a common feature in many houses that served as homes for the ruling authorities. The high standard of décor, elaborate space and warmth made it a stunning place and wonderful home for the Kothaka family. Though they had many homes across the world, this one remained the unanimous family favourite.'

Yes, this was the favourite of all the houses they owned. *Well done Jayagi!* He made a promise to himself to locate his copy of the book, it would be good to continue to read it from an adult's perspective.

The yawn went on for some time. He emptied the glass. *I think I will call it a day.* He turned off the fan and checking the room before switching off the lights. Mummy's sanctuary, my source of peace.

Darkness hid the contents of the room as Karthik headed to bed.

The coolest part of the day gave an unpleasant foretaste of heat to come.

It was late morning and the air conditioners struggled to maintain a comfortable temperature. Jayagi's decision to leave before midday had been eminently sensible. Heat added to the challenges of pregnancy. She relished the thought of giving birth; she did not look forward to the delivery so much as the freedom that would come afterwards. Trying to maintain her normal body temperature was almost impossible.

Karthik and Jayagi stepped onto the porch – the mahogany door closed behind them. Karthik was bathed in hot light – perspiration dripped from Jayagi's chin.

Both of them were dwarfed by the four silent Corinthian guards on sentry duty.

Their driver passed by the siblings, carrying the last of the suitcases to the waiting Mercedes. He was puffing as he struggled, bearing its weight on his head. The car boot shut with a satisfying thud.

Jayagi took Karthik's hand and gazed fondly into his eyes. With her free hand, she wiped her nose, sniffing intermittently. 'Well, little brother, it is time for us to part.'

'Indeed. But I hope that the next time we meet I will have a new nephew. I would quite like another nephew; the nieces outnumber them almost three to one.'

Karthik's smile extended across his upturned face. He was never afraid to show his emotions with her. Jayagi admired his openness and honesty. She moved closer. He smelt of cedar wood and musk; it was oddly masculine for her little brother. She rested her chin on his shoulder, hugging him with her eyes closed.

'I am so happy that you and Father have reconciled. He has been smiling all the time. I have not seen him smile since Mother died. You really lifted his spirit. I thank you for this,' Jayagi increased the pressure of her hug, trying not to overbalance as she sensed the tightness in her lower back.

'I'm happy too. I was wrong, you know. So wrong... You gave me wise counsel. I was ready to explode. I blamed him for not telling me about mother's death. I had no idea—' Jayagi's head jerked and he felt her stiffen in the embrace. 'What's wrong?' He pulled away to look at her face. She avoided looking at him. 'Jayagi… What's the matter?'

She struggled to answer, 'I… I…' Her gaze turned to her abdomen, both hands sliding from the embrace before resting limply by her sides.

'Tell me… What is the matter?'

Jayagi noticed his eyelids, partially closed, the skin around them crinkling. 'What did Father tell you?'

'What do you mean?'

His hands were open, both palms extended. Coldness spread from her lower back across her abdomen – the baby became restless, as if it knew.

'He said that Mummy told him not to tell me about her… illness.' Karthik's tone was measured, but Jayagi's face changed as he spoke. He watched the colour move from her cheeks, leaving them pallid; her top lip began to tremble.

'Is that what he said?'

The dull, flat tone of her voice heralded bad news. She told him everything.

Karthik lost track of time and space. He was dizzy, lost; his hearing temporarily suspended. *He had been lied to*. In his head he heard the words going round in a circle, reminding his childhood train set, watching the carriages complete the circuit. He blinked but saw nothing. *Betrayed by my father. Now. After everything*. A hollow and knowing laugh came from somewhere behind his right ear, growing louder before sweeping past him and away.

'Karthik, Karthik,' Jayagi shook her brother – he was staring blankly into the sun. 'What is going on?' She felt unwell, nauseous. Thick saliva filled her mouth, along with a metallic sensation.

Karthik gasped and drew a deep breath, his eyes re-focusing.

'What happened?' His hands grasped at his head, both palms viciously squeezing against his temples.

'What just happened to you?' She was scared. She had never seen him behave like that. She wondered whether it was the revelation, or something worse. Finally, Karthik moved. He wiped the sweat from his face, turning to her.

'He lied to me Jayagi.' His words were low, dull, almost hypnotic. 'Father lied to me.'

The sound of the driver's horn cut through the air. He did not want to get stuck in the traffic, and if they left any later that would be a real possibility.

We're still children. We're still the children we were. Even he knows it; even the servants know it. I am still in Father's kingdom. Betrayed.

'I'm sorry Karthik, so sorry. I thought that he would—'

'You knew?'

His piercing stare shook her. 'Don't blame me.'

Karthik watched the tears trailing down her face, meeting under her chin, forming one stream. She sobbed. He wanted to comfort her but the inner rage exerted its restraint.

'I had nothi—'

'But you knew?'

Karthik stepped back, staring at her. She hated the look. It was full of disgust. 'Karthik, Karthik,' she pleaded, 'Don't hate me. Please don't hate.' Jayagi reached towards him, he stepped back.

'No, sister.' Karthik's words were laced with menace. 'I will save all my hatred for him.' Inside, he felt something curl and turn ashen.

She cried out, 'No, Karthik. No hate.' Jayagi's knees weakened, she felt her body sinking towards the floor.

Karthik saw her falling and moved fast, embracing her; rocking his sister. 'Jayagi, be still.'

Together they negotiated the white sandstone steps; the driver jumped out of the car, running ran towards them. Her body seemed to flutter like a weakened bird. Tiny gasps escaped her pursed lips. Karthik supported her while the driver opened the rear passenger door; they both helped her into the car.

'We will take about this matter no more. I do not want our relationship to be spoiled.'

Mechanical words, his features now hardened. Horrible eyes, so harsh and dull. It made her shiver.

'Drive safely.' He barked the command at the nervous chauffeur. Karthik turned to his sister, taking her left hand, and kissing it tenderly. 'I love you, will always love you.' Her eyes were now red, blood shot but still pleading. He stepped back, then closed the door. The look of terror on her face remained in his mind for a long time.

The driver moved off slowly – Jayagi turned round in the back seat watching Karthik wave.

He spoke to himself in the quiet, midday heat. 'No I do not hate you. I will save all of that for Father. All of it.' He turned, walking up the steps. The feelings he had put aside were resurrected, newly empowered.

The mahogany front door opened before him. Normally, he would have thanked the girl, but he had other things on his mind.

+++

As the door closed, Dalaja leaned against it and sighed.

Mistress Jayagi was always so kind – and Mr Karthik, he made her feel as if she were more than a servant. Not like his cold hearted father. She glanced at the flowers in the vase; at their limp fading faces. She needed to get them sorted out before the master came home. He would not be happy if they were not the way her former mistress would have liked them.

THURSDAY 13TH AUGUST 1998 (BM, EWA, R)

Karl was screaming at the top of his lungs, shrieking with delight.

Brenda looked out at the three children playing together in the garden. Karl was on the swing, pushed by Darren. Jasper ran around waiting for his turn.

Their two sculpted lawns needed regular care, but Marvin enjoyed that part. Front and back. There was a lot of love in this place and Karl seemed to recognise it.

One month in, the final paperwork had been all been signed. The whole process took over eighteen months. She felt that they had been questioned and cross examined like criminals. At one point she almost pulled out. They wanted to know everything, she was glad she had no skeletons in her closet.

She sipped her coffee. Brenda understood that it was about making sure that they made the right choice. Today was a good day. Though they had two children of their own, Brenda longed for one more. Since the age of four, she had been adamant that three was indeed the magic number; at least when it came to kids. Marvin had a genuine love for children, added to which, Jasper and Darren were pretty excited at the thought of their having another person to play with. On the other hand, they were not so sure about the extra sharing involved with the new arrival.

There had already been tears and tantrums – the boys had needed a lot of convincing. They were good kids, but Karl needed help and support.

There was a risk that, as a family, they were not ready for his sullen moods.. He would often burst into tears for the slightest of reasons and at those times he was particularly difficult to consol. He would scream and shout for his natural parents. During such periods Karl would refuse to eat, even sweets were declined. Nothing could tempt him out of those dark moments. They had to be patient, waiting for the painful episodes to pass. Margaret had provided them with an excellent child psychologist though, and Brenda knew the number off by heart.

Brenda was shocked when she found the stash of food that Karl had squirreled away in one of the cupboards in his bedroom. Despite his refusals to eat, he seemed to possess an innate fear of starvation. it was the smell of decay that gave the game away.

When she'd questioned him about it he had shut down completely and had refused to speak for hours. But after that, he stopped storing food. Somehow, her loving approach had eased his fear. She promised him that there would always be plenty of food on the table and he could have as much as he wanted. He believed her.

Thankfully, he had stopped wetting the bed. That was their 'little secret' and those words became their code; something she would say when she needed to bring the matter up with Karl. It wasn't a big deal for her, at least not in isolation, but it worried Karl and that worried her in turn. He had been all smiles when he had managed dry nights for more than a week. His mini mountain seemed to have been conquered.

Karl loved the Disney channel and was practically addicted to *Bill Nye – The Science Guy*. He would sit there, studying the repeats. After recruiting Darren and Jasper as assistants, Karl had even started copying the experiments in their backyard. . Brenda soon realised that certain household items would inevitably end up being stacked up in the garage or used in the construction of yet another spaceship. Karl had once stated that he was going to be an astronaut. Everybody had agreed that it would be a good idea. The Kuhlman's advocated encouragement. It was a gift you could give to anyone; and it came without a price tag.

When it came to his experiments, Karl acted like a miniature policeman; he was a stickler for obedience, always following the rules and making sure that everyone else did the same. Jasper and Darren were kept in check by his antics and, strangely, their behaviour improved. He set a very good example when everything was running smoothly in his mind.

Karl's the natural leader.

Today they were playing well. She'd organised a barbecue for them today. Marvin could do the cooking when he came home. Brenda checked her watch, she had one hour to sort out the hot dogs, beef burgers and ice-cold Cherryade – Karl's favourite drink. Nobody else even touched the stuff but he could drink it by the bucket load. And, of course, the iced fruit tubes. He loved them. Not because of the taste, but for the science facts that were printed on the wrappers. He had a huge collection of empty tubes which he had washed out before archiving in his under-bed storage box.

As she placed the mug down, she witnessed the swap-over. Karl was now pushing Jasper. His little face was bright red... glowing. He looked so happy.

THURSDAY AUGUST 20TH 1998 (BM)

It was good to be back in the States... A new term, his junior year, a new challenge.

The encounters had reached double figures; today marked the tenth visitation. Each seemed to build on the previous one – a clear sense of progression. Karthik scratched at his beard thoughtfully. *Perhaps using logic and reasoning will help me explain and even understand each experience?*

A good strategy... But one that failed to explain this new reality. The timing and the information varied every time, but the experiences always seemed to happen when he was alone in his room; his moods seemed to make no difference. He discarded the emotional theory.

Eight – the octave, the end of a new musical scale. The eighth visit... A significant occasion. The conversation, if you could call it that, happened inside his head. Almost telepathically, he could hear and respond. Karthik selected a number of words to describe the voice – *calm, melodic, ethereal, clear and easy to understand.*

The words it spoke were few and weighty – *I am wisdom.*

Immediately, they were followed by a scene from the past. Like watching an old black and white movie, Karthik saw his mother sitting with him under her favourite mango tree, the familiar grounds of the Chelsea Place forming the backdrop. The fragrance of the mangoes wafted towards him, carried on an invisible cool evening breeze. His mouth watered, he almost tasted their sweetness.

Mummy; youthful, smiling and hugging him, while instructing him in English conversation. He heard himself struggling with a phrase, trying to get his tongue around the awkward pronunciation, Mummy patiently repeating the sentence for the third time.

Strange, so strange yet peaceful.

He gazed at the younger version of himself, feeling his innocence, sensing the inner hunger, recognising his receptiveness. *Why this scene? What does this that have to do with wisdom or previous visitations? Am I being listened to or taken for a ride?*

Before he could gain answers to his questions, the scene shifted. He was sitting at his desk writing an essay, the last essay one he had written; he read the title. Surrounded by books, his coffee mug half drained on the desk, writing vigorously, pausing, putting his pen in his mouth, pausing, then continuing to scribble. *How eerie* – watching himself creating, synthesising, and collating information thoroughly engaged by the activity. The essay grew, as if it were alive. The greys and whites of the scene limpid but lacking vivid colour.

Was the voice saying that he had been guided? Was it claiming credit for his creativity? A muse, a source of inspiration?

The third scene disturbed him the most. Karthik was still the external observer, able to survey and interpret the events. This time there were no familiar points of reference. This was a fiction: *a future?* Still in black and white, he saw himself standing on stage, behind a glass podium; he could not make out his words, but the audience… He heard their thoughts, and the few words they spoke! The audience consisted of people of prominence, people of significance –finance ministers, government leaders, celebrities, sports personalities, entrepreneurs, top academics and policy makers. His words captivated them, generating a catalytic sense of awe, mesmerising. The sense of frustration grew. He wanted to know why his words were having such an impact on the audience. He scanned the surroundings: no familiar features. His camera lens view took on a wide angle, rapidly closing into a tight head shot of… *an older version of myself.* A white trimmed beard, his face glowing illuminated by an inner light. The scene stopped, as if someone had hit the pause button on a VCR. It captured his eyes, the passionate wringing of his hands, his ascendant posture; both heels lifting from the ground.

The image faded. Karthik was back in his room. The voice spoke again – *I have wisdom… for you.*

Silence.

Karthik's impatience mingled with frustration – *why the long silence?* Then the thought popped into his head – *patience and wisdom are companions.* Academically, he considered himself a shark lethal and ferocious once the scent of fresh knowledge stimulated his nostrils. Some of his peers were unnerved by his aggressive style, indded, it had served him well in the debating arena and nowadays his methods were less confrontational. Yet that instinct remained. On this occasion and that of every other visitation it was not an asset. The presence seemed to work on an independent time scale, totally different from his, forcing a different learning approach, a change of style.

The whole experience seemed to be both in and outside of time. He had viewed the past, present and future. That authoritative, inviting tone, full of potential… *I feels like its student. It's a teacher then. The Teacher..*

But is it good or evil? Everything he heard and saw made logical sense, fitting within his framework of rationality, yet the supernatural element blurred the lines of logic. All the information was totally reasonable yet beyond the norm, outside of his comfort zone. He had nothing to compare the experiences with, no reference point, no plumb line.

Why me, why now?

Like Hansel and Gretel. The trail of crumbs… He pondered it; there had been a clear transition from a few words, to complete sentences, an increase in vocabulary. Changes in the amount of visual information, more intense experiences. Things were definitely advancing. The sound of the voice had changed as well, moving from the cold and metallic tones Karthik had first experienced towards something human in sound. The ideas had become more complex, involving clear scenes and time sensitive information. The visual component had also changed, from vague and blurry images to ones sharp in definition. The smell was usually the same though: musty, and damp. Yet the mangoes' fragrance had added a new note to it. Energy touches accompanied the encounters too – mini static shocks that he could feel all over his body.

The encounters had become more frequent too, showing an increase in duration and intensity. Curiosity grew with each encounter, as if some latent appetite had been stimulated. He wanted more; to know more about the nature of his instructor, to gain deeper insight into the source this intelligence, this wisdom. Alongside his studies, this became a private investigation.

The new term promised so much. Now he had to balance his time between his academic course and his own personal studies; his new source of inspiration.

Monday 31st August 1998 (BM)

Karthik was running, again. With no clear sense of direction, along the stony path made of hard, sharp pebbles that cut into his bare feet. Pain in every step; he left faint, bloody prints as evidence of his travel. Sweating, thirsty, cold and semi-clothed.

Pursued.

He saw only the outline of his predator, a grey shadow the size of a brown bear. It roared and beat its chest, before returning to all fours, set on catching Karthik. Its tiny red eyes shifted from side to side, long globules of saliva dripping from the ends of its mouth. Pointed yellow teeth, with a protruding green tongue.

The more he denied its presence the bigger it grew. Karthik did not want to admit its existence, denying it seemed logical. It fed on his failure to acknowledge its being. With time it began to change, becoming more ferocious, more blood thirsty, gaining ground. Every denial empowering its pursuit.

Terror, another wave moved up from his feet, hit his brain then descended. Branches grabbed at him, ripping his clothes, tearing into his skin. Each tear deeper, more damaging.

He continued to run.

+++

The same sequence repeated itself. Karthik faithfully recorded each episode. There was a clear pattern, the Teacher always appeared after the dream.

Was this his way of announcing the meetings, the exchange? Did he send the dreams, or were they self-induced?

The monster puzzled him. *Why do I deny it? Why does refusing to acknowledge it give it more power?* Logic failed to provide him with a satisfactory answer. Dreams were not his area of expertise; Freud majored on them however, and Sarah loved that kind of thing. Her view of the world was more all-embracing than his, she was more ready to accept the existence of a world other than that of their present reality. Despite the reality and his acceptance of these new experiences, the dream angle was a little too New Age for Karthik's taste. It smacked of the occult; a branch of metaphysics that he usually chose to avoid.

How would he talk about this without giving away his dilemma? He rubbed his beard, staring at the desk lamp. *Ah! Inspiration and hypothetical analysis.* They were the keys to this mystery. His own studies would seem to be a natural way of opening the debate followed by a session of 'what if?' *Karthik, you are brilliant.* He congratulated himself. *Coffee and cake, who could fail to take such bait?*

Judging by her weight, Sarah was particularly fond of cake.

WEDNESDAY 2ND SEPTEMBER 1998 (BM, EWA, R)

A trail of steam rose from the mug of Americano; a misty-thin ribbon, swaying from side to side. Similar ribbons rose from the white coffee beside it, though with less vigour, cooled by the heavy volume of milk that Sarah had added.

Karthik and Sarah sat side by side. Between them was a pale cream plate with a circular gold edge. In the centre of the plate lay the remains of a partially eaten slice of lemon drizzle cake.

Their favourite spot in the café – with two comfortable easy chairs, one covered in black leather, still pungent after nearly a whole term's use. Karthik always sat there. Sarah's chair was beige, torn in a number of places where students' bags had snagged the leather.

Sarah finished a mouthful. She seemed exceptionally pleased to be there. Dressed casually, she faced a day of lectures. Her course crammed the teaching in over two days, leaving her with five days a week for reading and research. Karthik looked her over discretely: blue jeans, brown suede trainers, a thick black woollen jumper with bobbled surface, the neckline stretched, exposing her grey polo shirt.

In contrast, he was neatly dressed, his beard trimmed – highly groomed, even on his off days. He had no extra demands on his time today, no lectures either, leaving him free to enjoy the meeting and concentrate on library work later that day.

It was quiet today, he had seen only five other people in the cafe. Nearby, a waitress was cleaning and tidying the tables. The place had a peaceful atmosphere, broken only by the occasional laughter from outside.

A girl on Karthik's right hand side sat alone, reading a newspaper, perched on a black leather stool. Periodically she turned the pages of the broadsheet that she held in front of her face. Her long brown hair was tied up in a ponytail that extended down to her waist. In between turns of the pages, she glanced at the two students, engaged in serious discussion. Karthik hoped that she was suitable engaged with her reading and, preferably, uninterested in their conversation. This was liable to be embarrassing enough as it was.

He picked up the mug of black coffee and sipped it.

'So, why metaphysics?' His eyes studied Sarah. She had a full, round face, smaller in proportion than the rest of her body. Her tiny eyes and mouth were punctuated by a generous nose, turned up at the end. *Mary Poppins* – the shape reminded him of the books that his mother had read to him as a child.

'Well, I wanted to delve into the realm of existence. My Undergraduate course barely scratched the surface. I wanted more freedom to follow my own lines of enquiry. Tackling the two fundamental questions—'

'Of what ultimately *is*, and what *is it* like?' Karthik cut her off.

Sarah tilted her head to quizzically. 'If you would let me finish…' The chiding sound of her voice made Karthik grin. Smiling broadly, he placed his index finger across his lips.

'I was saying,' Sarah eyed the remaining pieces of cake, then continued, 'that it's the question of being and the world that encompasses it. Origins represent the foundations of any future philosophical discussions. Always go back to your source.' She leaned forward and scooped the cake from the plate with her fingers, leaned back and pushed it into her eager mouth. Her eyes closed as she chewed.

Karthik lowered his hand, 'That is my area of interest. My focus is on the role of inspiration in philosophical development. So, in many ways, we complement each other.'

The expression on Sarah's face changed from pleasure to delight. *I hope you do not have any strange ideas. There is nothing romantic between us, Sarah. Besides, you are not my type.* He crossed his legs, then folded his arms across his chest before continuing, 'What about inspiration? What are your views?' He reached for his mug. .

Sarah's tongue slithered across her lips, back and forth. 'Everyone is influenced by their world and the things that happen or have happened to them. This will always play an important role in understanding our sources of inspiration. Take Plato for example: despite his great thinking he had an awful relationship with Dionysius the Younger.' She paused reached for her mug, cupping it in both hands, she slurped as she drank. 'Personal circumstances can make a big difference to our perception of the world. I wonder how his view of the world shifted after the heavy handed actions of Plato.' She placed the mug back on the table. 'Observations and what we make of them, that would seem to be the heart of inspiration. How we interpret those things is what makes up our world.'

Karthik heard the reader behind him turn another page. He glanced over in the direction of the rustling sound, seeing only the front pages of the *Daily Tribune*. Turning back, he saw yet more cake disappear into Sarah's mouth. *That was pretty quick. You must be hungry... Or just plain greedy.*

'What about inspiration from an artistic position. The Latin *inspirare*?' Karthik took a deep breath and used his hands to emphasise the point as he exhaled, moving them towards Sarah, tracing the path of his breath. Her plump cheeks flushed again.

'The idea of an unconscious explosion of creativity, to be breathed on by a Divine source. Think of the Greeks, the Norse religions, Hebraism, the Hellenists – breath from another place or a different dimension.' Karthik closed his eyes as he spoke, his mind drifted off, hypnotised by his own words. His eyes flickered back open.

Sarah was focused on him, her posture eager – both hands on the table as she leaned forward. Her lips pursed, full of anticipation. *I am not about to kiss you.*

'That... sounded so inviting, so powerful. You,' she pointed at Karthik, 'you're an amazing orator.'

He laughed, covering his embarrassment and brushing off the compliment. 'Shelley believed that inspiration came because the poet tunes into the 'wind' and then becomes a recipient of the information. Or how about Jung's idea of being tuned to racial memory, unlocking the archetypes of the human mind.'

He leaned forward, mimicking her body language. She responded. He reached for his mug. She reached for hers. Their eyes locked as they drank. She slurped, he sipped. Both placed their mugs down at the same time.

This was his moment. 'Supposing someone received information from an external source—'

'You mean like channelling?' Her chin pushed forward as her head tilted to the left.

That word is so New Age. Super spiritual. 'Receiving information like an antennae. How would you evaluate such an experience?'

'Has this happened to—' her words tumbled out, her voice increasing in volume.

'I am just hypothesising.' Karthik deliberately lowered his voice, hoping she would follow his lead.

'I love supernatural exploration. I read an article on telekinesis two days ago. Why, only last week I was in—'

She is not listening to me. This was not going according to plan. 'Sarah,' he did not mean to snap but her reaction indicated that he had. 'In such a situation, how could one remain objective?'

Sarah reached for the last portion of the cake, then changed her mind. She focused on Karthik, 'I guess one would need to assess the information and compare it with other sources derived in similar ways, or conventional understandings of the subject material. To be in the experience and at the same time assess it reflexively. That's my view. Why the interest in this topic?'

Her curiosity had been aroused, something he had not intended to do. Yet he wanted her opinion. 'I've been doing some research in this area and one of my interviewees claimed to be receiving information from an extra-terrestrial source. I thought it was ridiculous and would think that other intellectual people would also take a similar stance, but I had to check. I just wanted to know what you think.'

'I don't know Karthik.' The last piece of cake was hastily devoured. He watched her chew it slowly, reasoning between coordinated jaw movements. She swallowed. 'Some great ideas have come from unusual sources. Didn't Helena have some kind of spirit guide that helped her?'

'Yes, she did.' His hands were damp, he uncrossed his legs. Another rustle from his right. He tried to ignore it.

'Do you believe in prophetic inspiration Sarah?' Karthik watched her hands before lifting his focus to her face. There was a crumb on her upper lip. Without thinking, he reached over and brushed it off.

'I'm so sorry.' Her face turned red; the colour spread down her neck. 'I always do that for my sisters.'

Sarah smiled, the corners of her mouth crinkled. She then released an enormous laugh. 'I didn't know you cared,' her whole frame shook as the jovial nature of the moment tickled her. 'We seem to have covered so much ground over a cup of coffee.'

And a large piece of lemon drizzle cake. 'Indeed. One final question, Sarah.'

'Yes, but you'll have to make it quick. I have a lecture in ten minutes.' She reached for her crumpled green rucksack.

'What would you do it if happened to you?' He whispered the words, knowing that he was admitting his secret for the first time.

'Me? That would never happen to me.' She shook her head, hitting her chest with her right hand. 'Only special people have those kinds of experiences. If it did? Well…If it did, then I would give myself to it wholeheartedly… And I would probably write a book about it and make millions of dollars.'

Her laughter irritated him.

'Okay, Karthik dear.'

Dear? The sentiment is not reciprocated.

'I will have to love you and leave you,' she stood up, flinging her rucksack over her shoulder, 'but thanks for the coffee and the wonderfully stimulating conversation.'

Don't forget the lemon drizzle cake.

'I will see you around.' Sarah waved as she moved towards the entrance. Karthik sat back in his chair, rubbing his beard. *Has she worked it out?*

The copy of the Daily Tribune lay neatly folded on the stool behind him.

THURSDAY 17TH SEPTEMBER 1998 (BM, EWA, R)

'The drinks are on me. Let's celebrate,' Charles Ferrell strutted towards the bar, his arms swinging like pistons.

James smiled, raising his free hand in a mock salute. Charles noted the sharp knife in his other, neat rows of dissected limes behind the bar.

'Wow, you're... and some. Different from the hair bear days, eh!' James chuckled. 'Neat haircut, clean shaven... Amazing what a little grooming can do.'

'You knew me before the working life hit.'

'You used to have hair like a hillbil—'

'Watch and be amazed. But be warned, beauty like this only comes once in a life time,' Charles winked at him. 'Just try not to be jealous.'

Both of them laughed

Slim, with dark curly hair, James approaching his twenty sixth birthday, James was never short of female attention. He was a good friend. They'd known each other for four years. Every time Charles visited New York he would drop into the bar. Murphy's, right on the edge of Manhattan, had become a popular haunt for local young professionals.

James possessed an ocean of wisdom, generously ladling out glassfuls to anyone who would listen. He always had the right words for the occasion, listening to Charles with genuine attention. Then there was his amazing memory; recalling conversations from years back.

Charles and his drinking buddies were determined to have a night to remember; the place was buzzing. The evening would begin here, followed by a visit to one of the adjacent clubs and on from there.

The bar was full of music. They were playing *Come with Me*. Charles approved; Puff Daddy was, by far, his favourite artist.

Charles noticed that the look of the place had changed. The bar still had its oak serving counter but, underneath, were new panels; soft white plastic lighting panels resting on a thinner panel of red light. There was a new mirror, running the full length of the serving area. It made the place look oddly futuristic. Charles leant on the bar, opened his mouth to speak, only to find himself lost for words; glancing into the mirror above the bar, he caught sight of her.

The beauty sat perched on the fourth stool. Charles gazed at her reflection in the glass.

She is simply ra-vis-hing.

Something about her face seemed so familiar.

Have we talked – maybe even dated?

Her eyes glittered. They seemed so alive; it was – difficult to make out their colour.. At any rate, it called for closer scrutiny. *A bit of private in-ves-tigation.*

Long, straight hair reached down to the centre of her back – *perhaps chocolate brown?* It shimmered with every turn of her head. She sipped her drink through a straw whilst subtly grooving to the beat. *It looks like cranberry juice... Maybe raspberry?*

She must be around nineteen or twenty... Or even twenty one.

Her dress seemed modest for these parts: well fitted, but not at all tight or clingy. It rested just above her knees, its design made up of giant petals on a white background. Her slender legs were neatly crossed, the uppermost foot beating in time with the tune. He loved her sparkly, flat ballet pumps, studded with jewels.

Are they for real, genuine diamonds?

In this place you couldn't ever be sure. It served as a sort of middle ground. A watering hole for the wannabes and a tried and tested place for those who were already established. At any rate, he definitely wanted to buy her a drink. Charles made eye contact with James interrupting his flow.

'Who's that beauty on the fourth stool?' James' glanced down the bar before returning his gaze to Charles.

'No idea, Charlie boy. Not seen her before?'

'What is she drinking?'

'Cranbery spritzer, with a slice of lime,' Charles clocked the knowing smirk. 'Are you on the prowl, young man?'

'Never you mind.' James knew him too well. A beautiful face worked every time. He simply could not help himself.

Miss gorgeous had almost finished the contents of her glass. This was his moment to become of interest to her. 'Excuse me, I was wondering if you'd like to join us in our celebration?'

She turned towards him smiling confidently, then her head tilted to one side. 'What's the occasion?'

Her voice was both assertive yet soft. He loved the way her eyebrows rose as she spoke. *So cute!*

'I start my first job tomorrow. Tonight is cel-eb-ration time.' Charles sensed something very special about this woman; not something tangible though. *Call it gut instinct.* A weird, almost creepy feeling. Yet a good sort of creepy. Feeling jokingly quizzical, he asked, 'Have we met before?'

'No, I don't think so. I'm new to this area.' She returned to her drink. The slurping sound added a lighter touch to her otherwise sophisticated demeanour.

'May I buy you another one, Miss… ?'

'My name is Crystal.' Her eyes locked onto his as she extended her hand.

'My name is Charles, Charles Ferrell.' Her skin was smooth and silky, her handshake surprisingly firm. Charles felt the urge to kiss her on the back of her hand. So he did.

She pulled her hand away, her body shifting in the same direction. Her expression was a cross between bemusement and annoyance.

'Sorry, not trying to make you feel uncomfortable,' Had he overstepped the mark, lost his chance of making the acquaintance of this delectable lady?

'I'll take you up on that offer of a drink. I'll have another cra—'

'Cranberry spritzer. With a slice of lime.' He watched her mouth open, cute eyes revealing her surprise. A small smile crept onto her lips, before breaking into a full grin.

'How did you know that?'

'That would be telling.' Charles tapped his nose and winked. 'James, another cranberry for the lady.'

'Got it, and for you?' James placed his hands on the counter.

'Roederer…' He winked at his new acquaintance. 'Cristal – both my and Puff Daddy's favourite.' Charles enjoyed the obvious play on words.

'Of course.'

James disappeared from view. Charles propped himself on the counter, his elbows resting on the bar. 'So, you are new to town. Where are you from?' His question must have triggered something; her expression changed, frown lines forming on her forehead. The smile vanished.

'I'm… I'm from… Well, from quite far away.' She pulled on her right earlobe, focusing on the empty glass.

'Try me,' he rested his hand on his chin. *You are amazing.*

'It's overseas.'

'Where? I'm pretty good at geography.' The booze in his system gave him a combination of relaxation and boldness.

'Here are your drinks.' James placed them on the counter. Another customer called him away.

'So what are you planning to do in the future?' Her pointed interjection suddenly shifted the conversation from its casual start.

'That is a really strange question.' He stood up. Her eyes remained focused on him. Charles gulped twice.

'I'm working in copper mining at the moment, so I might…' He wondered why he was telling her this information, yet felt he should. Such a weird situation. 'I might stay in mining. Not really sure.' Charles sipped the champagne, tiny bubbles tickling his tongue. 'Who can say what the future holds?'

Crystal's eyebrows furrowed, then relaxed. She leaned towards him. 'Yes, who can.'

It was a statement, not question. Her voice was much softer now, as if she was weighing up her own words.

'Charles,' he turned around to see Ken standing behind him, 'Are you abandoning us for...' His head shifted in Crystal's direction.

'I'll join you shortly. Promise.'

Ken sauntered off, shoulders drooping. He turned back and gave Charles the familiar group symbol – palms slapped together followed by the twisting motion. They all knew what that meant.

Charles turned to Crystal.

She had gone. The half glass of cranberry spritzer remained. He stood up, searching. Nothing. No sign.

'James, where did she go?' His words were accompanied by frantic head turns, as he scanned the crowded room. Still no sign of her. 'James... help me.'

James had been preoccupied with cleaning glasses and stocking up beer. He cupped his ear, 'Sorry Charles, what were you saying?'

'Where did she go?' His hands were trembling. *Why did she leave?*

'I don't know. I was working, Charlie boy.'

'She never even said goodbye.' He gulped down another mouthful, the champagne had lost its taste.

Crystal – who was she? Why do I feel as if I know her?

'Charles!' Ken's voice boomed from the middle of the room. 'We're waiting for you.' He would not be dissuaded.

Reluctantly, Charles scooped up the flute, making his way to waiting crowd, feeling slighted, even cheated by the whole encounter.

FRIDAY 20TH NOVEMBER 1998 (BM, EWA)

If Brenda thought that she hated hospitals, Karl was even worse.

Karl's speech development seemed slow to Brenda. Of course he could talk but there was something about the way he processed and formed words that seemed odd. Their visit to the speech therapist identified an issue with his larynx; a minor operation would correct the fault.

Karl was terrified of the hospital but he could not explain why. She found him sleeping when she arrived to take over from Marvin.

Marvin stayed with him during the night while Brenda took the day shift. His swift recovery and improvement in speech after one month bore testimony to the success of the operation. They'd pulled a few strings to get a private room for Karl; Marvin knew the hospital supervisor from high school. The care they received at the Medical Center of Redford, Dallas was exemplary.

Bleak white walls, with cartoon characters on the curtains. Karl's bed stood next to the window. He looked like a little angel, peaceful and calm. No nightmares today. In fact they seemed to have stopped altogether. When he'd first arrived, he'd had regular nightmares, waking up screaming and begging for mercy. Brenda wondered what his little eyes had seen and what memories filled his mind.

She picked up one of the cards on the side cabinet next to Karl's bed. This one was from Jasper, it had a lovely picture of Karl in a hospital bed looking every happy. As she opened it she read, 'Dear Karl, you smell. I hope you get better soon. You can play with the Godzilla Rampage game when you get home. You have to let me play with your Furby. Love Jasper.'

Her stomach muscles felt as if they were ready to tear, the laughter came right from the centre of her being. *Why had Marvin allowed him to write that and give it to Karl?* The two boys had been told to write daily message for Karl to cheer him up. Tears streamed out of her eyes. *Boys!*

Karl actually thrived, enjoying the attention he received from the doctors and nurses, most of whom said he was a little 'cutie'. One particular nurse took a real shine to Karl, offering to take him home and look after him if Brenda got tired. Karl's toothy smile appeared every time he saw her.

She was so professional, caring and funny. She lit up the place with her twinkling blue eyes and luscious eyelashes.. Brenda wondered how she ever managed to keep her gorgeous brown hair in order; it was both thick and long.

Just how long is that braid?

She always had it up like a conical crown, neat and tidy. *How does she get away with that?*

Sunday 22nd November 1998 (BM)

On his last day at hospital the nurse made Karl a smiley face cake. Karl was so thrilled, he refused to eat it. On top of the cake she had written the words: 'To brave Karl who is so special, love Crystal.' He showed it to everyone; he was so proud of his cake. Brenda made sure she took pictures with him holding his special cake; Karl loved being in photographs.

Eventually it became rock hard. Brenda made it disappear discreetly, two weeks after his return from hospital. No child of hers would or could eat a sponge cake that had metamorphosed into a boulder.

Tuesday 1st December 1998 (BM, EWA, R)

'Daddy.'

Marvin looked up from his newspaper. Darren stood in front of him, looking contrite. That normally meant that he had done something naughty and wanted to confess before he was found out.

'Hello Darren,' he put down the paper extending his arms towards his son.

Darren sat in his lap; he cuddled his son. 'What's on your mind, buddy?'

'Did you know that Karl is a whiz at maths? He can do the most difficult sums like they were two times two.' He looked at Marvin with a pained expression and whispered, 'He's better at maths than me.'

Marvin gave him a strong squeeze, 'You know, son; that was a brave thing to say. Telling me that someone else is better at something than you are.' He kissed the top of his head. 'I'm so proud of you.'

+++

Sure enough, Karl had a natural talent for problem solving. Teachers at his elementary school soon noticed this; he became the school-champion in the maths challenge. Nobody could do calculations faster than Karl.

Reading was more of a struggle. Karl, not fond of books, preferred to watch things in motion. Brenda devised a method that motivated him;

rewards came in the form of science experiments. The longer he read, the greater the range and number of resources he could gather from the cupboard for the latest Bill Nye experiment. Needless to say, his reading skills improved.

Neither Marvin nor Brenda had attended university. Jasper was a talented soccer champ, while Darren excelled at swimming. Sports were a strength in the family, apart from Karl, who excelled on the academic front. He was fit and healthy but he lacked the physical confidence required of a sportsman – that, and teamwork was difficult for him.

Brenda and Marvin watched his progress closely all the same, often discussing his future. Now he had settled, his natural genius could shine. Each of the boys could be unique in their own special way.

They agreed that they had done the right thing, taking Karl in and making him part of their family.

TUESDAY 16TH FEBRUARY 1999 (BM, EE, R)

To: pbs@silverhurstmiddleschool.com
From: max1augustine@hotmail.com
Date: 16/02/1999

Hi Paul,
I am so sorry to hear about your wife. That must be shocking news to have to take in. My aunt died of breast cancer, so I am glad that she got it diagnosed

early. The best recovery rates are amongst those who get early treatment. I will light a candle for her. Give my love to your boys. Hope you had a happy Valentine's day.

How much compassionate leave have Silverhurst given you? If you need more time you make sure you get it!

I can hardly believe that I will be graduating in a matter of months. The time has flown by. I have taken your advice. I have a number of options that I can present to my dad when I speak to him. I thought I had better do it in person rather than on the phone or by email.

I hope to be in your area over the summer. I would love to meet up with you and your family. I think your twins are awesome. They have convinced me not to give up on football. Tell Ben that his kicking needs some working on, last time Archie gloated over his victory. Are they still competitive? I am still in competition with my brother. I have applied for a place on the five week summer school at Harvard Business School, it will involve research marketing and studying organisations. So I will have to fit you in either before or after the course.

I cannot understand why you are so fond of Wagner, I listened to Das Liebesverbot. I had to look up the translation (the ban on love). I just don't get him. I know that you don't like Berlioz, to me he is a genius. I am currently listening to *Symphonie fantastique*, just reached the third movement when he is thinking about his childhood. That piece gets me every time. It is one of my all-time favourites.

It is quite late, wanted to make sure that I acknowledge your email. Thanks for letting me know. I consider you a friend as well as being a great teacher.

Bye Paul,
Max

+++

Life was working out for him, his studies progressing well. Karthik's name would be remembered; he and his peers were pioneers, their work with HSTT had been ground-breaking. Everything was going well.

The thunder bolt came from nowhere. A heart attack. Father had died of a heart attack.

This time, Karthik heard within the hour. During an important business meeting, father had complained of chest pains. He stood up to speak, keeled over and stopped breathing. He died at the conference table in the middle of one of the biggest deals of his career.

Jayagi made it her personal responsibility to let him know. 'He never made it to the hospital.' She wept over the telephone.

Karthik felt confused, numb, hurt and distressed. All the pain flooded back. Mummy was hardly in the grave and now father was joining her. His father had left the world with so many things unresolved in his heart, so much pain, mainly due to rivalries and bitter feuds with old friends who were once his business partners; there had been rumours of bribery and corruption, deals that had gone sour and, of course, there were court cases still being worked out. But when it came down to it, none of that mattered anymore.

Dead in front of his colleagues. At least mother had managed the dignity of being surrounded by most of her family.

Except, of course, her favourite son. 'What happens now?'

'You are... You are coming home... Aren't you?' Jayagi's words were uttered between sobs.

Why does death come at the least convenient times? 'I am in the middle of my dissertation.' He paused, thinking for a moment. Recalling his last visit. Studies, though desirable, were less of a priority than family. He had learned that lesson. 'No. That can wait. I will book a flight as soon as possible. Where is Aahlaad?' He switched the phone to the other ear, clamping it to his face.

'He's on his way from Paris, Gilriraj should be in Delhi within the next hour. Shreya is here with me. Do you want to speak to her?'

'Does she want to speak to me?' They had rowed bitterly over the management of a trust fund set up in memory of Mummy. She had not spoken to him since then, almost three months.

'Shreya,' he heard Jayagi shout. There were some mumbles, a sharp exchange. 'Karthik, I'm sorry. She is not ready to speak to you. When you get home, you two will have to sort this out.'

She had stopped sobbing. 'Is there anything I can do here?'

'Yes, come home. We need you.'

Hearing that touched him. His family had admitted that they needed him. He had always felt like the outsider, spending so much time away from them. He had had little chance for any meaningful bonding. The last two siblings; he hardly knew them at all, Anjali and Chital.

Where have we gone wrong? Money could not compensate for this sort of dilemma. The realisation hit him like a truck. *We are a dysfunctional family.*

The family was outwardly successful yet inwardly, emotionally emaciated. He made a decision then that his generation would change this. The next generation would not go through the nightmare that masqueraded as family.

Praveen's death would have huge repercussions. He had built the conglomerate around himself. There would be fights, more court battles, accusations, money-grabbing and crocodile tears over the fortune; with Karthik having no choice but to be part of it. The next generation would not go through this.

The shaking was already beginning. He felt the ground moving.

THURSDAY 18TH FEBRUARY 1999 (BM, EWA, R)

Delhi... How things have not changed!

Their lives in a gated community had protected the Kothaka family from the harsher realities of life that lay mere moments beyond the walls of the compound.

Karthik resented being back in India deeply, but there was nothing he could do about it now. Despite his silent protests, he knew that the marriage of these tragic circumstances and a wealth of family traditions demanded his presence.

The long drive from the airport along the region's poorly maintained roads, along with the heat, noise and poverty; it all drained him. The contrast between the two cultures with which he had grown up could not be more apparent – East and West.

As the tinted windows of his BMW passed through the gates of the family compound, he thought of his mother and of how he still mourned her passing.

The old mango tree stirred his memory, reminding him of the late afternoons spent with mummy, learning the alphabet. It was dying; the talons of death swiping at its roots. The branches diminished, the trunk showing signs of age, beginning to sag, the whole thing bowing towards the ground. He wondered when it had last borne fruit.

It must be uprooted. He would talk to the gardener. *Mummy loved that tree, she loved the gardens. She kept the house running.*

Signs of her absence were everywhere; the bushes were turning brown here and there, the lawns had lost their manicured look, the sandstone building was greying, covered in a thin layer of dust. Neglect seemed to have touched everything.

The Kothaka Empire, a conglomerate of many successful and enterprising companies, generated an incredible fortune – now in the region of billions. The family tree had shed many seeds, spreading its limbs across a variety of nations. Now all of the Kothaka family were gathering here.

During the drive from the airport, Karthik had asked the driver what the local community were saying about his father's death. According to him it centred on the rumour that Mr Kothaka had died of a broken heart after the death of his beloved wife Mrs Sweeti Kothaka.

No one mentioned the relentless meeting schedule, nor constant arguments, back-stabbing and betrayal that had become part of his daily life. I will never become that.

He turned towards Chelsea Place, it seemed almost ironic that the family's situation could be considered the paramount reason for his demise. *Jayagi needs to update the book.*

Each of the seven children had become instant multimillionaires. Praveen had limited the resources available to his children while he was alive. He hated the idea of their being spoiled by family wealth. But now, in an instant, Karthik had attained the same degree of wealth as many of the young millionaires he had met at Harvard. More than them… he had leapfrogged up the Forbes rich list. The money was in his hands, his accounts; previously his father's.

From student to multimillionaire overnight. Karthik's life had prepared him for wealth management; now he too had contracted the *illness,* though much later than many of his fellow patients at Harvard. And the inheritance demanded care and attention – it was like a newborn child. One which would sap his time, distract his studies. He sighed inwardly.

Home sweet home.

THURSDAY 25TH FEBRUARY 1999 (BM)

The Teacher demanded extra time. He would wake Karthik at the most obscure hours, showing him specific events and people. Some were known to him, others complete strangers. Often there would be words or images connected with those people.

Somewhat to his own surprise, he had listened to Sarah's advice, faithfully recording the encounters, writing them down so that he could objectively assess the experiences. Recalling previous encounters had proved relatively easy; it was as if they had been imprinted into his brain, becoming part of his body.

Upon his return to Harvard, Karthik supplemented his lessons with reading concerning dreams and their interpretation – Freud and Jung added an interesting angle on the topic. Much of the time he had no idea of the meaning of the complex images he saw.

An understanding of symbolism helped as a starting point, he marvelled at the concept of self, and remained mildly amused by the thought of the id. He felt ignorant, an uncomfortable and distasteful sensation. An inner resolution to shed this covering catalysed his efforts.

The more he saw, the more his appetite increased. Slowly, he developed a sense of superiority. Not intentionally but fuelled by the fact that he was having these experiences whilst others were not. That made him special, unique. He was chosen. His grief was alleviated by the deeper level of his experiences with the Teacher.

The new reality continued to open up before him, it challenged his personal understanding of the world and forced him to question that which he believed to be real. The evidence became overwhelming. When predictions became real life events it only confirmed the fidelity of his convictions.

Mediation had once been a familiar practice for him. His background in the Hindu tradition had made it so. Now, he found that his experiences were enhanced if he engaged in meditation before the visitations. It became a regular feature of his daily life.

The Teacher seemed to appreciate his new level of commitment. The visions increased in their depth and detail.

Karthik was hooked.

WEDNESDAY 17TH MARCH 1999 (BM, EWA, R)

Sarah wrestled with guilt and lust.

There was no doubt about it, Karthik was avoiding her. She wondered if she had come on too strong, had she overwhelmed him with her attempts to show how interested she was in him? Not just as a friend.

His whole appearance seemed to be going downhill. He used to be so neat, so well presented – not like some of the hippies on campus. The last time she had seen him, he had seemed stick-like with masses of extra hair. They were meant to share a few classes this semester, but he seemed to be missing almost all of them. He would normally have sat next to her.

Then there were the calls. He simply did not get back to her. She had left numerous messages, even sending emails.

Nothing.

Men were a mystery to her – *why do they all have to be so complicated?* Even so, she did not became seriously concerned until he missed his fifth consecutive lecture. Still no response to her texts or emails, and her queries to his small circle of friends revealed a similar pattern.

Karthik was not getting back to anyone.

She recalled their conversation in the café: the cryptic questions and strangely supernatural topic. Karthik had said, 'There is no such thing as objective truth.' Now he seemed to be isolating himself, perhaps carrying out his own paranormal investigation? She had a strong sense that those pointed questions had been about him.

He had been through so much with the deaths of his parents. *Emotional overload, mental breakdown? Add the spiritual dimension and you have a recipe for disaster.*

Sarah was worried.

With a heavy heart she decided to make the call to the University authorities, stating her concerns and to see if they could get to the bottom to things. She hoped that, one day, he would thank her for this. But, cautious in equal measure, she asked that they keep her name out of it.

Surely there is enough evidence from the low attendance and the recent additions to his academic records for them to investigate? He's not been submitting work! It's totally unlike him! Maybe it was delayed grief from his mother's death? She was no counsellor though, and that was why they had professionals on campus. It was part of the student service that they all paid for.

She thumbed the student helpline card, turning it several times before dialling the number, sighing heavily.

One day you will thank me.

Karthik had no intention of opening the door of his dorm room, but the persistence of the caller and the fact that whoever it was knew that he was inside, forced him to raise himself from his bed and move slowly towards the door.

The security chain was locked into position. Karthik peered at the unfamiliar face standing outside the door.

'Yes,' he mumbled, scratching his shaggy face.

'Karthik Kothaka?

'Yes… that is me.' He did not know the visitor.

'My name is Alistair Forster,' a Harvard security card was held up for Karthik's scrutiny, 'I am the senior student welfare officer. May I come in?'

'I don't want any visitors,' he knew his room was a mess; the thought of someone seeing it in such a state was quite embarrassing. 'Come back another time or—'

'I'm here because you have not responded to my calls or kept any of the appointments I have made with you.'

Karthik checked over his shoulder, taking in the pile of letters strewn on his desk, unopened.

'I must have—'

'Karthik, the situation is very serious. You may be asked to leave your course. I need to talk with you today.' The voice rattled Karthik — *who is this person to tell me what to do?* However the message had hit home — *but I may be asked to leave Harvard?*

'Okay… okay. Just give me a moment to tidy up.' He closed the door partially , leaving the security chain in place.

'Where do I begin?' He stood in the middle of the bomb site, wondering. Alistair would need to sit down, so he scooped up the pile of cloths on the spare chair. 'Where?' The wardrobe option seemed best, as he opened it a pile of pots and pans tumbled out, mouldy and foul smelling. The clatter was unmistakeable. 'Sorry,' he shouted, 'I will be just a minute'

The idea came to him, *under the bed.* He knelt down and lifted the quilt. Food packets and three empty water bottles. One rolled towards him. He pushed it back wedging it in place with the bundle of clothes. *That should keep things in place.*

Karthik decided not to offer his visitor a drink. Besides, he had no idea where he would find any clean cups and he had no washing up detergent.

What else?

Opening the curtains allowed light to fill the room. The sudden illumination made him aware of his surroundings, *what about the smell?* No air freshener. *I'll open the window.* To reach the window he would have to clear the window ledge of plates and books. *Too much trouble, Alistair had better have a poor sense of smell.*

Karthik could not remember the last time he had showered or brushed his teeth.

He pulled the bathroom drawstring. Light revealed the piles of clothes strewn across the floor space. He picked them up making one pile in the corner. The bathroom cabinet was already open – no mouthwash. *Plain water will have to do.*

After a long gargle he spat into the sink; it was ashen grey with soap scum around the edges. The watery saliva stayed in the basin, its plughole blocked with strands of hair.

Karthik lifted out the artificial sink plug – *that smells disgusting*. He dropped the slimy toupee into the overflowing waste bin. It splatted as it hit an empty carton of milk.

One final check in the mirror: he had developed the hillbilly look – the same one he had criticised his peers over. Pale skin, gaunt cheeks, a full scruffy beard and moustache.

I am not looking my best today. One tug and the light went out.

The clothing offered no resistance to his kick, now there was a path between the desk and the front door. He removed the security chain and opened his room to the stranger.

+++

The putrid odour hit Alistair's nostrils. He resisted the gag instinct and the need to cover his nose, Karthik stood in front of him.

Dressed in pale green tracksuit bottoms, exposing his bare forest covered chest and hairy toes, both eyes grey and lifeless – *this did not bode well*. Judging from the facial hair Karthik had not shaved for a few weeks. His rank palpable body odour added to the awful array of smells.

'May I come in?' In reality, Alistair wanted to turn around and run.

This kind of thing happened frequently; he had dealt with so many such episodes during his time at Harvard. Top students who had suddenly crashed. The reasons varied: depression, drug abuse, relationship breakdown, unwanted pregnancies, family issues – so many situations. He had seen it all.

'Yes, sorry about the mess.' Karthik winced and stood to one side.

Alistair stepped across the threshold. *My report commences now.* The room disorganised and, chaotic. Mental health issues came to mind as he saw things in the wrong places, the general state of neglect. Dirty items stacked up, food items undergoing decomposition.

Probably a mental health case.

Karthik rushed ahead and pointed at the chair, indicating that Alastair should sit on it.

There were stains on the seat but he decided to accept the offer of hospitality. Building bridges with students was one of his top priorities. It felt uncomfortably sticky. He searched for a place to put down his satchel, deciding to use the bag to create a space by moving the several pairs of boxer shorts that lay near the legs of the chair. All the time maintaining a warm, professional smile.

Karthik collapsed onto the chair in front of the desk, turning it so that he faced Alistair.

With clipboard and sheets in place, smile secured, Alistair had already decided on the preliminary direction of the conversation. 'How are you Karthik?' *Always begin with care and concern. The client will relax.* He had memorised his training manual word by word.

Karthik appeared irritated; Alistair noticed his his frequent scratching and wriggling, as if he had fleas. 'I am fine. Not sure why you are here.'

Alistair wrote down:

Client is unaware of his present state. Possibly delusional?

He smiled warmly. 'We are very concerned about you Karthik?'

'We?'

'Yes, the student welfare office and some of your friends.'

'My friends, like who?' A note of menace tinged his voice while he rubbed his thigh vigorously, with long, rough nails.

'People who care about you, who are wondering where you have been. Your lecturers have not seen you for a while. The attendance records,' he turned to get out the printout but decided not to bother, 'show that you have missed a number of key lectures. Your assignments have not been handed in,' he paused to allow Karthik time to digest the information.

Karthik seemed to be staring at something immediately behind Alistair's shoulder. He checked to see what had distracted his client. Nothing there.

'Did you understand everything I said?'

'Yes, I understand.'

Alistair waited, no further response. 'What do you think about what I just said, Karthik?' A cruel smile erupted on his face followed by a frown, he nodded several times, then laughed.

The hairs on the edge of Alistair's neck created goose bumps, he felt them all over his arms, moving down towards his hands. Suddenly and to his surprise, Alastair experienced a powerful sense of dread.

He wrote:

Strange sensations. The client did not respond to the information that he was given. His behaviour seems bizarre, responding to situation in an inappropriate manner.

As his pen moved, he made a mental note of the type of security on the door and the nearest means of escape. 'Karthik, I note from your record that you have recently suffered a series of bereavements. You refused the offer of counselling. Is that correct?'

'Yes, I did not want help… Thank you.'

'Death is a very traumatic event, losing someone you love can be very difficult. There are so many stages to the grieving process. Counselling is not telling you what to do, it is helping you identify your feelings and finding ways to manage them.' *Almost word perfect, page 235 of the manual.*

Karthik continued to stare at Alistair, a dull empty stare. No response.

'If you do not need help, that is fine. We will not force you. However, there is the matter of your academic performance. If we cannot resolve this, you may have to leave.' He paused, then continued, 'You might consider,' his mouth felt dry, he swallowed twice; he considered asking for a glass of water but thought better of it, 'taking some time off and deferring this year of your course. You—'

Suddenly Karthik stood up, 'I have never failed at any aspect of my studies and I do not intend to start now.'

Alastair did not want to take his eyes away from Karthik. Something was very wrong here. Without looking down, he wrote:

Client responded to the possibility of leaving, has a strong sense of academic pride.

He swallowed his sudden thirst and tried to speak calmly. 'Please sit down, Karthik. You are not on trial. I am here to help you, not to accuse you or threaten you in anyway. I need to let you know about the situation that you are in and to try to help you to find ways of resolving this crisi… I mean, situation.' Alastair gulped. Where on earth had that come from? *Do not use language that might aggravate the situation. Page 142.*

Karthik sat down slowly, his head dropped. Both hands resting in his lap. Alastair watched him, still writing:

Client seems to become calmer, being at Harvard seems to mean a great deal to him.

'Would you like to say anything? Is there anything I need to know? Alistair thought compassionate thoughts, hoping that his emotions would convey compassion. *Page 45.* He had not been expecting the floods of tears, though the manual did repeatedly state that one should expect the unexpected, and he had always tried to work to that mantra.

Something broke. The sound came from somewhere deep within Karthik's bowels. The floor seemed to shake as he sobbed unashamedly. Globules rolled down the ashen-dry skin of his face, framed by matted strands of hair.

Alistair knew what the manual said about appropriate boundaries. The fact that Karthik was wearing only track suits bottoms made it even more risky. Against his better judgement he got up and put his arm around him, the smell was sickening. He baulked and continued his act of mercy.

'That's good, Karthik. You may have been bottling up your emotions. We can offer you discrete and professional help. No one is going to pry into your business.' Karthik's breathing became more regular. Alistair searched for tissues. None in sight, he had some in his satchel. He took his arm off Karthik, picked up the satchel, extracting the packet of tissues. 'Ah found them.' He turned round.

Karthik spoke, 'I may need help.' The haunting glare did not match the sentiments of the words.

Alistair handed him three tissues.

Karthik took them gratefully, wiping the mucus off of his face and hands before attending to the pool on the carpet. He seemed to wonder what to do with the wads of slime. Alistair watched as he crumpled them into a ball and threw it near the door.

Alistair reserved comment.

'Thank you, Alistair. I have been neglecting my studies. You are right, I have been suffering from emotional issues. Yes, grief. I seem to have neglected the stages of grief.'

Alistair nodded in agreement. Without taking his eyes off Karthik, he wrote:

The client has a real sense of clarity and seems ready to take action.

As Alistair left the room, he felt a genuine sense of achievement. Not only would Karthik attend an initial counselling session, he had promised to contact all of his tutors and resolve any problems with his outstanding assignments. He had even agreed to contact his friends and re-connect with his social life – and to tidy up his room.

Almost textbook perfect.

+++

Shock.

Karthik wrestled with the fact that for the first time in his life he might be labelled aa a failure. He considered the traumatic impact that his leaving Harvard would have on his family. He was the intelligent one, he had been given the privilege of being educated in America; of having thousands of dollars invested in his education. Now he might be asked to leave?

This would not happen.

Being told that he was no longer meeting the minimum standards laid out by the assessment criteria – that had been the deciding factor, the taste of failure too bitter. Karthik hated the feeling. The thought of his abilities being reassessed in the eyes of others was shocking. How would he have explained this to his father?

The door felt cold against his bare skin. His sweat felt like glue, sticking him to the surface. As he peeled himself away, the spiral of thoughts continued to revolve. He headed towards the bathroom.

Hillbilly. The face staring back at him would have shocked his mother. She had insisted on high standards at all times. Personal hygiene had been central to her precise world. Unkempt, unwashed and unreliable. *What has happened to me?*

It had taken a complete stranger to wake him from his spiritual slumber, with the threat of failure. 'You,' he pointed at himself in the mirror. 'You have to change, now!'

Where to begin?

The hair fell into the sink, the concealment came to an end. Karthik began to see himself again. The old Karthik.

Each stroke of the blade removed layers of natural growth and spiritual decline.

+ + +

The visit from Welfare marked the moment at which Karthik refocused on his studies and reduced the amount of time he spent in meditation. He locked himself into the routine of his counselling sessions, finding them helpful; they taught him new ways of tackling his suppressed emotions. He gained a deeper appreciation of himself and grieved that his father had died with so many issues unresolved.

After father's funeral, Jayagi had sat Karthik down into Mummy's room and told him the full story. She felt that she had the liberty, since father was no longer around. When mother's diagnosis had showed that there was no chance of recovery, she had begged father to allow Karthik to come home and see her before she passed. He had refused, mother had obeyed him.

Despite mother's pleading, he had believed that his son's studies were more important. Jayagi wept as she told Karthik. She had not agreed with the decision but had obeyed his orders. All family members were strictly forbidden from discussing the matter with Karthik.

When he spoke about this in the counselling sessions, the therapist helped him to see the judgements he had made about his father and himself. All of his life had been spent showing his academic prowess, judging others by his standards and finding them deficient. He valued knowledge, adopting a Western perspective, but lacked the ability to apply his knowledge and change his own behaviour; the view of Eastern wisdom. The realisation shocked him.

He felt ashamed of the way that he had dismissed and condemned those of less ability. It hurt to hear and work out for himself the truth, that others had seen and ignored or endured. His gifts as a strategist and planner made it easy for him to steam roll over others who he saw as being barriers to what he wanted to achieve. He had the potential for extreme behaviour, dominating and controlling others. He saw that in his father. Genetics had granted him the same weakness, but it was arrogance that had denied him the ambition to control those genetic traits.

He still regretted the fact that he had failed to confront his father. Karthik had kept his emotions locked up, feigning affection whenever they were in contact with one another. He never gave his father the chance to be free. That still plagued him.

The reading list that accompanied the session opened up new authors to him. Tackling topics such as the development of a healthy sense of self, ways of dealing with bitterness and forgiveness, understanding others, leading and managing oneself. He relished the new knowledge about people and the way they functioned. The pioneering work of Jung in his work 'Psychological Types' further developed by the partnership of Isabel Myers and Kathryn Briggs, gave Karthik a firm grounding in personalities and a framework for evaluating himself and others.

Inwardly, he felt his heart thawing.

It seemed strange, so unfamiliar. Frightening as well – he had to struggle with the risk of being vulnerable, instead of hiding behind his mask of pride and arrogance.

Looking back, he acknowledged that something powerful had happened in his life. In seeking a new spirituality he had disconnected from the rest of reality. He referred to Alastair as his electric shock treatment therapist. It was only half a joke. The jolt of electricity that he administered during their first meeting had woken him up from his deception. They would remain in contact for many years. Alastair already considered him one of his greatest successes with counselling.

Friends also noticed the difference, learning to know a softer, more genteel Karthik. Smiling became less of a chore. He recognised that he must have been so miserable to be around; though, when he broached this with Sarah, she denied that he had been difficult, just complicated.

Sarah was amazed at the change in him; it gave her hope, however, her efforts were still rebuffed.

Karthik re-engaged with his life and few friends. He was struck, suddenly, by the painful realisation that he had neglected them, and a new depth of understanding became part of his personality.

He redoubled his academic efforts and it began to show. Reconciliation became an important word in his vocabulary. He described himself as an 'emotionally maturing man.'

Karthik's spiritual experiences came to an abrupt halt though. The door of hidden wisdom had closed with a thud. His emotional growth seemed to dissuade the Teacher. The visions, dreams and hearings had stopped on the day that he commenced counselling.

He thought of throwing out the records of the meetings, or whatever they had been; even entertaining the urge to destroy his notes and exercise books. He came so close to doing that. But he had spent so much time cataloguing and gathering information and he half suspected that it might be useful to someone, someday. So he told himself. But he knew, somewhere, without admitting it, that he was reluctant to totally abandon his quest.

Secretly, even from himself, he grieved over the loss of such an intense and enlightening time in his life. On the other hand, the new level of intimacy with others, with real people; that seemed more than adequate compensation.

Even so, Karthik would never forget.

Data entry input: 265274655519
Programme: GWP
Level: 9
Accessed by C.

Thursday 22nd April 1999 (BM, EWA, R)

The fourth whisky.

Charles' face seemed gaunt. James felt growing concern for his friend.

This is a bad time for him.

He seems to have lost weight.

James saw the red eyes, dark circles underneath; the tense face layered with stubble.

He hasn't slept for a couple of days.

'How was the hearing?' James made his voice calm; soothing.

'What... the hearing? Do you really want to know?' Charles' body sagged while his neck bent forward under an unseen weight. He swirled the golden-brown liquid in his tumbler.

'It's over... Contocaro Copper Mining is no more.' He slammed the glass on the bar, sending the liquid into the air, straight onto his hand. 'Damn it, give me a napkin.'

'It's not your fault Charles.' James handed him the napkin, shaking his head as Charles daubed viciously at the back of his hand, struggling to soak up the liquid.

'Not my fault? Not my fault?' He pushed the glass aside, 'I was in charge of the company!'

'Charlie boy, you need to calm down.' James rested his hand on Charles.

'Calm down... How can I?' Charles spat out the words. James pulled away, noting the subtle tremors pulsating through the tense arm. *You need a lot of help. More than I can offer.* 'Have you spoken to your mother?'

'Oh yeah, run to Mummy... Ma I pooped in my nappy again, help me.' The mocking tone coloured his voice unpleasantly.

This was not like Charles. James had never seen this side of him. 'I'm sure she would be able to advise you.' He moved his face closer to Charles. 'She would help you.'

A vacant stare, spiritless eyes.

'I've lost everything... My company... People have lost their jobs, James... five hundred thousand dollars gone up in smoke!' His head dropped even lower, his body quivered. 'Pa's boy has flopped... I've let everyone down... Again.'

'Charles,' James leaned across placing both hands on his tense shoulders. 'You are a generous and compassionate person. You'll—'

'Don't you get it? I've failed again. First Harvard, with my lousy degree – barely passing – and now this.' Charles rubbed his forehead, sighed and closed his eyes. 'I might as well not exist.'

James tried to ignore the tingling sensation at the back of his neck. Charles was in a really bad way. Over the years he had seen too many people like this. It was part of his job, but an unpleasant part. For some, the consequences had proved fatal. And this wasn't just anyone – this was Charles. Suddenly, James realised that he was scared.

'Can I call someone?'

'Who ya' gonna call... Ghostbusters?' Normally the joke would have been funny but not tonight.

'Give me your mother's number,' James commanded, holding out his hand.

'No.'

'Charles, I need that number.'

'I said no!' A sullen expression slid across his friend's face. Charles pulled the glass closer to his chest, protecting it. 'Why should I?'

'Cos I'm your friend, and friends listen to each other even when things are difficult.'

Dull eyes peered back at him, followed by an angry scowl; the lips poised ready to challenge his friend. Then his whole demeanour collapsed and crumpled. Charles whimpered. He attempted to reach into his jacket pocket, missing twice. The third time proved more successful.

Charles pulled out his Ericsson cell and made two attempts to hit the speed dial button before shoving the screen towards James.

James took the phone.

'You make sure you stay here.' He pointed at the spot. 'Do not move.'

James returned a few moments later. Charles remained stationary, motionless.

Twenty minutes later, Icilda Ferrell arrived. James noticed her timid entry and rushed from the bar. They met in the middle of the noisy floor. The evening had reached its peak and bodies now filled every available crevice, undulating in time with the music.

'Icilda,' James extended his hand. 'I am so glad to see you. We've met before.' He spoke loudly to make himself heard over the noise of their surroundings.

A sophisticated lady. Charles' mother… *She's foxy.*

Every aspect of her appearance had been carefully planned, designed to blend together to make a single statement – the dark blue dress reaching past her knees, belted at the waist, a clutch purse under her right arm, the string of tiny pearls, a diamante brooch on what he thought might have been a mink coat.

You could have stepped off the front page of Vogue… Maybe twenty years ago you did. Somewhat surprised at himself, he felt a sudden hot flush pass over him. *Well now I know where Charles here gets his charm.* She was staring at him, her lips tight with worry.

'You're James.' Icilda studied his face. 'I owe you a great debt.' She scanned the room through a mask of rigid facial muscles. 'Where is he?'

'Over by the bar, did you come alone?'

'No, my driver is in the car. I will call him. I used to be able to lift Charles… ' Her eyes moved in the direction of the bar. 'When he was young, but not now.' Now her lips were close to his right ear. He smelt and tasted her fragrance.

Charles had his back to them, still draining his glass.

James waited while Icilda found her cell phone.

A tall, broad, dark skinned man appeared at the entrance to the bar. James guessed him to be in his forties; the driver. The man rushed through the glass panelled swing doors, surveying the room several times before spotting Icilda. He lumbered towards her, leaving several disgruntled guests in his wake. James watched him keenly. He really was huge.

Not someone I would like to meet on a dark night.

When he reached Icilda, James pointed them in the direction of the bar. Icilda followed, daintily walking the cleared path.

'Charles, hello… Charles.' She placed her hand on his shoulders and kissed his cheek tenderly. 'Ma is here. Let's go home.'

James observed them. *Will he flare up?*

'Oh Ma… I'm in such a—' He did not finish his sentence; instead, a stream of vomit spewed out. 'Sorry. I'm so sorry.' Charles half wiped his mouth with the back of his hand.

Icilda grabbed several paper napkins from the bar and wiped Charles' hand and mouth, manoeuvring over the deposit on the floor.

'Charles, it does not matter. Let's go home.' Her voice remained calm as she handed the napkins to James. Icilda's elegant nose wrinkled in disgust. She angled her head away from the reeking mess. James threw the things away, wincing. She was studying Charles. Eye to eye, mother to son.

How many times have I cleaned up vomit as part of this job?

'You get him home,' Icilda nodded and James gestured to one of the stewards behind the bar, using the familiar symbol – a finger moving up the stomach towards the mouth and then looping over and down. Universally known.

He turned back, inspecting Charles' face in the flickering light. His skin had taken on a yellowish tinge, his jaw hanging loosely. Both eyes were sealed tight.

'I've got a –' Charles stopped, grasping his stomach.

James knew what was about to happen. He was so used to this – another unsavoury part of the job. Unfortunately, Icilda lacked his instinct.

'Oh Charles… okay, it's alright, it's fine Charles.' Icilda's face cherry red, the edge of her coat drenched with vomit. Her eyes blazed, both hands resembling open claws. 'Do you *think* you can walk?'

The chauffeur pulled Charles' right arm over his shoulder gesturing with his head, instructing James to the other arm.

'Ma… I'm such a failure. I've let you down—'

'Charles, let's get out of this place. We can talk at home, not here,' she spoke quickly.

James sensed her deepening struggle to cope with the public face of the situation, Icilda's movements were rapid and erratic. A few guests had stopped drinking, watching the intimate scene.

As Charles stood up both his legs buckled, his body heading downwards. James moved closer to support him, Charles' upper body resting against his chest. A hard, cold object pressed into James' ribs.

Charles had a gun.

James fished inside the jacket's pocket and removed the Colt .45, handing it to Icilda. Charles remained oblivious to the action.

Icilda's eyes opened wide, her lower lip flopped down. Instinctively, both hands went to her throat. With one trembling hand she accepted the gun, holding it like a decaying thing, with the other she opened her clutch bag and dropped the weapon in.

Intense colour spread across her cheeks. She pulled her coat around her body, quickly.

Charles' eyes were still vacant – his appearance was pitiful . Both of his arms were suspended between the shoulders of his samaritans and he seemed to be groaning softly to himself. Between them, they took his weight.

Step by step, the trio made their way from the bar, still the centre of attention. Icilda trailed behind, her ringed hand shielding the right side of her face.

As they passed through the doors, James spotted a beautiful woman with long brown hair. *The girl that Charles had tried to chat up.* He recognised her straight away, but simply could not put a name to the face.

Who on earth is she?

He was normally good with faces, but tonight, Charles needed his full attention. They had to get him out without too much fuss and definitely no media attention. One phone call would send the paparazzi into a feeding frenzy.

They dragged Charles, his legs functionless as he continued to moan.

After all these years, James still could not abide the odour of vomit. He'd become an expert at deducing what clients consumed from the stench.

Vodka for hors d'oeuvres, whisky for the main course. *When had this drinking session started?*

Added to that was the pained expression on Icilda's face: her pinched mouth and cheeks – she looked haunted. It was not an easy situation for her to handle. She was out of her comfort zone, he supposed, and carrying a firearm of course. *Why the hell did he even have that thing?*

James felt the weight of the body pulling down on his neck, making his tendons strain, almost thrusting them through his skin surface while his lower back remained the fulcrum of the load. It was like someone had stuffed tight balls of rubber bands there, beneath the skin.

I'm suing him if I end up with back injury.

James smiled to himself. He had to make light of this somehow. If Charles had been sober he would have said it out loud, they would have laughed.

'Hang on in there Charlie boy,' James whispered. No response.

James heard the new tune as they reached the glass panelled doors. *How Deep Is Your Love* by Dru Hill.

An appropriate song! They don't pay me enough in this place.

The doors closed behind them.

+++

The girl sat at one of the tables just behind the stool, so recently vacated by Charles. She watched the whole incident, observing while sipping her cranberry spritzer.

Alone.

FRIDAY 23RD APRIL 1999 (BM)

Icilda sat, glaring at the gun.

Her favourite chair – the love seat. Designed by Helen, a personal friend; beige, with small brown squares, arranged in a chequered pattern, creating a gentle optical illusion.

The dull April morning did nothing to lift her mood. Natural light shone through the windows, contrasting starkly with the artificial luminescence of the ceiling spots. It felt cold and dismal.

Casper wandered in. Her dear pug, he always seemed to catch her moods; perhaps it was canine instinct. He trotted over, nuzzling her left hand, which hung limply over the arm of the seat. Casper licked it several times and Icilda glanced down before stroking his head.

'Hello Casper. Sorry dear, Ma is not in a good mood today.'

Casper paced away, as if he understood, sinking into the Aubusson carpet before jumping onto the pale brown footstool, opposite her chair. He laid his head between his paws, honey gold eyes riveted on Icilda, watching her.

She monitored the gun.

It lay on the coffee table, next to the latest editions of *Good Homes* and *Harpers and Queen*. Metallic, black and heavy – so cold. Just the sight of it delivered a freezing sensation from her mid-back to her feet, along with a dull pain.

How did he get it? Who did it belong to? How had it been used?

So many unanswered questions.

The gun remained silent. Unwilling to divulge any of its secrets. There were two bullets in the chamber, she had checked.

Two bullets – why two? One shot would be enough.

She did not share Ralph's pacifism; she believed in kill or be killed. Guns served a purpose. She would never use one unless the circumstances demanded it… but to protect her family? She would not have hesitated. Ralph had accepted her ideals years ago and had even offered to buy her one – for protection. She had declined, not wanting to violate his principles. They thought that this moment of compromise had set a good example for Charles.

And now this. This horrible gun… in her son's hands… sitting there. Cold, and waiting.

Where did we go wrong? They'd tried to do everything for their son. Even to avoid pampering him too much. Yet here he was, drunk and armed and, she balked at the thought, a danger to himself.

Their only son. Icilda had wanted more children, but pregnancy had been so difficult. Then preeclampsia had hospitalised her for the last two months before the birth; more children could be fatal.

He's always struggled with his identity.

No matter how much she tried to encourage him, Charles had always battled with what she supposed was a sort of sense of inadequacy. He was far from inadequate; she had told him as much in the past, and now she wished that she had told him more often. Always trying to prove himself. It was if he wanted to live life on his terms, never asking for help from his Ma and Pa.

They could afford the best, but he never asked.

Icilda recalled an occasion on which she agreed to pick him up from a friend's house; he had insisted that she wait three blocks from the house. Just after his tenth birthday.

Was it me or the car? What was the point in pretending to be poor?

As a boy, Charles had resented the privileges of wealth, preferring to associate with the less well off – those who were financially disadvantaged in one way or another. *Surely, having money means you can help those people, not that you should hide amongst them.* She had even insisted that Ralph make generous charitable donations every time profits were announced. It had never been enough for Charles.

How many times have we told him that we love him? Ralph was so affectionate, not like some of the men she knew. He could hug. Such a romantic, even after twenty three years of marriage.

The peonies sat on the table, a thank you gift from Ralph, for organising a charity function. The room scented by their tangible fragrance.

Education… Charles' struggle.

They had paid for private education ever since kindergarten. He simply took longer to pick up ideas; Charles jumbled letters, making reading difficult. The diagnosis of dyslexia helped to explain what he was experiencing but his frustration remained.

The solution had been extra private tuition. More hours on top of the time spent by other students. *Perhaps he resented that?* When others were having down time or fun, he endured extra lessons in the key subjects, Maths and English.

Getting into Harvard had seemed like an insurmountable hurdle, yet Charles had managed it. Ralph had pushed for special consideration and made a very generous donation to the scholarship fund after he was accepted, but it was a big achievement.

Tuition continued at Harvard; and although the final award had been nothing too outstanding, it was not to be taken lightly. Icilda suspected that he felt otherwise, never making a big deal of it. But then, that was Charles.

I should have worried more.

She'd given up her own promising career as a lawyer after she married Ralph. Now she spent her time doing so many things: helping others, organising events, charitable work. *Being a mother and a wife – that should also be included on the list.*

So many of her friends said that Charles was absolutely hilarious. She agreed. He was loved by guests, whenever she entertained at home. His timing and witty sense of humour had her in stitches every time; making her sides ache while tears gushed out of her eyes.

Comic? Charles, was a comic genius. When he was around being dignified went out of the window, oh, it was so therapeutic.

Undignified but therapeutic.

Charles simply brimmed with compassion – she remembered fondly that he had wept for days after watching *My Girl*. He also – immediately – developed a severe case of apiphobia that stayed with him until his teens. Thankfully, hypnotherapy had sorted that out.

Such a sensitive young man.

Wednesday evenings were sacrosanct – mother and son night. He kept that event every week, unless he was out of the country, on a job or ill.

They talked about many things; his hopes; his future plans. But this seemed to bring the whole thing into question.

How much has he kept from me? How much of his pain lies hidden?

She peered at Casper, then the gun and back to Casper, who yawned before closing his eyes.

Where did he get such a strong sense of justice? Always ready to take the side of the underdog.

Icilda folded her arms and sighed loudly, staring at the wall. Charles had given her that picture on her fortieth birthday.

A family photograph transformed into an oil portrait. He had known that she would love it – and she did.

The three of them, so happy and relaxed. Charles in the centre – their delight and great, great joy.

What will his father say? Should I – will I – tell him?

Today, a bleak day.

+++

Ralph as always, right on time. Icilda had checked her watch – exactly 11.30. The original plan had been for them to go out for a quiet meal, just the two of them.

Instead, she told him.

Ralph's face sagged, like a stroke victim. His natural colour drained away while his whole body seemed to sink. She was so glad that she had told him to sit down.

'What? He tried to kill himself?' Ralph's words were slow and measured, but they were accompanied by rapid, shallow breathing.

'Well… I think that… I'm not sure. I have not asked about the gun yet.'

'Yet? Where is he?' She sensed his alarm, but didn't know how to react this time. Ralph rubbed his eyes and buried his face in his hands. 'I can't believe this.'

Icilda hesitated, then spoke, 'He's in the guest room.' She paused, waiting to see his response.

Ralph returned from his momentary retreat, 'In the guest room? Our guest room?'

'He needed a place to calm down and get his head together.'

'When did that happen?' His normally calm voice was full of sudden fear.

'Last night. You were sleeping. I didn't want to wake you… I knew you had an early meeting today.'

'You took him in with a gun?'

He gazed at Icilda, a pained expression etched on his tense features. It made her feel awful.

'I have the gun,' she extended the Colt .45, holding it by the barrel, secured between her forefinger and thumb.

'Oh my God, be careful with that… that thing.' Ralph pointed at the gun, 'Where did he get it from?' He turned away, pushing his right palm towards her.

It won't go off dear. Icilda put it back on the table. It slid across the polished surface, coming to rest against the vase, knocking from its position. Icilda set the vase back in its place, ignoring the firearm. 'I don't know Ralph. I will ask him when he gets up.'

'When he gets up? I am going to wake him up now.' Charles rose sharply. Ready to head upstairs; judging by his gestures, a confrontation was inevitable.

'No, Ralph. Let him wake up by himself, talk to him later.' Icilda rested her hand on his forearm, stroking it.

'Well… this has ruined my day.' He folded both arms.

Ralph was hurt, blaming himself. Wondering what he could have done differently. A self-inflicted, deep wound. The recovery would be a long and drawn out process.

'We don't know that he tried to kill himself.' A note of hope tinged her words.

'Why would he have a gun? You know I hate guns? The fact that this is even in the house…' His voice trailed off.

'What shall we do?'

'Do? With him or the gun?'

'Both,' Icilda's voice was level and controlled.

'I need to think… This has totally thrown me.' He was pacing – *circular pacing*. That meant he was confused and agitated. 'Get rid of that.'

His finger shook, his face gained colour – warm pink.

'What do you want me to do with it?'

'I don't know and I don't care.'

Ralph stormed out of the room, leaving the door open. She heard his footsteps go up the corridor. The living room door slammed, shaking the walls.

Casper woke up, glanced around before yawning. His eyes on Icilda, tongue exposed, head cocked.

'What do you have to say about that Casper?' No response.

Distraught, Ralph Ferrell. Confused, Charles Ferrell. And me, in the middle.

Sunday 25th April 1999 (BM, EE, WD)

The solution to all his problems?

A document on his computer screen.

EMPLOYMENT CONTRACT

THIS EMPLOYMENT CONTRACT dated this 25th day of April, 1999

BETWEEN:

Ralph Ferrell of High Trees, Pilkington Tower, Manhattan, New York
(the "Employer")

OF THE FIRST PART

– AND –

Charles Ferrell of Studio Flat 2, 143 The Grove, Brooklyn, New York
(the "Employer")

OF THE SECOND PART

Employer and employee. The supposed warmth of father and son formalised into a document.

COMMENCEMENT DATE AND TERM

1. The Employee will commence permanent full-time employment with the Employer on the 26th day of April, 1999 (the "Commencement Date").

2. The Employee must successfully complete a probationary period of six (6) months (the 'Probationary Period') beginning on the Commencement Date. At any time during the Probationary Period, as and where permitted by law, the Employer will have the right to terminate employment without any notice or compensation to the Employee other than wages owed for hours of work already completed.

JOB TITLE AND DESCRIPTION

3. The Employer agrees to employ the Employee as a Fund Raiser. The Employee will be expected to perform the following job duties:
    Raising funds for IBC
    Recruiting new investors.

From CEO to fundraiser for Icilda Biotech Company USA, otherwise known as IBC-USA, one of his father's latest business ventures.

Biotech, what was that about? During his time at Harvard he had completed two biology modules. Most of them just went over his head. He enjoyed the genetic engineering stuff. Now he would be working for a company that specialised in gene splicing. That was pretty cool. Deep down inside he agreed with the idea of a better life for everyone. They had a duty to improve human life experience – yeah, he believed in that. *Maybe I could play a small part in the process.*

But, of course, it was one of the lowest paid positions in the company. *I'm a money collector, with embellishments.*

His 'skills' would be used though. He would have to convince prospective investors to part with their money and impart the vision to them. Persuasion and humour were both lethal weapons in the art of canvassing. Someone was going to have to sit down with him and get his bio up to speed.

Charles knew he possessed all the right qualities, with some extra bio lessons he would be fully equipped for the position. Still, it bothered him.

This is not happening to me. He shook his head.

A brand new company and he sat on the last and lowest rung, glancing up from the bottom of IBC-USA.

7. The Employee agrees to abide by the Employee's rules, regulations, and practices, including those concerning work schedules, vacation and sick leave, as they may from time to time be adopted or modified.

EMPLOYEE COMPENSATION

8. Compensation paid to the Employee for the services rendered by the Employee as required by this Agreement (the "Compensation") will include a salary of $20,000.00 (USD) per year as well as any compensation paid for Overtime Hours.

9. This Compensation will be payable end of the month while this Agreement is in force. The Employer is entitled to deduct from the Employee's Compensation, or from any other compensation in whatever from, any applicable deductions and remittances as requires by law.

10. The Employee understands and agrees that any additional compensation paid to the Employee in the form of bonuses or other similar incentive

compensation will rest in the sole discretion of the Employer and that the Employee will not earn or accrue any right to incentive compensation by reason of the Employee's employment.

No thrills. No special privileges. $20,000 – it was a pittance compared to his former salary which had reached the sum of $60,000 a year. A new lifestyle – *I'll be shopping at the 50¢ store.* He read on, moving the document with his mouse:

policy as in effect from time to time, including but not limited to, any travel and entertainment expenses incurred by the Employee in connection with the business of the Employer. Expenses will be paid within a reasonable time after submission of acceptable supporting documentation.

PLACE OF WORK

13. The Employee's primary place of work will be at the following location:
    - *IBC Office New York.*

14. The Employee will also be required to work at following place or places:
    - *All across the USA and other countries in the world.*

15. The Employer will inform the Employee in advance of the Employee being required to work at other locations.

Travel – he would be earning those air miles as he crossed the globe moving back and forth. That excited him – travel meant meeting new people, in new locations.

That's one of the better things about this job.

EMPLOYEE BENEFITS

16. The Employer will be entitled to only those additional benefits that are currently available as described in the Employer's employment booklets and manuals or as required by law.

17. Employer discretionary benefits are subject to change, without

compensation, upon the Employer providing the Employee with 60 days written notice of that change and providing that any change to those benefits is taken generally with respect to other employees and does not single out the Employee.

VACATION

18. The Employer will be entitled to four weeks of paid vacation each year during the term of this Agreement, or as entitled by law, whichever is greater.

19. The times and dates for any vacation will be determined by mutual agreement between the Employer and the Employee.

20. Upon termination of employment, the. Employer will pay compensation to the Employee for any accrued and unused vacation days.

Four weeks holiday per year.
People actually live on four weeks of holiday a year. Would he go mad? *Lots of work – and no rest.*

CONTRACT BINDING AUTHORITY

41. Notwithstanding any other term or condition expressed or implied in this Agreement to the contrary, the Employee will not have the authority to enter into any contracts commitments for or on the behalf of the Employer without first obtaining the express written consent of Employer.

TERMINATION DUE TO DISCONTINUANCE OF BUSINESS

42. Notwithstanding any other term or condition expressed or implied in this Agreement, in the event that the Employee will discontinue operating its business at the location where the Employee is employed, then, at the Employer's sole option, and as permitted by law, this Agreement will terminate as of the last day of the month in which the Employer ceases operations at such location with the same force and effect as if such last day of the month were originally set as the Termination Date of this Agreement.

TERMINATION OF EMPLOYMENT

43. Where the Employee has breached any reasonable term of this Agreement or where there is just cause for termination, the Employer may terminate the Employee's employment without notice, as permitted by law.

44. The Employee and the Employer agree that reasonable and sufficient notice of termination of employment by the Employer is the greater of four (4) weeks or any minimum notice required by law.

45. If the Employee wishes to terminate this employment with the Employer, the Employee will provide the Employer with notice of four (4) weeks. As an alternative, if the Employee co-operates with the training and development of a replacement, then sufficient notice is given if it is sufficient notice to allow the Employer to find and train the replacement.

A six month probationary period and a four week termination notice? That seemed harsh. Keeping him on tender hooks for that long? The silent threat. One wrong step and he could be asked to leave.

Part of him wanted to run, but he appreciated the opportunity.

Caged by my own Pa.

The studio block seemed especially quiet today. No noise coming through the walls. As if the world had gone to sleep. His room was a mess. A pile of clothes lay next to his bed, along with other pieces of his life strewn around the place.

It was 11.00.

He promised himself that he would tidy it up later. The screen waited for his next move.

The losses from the closure of the Contocaro Mining Company would be paid back over time, but the details seemed rather hazy. No mention of this in the written contract. Charles paused, thinking over the implications. Depending on his income, a percentage would be deducted. As his salary increased, the contribution would keep pace. A deal struck between father and son – in which the latter had his hands tied behind his back. He had agreed to it. A verbal agreement.

Charles studied the screen. The text coagulated, replaced by a single word: captivity.

IN WITNESS WHEREOF, the parties have duly affixed their signatures under hand and seal on this 25th day of April, 1999.

EMPLOYER:

Ralph Ferrell

Per: _____ (SEAL)

EMPLOYEE:

_____

Charles Ferrell

He'd so wanted to show that he could do things on his own. The mining position had offered itself as his moment of glory; he had pictured himself basking in the light of his achievements.

It had failed. He'd insisted he could manage things, asking for a hands off approach.

Now he faced a lifetime of close supervision, one without any 'special' privileges – though he knew that it was his own fault, after all, he'd insisted on being treated as any other employee, and not because of his name.

He hit the print button and waited for printer to churn out the document.

Charles paused before signing the contract. He planned to drop off the document at the office later on that afternoon. Pa had been so reasonable about the whole thing. Charles was deeply touched by the gesture, in fact, he had been astonished at his father's generosity.

They had sat down and talked – father to son – and they had left the matter of the gun to the very end.

No, he had not planned to kill himself. True.

No, the gun did not belong to him. He lied.

Charles asked for the return of the gun, only to be told it had been taken care of. Ralph Ferrell did not permit firearms on his property.

A deal had been struck. What a fall from grace; from the top to the bottom within one year of leaving Harvard. A new job meant a new chance, and Charles was determined to make the most of it. Tomorrow at 08.00.

Genesis.

WEDNESDAY 19TH MAY 1999 (BM, R)

Charles scooped up another mouthful.

'This beef stroganoff is delicious, how do you do it?' The meat was so tender that it separated into strands in his mouth. 'It's got a real kick to it today.'

He waved at his mouth with his hand, feigning pain.

Ma's laughter was full of music. Tonight she seemed happy, almost delirious.

'I had a coughing fit when I was adding the paprika. We've ended up with a little more than usual.' She scooped the broccoli onto her fork, using her right hand to bring it to her mouth.

Charles took a sip of red wine. *How many meals have we shared in this dining room?* He'd lost count. Everything in place and a place for everything. Two settings; every detail covered, glasses, plates, condiments, napkins and floral decorations. Colour coded, meticulously positioned.

'How did it go with Pa? It has been a few weeks.'

'What, you mean the contract?' He scrutinised every move. 'Pa did tell you about it?'

She hesitated, 'Yes, he did… that is, he mentioned it. How do you feel about it?'

He scoured his plate with his fork, pursuing the last piece of beef, avoiding the vegetables.

'At first I was furious, but I kept it inside. Later on I realised that it was kind. He could have been really nasty but—'

Icilda placed her hand over his, staring into his face, 'He loves you Charles. Pa only wants the best for you, we both do.'

Charles nodded. *Would she give away clues as to the real issues on her mind?* She sipped from her water goblet, avoiding his eyes. They could both read each other's moods.

A quiet room, apart from the occasional clink of cutlery against china.

'It's been so hard for me… I feel as if I've failed,' he tried to disguise the sadness in his voice. 'Like I've let you down, let Pa down. Everyone else is—'

'Why are you comparing yourself to everyone else?' Icilda's gentle voice was sheathed in firmness as she placed her manicured fingers over his hand.

'I can't help it… I always feel as if I have to prove something. I don't know why.' He dropped his cutlery on the plate, leaning back in his chair. The wine glass seemed like a suitable distraction. One gulp drained it.

I don't know why.

Rotating the empty glass helped him think; He completed two full circuits before he allowed it to rest on the table.

Tears glistened in her eyes. 'Oh, Ma,' Charles reached across for her hand, squeezing it. 'Don't cry. It's me that has got to work things out.'

The first tear trickled down, she sniffed while wiping it away. 'When you have children you'll understand that your pain is my pain.'

The idea of children frightened Charles. *How could I bring up a child? I still feel like one myself.*

'Your Pa does not blame you for the shutdown of the mining company.'

The tightness – it felt as if a giant rubber band had been strapped across his chest, then drawn in; the grip cutting into his flesh. His voice seemed to lose its strength, becoming faint as he recalled memories of failure.

'I blame myself.' As the confession left his mouth, his chin dropped.

'There were so many factors – economics, political upheaval in Bolivia, the list goes on. You—'

'But I was in charge. I was supposed to be the boss.' He grasped his right hand, wringing it. 'I should have known, what's the point of studying so hard if it proves to be useless?'

'Business is a tricky world Charles, it is not always predictable.'

'Yeah, but Pa is successful, grandpa is successful. And I'm the failure.' He gripped the table with both hands, feeling his energy seep away.

Ma was weeping. Such a display of grief pierced his ears and heart. Two streams of tears moved down her face. The quivering mouth, the low moan, her shoulders moving in rhythm with her distress. Charles pushed his chair away from the table.

He stood behind her, placing his arms round her trembling frame.

She responded, squeezing his hand. 'I hate to see you like this… To hear you talking like this,' her words were laboured, released between sobs. 'It's as if I do not… as if I do not know you. What's wrong Charles?'

'I don't know Ma,' his emotions were intermingling with hers; the lump in his throat moved towards his mouth. 'I just don't know.' Her shaking subsided.

'… And the gun?'

She had to bring that up again. 'I told you I was not going to use it. It wasn't mine,' Charles closed his eyes, tired of having to explain himself, tired of lying.

How could he tell her that it was for his protection?

He had this irrational fear that someone from the mining company would come after him, seeking their revenge. *Perhaps a disgruntled manager or a father who could no longer feed his children.*

Charles had bought a gun and had even gone to a firing range to practise his skills, or lack of skills; he was useless, an average of one out of each four shots had hit the target. The two bullets in the barrel were leftovers from his last shooting spree – he remembered having given up all hope before even completing the round.

He normally took his empty gun home with him – it would have been useless as a deadly weapon. The idea of having cartridges in his apartment did not appeal to him, so he left his spares in his locker at the range. He imagined pistol whipping any likely assassin, should he have to. It was better than a punch at any rate.

He explained that he had planned to go and blast some targets but he'd got himself too drunk to make the trip. Ma's breathing became more sedate.

Charles made his way back to his seat. Icilda wiped her tears with a lace kerchief then gently blew her nose. 'I always feel so much better after a good cry.' Her weak smile was at odds with her bloodshot eyes.

This is my fault. Should I have another glass? No, I'll leave it.

'I'm feeling so tired. All this travelling is taking its toll.' He spoke rapidly as the knot in his stomach dissolved. 'I'm up early, going to New Jersey. Pa is keeping me busy – three meetings in one day.' Getting things off his chest had helped, he'd made his point and she'd understood, or at least he hoped she had.

This inner restlessness, he could not explain it. It crept up on him when he was alone. Like he was supposed to do something, that his life was to amount to something. But he had no clue what or how things would work out.

Ma could not do it for him, neither could Pa.

My journey.

'If you don't mind, I'll skip dessert.'

'It's your favourite, apple crumble with cream.' Her offer sounded tempting. Icilda sniffed, pushing her plate away, focusing on him almost pleading.

'No thanks, Ma.'

'I'll put some in a dish, you can take it with you.' She rose grandly from the table. 'Don't worry about the washing up, or the table. I will take care of that.' Her voice trailed off as she went to the kitchen.

This is my problem, no one else can help. No one should have to. Me and my issues.

Thursday 3rd June 1999 (BM, R)

'Hello, Max.'

Lukas sat typing at his computer, surrounded by four different coloured files. He stopped work, his hand beckoning, the back of his black leather swivel chair still facing Max.

His home office is always immaculate, Max thought as he rubbed his wrist. He'd never seen the place look untidy.

'Dad, how are you?' Although his voice sounded calm, Max kept blinking.

'I'm fine, just going over some figure work at the moment.' He smiled, his hands resting in his lap. 'Do you need something?'

Max put one hand behind his back. 'I just wanted to talk to you.'

'Well I suppose I have a few minutes; what did you want to say?'

'I wanted to talk about my future.' He felt the pressure of his teeth on his lower lip, then rubbed the same area with the back of his hand.

'Future?' Lukas let out a deep throaty chuckle, 'that's already sorted out.' He leaned back, the chair groaned.

'I've got the contacts, everything is in place, got you a nice office, got you a nice position, everything is sorted.' He waved his hand at Max before returning to the screen.

Max shuffled his feet, seeing the wave as dismissive, distressed that his father had resumed his work.

'But Dad… that is not what I want.' In his ears, his voice sounded strained, on edge.

Stay calm Max.

'I'm sorry,' Max noted the look of bewilderment on Lukas' face as he rubbed his chin with the back of his hand. 'What do you mean that is not what you want? Your brother did what he was called to do, you'll be doing what you are supposed to do.'

'But that is not… I—'

'There is no argument, that is just the way things will be.' Max knew that tone of voice too well. The accompanying gesture – the flat hand halfway between his hips and his chest.

No argument required.

'I'm not interested in… pharmaceuticals.' Max placed his hand on his chest, pleading to be heard.

Lukas sighed deeply, then laughed loudly. 'You are joking aren't you, I get it – this is one of your… pranks.' The tough countenance softened. Max watched the gleefully wicked look slip into his eyes, 'You almost had me then.'

Max looked at the floor, one hand draped across his body, the other by his side. 'Dad, I'm really serious.'

Lukas pondered, as if recalling a memory, 'You've been hinting at this for some time. Thinking about it, I can remember certain little comments that you made. You are quite serious aren't you?' He leaned forward, gripping the sides of his swivel chair, gliding towards Max.

Yes. A sense of relief flooded through Max, he felt as if he were vibrating. *At last he is beginning to get the picture.*

'Tell me,' he questioned while folding his arms across his chest. 'What do you have in place of pharmaceuticals?' He was much closer now, Max could see the way his chest expanded and contracted.

The question gave Max renewed hope.

Perhaps he is trying to see things from my point of view?

'I have been thinking about… thinking about… biotechnology.' It was a struggle to combat confusion.

'Biotechnology?' Lukas repeated with disdain. 'What is the matter with you? Biotechnology?'

It's as if he's learned a new word.

'What do *you* know about biotechnology?' His thick finger pointed in Max's face, two hands width away.

'I have been studying'—'

'You have been studying *government*,' Lukas stated emphatically. The hand moved away returning to the arm of the chair.

'I went along to talks about… transhumanism and I really feel that is the way forward and that biotechnology—'

'Look son, you know my philosophy: drug 'em at birth, keep 'em for life. Our job is to produce products that will provide a regular income, that will keep people alive and keep them coming back for more. That is how we make our money, that is what your grandfather did, that is what I have done and that is what your brother is doing now and, no doubt, your sister, in time.'

He paused to make his point. Then returned to his work, 'And that is what you will be doing as well.'

From his perspective, the conversation was over. He shook his head as he tried to concentrate on the figures. He looked over his shoulder at Max, 'This is not a point of discussion; it is a point of fact.'

Max spoke softly: 'I'm not going to do it.' He thought if he said it quickly, it would minimise the impact.

'I beg your pardon?' He cupped his ear.

Since when have you been hard of hearing.

Max repeated his statement, 'I'm not going to do it.'

Lukas abandoned his work and stood up. The black swivel chair thudded against the filing cabinet, then toppled over. It lay on its side.

He stood face to face with Max.

'I've not put you through private school and Harvard for you to stand there and tell *me,'* Lukas jabbed his own chest, 'that you are not going. You will be working as planned, you will start you job and that is how it will be.'

Each time he said 'will' Lukas jabbed Max in his chest – hard, probing stabs at his sternum, forcing his upper body to jerk backwards.

The prods caught Max off guard, he stumbled. The physical protest was unexpected. He gathered himself, bracing his legs, adopting a defiant pose.

'I'm not doing it.' Despite the rising panic, his voice sounded confident.

I am not giving in to intimidation born of expectation and tradition – that old voice that always halts progress – the way it has always been done. No! I am the voice of the new generation. For a moment it was as if he were back in one of the stirring lectures at HSTT with Paul sitting next to him.

'I don't think you heard me, son. You are.' Spittle flew from his mouth landing on Max's top lip.

'No Dad, not this time… I'm making my own company—'

'You have got… Where did you get the money for that?' The look on his face was full of suspicion and hostility, accusing.

'I… I… I… Look, Dad, it's called praenumeration.' Max felt his confidence slipping away, his spine turning to rubber, his knees almost gave way.

Lukas rested his hand on his hips, 'I know a little about this concept. Pray enlighten me.' Then he changed his mind, 'In fact no. You go ahead, son. Go ahead and set up a company without me.'

He sounded mortally wounded. *It's your pride that is wounded. Little Max is not playing ball. That is the problem, this is not about you – it is about me!*

In a sudden flare of emotion, Lukas stepped towards Max.

'But how dare you? How dare you!' He pushed Max with both hands.

Max stumbled backwards, caught off guard. He gasped, not believing what had just happened.

Does he want to fight?

His stomach tightened, the same way he had always felt just before he'd gotten into scraps at school.

'The audacity,' his father's eyes were enclosed by slits of flesh, his neck extended, 'Who put you up for this? Did your mother–'

'It has nothing to do with Mother, she does not even know about it, we've not—'

'How dare you!'

Max started his apology, 'I'm so—' He never had the chance to finish it.

'Get out. Get out. Get out!'

Once would have been enough, but the accompanying finger jabs made it clear.

As he walked away, Max spoke loudly enough for him to hear, 'With pleasure.'

FRIDAY 4TH JUNE 1999 (BM)

None of it made any sense.

Berlioz did not help soothe his mind. Normally it worked, *Treatise on Orchestration*. Max heard the sounds but did not connect. He lay on his bed, in his bedroom; but neither creativity nor rhythm touched him.

At the university he'd developed a clear understanding of the connection between the hopes of society and the role of science in fulfilling those desires. Central to this understanding was his newfound academic appreciation for the hypothetical, practical potential of transhumanism. He believed that there existed in it a vast well of untapped potential for biological human development. Technology was advancing at an accelerating pace, and evolution was not *and had never been* static.

Of course, his thinking had changed. He laughed as the thought back to the early days.

A collision of ideas – that was how he would have described the first lecture he had heard on transhumanism. However, its underlying concepts seemed creep up on him, like a slow growing ivy. He loved engaging in discussions and debates with various gurus of the new religion – he would never forget the meeting with Max More. Seeing the impact of transhumanist discourse in its academic situation changed his thinking.

The string section pierced his thinking, stirring and full of emotion, soaring upwards. A moment of escape. Then the dark thoughts pushed to the front of his mind.

Fiscal potential – he found himself inexorably drawn towards its financial potential, and he loved engaging in an increasing number of conversations about this new philosophy as it accelerated towards its event horizon. An active observer, he predicted its movements: here was a way of thinking that would soon be a doctrine, a doctrine that could lead to a radical paradigm shift, paving the way as the old made way for the new.

Max believed rapid progression to new levels of human development to be held back by technical limitations and by minds that were not combatant in pushing beyond the boundaries of normality.

He turned onto his back – the restlessness would not be satisfied.

Max was not a scientist, but he admired those who dreamed of new possibilities; the innovators who would refuse to listen to those voices that were limited by ancient traditions and fading moral codes. He considered such credulity obsolete. After all, most people in the western world had no compulsion to adhere to these restrictions. The public were no longer guided by the moral codes that had influenced his grandparents.

A different framework governed affairs today. Max saw himself as a free thinker.

Combining chemical agents and nanotechnology had allowed the rapid acceleration of the transhumanist movement. The moment of singularity had presented itself, and by this time, he had opened the door and dutifully constructed a guest room to accommodate the most welcome of visitors. For the right price, of course.

Biotechnology was that door.

The rhythm of the drums matched that of his heart – synchronisation. Unity.

On returning from Harvard, he had become convinced that the family sagacity did not suit him. Expectation walked intimately with privilege all along the Augustine line. After all, it was Max's duty to continue in the footsteps of his ancestors.

He pressed his right forearm onto his forehead, both layers of skin felt rough and hot.

Maybe a long cold shower later.

It was so clear. His father did not share or even want to consider his perspective.

That meeting – if you could call it that – was awful.

His hero. His father. A blend of devastation, darkness and hopelessness swam around him, clinging to him like long strands of wet, decaying seaweed; this unwelcome emotional lodger, it delighted in dispensing torment.

He could still feel the prodding – blunt stabs that said his views meant nothing; his perspective, his dreams were nothing.

What a choice! He could toe the line and be a good little boy – making Daddy very happy. Or he could continue on this pathway, fulfilling his dreams. Living with the pain of rejection and without the support of those who he loved the most – he had never thought that would be part of the price. Being ostracised by the family… along with that came the unspoken threat of being removed from the will, a source of leverage and an effective weapon. Would any other member of the family dare to go against their father, even if deference meant the isolation of a sibling?

Dominant to the end, his father's iron grip threatened continuation, even after death – Max, caught in a never ending rigor mortis.

He turned onto his front, then gazed towards the window, faint moonlight trickling through the gaps in the curtain.

Mutiny was not an option. Max realised that he had always conformed – he had obeyed. But not this time.

The echo of his father's voice – the scary change in his tone. The deafening volume – eroding any possible pathway for communication. Only one way – his way. The solo booming baritone trying to fill the room. He shivered while remembering that moment.

Max felt proud of himself at the same time. He had been silent during the onslaught. A slither of moonlight lit up a small section of wallpaper, the faded stripy wallpaper, the same throughout the one bedroom apartment – he recalled its pale pastel shade.

He wanted to make a strong and memorable point as he left. He smirked as he remembered calculating the amount of force that had gone into the door slam, the crashing sound afterward – that was an added bonus. Part of him wondered what had caused the sound of breaking glass? But there was no way he was going back to investigate.

He used his imagination to create a caricature of his father at that moment? The veins on his neck ready to burst, his face beetroot like, swollen, looking like a bullfrog on helium, slamming his fists onto the desk.

Better the desk than me.

His father could be violent. Julian had used to stir up that part of his father's emotional spectrum and soon learned the stupidity of his ways. Nobody crossed father, in the family or in business.

I have gone and done just that.

By moving to New Jersey there was now some distance between them. Hiring lab and office space was costly. He chosen this place because it was cheap, the whole area was cheap. Right down to the décor.

There were some sections of wallpaper that had peeled off the wall revealing spotty black dots, faint dustings of black pepper on the bare wall; and the miserable landlord seemed reluctant to spend money on things like decoration. Keen to get his monthly income.

He considered his predicament. The repeated struggle with feelings of guilt and yet the sense of exhilaration. For once, he was fending for himself, no family net to catch him — *just me and my instincts*.

Would the rest of the family do as they were told? His mother had a way of dealing with father, she could work on him. What about Julian? Too timid to do anything but obey. A bit of a wimp in matters of family loyalty, though he could still whip Max in a fight. Little sis, still at high school. She dreamed of going onto the stage. If only his father knew how much she wanted that. He would have had another fit. Samantha would have to fight her own corner in the days to come. At least he would be able to help. Perhaps he would not be the only outcast.

What should I do?

Paul's face – the image slipped in front of his eyes. Paul would at least listen, and his advice was always balanced and helpful. *I'll send him an email.*

The music stopped. Normal everyday sounds replaced the beauty of genius: he was left with yelling from outside, car horns and barking dogs.

First I have to get my head round this thing.

SATURDAY 5TH JUNE 1999 (EE)

To: pbs@silverhurstmiddleschool.com
From: max1augustine@hotmail.com
Date: 05/06/1999

Hi Paul,

Help! My meeting with dad went so wrong. I stormed out and have not spoken to him since. Mom says that he is furious and has told everyone else not to get in touch with me until I come round to his way of thinking. What do I do?

You know that I have a couple of ideas of my own. I have heard of this new way of getting funding for projects. You invite people to make a contribution to your projects offering them some kind of return or reward. It cuts out the banks and allows ordinary people to get involved in supporting newcomers on the market. What do you think?

Sorry to sound so desperate but you were the first person I thought of.

Please say hi to all the family. Good to hear that Theresa is making great progress.

Max

To: pbs@silverhurstmiddleschool.com
From: max1augustine@hotmail.com
Date: 10/06/1999

Hello Paul,

Your advice was awesome. Thank you.

Dad is still not talking to me. My mother is disobeying his instructions and keeps in touch. He would go ballistic if he found out. The rest of the family are being obedient.

The funding idea has worked so well. I have enough money for a deposit on the business and plan to launch it by the end of the month. I would like you to come along as my guest of honour, I hope you will be able to bring the whole family with you. I hope that Theresa will be up to it. Thank you for investing in me – emotionally and financially. Your donation makes you a gold investor.

I am so excited. It is as if I have found my purpose in life. I feel so alive. I can see that our development as humans is held back by limitations in scientific techniques and minds that are unwilling to push beyond the boundaries of normality. We need to change the way we think – perhaps a paradigm shift to embrace things we can only dream of. Biotech is just one of the paths towards this goal. I hope my company will play a small part in this revolution.

Ben's video is fantastic, he has been practising his kicking. Archie looks a bit muffed in the background. Tell him to be glad for his bother.

Got a new car, you will have to wait to see what it looks like. Can you guess?

Well done on your promotion to deputy principal. You are the right man for the job. The kids are lucky to have you. Does that mean a new car for you too?

Bye,
Max

'I cannot believe you did that.'
Icilda buried a girlish giggle.

'I did and made it seem like a complete accident. A well placed nudge with the elbow,' said Icilda as she sandwiched the cordless phone between her ear and shoulder while she made notes on a writing pad. 'Poor little lamb, so terrified. Her eyes were like dinner plates and her little mouth… the way it trembled. Just staring at the red patch, she must have wondered if it was… her blood.'

'Icilda Ferrell, you are very wicked.' Marielle's words stern, Icilda's thoughts turned to Miss Eatteron; that woman had been a mean and hard spinster; one who had made life difficult at boarding school. Icilda had never quite worked out whether it was jealousy or hatred.

'A mother's got to do—'

'What a mother's got to do. I know the mother's code of honour.'

They both laughed, deep and loud. They shared a similar sense of humour, but not a common mind.

'But that was so risky. How could you know that Charles would—'

'He has been well trained, he knows all about the soda trick.' The view from the window was clear today, a bright and sunny day. Even the dog walker was out.

'Then what happened?'

'Well he goes over and stares at her all gooey eyed, mumbling about red wine and soda. She, Miss Mortification, was all ears and before you know it he has his hands all over her.' The pitch of her voice rose, she relished the memory, it gave her such a sense of satisfaction.

'Was that the ball for disadvantaged children? I think I was double-booked on that evening.'

'Yes, June 24th, that's right, you missed it. Lovely event.'

'Emerald dress with added wine spill – red wine at that. What did I say about you? Make that doubly wicked.'

Marielle's shriek made Icilda pull the phone away from her ear; the sound so discordant.

'Steady on Marielle, you nearly deafened me.'

'Now the rest is history. It has happened so quickly. When did you pencil in the wedding date? The day after the spill?'

'Marielle, give me some credit. Perhaps a week later.'

Both laughed hysterically. Icilda swapped the phone to her left ear, massaging her right shoulder as she moved elegantly from the window, before lowering herself into the love seat.

'Such a good family, such a good choice. However… a wedding in

September? Not really the weather for it.' Something about Marielle's comment irked Icilda.

'That is what we have chosen… It's been ages since we've spoken. I have been so busy, with arranging, booking flowers and hotels. ' She wanted to make a point, Marielle needed to be reminded who was who in their relationship. 'Colour schemes—'

'Is Mario Givetti doing the flowers?'

'Yes,' Icilda felt the smile – her golden shot.

'How did you manage that?' The woman's enunciation was coloured with wonder; it gave Icilda an inner glow. Top trumps.

'A few phone calls… It's who you know, you know.'

Marielle remained silent.

'Are we meeting next week?'

'Yes, Icilda. You have the date in your diary. I will be seeing Eleanor's mother tomorrow. Any messages?'

'No, everything is under control. We are having a meal on…' She picked her diary off the table and flipped through it. 'Ah, on the 25th of July. We've booked a table at Miguli's.' Another tiny stab. Stiletto sharp.

'Oh!'

The doorbell. The good old get out clause. 'Sorry Marielle. Got to go the wedding planner is here. Napkins and table decoration. See you soon. Ciao.' The conversation at an end. Icilda put the phone down and waited for the maid to open the door.

SUNDAY 21ST NOVEMBER 1999 (BM, R)

Charles applauded with vigour.

'That was fantastic – I'm ready for the second half.'

La Bohéme – his favourite opera. The show had been fully booked; getting a seat would have been almost impossible. Judging from the packed audience, a great many people shared his love of this production.

The box seats at the Manhattan Opera house came courtesy of his Pa. A thank you present for his hard work on behalf of IBC.

Eleanor looked stunning in her black chiffon gown, her hair up; the long red mane twirled and secured in an Audrey Hepburn style. Relaxed and thoughtful; such a gorgeous wife, his beauty.

She was a queen in her palace, surrounded by the ornate theatre; all carvings, chandeliers, plush carpets, and a live orchestra.

My beautiful wife. He kissed her on the cheek.

'Charles, we are in public.' She pushed him away.

The gesture of embarrassment surprised him. 'I wanted to let you now that I love you.' He felt silly, she'd misunderstood his intention.

'I know you love me, just don't create scenes in public. It's so common.' A brief glint flashed in her eyes. Then he noticed the childish expression that danced across on her face. Charles knew something was up.

She grabbed his right hand and placed it on her abdomen. 'What are you doing Mrs Ferrell? A public display of affection.' His shoulders moved up and down in an exaggerated manner as he teased her.

Eleanor's eyes locked with his; she moved in close to his left ear, whispering, 'A little Ferrell's in da house.'

Charles froze, glued to his seat. He told his mouth to speak – nothing came out. The room seemed to grow hazy, someone had trapped his lungs in a vice, then rapidly squeezed it shut.

Eleanor tried pulling him back into his seat, to shift him from his curious pose, right on the edge of the chair. He did not move. Still, motionless. Eleanor laughed, loudly. 'Sorry Charles. I could not resist that. Kiss me any time you like, I really don't mind.'

He did not remember a word she'd said. As he sat there, a single phrase kept going through his mind – *I'm going to be a Pa.*

Eleanor recounted the event the following day. It turned out that he couldn't remember anything else that had happened that night.

MONDAY 29TH NOVEMBER 1999 (BM)

As Eleanor opened the door, she felt her trembling heart bolt into her mouth. The dry sensation on her tongue combined with an air of foreboding, uncomfortable and unnerving.

The musty malodour of old books saturated the air, mixing with the fetor of years of cigars. Mr Peterson, known for being a compulsive smoker

– famed for his immense appetite for anything laden with nicotine. Added to that he was also the principal.

He should be more responsible, working with children and smoking – surely that poses a health hazard?

His busy administrative schedule limited his contact time with the kids – *thankfully*. Eleanor reckoned that sitting next to him or even engaging in a conversation was likely to increase a person's nicotine intake tenfold.

Mr Peterson sat in a leather-bound chair behind a huge mahogany desk. Neat stacks of documents were symmetrically positioned on the desk, leaving him with a clearly defined writing area. She noted the ink well on the right side of the desk – a relic from the past plus the fact that Peterson was leftie.

Imagine that, he still writes his letters and memos with a fountain pen.

The study suffered from light starvation. Mr Peterson's writing zone seemed to be bathed in a pool of pale yellow luminescence, emanating from an antique table lamp.

She had not missed the impact of her entrance. Once he saw her, the welcome smile slid from his face immediately replaced by a serious frown. He did not even attempt to disguise his displeasure.

'Hello Eleanor,' he stood up, pointing to the single chair in front of his desk. Mr Peterson's long, thin face, framed by a mop of tightly curled, once black hair, now greying, neatly cut in an archaic style that harked back to the 1950s. His black suit must have come from that era too; it needed a decent press. Mr Peterson's professional attire was both crumpled and saggy.

She sat, adjusting her carefully chosen and decidedly long skirt before making eye contact. Mr Peterson appeared stern, quite tense, his mouth thin and taut. Two bushy eyebrows confronted her, almost merging; red eyelids completing the tired expression. He stank of cigarettes. Pregnancy had increased her sensitivity to odours – *especially unpleasant ones* – she could taste tobacco. She sniffed several times in disdain, then crossed her legs.

Getting into Middleton Elementary school meant that parents and staff alike had to put up with Peterson's eccentricities and his awful personal hygiene. It was generally considered to be worth it; the school was widely acknowledged as a gateway into the top Middle schools – WM Diamond, Blanchard or Thomas Blake – and those schools paved the way to the top universities – Princeton, Harvard, Yale or Columbia. Middleton's impressive list of alumni was clear enough evidence that the institution's prestige was more than rumour.

In her mind his passion for collecting ancient texts contributed to the overwhelmingly musty smell. Overloaded bookshelves lined three out of the four sides of the room; the other wall was occupied by an empty fireplace. Several school trophies rested on the shelf above the empty log basket. Victories past.

She glanced away from Peterson, locking onto the faded oil portrait of the school's founder, hanging above the fireplace. Francis Middleton. Thoroughly miserable and significantly ancient; the crooked angle of the picture, so deeply annoying. Eleanor identified with his demeanour, his soul eternally immortalised on canvas. She wondered how many hours he had to sit to get that mood. Now here she was sitting with him and Peterson. This was one interview she wished she could avoid.

'I understand you have a bit of a situation.' Mr Peterson's long fingers formed a bridge, his forefingers tapping out an inaudible rhythm. 'First term and pregnant. That was not well planned.'

Something about his voice annoyed Eleanor, yet she clearly understood the predicament. Of course it was not planned, she was more shocked than anyone else including Charles. This was going to be a struggle, a struggle to suppress her own negative attitude; one that bordered on defiance. She accepted responsibility for the situation. Sure, contraception had been around for thousands of years, but she'd not imagined that it could happen to her so soon after marriage. They'd been using condoms; but the concept of the pill was not to her liking. A recent article in *Metropolitan* had questioned its toxic impact on the body, both short and long term, not something to which she wanted to be exposed. She was no lab rat.

Charles could be very spontaneous and very demanding, not that she minded. It must have been one of those unplanned moments. Inwardly she smiled, Peterson's face indicated that he was not amused.

She had ended up buying three pregnancy test kits. Periods were like clockwork, so she knew something was up when her October's run failed to arrive. She'd stood there for at least five minutes, staring at the stick, hardly believing the colour – the conclusion beyond doubt. After the second and third test it began to sink in.

The *La Bohéme* episode with Charles… she would always remember the expression on his face, only a snapshot of how she had felt; he was dumbstruck. She felt deeply shocked even traumatised. Keeping the secret from him had taken so much effort – somehow she'd managed it. That was all in the past. Now, more immediate matters demanded her attention.

'I know this is not the best of situations, it was... has happened. I have only just got married, I had not expected to get pregnant so early.' Eleanor chose her words with great care. 'My plan was to wait a few years, get ahead in my career and then have children.'

Her synchronised hand movements harmonised with carefully selected words. She wanted to say she was sorry, sorry for the inconvenience. Inside though, another part of her shouted: *tough, life happens you just have to go with it!*

Her plan: children after four years, some time out, then straight back into the classroom before becoming a senior teacher, a couple of years later a vice-principal and finally principal. All by the time she was forty.

Peterson's expression remained bleak, he gave no emotional cues. Eleanor crossed her arms, focusing on the ink well. *He's assessing me.* She'd felt the same way at the initial interview.

The room seemed eternal, even then. The streaks of light that did manage to find their way into the room only served to give it an ethereal glow. The dust and the awful smell – *have I been sentenced to a term in prison?*

Middleton. Getting a job offer for this place was a real accomplishment. Eleanor recalled the sheer delight she'd experienced upon opening the confirmation letter; she'd jumped on the spot and screamed. It was an achievement, her second teaching post.

'I have—'

'Our situation,' he sneered as he interrupted her, 'demands that we think ahead. We will have to recruit a kindergarten teacher to cover your class during your maternity leave; which means advertising, interviewing and all the things that go along with the acquisition of a new member of staff.' His eyes focused on something above her head.

What is he staring at? Lost in his own little world. He's so rude. No wonder the staff say he's a long lost relative of Attila.

His nickname, Commandant Hun, abbreviated to CH. *Bold, tough and ruthless, our dear CH.* It was hard not to despise him.

She pushed out the breath, turned towards the fireplace. Gurgling sounds rumbled in her stomach, accompanied by a queasy sensation.

'When's it due?'

Eleanor sat up. The use of the term 'it' triggered something, prickly heat moved along her abdomen. When she spoke her voice quiet yet menacing: 'Did you say… it?'

Peterson's reaction, so comical – *that caught him by surprise.*

His face turned pale pink. 'I meant… Ah your bab… child.' That voice sounded so different from the condescending air of their earlier conversation.

'I'm due in June.'

All the initial reservation vanished, replaced by open defiance. *Let him say whatever he has to say* – she knew her rights. Sure, she would not be able to claim much in the way of maternity compensation but the law gave her some protection, she'd done her homework.

Charles' salary would hardly stretch to cover the loss of her income though and things would be tough. If the worst happened… *if things get too tight… well, we can always raid his family's huge vault.*

Though to his credit, Charles never made reference to that. Or her parents would make a contribution.

They had no mortgage worries – the apartment belonged to them. Legally, the school had to cover her absence and hold the job open until the end of her maternity leave. 'Do you have a problem with that?'

Peterson shifted uneasily on his seat before sinking into it. Those bright pink cheeks – *a touch too much rouge.* She wanted to smirk.

The gossip in the staffroom suggested that he had only just survived his second marriage. His way with women was not well defined – in need of remedial assistance; long serving female teachers could testify to this. Some said he had a real phobia of strong, independent women, which made it ironic that he should have chosen to marry several of them.

What was the phrase that Sonia, the head of maths used? Yes that was it, 'emotionally undeveloped, academically brilliant'. Thank God I'm not married to him.

She only half-accepted that he had called the baby an 'it'. At least, the baby was an 'it' to Peterson. But she felt defensive all the same; this was their 'it' – the unknown child of *their* union. Next week would be her second scan. It was too early to find out the sex – that would provide a bit more information about this unknown little one.

He has such a nerve, using the term 'it' – ignorant, pompous and out of touch with modern life, and now he's squirming on his comfortable chair!

Peterson's face returned to its usual hues, he continued: 'We know that you are an excellent teacher. We would be sorry to lose you, so we will do everything that is legally required to meet the demands of the situation. This will be very sad for your kindergarten class who are just getting to know you—'

'I'm pregnant, not dying.' The honesty of her voice worried her – *did I really say that?* Perhaps the hormones were unsettling her normally rock solid response to pressurised situations. 'I will be at school until my maternity leave.'

'Have you been pregnant before?'

Legally she knew that was none of his business. She wanted to make the point but decided in the circumstances not to aggravate the already tense situation. 'No.'

That little revelation seemed to encourage his boldness, he leaned forward, 'There are many unforeseen sides of pregnancy that can impact teaching. Have you thought about morning sickness, standing up for long periods... lifting children?' The new advantage seemed to increase his confidence, the finger bridge returned.

'We might need to have a temp on standby.' His head moved up and down as if he were agreeing with himself.

That's your problem not mine. I have a class in twenty minutes. I would like to go right now.

'But that is our problem, not yours. Come and see me if there are any particular issues. Have you notified the school nurse?'

Those unkempt eyebrows were ready to mesh together. Eleanor's growing sense of agitation – fuelled by the fact that she still had not finished hanging up the art display, knowing that the students would be arriving within the next twenty minutes – pushed her towards rage; insolence now a neighbour to resurfacing anxiety.

'Yes, Christie knows. I will let you know if I have any problems.' She was determined not to have any 'problems' and would do everything within her power to avoid them.

'Okay Mrs Ferrell, we will talk again. Anything else on your mind?'

No, she thought, then after a short pause she reconsidered.

How did an idiot like you get to be principal?

Both of them were mesmerised by the screen; a miracle before their eyes.

Today they would find out the sex of the unknown one. Eleanor had convinced herself that it was a boy, Charles believed they were expecting a girl. Today would reveal who was right and who was wrong.

Charles had cancelled all his morning appointments. Eleanor's controlled rage prompted this move as he'd missed the previous two scans. Her poignant accusation – he put his work before his family – had infuriated him. She then added that this was not a good omen for their life together. It took a while before he managed to calm down, at that point Charles promised to attend the next session.

True to his word, he sat next to her, holding her hand.

The baby was now in its fifteenth week of life; the sonographer, Friya Prigg, hummed as she worked. Eleanor relished the wonder on Charles' face, sharing his moment of awe.

'We are not usually sure about the sex of a child until about the fourteenth or fifteenth week. By now the baby's sex organs will have grown so we can see for ourselves. Let's hope that baby will let us have a peek.' Friya turned the screen to face them.

Bloating! Not due to pregnancy, it was all that water she had consumed in preparation for the scan. So awkward, her extended bladder ready to explode. Having the ice cold jelly smeared all over her abdomen was also rather unpleasant part of the process. She took some comfort in Charles' firm grip.

Eleanor's fascination overshadowed her discomfort. Friya took many measurements and showed them the inner world inhabited by their child.

'Would you like a picture?' Friya asked.

'Yes please,' they said in unison.

'Judging from the way things are developing, your due date is correct.' Friya completed the paperwork as she spoke. 'Do you want to know the sex of your baby? That last somersault gave us all the information we need.'

They nodded.

'You are having a little...' Friya seemed keen to reveal the mystery. Eleanor pushed herself into an upright position while Charles squeezed her hand, 'A little girl!'

Charles moved his shoulders up and down, gloating in his moment of victory. Eleanor simply huffed, equally delighted.

A baby girl – how exciting! Tired yet happy, she soothed her little girl with gentle circular strokes. An early Christmas present.

Saturday 22nd January 2000 (BM, R)

Bethany woke angry; her mood exactly the same as when she had gone to bed. Those nasty words would not go away. Peggy Su had voiced her obnoxious opinion the previous evening, during their girls' night out.

Frank and Bethany believed that they were destined to be together. After all, they were childhood sweethearts. Others, Peggy Su included, were not so sure.

Both of them went along with that assumption even though they sensed that serious issues bubbled just beneath the surface of their relationship. Perhaps that was part of the problem...

They'd grown up in the same neighbourhood in Phoenix, Arizona. Bethany had lost count of the number of times they'd split up and got back together; somehow, it seemed natural. Call it gut instinct, she often said, but they needed each other. Nonetheless, nothing they did really helped to resolve the tense undercurrents and they continued to have bitter arguments with one another over the most trivial matters.

When Frank proposed to Bethany a number of concerns surfaced... Would they end up fighting all the way to the retirement home? How many of her angry slams would the door manage before it fell off its hinges? Silly things like that. Sure, they had great times; but the low times in between, they were mentally wearing. Was she ready to sign up to a life of strife?

Back then, Bethany had confided in Peggy Su, her best friend in the world. Her advice: 'Follow your heart, Beth.'

And so they were married in the summer of 1991. Bethany had just turned twenty. Miss Greaves became Mrs Bartell. It was a beautiful sunny day and the small Methodist Community Church in Phoenix was packed with hopeful onlookers. Saturday 22nd June.

Everyone went home agreeing that it had been a good wedding. Nonetheless, it was followed by ten years of stress and discontent; despite the best assistance that science could offer, Bethany failed to become pregnant.

They'd both come from large families and had expected to have lots of kids. Bethany assuming that she would have four or five kids for most of her life and as a girl she had played somewhat overzealously with the plastic family of Barbie, Cindy and Ken. In her teens she'd dreamed of a large family, hovering about in the background of her life; something along the lines of the *Brady Bunch* or the *Partridge Family*. She adored those classic shows, sitting there, glued to the golden oldies channel, back then.

The stark reality of her condition was a barren womb; it was like a wound, throbbing, reminding her of its presence, right there at the core of her identity. Babies – she loved them yet dreaded being around them, forced to witness and feel the internal boxing match between guilt and shame, a relentless pounding of blows inside her stomach that arose whenever she spent time around children.

Bethany loved her parents, but the subtle comments that they made were getting worse; increasing in frequency since her last birthday. Their retirement plan in place, they wondered what to do with the portion set apart to accommodate grandchildren. Though their words were meant to be lighthearted, those comments cut like a silent stiletto knife each time she heard them, on the phone or during their infrequent visits from California.

Both she and Frank had undergone extensive testing. His sperm were fine and there were no obvious problems with her plumbing. They were encouraged to try IVF. Those nasty cycles – even the memory made her bladder muscles relax. Another painful addition to her life.

Bethany and clomifene did not get on; an alternative medication proved to be more effective and with fewer side effects. After six cycles of treatment, she had seen no improvements – it was not working.

Conversations about adoption quickly reached an impasse. Frank wanted to have his own children and refused point blank to look after the offspring of a stranger. The whole thing turning out to be a source of further heartache – like a cruel marathon, run for over a decade and with no finishing line in sight.

Her job as a supervisor at the local supermarket provided a little distraction, at least it kept her mind off her own problems. But at the same time, it placed her right in the centre of other people's lives. Every few weeks there would be an under delivery of diapers or an incorrect order of pregnancy tests or a pile of smashed baby food bottles on aisle seven. That or some other reminder. On top of that, the workforce was mainly female and mostly conversed about one another's children, good and bad relationships and their plans for transition into the world of motherhood. It was one part holiday from home (at least she didn't have to listen to Frank's complaints) and one part living hell.

Then there were the times that her colleagues became pregnant, the bodies advertising they were knocked up again, as they smiled gleefully, submitting the paperwork that would ensure their maternity leave. It was always their second, third, or fourth. Never her first. Bethany thought of leaving and working in a retirement home, but she disliked seeing people die on a regular basis and the thought of coping with dementia and Alzheimer's and all of that was just too much. Besides, she had concluded, there would always be a plentiful supply of visiting grandchildren who would serve to remind her of her empty womb. The canteen was the worst... If only she could skip that part of the day. She smiled and laughed heartily as she listened to their stories; but on the inside, jealousy smouldered along with envy in a slow burn.

That pain ran deep. As time went by and people realised her situation, it began to feel like her flat stomach served as a public declaration of failure; it was as if she had let everyone down, unable to do something that everyone else seemed to take for granted and even expect of her, a secret deal made between men and women; unspoken but assumed.

Bethany managed to avoid invitations to events involving children; her main excuse was Frank's guests. Her busy hospitality schedule made it impossible to accept their kind offers.

The truth was that Frank never needed her services as a hostess because no one at his workplace became more than an acquaintance. He remained painfully shy when it came to forming in-depth relationships with other people – she was something of an exception. He could cope with the sales pitches and was able to close on deals, but long-term relationships? Well, they caused him a great deal of anxiety, so he avoided the challenge. She could count the number of people he called friends on the fingers of one hand.

Sometimes, the undercurrent lurking beneath the surface of their relationship would surface like tidal wave; arguments and harsh words always followed. She gave just as good as she got and the violent exchanges were followed by increasingly lengthy periods of silence. If no words were spoken, there could be no argument. This was her strategy for survival.

During these emotional storms, she would thump her way around the house, bashing the iron on the ironing board in the spare room, or shoving the broom noisily around the backyard. And they were just two of her hiding places.

They both enjoyed bowling and they attending the same country-dance group at their local school hall. Such moments were the glue that held their fragile relationship together. Shania Twain's *You're Still The One* – that was their song. Bethany swore it had been written just for them. No matter where they were, they would always find each other, even if they had just rowed. Cheek to cheek, it was their way of saying sorry, admitting their need for one another. Bethany meant every word that she sang along to; and she knew that Frank enjoyed the sentiments of the lyrics just as much as she did. They sang in tune, but not in harmony.

Frank and his company car – the thing allowed him to travel to his clients without being a burden on their household's budget. She admired his progress within the refrigeration company but it meant that he was often away on lengthy business trips. It was hard at the beginning, but in truth, those absences gave them time apart – and they needed those breathing spaces. Regular chances to consider the reasons for which they were still together.

During the pauses, she could see her friends and have Peggy Su over. How she enjoyed those girls' nights out – like yesterday. It provided her with a chance to dress up and act as if she was single. She never went too far though; just a bit of flirting, nothing too serious. Always under the watchful eyes of her friends.

And Peggy Su, well, she knew all of Bethany's little secrets.

SATURDAY 6TH MAY 2000 (BM, EWA, R)

The day that Momo died.

Brenda wondered if Karl needed additional counselling. There were no tears or any expression of emotion.

The Kuhlman philosophy included teaching the boys about being responsible and learning to care for others. They were allowed one pet each: Jasper had an albino corn snake, Darren kept a pet tortoise. When Karl joined the family, they had spent over two hours in the pet shop before he made up his mind. He settled for a pet hamster, promptly naming him Momo.

Karl chose the cage and a good selection of toys. He kept the cage scrupulously clean, making sure that Momo had plenty to eat and drink. Due to his frequent handling of Momo, the hamster became accustomed to human contact. Karl kept a diary of Momo's life, measuring his growth, weighing him and keeping written records. Soon becoming a mini expert on hamsters, learning unique facts and interesting information about the species.

Momo featured in all of his animal behaviour experiments. Karl believed that animals could be trained and educated, thereby boosting their intelligence. He designed various experiments to test out his ideas, creating a series of test circuits for Momo to navigate through, while he recorded the timings, compared the results and meticulously plotted them on his graphs. Momo seemed willing to participate, the two of them enjoying their time together.

The memory circuit seemed to challenge Momo the most. Brenda recalled being amazed at the experiment, there were four mini tests that needed to be solved. Karl made sure that he rewarded improved times with extra treats – Momo really liked carrots. After each successful run, a delighted Karl would hug the hamster and give him a carrot stick while praising him with generous words. Momo's whiskers twitched as he displayed his incisor teeth, almost as if he were smiling. Fun and science were the names of the game. Everyone could see they were devoted to each other, Karl loved Momo and Momo seemed to adore Karl. He shared his thoughts, even his secrets, with his furry friend.

Karl begged Brenda to get another hamster, he had read that they were social animals and did much better if they had company. She reminded him of the one pet one child rule. Karl threw a strop, stamped his foot and shouted at Brenda calling her wicked and cruel.

By Kuhlman standards they were pretty harsh words; she'd tried not to take it to heart. Even so, Brenda remembered how shocked and hurt the outburst made her feel. Karl was sent to his room while she waited for Marvin to come home; too confused to trust herself to respond.

As soon as Marvin stepped through the door, she rushed into his arms, crying. It wasn't the first time they'd been talked back to by their children but the venom in Karl's voice had shaken her. It was like an unpleasant echo of something half remembered – something that reeked of his life before the Kuhlmans. Brenda had a sneaking suspicion that he would have used other, forbidden words, had he ever had chance to learn them.

Marvin supported her and spoke sternly to Karl, who had managed to calm down.

Afterwards, he apologised for his words and hugged her before telling her that she was neither cruel nor wicked. A little reluctantly, he confessed that he had wanted to hurt her and those words had seemed best. Though she appreciated his honesty, his callous streak frightened her, something nasty even sinister lay beneath the surface.

She told the rest of the household not to accept any similar outbursts before interrogating the other boys to make sure that they had not enter into any secret pacts with Karl. There would be no covering up of unacceptable behaviour. They seemed genuinely shocked that she would think them capable of such deceit. That pleased her, Jasper and Darren were honest, but they were not spiteful.

A year later Karl found the body in the cage, cold and dead. He seemed to go into a trance, speaking in a slurred manner while hyperventilating. She'd wanted to call the doctor but Marvin had told her not to. He carried the Karl up to his room, laying him on his bed.

Brenda sat with him. He started talking about science and hamsters. He was regurgitating various facts, snippets of information, all the while avoiding any mention of Momo. They all knew about his mother and the tragic nature of her death.

Did this take him back to that event?

Discussing his parents? Karl never did. Carlton managed to send birthday and Christmas cards though. He' been refused all access to Karl, the letter arriving via social services. Karl read them, shaking as he deciphered the awful handwriting, then he threw them into the bin. Straightaway his mood darkened; his frustration taken out on any of the boys who came across his path. It would take him days before he calmed down.

Karl kept two photo albums in his third underbed storage box. They were full of photographs of his life with his mother and father, social services retrieved them from the suicide scene, it was agreed that Karl should be allowed to keep them. Brenda asked him to let her have a look at them; he refused every time, shaking his head vigorously. To Karl, they were his secrets, his private life. Of course, when he was not around, she had gone through them. The photos showed painful things, often masked behind fake smiles; photographs depicting a bleak life on the edge of poverty, full of what looked to her like sadness. That woman's sunken eyes... his mother's. Brenda had mentioned this to the psychologist, who had advised her to until Karl told her that he wanted to bring things up, to wait until he was ready.

She sat listening to his scientific talk, waiting for a moment to ask him about his feelings and what he wanted to do with Momo. He just kept going, non-stop – fact after fact – accurate but cold information. Brenda held him in her arms rocking him as he talked. He eventually drifted off to sleep.

$$+++$$

'Do you want a brandy?' Marvin headed towards the drinks cabinet.

'Are you kidding me? If I start with one glass I might finish the whole bottle.' She raised her hand, shaking her head.

Marvin stroked the side of his face, deciding to abandon his dry martini, 'You look shattered.'

'I'm exhausted,' Brenda dropped into the easy chair, kicking her slippers off then bringing her knees up to her chest, hugging them. Marvin thought of a slow puncture on a tyre; Brenda close to running on empty. 'Did we do the—'

'Look Brenda, we've been down that road,' he sat in the opposite chair, leaning forward. 'We can't do this every time things get tough.'

Brenda put her legs down, flopping her hands in her lap, 'I know but, sometimes I feel so desperate so helpless,' she rubbed her left wrist with her right thumb. Her tick.

'We,' he pointed at himself then Brenda, 'cannot undo all that Karl has been through. All we can do is provide an environment for him to come to terms with the past and heal.' Marvin folded his arms, leaning back in the chair.

'I wish I could do more.'

'Well you can't, perhaps you'd better stop trying.' He checked his watch, 'We have two other children to care for.'

'Karl needs so much time and attention I…' Brenda's voice was strained, lacklustre.

He hesitated before making his next statement, 'Brenda, you are not the fairy godmother in this story. There is no magic wand or instant fix. We'll keep loving him.'

It hit home. She looked away, tearful.

'Are we agreed on this?' No response. 'Brenda!'

She looked at him. 'Yes, we'll do what we can.' She brushed away her tears.

'Shall I cook tonight?' He disliked that particular chore but on this occasion, being helpful was more important than being macho.

'Yes please,' she sat back in the chair. 'Thank you honey.'

Brenda sat alone in the living room with her thoughts.

+++

Marvin worked on the meal while Brenda called the psychologist, who promptly advised her to book Karl in for a bereavement counselling course, alongside his monthly therapy sessions. In some ways this tragedy was a blessing as it provided a way of dealing with his mother's death in a non-direct manner. She praised the Khulman's for their parenting skills. Her words flowed over Brenda, like a soothing balm; words of inspiration and encouragement were just what she needed.

Karl decided to bury his hamster in the back garden, underneath the rose bushes, near the back fence. He insisted on digging the hole, wrapping Momo in white dishcloth before placing him in the freshly prepared grave. Nobody else was to be involved; he wanted to do it his way. Marvin and Brenda agreed, watching the sombre ceremony from the kitchen window. Jasper and Darren were in the playroom watching videos. They knew Momo was dead and felt sad; Jasper's snake had died a few weeks before Momo. The little guy had cried and cried for hours, before deciding to bury it under the apple tree in the centre of the garden. All of the family had been invited to that ceremony, but Karl had decided not to attend.

Karl never cried. That worried Brenda the most. Not one tear. From that day onwards there was not one mention of Momo. The bereavement sessions would go on for six weeks. After discussion, they decided that Marvin should attend with Karl. He promised to give her updates on how Karl was doing.

After an initial assessment, the counsellor suggested that Karl had compartmentalised the death of his mother in order to survive; he lived with the grief but had held it at a certain depth. This was not uncommon in such cases of trauma. Momo's death allowed her to tactfully confront Karl about bereavement issues, giving him the chance to think about his mother in a controlled manner, to release some of the buried emotional energy.

After the final session, Marvin came home needing counselling himself! Listening to the shocking experience of a four year old boy, strained through the trained mind of the bereavement counsellor, left him feeling traumatised. The true extent of the cruelty inflicted on Karl by his father released pure fury in Marvin; an emotional state he didn't quite know how to deal with it. It had shocked him.

Now he understood the relationship that Karl had with his teddy, who he called little Karl. When he had arrived, the bear had already looked tatty and battered. Karl went to sleep hugging the bear every single night. It was his principal source of comfort. The counsellor explained that Karl talked to the teddy, feeling able to share his deepest and most intimate secrets. This strategy helped him to survive in the wake of his mother's death; enabling him to step beyond this traumatic past. As far as Karl was concerned, the bear understood. Brenda could see that Momo had been a living version of the teddy too; another being, capable of listening to the boy's fears and dreams without ever judging or condemning Karl.

Marvin reflected on all the love that Karl had poured into his friendship with Momo. Losing him had been like losing a best friend; your most trusted companion. Brenda seemed to have understood it all straight away but he'd had to think about it before it had made any sense.

The details of the sustained abuse come to light during those sessions; the naked, unrestrained cruelty of Karl's father. Brenda tried to explain to Marvin that beating up the man would not solve the problem. Even so, Marvin was so angry, livid even. From that time on, he dealt with Karl with much more compassion; going out of his way to show him patience and understanding. In fact, he redoubled his efforts in praising and encouraging Karl. He held him more too. Brenda liked the change in her husband.

Every anniversary of the death was marked by Karl. It was always a private ceremony. He kept that up for five years, until he was twelve.

Sitting in the living room felt uncomfortable. In fact everything that she used to do before getting pregnant was entirely awkward or otherwise difficult. She adjusted the cushions. Eleanor leaned back, then decided that they were still not right.

Last night had been sleepless. For the last two nights rest, no rest. Conscious of Charles, snoozing away beside her, quite contentedly, she tried not to toss and turn too much. Knees up, knees down, hugging pillows, on the side, then turning and trying the other side – the mound kept growing week by week. Observing the changes in her body, they were both scary and mysterious.

Her regular keep fit routine stopped after about week sixteen, she read it was too risky for the baby. So then she had tried swimming, finding it relaxing, an added bonus she'd got to know a couple of other moms who were also expecting.

Let nature take its course while my figure goes off course.

Her bra was wet again, both breasts seemed to leak at intervals as if they took turns to seep the watery secretion.

I should have put the pads in – the wetness has gone straight onto the material. Too bad.

She turned the pages of *Baby and Mother.* There were so many conflicting accounts about childbirth. If she was honest, it frightened her. Pain – she could take it but *that* pain? Everyone had their own take on what or what not to do. She had already worked out the birthing plan. Their midwife was so supportive, ready to listen to her ideas and take them on board.

Eleanor reached for the glass on the table, her breathing seemed to stop momentarily. She panted for a few seconds.

Temporary breath cut off – coping with shortness of breath still made her anxious.

Sipping soya milk, she used to hate this stuff but since getting pregnant she consumed it. Charles would be home around 6pm, that left her two hours before she would need to think about being in the kitchen. Tonight he would have to make do with a frozen lasagne and salad, she felt too tired to stand on her feet and cook something from scratch. He was good in that way, he never complained about her food provision.

Charles loved her new curves and keeping his hands off her boobs seemed like a full time job. Making love had become more difficult in the last couple of weeks; she was too tired to be passionately involved, he still seemed to love it. Sex bomb Charles had not changed. Even her warning that it might trigger the birthing process did not deter him.

The light was dimming, the traffic sounds rising as people made their way home. The gurgling sound moved from on one side of her belly to the other. Today her daughter seemed to be having a gymnastics session. Eleanor whispered, 'Not long my lovely one, not long'.

If the estimates were right, she had four weeks before the day arrived. The video on giving birth stated that the first child was always unpredictable, late arrivals were more common than timely ones! She belched, and rubbed her sternum – *heartburn again.*

Pregnancy and the problems it caused, she could write a book. She certainly did not relish haemorrhoids – swollen, tender bubbles of flesh that made going to the bathroom something of dread. How they itched. It was so embarrassing when she was in company. The ointment stopped the bleeding, and seemed to reduce them a bit.

The bathroom was calling. With careful manoeuvring she pushed herself forward, then perched on the edge of the sofa. If she moved forward with purpose she could do it. The new position made her aware of backache. Instinctively, she moved her hands onto her back. 'I hope you appreciate all this hard work young lady.'

The young rebel seemed to kick out her response. Eleanor's bladder took control, she had approximately thirty seconds before she would need to change her underwear. Past experience had taught her that timing was everything.

The race was on. It was an event that Eleanor was determined to win.

WEDNESDAY 28TH JUNE 2000 (EE, WD, PA)

NEW YORK TIMES
BIRTH ANNOUNCEMENTS

Charles and Eleanor Ferrell of New York are proud to announce the birth of their daughter, Miranda Ferrell on June 28 2000 at Lister Hospital.

Miranda weighed 8lbs. 7oz. and was 20.5 inches long. Maternal grandparents are Sheila and Dwight Raddison of New Jersey. Paternal grandparents are Icilda and Ralph Ferrell of New York.

TUESDAY 8TH AUGUST 2000 (BM, EWA, R)

Icilda was on her way, the impending storm complete with rain sodden clouds.

Eleanor tolerated the churning stomach that accompanied the idea of occupying the same space as her mother in law. She felt jumpy, on edge. After the fourth check of her watch, she had about ten minutes left before the witch of the East arrived. Though the late afternoon sun warmed and lit the apartment, that woman's visit threw a damp blanket on everything.

Maybe she was being unfair on Icilda? Charles loved his mother and she doted on him. Being an only child… it only seemed natural for her to devote her life to him. Charles – a her pride and joy.

She's struggling with the fact that Charles is married to me now. She just can't to let go.

Always offering advice when it was not called for, making frequent comments that implied that Eleanor was not doing things right, according to her view of right. Eleanor found herself constantly having to counterattack her quips.

Very tiring company… I hate feeling like this.

Eleanor scanned the apartment. Everything was in place. Miranda was clean, the kitchen was spotless, the living room had been vacuumed twice. Cushions were plumped up and set in place.

Maybe if Icilda had to do these things for herself she would be kinder? Her lifestyle was characterised by the presence of maids and servants, carrying out her every whim. Had her tender hands ever actually known what is was like to be ordinary?

I wonder what she did before she got married? Maybe she thinks I married Charles for his money? My family are not poor. Why would she think that?

Such worrying questions made Eleanor analyse her relationship with Charles. Did she have a hidden motive? That tormenting inquisition went on when she felt melancholy or they had a fiery argument. Working out the truth was so difficult.

Her conclusion – a she married him simply because she loved. *Why was it so hard?*

Charles would not hear one bad word about his mother. In his eyes she was an angel, without blemish or fault.

The saintly witch from the East.

A sigh escaped from her lips; she rubbed her elbow, pacing.

+ + +

'Come in Icilda,' Eleanor pecked her on the cheek.

That was a light touch kiss, obviously not one for affection. Charles always kissed her properly. 'Thank you my dear, how are you today?' The scrutiny began the minute she stepped across the threshold. On her last visit Eleanor had seemed rather glum, even melancholy.

'I'm well, had some sleep last night that always helps,' her daughter in law shifted her fringe.

Yes, she appears a bit fresher.

Icilda surveyed the corridor as she handed her coat to Eleanor. Neat and tidy, they had decorated since she last visited. Very nice in a kind of bohemian manner. *This must be her choice of colour, the décor is certainly not the style Charles would have chosen.*

The plain walls, cream, with a few large framed photographs making it seem less bleak. The dark runner leading down the corridor, *perhaps in need of a dry clean?* Icilda made a mental note to recommend a suitable carpet cleaner.

'Do go into the living room, I'll just put your coat away.' Eleanor smiled.

'Thank you dear, it would be nice to sit down, today has been pretty hectic.' As she glided towards the living room Icilda commented, 'I can see you have had some work done,' She raised her voice, so that Eleanor would hear her approval.

The bright afternoon light made the room feel airy, though it was bijou and compact. The young architect had made good use of space and they had not cluttered the place with too much furniture; this was an excellent wedding present for the couple. Hopefully by now Charles had acted on her advice, deciding to rent out his bachelor pad – it was in a prime location and was capable of securing a top rental rate.

This place is so suitable for a first home. She smiled, knowing she had persuaded Pa to push out the boat, after all they only had one child, one son.

She decided to sit on the sofa.

New curtains, flowers on the table, she overcame her instinct to go over and check that they were real – instead she monitored the air. No discernible fragrance. *Probably artificial.* She had always opted for fresh flowers.

'Miranda, Granma is here.' There was no response, Miranda seemed docile in her mother's arms.

Icilda stood up reaching for her grandchild. 'Hello Miranda. How are you today?'

She seemed much heavier than on her previous visit. *What is Eleanor feeding her? Has she already put her on formula? Breast milk is always best.*

Miranda's fragrance was so sweet, baby fresh. Clean and pure. Icilda clasped Miranda to her chest, observing her intently. Two glazed eyes swivelled from side to side intermittently.

'Has she just woken up? She seems sleepy.'

'No, she has been awake for at least an hour,' Eleanor cleared her throat then wiped her forehead with the back of her hand.

Icilda sat down. 'How has her sleeping been?' She clasped Miranda, resting her chin gently on the curly brown locks.

Eleanor flopped down, 'Miranda has been much better. She sleeps for longer and wakes up in a much better mood.' Her voice sounded brighter than last time, both hands secured in her lap, as she sat upright in the easy chair.

'Lovely, Charles mentioned that she was not settling.' That particular piece of news caused a scowl to play across Eleanor's face, quickly replaced by a thin smile. Nothing passed Icilda's scrutiny. 'Babies, so unpredictable, you never can… I think Miranda has leaked a little.' A growing dark patch on her light grey dress indicated that her statement was true.

The horror on Eleanor's face startled Icilda. Her memory went back to the last time she had seen that expression – when red wine had been 'accidently' spilled on Eleanor's dress, back at the eventful ball.

'I am… Let me have… I will get a cloth for your dress.' Eleanor's words were jumbled and rushed.

'No problem dear, all babies are prone to being leaky.' Icilda held out Miranda, Eleanor promptly scooped her up.

'There are some wipes on the table next to you. I will just be a moment.' Eleanor rushed out.

The dabbing seemed to make things worse. What a relief that she had no other appointments that day. This was one of her favourite dresses. She blamed herself for wearing it knowing she would be spending time with a baby.

Disposing of the wipes? She surveyed the room, opting for the stainless steel pedal bin in the corner, next to the writing desk.

The bin revealed its contents – a number of wipes that seemed to be fermenting along with an isolated nappy.

How offensive, how disgusting. 'Ooh,' she dropped in her contribution, blocking her nose.

The smell rapidly diffused throughout the room. She searched round for an air fresher. Nothing. *That was poor household management, Eleanor needed to improve her housekeeping skills. Perhaps a quiet word would be in order?* She had some perfume in her handbag.

She did not mean to do the dust test, but could not help herself. With one finger she swept along the edge of the mantelpiece. The result spoke for itself.

Icilda considered using another wet wipe to remove the thick layer of dust on her finger.

No, I will use my *handkerchief and sanitising spray,* she reached for her handbag.

Three squirts and then the clean-up, then she used the soiled handkerchief to attack the stain on her dress. The patch accused her. *So annoying.* She promptly bagged it, meticulously sealing the plastic sachet before placing it back in her all-purpose handbag.

Eleanor returned with Miranda, flustered. 'I am so sorry Icilda, I changed her less than twenty minutes ago,' the sincere apologetic note registered with Icilda. 'The patch is still there… let me—'

'It will all come out in the wash. Not a problem. Come and sit down with me. Tell me how you are?' Icilda patted the seat next to her.

An unfamiliar sweet fragrance filled the room, masking the fetid scent – Eleanor knew that underlying odour, so distinct. One thing caused that… a soiled nappy. Tiny waves of panic swirled around her ankles. Now she could expect a severe scolding from Icilda; perhaps she might call her an unfit mother? *How had the nappy escaped her?* She scanned the room, feeling the sense of panic shimmering in her stomach.

It suddenly clicked into place – the pedal bin in the living room.

She had told Charles so many times, he was not to put soiled nappies in it. He always opted for the nearest bin, despite her numerous requests. That one must have been there for a day or two. In her haste she'd missed that bin.

Eleanor's flight response kicked in, she wanted to run and hide, not to sit down. The only thing she could do now: mental preparation.

She sat down cautiously, glancing at Miranda then Icilda.

'I am okay, being a mum has not been easy.' *Just say it, just get it over and done.*

'Tell me about it, dear. I have been Charles' mother for a rather long time, and I can tell you now, it does not get any easier.'

To their collective surprise, they laughed together.

Friday 18th August 2000 (BM, EWA, R)

Eleanor wrestled with her foul mood, then decided to give in. The combination of family life, sleepless nights and needy, childish Charles; life bore down heavily on her. She had no intention of responding to the call, allowing the answering machine to take over instead. Six rings was all it took.

After the fourth, something told her to answer it.

'Hello,' her voice, abrupt and snappy.

'Well hello sunshine,' the cheerful voice of Danny Fordham. She attempted to remain angry, but the very sound of his voice shifted her mood a few degrees.

'Sorry Danny, having a really bad day.' She could be honest with him.

They'd met at her first teaching post, both of them newly qualified teachers. A natural bond had formed, possibly out of fear and desperation, they became frim friends. Danny had remained in touch even after she got married, so many other close friends seemed to think that the union disqualified them from her life. The loss bothered Eleanor.

'Just checking up on you, I wanted to find out how you were?'

'Do you really want to know?'

'Yes Ellie, I do.'

Danny, such a fantastic listener with a genuine connection with people. Children loved him as did most of the staff, not everyone could cope with him.

Although he was naturally quiet, he carefully considered things told to him in confidence, reflecting on them – *a right little Yoda. And he's totally trustworthy.* Eleanor could say this with some certainty; she'd tested him with some minor bits of information that would normally spread rapidly around the gossip table in the staffroom. None of it got back to her, he'd passed with flying colours.

'I am fine,' The lie passed through her lips so easily, she even surprised herself. Things were getting to her, as if her upright, moral streak had been weakened, replaced by a more flexible and laissez faire approach to life. The path of least resistance felt false; as if she'd betrayed herself again.

The pause.

She wondered, *will he press me for information or take the bait?*

The pause continued and then he spoke. 'Who are you trying to kid? That was as fake as… as fake as the tan you claimed to have got when you went to Europe.'

Eleanor burst out laughing. The memory was vivid. She had boasted of this wonderful trip to Europe and it had rained the whole time. Feeling that she had to live up to expectation she had used tanning lotion to get a holiday glow. Danny had taken her to one side and made her confess.

'Well, what is really going on?' He spoke slowly, a detectible sincerity in his words. Eleanor's guilt surfaced.

'I… I am really struggling.' The confession was genuine, it came from her heart. Danny was the first person she'd been truly honest with. Not even Charles was privy to her real feelings about things at the moment. She was hit by a mixture of relief and guilt; relief the truth was out, guilt that she was telling a friend and not her own husband.

'What is happening? Is it Miranda or Charles or is that witch riding her broomstick through your living room again?'

'No… well,' her words tumbled out, 'it's everything. Lack of sleep, Miranda, Charles being away so much. It's as if… It's as if I am bringing up Miranda on my own.'

The clock on the mantelpiece served as the only indicator that as much of the day had already passed by. It seemed as if she had achieved so little. Now she was dishing out gossip about her husband.

Accusation and feelings of guilt collaborated with her revelation – an uncomfortable trio. Charles would be so hurt if he knew she was discussing him with a stranger. *Family business stays in the family*, that was how Icilda operated and Charles might as well have chanted the same mantra.

'Have you talked to him?'

'I would but… he is so busy.'

'Ellie, you are busy too. Caring for Miranda and him. He's not the only one who is working.'

A true statement, however her efforts simply couldn't be seen on the same level as Charles' work.

'I am at home, he—'

'Let's stop the prehistoric rhetoric. As if woman's place is in the home! Both of you are working.' The pace of his speech accelerated as he spoke. She could imagine him waving his arms, echoing the undulating volume of his animated voice.

Eleanor failed to respond.

'Ellie, are you still there? Hello…'

'Yes, Danny.' A familiar sense of heaviness and exhaustion rolled over her. She was unhappy. Today she'd snapped at Miranda, yesterday she'd snapped at Charles. She'd even deliberately ignored Icilda's unwelcome helpline calls and given her own mother a load of happy family codswallop.

'Ellie, you can get help. You need to talk to someone.'

'I am… I am talking to you.' She slumped onto the sofa.

'You sound awful.'

'You try staying up four nights in a row and caring for a demanding husband.' Her whole body trembled with resentment; he had vented the volcano, now the larva was running.

'You need some time off. How about getting in a sitter once a week?' The suggestion only fuelled her anger.

'Are you saying that I'm an unfit mother?' She heard herself scream into the phone.

'What?'

He sounded so shocked. Now another set of guilt weights were stacked onto her personal yoke, it was pulling her down, almost crushing her. *You could destroy this relationship.* Part of her could not have cared less. Yet she listened to the part that felt strongest. It was full of fear; fear that she might be about to lose a true friend.

How can I make up for that outburst?

Danny continued, 'I am making a practical suggestion, not assessing your ability to care for your child. What's got into you?'

Eleanor pressed her hand against her forehead, sighing. *Why did I scream at Danny? This is not his fault.*

'I am sorry Danny, I… I am so tired.'

'If you won't talk to Charles I will.' He sounded definite, she knew him to be someone who would never pass up a dare.

'That's very sweet of you.' A deep sense of calm ministered to her heart, she appreciated his concern and willingness to listen. 'I should—'

'But you won't.'

'I will find the time, now I have spoken to you.'

'Is that a promise or an avoidance tactic?' The sarcasm made her smile. 'You sound weird Danny. Stop it.'

'Well if it gets you to take action, I will continue to be weird.'

'I really appreciate you, Danny.' She knew that she meant it and hoped he would know too. *What would I do without you?*'

'Remember you married Charles.'

'I would have married you but…' She stopped.

'I'm gay Ellie and there is nothing you can do about it.'

Eleanor's guffawing laughter made the phone cord quiver. His coming out had been such an event – Daniel Fordham had been terrified of his parents' response, about the impact it might have on rest of the staff and about his unenlightened friends' opinions. He'd talked to her in depth before deciding on the time and place of the revelations, even getting her to edit the three versions of his speech, each appropriately modified of one of the three target audiences. Now he seemed to be repaying the favour. They were equal, the debt paid in full.

'I want the best for you, even though you're not my type,' his voice was deep with an affected machismo. It was Danny's best attempt at a gravelly caricature. It wasn't very good. *I think not*, she smirked.

The foul mood had totally lifted and she was hit with an instant relief, free from that dreadful sense of being pinned down. It felt so much better. Wiping several tears from her eyes, Eleanor breathed deeply and freely.

'I really needed a friend.'

'And one came along at the right time.' His voice was back it's normal, sedate sound. 'I had such a strong urge to call you, but I put it off for a couple of days. Next time I will act on instinct, right away.'

'I nearly didn't answer the phone. I was just not in the mood to talk.'

'Well that's amazing, we must be psychic.'

Eleanor nodded. They shared a real connection. It really was too bad his interests lay in another direction. *At least he'll never have to deal with a pregnancy! Good for him.* She smiled to herself.

'So will you call me and let me know what happens?'

'I will, I promise.' Eleanor's words were genuine.

'Okay, I will have to love you and leave you. Got a hot date tonight.'

'You, a hot date? That will be a first.'

'You're not the only one who can get lucky.' Eleanor knew he was referring to Charles and his family connections, not to mention his fortune. Danny often claimed that she had a lucky charm, that she carried around a rabbit foot or something in that line.

'No need for catty remarks,' she scolded.

'Sure, as if my claws are out,' Any signs of machismo had since departed.

'Danny I really appreciate you, I do mean that. Will you call me to check?' Hope surfaced from its slumber. *Perhaps there is an good way out of this situation.*

'I will, got to run. Love you Ellie.'

'Love you Danny.' The silent phone rested in her lap. She wondered if the room had gotten brighter. Or was it her change of mood.

That call changed my day. My mini miracle. Then she realised that Miranda was still sleeping, despite her loud laughter.

Two miracles in one day.

MONDAY 28TH AUGUST 2000 (BM, R, EWA)

The fifth day in a row.

Bethany had been feeling unwell; waves of nausea rose then subsided. For the second time she left the staff canteen to visit the bathroom. Knowing she was going to be sick again.

Suzy smiled broadly when she returned. 'Why Bethany, you look like you have seen a ghost. Morning sickness perhaps?'

Bethany stared back at her blankly. 'What do you mean morning sickness?'

'Are you *pregnant*?' mouthed Suzy, silently, not wanting to alert other listeners. Bethany appreciated her, she was kind-hearted and considerate.

Not like some of the others known for their readiness to divulge the secrets of anyone who came on their radar.

'Me, pregnant?' Bethany sneered loudly.

A couple of adjacent heads turned and looked in their direction, Bethany knew they were on the lookout for juicy information for the late afternoon's gossip update. She ignored them. 'Don't make me laugh. I'm not feeling well that's all. It must be a tummy bug.' Bethany's sense of conviction shaded her tone as she sipped her second cup of peppermint tea.

Suzy rolled her eyes. 'Will you go and take a pregnancy test? Aisle twelve has some of the best on the market. Seriously. Try 'Positive Plus'.'

Bethany felt annoyed, Suzy's obviously felt that her vast experience in the area gave her authority. She already had three kids, often talking about her plans for at least two more.

'I'm not pregnant, Suzy,' insisted Bethany.

She was wrong.

Three hours later she came out of the bathroom stall, pale and trembling. Two successive tests had proved positive.

TUESDAY 29TH AUGUST 2000 (BM, R)

Frank roared with laughter as the credits rolled on the screen. Bethany sat next to him on the couch, arms looped, yet she remained tentative. The air conditioner clanked away in the background, keeping the room well below that of the outside world.

The right moment was crucial.

He turned towards her, kissing her gently on her cheek. They'd enjoyed a lovely meal and his favourite comedy show had just finished.

It felt like a really good moment.

'I have some news for you honey,' Bethany's insides quivered, he leaned his head on hers. 'I found out that I'm…' she paused for a second, preparing herself, 'pregnant.'

Frank jumped out his seat as if hot coffee had just been dumped in his lap. 'What did you say?' He spoke loudly, unaware of how ridiculously noisy he was being, not believing his own ears. Wide pale blue eyes displaying disbelief.

'I'm pregnant!' The width of her smile broad enough to accommodate an ocean liner.

'But how, Beth?'

She watched him struggle, enjoying the way his mind was trying to process the startling information. 'Biology classes at High School should have sorted out that question,' Bethany teased him, and he knew it. She placed his right hand on her abdomen.

Frank flopped down onto the couch, she felt the tremors in his hand. Poor, shaking Frank.

'Are you sure? I mean… this means… we're having a baby.'

He started crying, laughing at the same time. Wrapping his arms around Bethany. She wept beside him.

It was a miracle: their miracle.

TUESDAY 5TH SEPTEMBER 2000 (BM, EWA, R)

'Danny, you didn't return my call!' Annoyed and irritated, Eleanor decided to be honest about her feelings.

'You sound like a school teacher.'

She laughed, though she was still annoyed. 'Honestly I was worried. How was Mr Hot Date? And I am a school teacher, you fool.'

'He turned out to be a real sleaze ball actually. Not nice, not nice at all.' She realised that he sounded dejected, unlike her normal, cheerful Danny.

'Will you see him again?'

'Are you mad? Do you think I'm a masochist?' Eleanor reserved judgement, his private life was his business.

'I wanted to let you know that I took your advice. I'm having at least one evening off a week. So when are you free?'

'Does Charles know you are going out with another man?' His voice, heavy with mock insinuation.

'Yes, he does and he is not jealous.' That was true, actually. Charles trusted her, never seeming to worry about her conduct with other men. She chewed her lower lip; she did not feel the same about him. He always noticed beautiful women then made some little quip about them, feeling it was okay to share his inner workings – *his attractions* – with whoever was in earshot.

Perhaps he thinks that honesty will make me feel less suspicious?

In truth it caused her to experience a deep insecurity; and despite sharing her discomfort with Charles, he continued to allow his eyes to roam too freely. That part of his personality hurt her like crazy. He didn't seem to be able to change – or even want to. She knew that he never acted on any of it but that certainly didn't stop her worrying on the inside.

'So when are you free?'

'Can I call you back, I've got loads of marking to do, struggling to get back to school mode after the long recess. I'll send you an email later tonight. You do still check your emails?'

Eleanor submitted to a sense of dejection, she had her diary in her hand ready to write in the date, to book her first evening off.

'Okay.' Her voice was low, monotone. Normally Danny would have picked that up, but today he made no comment.

'I will touch base later. Bye.'

'Bye.' She stabbed at the off button. Icilda would be visiting that evening.

WEDNESDAY 20TH SEPTEMBER 2000 (BM, EWA, R)

'When did you discover fish?'

'Since I read that it keeps you slim and is great for the brain. Got to stay sharp.' He handled the fish fork with dexterity.

'Wow, this steak is gorgeous, just the way I like it.' She chewed – not that she really needed to, it was so tender.

'So what's this about more children?' Danny quizzed her with his words and eyes.

'Charles had been going on and on about having another child. I told him no. He just won't drop the subject.' She put her cutlery down then rested her chin on her hand.

'Well is *he* going to have them?'

'No!'

'Then it's your decision.' He chewed slowly.

Eleanor paused, considering the weight of what she was about to say. She lowered voice. 'I had my tubes tied.'

'Sorry, you whispered that.' Danny had his mouth full, he stopped chewing. His expression, quizzically. 'So what's the secret?'

The presence of the waiter made her jump. 'Is everything alright?' Though his manner remained attentive and congenial, she wanted to tell him where to go.

'Everything is fine,' she snapped. The scared waiter retreated from the scene. Eleanor watched Danny's eyes follow the waiter, seeing the little smirk on his face. She leaned forward and spoke quietly. 'It's just… well I've had a tubal ligation.'

Danny's confusion distorted his face. He swallowed, pondering for a second before speaking. 'Then you won't be having any more children unless the tubes untie or miraculously re-grow.'

She hesitated, 'Charles doesn't know.'

He dropped his fork. 'Rewind. How come he doesn't know? You did it behind his back?'

'Keep your voice down, I don't want everyone to know my business,' the sharpness of her voice made him wince. Danny said nothing, his wide eyes accused her while his partially open mouth, further proof of his disbelief.

'Well aren't you going to say something?'

He's shocked, really shocked.

The quiet evening shift, there were only a few people in the restaurant. This, being mid-week might have accounted for that. The mood around them could be described as relaxed, there was even soothing background music. All the same, she was overcome by a wave of anxiety.

Is he judging me?

'What do you want me to say? Well done on deceiving your husband.' He pushed his plate away. 'I've gone right off that.'

Eleanor twisted her wedding ring. She hated secrets, yet had not shared her procedure with anyone apart from the healthcare professionals who had been involved in the operation. Even they had questioned her as to whether she had discussed this with her husband. She remembered making up some lie about her husband's busy schedule and not being able to be with her. They asked if there was a next of kin who would stay with her, another story appeared like a bunny rabbit from a hat – the whole thing without effort, like a professional. At the time, she wondered if they would carry out the chop without someone else's assent; the authority of her gold card silenced any further questioning.

In her mind, she knew it was wrong to go ahead without consulting with or even informing Charles. After all, he had always expected a large family – but she could not face the thought of having any more children.

During her recovery she blamed her bed ridden state on terrible food poisoning. The doctors specifically told her to rest for a couple of days. Thankfully, her mother had been able to take Miranda as Icilda had been on holiday. Charles had wanted to take time off from work, of course she declined his offer. Coping with the guilt when he was around was more than enough for her – *more time with him? No thanks.* She had gotten through that episode but her conscience kept records, always ready to remind her that seeds of deception bring forth a harvest of betrayal. *That and who knows what else?*

'I'm not a bad person.' She whispered.

'No, you are not,' he paused, 'but on this occasion you're acting like a *terrible* one. You're turning into a bare faced liar, and it's both dishonest and deceitful.'

Buzzing, stinging words; she could feel her mouth opening of its own accord. Cold air rushed in, ramming into the back of her throat.

'What did you say?' Her hands hovered over her plate, the tightness in her shoulders pulled on her upper back. Who was he to question her decision? *I made up my own mind.*

'Since when did you have selective hearing, I thought only the kids at school suffered from that?' Danny stated.

Eleanor's lips moved, no words came out.

'Ellie, I love you, but that is a recipe for disaster; secrets do not make a happy relationship. Have you really changed so much?' He picked up his napkin, then dropped it onto the plate.

Danny's response generated a deep fear – the sinking sensation pulled at her abdomen. *Did I do the right thing?* It was too late now though; the decision had been made; she would have to live with its consequences. If Danny did not like it. He could do whatever he liked. His reaction baffled her, she thought that he would support her, that he would stand by her side. *It is my body, my choice, my future.* He didn't understand the pressure she was under, the daily anxiety she faced.

Since when did his lifestyle make him an expert on heterosexual relationships? He didn't even have a steady relationship. *Who is he to judge me?*

'Yes, I guess I have changed.'

Danny paid for the meal; they did not talk further on that subject or indeed on any subject for a while. Eleanor allowed three weeks to pass before she returned his messages, ignoring the voicemails that called her immature and dishonest – even from a friend, the truth was just too close for comfort.

SATURDAY 23RD SEPTEMBER 2000 (BM, EWA, R)

Eleanor applied another generous layer of wine-stained lipstick, she completed the transformation with thick cat eyes and a faint application of blusher. *Was the fashion article right?* According to the magazine, the deep colour would complement her hair. After examining the reflection, she wondered. *This is* definitely *not my normal image.*

Her conclusion – it really worked. 'Charles, what do you think? Am I okay?'

He wandered in from the bathroom, still buttoning up his white shirt. Both feet clothed in dark socks, his favourite funky boxers on display.

'Wow!' He paused momentarily, before making a beeline in her direction, both arms outstretched, an amorous expression dancing across his face. 'Who's the honey in the mirror?'

Eleanor extended her right arm in his direction, preventing his approach, 'I have worked too hard and too long on this style for you to mess it up Mr Ferrell, you sex bomb!'

The expression spoke volumes – his disappointed eyes, his jaw hanging down, his shoulders slouching. He immediately headed back to the bathroom.

'Maybe later,' she hinted. *No promises though.*

It had been a restless night for Miranda and a restless night for Eleanor. Truthfully, she wished there was a way of getting out of the dinner, except they were hosting it. Icilda and Ralph agreed to take care of Miranda for the whole night. For her and Charles a rare treat – a night alone. Delicious thoughts flitted through her mind – hours of unbroken sleep. *Maybe they might…*

One final brush, her hair – simply gorgeous. She chose the silver necklace. Another makeup tip from the article. She used to know everything about fashion and makeup, these days she was either too busy or too tired to care about being glamorous.

Tonight was an important evening for Charles. He'd hand-picked the guests, many of them were on the edge of investing in *IBC*. This little soirée was carefully designed to push them over the precipice. The caterers and the servers were all hired in, leaving them free to host. All paid for courtesy of *IBC*.

If *IBC* were paying then she was certainly going to enjoy herself. As she contemplated her image, a sigh slipped out. *Honestly, this is not my type of affair.*

She considered herself to be fairly reserved by his standards. Other people tended to view her as cold even unemotional. Luckily, Charles had not made that assumption when they met.

It was true to some extent, but not to any great degree. It represented the outer coating of her personality. She simply preferred being in the background, working behind the scenes. A natural organiser. *Teaching works well for me,* the children were usually appreciative of her efforts. Adults – well she could cope with them but would not describe herself as particularly confident. In her mind she knew that being a principal meant being a good manager, demanding strong people skills that were appropriate for dealing with all sorts of individuals – she could do it but would prefer not to. Not like Charles. He seemed to thrive during these occasions, his warmth and funny ways cutting across the barriers of class and social standing. Sometimes she wondered how he got away with a sense of humour that was so close to the edge. In many ways she envied him. His freedom and natural confidence had rubbed off on her. When she was around him, she felt different. Something about his unwavering support allowed her to flourish and push the boundaries of what she formerly considered normal.

Me, the calm and practical one; he the energetic fireball that makes things happen. Even in their care of Miranda their personal differences were clear.

Eleanor dabbed Chanel No.5 onto both wrists, at the base of her neck and then just under her earlobes – that final application, well that was just for Charles. He had worked out that this was one of her most sensitive spots, how he loved to kiss and caress her there, knowing what it did to her. The memory sent a shiver up her spine, there could be some passion tonight.

Things had got so much better in their marriage. At the start Charles seemed determined to change her, trying to make her into a female replica of himself. Foolishly, she went gone along with it, just to keep the peace. It only took a couple of weeks before the strain of it began to show. This brought about a roaring argument that ended up with him storming out, running to his mother's side. Icilda's response had surprised her. She sent him straight back home under strict instructions to make peace. For a moment, she reflected on that shaky start. She shuddered. Back then she had seen herself as an Eliza Doolittle – his Pygmalion project.

Yes, he was much better now; things were much better. She had room to be her own version of Eleanor, not feeling the need to apologise for that. In some ways, Charles still seemed to mentor her, encouraging her to try new things, to launch out. She liked it that way.

'I'm ready!' Her voice was triumphant.

Shaking her head caused her auburn locks to flow, luscious and full. Pregnancy had done wonders for her hair as well as her boobs. Charles could hardly keep his hands off them when she let him, only if she had time and was not close to exhaustion.

Mrs Charles Ferrell, wife, mother and hostess extraordinaire. *You will invest your money in IBC.*

'Charles, they will be here soon, especially if they're punctual. We need to be ready,' she forced herself to sound calm, though inwardly her stomach wobbled.

The click of the bathroom door, revealed her handsome and ravishing husband, full attired apart from his missing shoes.

'Mr Ferrell, we had better get out of here, before I tear those clothes off you!' Eleanor teased.

'Mrs Ferrell, I like it when you talk dirty.' He strutted towards her.

'Ah, ah, no you don't, no touching.' Her hands still acted as buffers, preventing any contact that could lead to other things. His brow crumpled as she watched his head droop.

'Maybe, just maybe…' Her voice was low, yet tempting. Its promise hung in the air.

+++

'So how many children do you have?'

Major Hamilton's red face was punctuated with a bulbous nose. *He drinks far too much – I hope that's not true while he's on duty.* She smiled. 'Just the one, her name is Miranda.'

'Miranda, ah. Great name, how old is she?'

'Nearly three months,' Eleanor feigned, her best plastic smile stapled to her face. He was one of the clients that Charles was keen to recruit. Normally she would have avoided such a character. Odious – a strong term but one that described him accurately.

'I must say you are lovely.' *He's almost slobbering all over me.* Everything about him made her skin crawl – an overly familiar approach, no sense of respect for her personal space, openly ogling her – he could hardly keep his eyes on her face. *If he lays a finger on me I'll kick him right where it hurts, even if this whole thing is for Charles.* She comforted herself with a clear image of him staggering away with his hands gripping his crotch.

Major Hamilton moved in closer. His drooling disgusted her, the way his eyes lingered on her breasts. She glanced around feverishly, hoping to make eye contact with Charles, who was deeply engaged in a heated conversation in another corner of the room.

'Tell me about your time in Iraq.' The major had mentioned the war, then swiftly moved onto another subject.

'Iraq. An awful time.' He grimaced before wiping his forehead several times. A pale sheet moved down his face, as if reliving a nightmare. After a few seconds he continued, 'It's not something I want to talk about… if you would excuse me.'

He could not get away fast enough. *Fantastic. Well done!* Eleanor breathed a sigh of relief, that had worked out quite well. She checked her watch, only 21.30 – the night was still young. *I wonder how Miranda is doing?* Icilda relished spending time with Miranda, overjoyed at a chance to help out. Eleanor gave her a list of tasks and had suggested a timetable of events to make sure that Miranda did not break her routine. Having got to know her mother in law, it became increasingly clear she was not one to listen to advice. Miranda might end up being confused, it could even upset her sleep. *Guess who will be left to pick up the pieces and stay up half the night until she gets back into a rhythm again.* She gripped her elbow. *I am going to be the one left to carry the can.*

The night turned a little sour, despite the striking city centre location and the expensive hotel. None of that really impressed her. A whole lot of glitter and grandeur. Instead, one thought now dominated her mind – going home.

The thought reverberated, obscuring all the noise in the room. She just wanted to go home now. Suddenly fed up with the trivial nature of all the conversations taking place; the superficiality of the whole event, the irritating potential investors trying to make up their minds, the need to be charming. It all seemed futile.

One of the female guests had really annoyed her, making loud and derogatory comments about IBC. Criticising their pioneering work, calling it 'meddling on the borders of the obscene.' If she objected to the work, why had she accepted the invitation? Obviously a cheapskate who wanted a free meal ticket in glamorous surroundings. Eleanor squeezed her clutchbag throughout the entire conversation, biting her lower lip. Straight after that, she'd gone to the bathroom, feeling sure there would be lipstick on her teeth. She'd been right.

For Eleanor, the research and techniques helped make people's lives better. What was wrong with that? No one in her family had any real health issues, she felt sorry for those who had to struggle with a disability. Her belief – everything possible should be done to help those who suffered, that society should offer support to those who cared for the disabled. A student in her class had cystic fibrosis, Missie Stornorway. She missed so much school due to frequent chest infections and complications with the numerous medications that were part of her daily life, and the hospital appointments – she was so thin. The other children loved her dearly. If she lived to twenty, she would have done well. Sitting in on the social services meetings had been depressing. Thinking about the Missie's suffering saddened Eleanor. She couldn't begin to imagine what her parents were going through. However, she loved Missie as much as any of the other children.

Helping these people is not dabbling on the edge of the obscene.

The touch on her elbow, so familiar. 'How are you coping Mrs Ferrell?' Charles sounded happy.

'I'm fine, thanks, Charles,' she lied to avoid spoiling his evening. He read her too well.

'How are you really feeling?' He moved in closer, studying every detail of her face.

She swallowed, 'I'm feeling so tired. Some of these people are… so irritating.'

Sad Charles.

She wanted to cover up her emotions more fully, she had no desire to be the perfect hostess anymore.

'Can you hang on for…' He checked his watch, 'Another two maybe two and a half hours?' The grip on her elbow softened turning into a stroking motion. 'I really need the time with these people.'

'Okay, I can do it. Just keep me away from Major Hamilton and that anti-*IBC* prophetess of doom.' She spotted Hamilton in a corner, closing in on some other poor female victim. The prophetess had gathered another group of devotees in a corner. *Awful man, awful woman.*

'Oh him, he's harmless. Loads of money, three divorces and searching for wife number four. As for Miss Dewey, she is yet to be convinced. Watch me work on her.'

Okay, Charles, let's see you work your magic. She smiled at him, suppressing a yawn.

Charles kissed her on the cheek, whispering in her ear, 'I'll make it up to you later.' He brushed the edge of his forefinger just behind her ear, right where she had applied the perfume. She shivered with delight.

Maybe, just maybe.

TUESDAY 17TH OCTOBER 2000 (BM, EWA, WD, PA, R)

ARTICLE FROM THE DAILY TRIBUNE
(EDITORIAL COMMENT)

'… The good city of Philadelphia warmly welcomed her latest business venture as signs of fall appear, despite the inconvenience. The grand opening of the first Icilda Biotech Company site (IBC-USA) had almost shut down one of the city's key highways.

The auspicious event had been well publicised and celebrities and influential people gathered to be part of this occasion. The publicity around IBC generated a mixed response. Many associated the aims of the company with the legacy of eugenics, others heralded the breakthrough in disease management and improved social wealth for the future.

The company motto: inspiring future hope…'

Excessive quantities of liquor seemed to have the same predictable effect on his mother as always; she lost all sense of confidentiality and decorum. It was one of her few flaws.

The opening night of IBC-USA. Charles smiled. Eleanor stood next to him, their arms entwined. The tours were over and Pa's speech was the last one on the list before the real party began. Now on his second glass of wine – a good quality one.

Is this French or German? It's definitely European.

'Thank you all for your attention, and for making this such a wonderful occasion.' Ralph's easy rapport was infectious and his voice commanded attention; the chattering guests stopped their conversations. A team of liveried servers ensured that wine glasses were quietly filled. 'Birthing IBC reminds me of the way that Charles came into the world – a long drawn out labour, but a beautiful outcome.'

Charles could not decide whether to be delighted or abashed at the public expose. Pa was elevated, the stage raising him above the crowd, Nicholas Cecil stood beside him.

Nicholas had visited their family home on many occasions, showing his generosity by giving extravagant gifts, every occasion counted. Christmas, Easter, Thanksgiving, Independence Day and birthdays. There were always gifts from Nicholas. He and Pa were faithful business partners and loyal friends. Charles squeezed Eleanor's arm, she returned the gesture. *What other pieces of private information are about to be exposed? This fake smile demands more energy to sustain it compared to a real one.*

Ralph continued: 'Everyone needs a second chance – or a third, or fourth chance.' Nicholas seemed to nod in agreement.

Charles felt tearful, something was sweeping over him for no discernible reason. A sudden, brutal rush of emotion – sadness.

'Personal failure has been responsible for the destruction of many once great individuals in this business; people whose potential has been quashed by failure's ability to destroy hope, tearing people away form once promising lives,' Ralph paused, establishing eye contact with his audience. 'History is strewn with the wreckage; casualties of fate who missed their opportunities; those who fell short of expectation.'

Sadness transformed into paranoia. Charles fought the desire to run.

His right hand dropped from chest to waist level, the stem of the wine glass clenched precariously. *Just let go of Eleanor's arm and take off. What are you waiting for?*

He ignored both the suggestion and the question.

Where is this going? Why is he having a go at me? Another inspection of his shoes, his body weight shifted from one foot to the other. Eleanor's body pressed against him, even closer. He started to turn his face towards her but stopped midway, resuming the shoe inspection. Black patent shoes, gleaming, polished to perfection.

'For others it can be the springboard to success. They grow sharper, wiser and softer, recognising that they do not know all the answers.'

Charles glanced up briefly to see Nicholas, still nodding. Black shoes again.

'Many of you know about my son's history.'

Their eyes met. Charles shuddered while his stomach registered pain, as if he had been kicked in the gut. The wine glass slipped out of his hand, spilling its contents as it fell. The mini explosion scattered glass fragments.

I'm being publically chastised by Pa. Everyone is staring at me. Fighting the urge to run took all of his strength. If Eleanor's arm had not been wrapped around his waist, he would have fled. A waitress stepped forward, keen to sweep up the wet shards.

'Demand for copper has entered rapid decline in recent years,' Pa smiled, Charles recognised that expression – he used to flash it when they were horse fighting. *This is not a horse fight. I'm not seven years old. You're killing me. I'm being publically humiliated by my own Pa.*

The twisting in his stomach grew stronger, pulsing miserably. Charles wiped his forehead and smeared the moisture on his trousers. Eleanor's grip tightened.

Perhaps some of the people in the room might have been investors in the failed copper business? Maybe they were personally impacted by my failure?

Pa coughed several times, lifting his hand up to his face. After regaining his composure he continued, 'True character is tested and tried. Gold needs refining before its true worth is established. Intense heat is part of that process.' Nicholas placed his hand on his throat, visibly moved.

He's staring at me.

'Son, you have overcome many setbacks. You did not give up,' Pa's voice seemed tender and gentle. 'I have never been more proud of you than I am today. The way you have handled yourself over the last few years – it is nothing short of incredible. I have watched you turn from boy to man.' A tear tricked from his right eye.

Transfixed, Charles stood motionless. The words were swirling around in his head, knocking on doors that had 'no renovation' signs etched on them. Hidden hopes, a chance to believe? His concealed dreams; he had given up hope a long time ago. *Maybe… Maybe…*

Eleanor's grip intensified, the comforting touch of her head on his shoulder felt like reassurance. Intense pinpricks stabbed behind his eyes. The muscles in the back of his legs felt like rigid, hot rods.

'In view of your performance, and *not* because you are my son.' His beaming smile directed, sent with love. 'I am indeed going to keep you on the payroll.' Waves of laughter soared through the room. 'And, son… the debt is cancelled.'

From his peripheral vision Charles caught sight of his Ma laughing loudly, swaying from side to side. *Too much booze*. He hoped someone would take care of the situation. Other things were on his mind.

'Yes, Charles, not only are you going to continue in your current role, you are going to need a couple of new suits. Welcome to the board.' Pa's face was radiant with *pride*. 'Ladies and gentlemen, may I introduce you to the latest CEO at IBC-USA, Charles Ferrell.'

Applause, free and spontaneous. Cheering too. Someone even wolf whistled. Nicholas was applauding with great enthusiasm.

Charles sensed his hand move to his lips, possessed by an inner life while the left side of his face tingled. Eleanor flung both arms around him, shielding him as he digested the information. He appreciated her affection but was unable to respond. Inside, he felt lost and found at the same time. Numb yet deliriously happy. Humbled, stunned and elated.

Eleanor's hugs assured him that this was not a dream. 'I'm so proud of you too, my darling.' She kissed him on his right cheek, tenderly. His whole body trembled.

The other announcements continued. Charles struggled to explain his feelings; he was truly lost for words. He felt as if he had been cleansed from head to toe. The past, once ominous and tormenting, was gone. His failures, his shame; they were wiped away in a moment.

Eleanor's fragrance offered comfort. She held him, gentle waves of scent wafting upwards. Her favourite, and his. He closed his eyes as he absorbed the scent and the moment.

Just to savour that special moment. Eleanor, friend and lover. Both of them shared an enduring bond, they had gone through so much. Enduring many battles yet still united, still together.

+++

Quivering and trembling with sheer delight, Eleanor's ecstasy increased with each kiss Charles lavished on her.

It had been so difficult for him, feeling that he needed to prove himself. Always worrying, checking his performance figures again and again. Now the past could be laid to rest.

When he finally let her go she clapped her hands together, her broad smile displaying her delight. Her soul seemed saturated, full of happiness. Total fullness, brimming over.

All she wanted to do was dance, wild expressive dancing. Maybe slightly vulgar, a little bit of teasing. She still knew how to make Charles go weak at the knees.

As if on cue, the band began playing Charles' favourite tune – *I'll Be Missing You* by Puff Daddy and the Family.

Time to boogie! These heels have got to go.

Shoes in hand, she led him to the dance floor.

+++

As soon as he separated his friend from the eager, now loquacious individuals queuing up to engage with Ralph, Nicholas quizzed him.

'So when did you plan to tell me?' Their faces were close, his tone playful.

Ralph's face was somewhere between sheepish and coy.

'Sorry Nicholas,' his eyes shifted from side to side. 'You ask too many questions, awkward ones no one else asks and you get to me.'

Nicholas knew this to be true. After many years spent working alongside Ralph, he knew how to probe beneath the surface of the man's ideas and business strategies.

He had listened intently during Ralph's speech. Many memories had been stirred by the depths of its sentiment. Over the years, many seemingly bright stars had fallen. A few did manage to come back though, and they often made the best employees. He thought of Jane Petrier, who had struggled with depression – now assistant director – and Henry Cavendish, who battled with alcohol addiction – now flourishing as the head of marketing. Both of them were excellent employees; they were totally committed and were entirely faithful to IBC.

Nicholas recognised that Charles had not been given any special favours because of his family connection. Reports about him had been favourable, even positively glowing. Charles beavered away for long hours and was by far the best at recruiting investors. He alone accounted for well over $4 million in shareholder's equity. Charles could charm money from the poor.

However, he had his suspicions that Ralph was up to something. Thinking about it… Ralph had fended off a few pertinent questions; documentation for recruitment at that level should have been sanctioned by Nicholas. How had Ralph managed to side manoeuvre him on this occasion?

'I thought,' Nicholas turned his head sideways, then swivelled his eyes towards Ralph, a mischievous ring colouring his words. 'Friends did not keep secrets from each other.'

The response was a big grin. Ralph swallowed hard.

'I'll let you off this time but…' Ralph's grin expanded across his face. 'I would not have told him. You can trust me.'

'Sorry Nick, I wanted to surprise you, both of you.'

'You certainly achieved both goals.' A hand grabbed Ralph's arm, summoning him elsewhere, for a brief consultation or family diagnosis.

'Catch you later,' Nicholas nodded as he watched Ralph being dragged to another appointment.

+++

The hug.

Charles heard later on that those who witnessed it had, in good humour, described it as being more appropriate for a sports arena than for the opening night of a new business venture. Later, Pa displayed the bruises on his ribs as trophies; they were still there two weeks after the event.

Ralph's feet left the floor as Charles swung him around, fervently kissing his cheek.

'Thank you Pa, thank you, thank you.'

+++

Ralph revelled in the moment. He breathed again.

Reconciliation and restoration. *Erasing the pain of yesterday so that tomorrow may be embraced* – what a fantastic and memorable evening this had become. Ralph relished his sense of accomplishment. He'd freed his son from a personal prison. There was no price on that; neither could he describe the emotions that pulsated in his heart.

Liberty bells were ringing from four corners of the room.

His shining countenance gave hope to many who knew of his earlier troubles. People needed a second chance. Quiet discussions in between canapés revealed that many executives and celebrities had family relationships that were nonexistent or on the edge of breakdown. Ralph willingly shared his personal insights, grateful for the fact his wise response to failure allowed his son to dream again. Now he could flourish.

Proud, he was so proud.

The festivities continued late into the night.

+++

Icilda witnessed the rapid pace of activity that characterised Charles' new corporate life. Selfishly though, she missed the Wednesday evening meals; marriage had quickly put a stop to those special moments. Charles loved to talk; he was wonderful company – very comfortable with people.

Eleanor owed her a great debt. Icilda congratulated herself on bringing up such a well-balanced and considerate young man.

The coincidence of two major events in the same year had turned her son's life into a hectic array of meetings, nappies, late nights, bottle feedings and conferences. They could have hired an au pair, but Eleanor did a great deal of good work by herself, keeping their home together and taking care of Miranda.

Icilda observed from a distance, making the odd comment when she felt things seemed to be moving in the wrong direction. She used Ralph as a model of good practice – despite his workload he always made put his family first.

When Charles disclosed his concerns about Miranda, Icilda responded with disbelief. Eleanor had noticed that things were not going well in the arena of Miranda's physical development – she seemed distant and unresponsive. Initial worries turned into fears.

Something was very wrong. Miranda frequently fell over and seemed unusually clumsy; basic tasks seemed to take too long. The diagnosis of muscular dystrophy, devastating news for everyone. Without any history of the genetic defect in either's family, there was no precedent; slowly but surely, her granddaughter's ailment became a burden for both sides of the family.

Icilda often cried alone when she thought about Miranda. Though she knew that chance alone had been responsible for the girl's condition, she hoped that the top doctors and world renowned specialists they had on board could fix it.

Not this time.

She continued to watch.

+++

Charles' work with IBC became crucial to his family life. He ceased to view his work as business and the company's research began to change course. The destruction genetic diseases became a key part of IBC's vision.

Charles believed that his company held the key to a scientific breakthrough, the sort that might transform lives like Miranda's. He hoped, even prayed that they would find a cure for her condition as he watched her slowly deteriorating before his eyes.

Miranda remained joyful and contented, despite her physical limitations and the painful therapy. She laughed all the time and showed a great deal of affection towards others.

Charles continued to hurt inside.

+++

Eleanor knew she was struggling.

Miranda's cheerfulness became Eleanor's shield; she hide behind it, giving her close friends and relatives the impression that she was coping well. Smiling and confident, she seemed to be dealing with the challenges of daily life and those trials associated with her daughter's health; Eleanor, mother and wife of an influential man.

Internally however, she was wracked by a deep and unavoidable pain. Comments made by guests during her frequent dinner parties showed their lack of understanding of the issues surrounding disability and the emotional toil it took on carers. She found herself having to explain over and over again why Miranda would not get better and why no specialist could do anything apart from slow down the deterioration of her body.

She knew they did not mean to be unkind – their nonchalant words infuriated her. There were too many times when she had to leave the table – so close to the edge of losing control. Charles worked so hard. This was no longer just a job, it was personal.

Under the weight of her daughter's condition and his frequent absences, Eleanor began to express symptoms of depression. Her dinner parties dwindled in number and frequency and, though Charles was sympathetic towards at first, he grew irritated at her sullen behaviour. The increasing emotional distance between Eleanor and Charles stoked her symptoms, the condition deepened.

To avoid herself, Eleanor lavished all of her attention on Miranda. Her efforts did not go unnoticed by Charles, who felt increasingly excluded.

All her life, Eleanor had tried to be perfect.

Perfect teeth, perfect grades, perfect hostess and perfect wife.

However, after Miranda's diagnosis, she realised that she was not a perfect mother, she had brought a defective child into the world.

The accusing voice of guilt whispered in her ears every time she went near Miranda. The pain seemed to grow over time, becoming excruciating. Eleanor reasoned that other people must think less of her. She misinterpreted compassion for condemnation, feeling judged by all who laid eyes on her daughter.

All expressions of sympathy judged dark and scornful. Eleanor could not bear it; and retreated into a private world.

As much as Charles tried to provide for Eleanor and Miranda, his new found position and wealth proved ineffective: his busy workload heralded no solutions, only demanding a greater investment of his time. His absence merely meant that Eleanor was left to bear her child alone.

She continue to experience more pressure Charles wanted another child

– Miranda was now eighteen months old. They tried for months and the fact that Eleanor did not become pregnant again baffled him.

She refused to talk about it, saying that nature must have decided that one was enough. She also refused his insistence that they consider fertility treatment, always managing to side-step any deeper enquiry. Her guilt secret remained hidden.

Her stance of 'natural, or not at all' became her adopted cover. Eleanor gleaned evidence from any source she laid her hands on, proof that might explain their failure to conceive.

As time went on, the relationship experienced frequent periods of stress, the product of their unresolved anger. Initially, Charles would not let the issue go, the heat of conflict white hot during that season.

With time, he brought up the issue less frequently.

Over the course of Miranda's life, Eleanor campaigned tirelessly for funds to eradicate genetic diseases and to make testing for these conditions more widely available. She turned her personal pain into passion, a passion that pushed her towards a newfound confidence. It overcame her natural reluctance to avoid confrontation and adult interaction. Eleanor found her voice, speaking from her personal perspective on issues she felt strongly about, stating the truth about disability, genetic disease and the impact these things had on the carers of innocent people.

Charles often commented on the transformation he saw happening before his eyes. It released in him a new sense of respect for his wife. This served as a bonding agent between the two. They grew closer. The new voice trumpeted its message. With Eleanor as a catalyst, Charles developed the motivation to intensify his building of the funding arm of IBC. Thoughts of returning to teaching diminished. Ultimately, their shared vision of a common cause, moving towards a common goal, brought them closer together.

Eleanor eventually accepted that she needed medical help. The late diagnosis of post natal depression gave a name to the swirling madness that threatened to drown her. A combination of antidepressants and cognitive therapy improved her self-image and the health of her marriage.

Things appeared to get better, less bleak, more hopeful.

SUNDAY 1ST APRIL 2001 (BM, EWA, R)

Bethany looked at her daughter and whispered, 'She's got your eyes.'

Frank stood next to her, beaming. After nearly ten years of trying for a child, the impossible had become possible – perhaps that was just nature's way. Once they'd known they were expecting a daughter, they'd had little difficulty deciding on a name; she would be called Chloe, after Bethany's grandmother, a woman who had never given up; who had fought to the end.

Chloe arrived slightly earlier than expected, on April 1st 2001. Three weeks ahead of schedule! Bethany wondered if that was significant, would she be a woman ahead of her time?

Bethany sensed the shift in her chest, a geyser of emotion. Chloe appeared to be staring at her. She coughed several times before crying.

'There, there. It's okay, Chloe. Mommy's here.' Bethany pulled her close, cradling her. Welcoming tears flowed softly.

At last, her dreams had come true.

MAY 2001 (BM, R)

Wet diapers, filled with green and brown offerings, feeding bottles and sterilising tablets, vomit and tiredness – life changed overnight.

Suddenly, Frank was no longer the centre of Beth's attention. The resentment chewed away deep on the inside. He'd grown used to being at the core of her world. Little Chloe needed her mommy's attention and time. Bethany was too tired for him, too tired to go out; too tired, full stop.

The habits of life before Chloe seemed to be slipping away. Now he faced the option of going bowling or attending the country-dance classes by himself. Beth always said it was okay.

But, for Frank, it was not okay.

He thought he was ready for parenthood; they had been waiting for ten years. The reality was much more hard work than he'd expected and the endless crying interrupted his sleep, which impacted his performance at work. His manager had already commented on his slipping sales figures. Frank responded by stating that this was just a blip, things would be sorted out.

The answer lay in the spare room. He slept in there now, with earplugs.

The hidden costs were an unwelcome addition. Their budget was just not stretching far enough. They were down to one salary and their dwindling finances were draining away quickly, what with all the stuff they had to buy – including the expensive stroller that Beth insisted on having. They were arguing much more and he was getting tired of the whole thing.

He just did not feel happy anymore. The family unit and its relationships should have all been fine. He could not understand why it was not enough – him, Beth and Chloe.

Sometimes he wanted to explode, to just walk out and never come back. Frank hated the feelings of confusion and uncertainty. The thought of talking to his mom was soon quashed. It seemed far too much like admitting that he could not cope. His own dad had left the family when he was a crying baby. Maybe he was the smart one, bailing out right at the start.

Growing up without a dad had been tough too. Mind you, he'd got by.

Cassandra, the new typist at work; she listened to him, paying him compliments and telling him that he was doing a great job. Beth did not even notice him anymore, she was so busy with Chloe.

Yes, Cassandra had time for him. It was odd at first, having a friend who happened to be a woman. He'd not really even had many male friends over the last ten years or longer, let alone female ones. He even thought of inviting her to the country-dance group. If Beth was too tired and too busy, he'd have to make alternative arrangements.

JUNE 2001 (BM, R)

Cassandra was a better dancer and, it turned out, a better kisser than Beth. It only took three sessions at the country-dance class for Frank to come to that conclusion.

Beth had used to be slim, but since having Chloe she had piled on the pounds. No longer fitting into her dark denim jeans; she'd used to look so sexy in them. Beth's once statuesque face had taken on a rounded look; she didn't seem to mind though – rarely wearing make-up and spending all of her waking hours in a bathrobe. She expected him to come home from work and spend time looking after Chloe. Of course he did, Chloe was his kid, how could he object to looking after her? Yet he did so with an attitude; just so Beth would know how inconvenient it all was.

With Cassandra, he could be himself. She even laughed at his feeble jokes. Beth just raised her eyes, in that familiar condescending manner. Yeah, she's grown accustomed to him. Cassandra made things exciting, she had a spirit of adventure, ready to explore. Not like Beth who seemed to be happy with the mundane, ordinary life.

Do I still love Beth? Yeah – but in a familiar, comfortable way, like a pair of comfortable slippers, well worn. She knew him and accepted all his ways, that gave him a sense of calm when he was with her. She did her best, but it was not enough. In the past it worked, but not now. The spark of a the tinderbox, the edge of the match box – now worn away, smooth. The only heat they generated happened when they rowed, which now seemed to be every other day. He hated the long sulks, the bashing and crashing that spoke of her inner frustration. Him, he just kept it inside.

Cassandra made him talk about things, right from the start. That was new for him. He resisted it at first but she could be determined, skilfully persuasive. The reward seemed to be increased passion, expressed in fiery emotions, wildfire. Just the memory, made his insides ignite.

Do I love Chloe? Kind of, she was cute. Lovely bundle of affection. Glad to be in daddy's arms. Chloe relaxed when she was in daddy's arms. Beth's face took on an annoying look – the corners of her mouth descended downwards. Chloe fell asleep in his arms, almost instantaneously every time. Yeah, Beth hated that effect, especially if she'd been struggling for a while.

He had no regrets about having Chloe – sure their life got turned upside down but it was worth it for her. He just was not sure what a father is meant to feel. After all he had no role model or pattern to follow. It was not as if he had any close male friends to share with.

In a way, he did feel guilty. His relationship with Beth had grown stale, and Chloe was great but that combination did not glue him to home. He had a right to be happy. Once upon a time that would have been with them – *but now… now, Cassandra offered an appetising alternative.*

July 2001 (BM)

Frank looked miserable. He mopped around the place and grumbled whenever she asked him to do anything. He still could not put on a nappy without leakage. In fact, she had decided, he was a hopeless father.

He left her to do the housework and the bulk of the childcare. Sure, he paid all the bills and made sure the paperwork was in order and sure, that was his skill, but she couldn't help feeling that a father's role required more of a man than a knack for administration.

August 2001 (BM, EWA, R)

Cassandra accepted his offer to accompany him the first time he asked. That was when it became an affair; it was the trip to Hawaii, during the heatwave at the start of August.

She was petite, with shoulder length, dark brown hair and the biggest green eyes he had ever seen. She laughed a lot, unlike Bethany, who had grown to look as if she was always sucking a lemon.

Cassandra said she had been married before, but that her husband had left her… for a man! They had no kids and they had been married for just two years.

That had crushed her confidence; she'd divorced her confused husband and moved states, ending up in Phoenix. Getting a job had proved to be quite easy as she was a trained legal secretary. *Arctic Freeze Refrigeration Inc* had been the first people to offer her a job and, new in town, she had accepted without much hassle. Cassandra told her story while she was resting in his arms in their four star hotel room, glad that she accepted the *Arctic Freeze* job.

Frank remembered everything about that trip, even the request for an extra fan as the air conditioning was not up to standard.

Hawaii was passionate – no, red hot. And that's what's missing with Beth.

At the beginning he'd felt guilty, but Cassandra had showed him that life could be different. Perhaps marrying Beth was a mistake? Their relationship had arisen out of convenience, after all; they were used to each other. Cassandra did not argue with him in the way that Bethany did. He'd even begun to think that the violent rows were normal.

Yeah, Cassandra had showed him that life could be different. In the end, it took him three months to make his mind up.

TUESDAY 14TH AUGUST 2001 (BM, EWA, R)

Two long years had passed. Max reflected on this. Two years of isolation, pain and success. No communication. The thing that made it sting today. His father's birthday.

The next appointment was an hour away. Max had time to kill and the park seemed like as good a place to go as any. The space was owned by all; shared by many. The guard on rollerblades felt they were the kings, others needed to get out of their ways as they zoomed past. The mothers, with children grateful for the fresh air and a chance to get out of their boxes. People on lunch break, eating and reflecting.

Like me, he thought as he bit into the pizza slice.

The weather team had promised sweltering temperatures. They had lied. It was pleasant, the kind of weather Max enjoyed. The park showed signs of water deprivation; the grass had lost its green lustre and had taken on a yellow-brown tinge. The nearby pond, drawing people and the few ducks being fed with stale bread thrown by wide-eyed children.

Max reflected on his adventure into the world of biotechnology. It had been a hectic ride. Despite his father's complete refusal of financial support, he had been able to make the most of his own background in business; more than that, he had honed his skills. His ruthless pursuit of financial goals had drawn opportunities to him from places he had never expected. In very little time at all, he forced his own name into the biotech community. He still struggled with the fact that his father had cut him off though. That was bad enough, but the fact that Julian and Samantha had followed his lead, that quadrupled the pain. At first they had been too scared, too controlled by their father to dare push his boundaries.

Scared.

Max didn't know whether to feel sorry for them or hate them.

A slender young lady passed by, smiling at Max. He checked her out through his Prada sunglasses. *No – not my type.*

Mother – she had acted as the secret go-between. Lukas had known nothing about it – that made Max smile, smugly. He admired her spirit; she was a tough woman to marry his father, to have coped with his moods and his controlling nature.

She assured him that no one, not even his father, would stop her from loving and caring for her children. She asked him to love his brother and sister – after all, she had said, they were torn between their love for Max and their loyalty to their father.

Julian had been put into position by his father and he could hardly throw it back in the man's face because of Max. She had advised Max to see things from a practical perspective, not to get sentimental about it. Samantha – she still needed the financial support that her father provided; she could not become a rebel or a renegade, at least not yet.

Max had listened carefully during that phone conversation. His mind at ease – she had promised to keep both Julian and Sammy in the loop. He remembered the long pause. It preceded her hint that his father did not have control over the children's use of the internet or their mobile phones, nor over any future clandestine meetings – at least not at that moment in time.

After that phone call he had reopened a dialogue with Julian and Sammy. They now spoke frequently, via text and email and the occasional discrete phone call. He tried to make sure that he did not influence them one way or another, leaving them free to make up their own minds about their father.

Losing out on them because his father wanted to control him – that was wrong.

He wiped his mouth with a napkin and checked his watch.

No communication with his father. It still hurt. It was like an inner wound that would surface at the strangest of times – hearing a voice. Someone would mention their father, Father's day – it would surface like an iceberg in the night. Then he would feel the inner lingering pain. Sometimes he thought that it would have been easier if his father had been dead, that way he could at least have closure. But no, this pain went on and on.

He still had fifteen minutes in which to cover the five minute walk to his meeting. Too much time to think. He wished that he could shake the feeling of dejection, that he could get into the meeting room already and focus on his work, but it hung over him like a grim cloud.

Somehow, they had managed to stay out of one another's ways. It was for the best that way.

FRIDAY 17TH AUGUST 2001 (BM, EWA, R)

It took a lot of planning, a lot of soul searching and a lot of hinting. Lillian arranged for the two to meet at a civil function, neither realising that the other would be present.

She knew it was risky, but Lukas had been diagnosed with prostate cancer. His annual health check had turned into a major event and he was already undergoing treatment.

Suddenly, life seemed to have a timer on it; she would not go the grave knowing that she had failed to help her son and husband resolve their issues. She could not force them back together, but she could provide the right environment for reconciliation. A public setting, which would influence the way they both behaved. It would be a small step. She remembered the moon landing. Max knew about the treatment, she made sure he did.

The event. She sold it to Max, describing it as a civil reception, a wonderful chance for networking. He had done well to establish himself within the industry but he would need a whole lot of new, external contacts if he wanted advance with his fledgling biotech company. Thankfully, he listened to her.

My poor nerves – both hands were sweating, she found herself feeling awkward, forgetting the names of people that she knew, fighting back tears.

This had better work out well.

She kept Lukas busy, meeting and greeting. When he was otherwise occupied, she sent a text to Max, reminding him that she was looking forward to catching up with him. He replied, saying he would be there.

Lillian hoped Lukas would not be too angry about her deception. Now, here, in public, it felt like she might have made a mistake. She steeled herself.

Your nerves are getting the better of you, Lilly.

She drank her third glass of champagne. It had no effect.

Perhaps brandy would have been a better choice.

Movements in her stomach told her that all was not well. She smiled through it, beaming at the various guests and delegates.

I'm going to pass out if it's not over soon. What if I do?

Secrets, she thought; they were awful things; they consumed you in the innermost of places and then surfaced like icebergs, threatening to shipwreck everything above the surface. Hidden vessels full of danger.

She looked at the back of Lukas' head, still full even at this age. How stubborn he had been.

He turned to her, his eyes tired, more crinkles around their edges. *Still strong, still hurting.* She kissed his cheek, he hugged her. *He's going to be livid.* Her eyes scanned the room, half listening to the conversation between Lukas and his business partner.

Lukas turned and whispered in her ear. 'Are you alright dear, you seem distracted?' Lying would be pointless, so distraction seemed the better option.

'Look, there is Cole Decasse, he's good friends with the mayor. A chance to connect; go over and say hello,' she pushed him in the direction she was pointing. Grateful that her memory had not let her down. He let the question hang but moved off dutifully, his hand extended in greeting. She released the long sigh.

I'm not sure how much more of this I can take. She rubbed her forehead, feeling weary.

Lukas and Cole were joined by the mayor. That kind of connection could not be planned. A moment of respite. At least clutching the champagne glass gave her hands something to do.

Lillian spotted Max the same time as Lukas. He had just turned to speak to the Mayor. Her hand moved to her mouth, covering it. She looked at her husband, then at Max.

Max walked into the room, entirely unaware. *Innocent*. Like a lamb.

Lukas' complexion changed suddenly. He resembled a clean, stretched out linen sheet; the tightly clenched jaw, the way the champagne glass became trapped in his fist. She was sure, for a brief moment, that his breathing had stopped. His whole frame was shuddering – they were tiny and almost imperceptible tremors. Lillian felt dreadful.

Oh God, help me. Before she could be consumed by her own feelings she registered at the reaction from Max.

Max was clearly unnerved at the sight of his father. She sensed his pain. Two years had passed in which there had been no contact – no Christmas cards, no presents. No communication. She knew how it was: Max felt that he was dead to his father.

Though Max loved his father, he had a dream and he wanted to try and pursue it. She understood him. She saw him looking at the floor; that was his thinking pose, his mind now in problem solving mode. That gave her a small window of opportunity. She moved swiftly.

+ + +

Max's mind was in overdrive and yet all he could ascertain from his panic was a simple question: *Should I walk away or stay?*

It repeated itself incessantly inside his head. Seconds felt like fruitless hours. Suddenly, he made his decision.

As he was about to pivot, a hand grabbed his left elbow, tightly. The perfume – lavender blended with cassia – was immediately recognisable.

Mother.

'Mom,' he paused, his whispers low and quiet. 'You did not tell me that he was going to be here,' Max was livid, his rage concealed by the lowness of his voice, 'I would not have come.'

Lillian leaned forward, kissing her son on his forehead. 'My dear, dear son.' Tears began to well up in her eyes; she stared at him. 'How I have missed you.' Her mascara mixed with the tears and formed rivulets that flowed down her cheeks. Max took the white handkerchief from his breast pocket and handed it to his mother, wanting to spare her any public scrutiny. He glanced up then down again, trying to see what was going on around him without catching sight of Lukas. The man had moved, quietly and quickly out of his line of sight.

She received the handkerchief gladly, dabbing at her stained cheeks, still covered with black streaks. She gestured in the direction of the corridor.

As they headed there, Lukas stepped in front of them, blocking their retreat.

Neither men spoke. Lilian sensed the dam of tension, an invisible force field, seemingly impenetrable; a wall built of pride and ego and the foundation of their separation.

It was now or never.

She spoke softly, 'Well aren't you both going to say sorry?' Like father, like son – both stubborn, irascible, sometimes prickly and driven by passion.

'I'm...' Both responded at the same time.

Max felt a searing, wet heat stinging his eyes. He did not want to cry, but deep down inside he missed his father. He still remembered the pushing and shoving, the threatening and the sound of his voice; the violent anger on his face.

So different from the frail, scared look that held stay there now.

Part of Max wanted to square up to him, to tell him that he could not intimidate him anymore.

I have done it. I have done it without you.

Yet he knew about the cancer and the possibility of the man's death, maybe sooner than expected. So many things were swirling around in his head; conflicting emotions, fuelled by the past and now airborne in the present.

Lukas felt his heart soften. His son, Max, was close to tears. Yes, he had been angry, in fact he had been furious at the boy's determination to pursue his own path. Lukas had sincerely believed that Max would buckle under the pressure. Now he knew that he had been wrong. It was just that... it had seemed so weak to apologise. *It scared me.* But seeing him, like that.

Compassion overcame anger. Lukas grabbed his son and drew him into a tight embrace, feeling himself choking on the inside. He had been wrong.

Max was stiff, poker straight in the embrace. Lukas wondered if he was feeling uncomfortable with this public display of affection, or was it the bad memories? This was new territory for him as a man, as a father; he was not one for public displays of affection or indeed any affection at all, but recent events had forced him to re-evaluate those things.

Lost in the embrace, the intensity of the moment passed by his defence mechanisms. Max softened, all of his carefully built defences were at once obliterated; two years of pain and isolation burst out into the open. He had not expected this today, nor had he planned for anything of the kind to ever take place. It just happened.

They wept.

Lukas struggled to expel the words. Tears continued to fall. 'Please—' he coughed, the words catching in his throat. 'Please forgive me.'

He could not look at his son. He felt ashamed. He felt that he could not pardon Max, nor release him from the sentence that he had imposed when he told him to go that day in the office. It was burned into his mind, replayed countless times. He would never have behaved like Max had; he'd never stood up to his father on any matter, even when he wished that he had done so. Perhaps that was why he had been so furious with his son. He was the truly brave one.

He's braver than you and you resented that; you resented your own boy.

And suddenly he understood.

He's strong. He's so much stronger than I ever was. I love him.

The admission allowed him to pardon, gave him permission to reconsider his verdict and cancel the sentence – the moment made redemption possible. Not only Max's but his own. By the admission of fault, he released his position as judge and jailor. He placed himself at the mercy of his son. From the place of the judge to that of one seeking mercy – *even clemency?*

Max wailed; deep rivers of pain rose to the surface.

The fact that this was a public reception had seemingly slipped their minds.

A third person joined them, putting both of her arms around her men.

SATURDAY 20TH OCTOBER 2001 (BM, EWA, R)

Bethany winced as she turned and inspected her image in the bedroom mirror. There was no doubt that pregnancy had left its mark on her once taut figure. Those extra pounds would just not go, and the stretch marks were like angry red ridges of extended skin; old looking and wrinkly.

She sighed wholeheartedly.

She had given her word and so tonight she would go to the country-dance group. The baggy eyes could be hidden behind a good concealer and she'd purchased a new colour of lipstick, it was on a special deal at Walmart. Her newly dyed hair was much brighter than before, it really lifted her skin colour. She had spent so much time indoors at the beginning, taking Chloe out for daily walks, twice a day if the weather was good. Twenty minutes sessions; a sure way to boost her vitamin D levels.

Though she was tired, Bethany was determined to make an effort. She could not remember the last time she had attended. Frank had stopped asking, so her request had caught him by surprise. The way his eyes had opened, the actual shock that had run across his face – he'd almost dropped the plate he had been holding.

Peggy Su told her to make sure she did not neglect Frank for Chloe. In reality, she knew that she was guilty of doing just that. She was glad that Frank, for his sins, was tolerant and loving, even if he was grumpy about it. All the same, she had been giving her full attention to her daughter and Frank had been left on the sideline. Nothing was too much, interruptions in the night, the leaks from both ends, the swollen nipples, and overwhelming tiredness that stayed with her all the time. Motherhood had its share of highs and the lows but – as she had been warned – she could not afford to neglect her husband.

The top button would not remain fastened. The dark denim jeans were straining. She was fearful that if she moved or bent down unexpectedly a ripping sound would be heard, followed by bundles of flesh emerging. But she hoped that the long checked shirt, would conceal that – it was one of Frank's.

She turned sideways. Yes, she could just about pull it off. Would she remember all the old dance moves? Maybe it would be like riding a bike, once she got into the rhythm. she would be fine.

Now for the make–up.

When was the last time I put any on?

It had been a good while ago. She smiled at herself in the compact mirror.

Frank had better appreciate the effort she was making.

+++

As they made their way home, Frank remained quiet.

Bethany had laughed and chatted during the whole event, obviously excited. Frank kept quiet for most of the evening, giving an occasional grunt and monosyllabic response; the whole event triggered feelings of sadness, reminding him of funerals where everyone is trying to remember the good things about the corpse in the fresh grave. Their song had played; as they clung to each other he'd realised that she was no longer the one.

The roads were largely deserted. Phoenix was having a quiet night. Beth made some comment about it being unusual for a Saturday, then she questioned about the lack of local drunks and revellers, wondering where all the patrol cops were hanging out.

Yeah, the night felt so... different. He kept his eyes on the road.

For him, it was over. Too much, too late. He needed to find the right time to announce the end.

Not tonight though. Not tonight

FRIDAY 2ND NOVEMBER 2001 (BM, R)

Frank put Chloe back into the playpen, she made her way towards the spinning top, lifting it up and showing it to him.

The living room needed tidying. Beth could do that later.

Chloe was such a lovely kid. She was really no trouble. She'd settled down and made it through the night without a peep.

Frank had been asking himself the same question for days now. *Life without a dad? How will she cope? What will this do to her?*

He'd held back his tears at High School when people had talked about the fun they had with their dad or the way that their dads showed them how to do things or the arguments they had with their dads, who seemed to know so little about what it was like to be a kid these days. He'd just put on his tough face and had walked away from it all.

He had talked to himself. *It doesn't really matter,* he had thought, *I'll make my own way, I had to once, so will she.*

Having a bigger brother had helped. Richie filled in some of the gaps. He'd been a role model, showing Frank how to do stuff around the house.

Dads. Maybe they were expendable. He'd turned out alright.

Chloe had reached the bars of the playpen, gurgling happily, biting onto the plastic keys, dribbling.

I hope you'll be okay without me, Chloe.

SUNDAY 4TH NOVEMBER 2001 (BM, EWA, R)

'Do you want to go to the country group next week?'

It had been a few weeks since their last visit. A fun evening. Frank had seemed a bit moody but he'd still managed to laugh here and there; and he was a really great dancer.

'No.'

That surprised her. They'd grown up dancing together and he was so keen on it that such a refusal was completely unheard of.

'I thought you—'

'Sorry, Beth, but you thought wrong.' He kept staring at the television screen. That was unusual; he normally looked at her when she spoke. Chloe was sleeping in the playpen.

She stood between him and the television. 'Is there something wrong, Frank?'

'Wrong? There's nothing wrong. I just want to watch the game in piece. Would you please move out of the way?'

Bethany sensed her heart racing, there was definitely something wrong. She could feel it – this standoffish attitude was about avoidance. He was not saying something. She would have to get it out of him though, or this could continue until the morning, turning into a nasty row – she knew that too well. He hated being confronted, but it had to be done.

'If there is something you want to tell me,' she moved towards the kitchen, 'you know where to find me.'

The evening meal was still in process, the roast was in the oven, the vegetables would soon be ready.

I'll make this a good meal for him and hopefully he can chill out a bit. I hope it's not about his work. God, please let it be about anything other than his work. We couldn't cope with a pay cut… Oh, no; maybe it's his mother. Oh, I hope not. Perhaps he'll spill the beans later.

She heard his heavy approach, Frank leaned against the door frame. 'Actually, Beth, there is something I want to say.' He scratched his head and sniffed.

I need to darn that hole in his sock – his toe's poking through. She put the pot of peas back on the stove, deciding to drain it after he had finished.

'I'm listening.' She really did wonder if everything was okay a work, he had been spending a lot of time on visits and extra trips away from home. He must be so important in the company if they had him on the road so often. It couldn't possibly be redundancy. But he seemed to be so down. The tension was killing her. She wished he'd just tell her now.

What the hell is it, Frank?

'I'm leaving Beth.'

Oh. She looked at him questioningly, her head cocked to one side. She had been expecting something… more. She spoke, careful to keep her voice calm.

'You have another trip? You've only just got back from the last one. Where are you going? When do they need you to go? I mean—'

He shook his head, 'I'm leaving Beth. I'm… I'm leaving you.'

'What do you mean?' For a moment her mind felt fuzzy, the words hijacked on route through her brain.

'Do I have to spell it out for you?"

It was like an echo. It was like all the times he'd uttered those words as a teenager. All the on and off moments. The things she hadn't heard for more than ten years. Suddenly, it was like he was a ghost. She felt sick. She didn't really follow.

She looked at him, imploring time to turn back a few seconds, wondering if she could wipe away what she thought she had just heard.

'What, sorry? Frank?'

'I am leaving you for,' he licked his lips and looked down at the floor. 'It's for someone. Another woman, Beth. For someone else.'

Everything went still inside her. Suddenly she was filled with the most startling sense clarity. Her motherhood was forgotten. All over again she was an angry young woman, a man, her man, stepping in her way. And for what? The words thumped in her head.

Another woman.

He looked confused. She exhaled slowly, feeling as if her face changed, losing its roundness. She spoke, quietly at first.

'Who is she?' She turned back to the cooker hiding her face in the steam. At first she thought that she was hiding tears. Then she realised that she was aware of the changes. She was hiding her age. Her tiredness. Her sadness. In the steam, it turned to rage.

And then she was screaming at him.

'Who is she? Who is the little… whore?'

Chloe started to cry.

'I want to make this as painless as possible—'

'Painless… What do you know about pain?' She was close to picking up the pot of peas and throwing it at him. She realised that she was gripping its handle, her hand raw red with tension.

'I knew you'd react like this.' His head shaking had increased, he looked up at the ceiling.

'Like what? What did you think I would do? Call Oprah and let the world know. You're dumping me? What are you, Frank? Who the hell are you? You're not a teenager! You're a husband. You're a father! Frank!'

Here he was. The one she had trusted, the one she believed in, the one she turned to, the one she kissed goodnight, not every night, not anymore, she knew that too well, but the one she had loved.

The bastard's leaving.

'What about Chloe? What's going to happen to her?' Her little cry morphed into wail, Chloe was so sensitive. She had crossed from worry to hysteria.

'We'll work it out.'

'Work it out. This is not a business deal. This is your daughter we're talking about.' She'd been such a fool, letting her guard down, allowing him to get into her heart. Now it was trampling time, her emotions trodden down into the gritty ground.

How many of those trips were business trips? I bet he was with her.

She pressed the back of her right hand against her forehead. 'I just can't deal with this now.'

'You wanted to talk—'

'But not about this! I…' Chloe was hyperventilating. 'Move out of the way Frank, Chloe needs me.'

She barged past him, making straight for her distressed child. Behind her, Frank said, 'She'll learn to live without me.'

'Chloe, Chloe, mommy is here. Shh, it is alright.' She rocked and stroked her, tears rolled down her little face. Seeing Chloe's blurry face, she uttered the three words she would repeat in the coming years.

'Mommy is here.'

The slamming of the front door told her that Frank would not be eating her roast tonight. On the stove, the peas boiled over. By the time she noticed, they had burned to the bottom of the pan.

2002 – 2005

'Good girl Miranda.'

Eleanor hugged the delighted learner, kissing the top of her forehead. After the fourth attempt she had managed to tie her shoelace.

'Mummy is so proud of you.' The broad teeth revealing smile from Miranda made her glad. Even small things meant so much.

'Daddy will be very happy too when I tell him.' Her smile grew even larger.

'Will Daddy be very happy?'

'Yes, Miranda, he will'

Miranda clapped her hands together and squealed. Then she seemed to forget what she had been doing, a blank expression replaced the smile.

Eleanor felt her heart sink, another episode. Emotional memory loss was another of the increasing list of symptoms. She hid her pain behind a smile, giving Miranda another hug.

Charles would be on duty tonight, it was her night off. She had left a list of things that needed to be done, including her bedtime and bathroom routine. He often needed reminding of how things needed to be done;

routine was absolutely essential to Miranda. Without it she would not get a good night's sleep, and when she slept well it meant that Eleanor had a good night too. Miranda's learning routine had to be maintained. Eleanor's brief years as a teacher had provided her with the principles and procedures needed for effective learning. She knew what was best for her daughter.

'When is Daddy coming home, Mummy?'

'Daddy will be home soon honey,' *while Mummy will be going out to play.*

+++

'Mummy says I must not do that.' Miranda felt very confused.

'Miranda, watch me,' Miranda obeyed. 'If you want to be messy then Daddy says that it is okay.'

'But—'

Daddy put his finger on her lips. 'Daddy says messy is okay.'

A huge white plastic sheet covered the living room carpet, Daddy had moved the big table to make space. There were lots of paints in lots of lovely colours. Daddy had let Miranda choose any colours she wanted.

She was happy. Daddy put large pieces of paper on the floor next to Miranda.

'I want you to make a lovely picture for daddy.' Miranda nodded her head. 'You can use your fingers to paint like this.' Daddy dipped his hand into the dish and covered it with paint. He then slapped it onto the white paper leaving a print. Miranda clapped her hands.

'Miranda turn, Miranda turn.'

'Yes, Miranda turn.'

Miranda giggled as she made her picture.

Charles loved to see Miranda at play. He believed in freedom of expression. No rules or regulations: *let her have fun.* He knew Eleanor held a different point of view, but his night, his rules – and if that meant no rules at all then that was what it meant.

Miranda was concentrating on the task at hand, her eyebrows twitching away as she focused on the paper, then the paints, then her hands.

'Go for it Miranda, make it special for Daddy.' Mummy might have a fit if she saw the mess. He would manoeuvre around that bridge when he came to it.

Charles nodded in approval.

'Hello Ma, how are you?'

'Hello Charles, I have called a couple of times. You have been out. How is work?'

'Fine, no problems. Ellie sends her love and Miranda is waving at you.'

'I want to speak to may granddaughter in a moment. Charles, that picture she did for me is amazing. Did you help her?' She heard him chuckling.

'No Ma, that was all her own work.'

Icilda hesitated before making her next statement, 'That is better than what you produced when you were… seven.' She paused waiting to see if her words ignited a response.

Charles chuckled again. 'She is better than I will ever be. She has real talent Ma. Her painting will be world famous.'

Icilda breathed out, 'I have it on display in my quiet room.' She'd had the picture framed. It sat next to the family portrait that she so adored.

'Keep it. One day it will be worth millions.'

'Is that prophetic, Charles; or are you just a proud dad?'

'Time will tell.'

+++

As the years passed, Eleanor watched Miranda struggle with the progression of her illness and the onset of its more limiting stages.

Eleanor and Charles made a concerted effort to spend more of their time together with Miranda, ensuring that her last days were her best.

They had no clear idea how much time they had.

Data entry input: 366343963711

Programme: GWP

Level: 6

Accessed by C.

It was now official. They were divorced, the final decree lay there in her trembling hands. The sweethearts, a failure – how right they had all been. Bethany leaned against the wall, in the corridor. It was the place she called home.

We *used to call this home.*

The residency requirement: three months, after filing for divorce. From July to November.

She had been granted full custody of Chloe, he was allowed visits once a month and could have her for weekends once every three months. The interlocutory divorce decree spelled out the grounds for the divorce – adultery.

He never contested her claim, which actually made it quite easy. He had child support to pay as well as spousal support. That was good, meaning she could spend time with Chloe and stick to her original plans; she could to go back to work when Chloe was ready for kindergarten.

He'd left the house in December 2001, before Christmas. Bethany heard that he'd moved in with his strumpet. She wished them nothing but grief. It was difficult to put into words the pain and the shame that she would now have to live with. If they wanted to tie the knot, now they could. She would stay here with the man's daughter.

Her parents were shocked, wondering why she complained about his antics – saying that she should just get on with things, forgive and move on. Put the past behind you, sort out the issues, let the past go, reconcile for the sake of Chloe. Bethany did not see herself as a pale Tina Turner – *Let's stay together.* No way. If that was how their generation coped, she had no intention of following their advice.

His mother – she had no idea how she was coping. She could contact Ginny now that the divorce was finalised. Ginny had a soft spot for her, she could tell. She still needed to have access to their granddaughter; why should she suffer because of her son's stupidity?

As for Frank's dad, he was still on the run from responsibility. Nobody had any idea where he could be found, even if he was still alive. What a loser… just like his son.

Peggy Su was as solid as a rock. Standing with her all the way.

As for Shania… she could get stuffed. Bethany could hardly bear to hear that tune now, knowing all the history that it brought to the surface.

From now on, Bethany decided, she would do things her way.

December 2002 (BM, R)

Adrian was seven years old when Louise was born, his condition in its early stages.

Anne had almost finished cleaning the living room; now her focus was on dusting the mantlepiece, carefully working around the family photographs. Not one for clutter, she only allowed a few photos be displayed at any one time. She picked one up: a permanent fixture, Adrian with Louise. She was just a few hours old. He had still been able to hold things then.

Louise's expected date of delivery – January 1st 2000. Anne had been looking forward to the tidy sum of one thousand pounds which had been promised to all Millennium babies, those children born on the first day of the new century. Back then she had thought it was an omen; hopefully promising future good luck. However, Louise had arrived late, born on January 25th 2000.

Looking back, the whole pregnancy had been overshadowed by a deep sense of foreboding which gradually transformed into periods of mild depression. She could call it that now, but then she would have vehemently denied it. Sleepless nights, feelings of insecurity and being overwhelmed; niggling thoughts and her persistent crying, over the smallest things – each was a miniature clue about the state of her inner self.

Of course, it was nobody's fault that Adrian had inherited SMA. She looked up every definition for spinal muscular atrophy, becoming something of an expert on the condition. Like taking part in a genetic lottery, it could be you! In their case, they had lost, badly. It was so cruel.

A random mutation struck at their son, threatening to slowly rob him of his mobility and them of their firstborn child. Nothing was fair about it. A kind of daylight robbery, the theft of a life by nature tampering with their son's genetic code.

Nonetheless, the intense feelings of guilt remained. She tried to congratulate herself for hiding the stress so well though. Patrick had been largely unaware of her anxiety while she was carrying Louise.

Dear Patrick, her granite support, her anchorage. She never believed in love at first sight until it happened to her. She had known, from the day she set eyes on him, that they were destined for each other. The way that Patrick stepped in, quietly supporting her, offering wise words of assurance; those words were few, but weighty.

Thank God it was a short labour! Adrian's arrival had gone on for days, a tortuous personal eternity.

Louise was a beautiful child, with gorgeous eyes. Patrick insisted on being at the birth of his second child. His work commitments had robbed him of his place at his son's arrival, that exclusive meeting with the Peter Jones Group had taken months to organise. Thankfully, their upmarket 'Dalton' kitchenware could now be purchased at stores up and down the country. The coffee morning group were impressed. Anne understood the hidden costs of running one's own business.

She smiled contentedly as she recalled his teary eyes, welling up as he whispered words of love over Louise, blessing her as she lay in his arms. 'She's beautiful, just like her mum.' He kissed Anne on her forehead, still damp with perspiration.

'Is she going to be okay? Does she have…' Her anxiety lent power to her vocal cords, forcing the words out.

'The medical staff have said that all the tests are negative, no signs of any issues. She is a healthy little girl.' Patrick's words stemmed the rising waves of panic, she gripped his hand.

'Your mum will be here shortly. She was delayed by the snow. It's almost shut down the whole area. It's a good thing she left her home when she did or she might have ended up stranded like all those other poor people.'

Both of them had heard about the unfortunate cases of travellers trapped in their cars, imprisoned by the most recent snowdrifts. There had been three fatalities so far…

'We just need to borrow your daughter for a while.' Sarah, the midwife, carefully took the bundle from Patrick. 'A couple more checks and she'll be back in your arms before you know it.'

The words and actions terrified, 'What tests? She already had some earlier on today. What are you not telling me?' A wave of dizziness moved across her abdomen accompanied by a deep throbbing in her chest.

'This set of tests will check her reflexes and senses. Please don't worry. You need to rest.' Sarah was well aware of the Dalton family history; she had been on duty when Adrian was born.

The throbbing continued.

That was how it all started – Adrian's checks. Early tests had revealed that there were serious coordination issues; an ominous warning about things to come. Then the devastating blow to the family. Their joy turned to shock and then fear, leaving them with a deep and numb lack of feeling.

Sarah repeated herself then added, 'Your daughter is going to be fine, just fine.'

Her calm voice and carefully chosen words did nothing to deter the dread, radiating from the moment she discovered the truth about Adrian's condition.

Despite her forced smile, Anne still wanted reassurances. She trusted Sarah even confiding in her during her pregnancy. Back then she consumed every book she could find on genetic conditions and inheritance; it become a personal obsession. However, increased knowledge did not bring comfort, only generating further questions.

Even one child with a condition was more than she felt she could handle. Discovering she was pregnant for the second time released intense feelings of joy and stark fear. Would this child be the same as Adam?

The amniocentesis test indicated that all was well. No signs of genetic abnormalities. Now that her daughter had arrived, subconscious fear surfaced. Sarah did not consider herself a religious woman, yet she uttered a silent prayer. *God, let her be alright.*

'Annie, just going to give Danielle a call to see if Adrian is okay.'

'Oh yes, you do that. I'm just going to have a little rest. I've got a bit of a headache. Could you ask the nurse for something?'

'Yeah, will do.' He stared into her eyes. 'For you, anything.' He kissed her again.

Anne remembered closing her eyes, irritated by the constant noise of the ward, so tiring. She just wanted to be at home with her family.

Louise – her arrival would give them a chance to alter their lives, a new perspective. She changed everything they considered normal.

Hard to believe she was almost three. Adrian had another appointment this afternoon. Anne still struggled to cope with the time management issues of hospital appointments, NHS bureaucracy and a mobility adapted car.

Anne put down the photograph, then checked the grandfather clock. 11.45am. She certainly did not want to get stuck in the lunchtime traffic, especially since they had closed her favourite short cut – part of the so called road improvement programme carried out by their local council.

Fingers crossed, Louise would still be sleeping, Adrian in his room on that computer of his, enthralled by his latest video game. Time to mentally prepared for the "get the kids in the car manoeuvre".

As she picked up the car keys, she thought, *my life isn't easy; but it is strangely beautiful.*

MONDAY 17TH MARCH 2003 (BM, R)

What was the plan again?

It was clear to Bethany. Frank might have disagreed, but she would look after Chloe until she was ready for kindergarten and then return to work.

Frank had been ordered to pay regular maintenance costs but no money ever materialised. She knew she could go through the courts – getting what was due to her – it was her right. Yet something in her had lost the will to fight. Perhaps it was the sheer effort of looking after Chloe alone. She remembered resenting Frank for his doing so little with Chloe. That was fair enough, she thought; after all, the man was an adulterer and a runaway. But she also knew now that she hadn't really noticed his reluctant contributions, somehow that had helped her take a break here and there. Even if it was for all of half an hour a day.

She simply had no time. No time and no money.

The finances were now her responsibility. Life was just stress upon stress; things becoming more and more difficult by the day. The mortgage payments were eroding the last of her precious personal savings – her fear of her growing arrears played on her mind all day every day and often at night, keeping her wake. The thought of repossession was unbearable. Bethany imagined their losing the roof over their heads, her and Chloe out on the street and all because she couldn't face yet more time spent wrangling over money with Frank. She just could not. No courts. No contact. No Frank.

There was no other option – she would have to go back to work now. When she rang her former manager, Roland, he sounded so enthusiastic it left her smiling. Bethany prided herself on being a hard worker. She had just enrolled on the management training programme, then she fell pregnant. To her surprise she was given her old position back.

That was one headache solved. Now for the other – childcare for Chloe.

Why did women have to make the choice between financial provision and looking after their children? It was so unfair. She did not want to hate Frank but she came so close to the line. The coward had abandoned her and daughter.

Bethany wanted Chloe to have the very best in life. That now looked like a life without Frank. As far as she was concerned, that was okay.

SATURDAY 10TH MAY 2003 (BM, EWA, R)

'Where's Daddy?'

Chloe repeatedly asked the question out aloud, usually as she played alone in the den. Bethany would hear her daughter's voice, lost somewhere in the middle of her childish rambling. Even if she was in the kitchen, like today.

'Daddy used to play with me and all my toys but not anymore.'

Bethany went into the den, watching Chloe, playing with her toys as if they were part of the conversation, understanding all the issues, sitting, listening attentively. Chloe's little family.

Bethany knelt down and tried to explain that Daddy was busy, that he'd had to go away.

She tried not to cry.

FEBRUARY 2004 (BM, R)

Louise realised that Adrian was not like her when she was four. He was so clumsy all the time and he needed to be helped around. She was faster than he was and she could beat him in any race. Adrian sometimes needed a special chair with wheels and he sometimes let her ride in it. He could not play for very long and would become very tired, often needing to lie down. Louise felt stronger than he was.

She would soon realise that the condition was responsible for this lack of mobility. The wheelchair was one of the first signs that Adrian was losing his fight to remain independent. By the time Louise was eleven, Adrian had lost the use of his legs, becoming totally reliant on his wheelchair.

WEDNESDAY 19TH MAY 2004 (BM, R)

Two days – it was the only time that was ever allowed to pass before one of them contacted the other. A stark contrast to the two silent years.

Having lived without his father, Max set about making sure that every moment counted. He wanted to absorb the wisdom and knowledge that his father possessed. Thinking of it as an investment for the future, a hidden legacy that was passed on from one generation to the next. The silent timer gave no indication as to when the final alarm would trigger, no one could know when that fatal moment would fall. The closing of books, the end of the account.

It was not just a matter of talking. Max viewed this newfound relationship as an act of sharing, drawn from the heart; the deepest type of communication. He had a ferocious appetite for it, like a starving man allowed into an eat-all-you-can buffet. Looking back, Max saw it as a time for apology, a time for appreciation, a time for understanding and at time to grab precious moments before they were cruelly snatched away.

Yes, his father spared no punches, revealing insider knowledge about the things that had made their business so successful; including many of the murkier aspects that were never to be discussed around the conference table. Max's initial shock seemed to amuse his father. Lukas would remember that moment for the rest of his life, how he had stared straight into Max's eyes and said, 'You need to know this, son.' It was something he had always imagined he would do; something he had then imagined lost, now regained.

Max learned that his grandfather had been no saint. Deals had been made behind closed doors, broken covenants, the consumption of smaller companies whenever the opportunity arose – ruthless and hard, that was the Augustine way. The family fortune was streaked with dark smears. Armed with that knowledge Max recognised and began to fully understand the man he called father. His views shifted. It was as if an optician was at work behind the scenes, changing the lenses during an eye test until Max could see the images on the chart clearly.

Another revelation – his grandfather not only used his voice, he spoke with his fists too. Lukas confided that he had lived his early life with many bruises and black eyes: the price of disobedience. The memories seemed to be too much for him; he'd broken down and wept loudly, apologising for the prodding and the pushing. In his mind it was like watching a movie about his relationship with his own father, but the PG version. Max understood and told him that he forgave him. He wept more.

Lukas had promised himself that he would be nothing like his own father, yet over the years he had noticed many of the same traits in his own behaviour. It scared him, despite his efforts to fight what seemed inevitable.

Like father, like son. A destiny written in his DNA.

Max's grandfather had died when he was three. Black and white photographs helped to create a physical image of him; their talking about the stern, austere man with cold dark eyes helped to fill in the emotional and social details. Max learned that he was a determined individual who had lived for money and power. His father's mentor. As he listened, Max wondered if he was destined to continue down that line, extending existing branches or starting new ones.

During these times, Max felt a strange tenderness towards his father. The man's body had begun to yield to the silent invasion of the cancer. His once-strong frame was now sunken and vulnerable.

In Max's mind this had been the journey of lifetime – from outcast to closest son, even friend. Julian still stayed away from their father. Max concluded that he either did not care or was too consumed by hate and bitterness to enjoy the relationship. Max knew that he resented their father. That was something he had picked up during his exile, part of the many conversations the brothers had held in secret. All his life, Julian had felt bullied into doing everything his father wanted, and now he was stuck in a life he hated. Trapped in the serval cage at the zoo, when he dreamed of being in the lion enclosure. And now, despite Max's best efforts to convince him to change, Julian refused to let go of the past. Max knew that the situation was further aggravated by his reconnection with his father.

Nonetheless, that reconnection had taken place. It was taking place every day. For both of them, it was shocking yet life enhancing. His mother seemed to agree, talking about the reconciliation as the defining point in the two men's relationship. He was glad she had been spared the more sinister content of their conversations.

It was a brief moment.

DECEMBER 2004 (BM, EWA, R)

Lukas Octavius Augustine died on November 20th 2004, just before the Christmas sales reached their peak and the weather turned bitterly cold. Heavy snow fell that year.

Max commissioned an oil portrait based on his father's favourite photograph. The one with him standing beside the fireplace, looking relaxed and happy. From the day of its completion, the painting followed Max, occupying a central position in each of his main offices whenever he moved. Somehow it helped to keep the memory alive.

The funeral attracted many dignitaries, celebrities, those in public office, business people and members of the community of differing shades of respectability. Max struggled to control his emotions that day, relying on Julian for physical support. During his time of exile such a display would have been unthinkable. Now it seemed only right – a rejuvenated bond between father and son. A lost mentor; a friend as well.

The calm after the storm – extremely bitter sweet.

He jolted himself out of thought, surprised to see someone he half recognised moving towards him, right hand extended. *Who… Ferrell? But he looks so much older.* Almost automatically, he raised his own hand, ready to shake.

Max recalled meeting Charles Ferrell again for the first time since Harvard, catching his eye across the casket. Charles acknowledged him with a nod.

Lukas had been good friends with Ralph Ferrell. The two boys had attended various social functions as they grew up. They knew each other's names and family connections, but they hadn't met formally until their undergraduate days. Charles had been a year ahead of him and had kept his distance back then. Indeed, they had shared a passion for transhumanism and had both been keen members of HSTT. They had kept strikingly different social circles. Max often thought that Charles had harboured some rather questionable friends. *As for his politics… he was always absurdly leftist for a man of his wealth.*

At the time, the man had been a close friend of that Indian fellow. Kothaka. Max was never quite sure what to think of him. On the one hand, he'd seemed like an arrogant and ambitious foreigner; another person trying to make it big in America, using Harvard – clinging like a lost puppy to Charles. On the other hand though, there was no denying that the man was a brilliant academic; he had possessed exceptional debating skills. He had even stepped into the leadership of HSTT with relative ease, but Max had kept his distance after that. The man had seemed to have an agenda and Max had never quite worked out what his game might be. Himself, he had opted for a back seat within the society, watching and listening but never pushing like the others; his own business ideas always needed fostering and that was where he had devoted his spare time. Max understood that the man was heir to an almost insurmountable offshore fortune. He had been haughty and distant. *Like royalty.* And something about that had bothered Max.

Despite the family connections and the fact that they had attended many meetings and discussions together, Max had never felt particularly drawn to Charles. In the end, he had left and Max had failed to keep in touch with him.

Charles Ferrell took his hand. 'I'm so sorry about the loss of your father, Max. He was a great man.' Charles' grip was firm; he was making his presence known without being overpowering about it. Still, Max appreciated the sentiment.

'Thank you, Charles. It is very kind of you.'

'How are you doing?'

'Difficult to say, one moment you're okay, the next…' Another wave of emotion swept through him, terminating in his bowels. Charles moved quickly and Max found himself in the embrace of someone he hardly knew. Gripped by embarrassment, his body stayed rigid throughout the gesture of compassion.

'Thank you.' They stood apart, Max putting as much distance as he could between himself and his comforter. Polite distance.

Charles handed him a clean handkerchief. 'I always carry spares at these events.' His smile seemed genuine. Max accepted the offering, carefully wiping his eyes.

'That will go on for some time I am sure,' he smiled at Charles before continuing, 'Anyway, how is your own father?'

'Pa is fine, he is around here somewhere. I wanted to say that I am really impressed with what you have done with BioFuture. I have been watching the growth of your company with some interest.'

Max was a little shocked. *Is this guy making a business proposal at a funeral? Do some people have no shame?* He said nothing.

'Perhaps I could get you to share your thoughts and ideas at one of our encouraging new meetings, as part of IBC's Progress In The Community Programme?' He handed Max a business card, 'Give me call… when you have time, of course.' He gripped Max's elbow, firm but not imposing. 'And Max, I really am sorry about your father.' He moved off.

Max put the pieces of the business card into the nearest bin. He was annoyed and worse, he felt as if he had been disrespected by Charles Ferrell.

A part of him wondered if he was wrong though. Perhaps he had simply misjudged the man's motives?

After all, there was every reason for Charles to admire him; perhaps the man was drawn to the fact that Max had built up his company from scratch, without his family's help. His style of management had revolutionised the productivity of his workforce and was, he suspected, admired by many in the industry. Maybe Charles had recognised this and maybe that was all that lay behind this strangely timed proposal.

Perhaps it would be worth following up? Too late the pieces were already in the bin and he did not fancy being a refuse picker today.

He walked back into the event.

+++

Looking back, Max realised that he had changed. The death of his father had seemed to spark a dramatic loss of compassion in him. He became much more ruthless and demanding in his business activities. Perhaps a part of himself had been buried in the casket alongside his father – *my empathy*.

Security was now a top priority. His efforts went into the expansion of his enterprises and the preservation of his position in the industry, while at the same time sharing his thoughts on transhumanism. Cancer had robbed him of his father, now he would spend his life fighting against its power over human life. That would require money for research and in that fact lay the key to scientific progress.

Yes, he spent more time investing in work and business, less time into Max. He must have been so close to the edge. Almost losing sight of himself and becoming obsessed with this goal. The more he chased, the less of him remained. Driven, he could not make enough profit, or speak to enough people, or build enough management structures. Meetings after meeting. He knew he was close to exhaustion, life became flat and stale. His personal productivity decreased. Yet he could not understand why.

His mother had tried talking to him – so had Julian and Sammy. He'd brushed them off and continued.

After Dad's death, the work of *the Light* had synchronised with Max's new goals. His family enjoyed a long and active membership but the organisation's work became even more significant to Max than it had been to his father. The consolidation of power was now central to their basic doctrine. The group of industrialists, philosophers and public speakers worked together to ensure that the powers behind various nations remained in the hands of those who possessed superior understanding and a highly developed knowledge of the world.

Within their circles, Max's leadership skills were appreciated, and his progress within the organisation seemed guaranteed. As time went by, he found that he often bumped into Charles and Ralph Ferrell at the organisation's events. They would always exchange civil comments. He sometimes thought about the business card.

What had been the deciding moment in all this? *When did I change?*

That was it – he thought – *I lost my sense of humour.*

It came right back to him. He had been at a business function and someone – he struggled to recall who – had told him a hilarious joke. He had just stared at them. Previously, he would have been in stitches; everyone around him was laughing but not him.

He had made a feeble excuse to get away from the situation, just to be alone.

It was not long before solitude became his sole companion.

FRIDAY 20TH MAY 2005 (BM, R)

Max stared out across San Francisco Bay. The clear night gave him a wonderful view.

It meant nothing.

The Golden Gate bridge was striking, its famous orange vermillion complementing the rest of the vista. The mound, topped by a plateau in the background, hiding behind the bridge, made up of hills and fairy lights; reminding Max of a Christmas tree. If it had been foggy, he would have seen nothing. Some would say that this was the view at its best. Yet it did nothing to lift his spirit.

Dull, dull and very dull.

'I take it you are not impressed,' the voice sounded like small bells all ringing at once. For a moment he was transported back to childhood. He thought of reindeer and Santa. That voice, it sounded like... *Tinkerbell.*

He turned round to find himself staring into the face of Snow White. She was dressed in a long and flowing white, jewelled gown; her gleaming raven hair topped by a glittering silver tiara, her hands gloved up to the elbow. A vision from heaven.

It took a few moments for him to realise that he was staring – saying nothing. She looked bemused.

'I thought... I'm sorry... I thought I was seeing a vision. Are you for real?' He pinched her lightly on the arm.

She squealed, the edges of her mouth crinkling. Surprisingly Max found himself laughing too.

That's the way I used to laugh.

They enjoyed the moment.

'I bet that happens to you all the time,' Max leaned in, his heart rate increasing.

She whispered in his ear, 'Normally they don't pinch.'

He covered his mouth, 'Sorry, I always have to check to see if my dreams are for real.'

She laughed again. *It's a musical sound – and it's honest laughter.*

They were alone on the balcony.

Max had been invited by Ivan, his business partner. Not really wanted to be there, Ivan made him promise that he would attend. Max was trapped. Ivan knew some amazing people; the exclusive apartment loaned from a Hollywood director.

Nestling on hill next to Glen Park and Noe Valley, there must have been fifty guests, in the ten bedroom luxury condo. How Ivan managed to get the place still baffled Max.

Max felt out of place from the moment he arrived. Brushing shoulders with celebrities, not his thing; business people, yes, celebrities, no. He promised himself that he would stay for one hour, then make an excuse to go home and watch the latest episodes of *Grey's Anatomy* and *Prison Break*.

There had been only fifteen minutes left when Snow White walked into his life. His plans changed.

'I know who you are,' he turned away and considered the view, which seemed different, more alive. 'You're more lovely in real life than on the screen. You remind me,' he paused, 'of an angel.' He suddenly felt stupid.

Is that the best you can come up with Max?

Her hands were crossed, her jewelled purse dangling. 'And who do I have the privilege of being in the company of.' *Her perfect smile.* Max's insides were suddenly hot; like liquid fudge had been poured into his gut.

'My name is Max,' he bowed low and deep. 'Max Augustine, at your service.'

She extended her gloved hand adorned with an elegant diamond Audemars Piguet watch, 'Michelle, Michelle DuPont.'

Max lifted her delicate hand and kissed it twice. As he analysed his own behaviour, something told him that he was being stupid. *What's the matter with me? Why am I acting so weird?*

She removed her hand then rested it on his shoulder. Close, intimate.

'I want to hear all about you, Max.'

He felt his face flush. *Why would you want to know about me?* He had nothing to boast of in the looks department, he was okay looking but was neither beautiful or handsome. The same questions kept going round his brain: *why is she paying attention to me? Is she after something?*

'I'm pretty ordinary.' Max smiled wanly.

'Ah, ah,' she said. 'No such thing as ordinary, only extraordinary people who are yet to be discovered. Are you a poet or a philosopher?' The sound of her voice was doing something to him.

She threw back her head, then smiled, displaying her dazzling, pearl-white teeth. Her trademark gesture. 'You are so genuine. That is refreshing, Max. I am so used to fakes; I meet them all the time.' She studied his face, pausing for a second before going on. 'But in you I see someone who is real. Are you for real Max?'

It seemed as if she was searching, hoping to find the right answer. She, whose face had been a key part of the Prada campaign, she, who had won the hearts of the nation with her portrayal of Snow White, she was asking him if he were real.

He turned back to the view. 'What you see is what you get with me. I have no time for fakes.'

She stood next to him, sharing his view. 'Then we should get on just fine.'

MONDAY JUNE 13TH 2005 (EE)

To: principal@silverhurstmiddleschool.com
From: max1augustine@hotmail.com
Date: 13/06/2005

Hello Paul,

How are you and the boys? I thought I should let you know that the most amazing thing has happened to me. I think I am in love! You will never guess with who? Snow White!

I met Michelle DuPont a few weeks ago and we have been dating ever since. I cannot believe this is happening to me. She is real, I think. I have pinched her a number of times just to check. I keep wondering if I am dreaming.

She makes me laugh. I have found laughter again. Since father died, I have been consumed with work and have been keeping myself busy. Michelle has changed all of that. She is funny and caring. She listens to me going on and on about myself. She called me amazing, can you believe that?

Paul, I know that you know about true love. I saw that in the way you loved Theresa right to the end. What makes true love? What should I be looking for? What are the signs that mean that this is for real? I keep smiling all the time. Some people keep asking me if I am puffing something illegal (joke).

Sorry to be talking about myself again. How are Ben and Archie? This summer they can some and spend some time with me. I should be in the states during their vacation time. I can hardly believe that they are in the 8th Grade. That is where our story began.

I need lots of wisdom. I am trusting you and Mom to guide me in this one. Love has come late in life for me and, to be really honest… it is pretty scary. I don't want to mess this up. In business I know what I am doing, I have an instinct. In love, I am a complete novice.

Write soon,
Max

WORLD EXCLUSIVE: Michelle DuPont marries business phenomenon Max Augustine.

Michelle DuPont has married sweetheart, science entrepreneur Max Augustine, in a ceremony featured exclusively in *SCOOP!* magazine.

The highly successful biotech mogul exchanged vows with Michelle in Grand Bahia resort in Runaway Bay, Jamaica. Max says the arrival of his bride – dressed in an exquisite gown by Vera Wang – took his breath away.

'Seeing her in that wedding dress… For the first time, smiling and walking towards me… I was breathless… She looked like an angel from heaven,' Max told *SCOOP!* in a world exclusive.

'I was trying to make the most of the moment and somehow store it in my memory. My eyes were fixed on her, and that beautiful smile. It really was a perfect moment.'

And his bride felt the same. 'I was shaking with nerves and everything seemed a blur,' Michelle told the magazine. 'I looked at him through a veil of tears. I was just so happy. I am so fortunate to have him in my life. I couldn't ask for a better partner. He is the most amazing man in the world. We are going to live happily ever after.'

Max responded, 'The ceremony was everything we hoped it would be. Our family and closest friends, together, in a beautiful setting, in celebration of our love. It was truly emotional. A day we will never forget.'

The ceremony took place just days after Max's bid to takeover TransGenomic was approved by the mergers and acquisitions authorities. 'This means more to me than any business venture. I am truly happy. I only wished my father could have been here to see this day.'

A total of 200 guests attended and were given a rousing steel drum session before and during the ceremony.

'I walked down the aisle to the *Wedding March*, after we exchanged vows and kissed, the steel band played Bob Marley's *One Love* — it was a dream come true. It combined the traditional with the flavour of the tropical,' said Michelle.

The ceremony was held on the sandy beach, under clear blue skies with an ocean breeze. 'The smell of palm trees and the beach — it was my childhood dream in front of my eyes,' said the bride.

After the outdoor ceremony, the wedding party continued their celebration on the beach then had a lavish dinner in a nearby restaurant, overlooking the ocean.

MONDAY 3RD OCTOBER 2005 (BM, R)

The wedding photographs arrived.

A month had passed. The wedding had brought in a tidy sum and gave a burst of publicity to their married life. Max considered it a good deal – profitable to both himself and Michelle. Enough to refurbish the kitchen and the bathroom of the Manhattan apartment all by itself. Of course they had traded their privacy in return. Michelle was used to that but Max found the whole thing distasteful.

They sat together concentrating on the official *SCOOP!* Wedding photographs. Max was impressed with the quality of the shots. Michelle was less complimentary, bordering on scathing.

'I look so fat in that shot… and in this one,' she pointed at the adjacent photograph. 'Who took that one? That's awful.'

Max kissed her on the cheek, she hardly seemed to notice.

'Thank god they did not publish that one.' She jabbed at one of the pictures. 'Work would dry up immediately.'

As they sat on their plush white 'Marc Newson' couch, a cool breeze blew through the open balcony doors. The apartment belonged to Michelle, set in the heart of Beverly Hills, near the corner of Burton Way and Almont and really close to Doheny. Max liked the polished hardwood floors and the exquisite use of marble throughout the unit.

After a late breakfast, the *SCOOP!* despatch rider altered all of her immediate plans.

Max's eyes were on her, a dream come true. His angel who had taught him to laugh again.

'I still think you look like an angel.' He kissed her again, not too bothered about the pictures.

Michelle brushed him off. 'Not now Max.'

For a fleeting moment Max felt like squeezing her neck, just a little. Enough to cut off her breath for just a second. Then she would understand that she needed to pay attention to him and not always focus on herself. He was a little shocked but allowed the thought to pass without further scrutiny.

'Who is she?' She screeched, holding up the offending photo, shoving it under his nose. 'Is she one of your friends?'

Her little scrunched up nose, reminding him of a worried rabbit, not a view she would allow any camera lens to see. 'That is not someone I recognise. Maybe she was a passer-by or a guest from the resort?'

'What is she doing in *our* photos, at *our* wedding?'

Max realised that she was genuinely angry – her normally soothing voice raised an octave. Whoever she was, she was an undeniable beauty; the sort of woman to make other women, even attractive women, feel inferior.

A stunning woman with a bronze tan and beautiful, limpid blue eyes. Gorgeous facial structure, simply perfect, long brown hair cascading down around her face and body. A simple, sleeveless white dress, cut low to show an amethyst pendant around her neck. She stood out from her group by several miles.

'I hope those are extensions, not her real hair. She is…' Michelle struggled to admit the obvious, 'She's gorgeous. She's photogenic and elegant and good enough for…' She paused, deep in thought.

'A part in a film.' Max finished off her sentence.

He turned away, concealing a smirk behind his hand. Michelle possessed a very sensitive side, bordering on jealousy – *perhaps insecurity?* No, he had no idea who the beauty was but she clearly unnerved his new bride.

'I have an audition today, Max. Will you put those photos away?' Michelle stood up, showing no further interest in the photographs.

'Of course,' he said watching her leave the room. Obviously irritated, her pace a little faster, her movements less fluid than normal.

Max studied the image again. There was something about those eyes – deep and engaging, framed by a long mane of brown hair.

He stroked her image whispering, 'Who are you, lovely?'

2006 – 2010

Michelle would not be home till late. Max accepted her busy schedule; her way of life was so different to his, and he was fine with that, but it still irritated him at times like this. He had even taken time off to be with her.

I'm actually bored.

It shouldn't have surprised him but it did. In fact it annoyed him. He had absolutely nothing to do. Not even phone calls. Nothing. He needed to be in his office; he had none of his things with him. He was just... waiting. It began as an idle task, something to take up a little time: he decided to investigate his wife's life. He'd start with the bedroom, before moving to her walk-in wardrobe.

Max searched box after box, drawers, anything that was not locked or required security codes. He went through documents, folders, anything that would reveal more about her – the real person.

Of course he had not asked for permission; after all they were married and he felt that there should be no secrets. They had agreed, early on in their relationship to be open and honest. It would be their foundation for living.

The brown A4 sized box was marked simply: scripts. He wondered if this was where she stored the old texts, from all the different parts she had performed.

That might be fun. A chance to see the lines before they ended up on the cutting floor.

Max lifted the box down, placing it on the hardwood floor. There were about twenty manila folders, bulging with sheets. He took out the first folder – the title read – *The Time of My Life* the next line surprised him, *written by Michelle DuPont.*

She never told me that she could write.

He flipped open the folder and sat for the next hour, mesmerised.

Tuesday 11th April 2006 (BM, R)

'Can I speak to Miss DuPont?'

Max called to her from the living room. 'Michelle, it's for you.'

She emerged from the bathroom, towelling her hair. She was wearing cut-off jeans and a checked shirt. He handed her the phone, winking.

'Hello'

The conversation continued but he could only hear her side of the conversation. *This sounds interesting.*

'I don't understand, what script are you talking about?' She swapped the phone to the other ear, still towelling her hair.

'*The Time of My Life*? What are you talking about? Is this some kind of prank call?' Her voice had lost its smooth, professional edge.

Temper, temper dear.

'Look mister, I have never submitted that script, so I think you have the wrong girl.' She was annoyed.

'I don't care if got my name on the front.' She stopped mid-sentence, slowly turning and looking straight at Max. She covered the mouthpiece, 'You did not—'

'I did… and *you* need to finish your conversation.'

The look told him that he was in trouble. Judging from the size of her wide-open mouth. *Hopefully gigantic trouble.*

'Okay, so you like it.' Her naturally brown hair was still dripping, towelling forgotten.

'You want me to come in and talk about it?' Michelle was sitting on the sofa now, shaking her head clearly in shock.

'Okay, next Wednesday at 10.00. Meeting with Greg Carmichael.' She rubbed her forehead, blinking.

'Bye'

The long bleep.

'Max, what have you done?' She stood up her hands on her hips, accusing him.

I hate that pose. He thought it best to confess, 'I sent in one of your old scripts to one of your agency friends. I thought it was pretty good. Sounds like they agree with me.'

'How did you…' She moved towards the walk in wardrobe. 'Were you looking through my things?'

The actress is on stage – boring.

He had hoped that she would be delighted; the contorted mask on her face told him that he was wrong. Those wide eyes looked cold, even cruel.

'How dare you go looking through my things!' Her voice, loud and shrill. Michelle's collagen thickened lips stuck out, both hands held in front of her body, complete with trembling open palms before she placed them on her hips, in that petulant manner, it annoyed him so much.

Shakespeare would be pleased. What happened to openness, to honesty?

'But Michelle, it was were really good. The world deserves to know the talent you possess. Remember about potential, extraordinary people; our first meeting?'

The magic words seemed to have an effect, her lips returned to normal, both hands dropped to her sides. The voice now quiet.

'But you went through my things.'

'Yes, I did, but in doing so I discovered that my beautiful wife is also a talented screen writer. I am sorry if that is so wrong.'

He knew he was pleading, still, he did not want to sleep on the couch.

She pondered, considering his assessment of the situation.

You know you're thinking about it, stick by your own philosophy. Let me off the hook. Please!

Then the face of Snow White reappeared. She rushed over, giving him a warm, passionate hug.

'I'm sorry for being upset. You have… you have done something wonderful for me. You are so real Max. And look, I'm sorry for not trusting you.'

He absorbed her love, drinking in her affection and devotion.

'You are more than a pretty face Michelle. You are amazing.'

Inside, he breathed a sigh of relief. He had just about got away with it. At least this time.

June 2006 (BM, WD)

Despite the frequent trips to the hospital, the ongoing physiotherapy and a great deal of medication, Adrian considered himself to be feisty and full of life. He loved to play tricks on Louise, like the time he replaced the sugar with salt just before she sprinkled it on her porridge, she loved to spoon on generous amounts of sugar. He had laughed so much that he'd had to change his incontinence pad.

He cherished any time he spent with his little sister. Adrian struggled with the fact that his disease was progressing at a faster rate than the medication could handle. Time, slowly running out. Mum and Dad tried so desperately to shield him from the inevitable truth but he had already worked that out for himself.

If he lived to twenty he would have done well.

The numbness in his legs lasted for longer periods than before and ebbed away more slowly than ever, then normal sensation returned. It was becoming more difficult to do ordinary things without exhaustion. His muscles were losing strength, though he felt the same as ever in his mind; his body succumbing to the symptoms of the condition.

Louise was unusually bright. Her reading age had been that of a twelve year old when she was only eight; she loved books and retained information like a human sponge. Adrian enjoyed their discussions about science and nature – Louise was special. They spent a lot of time watching a variety of programmes on the television and listening to radio broadcasts. Louise would always ask questions right in the middle of the most important points. Though there was a seven year age gap between them, they were friends, most of the time.

Adrian really appreciated the fact that Louise never made him feel weird. If he had chores to do then they had to be done unless there was a genuine reason for assistance. Louise made life normal.

When he found it difficult to carry out tasks, she would step in for him but only if necessary. She never complained or made a fuss; not that she allowed him to wallow in self-pity. She could be tough on him.

He knew too well the look of pity that crept into the eyes of people who met him for the first time. Too often, that pity became a filter for their vision; they lost sight of him, seeing only his disability.

Tuesday 13th June 2006 (BM, PA, WD, R)

The tabloids were the first to realise that Snow White no longer seemed to whistle while she worked. Her normal, cheerfully calm demeanour replaced by that of a tearful and moody prima donor, a woman whom directors found hard to control. Fellow actors and actresses criticised her shaky performances. The fairly-tale seemed to be going south.

Before his marriage, Max had never even glanced at a tabloid. Now they were part of their life, alongside his copies of the *Financial Times* and the *Economist*.

He had been drawn in, seduced.

At first he ignored them. Michelle left them all over the place; she lived by them. The ever present temptation weighed over him; his biggest mistake, giving in and reading one. He had seen a feature on a friend of Michelle, Jasmine; he glanced at it, then decided to read it. The point was that he knew her, half understanding the challenges that she was facing in her second marriage. The cutting and malicious comments were outrageous, they were so far from the truth, yet they were right in front of him in black and white. From then on he read everything. He had fallen; the cruel mistress of gossip claiming another victim.

He became afraid: one day it would be about Michelle. Max was not sure what he would do when that day came.

The day arrived.

Of course Max noticed a change in her. She seemed sullen and distant. Whenever he tried to raise subjects, she declined conversation, preferring to remain silent; never talking about the issues he brought up. He was worried. His work demanded frequent travel, her work as well. They found themselves making appointments to have a relationship.

Four months into the marriage things started changing for the worse. His attempt to make her happy by exposing her writing talent proved to be nothing more than a temporary aid. Michelle's writing career skyrocketed. There was talk about her first movie as a screenwriter. Max thought she would be delighted and she seemed to be at first, then the excitement turned into something else.

She said she needed time to think, to write.

When they first met he had thought that she was simple enough a person. But it seemed that her persona concealed a complex and emotional child, something else buried beneath the image she projected on the balcony. She was, Max thought, forever the actress, both on and off stage.

Is she jealous of me? She has her own money, her own prestige, her own career, houses and life. She's in the spotlight, but so is the company. Does she not realise just how similar we are? And after all that, is she jealous of me?

He just did not get her. His initial strategy was to say yes to whatever she said. That resulted in flaming rows about his lack of communication. But he didn't know what to do, and bitterly, he kept on saying yes, enjoying her loss of control.

Now the media were coming up with explanations for her personality change. Comments were thrown around. A line from one or another tabloid stuck with him: '… beauty and the beast are no longer in harmony.'

Of course Max knew that they were referring to him. He'd been typecast by the entertainment industry without ever having tried for a role. The media loved her, she could do no wrong in their eyes. Celebrated for her work on HIV awareness campaigns and for starting a foundation for the children of AIDS victims from all around the world. Michelle won the hearts of many in the wider community, even those uninterested in celebrity gossip. Yes, the media would take her side in any argument. And that infuriated Max.

He lay awake some nights wondering if any of the reporters who sang her praises actually knew what his work was funding; whether they ever even considered the value of the research his satellite companies were doing – working to end the sort of things that his wife could campaigned about but never actually prevent.

Do they care about the man behind the wheel? No. They care about the woman smiling from the passenger's window!

He found it hard to see how they could fail to care, but he knew that they didn't. He could have raised his media profile. He knew he could, yet he did not. Part of him allowed the bitterness to grow. It was, after all, not the first time his work had been ignored, unwanted, shut out. More and more often he found that his disdain for this unwanted publicity fuelled his other thoughts, keeping him awake; giving him more time to formulate business strategies that no celebrity paper would ever be interested in. In the dark, it guided him, while she tossed and turned beneath the covers.

Some nights he did sleep well though. Last night, in fact. She had slept in the spare room. He had no idea why. In the morning she'd left early, leaving his breakfast on the table and a note beside it. They had agreed that the Manhattan apartment would be their main residency, until they found somewhere they both liked. It worked out surprisingly well for both of them. Now he wondered if she missed her freedom, her various pads around the country.

Paul suggested that he give her plenty of space. Mom said they needed to talk about the issues they were faced with. So confusing.

It didn't help that he was living through her – everything beyond the confines of his work seemed to be channelled through her public status. His home life was being falsified by journalists, written around him. Part of him wanted to cry, part of him wanted to cause her pain. Perhaps then she would understand how it felt to live vicariously.

All his life things had been tough; he had never wanted for anything but he lived under the shadow of expectation, of his father, and now that the old shadow had been understood and accepted he found that he was living under a new, moving darkness. Hers. He had thought that she would change everything for him, but that had been back when it all seemed to work.

Cameras were everywhere. It was like 24/7 CCTV. She had no control over it. Paparazzi captured her, carrying her away with them. Writers mocked or praised them publicly, made things up about them or otherwise discovered, then published, difficult truths. And there was nothing he could do about it.

Personal grooming had become part of his morning ritual – shaving his nose, his ears, shaping his eyebrows – along with other things that he never used to do. Even his clothing looked much sharper these days.

He looked at the breakfast she had left and it struck him that they had stopped laughing.

Max shook as he read the toxic article. They had not spoken for weeks now, not since the last, bitter argument. He was furious.

She's gone to the media for sympathy.

The piece, *if you can call it that*, was titled *An interview with Michelle DuPont*.

'My marriage has left me emotionally devastated and spiritually disillusioned. I thought that I married Prince Charming, only to find he's the devil's first cousin.'

The interview seemed a little overeager to slate Max. It called him cold, ruthless and unappreciative. Claiming that he was obsessed with money and power, that he never communicated, she was hurt by his silence. It argued that, to him, she was simply a possession that he wanted to control, a negotiable commodity.

She certainly knows how to use her acting skills to the full.

The reporter claimed that she had broken down in floods of tears at various points in the interview. She simply wanted some security, and he had taken that from her. Max, she said, left her bereft and alone.

She would settle for $30m and legal expenses. The life of luxury she was accustomed to, her possessions, a share in his estates filled with antiques, some of the furniture and most of the expressive jewellery. Nothing too much. She was not interested in punishing him; she just wanted an exit and a fair deal.

The lawyers would have to deal with this one. They hadn't even reached the end of their first year of marriage and they were heading for the divorce courts.

Max had once believed he had married Snow White. She had, he thought bitterly, morphed into the wicked queen. He could see her dressed as a crone, offering him her poisonous fruit, 'Would you like a bite of my apple... Max?'

She is an unstable, sultry seductress.

How do you carry out the autopsy of a marital breakdown? So much is happening so fast. This is like a high-speed car collision and it's being laid out before the world. There's no hiding place. There's no safe cover.

Everyone had an opinion. He was sick of it. And to think he had thought she was worthy of his personal investment. That time, that love, that effort;

it was all work. It was all something he could have put into something else more worthwhile, less painful, positive, important. And now this. It had become pretty clear early in the marriage how wrong he had been but he had held on. *And for what?*

He stroked his hair, for the umpteenth time. Whenever he considered the situation he got nervous, it was an inner, shaky kind of feeling. Hair-rubbing, that was his tick.

Now the media seemed to feel his personal life served as public fodder.

This would not continue. Something would have to be done. If Michelle thought she was going to get away with this outrageous behaviour she had another think coming.

Besides, he knew…

Apparently they had met during one of her lonely moments. He was a nobody, a pick-up at a bar, an aspiring actor. Yet something had developed. Something nasty and distasteful. Maybe the fool had put her up to this. He had a name – the Private Investigator had told Max all the sordid details.

It was the same PI he had employed since he and Michelle had first met, back in San Francisco. The files were extensive. She would have no chance at all in court.

However, more drastic action would be required and she would not go unpunished. The words hung over his head like a sickly crown. *Cold and ruthless.*

TUESDAY 10TH OCTOBER 2006 (PA, WD)

WORLD EXCLUSIVE: Snow White Lost in Tragic Car Accident

We are shocked to announce the death of Michelle DuPont, 27, in a car accident yesterday.

Married less than a year, broken hearted, Michelle publically expressed her pain at the forthcoming divorce and spoke openly of her new relationship with aspiring actor, Jeffery Palmer, also killed in the accident.

Husband, Max Augustine, 29, was unavailable for comment.

The crash occurred on the New Jersey Turnpike, police said. Jeffery Palmer, who was 28, lived in Queens, New York, was riding in the Chrysler 300 with Michelle.

At least three other people were hospitalized following the crash, around 1 a.m. local time near Cranbury Township, New Jersey State Police spokesman Myles Beard said

After the collision, a sport utility vehicle and three other cars, their vehicle was thrown onto its side, said Myles.

Michelle, loved by everyone, found fame as a Prada model before making the transition to the screen. Her role as Snow White won her worldwide acclaim.

The circumstances around the accident remain unclear. Preliminary investigations are being carried out.

A spokesperson for Gemstar Film studio said: 'Her death is a great loss to us all. She was a sweetheart. Her charity work has touched the lives of millions. Everyone loved her. We will all miss her. She will always live on in our hearts.'

WEDNESDAY 11TH OCTOBER 2006 (BM, R)

Max felt a sense of satisfaction, rather like the closure of a tricky business deal. Intense negotiations, back and forth, and then the terms are reached.

It was all done.

He put down the article and sighed heavily, nodding to himself. He felt no remorse. Things had to be sorted out... he had done what was necessary. He thought back to his father's office. It really was the Augustine way.

The phone was off the hook, he had no comments to make and would not be doing any interviews. He was no longer a significant celebrity. That car crash effectively ended his time in the limelight. He was grateful for the corporate PR department, who were handling the whole situation.

He smiled to himself, thinking much more clearly now. He could hear his own voice again. It said something inside him and he relished it.

From now on, you're behind the scenes, Max, it said. *No more cameras. Only business. Only work.*

Suddenly, he spoke out loud. 'And I am the work.'

The apartment in Manhattan was glowing, bathing in morning light. All the furniture had been returned to their original positions; the way they were before she moved in. Back the way he liked it. The view of the Atlantic less obscured, she failed to share his love of the sea.

Before his had father died, they had talked about the darker sides of business. The types of transactions that needed to be made, that not everyone was ever going to be comfortable with. One of the many companies his father used – a company capable of such operations – run by a man known as Mr Henderson.

He was a talented individual, who could get things done. Leaving no trace, no blame and no connections. Some people might have called him a gangster or hit man, Max preferred to avoid such terminology. Those were words for the papers and he'd had quite enough of the papers. No, he was none of those things, or if he was, it didn't matter. Mr Henderson simply knew how to get things done, for a fee.

In this case he had earned his fee. The lawyers would deal with all the nitty gritty and the various loose ends. Max sipped his cup of coffee, sniffing at the spicy aroma, feeling a slight kick in his system.

He felt an intense, perhaps even sublime sense of satisfaction. It was all done.

The police had questioned him but were satisfied with his alibi. They said they would be in touch if they needed further assistance; given the circumstances, he had to be in the country for the next week – although a couple of calls had reduced this to three days – and that this was all normal. There was no blame being levelled at anyone, he would be allowed to grieve in his own time and that they were sorry for his loss. It had not been a particularly genuine conversation.

He hoped she didn't notice his smirk, he remembered the look he had been given by the lead investigating officer. He could tell that she believed he was guilty. But proving it? That would be a lot more difficult. *In fact*, he thought, *that will be impossible.*

This deal is closed.

He had a flight to Europe in two days.

There was the possibility of a new business venture… one even more profitable than the last.

'You have a call on line two from Charles Ferrell, CEO of IBC-USA.'

'I'll take it, send it straight through.'

What does Charles want?

They had spoken a couple of times since his father's funeral, he'd even sent a message of condolence after Michelle's cremation. But Charles, well, he could hardly be described as a faithful member of *the Light*. His attendance intermittent at best.

A call out of the blue? There had to be a motive, an angle. Still, Max was interested enough to listen. There was no harm in listening.

'Hello Charles,' Max kept the tone professional.

'Hi Max, how are you?'

'Not bad thanks.' *Why doesn't he get to the point?*

'I was wondering,' *here we go,* thought Max, 'if I could ask you to do some consultancy work for IBC-USA?'

'Why would you ask me, we are rivals in that field aren't we… business rivals?'

Charles' laugh sounded real enough. 'We don't have to be. Besides, I think we are aiming for slightly different fields, Max. There's some common ground, but there are a lot of different directions over here and we could use your expertise.'

'Tell me more then, Charles. You've stirred my interest.' Max rolled his fountain pen between his forefinger and thumb.

'We're expanding, looking to build up our management structure, and I thought you would be the man for the job. I have seen how your companies work and they are sleek.'

Flattery or honest observation? 'Are you sure you can afford my fees?'

Charles gulped dramatically, then chuckled. 'You name your price, we pay.'

Max looked at his watch then reached for his diary, fountain pen ready. 'When are you thinking of doing this?'

It would be an ideal chance to get to see how the competition works, and an opportunity to get an inside angle. Strange as it seemed, he thought of taking up on the offer.

Charles said, 'The sooner the better.'

IBC-USA, sounded like it could be profitable. 'Five zeroes at the end. That's short term, as a deposit, Charles. We'll see where it goes from there.' He doodled on his jot pad as he spoke. Large, round zeroes.

If Charles could see the huge smile on his face.

Charles remained silent for two seconds, then said, 'You're the one we want. You know that, Max.'

Good, look inside the guts of my rivals, whilst being paid to take the tour. I think so.

I could do with a laugh after the way things have been.

Data entry input: 259476199529
Programme: GWP
Level: 6
Accessed by C.

APRIL 2007 (BM, R)

By the time he was fourteen, everyone could see that his body was failing. Despite his brave smile, inside he struggled with isolation. After one sleepless night, Adrian had a brainwave: he would start recording his thoughts.

Morbid? Not really, he thought; after all, it was about seeing the reality of the situation and responding with clear thinking. He begged his parents to buy him a hand held VCR for his fifteenth birthday and aided by his wonderful camera assistant (Louise of course) he began regular open-heart sessions. During these times he would share his high points, low points, best jokes and his desires for the success of other members of his family and his close friends. Some of these sessions were recorded with Louise, others in the secret confines of his bedroom.

Louise called him a sage, saying that he possessed wisdom well beyond his years. She saw those private moments when things became too much and his frustration expressed itself in destructive rage. Yet he discovered an inner strength that helped him, rising up like a silent comforter. When his body failed, that power seemed to sustain him. Louise told everyone he was a living hero, *her* living hero.

With her help, he wrote many letters to newspapers and to their local MP, demanding more rights for those with disabilities. The idea that they had nothing to contribute was at best a misconception and at worst an outright lie. He knew that it only reinforced the stigmas; fuelled the preconceptions of those who could not cope with the idea of a life outside the limits of 'normality'.

As an avid supporter of the SMA society he raised thousands of pounds for research into the condition. Going on wheelchair sponsored races, with Louise pushing him; that worked well. They had managed to raise over two thousand pounds from one race alone.

Louise called him a warrior, true and brave. Sometimes at night he felt like a fraud, battling feelings of weakness and frailty. Tear stained pillows supporting his floppy neck.

July 2007 (BM, R)

'What is cloning?' Louise leaned against Adrian on the sofa.

'Louie, if you listen, they will explain it.' The programme on genetic modification had captured both of their attentions. Louie and her annoying habit – questions at the wrong time. This moment being one of them.

As if on cue the presenter used a series of diagrams to explain the process, starting with the story of Dolly the Sheep.

'Is this right?'

'If you carry on talking I'll ban you.' The tone of his voice indicated his annoyance.

'I just want to know if this is,' she paused to consider, 'Morally right?' she sounded hurt.

Was I too rough? He thought. Louie held up the justice beacon all the time, she just had to get involved in issues; speaking up for those who could not, taking a stance. He admired that quality in her. Without her, the letter writing campaign would never have happened – he dictated, she wrote. He remembered her twirling on the spot when they'd got a reply back from Prime Minster Cameron.

'Can we talk about his later?' He wanted to keep up with the presenter, who had moved onto to the idea of genetically engineering mice, making them glow in the dark using the genes from jellyfish.

'Okay.' She did not ask any further questions.

JUNE 2009 (BM, R)

Adrian received a solid gold signet ring for his sixteenth birthday, bearing the family crest. It had to be adjusted as his fingers got thinner, the disease eating away at his muscles.

Daddy researched into their family history, uncovering all kinds of information. Like the family motto – *Tristus et fidelis* – meaning sad and faithful. Louise felt deeply disappointed, wishing the ancestors could have come with something a bit more jazzier than that.

The only thing she liked about the crest was the dragon on top of the silver central helmet. She nicknamed him Smoky.

Adrian loved the ring, wearing it whenever he could. Once his fingers had constricted into a permanent claw he wore it on a gold chain around his neck.

DECEMBER 2009 (BM, R)

Mum had told her numerous times not to drink too much water before she went to bed. Tonight Mum was proved right, again. Louise's bladder was close to bursting, that meant the journey across the landing to the bathroom.

She had already turned off the bedside lamp; the room was shrouded in darkness.

Somewhat annoyed, she switched it back on. The glow illuminated her untidy room; Mum said she needed to work on being neater. Then again, Mum was ultra-fastidious; *a cleaning Hitler. The Arrival* by Shaun Tan – her current reading project – lay next to the lamp, the green dragon bookmark protruding like a long, odd tongue.

She pulled back the covers, shuffling her feet into her fluffy slippers.

As she opened her door, she noted that Adrian's light was still on, his door slightly ajar. As she walked past she heard him talking quietly followed by slight pauses. All thoughts of the bathroom vanished.

Who is Adrian talking to?

She moved closer, creeping towards his door. The floorboard squeaked. The conversation stopped.

'Who's that?' Adrian's voice sounded alarmed. Her cover blown, she barged open the door.

'Who were you talking to?'

'I was not talking to anyone? Do you see anyone here?' She knew when he was lying.

'I heard you talking to someone.' She stood at the door, 'Who was it?'

'Louise, number one, I was not talking to you,' his left eye twitched as he spoke, 'and secondly, I don't remember asking you to come into my room. This is my private space.' He only called her Louise when he was annoyed.

'Sorry,' she knew that she had stepped over the line. He was right. She hated it when mum did that to her. Then a thought popped into her head, 'You weren't prayin—'

'Louise, go to bed!'

'Okay,' she retreated, closed the door.

As she leaned against the bathroom door, she wondered why he had lied.

Who was he talking to?

JULY 2010 (BM, R)

'What is that Louie?' Adrian pushed the control stick, the electric wheelchair headed towards Louise, who was perched on the edge of the sofa, hunched over the device in her hands; not moving, apart from her rapid, jerky hand movements.

'It's a game, don't disturb me.' She continued staring at the screen.

'What game?' Adrian felt a moment of revenge coming on. She always asked questions at the wrong times. *Perhaps a taste of her own medicine?*

'Oh, blast!'

She looked up at him, annoyance blazing from her eyes. 'You've spoiled it, I was just getting to the next level. Adrian, you can be so annoying.' She pointed at him, waggling her finger.

'What's it called?'

'Osmos, if you must know.' She stuck her tongue out at him.

'Okay, Louie, sorry to disturb you' Adrian turned away, heading for the kitchen, smirking.

Two all, I think. Now they were even.

Thursday 21st October 2010 (BM, EWA, R)

'Karl, you only do this if you want to.'

Brenda had her arm around his shoulder as she placed the mug of hot chocolate next to him. A wide circumference of clean white light bathed him and his latest difficult assignment.

'Mom,' she loved it when he called her that. It had taken a long time. 'I really want this.'

She hesitated, 'We can't afford any extra tuition for these exams.'

She rubbed her forehead, painfully conscious of the fact that other parents paid huge amounts for their children's preparation but their finances were already stretched. Marvin earned a good income as a supervisor at Redford Trucking company while she worked a part time shift at the Laundromat between looking after the house and the boys. She went in three, sometimes four days a week.

'But we'll always be here for you Karl.' She tousled his hair, he left it scruffy. At the start of his teens he had hated it, immediately smoothing down the hairs that were now out of place, mumbling about losing his hair style and complaining that all his gel work was going to waste. He had changed so much. His boyish looks had started to give way to those of a stunningly handsome young man.

Karl rubbed her hand, then continued with his work. 'You don't have to worry about extra help. I will do this because I want to.'

'I am sure you will.' As she turned to go, she looked back at him. 'Karl,' she waited until he returned her gaze. 'We love you, we believe in you.' She felt a sudden rush of emotion spreading up from her stomach, the room became slightly blurry. 'We love you.'

Karl jumped up from the desk and threw his arms around her neck. His sobs started slowly and then increased in both volume and intensity. Brenda held him, weeping gently.

He said nothing.

2011 – 2014

Tuesday 4th January 2011 (BM, EWA, R)

Adrian had another chest infection, this would be the third in the last four months. He looked so thin, not really eating the way he used to.

He seemed more tired than usual, less chatty. The antibiotics were not responding as well as they used to, the hospital had prescribed him some new ones but they made his drowsy and gave him stomach cramps.

Louise found herself stuck in her books, she had no life; her time taken up with constant revision for entrance exams. There was a good chance she could get into the top grammar school in Beckenham but Mum wanted her to try for some of the private schools that were in commuting distance – Alleyns, JAGS, Dulwich and Emanuel. That meant a barrage of exams, extra tuition and endless mock interview practices. All her friends were doing the same thing. Mum and Dad had sent her to a state school for primary education but considered the private option for secondary school.

This week she had three exams: one yesterday, one tomorrow and the finally one on Saturday. It was too much. Dad was not bothered but Mum… she seemed to think it mattered a great deal. Going on about opportunity and choices in life. At times Louise felt she was a bit extreme. Even making her learn two instruments – the piano and the cello. Of the two, Louise enjoyed the cello the most; practice was not problem there. The piano though, that required a great deal of effort.

Adrian was coughing really badly. He looked ashen, so grey.

'Do you want me to get you anything?' She held his hand.

After recovering, he waved at her, 'No. Thanks. I'll be fine. You go and hit those books.' Another coughing fit. She squeezed his hand, feeling his pain.

'If you need anything just holler,' she kissed him on the head before leaving his bedroom.

Worried.

Friday 7th January 2011 (BM, EWA, MR, R)

The doctors decided to hospitalize Adrian. The antibiotics were not working and his lungs were congested, adding to the complications of SMA.

Beckenham General Hospital, a familiar place for the whole family. The sprawling unit just outside the town centre coped with a growing young population, resources stretched to their limit. Mum had an opinion about everything – she was very positive about BGH and their care of Adrian.

Adrian was the youngest on the ward, the other patients seemed ancient in comparison to him. Louise was not fond of hospitals. They had come straight from school, Dad picked her up.

Visiting hours were until 7.00pm, the plan was to let Louise see Adrian, then get her home to have something to eat and a good night's sleep. After all, she had an exam the next day.

Louise walked behind her father, as they headed towards the corner bed, near the large wall of windows. Other patients looked up as if they were expecting visitors. On seeing them, their faces dropped, they seemed so sad.

'Hello Adrian, how are you today?' Dad's voice seemed subdued, low.

Adrian's voice was barely a whisper, 'Tired today Dad, bone tired.'

As her father stepped aside, Louise gasped at the sight of her bother. He looked weak, his whole frame emaciated, half the Adrian she used to know. His body would spasm then relax. The effects of SMA intensifying over time. She hated seeing him like this.

He looked at her, smiling an effort.

'Louie… how's school?'

She kissed his forehead, 'I'm far too grown up for that baby school, can't wait to start secondary school… if I can get into one.' She wanted to sound convincing but part of her wanted to break down and cry, seeing him looking so frail.

'You'll be fine, you—' He coughed violently, making the bed tremble. The way his face contorted, squeezing tears out of his eyes. Louise wanted to run.

Louise looked at her father. He was trying to be brave, he had his strong face on.

Adrian relaxed. She sat down, moving the magazine from the chair next to his bed. 'Since when did you start reading *Secret Life*?' Dad remained standing.

'In here, things can get really boring, Louie.'

You had to pay for television by the hour. Slot in your television card and then you could view. No money, no view. Simple really. Louise thought it was a bit heartless, extracting money from sick people.

'Got another exam tomorrow. I seem to have done so many.' She sighed, like an adult.

He attempted to lift his arm, she could tell. The movement got lost en route. The arm trembled. It was not fair, this disease was so cruel. Stripping away his life, taking his dignity, making him wear incontinence pads at his age. He should be having fun.

When they were young, mum had insisted that they go to church; a part of her strategy for getting them into the local Church of England primary school; it was highly rated in the league tables. Louise had found the whole thing so boring; all these rituals and candles, and of course the adults, particularly the men, playing dress up. All the prayers, long boring songs, quite depressive and painfully lengthy talks. Sunday school had been fun though, lots of play activities, songs and stories. Bible stories admittedly, but she enjoyed them.

Now in her time of need, God seemed a long way off. Adrian kept quiet about his beliefs and she simply did not believe in anything. She was something of a trainee agnostic, not quite an atheist but very close.

Looking at Adrian, she felt more like an atheist than ever before.

'This will have to be a short visit, Adrian. Louise has an exam tomorrow and I need to get her something to eat. Mum will be in later this evening though.'

Dad's hair needed a cut. His strong features strained, the skin around his eyes more wrinkled than Louise remembered. They had all aged over the last few years, living with SMA.

'Okay Adrian, see you tomorrow.'

'Okay, Louie, I promise I won't die.' He laughed as he said it.

She loved his dark sense of humour. 'You'd better not.'

It was the last time that she saw him alive.

SATURDAY 8TH JANUARY 2011 (BM)

Adrian died on Saturday 8th January 2011. He did not reach his eighteenth birthday and he missed Louise's eleventh.

Louise spent many hours crying. His eulogy script was drenched with bitter sorrowful tears. It was a message from the heart. Her parents said she did not have to do it, but she insisted. She wanted the world to know the untold story of her amazing brother, her hero.

Yet she held him up for one thing: he had not kept his final promise.

TUESDAY 18TH JANUARY 2011 (BM, EWA, WD, R)

Adrian's passing has left a gaping hole in our family, the Dalton family. Adrian's legacy cannot be measured in financial terms, however, the richness of his love made others value and appreciate those things which they normally took for granted.

Adrian Dalton was a genuine person and one who always overcame the limits of his wheelchair, challenging ideas that often remained in the minds of others. I loved him, I love him now and I always will. If I could have swapped places with him I would have.

I will never forget him, nor the things he taught me. Watching his suffering has had a profound impact on me, and it has served to strengthen my determination to change the world for the better. I would like to live in a world where genetic disease has been eradicated.

Adrian never wanted things to be about him, but I think that this is the time to honour him and to commit to his ideals. Therefore, as he would have done himself, I dedicate myself to ending the plight of those with disabilities. I envision a world in which no one is born to suffered. Not in the way that Adrian suffered. Not in the way that I and the rest of my family have suffered. I will live to make this goal – his goal – our goal – a reality.

She read it through one more time. Her turn next. She knew the programme off by heart.

The packed church, the one they had stopped attending once she'd got into St. Stephens. It was full of people she knew – and strangers too. The old building was like a living tomb. It was part of an ancient world with which she was no longer familiar. The strange, acrid smell in the air was incense. It made her feel sick.

Adrian had insisted on bright colours at his funeral. His wish had been granted, she looked around at the jovial array of clothing. He would be happy. Mum had her veil on, its black lace contrasting with her bright red dress. Dad was in a sharp suit, bought for the occasion. The colour was not one of his usual choices: deep purple. Grandma and Grandpa had stuck to the dress code, showing their wholehearted support of Adrian's wishes. Grandpa wore a plaid kilt and looked hilarious with fake red hair attached to the tartan beret. Grandma was in full make up and a polka dot dress from the 1950's. Dad's parents, well they had gone ahead of Adrian. Probably dressed in colours, watching from above? Who could say.

The Dalton family were crammed into three rows. Aunts and uncles, nephews and nieces. A selection of the rainbow on display. Louise nodded, approving of their efforts.

She sighed nervously, not knowing if she could read her sheets without breaking down. She had three copies. Sasha had one and was on standby, just in case it got too much. Louise touched the gold chain around her neck, sliding her fingers down its length till she touched the signet ring. Adrian's signet ring. *This is not the way it is supposed to be.*

When she had asked to be allowed to keep it, Mum had been reluctant however Dad agreed. Now she would have a part of him close to her, near her heart. The crest, its surface etched in her mind deeper than the image on solid gold ring. Sad and faithful, yes she could fully identify with that.

Thank goodness for Sasha. Her love and support was invaluable.

Her time was up. The walk to the lectern seemed perpetual.

Karl studied intensely, working long into the night. The scholarships at MIT were very generous but they were hard to win. Brenda and Marvin encouraged him to the best of their ability, knowing they were out of their league. Karl was up against complex equations and long essays. All the same, he frequently told them that their love and support spurred him on.

Mr Griffin – he was a godsend. The man had spent a great many hours working with Karl, giving him free tuition. They were great friends; he seemed to understand Karl and clearly wanted the best for him. Brenda sent him a bottle of champagne at the end of Karl's time at Beaton Place High School.

They were so proud – he would be the first person in the family to attend a top academic college. Deep down inside, they knew they would have been proud of him whether he went to college or not, yet it was still a significant thing for their family. Karl was unprecedented and that made them feel special too. They tried their best to take the time to reassure him, to pour love onto him, telling him repeatedly that they were for him and not against him in all of his decisions.

But his sense of isolation held a secret power over him; more so than his surrogate family might have suspected. He felt the most wanted when he won – that was something he had learned early on – and competition excited him. There was only one position that mattered though.

The desire to win had become his compulsion, his drug.

FALL 2011 (BM, EWA, R)

The journey from Oak Lawn, Dallas to MIT.

One thousand one hundred and seventy five miles, six stops, passing the halfway point at Hales Crossroads, a horrible hotel in Knoxville Tennessee and the arrival. The driving shared between Jasper, Darren, Marvin, Karl and Brenda. Jasper's driving was in a class of its own.

Thirty five hours, twenty seven minutes.

Brenda, Marvin, Jasper and Darren – all of them accompanied Karl to the Massachusetts campus during the Fall of 2011, giving him the biggest group bear hug they could manage just before they left.

Alone in his single dorm room, Karl wept profusely, knowing he had people on the earth who loved him – despite his flaws and his weaknesses. It was one of those rare moments in his life in which he knew, really knew, that someone actually cared about him.

SEPTEMBER 2011 (BM, EWA, R)

MIT challenged Karl on every level. Nothing was easy, hard work and dedication were only two of the components of success. You also needed money.

She approached him as he sat alone in a corner seat in the student bar, at the end of the first week. He was flattered. She made it abundantly plain that she had been watching him and thought that they might make a lovely couple. She tried to smile as she spoke but it seemed strained. Later on Karl found out she was still recovering from the effects of plastic surgery. Much of the summer vacation had been spent being chiselled, stretched and filled. The full use of her facial muscles came into play around October of that year, restoring her full smiling range.

As he got to know Melissa Moore-Bridger she confided in him. Karl learned that she did not want to be ugly at 21, so she'd got her parents to fund extensive work on her nose, had facial enhancement, jaw reduction and teeth veneers. She even opted for bigger breasts. All of that for just under $30,000. A bargain! A very special birthday present, albeit one with long term effects. She often asked Karl if he liked her looks. He would nod vigorously, hardly believing his luck at landing on his feet at MIT and ending up being the love interest of a wealthy heiress.

On her twentieth birthday, her portion of the Moore-Bridger trust fund become available to her. She had $100 million at her disposal, released in batches of ten million by the Moore-Bridger Foundation board of trustees every five years until she reached her fortieth birthday, when the remainder would be hers. Karl didn't really understand the gravity of those figures and he tried to ignore her money to begin with.

She wanted to know if his looks were natural and pestered him often. When he gave in and told her that he was completely unmodified, envy took over. She was rendered silent for almost twenty minutes, quite a feat for her. In all their photographs they looked like the perfect couple; they were like something out of Hollywood. Young, beautiful and present at all the major events where people wanted to be seen.

They became intimate friends.

+ + +

Melissa introduced Karl to the world of fine dining, exclusive events, art exhibitions, private planes, exclusive skiing resorts and designer suits. She took him on like a project, training him in matters of etiquette, building up his social contacts, showing him what to look for in a piece of art and displaying generosity at a level he had only dreamed of.

She awakened something deep within his being. Her money gave him the keys to a new world, one he really liked. People treated him with respect and dignity, calling him sir, pandering to his every whim. Melissa's parents were kind as well, treating him well, admiring his academic ability.

Melissa loved shopping and Karl became used to spending hours waiting for her to choose a single dress at a time in some of the top boutiques in town, and when they had nothing that caught her eye in town, she would hire a plane to search elsewhere.

All he had to do was say that she looked good and give copious quantities of praise; she seemed to beam with delight. Melissa called him her handsome hero – her generosity really could only be described as astounding. When she offered to open up a private account for him, he declined. She expressed genuine surprised, Karl told her he loved her for who she was not for her money. Of course, by then, he knew that he was lying – but she seemed none the wiser. Melissa purred like a content pussycat. That earned him three more designer suits.

Her passion for Tiffany jewellery bordered on the insatiable. Every month she would get an email alert describing the latest pieces on the market. He could tell from her facial expression whenever those alerts arrived. Privately, on days when she annoyed him, he called her the 'Tiffany slut,' entertaining the thought that she would do anything to land her hands on the latest collection.

Of course, he tolerated her vanity, after all, her wealth was so enjoyable. Karl considered himself a fast leaner, able to hold conversations with people of influence, updating them on the latest scientific developments or setting them right where their knowledge of genetics seemed elementary. They taught him about business and their private worlds of finance. As far as he was concerned, it was a mutually beneficial arrangement.

Poor Melissa though; she lacked intelligence beyond a certain point. Karl often wondered how she had ever worked her way into MIT, wondering how she had achieved a place in the school of Humanities, Arts and Social sciences. Perhaps Daddy had organised something in a brown package slipped under the door of the Dean's office? He had his theories. He did love her, it had been far more personal in the beginning. Money had started to eclipse that in a way. Once you pierced the veneer of charisma, she was shallow, self-absorbed and actually quite boring. She pretended to be interested in his studies, but he soon came to know the precise moment when her eyes seem to be veiled with a layer of saran wrap. Any conversation beyond that point, a waste of time.

Melissa said that one of the things she adored about him, apart from his gorgeous looks, was the way he kept her in order, making sure that she got things done. She had actually called him her personal PA – but that came to light after they split. She relished the way he was always trying to stop the breakdown of society, almost feeling it was his duty to uphold justice and moral standards. She found it hilarious; having such a different perspective on life. Karl, as reliable as clockwork, doing what he said he would do and making sure everything was done on time, punctual to a fault. Her notion of time was loose, feeling the occasion was more important than its timing.

Amongst her close friends, she disclosed that Karl was so shy in the bedroom that it was often embarrassing. He needed a lot of help to manage the tasks that she demanded. Her little, handsome virgin. That gave her such a childish rush of pleasure.

Later, Melissa would describe Karl as both cold and calculating. Initially, he seemed the perfect gentleman – opening doors for her, standing up when she entered the room – then his determination to get his own way emerged.

They were at an art exhibition when she told him that she was pregnant. It was a casual comment in between the Bossun still life and the Matthewson snowy landscape. Karl stopped in front of the Bossun, looking at it but not registering the view. She took him by the arm and told him it was alright. These things just happen.

The next day she miscarried. Saturday April 21st 2012, just after her manicure session. Her five week pregnancy at an abrupt end.

Karl visited Melissa in her deluxe room at the private hospital. It was then that she realised that their relationship was in trouble. He simply asked if she was okay and if she had planned to keep it. She declined to answer. He never brought up the subject again. Carrying on as if nothing had happened.

She remembered thinking about it – *is this the end of the beautiful relationship?*

They managed to keep things going for one year, then Melissa decided to dump him. Though she had enjoyed being around him, his intense control issues grew to be overpowering. In her mind she wanted to be as kind as possible, knowing how sensitive Karl would be.

She carefully choose the time and location; a lovely exclusive restaurant, allowing him to order his favourite dish, mille-feuille of beef tenderloin and chanterelle mushrooms. He was particularly chatty that night, talking about his latest project or assignment, she could not remember – as she switched off after the third minute of his babbling.

Melissa looked him straight in the eyes, 'Karl darling, I am sorry to tell you that we are at an end. I have loved every moment of our time, but for me,' she looked away, then twisted her latest Tiffany bracelet, 'things are not working out.' She stared into his captivating green and hazel eyes, 'I have found someone else. I wanted to tell you to your face.' Her brief, weak smile replaced by a feigned look of surprise.

She reached for her handbag and opened it. 'I have something for you,' she pushed the gift box towards him.

Karl said nothing. The look on his face a mixture of shock and disgust. She told him that she was sorry and hoped that things would work out for him. It had been fun.

She left first. When Karl opened the box, he gawped with amazement – a 1925 Grogan Patek Philippe watch, engraved with the message:

'To Dear Karl, In memory of our time together, love Melissa Moore-Bridger.'

He did not know what to do. He finished his meal and sat in silence.

Karl could not let go and would not let go without a fight. In his mind she was keeping him from what was rightfully his, a different way of life, access to opportunity and especially security; something he had craved all his life. Karl pictured himself dressed in a bespoke Domenico Vacca suit, watching it being stripped from him piece by piece, leaving him standing in his Calvin Klein briefs.

He stalked her from that time on. Not in an obvious way, but subtly.

Who had replaced him?

It did not take long. A student from the same school as Melissa. A muscular man with high cheek bones, dark and brooding eyes, striking to look at. Melissa obviously liked her men fine. She laughed with him the way she had used to laugh with Karl. Justin Tennant – his substitute. Karl despised everything about him, making an inner vow that by the time he had finished with Justin, those looks would be quite different indeed.

He hunted his prey, getting to know his moves, his favourite places, when he was not with her. Karl made sure that they accidently bumped into each other on a few occasions, talking and sharing time together. Just to build a foundation for his plan. A well thought out plan, meticulously executed.

True, both of them drank heavily that particular night, but Karl retained his purpose. As he pasted his opponent outside the bar in the alleyway, Karl tangoed with the stirring rage which had lain dormant for several months now. Even after several days, he found it difficult to work out how much the alcohol had contributed to the situation.

Raw and destructive power. He looked through a veil of blood as his arms moved like a machine, set on destroying the target. The three men who pulled him off probably saved the man's life, not to mention Karl's career. Justin's face was a bloody pulp, his nose broken. Later, the surgeon called it a vicious attack. He needed plastic surgery.

Both young men received cautions from the police. The Dean did not take the matter lightly. They were reprimanded and warned that, if they were involved in any further incidents, they both faced being asked to leave their respective courses. The fact that his opponent was one of the soccer jocks had not gone unnoticed by fellow observers. The victim was almost a two feet taller than Karl; his latent anger levelling the playing field.

Justin did not press charges, he could not remember why they had fought and considered Karl to have been an acquaintance. In his mind's eye they got on well before the incident, however, they no longer talked from that day.

Karl kept his head down afterwards, avoiding Justin, Melissa and the limelight, choosing instead to focus on his studies.

He was miserable though, deep down. He'd really liked Melissa.

Expressing his emotions… it was so difficult. He seemed to lack the appropriate words and gestures for love. The incident did make him reflect on his behaviour though, forcing him to revisit some of the things he had learned during his counselling sessions at the Kuhlmans. He decided to make an appointment with the college counselling service.

The societal trappings of his relationship with Melissa were part of a lifestyle he now craved. He felt like an addict, facing the horror of going cold turkey.

Money had meant nothing to her, she had been unwittingly generous with her cash. He loved the experiences she facilitated, the exclusive dining and the sense of belonging – of being one of them. And in her presence, then afterwards, more strongly in her absence, his craving intensified, along with an appetite for the finer and indeed the less accessible things in life.

Many lonely evenings were spent looking through his collection of photographs on his computer – remembering and sorrowing over what could have been.

He never told Brenda and Marvin about the incident, feeling ashamed of himself and his dangerous behaviour. The storyline when in contact with them was always the same.

'Everything is fine, MIT is wonderful and I miss you loads.'

AUGUST 2012 (BM, EWA, R)

Chloe loved Hannah Montana.

Bethany blamed herself for that. She had got a copy of the video at half price, using her manager's discount. From that day forth, Chloe watched every episode of the television series religiously. She was nine years old at the start.

Bethany started watching the series with her, they both observed Hannah growing up, almost studying the complex life she lived; having two images, the superstar Hannah and the alter ego Miley Ray Stewart. Two very different lives.

They had some great conversations after the episodes. Chloe was also going through her princess phase, begging her mother to buy anything with a ballgown and tiara theme. Bethany enjoyed those girly moments; the two of them bonded and laughed together. The only point of contention was around make-up. Despite Chloe's complaints, there was no way that Bethany was about to allow her daughter to wear make-up at that age. She already believed that girls were encouraged to grow up too quickly. She didn't need Chloe getting into that mindset and ending up in the position into which she'd gotten herself.

A sense of concern emerged in her mind as she watched the real life star Miley Cyrus undergoing a complete metamorphosis in front of the world. Bethany was horrified to see her thrusting herself against Robin Thicke at the MTV Video Music Awards in August 2012. If she had known what to expect, that show would have been the first thing that she would ever have forbade Chloe from watching. No doubt, they'd have had a bitter argument about it. As it was, she didn't realise until it was too late. Both she and Chloe had borne witness to that outrageous episode. The whole thing made Bethany feel sick. It was just such a vulgar and public destruction of the image over which the two of them had bonded.

Bethany took the opportunity to express her disgust at the performance, telling Chloe that it spread a dangerous message; that it told young girls all over the world that women are valued for their sexual appeal rather than their talent. She did not hold back. She didn't think she needed to.

I should have known, Bethany thought; she'd had to listen to Thicke's ridiculous, even dangerous, music on and off all day, every day at work, over the speakers, and she should have seen this coming. She tried to do a good job, being honest with Chloe.

Chloe remained silent through both the whole televised performance and her mother's review. She seemed to be giving it all a lot of thought. Bethany hoped that she was not going to be the quietly rebellious type.

MONDAY 15TH OCTOBER 2012 (BM, WD, EWA, R)

Karl met Dr Esther Cohen, during his sophomore year at MIT. At the time, he knew she was an assistant Director from IBC-USA.

The 2012 science Fair brought together the best minds in science for debate and competition. It was served as a recruitment platform by many of the companies who sponsored stalls. From his conversations with Dr Cohen, Karl found out that IBC championed young talent in the sciences. Esther mentioned that they were about to begin a recruitment wave.

Esther sat down with him and explained how she had left her home in Tel Aviv and moved to the States to join IBC-USA in March 2011. Something about her enthusiasm and tremendous energy made a lasting impact on him. They shared a common love of science.

Esther handed Karl an application form, suggesting he filled it in. Her reasoning – if IBC had his details they could keep in touch with him as his career developed. He gladly accepted the form.

Later that afternoon, he sat in the café, thinking about his response to the questions – what were his main areas of interest and what were his plans for the future?

He identified the fact that boldness was one of his stronger traits. For the second question, his answer read:

'*I intend to head a department at IBC-USA, preferably the Human Technology Division.*'

MONDAY 26TH AUGUST 2013 (WD)

Monday 26th August 2013

Dear Diary,

Mom is so old fashioned. She nearly had a stroke when she saw Miley twerking today. Going on about women and sex appeal. She has no clue! What is wrong with a woman using her body in any way she chooses! I think modern girls are freer than her generation, we don't have to follow the rules she did. I am not getting married in my 20s! Miley is cool. I luv the video for wrecking ball – go there sister! She is brave and free – Hannah Montana is dead and buried.

Miley is a smart woman who understands how to use the media for her own ends, slick marketing – she is not too bad as a singer.

Don't' get me wrong I liked Hannah, we even had some things in common, a love of camping and a hatred of spiders. Even the idea of living a double life. But Miley is like a real person now, alive and in your face.

I luv flappy bird. I'm an addict!

THURSDAY 5TH SEPTEMBER 2013 (WD)

Thursday 5th September 2013

Dear Diary,

Super embarrassment – why do things like this happen. Arrgh…

Mom knows that she should knock before entering my room. Well she didn't. She walks in and finds me twerking and lip-synching along with Miley in front of the mirror in my undies! She looked like a ghost. She said nothing, promptly closing the door. I thought, Oh no, there's gonna be trouble!

Sure enough she waited to meal time. Then gave me the lecture about decency and moral standards. How things are so different from her day (you bet they are!) and that young people needed good role models. I just asked her if she had a problem with young people being sexual or did she think we don't talk about that issue. She went white, almost choked on her broccoli.

Why are parents so difficult?

OCTOBER 2013 (BM, R)

Louise heard that song again. Her mother seemed to be in love with the song or the person who was singing it.

Louise knocked and opened the living room door. 'You're playing that song again, Mum,' their eyes met. 'Got any others?'

Her tone mockingly scolding, Anne responded, 'I will listen to whatever I like. Do I get involved in your musical moment or when you spend hours playing flappy bird?'

Louise rolled her eyes, 'Louise Dalton, stop that annoying habit.'

'Yes Mum,' she closed the door. No wonder she called Louise 'Bachelor girl', she was forever listening to that annoying Cliff Richard's song – *Bachelor boy*.

TUESDAY 10TH JUNE 2014 (BM, EWA, R)

Sasha and Louise were so excited, being in London, at such a world changing important event – a teenage dream come true. However, at this precise moment, Louise desperately needed the bathroom.

As they waited by the coaches, Mr Russell had dryly read out the riot act, the rules for the day. They had to stay in pairs and notify member of staff before going anywhere. Blah, blah, blah.

So Louise made sure she asked permission to go to the bathroom, dragging Sasha along for company. Mr Russell agreed. Louise did not want any blemishes on her character; she needed a glowing character reference from Beckenham Grammar if her aspirations were to become a reality.

Her and Sasha chatted as they turned the corner having made use of the dirty, crowded loos, they stopped abruptly as they came face to face with Angelina Jolie.

Louise felt overwhelmed and overloaded. Here she was, standing in the corridor at London ExCel, during a loo break, and in front of her stood a living legend, a film star. Angelina, beautiful and elegant with passionate, with piercing green eyes. Louise felt goofy, almost embarrassed to be there at all.

Angelina smiled graciously – that put Louise at ease. Before she could think about it, words blurted out, 'I have an idea, Ms Jolie. What should I do?'

Angelina continued to smile, 'No matter how small, do something!' She pointed her finger directly at Louise's heart, her eyes suddenly fiery. Angelina walked on, then turned giving them a smile and wave.

She was gone.

Sasha punched Louise on the shoulder, 'How did you do that?'

'Do what?

'You spoke to a… superstar… God, you are so brave!'

Their animated chat continued as they made their way back to the main arena.

+++

Angelina concluded her speech:

'I will work on this for as long as I'm alive. As long as it takes.'

It was a repeat of the same line that she started her speech with. The quote burned into Louise's ears, searing a pathway from her ears directly to her chest – a trail of poker hot heat. A spoken word living inside her, becoming part of her inner mantra, fusing with the promise she made at Adrian's funeral.

Angelina urged them, as young people, to make a difference in the world, to engage rather than simply sitting around doing nothing; she encouraged them to get involved and to do something positive and effective.

In Louise's mind, Angelina's presence added fairy dust to what was otherwise a stuffy occasion, mostly populated by heads of government, the executives of NGOs, lawyers and doctors. All the same, it was an extraordinary summit, aimed at looking for an end to sexual violence in conflict.

Angelina had added an air of glamour and for Louise it created a sense of mystique about the whole thing… being in the presence of a goddess. Yet a goddess with flaws – Jolie, a sex symbol and Madonna, from being a rebellious child star to self-giving way to a kind of overflowing maternal spirit with unusual empathy. Louise had read all the blurb in the handouts. Hollywood at its best.

Louise particularly admired the way that she used her status to draw attention to important issues. It was a wise, kind use of fame.

Beckenham Grammar School (BGS) had organised the trip as part of the Personal, Social and Health Education programme. The summit coincided with their current study module on the role of women; Louise had jumped at the chance to attend. Somehow the BGS group secured great balcony seats in the main arena, giving them a clear view of the stage and the speakers.

The Greatest Silence: Rape in the Congo. It was a film that changed lives. Louise felt jittery as she waited for the film to start, Sasha whispered nervously to her, 'I hope this is not too harrowing.'

The camera shots and presentation suggested this was a low budget production. Interviews – women and girls in front of the camera telling their stories, all from the Democratic Republic of Congo. After the first interview, Louise noticed the numb sensation in her hands, as if she'd lost feeling in them, they tingled. Soldiers were supposed to protect yet they raped, tortured and mutilated the women. Lisa Jackson, such a brave woman, Louise knew she was a survivor of gang rape, sat with the women and listened to their stories, recording them faithfully. Every emotion, reliving trauma and recording every tear.

Louise sat motionless. Lisa interviewed peacekeepers, activists, physicians and most shocking of all the indifferent rapists themselves.

The honesty and immediate nature of the recording, made you feel as if she were part of an intimate discussion, hearing every detail up close, so personal. The stars were the women who showed resilience, courage and grace in the midst of their trauma. Some even choosing to keep the children of their abuse.

As the credits rolled, Louise burst into tears, the tension too much for her to handle. Sasha comforted her, hugging her as she sobbed.

By the time they were back on the coach, she reflected on her day. They spent the morning looking at the giant sculpture of an upside-down toy aeroplane by London artist Charming Baker. It was centre stage at the global summit, called *Love Revolution*, measuring eight metres long six metres wide – three metres off the floor – a visual representation of 'the fear and powerlessness of victims of war'. Louise loved it

Sasha preferred another piece, *Faith's Leap* – a cast of a girl wearing a mask, showing the terror felt by the artist' daughter when experiencing turbulence while flying.

By the end of the first section, Louise understood that children carried the trauma of war for the rest of their life.

One of the invited exhibitors display told the story of children born to mothers who worked in state brothels in China, all of them abandoned at birth. Care Out Reach (COR) provided homes, lots of love and education for the rejected babies. Something about that registered with Louise.

The day was almost complete. Louise could barely keep her eyes open, the early start and emotional day literally drained her. She wondered if she would be able to sleep on the coach journey back to Beckenham. Sasha was already snoozing.

A seed had been planted. Angelina's words meant a lot to Louise. The hum of the engine sang a gentle lullaby; one minute later she snored in rhythm with the deep throb.

2015 – 2018

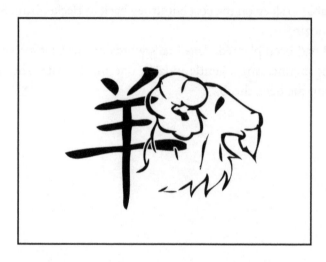

Monday 7th September 2015 (BM, R, WD)

Dear Diary,

Why does life have to be so complicated? High School years are meant to be the best years of your life? Somebody lied.

Why do other girls have to be so bitchy? Snide little comments about me behind my back, some brave enough to say things to my face. Who is on my side?

The boys seem to be queuing up to ask me on a date. Let them queue. I am still deciding which group I want to belong to. Either the Keystone Kitties or the Goth Gang. Dyeing my hair will not go down well with mom. So I guess… the Kitties it will be.

Mom and I fought over chores – that is so stupid. Why does rubbish have to sorted out in such a specific manner? We seem to be fighting a lot more lately. She realises I am growing up and wants me to remain a child.

Why are adults so… annoying? The new maths teacher is cute – he must be around 24. He's the hottie at the moment. The kitties have selected him to be the new pinup boy. Flavour of the month – Mr Ned Hurley – yum, yum!

+++

Chloe loved the assignment. As part of her creative writing project she opted for the creation of a two week diary. Writing her inner most thought proved to be liberating. Of course, she had done it every now and then in the past, mainly to blow off steam, but doing it daily was kind of therapeutic.

Of course she would only hand in an edited version of her inner ramblings. Some of the material too sensitive for teachers' eyes.

Perhaps this could turn into a habit. I could make it into something someday. It might actually help me work stuff out.

FRIDAY 18TH SEPTEMBER 2015 (WD)

Dear Diary,

Wyatt Hogan – not only has a stupid name, the boy is a complete jerk. After making out he had the cheek, to tell everyone. I was so stupid allowing him to stick his tongue down my throat.

He's dumped. If I can't trust a guy then how can we have a relationship? Now the rest of the kitties are teasing me. They all claim to have done 'it', calling me the blonde virgin. I don't care what they say. Some of them are lying. I hope this will blow over soon. Other guys think they have a chance.

Reputation is a fragile thing.

TUESDAY 6TH OCTOBER 2015 (WD)

Dear Diary,

It's happened again! I need psychiatric help.

You would think I would learn from the past. He seemed so sincere, so real. Jagger Waley-Cohen. He's popular, handsome, wealthy and a complete narcissist. We dated three times, he behaved like a complete gentleman. So when he asked if he could kiss me a little more I thought he meant longer, not deep penetration with his nasty tongue.

I wanted to bite it off. If I did not give permission, why did he feel he had the right to behave like that? He can join Wyatt on the dumped list. I am staying away from boys for a while. My reputation is hanging on a thread.

Been promoted within the keystone kitties, now second in command. That means they answer to me and I answer to Jade. Need to ask mum for new shoes, kitten boots are in, the sign of membership – pink is out, lime green is in.

Maureen tried to ask Mr Hurley for extra help, he told her to get a tutor. Haha.

SATURDAY 24TH OCTOBER 2015 (WD)

Dear Diary,

How did she hide it so well? Found out that Sylvia has been spreading nasty rumours about me. When I confronted her, she denied it. So I brought some witnesses to support my case. She burst into tears and ran off. Why did she do it? Is she jealous of me?

Mum went on a date yesterday. Yuck!!! She looked really good, her latest diet seems to be working. She has lost pounds, food at home has become pretty dull. I am not into this low carb stuff, thank god for haribos.

Dad called me yesterday. He sounded really down. I agreed to meet him next month, I am not looking forward to staying with Cassandra, the side bitch. Her little sprog, Kim, cried all the time on my last visit. Ian is fun, he makes me laugh, having a half-brother is alright.. Last time Cassandra tried to be super nice… not a chance in hell.

MONDAY 2ND NOVEMBER 2015 (WD)

Dear Diary,

I hate Miss Cleveland. She is a horrible person. Imagine calling me fickle. She has just arrived at Fairfax this term and she thinks she knows me. I am not going to try on my assignment. If she thinks I am fickle, I will show her what fickle means.

Voting happens tonight. Could be the new leader of the keystone kitties. I'm ready for the top job. Will change the look – hairbands are in, bracelets are out.

Mom wants me to go to the hair salon and get my hair sorted out. If I am going to keep it long I have to be more responsible. I wonder if a short cut will be too drastic? Dad offered to pay for a treatment this time. I am wondering if his budget will stretch to highlights?

WEDNESDAY 11TH NOVEMBER 2015 (WD)

Dear Diary,

Miss Cleveland has found me out! She asked a difficult problem in class, I worked out the answer and wrote it on my sheet. She gave the answer on the board and I told her that it was wrong. She went ballistic. She must have checked it, turned bright red and told me to see her after the class.

She asked me how I worked it out, I told her I did it in my head. She accused me of lying. Asking me if I used a calculator. I said no. She didn't believe me. I asked if I could go.

She's the teacher, she should know the answer. It is not my job to teach her.

As the leader of the keystone kitties, the girls all answer to me. I think we need some new blood, I have a couple of new recruits in mind. I think the initiation ceremony needs to be changed, kissing a ugly boy is not cool.

TUESDAY 17TH NOVEMBER 2015 (WD)

Dear Diary,

Changing my mind about Miss Cleveland. Not only is she gorgeous, she is so smart. She gave me such a high mark on my last assignment, the highest in the class. I was thrilled. She asked me to see her after class. Told me I had been wasting my talent, hiding my light under a bushel? I think that was the phrase she used.

She offered to give me some extra help to improve the standard of some of my earlier assignments. That could mean that I get some high scores in my science grades. That will be a first.

Mum had a go at me yesterday about my clothes. Asking me where I got them from. Told her dad brought them for me. She told me they were too slutty. I told her everyone is wearing them, she is out of touch with young fashion. We agreed to disagree.

Monday 23rd November 2015 (WD)

Dear Diary,

Can you believe it? Miss Cleveland made me the leader of the group science project. Everyone, I mean everyone was shocked. Blonde Chloe, leader of the keystone kitties, leading a science group – some people laughed out loud. Part of me wanted to say no, but I didn't want to let her down.

Did some extra reading and think I know what to do to make a first class experiment. Am really enjoying science.

The new girls are causing division in the kitties. Need a group meeting to iron out the disagreements. Maybe my idea was not that great after all. Last thing I want is a massive split, especially under my leadership.

Decided to accept Albert Carmichael's offer of a date. That boy is persistent. And not bad looking as well. Going to lay down some ground rules, stuff about boundaries and appropriate behaviour. Have learned from the past. I am a slightly older and wiser Chloe.

Wednesday 16th December 2015 (WD)

Dear Diary,

My scorecard is amazing. I've got the best grades ever! Mum is shocked, asking me how I did it. Dad offered to buy me a new dress, something really modern. I approve.

Miss Cleveland has changed my life. She's such a positive role model, beautiful and smart. The two can coexist in the same body. I've got living proof of this.

Wondering if I can continue to be part of the keystone kitties? Spending more time studying and less time with them. Might hand over the reins to Monica who is so keen to rule. She's a little minx, does she know that I know that she talks about me behind my back? The girls will be hurt, they all look up to me. Some think I've become a bit of a nerd. Me a nerd? That's hysterical.

FRIDAY 18TH DECEMBER 2015 (WD)

Dear Diary,

Awful – mum caught me lip synching to Miley again, not twerking this time! She went ballistic, shouting at me, calling me horrible names. What is the matter with her? If she had her way she would keep me in the house away from all human contact, especially boys. She sees them as an alien species.

When I ask her why she does not want to talk about it she goes all silent. I think she met Dad when she was young. She's worried that I will make the same mistakes. I'm so angry.

Handed over control of the group yesterday. Some members cried, other looked like they couldn't wait for me to go. Have decided to focus on my work and still have a social life but not in the way I used to.

The parent-teacher association evening is next Monday. Mom is coming. I hope it will be positive. Dad says he will come if he gets back from his trip on time. That will be weird to have them both in the same room, how long can they last before they start rowing?

Nearly Christmas!!!!!!

MONDAY 21ST DECEMBER 2015 (BM, R)

Miss Cleveland rubbed her bottom lip as she read the competition pamphlet; the High Schools launch of the International Genetically Engineered Machine (iGEM) competition presented an opportunity that should be taken up by Fairfax.

During her studies at Berkeley, iGEM provided a focal point for the summer vacation and their team almost won the regional finals. The aim of the competition – to encourage students to build simple biological systems starting with a kit provided by the programme. Success required an extensive knowledge of genetics and programming.

Basically giving students an opportunity to create synthetic life – designing and manufacturing cells that could carry out unique and interesting processes, well outside the scope of their normal function. Genetic engineering for teenagers.

Miss Cleveland knew the ideal person to lead the team.

Monday 21st December 2015 (WD)

Dear Diary,

What a fantastic evening. They all got on okay and the reports were amazing. Miss Cleveland was full of praise, saying that I had real talent. I love that woman.

Have been asked to lead the iGEM entry for Fairfax, that is going to take a lot of time over the summer holiday. Having to manage others when they are on vacation? That will be a challenge with me leading a team of six including me.

MAY 2016 (BM, EWA, R)

The iGEM project became Chloe's all-consuming passion. Possessing rudimentary leadership skills, she chose to charm and bully the other team members into action.

Once their entry had been submitted, team Fairfax faced a nervous two week wait; they shared the moment of delight on receiving an invitation to present their work at the regional heats, scheduled for the end of August 2016. Bethany was ecstatic. Chloe lacked words to describe the confidence and pride that accompanied her new persona. The Fairfax Principal, Elvina Wheatley, ensured that the exciting news appeared in the newsletter and arranged for an interview with Chloe's team which was published in the school's online prospectus.

For some of Chloe's former gang, the transition was too much – her status as *Keystone Kittie Babe* was replaced with the somewhat less savoury *Blonde-Nerd.*

Chloe allowed it to pass by. Her newfound potential was more than sufficient to compensate for any loss of schoolyard notoriety.

THURSDAY 11TH AUGUST 2016 (BM, EWA, R)

Nervous and excited, the team hugged one another, trembling as they waited for the final results of the judges on the iGEM committee.

The three star Phoenix Central Hotel sponsored the event, keen for the publicity. Each student wearing a purple t-shirt, bearing the hotel's logo along with the iGEM symbol. The local press were clicking and scribbling away, making it a big occasion for the area.

The ground floor conference room barely accommodated the large crowd, some spectators even had to stand at the back.

'The winners of the regional heats are…' The judge lingered over the anticipated announcement, allowing the anticipation to build, 'Fairfax High School—'

Their screams pierced the atmosphere as the teenagers pogoed up and down with joy, hugging and backslapping one another. The rest of the announcements were lost on them.

Chloe shouted, 'We've done it!' She personally congratulated each of the five team members – Kendra Phillip, Albert Carmichael, Winnie Schumann, Jenny Leach and Laura Dubuis.

Miss Cleveland cried. *My team, they are my team.*

Bethany covered her mouth, 'Oh… Oh wow…' And as if it had only struck her: *Chloe is brilliant. My daughter is brilliant.*

MONDAY 5TH SEPTEMBER 2016 (BM, EWA, R)

The victory at the regional heats became a catalytic point for Team Fairfax. Their successes doubled and redoubled as they went on to conquer the national finals and then to represent North America in the World Championship. Tokyo, chosen as the destination for the young men and women fortunate enough to reach the final rounds.

The principal gave them authorised absence from school as the new term was under way. Other students responded with snide comments, but inwardly they were jealous; the team knew it full-well.

Chloe, her team and Miss Cleveland were flown first class to Tokyo and put up in a five star hotel, the like of which Chloe had never imagined. A new way of life unfolding before Chloe.

She stood in her hotel room, staring out of the window at the unfamiliar territory when she realised that the competitive streak she had developed as a member of the long forgotten Keystone Kitties could be married to her affinity for scientific thought; she suddenly saw that the two might be used together in a life changing and financially rewarding manner.

Oh wow. I could actually do this.

It was as if all this new energy had opened a door for her. A new motivation for her life.

TUESDAY 6TH SEPTEMBER 2016 (BM, EWA, R)

The iGEM competition drew international attention; the various teams secured interviews with TV networks from the participant countries, allowing them the opportunity to present their research and ideas to the world.

After speaking to a Japanese television station, Team Fairfax were duly escorted to a luxurious buffet at the International Tokyo Centre.

Chloe was introduced to a high-flying businessman called Max Augustine. She thought that she might have heard his name somewhere, but she had never heard of his work. Not many teenagers from Fairfax had any real interest in the commercial or financial worlds. What surprised her was how keen Mr Augustine seemed to be about Team Fairfax and their project. Added to this was the shock that came when the team was asked to present their research at IBC-USA, out in Philadelphia.

Miss Cleveland revelled in the honours laid on Fairfax. Professionally, it was great for her career, but for the students... well it was life changing. Teenagers being made the centre of attention, talking about science, being role models to counterattack the negative image often presented by the press – the list could go on. They had achieved something that put them on the level of the adult world – in some ways overwhelming the teenagers. Not one of the them older than eighteen.

To their dismay, the team did not win the overall competition. All the same, Fairfax were highly commended for their ideas and final report. Their entry – they devised a unique design whereby genetically engineered bacteria were able to detect the presence of toxic ions such as mercury and cadmium in polluted water.

Chloe and the team agreed that the winners deserved their place, though they struggled with the sense of disappointment. A team from Russia took first place for a project involving GM bacteria that could manufacture artificial blood products specific to blood types.

Fairfax came in third.

+++

A tearful but elated group of teenagers departed from Tokyo, angry and at times indignant, but looking forward to the future's challenges.

Miss Cleveland could tell they had been changed by the experience. Disappointment tasted bitter after the giddying successes of the earlier competition.

Preparing students for life. The highs and the lows – all part of her job.

JUNE 2018 (BM, R)

Karl's satisfaction – there were no adequate words to express it.

Not only had his work on stem cell research and recombinant animals been highly praised by his peer review group, his double Doctorate was assured. All the years of hard work, sleepless nights, cups of coffee and living on cheese baguettes had finally paid off. The accumulated debts, it would take a lifetime before they could be paid off. However gaining grant sponsorship had been easier than he had anticipated, that helped reduce the overall yoke of debt.

Surely the Kuhlman family would be proud of him, of his achievements.

Data entry input: 782951533192
Programme: GWP
Level: 6
Accessed by C.

2019 – 2022

MONDAY 2ND SEPTEMBER 2019 (WD)

Dear Diary,

I am torn between MIT, Standford and Berkeley – the thought of California is tempting. I could see my grandma more often! Miss Cleveland favours Berkeley because she went there. However I liked the feel of MIT, I prefer it to Berkeley. Standford was good but I felt more at home at MIT. I want to make the world a better place – right in line with MIT's mission statement. The idea of collaboration and cooperating with others appeals to my way of doing things. Creative thinking along with risk taking. I think it is going to be MIT.

Have booked my SAT for 11 October, so nervous. Read all the advice, books and website information and getting some great help from the regional school college/university teacher. Will do my best.

Thursday 31st October 2019 (WD)

Dear Diary,

Amazing – Critical reading 780, Mathematics 800, Writing 780! Almost made the triple 800. Good enough for MIT. I could re-take – very tempted. Mom is delighted, Dad offered me a car! Thinking of doing some subject specific exams, will contact the MIT admission to see if I really need to put myself through this. Someone should have told me earlier, this is freakin' me out. Stress, stress, stress!

Sorting out all the paperwork now, so I can get ahead. I hate those essays! Sure Miss Cleveland will give me a glowing reference. Hope my tutor will go out of her way to recommend me. I have been sucking up to her for a few months now. Even getting her daily coffee injection.

Have organised an interview in December, my interviewer is an alumni. Hope that will go well, if not, game over.

The January deadline approaches – Com'on teachers! Press and send, it's so easy.

Monday 9th December 2019 (WD)

Dear Diary,

Interview seemed to go well. He asked me lots of hard questions and wanted to know all about me. I talked a lot about iGEM, that was a great investment of time. Coped well with most of the questions, he asked me about the British Royal family – how random is that!

Will have to wait and see. Fingers and toes crossed.

WEDNESDAY 18TH MARCH 2020 (WD)

Dear Diary,

I have done it! MIT have accepted me. Miss Cleveland cried, Mom shouted, Dad mumbled something about being proud of me. Wow! Life has just got better. Can't wait to finish High School and start my new adventure. Boston here I come.

OCTOBER 2020 (BM, R, WD)

The move from Fairfax High to MIT required a dramatic house-move, as well as a major shift in her thinking.

At Fairfax, Chloe had grown accustomed to being the top of her class. Now, she faced the challenge of being among intellectual giants – success was no longer guaranteed. Everything demanded focused attention and consistent effort – natural intelligence soon proved to be little more than a common trait at this level of the academic world.

Suddenly, identity from excellence was snatched away. Her first grade barely achieved 20% and came alongside a damning comment about her sloppy writing technique and poor research methods. She tried not to cry but the tears oozed their way out. After making up an excuse to leave the seminar room she retreated to the bathroom.

Leaning against the stall door, she cried. The best mark amongst her peers was only 32%. That was not much better than hers – however, hers was not the best. Such a blow.

She had always been the smartest, accepting it but not thinking that it mattered that much. Now it did, she was amongst those who were equal and even more threatening beyond her ability. Feelings of vulnerability bubbled up, along with this irrational sense of being threatened, a kind of inner deflation.

Of course she had a competitive streak, not serious but present. Part of her wanted to challenge the marking criteria and loudly justify her work. Chloe considered talking to her personal tutor but decided not to.

Instead adopting a different strategy: she would brush it off. It was no big deal.

Back in the seminar room, she whispered a disparaging comment about the course tutor to the students on her row. They agreed with her, equally wounded. The foul mood passed.

Unknown to her, the faculty's unofficial marking policy went along the lines of "stretch them, humble them, then educate them" and certain members of the academic board felt that a little belittling was necessary in the making of compliant and pliable students.

Three weeks later, her next essay was better, this time 33% – the comment suggested she had improved her writing style and showed a better understanding of research. Still, it did not make her feel any better.

Making genuine friends proved to be harder than she had expected. Everything so unfamiliar – new surroundings, new people, new living arrangements; she ended up in a single room in an all-girls dorm. Her few square metres of sanctuary.

Yet she found herself surrounded by people who wanted to date her – male and female. That was shocking. Something about her looks seemed to draw people in. She could not understand it. As if she generated a powerful magnetism whenever she walked into a room.

The comments and suggestions shocked her at first; she soon learned to read the faces, working out those who were jealous from those who were in awe. In her eyes she was okay, pretty but not beautiful. She got used to the attention, working out her own way of dealing with the interest playfully and, in time, she thought, quite skilfully – discovering her own dark sense of humour, thinking in some way it might be useful for her own entertainment.

Perhaps out of insecurity, she reverted to the old Keystone Kittie Chloe. Once again, she was the popular party girl. Hannah Montana had two sides, so did she. Chloe threw off her restraints and decided to resurrect the alter ego. Yes, she had her nerdy side, but she suspected the same of most of the people at MIT. On the other hand, she possessed a confident persona; she could also be the girl who knew how to have a good time, who could lead the way, the centre of attention.

A strategic manoeuvre? Later on Chloe would consider it to be an ill-considered one. Such a life was made easier by the artificial stimulants she started to take, they facilitated her transformation into someone else.

The combination of wealth, beauty, opportunity and the pursuit of adventure – a business opportunity jumped on by the Creative Stimulant Laboratory (CSL), a branch of the invisible business community – they even produced business cards with the logo embossed on a glossy finish. They simply recognised a niche moment and provided the goods. Designer drugs alongside more common items like cocaine and MD. Chloe found sponsors only too willing to provide her with the means to explore the goods on offer. She had her suspicions that one of the top chemistry students headed this organisation.

With a much wider field at her fingertips, the MIT frat party scene offered new areas for exploration. The combination of music and drugs – *and the sort of activities that require one's status as a consenting adult* – the sort that took place far from Bethany's watchful gaze – all took precedence over Chloe's academic studies.

SUNDAY 18TH OCTOBER 2020 (WD)

Dear Diary,

Am I havin' fun or what! Have not slept for three nights. Keep alive by poppin' a couple of uppers. One more invitation has just come in. My phone is hot, buzzin. Can hardly believe that this kind of life is possible. Still managing to get my work done, just about. Missed a lecture today – oops. Told them I was sick, sick of being in that dull class. Hahaha.

FRIDAY 19TH MARCH 2021 (WD)

Dear Diary,

Just heard Mom's message. Why does she bother? I feel so bad when I disrespect my Mom and I do quite often. Did not return her last call. Why do I feel as if I need to punish her? What has she done to deserve such a horrible daughter?

MONDAY 29TH MARCH 2021 (WD)

Dear Diary,

Colin is not even remotely interested in a long term relationship, why is he such a child? I am on the verge of breaking up with him anyway. I am sure he spiked my drink at Olivia's party, I woke up with such a weird head and in his dorm. I had no memory of the evening beyond drinking that glass of so called champagne. I was really sore down below. Not sure what we did but… I always make him wear a rubber despite his protests about loss of sensation. The man is a complete idiot. Rich but dumb.

Dear Diary,

Dirty hell! I'm pregnant. A disaster. Made an appointment at the Planned Parenthood Organisation in town, don't want this to get around the campus. What a mess. My life is complicated enough as it is without this.

Help, help! Oh god. Mom would go crazy, can't tell her. Will have to deal with this on my own.

What a mess! No point in mentioning this to Colin, he only cares about himself and his trust fund.

I'm in trouble. Double crap.

WEDNESDAY 14TH APRIL 2021 (BM, EWA, R)

'Chloe, Chloe Bartell?' Hearing her name broke her daydream in two.

There was kindness in the voice. She turned to face the source of compassion. A young lady, early twenties, with wonderful eyes; her warm smile and radiant face was almost angelic. Long brown hair was neatly braided, reaching right down her back. Chloe wanted to ask her what conditioner she used, they obviously shared the same hair issues.

'Your appointment is next, you go through the double doors and take the first door on the left.' The smile continued, 'Do you mind if I sit next to you?'

'No,' Chloe mumbled her mind preoccupied with other things.

'It can be quite nerve-wracking for people, being here... in this place.'

'Do you work here?' There was nothing so suggest that the woman was a member of staff. Chloe wondered how she knew her name.

'Yes, I help out sometimes; just about to start my shift. I'm a volunteer.' She touched Chloe on the arm, 'Don't worry, things will work out okay.'

That smile – something about it seemed so comforting, so genuine. Chloe managed a weak smile in response.

'Got to go.' She headed towards the double doors.

Chloe's number appeared on the appointment board. *Right on time*. She picked up her bag, clutching it.

My turn.

+++

As she passed through the double doors, Chloe felt happier.

Tasmin Oliver, her counsellor, talked through all the option with her and discussed the pros and cons. She really understood, they had chatted and it turned out that Chloe was not the first student to get caught out. Tasmin confided, off the record, that she'd gotten pregnant at college and ended up having an abortion. Now she was a mother of two. That gave Chloe confidence, it was not the end of her life. Pregnancy had been so hard for her mother. Was this some sort of sadistic irony? Tasmin did emphasise the importance of contraception and she talked Chloe through some of the latest ones on the market.

The obvious decision seemed like the right one. Two days from now. They both agreed

She saw the helpful young lady putting some magazines into a rack in the foyer, humming as she worked.

'I just wanted to thank you for your kind words,' she turned towards Chloe. 'They really calmed me down. I'm not sure how but you made me feel so much bet—'

'Kind words cost nothing.' The woman smiled suddenly, and laughed warmly.

Chloe read the identity badge: volunteer and coordinator, and beneath that, her name.

'Thank you, Crystal. Thank you very much.'

WEDNESDAY 21ST APRIL 2021 (WD)

Dear Diary,

Wrestling with such a sense of guilt. The 'op' went well, recovery was fine. Back on my course. I've wasted so much time and squandered a unique opportunity.

Booked an appointment with my personal tutor and told her most of what has happened, left out he drugs bits. She was so supportive. Gave me some great advice and told me I could have spared myself the isolation by using the facilities on campus. I suppose she's right, I didn't want my private business all over campus, I guess it is confidential but didn't want to take the chance.

Catching up with all the work that I have missed, got some extensions from the lecturers – phew! Spoke to Mom, told her the selected highlights of events. We seemed to connect in a different way. Maybe the event has changed my perspective? Felt softer on the inside towards her.

Decided to drop the party scene and step up the academics. I am going to take MIT for the serious challenge it's supposed to be.

Can I still make up for lost time? Exams are just round the corner.

May 2021 (BM, EWA, R, WD)

Chloe's metamorphosis drew the attention of the tutors on her course. Despite a poor track record, it was unanimously agreed that Chloe should be allowed to try for the annual scholarship offered to those students who displayed academic prowess. In her case it was a raw and an innate sort of power, but it was potential all the same. Successful applicants earned generous reductions on fees, free accommodation and access to summer courses and placements at a number of international destinations.

Feeling somewhat flattered to be considered for such a prestigious award, Chloe felt obliged to make the most of this opportunity. It was like High School all over again.

Summer scholarships required candidates to submit a dissertation and then to appear before an external panel. A group of academics and professionals would judge each student's work and then ask probing questions. The winner would be selected from the field of invited applicants.

Chloe just managed to complete the dissertation by the May deadline; only the interview remained.

Tuesday 1st June 2021 (BM, EWA, R, WD)

Chloe could see the pensive look on the applicant before her. The corridor had four chairs, dull and nondescript, a containment area.

She studied her hands, before wringing them – the corridor felt hot, really hot. The external panel would include academics as well as those who were influential in other areas of life. In the past, local congress members and governors had taken time out to come and see the new talent at MIT. Chloe struggled to swallow the lump in her throat.

As she entered the interview room the air felt stale, thick and warm. Chloe coughed twice, then sucked in as much air as she subtly could. On exhaling she remembered to smile. Six tired faces peered at her.

'Please sit down Miss Bartell,' encouraged the Dean of the Faculty of Sciences, Professor Clara Harris. 'We're here to ask you questions about the research that you have submitted. Please feel at ease.'

The next thirty minutes were gruelling; she watched her hypothesis being torn apart and reassembled. There were questions about her understanding of ethics and the future of human life on earth.

All the same, Chloe focused on remaining calm during the ordeal. When she felt anxious, she summoned up that version of herself who had once beaten challenge after challenge at High School.

Her interview notes read:

"The student showed remarkable control, remaining calm at all times. She gave intelligent and carefully thought out responses, evidencing a genuine appreciation of the complexities behind central and surrounding ethical issues in her work – very impressive."

Tuesday 8th June 2021 (BM, R)

Chloe sat on the edge of her bed as she opened the letter from the scholarship committee. It was so nerve-wracking… even worse than the interview.

She screamed with delight – the scholarship was hers! Three weeks at Oxford University, England, all expenses paid. Yippee!

Chloe jumped up, twerked and clapped her hands simultaneously, grateful no one was watching.

I've got to let Mom know… and Dad.

Yet another door of opportunity swung open. Later that night, Chloe recorded every emotional detail in her journal.

FRIDAY 12TH NOVEMBER 2021 (BM, EWA, R)

"Transhumanism is a class of philosophies of life that seek the continuation and acceleration of the evolution of intelligent life beyond its currently human form and human limitations by means of science and technology, guided by life-promoting principles and values." (Max More, 1990)

The final quote stirred Louise as she departed from the Martin Wood lecture theatre, clutching the bundle of leaflets strategically laid on the chairs.

Something in her thinking and her personal philosophy had changed. Many of her own vague ideas now crystallised and expressed in a way that surpassed her own powers of articulation – new vocabulary, new concepts and new possibilities.

Yes, despite all the rhetoric, human beings were on a path of development. Her mind raced, processing the lecture.

The next steps in our natural and technological development will be crucial, it will be a keystone in our progression towards perfection. Evolution was far from over. Why allow ethics and moral dogma to stop this transition towards who knows what?

She did not go along with those who opted for a world with no morality. That seemed crazy, dangerous. There was a need for shared morality, an agreed code of conduct that focused on the good of all, the improvement, and protection of all in society. In the past religion had provided the framework that underpinned Western societies, but now in a postmodern world the concepts needed to be separated from their origin and viewed as ideas in their own right. Once there are agreed common ideas, the shared morality could then be incorporated into decision-making. It made sense.

She thought back to the time David Cameron had spoken about British values back in… *when was that ? It must have been 2013 or 2014.* Cameron described the values that make democracy work, the rule of law, individual liberty and the mutual respect and tolerance of those hailing from different faiths and beliefs. Beckenham Grammar School had taken the programme quite seriously, as aspiring academic students they were forced to write essays and engage in vigorous debates to investigate what all of this could mean in practical terms – trying to work out what it looked like in everyday life.

Yes, the work of Max More certainly needed further investigation; she would definitely look for the original version of today's ground-breaking lecture on YouTube.

What was it called? The Singularity o—

Her collision was eminently foreseeable. However, Louise was so deeply wrapped up in her personal epiphany that she missed all the signs. Listing slightly to the right and directly into oncoming human traffic, she had ended up in the path of one of the greatest living minds in the field of biology and genetic advancement. Louise bumped into him clumsily, almost dropping her things.

'Oh, sorry! I'm so sorry.' Louise felt the warm flush on her cheeks.

She noted his laughing eyes, Professor Sutcliffe pointed to the pamphlets in her hands. 'What did you think of the talk?'

'Oh, I thought it was brilliant, it summed up a lot of what I have been thinking and I realised that I wasn't the only one thinking along those lines.'

'Well, there are a number of us who believe this to be the only way forward. Have I seen you somewhere?' Professor Sutcliffe focused on her face, his scrutiny only encouraged the sense of unease building in her stomach. She hated being stared at.

'You did a couple of guest lectures as part of the ethics and morality unit during my first year here.' She blurted out her confession.

'Ah, my bread and butter for earning my keep. And your name is…'

'Louise, Louise Dalton.'

'Louise. How did you get on with the unit?' Sutcliffe seemed unable to contain his curiosity.

'It was thought–provoking and challenging, but nothing quite as revolutionary as what I just heard.' Louise considered herself forthright, but on reflection, she wondered if that had too much information.

Professor Sutcliffe nodded casually, looking slightly deflated. 'If you really want to grow in your understanding, you should join the transhumanism movement. Let me have a look at the leaflets.' He picked out the grey sheet titled 'Changing the World – Transhumanism.'

'This one has contact information and the main email address, there are regular meetings and we are always on the lookout for new talent. There are creative minds at all academic levels here, as I am sure you know.'

Her mother had always told Louise that it was rude to maintain eye contact for too long, but then there was something about Professor Sutcliffe that intrigued her, plus he was really dishy; a handsome mature man. She didn't really know what to say.

God, I wish I still had some of the courage I did a few years ago. Like the time I met Angelina Jolie. If only I could…

Louise sensed the depths of charisma radiating from the professor. And on top of that, there was the fact that he was a living genius. It was powerful, like seeing herself being swept along by an invisible wave. She gulped her words out. They sounded surprisingly clear to her.

'I'll do that.' Louise nodded emphatically.

'Good. Then I hope to see you again.' Before she could reply Professor Sutcliffe had moved swiftly down the busy corridor.

That was amazing.

Louise stood still clutching the pamphlets.

Data entry input: 191851842175
Programme: GWP
Level: 6
Accessed by C.

DECEMBER 2022 (BM, R)

Chloe read the course description:

"The PhD programme, specialising in genetic manipulation in mammals, will require four years of study and surrounding research. You will be required to spend a residential period at Oxford University, England."

That would make me a Doctor of Science. A perfect course, tailor made for me. This incredible opportunity would give me the potential to cut another new facet into my life experience. Plus an untapped opportunity for scientific development.

Oxford had been such an amazing place. You could almost feel the history of it all as you sat in lectures or walked around the grounds; steeped in academic energy. The Brits had an accent and some of them... well, she thought... they had an attitude. So proper, so suppressed and reluctant to say what they were thinking.

She recalled some of the looks that she had been given by the natives during her time at the Summer school; no doubt they had seen her as another loud American. Yes, she knew how they thought.

Still, it had been a great experience; she still kept in touch with two students from the course. People were not the only factor in the equation. It was about her future, her plans.

Mom had cried when she'd heard about the long-distance move, but offered her unfailing support, Dad seemed impressed, he was busy with his family so Chloe did not bother him with too much detail about her life...

A doctorate by twenty five, it was an achievement by anyone's standards. All of that said, it had come at a price.

Sharp as a diamond yet steeped in debt. She had thought to herself – *I'm going to need a highly paid job when all this is over.*

Chloe's reflexive chatter was a comfort. Stirring her expresso in the MIT refectory, she mulled over the possibilities.

Four more years...

Data entry input: 525256937982
Programme: GWP
Level: 6
Accessed by C.

PART III

THE ICILDA BIOTECH COMPANY (2000 – 2026)

I B C - KOREA

Icilda Biotech Company – Korea
Inspiring future hope

CHRONOS

A VISION FOR THE FUTURE

FRIDAY 8TH DECEMBER 2000

As Charles prepared the finishing touches on his speech, he reflected on the events leading up to this key moment. Things had certainly progressed since leaving Harvard. Pa's promotion putting him into a managerial role. His new role as CEO gave him influence over more of the company than he had ever expected. It was, he concluded, somewhat scary. *Thanks Pa!*

Keeping things in the family. Well that made sure that wealth remained in strong and capable hands – he sometimes joked about the irony in that – and that it could be protected by wisdom accumulated over many generations. Of course, it also boosted the family's ranking on the rich-list. *Up ten places! Rapid progress.*

Charles still remembered the retirement speech given by the headmaster at his prep school, Thornton Middle School. He'd just turned thirteen. With a loud booming voice, Mr Graymere said: "Power belongs to those who recognise the fleeting opportunities; destiny is never an accident. Careful preparation is essential." The words had stuck with Charles, becoming part of his core value system.

Having Max on board was an added bonus. They had a similar outlook on life, better yet, both of them believed in the improvement of human existence and the role of financial posturing in making that a reality. Neither of them had a background in the sciences, but they understood that money could purchase knowledge. A mutually beneficial arrangement – their cause needed scientific knowledge, the sciences needed their funding.

Yes, Max was a wonderful leader, convincing him to come on board as President at IBC had cost them though. Still, it was immensely satisfying to see the outcomes.

Thinking about it, Charles viewed Max as a friend. Sure, it helped that they were part of a common social circle, but there was more than that too it. Yes, they had grown closer.

Their family's long history with *the Light* had cemented their covenant, giving them a shared ideology that opened up new possibilities. He sometimes thought that these ideas might be uncomfortable for those accustomed to traditional morality models. Still, it was hardly the greatest of his concerns.

At the root of it, Charles admired Max. Mostly for his breaking free from his family's influences and his early, lonely business pursuits, those that had forced him to develop his independence, readily acknowledged by other industry leaders.

Max has a lot of guts – far more than me.

Careful, tenacious and resolute, he did not fall back on his money. Instead, Max invested it cleverly. Charles could not help but secretly covet his friend's growing understanding of biotechnology.

IBC benefitted from Max's wisdom, something he'd gained through his own suffering. They'd talked about his time in exile quite often. Putting his money where he thought it would grow, he'd invested in IBC. The sum total of that investment was now incredible; close to $50M. Max was an asset. That was indisputable. His was a hard working and infectious enthusiasm. Charles checked his Breitling – he still had plenty of time.

Another benefit of their shared values – certain controversial matters were easier to manoeuvre around. Everyone understood that the lines could occasionally become blurred, the lines between business and personal beliefs. However their mutual understanding helped them to come through sparkling clean. They agreed, morality could be negotiated, profit could not.

One of his brain waves... Max had invented the silence clause that prevented ex-employees from sharing trade secrets. Should they do so, the legal consequences would be devastating. Some of the country's finest lawyers had worked on creating a set of severe measures and effective means to stop disclosure. So far, IBC had not needed to utilise this facility. Loyalty, that could also be purchased – if the right price was on offer; silencing the cries of conscience, an inner voice easily stifled behind the walls of comfort and ambition. Charles smiled, as he considered all that he had achieved this far.

His New York office seemed pretty quiet for mid-morning.

Today was another chance to bring in more investors. After checking his emails, Charles realised that Karthik was flying back to the States. He hoped to attend the meeting despite the distance. It would be great to catch up with him.

Charles felt ready, the speech carried the right tone. He picked out the golden fountain pen from the organiser on his mahogany desk. A gift from his father on his thirteenth birthday. He added a final sentence. Yes, the voice of his headmaster would be heard again that afternoon. One hour to go before the short trek to Newark airport, then the flight to New Jersey.

He'd told Miranda that he would get her some new paintbrushes, at this rate it was going to be a tight squeeze. Still, a promise was a promise – and yet another job for his PA.

+++

The beating in his chest made Charles wonder if he was close to having a heart attack. One final paragraph to go. He desperately wanted to convey his passion and commitment to the potential investors. Somewhere in the back of his mind, he frantically hoped he'd reinforced his words with the appropriate body language.

How do you show hope in words?

Their money was crucial to the continued development of IBC-USA. Miranda's face flitted in front of him… *If only things had been different.*

There it was again. *The mantra.* He lived with the pain of her daily battle to survive. Along with Eleanor.

IBC banners were strategically placed around the room; two near the entrance, one in each of the corners and two more flanking the speaking platform. Charles was pleased to see that the colour scheme had changed.

Eleanor had commented that the old colours were a bit dull, he'd passed her comments on. Good to see someone was listening.

The room could have held one hundred and fifty people – he guessed there were around a hundred or so present. That was a good turnout for the area; not exactly a stronghold of support for IBC. The age range in the room, probably around thirty five upwards – not many young people. That was disappointing. *So disappointing.* The next generation were the lifeblood of tomorrow. They'd have to work out how to appeal to more young and upwardly mobile professionals.

He scanned the faces. Most of them were personal friends, some relationships went back further than he could remember. Others were new acquaintances; influential people who were keen to increase their net wealth, looking for that business opportunity that would be missed by many but recognised by the astute few. He spotted Karthik, on the front row, looking jet lagged, just in from Delhi.

+++

Oddly familiar, as his eyes connected with Charles, an experience from the past flowed through his mind. The air changed, becoming – *crispy* – full of static. A waft of cool air brushed across his face, making it tingle. Tiny whispers circled around his ears: unclear mutterings. It was a presence from the past – that of the Teacher.

The widescreen spanned his vision, reminding him of the cinema he'd visited as a child, his stomach tightening in anticipation; he trembled, becoming aware of his intense thirst. Something like a feature film commencing before his eyes.

Grotesque faces moved in and out of the screen. Like a 3D film, full of twisted and cruel expressions on skeletal frameworks, toothless half smiles, bulging eyes veiled by fine muslin. Then a row of chemical symbols emerged, a lesson from his school days, drumming the first twenty elements into his brain; now those symbols were combined in long strands. Compounds, old ones, new ones? Then there were strange organisms in front of him, yet he had only seen such creatures on movie screens: centaurs trotting on four legs, merfolk diving into pools of tranquil water, walking and talking plants; a succession of half human, half animal and perhaps even half alien beings. All in rapid succession, one image then the next.

A book covered in gold leaf, shining, gleaming. It opened as if turned by an invisible hand. New inventions, new devices. The images were all unfamiliar.

Somewhere behind it all, he could still hear Charles.

Both hands trembled as hot and cold flushes moved up and down his back, the hairs on his neck bristling – almost rippling.

This was incredible. It was genius.

Newspapers materialised – dated from the future. He could see the headlines: national situations, financial events, IBC breakthroughs, global catastrophes, even world peace. Each paper quickly replaced by another; all in detail. He wanted to make it stop, to slow it down so that he could read it all now; his mind stored each image though, then it moved on, as if the source knew he would be able to retain the information for a later date.

Let me grasp the full extent of this wonder.

He gasped at the spectacular sight. The extent of its detail was simply astounding. This was something more than usual. Past visions had lacked this level of precision. And the whole vision was in colour this time. He remembered the scene from the *Wizard of Oz*. The point at which the film switched from black and white to Technicolor. The audience had gasped during the transition. This was that moment.

The sound of clapping.

He jolted forward slightly, blinking rapidly. He was back in the auditorium; the audience were applauding. Somewhat startled, he gasped for air, looking nervously at his neighbours who vigorously displayed their appreciation. He managed a few feeble claps. Mechanically slapping his palms together while his mind spun in circles.

Shaken and confused, he wondered if anyone else had witnessed his encounter. Judging from the expressions of the other attendees they were unaware of his transportation. Their eyes were fixed firmly on Charles.

The meeting was over – conversations started all over the room. Karthik sat for a moment, collecting his thoughts.

What was that? What did I just see? What was that about? Why now?

The Teacher was back.

+++

Charles stepped down from the platform, carefully negotiating the small steps. He walked confidently towards his friend. Karthik seemed somewhat preoccupied. Charles stood in front of him – he hardly seemed to notice.

Charles cleared his throat and spoke, 'Karthik, are you all right?' He placed his hand on Karthik's right shoulder.

The voice interrupted Karthik's thoughts. He gasped and looked up at Charles.

'My friend Charles…' The heat from Karthik's hand mingled with a slight tingling sensation, reminding Charles of a vibrating thermopad. 'Something strange just happened to me, while you were speaking.'

'Oh? Tell me more.' Charles sat next to Karthik, keen to hear about his friend's experience. He'd meant to ask about the journey and perhaps about his own presentation. The room still populated with people, at least they had not rushed off. The buzz in the air that was a good indicator of their interest and his success as a speaker.

'I just had the most incredible…vision. Only briefly, but it was amazing.' Tears filled Karthik's eyes. 'What you are involved in is very important. I am not sure why, Charles, but, you know, it really matters.'

Karthik's stare would have unnerved him if they were not such good friends; the look somewhere between wonder and terror.

'I believe in what I am doing. It's something deep inside.' Charles pointed to his heart. 'You know it, I suppose. It isn't about the money,' he gestured to the room at large, speaking softly. 'But there is a purpose that needs to be fulfilled. I cannot put it into words. It's just something I have to do. I guess you know that too.'

Charles felt the repeated prod on his right shoulder, he turned to see an extended, huge and hairy hand. He shook it firmly before looking into the face of its owner.

'I'm right with you Charles. My transfer will be with you by tomorrow morning. Impressive!' Charles scanned his mental address book for a second, then snapped out an appropriate response.

'Maurice! That's wonderful.' Maurice Bizet, an extremely wealthy oil tycoon, successful, married four times, had a real aversion to anything that was not solid. Except oil, of course. Charles suppressed the wicked thoughts passing through his head, about the man's infamous love life; after all, he had cheated on all of his former wives. At least he had a better reputation for loyalty in the corporate arena.

'Thank you Maurice, you'll not be disappointed.' Charles smiled gratefully, glad that this behemoth had acknowledged his mission. His skills at persuasion were improving. Maurice avoided almost everything that sounded remotely experimental, preferring tried and tested investments.

Charles turned back to Karthik, tears filled his eyes. A few broke free, creeping down his cheeks. He wiped them away. 'What's the matter Karthik? Are you alright?'

'I just know.' He cleared his throat before continuing, 'Charles, I know that I am to be part of this; this revolution of yours. This is not a business opportunity, Charles. It's a revolution.'

Karthik decided that it was time to tell Charles. 'That vision, Charles. That vision is just a glimpse of what is about to happen. You already know it here, my friend,' he tapped his forehead, 'But you need to know it here,' and then his chest. 'Charles, consider it, but feel it too. You are about to change human history in accord with everything we spoke about at college; human history and even,' Karthik paused again, this time to wipe away the last of his tears, 'even human evolution.'

'What do you mean?' Charles smiled, nervously.

'I've spent so long sorting out everything at home, Charles. But your speech today, and what I saw while you were talking.' He paused for a second, breathing deeply before continuing, "Sorry, I'm still in shock at the moment. Charles, let's meet in the next couple of days. I am here for long enough for us to discuss matters properly.'

Karthik struggled to convey his emotions and the words tumbled out. 'I will give you a call. This is momentous, it's a real shift in the direction of your work, and our history.' Intense heat coursed through his body, Karthik knew that sensation. It was like the old days back at Harvard, the touch of the Teacher.

Now his insides were trembling alongside his major worry – at any moment, a tidal of power wave could break loose, sending him straight to the floor. He often lost consciousness when the power surges reached their peak. Waking up to find himself in the weirdest positions, sometimes bearing large bruises from the falls he suffered when fainting.

Charles wiped his forehead, a hot rush moving through his body. He felt confused but at the same time happy. Yet concerned for Karthik, he could not shake it off. He knew about Karthik's fortune, but that wasn't what sustained the friendship. Now he seemed to have some unique insight into the work.

'Of course. I would love to.' Charles smiled. Karthik continued to wipe his eyes, smiling back. In that moment, the two felt united, like they were in the old days.

Charles, glanced at his watch. As much as he would have liked to continue the conversation, he was becoming increasingly aware of his PA. He had that hovering stance, his nervous expression covered by a thin but professional smile, sending frequent glances towards Charles, while fidgeting with his clipboard.

'You make sure you call,' insisted Charles, noting his old friend's shallow breathing. 'I will be sure to answer. And Karthik, I'm looking forward to it.'

Karthik watched as Charles disappeared, swallowed in the midst of a sea of hungry billionaires. Each of them was ready for a slice of human history. The moment had arrived. Charles might not know it yet, but his work was a herald; it would bring about the dawn of the next stage of human development.

Karthik knew it.

MONDAY 11TH DECEMBER 2000

Karthik placed the envelope into Charles' hand, smiling confidently.

'What is this?' Charles turned it over twice. Noting the neat handwriting, Karthik's work.

'I have been shown the future of IBC. Here is an outline of that which I have seen.' Karthik seemed to look straight through Charles. His stare had always been so piercing.

'Future? What are you… psychic?' Charles laughed gently as he said it, but the serious look on his face made it clear that this was not a trivial matter. Charles allowed himself a moment and then put on a more professional persona. 'I'll look at this later.' He put the envelope on top of the stack of manila folders on his right-hand side. 'Are you in Karthik?' The real business needed to be discussed.

Charles watched Karthik open his briefcase. He presented the cheque. $20.2M .

'That's very, very generous. Thank you, Karthik.' He placed it in the top drawer of his mahogany desk. 'Thank you for your confidence.'

Karthik rubbed at his white-trimmed beard, thoughtfully. 'Charles, the vision is the reason for my confidence. We have much to do and all within a fairly inflexible time frame.'

Karthik seemed strangely driven. He had always been a little intense but now… *there's something about his manner, his body language.* Charles could not put his finger on it. A thought surfaced – *The Muppet Show.* Karthik reminded him of one of the characters, the dopey one. The specific name escaped him. The man moved normally but his eyes told a different story – blank, vacant spheres.

Those carefully orchestrated actions were a little eerie; he had loved the puppets when he was young, but inside he'd always felt sorry for the marionettes, working out that they had no real life of their own. Karthik's mannerisms took him back to those days. Like he had no agency, no real self.

Charles was concerned. Things had changed so much since their student days at Harvard. He allowed himself a moment to reminisce, putting his worries to one side.

Karthik continued, a deeper urgency in his tone. Charles thought there was something pedagogical buried in there. A subtle tone or texture that was perhaps, even, a little arrogant. A little too knowing.

'Charles, this fits in with everything that we stand for as members of *the Light.* It is far bigger than you can imagine.' As if out of nowhere, Charles realised that he was scared. He could feel a strange energy crawling on his hands and shoulders. Karthik's words were wrapping themselves around his body. There was an unusual sound in there. Something other, resonating inside and around a familiar voice. It was his voice and yet not his voice at all. Charles breathed in deeply, the air tingled as if it had been filled with electrostatic pulses from a Van der Graaf generator.

Karthik smiled suddenly. 'I am meeting with *the Light* central council tonight to inform them of the pathway I have seen and to encourage them to join with IBC. Without hesitation. Thank you for opening the way Charles.'

He extended his hand towards Charles. Charles reached out to meet Karthik. The two hands connected, firmly. A surge of power jumped from Karthik to Charles who winced in pain – it was as if he had touched an electric fence on a farm. He let go immediately, visibly shocked. Something strange was happening.

Karthik did not seem bothered by it. *Perhaps it was just… static?*

Karthik continued to smile at Charles who studied his face for a second. Karthik's progression within *the Light* had made perfect sort of sense. His leadership skills and philosophical wisdom were recognised by everyone. It hadn't been long before he had been asked to take a leading position on the group's guiding council. However he had never used his status as a means through which to dominate others. Charles admired this quality about him.

His youthful hardness and brash attitude had simply matured into a more caring and compassionate disposition. They shared a mutual respect. Regardless of the strange formalities and the esoteric lecture, Charles still had faith in Karthik. Friendship was friendship and business was, ultimately, business. Now Karthik was going to promote IBC at the council? Max and Charles hadn't even discussed the idea, it would have seemed outlandish, too much like asking for favours.

Yet here is Karthik. Karthik and his strange behaviour – and his position of influence on the council. *Why is he so adamant about all this? Was I that convincing? No… He knows something we don't.*

However, he was an old friend and Charles didn't want to come across as an obsessive. Anyway, a full schedule lay ahead. He decided to put his questions to one side and resolved to read the letter as soon as he got a moment.

Karthik promised to stay in touch. Charles told him that he would be unable to attend the next meeting of *the Light*.

'I've got a crazy schedule, Karthik. But thank you.' He seemed disappointed, but seemed to understand. They parted with a warm handshake – no shock this time – and with smiles on their faces.

Before he left the office later that day, Charles slipped the letter into his attaché case. He had meant to open it there and then, but, as usual, he was almost running late.

Two days later he came across the letter while sorting out his case. He had just arrived in Cleveland and checked into the luxury International hotel. It was to be a short stay, a stop-off before heading to London.

He read its contents. As he did, his hand trembled violently.

Suddenly, he understood the gravity of Karthik's words.

+++

Charles hated it when his lips trembled. He read the document for the third time. Emotions danced around inside his mind, confusion and elation both partners in a frenzied duet. He could hear his heart beating through his stomach, rapid deep thuds. The dryness in his mouth seemed to demand immediate attention. He poured another glass of water – his third in the last hour.

What was this; prophecy? The future had been laid out in the letter, apparently dictated to Karthik. *But by whom – or by what?* Charles rubbed his head. *Can I take any of this seriously? It's hard not to take twenty point two million seriously.*

He could feel Cleveland getting ready for the night, they sky turning from bright blue to azure, then to an orange, purple hue. Time had slipped away while he was reading.

His jacket still lay draped across his untidy, temporary desk. He'd taken off his tie, throwing it down next to the jacket. He sat there, staring at the letter. The world seemed a whole lot less certain than it had this morning – *is Karthik insane, surely not?*

Strange thoughts flitted through his head but, strangest of all, he couldn't stop thinking about *Back to the Future II.*

And this is what Karthik's taking to the council?

The letter outlined the expected development of IBC over the next fifty years. It was a business plan to die for. Some sections lacked specific dates and details, but key points in the company's future were described at sufficient length as to make them a manageable reality.

It would be easy to stay quiet and watch developments over the next few months. To see if any of this happens. What about Max though?

It was now completely dark outside. Time seemed to be passing strangely.

Marty goes into the future and brings back a Sports Almanac. The movie kept tugging at his memory.

This is what he's taking to the Light? He could feel the hair on the back of his hands standing up.

The Almanac gives all the race results, from the 50s through to what would have felt like the distant future. *Marty's* rival, Biff, gets hold of it and alters the present. It threatens Marty's future.

Can it possibly be true; can it really happen? It's so detailed though. So realistic. So, convincing!

He sighed, rubbing his forehead. His head ached. There were too many conflicting thoughts. He realised that he'd drained his glass again.

Charles relied on others to make the decisions about planning – principally Max. He knew his limits. But this, this plan, it could change everything. If things did not happen as stated, well then it could be thrown out. But if they did… *well I will* have *to take it to Max.*

Clearly Dr Karthik Kothaka had no formal training in the sciences; the terminology reflected his university education, and his lack of specific knowledge. The idea that IBC would expand beyond the border of the USA was the first thing that struck Charles. In the opening section of Karthik's vision, South Korea was mentioned by name and a specific location followed – Pohang.

'So where is Pohang?' Charles spoke to the air as if expecting an answer. South Korea, he supposed. Charles had no real knowledge of that part of the world. He knew full well that the country was hugely invested in the computer science industry – *but biotech? And how are we meant to get into South Korea?* All the paperwork and documentation, the investment projects, the staffing… it would need a whole lot of organising.

The rest of the vision highlighted key areas in which IBC-Korea would pioneer new technologies. These included a breakthrough that would see the end of terminal muscular dystrophy. Charles stopped reading at that point and thought of Miranda. MS and muscular dystrophy were similar diseases, considered incurable by science. The future looked bleak for sufferers – even the best tailored medication only slowed the progression of the disease while its symptoms continued unabated.

Can this be true?

He recognised the gripping sensation in his stomach, switching on and off. That only happened under extreme stress. Instinctively, he placed his hand over the dull pain.

Dr Kothaka used Chinese astrology symbols throughout his work, describing particular years in words and the animals linked with them. Charles did not understand the symbolism, and the association was lost on him.

The section of the letter that discussed the coming genetic revolution was mind blowing.

'This will change the course of human history,' Charles spoke aloud. His hotel room was plush and comfortable – it wanted for nothing. The background sound of the LED TV was low, but comforting. It provided a strange sense of companionship. Eleanor and Miranda were many miles away.

He had to tell Max. There was no choice. He reached for his Nokia 7110 and hit the speed dial button.

Within a few seconds he was deep in conversation with his friend. Charles agreed to fax the document to him from the machine in the reception. He made it clear that nobody else was to know about its existence. At least at this point in time.

He closed his phone, the TV was his only company.

Charles was still trembling.

MONDAY 11TH DECEMBER 2000

That's a call I won't not forget in a hurry. Max shut his flip phone. *Is Charles on something?*

Knowing Charles, he pushed aside that possibility. *What about the source of the document?* That worried Max. He was not one to be fooled.

Visions. Visions, that applied to business practice? It was a totally new concept for him and not one he was ready to accept. This was ridiculous... *wasn't it?*

Charles seemed to have been taken in by the whole thing. That meant that its progenitor must have packed some punch; there had been no mention of the document's author over the phone despite Max's asking. Just a hurried explanation and the promise of a fax.

Knowing Charles and his business practices, it meant that person or people responsible for the document were established and respected – otherwise it would have been dismissed as lunacy. Someone of industrial importance was behind this, evidently. Max decided to reserve all further judgement until he was presented with the facts.

An hour later, the fax machine in his office whirred into action.

Max was unable to complete any of the tasks that needed his urgent attention. He too gripped by the details of the vision. The developments described would put them at the top of the biotech industry – investors would come flooding in. Expansion would be possible – and on an international and indeed global scale. The transformation of human life was also described as a part of the equation – the new man would be a step closer. He read the document again, scanning for particular sections. He re-read them and highlighted key points.

At times, he laughed out loud. Yet something made his skin crawl with anticipation. There was a tone of certainty to the writing. *Can this be a possibility?*

Of course not. *Certainly an astute director could plan for some of this but this seems so sure… how could anyone know?* There were background details in the document that described very specific business decisions. Ones which linked to current and ongoing projects. Things that were meant to be kept quiet. This was some forecast!

He had a meeting with Charles scheduled for tomorrow afternoon. Judging by the arrival of the document, he figured that lunch would be a long affair. Max remained acutely aware of the list of urgent matters still sitting on his desk.

Excited, sceptical and considerably worried, he put down the faxed pages and began to deal with more practical and immediate matters.

Someone is definitely watching us, he thought, staring at his desktop. *I'm not sure who or how, but someone is.*

TUESDAY 12TH DECEMBER 2000

Max was pleased with the choice, a central table, against the back wall, surrounded by small booths; cosy and private in what was an otherwise busy location.

The International Hotel, London, England; the Michelin star Indian restaurant was always booked months in advance. Charles' PA had done a sterling job.

Max was travelling to Berlin, from New York, while Charles was on his way to Russia. London almost in the middle.

The ambiance and the excellent service always made it a pleasant experience. The air was full of the pungent odour of cumin and curry leaves. The waiters were all excellent at their work.

Max noted the table settings, every detail had been meticulously covered: napkins, plates, cutlery, authentic music, décor and floral arrangements.

Max decided to go for the house red, Charles opted for mineral water. 'Are we agreed on the starters, main dishes and desserts?' Charles nodded. 'Well, that was pretty straight forward.'

Charles was so easy going – he never made a fuss of anything. A calm and straight forward, regular guy. Not that Max envied Charles, he was an excellent fundraiser and a social genius, but lacked the ruthless focus Max admired. He didn't have that killer instinct, the sort needed for really successful business ventures.

The poppadums arrived with an assortment of condiments. Max thought that he would be adventurous and try the Bombay special. He soon regretted it, only the cooling effect of the yoghurt stopped him crying out in pain. Charles seemed to find the whole thing hilarious, opting for the safer choice of mango chutney, shredded cabbage and mint.

Max asked the waiter for two bottles of Tiger. 'You've known him since Harvard. Still, why would you put weight behind anything that he says?'

'Even then it was pretty obvious that Karthik had charisma and a real air of dignity. I always thought he would be something special.' Charles bit into the poppadum, which exploded into fragments, leaving him scooping up the pieces.

Max smirked behind his napkin, now fully recovered from his painful episode. The beers arrived. He probed, 'So you took him on as what… as a special project?'

'You know me, I see talent and nurture it. But you know as well as I do that it was sometimes the other way around. Karthik has a way of convincing people to agree with him, even I don't have that degree of influence, not at that level. And look at our funding successes.' He sipped the Tiger beer straight from the bottle, Max poured his into a glass.

'That is what concerns me Charles. You seem so ready to believe in visions rather than real business plans? In truth, I am surprised.' Max eyed him over his glass. He watched every moment, trying to read his partner's intentions. 'It is an enticing presentation. A lot of it makes sense. But a lot of it does not. I believe in dollars and facts, not lucky rabbits' feet and vibrating jade stones.'

Charles looked a little hurt. He dabbed at his lip thoughtfully and took another swig of his beer. 'Opportunity only knocks once, Max. Are you,' he pointed at him, 'Are you ready to allow this to pass you by? And why? Maybe you are scared of the tone of this document?' He looked nervous, pausing before proceeding. 'Because something is outside your comfort zone. Rabbits' feet and all that.'

Max could have sworn that Charles was smirking at him.

'Supposing – and I know it's a long shot and an odd one at that, but Max – just supposing this was the biggest scoop going and you missed it because you're scared to have a little faith.'

Charles, you have a cheek. His thoughts were interrupted as the main course arrived. Max had chosen the Chicken Jalfreizi, Charles the mild Lamb Biryani. They'd decided to share a plate of pilau rice with almonds. Max thought it was mildly ironic that they were sat here of all places, eating Indian food, discussing a mystical business plan. *Rabbits' feet.*

'I am not one to fall for a scam Charles.'

'Why not test it? If it fails, we can respectfully write Karthik off and I will talk to him about it all – and yes, you can tell me that you told me so. If it works, IBC could be at the top of the list. Imagine what that would do for *our* shares, Max.' Charles smiled wryly.

Charles had him, the thought of the company being at the top, his role in that, the investment, the potential. With the technology that the new funding would go on to develop, they could accelerate evolution; double it, perhaps even triple it. This would put them right at the top of the wave.

'Okay, Charles. Going international is something that we have thought about. But to go to an unknown destination and set up a new company, Charles that is,' he paused to make his point. 'Well that is a gigantic risk.'

In many ways he was not alone in the venture, a chunk of his finances were tied up in the company. This was so very much outside his comfort zone. Max tugged at his collar, feeling hot.

'Why not try some of the local issues first before venturing overseas. Test it out and see for yourself. Arrest your scepticism. I know I have more faith in Karthik than you ever did, Max.' Charles put his fork down, draining the rest of the bottle.

'However, you know me better than to think I'd take any leaps of faith here. I just trust him a little more than you is all. I am sceptical too, you know. But you have to have a little confidence. After all, he took it to the council didn't he? And if you'd have seen him, if you'd been there, you might be more inclined to try this. It was, well it was so strange. And I want to test it. I want to see.'

Their plates were removed.

Giving control to that immigrant? Max still disliked him.. His rising empire in the East, his influence within *the Light*. He was as much a guru as he was a businessman. Max did not like to admit that he was scared of Karthik. He could swallow his pride; it would not hurt to indulge his partner's fantasy's. Perhaps, in doing so, he would remove Karthik from the equation. Two birds with one stone.

After all… the man is a powerful investor and he's already given us the money.

'Well, we can see, can we not?' He smiled at Charles. 'You know, I heard him speak at the last meeting of *the Light*. He virtually told the fellowship to plough their money into IBC. Since then, it is indisputable, there has been a flood of investment.' He held off adding more. He wanted to add that the masses had done exactly as they were instructed.

Charles smiled back, practically beaming. 'Max, I knew you'd come through. It's too good to believe, right? And if any of it is true then we'll have some serious questions for our friend in India. But it never, ever hurts to try. I'm glad you see that too.'

Max took a swig of his beer. 'Indeed.'

Charles and Karthik had always been a convincing pair. Max was less interested in the faith of others and more in the numbers. However, as much as he hated to admit it, where he ruled by force, Charles motivated by inspiring confidence, Karthik simply spoke and was followed. He was either insane, or had an agenda. Max watched Charles who was preoccupied with dessert. *What are we being played for?*

He wondered why Charles put himself through the torment of the mango ice – he had always had such sensitive teeth. Max's strawberry cheesecake, was not in the least bit Indian. He sliced it with his fork, pushing a small portion of it around the plate, considering its layers. It was just something he enjoyed.

'Anyway, how are the girls?' said Max as he finished his beer.

'Everything is good. Miranda misses me a lot.' He scooped up the last spoonful of the sorbet, wincing before he swallowed it.

By the end of the meal, Max had promised to choose a couple of events on the list and try them out. If they proved to be correct, he was in. If they did not, then he could defame Karthik and win Charles back over to the side of reason.

It occurred to Max that this was quite possibly a win-win situation. Something about that made him smile for real as he shook Charles' hand and wished him luck in Russia.

JANUARY/FEBRUARY 2001

Three out of three, this was becoming more than a little spooky. Max had deciphered the messages and acted on the business aspects that went along with the premonitions.

In the first instance the vision stated that there would be a major shifting in the balance of power from the West to the East. He'd brought shares in Chinese companies, they had continued to climb in value. He was mildly interested.

Secondly, that a new concept in music technology would revolutionise the way that sound could be processed and heard all across the world. He struggled with the strange symbol of an eye next to a singer. He hated the symbolism. Without someone to explain the images, it meant little. The written statements were often clear enough. *And why all the Chinese zodiac business?* However, his now frequent calls to Karthik were always met with patience and kindness. His view of the Indian was altering just a bit.

Max took the advice and made investments in various ongoing digital distribution technology projects in the US including, one suggested by his secretary who knew the assistant manager of a popular company computer – Apple. Max had met the founder, Steve Jobs, on a number of occasions at various social functions.

Max wondered if Karthik only gave out an edited version of his encounters – that really bugged him. Did Karthik retain full knowledge for himself? It made him vital to the whole thing. Smart business sense, but Max continued to hold some reservations.

On Tuesday 9th January 2001 iTunes was launched. He was interested. That was more than just an accident. His investments were making returns.

There was one section marked February 2001. It spoke of a major earthquake, stating the actual Richter scale value that it would measure. Checking that one would be easy.

On February 13th 2001 an earthquake hit El Salvador. Max was all ears. The newscaster stated that the reading was 4.2 on the scale. The vison was wrong. *Yes*, Max felt elated and vindicated at the same time. Perhaps he had simply made good decisions regarding Apple and the Chinese businesses. After all, he was an expert investor. Now he had concrete evidence they were not accurate.

The number of deaths was estimated to be about two hundred. The vison stated over four hundred. Small details, yes, but they were wrong. He wanted to ring Karthik and Charles to let them know that accuracy seemed to be an issue. He almost made the call but an urgent meeting required his attention.

Later in the day, a broadcast announced that the initial reading for the earthquake was incorrect, in fact the quake had registered 6.6. Max gulped as he listened. It was as the predictions had suggested, and the number of dead had risen from two hundred to over four hundred. A shiver rippled up and down both arms and one word exploded in his mind.

Supernatural.

TUESDAY 11TH SEPTEMBER 2001

Max remained sceptical until he could no longer avoid the conclusive evidence. The point at which he could no longer ignore the implications;

in September, 2001, a single event both confirmed the visions' reality and strengthened his beliefs that acute financial investments could be made off the back of the predictions.

The vision stated that, in September 2001, there would be an attack at the foundations of the Western world. Forces from the East would destabilise the integrity of the United States. The phrase 'like a pack of cards' was repeated three times. Unprecedented action would be taken, due to the severity of the incident, leading to a new war in the Middle East. The market would crash, the dollar heading downwards. Great quantities of wealth would be lost overnight. People would accept greater levels of surveillance in order to protect themselves from the threat of future attacks.

Reading it, it meant very little. Then on Tuesday 11th September 2001, it became a reality.

The towers fell. Like a house of cards. Max watched the rest of the vision unfold over the next few years, having made numerous investments in line with the predictions, watching the revenues come rolling in. How he relished the blossoming of his chosen companies in the surveillance industry and weapon technology sector, allowing him to make millions, as the world moved close to the edge of chaos.

Charles struggled with the moral implications of their foresight, arguing that if they knew events were going to take place surely it was their duty to try and save lives or minimise the effects? The Twin Towers being a case in point, so much devastation, such a huge loss of human potential.

Me, becoming a superhero? He harboured no desire to be *Spiderman*, the active hand of the social conscience. He listened to ongoing Charles' concerns, sympathising. Even Karthik agreed with Max, the information had been trusted to them for their purposes. To intervene might mean tampering with history, creating some kind of time anomaly. Sometimes the symbolism concealed the event until it took place, then they understood. It was not a case that they always knew in advance the exact nature of the predictions.

Charles would have to learn to live with him conscience or back out of the project. Lives were lost every day, the fact that they knew before hand in some cases, sad but all to their advantage. It did not rest easy with Charles; too much compassion, that was one of his biggest problems.

Creating wealth on the back of such wild predictions – it was a satisfying yet risky enterprise. The dividends were vast.

Max considered himself a believer.

POHANG WELCOMES IBC – KOREA

Pohang was a seaport city, situated in the Daegu-Gyeongbuk region of South Korea. Now vast and sprawling, it started life as a small fishing village, before its development into a significant harbour in the 1930s.

The outbreak of the war between North and South Korea brought both bloodshed and international attention to the once sleepy area, between August and September of 1950. The rapid growth of the fishing industry in the 60s saw the population swell to 50,000. It was a short lived expansion.

A flourishing market was threatened and undermined by revisions to the UN fishing quotas which were made during the 1970s. However the decision of Pohang Steel Company (POSCO) to base their main plant in the area brought industry to the town and, with it, the promise of prosperity. POSCO was a world leader in steel production. By the end of the 20th century the role of steel in the world economy had shifted and Pohang needed to survey the global market for other opportunities. It was that, or face the threat of economic extinction.

IBC made excellent use of the improved economic relationship between the USA and South Korea. The newly elected government desperately wanted to encourage foreign investors – their package of tax incentives and preferential planning permission proved attractive to the management team at IBC. Internationally, the strength of the dollar surprised many and only added to the appeal of this particular venture. The ultimate decision to open IBC-Korea in Pohang offered a much needed hand to a faltering economy.

Construction commenced in March 2010 and the central base for operations opened in September 2013. Boasting some of the latest hi-tech laboratories and a revolutionary nanotechnology suite, IBC-Korea sparked a wave of excitement amongst the international scientific community. Once again, Pohang showed its ability to adapt to challenging times. Pohang University of Science and Technology (POSTECH) was happy to supply these new investors with the sharpest academic minds that South Korea had to offer. It was their chance to lead what was rapidly being referred to as the start of a genetic revolution; one happening right on their doorstep. IBC invested in POSTECH by sponsoring a generous scholarship programme and providing work experience for the institution's top students. As a result, there was always a growing list of potential candidates on the books at IBC.

IBC's recruitment policy had been crafted for the recruitment of the best minds from across the world. International interest in this technological breakthrough would see the migration of talent from across the world, including graduates from the USA, the UK, Israel and Japan.

Pohang was about to change forever.

NEW RECRUITS

The 2012 science Fair brought together the best minds in science for debate and competition. It was also used as a recruitment platform by many of the companies who sponsored stalls. It was during this event that Dr Esther Cohen met the aspiring Karl Winwood.

Her convincing rhetoric seemed to have brought him around to the notion that IBC had a real passion for young talent in the sciences. Esther had many ambitions and was full of hope for the future.

She chuckled as she read his responses from her seat, on board the plane back to Philadelphia.

Just the kind of candidate we need.

TUESDAY APRIL 5TH 2016

The death of Miranda Ferrell on April 5, 2016, brought Charles and Eleanor an added dimension of intimacy.

United in grief, their relationship became a source of comfort; a place of mutual understanding and support. Miranda's funeral was attended by family, friends, business associates and people of standing within the community. Everyone who had known Miranda fell in love with her.

The thoughtful eulogy gave many attendees a chance to reflect on the joy that Miranda shared with everyone who spent time with her; regardless of their status in life. Miranda loved people. Despite her personal pain, she could make light of the most serious of matters, releasing childish giggles at the most inappropriate of times. She had never respected social order. From the Mayor to the maid, all strata of the neighbourhood grieved; her joy had been overwhelming. Many staff from the local private hospital, normally hardened by their daily exposure to suffering, openly wept as they considered their loss. Lovely Miranda had left them.

The invitation requested that attendees brought any of Miranda's artwork to the funeral. She had loved drawing caricatures and cartoons of people, hilarious and insightful. She would write a personal comment before signing each work, always finishing with the phrase: *with lots of love, Miranda*.

As her motor skills had deteriorated, she had drawn by clenching the pen or paintbrush in her teeth. Eleanor commissioned a special easel made so that Miranda could remain in her chair whilst working. The painstaking task was always undertaken in a cheerful manner, each piece taking hours, leaving her exhausted yet elated.

It seemed only right to Charles and Eleanor that their daughter's work should appear at her funeral. They were so proud of her.

Icilda clutched her son's arm. She reminded Charles of a comment he had made about Miranda's work when she had been little more than a baby – it had come true. She lifted her black veil, dabbing her eyes; always elegant. He remembered, nodding tearfully. His gifted daughter.

In Charles' mind, Miranda's life ran parallel with the development of IBC-USA. Charles could mentally chart key events in her life alongside important stepping stones in the life of the company. Her third birthday coincided with the completion of the Cryogenic Division. She had just turned five when the same section experienced a power failure and lost valuable data relating to the impact of nitrogen gas assisted freezing on human tissue. To think of Miranda was to think of the history of IBC. The two were forever linked in his mind. But now, Miranda was gone while IBC lived on.

+++

As time passed, Charles came to understand that the grief had revitalised his resolve. As if his motivation turned over ten-fold, he felt more compelled than ever before to share the vision of IBC. He did so with greater zeal, encouraging the super-wealthy to invest more and more money in his work. Eagerly, he took on extra hours, covering hundreds of thousands of miles by plane and road alike; all in order to talk to potential investors.

They wanted to keep her memory alive; Charles had the Miranda Ferrell Auditorium designed by a top architect. She would be a permanent part of IBC. The look would be one of dazzling brilliance, with the extensive use of crystals to create light that changed colour. A breathtaking statement.

Eleanor established an art foundation aimed at giving disabled people a platform for developing their creative skills and displaying the work to the wider public.

They were working together, as husband and wife.

Despite their newfound intimacy, Charles had concealed something from his wife. Miranda's body had not been buried.

Charles arranged for Miranda's body to be frozen and stored at IBC-USA, even organising the swapped coffins before the committal. His covert plan covered every detail and possibility and only a handful of individuals knew anything about it. His little team.

Two head technicians in the Cryogenics Division knew that his daughter was client 44057, on the second floor, third pod from the right. They were rewarded for their discretion. Each had been given a car of their choice as a thank you gift.

He dreamed of bringing his daughter back to life at such a time as it was made possible by the unstoppable progression of technology. He would raise the dead.

Prior to Miranda's death, Charles had also arranged for a record of her brain map to be taken. This involved the recording of the neural pathways contained in her brain as well as the electrical impulses with which they were associated. He hoped that, when Miranda could be physically resurrected, the brain map could be used to restore her personality, thoughts and memories.

Many members of *the Light* had opted for this storage process. Charles could see it being a very profitable arm of IBC's operation. The initial treatment could cost anywhere between $135,000 and $255,000, and then there was the annual $20,000 maintenance fee, to be paid in advance – in terms lasting from twenty to one hundred years. The list of willing and wealthy clients continued to grow. Extended life was proving to be a dream worth waiting for. The possibility of their coming back in the future took the edge off people's fear of death.

Of course Charles felt guilty for withholding the truth from his wife. But he knew she would resent his decisions if he told her. All he wanted was to develop a way to connect with Miranda. Nothing in his life had been more painful than her passing. He could not accept it.

When he had time, Charles would slip into the Cryogenics Division unannounced. There he would spend time with her alone. He talked to her warmly, observing her frozen features through the viewing panel. One day he would bring her back, and he frequently told her so.

On September 4th 2024, Dr Karl Winwood became one of the youngest Directors of Natural Sciences in the history of IBC. His extensive range of qualifications and laboratory experience had already impressed everyone who met him.

At his interview he charmed the panels at each stage of the selection process. The final decision had been unanimous.

Karl completed his eight years at MIT with a degree and a double Doctorate. Securing a top research job in Switzerland was easy, followed by two years spent leading a project on genetic manipulation in Sweden. He had become one of the world's youngest leading lights in the world of genetic alteration.

TUESDAY 10TH SEPTEMBER 2024

IBC-Korea made contact with Chloe during the second year of her PhD course at MIT. Flattered by the interest, Chloe outlined her research plans and promised to give IBC a call at the end of her studies to see if there were any openings. During the long conversation, Chloe was shocked to hear that Max Augustine recalled meeting her at an iGEM event in 2015 and that he extended his warmest wishes.

Chloe felt like spreading her wings and taking off once the call had finished. Such an incredible honour. She could see no other career for herself except in the unique fields of biology practised at IBC. New horizons appeared as often as the technology jumped forward – genetic manipulation could well be a future tool for the development of the human race.

I hope so.

PROBLEMS WITH CROSS SPECIES MANIPULATION

WEDNESDAY 23RD OCTOBER 2024

Was this the end of the road? Karl faced a challenge; the sort of challenge that that could jeopardise his future at IBC-Korea. To make matters worse, it was only his first month.

As the Director of Natural Sciences, problems always headed in his direction, especially when other team members ran out of ideas or could no longer see a way forward. Karl loved challenges. That brought out the best in him. However, lately, nerves had kicked in, along with an underlying sense of anxiety; doubts about his ability; the innate fear that he would be found to be inadequate. Little mental niggles. Winning the contract with IBC-Korea, that had been a dream come true; applicants had come in from all over the world, yet he had been chosen to lead this entire division. Now the weight of the crown hurt his head.

The issue – the genetic information found in rabbits. The Chimpanzee genes had responded well in chromosome implantation. However, the rabbit sequences were accepted on the host chromosome, but remained inactive; no proteins were being made. No amount of cellular or chemical stimulation would wake them from their dormancy. Every single attempt ended in failure. The team's frustration was almost tangible, displayed on their downcast faces.

Karl and his ideas represented the final stage before defeat; if he could not solve this himself, the failure would become official. Karl hated the thought – and his seniors would hold him accountable. It was not an option.

Sitting alone in his office at midday, Karl remained motionless. *This is so irritating*.

The sleeping hypernet portal woke from its inanimate state as he waved his hand. Karl typed 'rabbit' and 'cross species manipulation' onto the virtual keyboard; the letters were projected onto his desk. The latest research and academic information was readily available to all scientists at IBC. Tools to enable them to get their jobs done.

After all, any and all scientific knowledge contributes to the overall progress of the discipline.

IBC had forged affiliations with many of the leading voices in industrial science, creating some unique and incredible links with top universities around the world. Grants and scholarships enabled talented but cash-strapped students to join the scientific community. Such financial assistance also replenished the coffers of struggling deans, and IBC was very generous.

Four journals appeared on his screen. The third one caught his eye. Scanning through the abstract he felt confident that he may just have found the missing keys. 'Download.'

Karl pointed at the journal. The portal responded immediately.

Twenty minutes later, Karl completed the request for further information link at the end of the article. Addressing the enquiry to Louise Dalton at Oxford University, Karl despatched the request with a touch on the plasma screen. Karl had visited Oxford on one occasion, as part of his studies during his time at MIT. A sacred and historical place.

+++

Karl was glad to be back in his office, the team meeting had been so tense. An incoming message flashed in the corner of his screen. He touched the image immediately. Louise Dalton – the header of the email added to his excitement. By the time Karl had finished reading the article, he knew beyond a shadow of doubt that IBC could break though the ominous barrier.

During her M.Sc. at Oxford, Dalton had solved the inactivity problems associated with rabbit genes. Two keys were needed to reactivate the genes: temperature control and the presence of an inhibitor that would stop the action of the regulator genes. Such regulator genes turned off the activity of the main genes responsible for making all the structures in a rabbit. So simple; yet for the uninitiated, a hidden mystery. And one missed by Karl and his team. Epigenetics at work.

He fired off a quick reply to Louise, thanking her for her speed and efficiency, and for solving his problem. He agreed to let her know how things progressed. A copy of the journal was sent to all members of the project team at IBC along with a reminder that if they wanted to stay ahead of the game, they should not forget the basics of gene operation. He smiled to himself – *another problem solved*.

Thanks Louise! After a little consideration, Karl sent an email to the Human Resources Division. It recommended Louise as a potential recruit.

THE CURE FOR MUSCULAR DYSTROPHY

Despite the dazzling effect of the flashing bulbs, Dr Winwood continued to smile as he looked in her direction.

'Would you mind explaining how the treatment works?' Angela felt so smug. Her appearance could be described as professional yet alluring, her prime position in the room giving her a great opportunity to make an impression very time she spoke.

What a scoop: to be the lead person in the questioning section of the presentation! And a meal with Dr Winwood, an extremely handsome man, and one with a great deal of influence.

'In this treatment we have combined nanotechnology with a traditional vaccine. Let me take you back to the relevant section in my presentation.' Karl eye-scanned the presentation section of his Generation I tablet. With three swipes of his right hand the slide-show moved onto the first picture of a nanobot. It took on a 3D aspect. Angela watched as Karl rotated the virtual image until it was central to the viewing panel; the screen mimicking the activity of the Generation I tablet.

'Nanobots are miniature robots which are nanometres in size. You can see a typical bacterium in the right hand corner of the slide so that you can get an idea of scale. We cover them with cell membrane which is made up of phospholipids. Once they have been programmed we inject them into the bloodstream where they will migrate to their assigned areas.'

Karl's voice filled the auditorium with slow and measured tones; his command of the technical language was more than indicative of his experience in the field; it was also a show of his authority.

'We can use a scanner to monitor their progress – and to make sure that they do not get lost.' The crowd laughed, Angela too.

'The nanobots reach their chosen area, enter the nucleus and then begin to repair the damaged DNA, replacing defective sections with functional ones.' The visual display illustrated everything he described.

Angela could not help thinking that Karl... *well, he's unavoidably hot.*

'The new DNA is then read and the correct protein will be made by that cell. We use the colour absorbance and individual frequency of these correct proteins to show that the treatment has been affected. The protein song changes when the nanobots have done their job.'

She raised her hand, 'What happens to the nanobots after the treatment?'

Karl's pre-presentation coaching session had included the order of the questions. She was happy to play along with his forceful manner. He'd agreed to take her out to the Beethoven Bistro in Pohang. Getting a reservation at that place was almost impossible; bookings were made up to three months in advance. The food though, was truly heavenly. Angela could feel her mouth-watering as she toyed with the thought.

'Once the nanobots have finished their task, they are deactivated and the membrane coating begins to break down. The normal cellular responses take over and the nanobots are eliminated by way of the most suitable bodily fluid – sweat or urine.' A few flashes from the cameras of the audience made Karl wince. He continued, 'During the treatment we use immune suppressor drugs to reduce the likelihood of this happening before this stage of the process.'

Another group of reporters extended their hands. Karl picked out Hugo from the Herald Tribunal, her rival. 'Why do you use vaccines?'

'Vaccines are central to this whole process. We use them to enable the body to destroy the viruses that cause the damage in the first place. All of our hard work would be undone if we failed to deal with the initial cause of muscular dystrophy. Both treatments take place alongside each other.'

'What about the cost?' The question was firmly spoken and came from the back of the auditorium. She turned to look at the speaker.

'Though initially more expensive than conventional treatment, our outcomes are permanent and allow normal life to be resumed. No drug on the market offers this hope. With intensive therapy, normal muscle function can be restored.'

Karl glanced down at the figures on his sheet. *He's probably checking his figures.* Her assumption seemed to be correct.

'Treatments start at five thousand dollars with maintenance coming in at around five hundred dollars every two years. Compare that with two to four thousand dollars per year on conventional drug therapy – conventional drug therapy with very limited results, taking place while the patient undergoes a slow and painful death.'

Yes, Karl was interesting. A measured and persuasive speaker. She wasn't sure which she was looking forward to more – the food, or the company?

+++

Louise sat transfixed by the broadcast. *We finally have a cure for muscular dystrophy*. She wept unashamedly as she remembered her promise to Adrian. IBC had fulfilled one of her lifelong dreams. She felt indebted to them, almost overwhelmed by a sense of gratitude. Somehow she secretly hoped to find a way to contribute to the future success of this outstanding biotech pioneer.

During her time at Oxford, IBC had funded a number of scholarships for talented students in the area of biomedical research and genetics; and to top it all her recent correspondence with Dr Karl Winwood had been pleasant. *Good for them!*

The science item soon replaced by a piece on global fuel development. She made a mental note to get hold of the data on muscular dystrophy and to scrutinise the results for herself. Still, this was truly amazing.

She had a lecture with undergrads scheduled for the afternoon. Realising that she needed to get her act together; her factsheet still lacked some key information. There would no way she could fool them; like generations before them, they were too smart for that.

+++

Karl was glad that the ordeal was over. Though he loved the limelight, it intensified his feelings of insecurity and his sense of vulnerability tended to go off the Richter scale. His breathing was returning to normal. He felt sure that tiny beads of perspiration had coalesced all over his body. He'd been worried that the mini rivulets might create streaks in his light-touch make-up.

A heavy hand rested on his shoulder. 'Well done Karl, you were great.' He turned, seeing a beaming smile on the lips of his line manager. Deep down he wanted Max Augustine to mentor him, show him the ropes, be like an older brother. But it was just a dream, of course.

'Thank you, thank you Max.' Karl felt tears sting his eyes. He'd done something right.

Was he was accepted?

His mind slipped back to his childhood; Once Daddy had come home, only to announce to his frightened mother that his son would amount to nothing. He remembered that Daddy had been drinking at the time. The success of the moment, here, now, seemed to ease the memory back out of existence.

Karl smiled back, unaware that he had paused for a second, expressionless.

Max studied the younger man's face for a second, smiling, before continuing. 'The shareholders are delighted and the share price is going through the roof. More projects are in the pipeline.' His tone revealed his exuberance. 'More finance to explore new areas of uncharted frontiers. Karl, we are on the way.'

Max leaned towards Karl, staring into his eyes. The look was dark and piercing; a strange coldness inhabited what should have been a close and personal moment. Karl felt the chill and a sudden sense of fear.

Like he was an object on sale; handled, evaluated then owned, the property of IBC. *What? That's a weird thought?* 'I owe you so much. You—' Max interrupted Karl with a brush of his hand.

'We are glad that you work for us, Karl. You have a great future ahead of you. Very bright. Maybe a raise is in order. Come and see me when things quieten down. Let's keep this between you and me for now.'

Karl nodded. Feeling confused, elated, exhausted and excited all at the same time. He wanted to lie down but knew that the adrenaline kick would keep him upright during the looming party and probably into the early hours of the morning too. Icilda Biotech Company – now firmly on the genetic manipulation map. After twenty four years, their moment of glory had arrived.

He and Jim Beam would celebrate later. Maybe Glenda could join them.

EYES THAT SEE

FRIDAY 25TH APRIL 2025

Ahn Jong-kyu thought fondly of his two sons at home. He should have been concentrating on the meeting of the Business and Finance committee, taking place in the central meeting room at IBC-Korea. The combination of the air-conditioning and the monotonous tone of the speaker from Bio-clothing Inc. caused his concentration to drift.

Dong-Sun was six, while Du-Ho had just turned four. Lively and inquisitive, having them brought joy and happiness to the lives of Ahn Jong-kyu and Eu Mi. A pertinent question from Charles brought him back to reality.

'What do you think, Ahn?'

Ahn Jong-kyu swallowed hard, before responding. He could tell, from the tapping of his pen on the desk, that Charles was eager to hear the figure work before proceeding with this new venture.

'Ah... sounds pricey.' He paused giving himself time to gather his thoughts. Shuffling through the papers in front of him he spotted the relevant column of figures relating to the last time the uniform at IBC-

Korea was altered. 'This will necessitate an increase in the budget of almost ten percent.'

His confident response reassured the Finance committee assembled in the room. Those in attendance included Max, Charles and a number of familiar faces from the IBC Executive Committee, some of them belong to the organisation called *the Light*. Ahn had never been offered membership. In some ways that irked him. Members were known to have a great deal of benefits and favours.

The rep was far from defeated. With evangelistic fervour she expounded the immense value of biosensors in monitoring the welfare of staff. The biosensors, which could be incorporated into the clothing, monitored the bodily functions of the staff members such as skin temperature, heart rate, breathing rate and other important indicators of health. When employees enter the premises by undergoing retinal scans and fingerprint analysis, the biosensors in the clothing would be activated and begin recording vital information.

As employees logged out, the personal information could be downloaded and stored on the central database. The vast quantities of data were instantly analysed by the health awareness software programme. Should there be any signs of health issues, the programme alerted a hospital technician who could then initiate further investigations. The new range of clothing included enhanced microbe resistance further reducing the chances of bacterial or viral infection. Another rep modelled the laboratory coats – in a range of colours styled for male and female members of staff.

Charles liked the concept but wanted to know how much the bill would be should they decide to take on the new clothing range.

'As we are a long-standing client, what kind of discount could we hope to secure, especially if we are bulk buying?'

The gauntlet had been laid.

Somewhat flustered by the direct questions, the rep looked down at her notes, wishing that the relevant figure-work would jump enthusiastically in her direction. It did not.

The meeting ended shortly after this exchange. She left unsure as to whether she had been victorious or not while Charles talked the matter over with Ahn Jong-kyu, who, on this occasion, paid full attention to the conversation.

Dong-Sun and Du-Ho jumped on their daddy the minute he came through the door.

'Daddy!'

They screamed it at the top of the voices. Eu Mi told them to be quiet and not to disturb their father. Ahn Jong-kyu was quietly delighted by the affectionate welcome. Chung Cha smiled as she greeted her son-in-law, bowing before him. He bowed in response. Chung Cha had come to visit them and would remain for a few days.

Ahn Jong-kyu loved his mother-in-law. She was cheerful and good natured. The boys adored her; she loved them, and she told them so every possible occasion. This generous outpouring of love felt foreign to Ahn Jong-kyu who came from a much more reserved family. However, her impact had forced him to reflect, he now showed much more emotion towards his children. Even Eu Mi took on the task of daily telling her children how much she valued and loved them.

The death of her husband had wounded her deeply; she had relied heavily upon him in most matters of life, including finance. Suddenly she was alone and important decisions required her attention.

Then Chung Cha had started attending that strange church in central Pohang, and, since then, she seemed to have changed. Before that encounter she had been engulfed by her depression; becoming a recluse. Even her grandchildren had been unable to bring her back from that place of isolation.

One of her neighbours invited her to a religious service at the church; a lively, spiritual gathering, near the bustling market. From that time she became a new person. Even Eu Mi could not believe the transformation. The gentleness and love that flowed from her surprised her daughter. Her childlike laughter filled the house; Eu Mi enjoyed her visits so much. It was like having a new mother.

Later that evening, Chung Cha asked Ahn Jong-kyu how things were going at work. He responded politely, not wanting to give too much information away.

'I am an old woman, widowed and retired.' She spoke with sincerity, but he noted the girlish sparkle in her eyes, 'I have many hours to spend with the Lord, in fellowship and prayer. I have been given many dreams and the gift of dream interpretation. Some call it a spiritual gift; before I knew the Lord I used to dream, I had many dreams, lots of them. None of them meant anything. Since meeting Him, I have been able to understand many things from the past,' she paused and smiled slyly. 'And then there are the things He is teaching me now.' She hesitated before continuing, 'You could say that I am a mature student.'

Peals of laughter filled the room as she rocked on her seat. Ahn Jong-kyu could not help joining in. She had changed so much. Still, a part of him wondered why she was disclosing this information.

Eu Mi poured her mother a fresh cup of ginger tea, her favourite. The steam generated a gentle mist, its fragrance filling the room. Chung Cha sipped from her cup, quietly thanking her daughter who bowed gently before returning to the kitchen.

Chung Cha continued, 'Since I asked the Lord into my life, more dreams have come. Some for me, some for the church, others…' she pointed at Ahn Jong-kyu, suddenly sincere again, 'for people who do not yet know Him.'

Her words caused an internal wall to spring up causing him to struggle with the new sensations that surfaced, suddenly he felt the need to defend himself. His beliefs were in the ancestral gods; he even made regular sacrifices at the local temple. Chung Cha had left the ancient path to follow one called Yeshua, a Jewish teacher. Departing from the old ways was unheard of in their culture, unheard of in their family history. However the whole family had judged her conversion only by the transformation it had brought about – but he was uncomfortable with this new direction she had chosen.

And what exactly does she mean by "other people who do not know Him?" It's as if she's talking about a real living person, not a god.

She'd never preached at him before; instead she politely answering any questions that he'd had for her but nothing more. It had been encouraging. Eu Mi even suggested that they visit the woman's strange church out of respect, but he had declined. He was happy with what he had always known. It was good enough for his ancestors, it would serve him too. Still he listened attentively, curious.

'My church has run a number of courses on dream interpretation. I seem to have picked it up very easily. Can I explain the process to you?'

Ahn Jong-kyu nodded, his mind racing. Something in him felt excited, yet the internal resistance remained.

'There are three stages to understanding dreams. The first one is the dream itself, the second, understanding the symbols used in the dream. Each dream is personal, so you need to understand the person who has the dream and the unique meaning they attach to the symbols. The last stage is the most difficult, this is application. What do you do with the dream?'

She paused and looked at her watch before continuing, 'There is a famous dreamer in the Bible called Daniel – he had many dreams and understood them. As a result he was able to guide many kings and make wise decisions. He lived in the era of the Babylonian kingdom, where the Jews were being held in captivity.'

Eu Mi continued cleaning up the dishes from the meal. Ahn Jong-kyu knew she was listening. The elongated pauses between the sounds of her clearing the plates and dishes from the dining room gave her away; it was not like her.

'Now let me tell you about the dream that I had… about you.'

The tips of his ears burned. He swallowed twice. Part of him wanted to know, part of him wanted to avoid the knowledge.

She described how in the dream she saw Ahn Jong-kyu sitting at his desk, working on some accounts. A stranger walked in and handed him three scrolls. When he opened them words and music jumped out; lively, cartoon animations dancing before his eyes. The symbols descended, forming a message on the scrolls. Words such as "deceit," strange creatures and images of death now visible on the scrolls. Two diagrams stood out, one of clothes covered in eyes and the other a ladder descending down towards a pit of shadows. The dream had ended at that point.

Ahn Jong-kyu struggled to breathe as he listened, covering his mouth with one hand, hiding his trembling lips. He felt a draining sensation on his face, a warm shift downwards.

It was the same dream… the one he had been having for almost three months.

She smiled at him and stood up, walking towards the kitchen eager to help her daughter.

He leaned back on the couch, grateful that Chung Cha had left. To hear that someone else shared the experience shocked him yet also filled him with wonder. He had not even told Eu Mi. This experience felt unnatural, nothing in his rational mind could make sense of it. *A shared spiritual experience? Why would it happen to her and to me?*

Time to think. An accountant at IBC-Korea – a dream job. The salary, the opportunity and the security. Now he was confronted with the suggestion that there might be something sinister going on. *But only in the form of a shared dream!* He considered himself a man of honour, one who helped others, one who believed in respecting all. Now he began questioning everything.

Of course, there had been times when he queried some of the financial matters, some of the decision making; but he had never felt as if his morals had been compromised. In the past it had simply been a matter of perspectives, the views of the West contrasting with the views of the East.

They emphasised the individual and their rights, he believed in the considering the impact on the group. It sometimes resulted in different conclusions about strategies and objectives but it never made him feel uncomfortable.

Chung Cha returned, still smiling. She sat down and asked him for permission to continue. He nodded.

'I will begin with the symbols first. The stranger represents someone who you do not know. But, perhaps in time, you will get to know this person. All friends were once strangers who we become acquainted with.'

He nodded again, that made sense.

'What do scrolls mean to you?' She asked.

'When I think of scrolls I think of learning and books… that means knowledge.'

She winked playfully, 'I agree with you. Our search for knowledge is often symbolised by books. The fact they were scrolls suggests that it is ancient knowledge, we do not use scrolls anymore. Had they been computer files I suspect you would have felt at home. Perhaps these are things of more or older importance.' She paused to sip from her cup of ginger tea. 'Our desire to look into these matters can show our inquisitiveness about things or even our need to know we are moving in the right direction.'

Eu Mi sat next to him, squeezing his hand as she leaned against him. She looked tired. Tonight she had taken the boys to bed, despite their requests to stay up with Grandma.

'Three scrolls, this is interesting. Three points make a triangle, or symbolising unity. Such as the Three in the Godhead.'

Another preposterous belief that she held. *How could there ever be three gods, one of them becoming a man and then being raised from the dead?*

'I am not sure about that meaning here,' Chung Cha rubbed her finger along her bottom lip, 'I will continue to ponder on that.'

Eu Mi snuggled closer to Ahn Jong-kyu, eyeing him; he sensed her interest in their conversation.

'The words and music, it seems as if there is life in the message. This is a living message, something that is real; something that is growing, unfolding. It possesses life. Well perhaps it has been given life and now it lives.' Her voice trailed off.

He wished that he had recorded her words, but he felt too embarrassed to ask her to stop and start again. He would try to remember everything she said.

She clapped her hands, causing him and Eu Mi to jump. 'I see. Thank you Lord!'

What? It was as if she was having a conversation with an invisible person.

There it was again, that sparkle in her eyes. 'The words are very clear, though I am not sure about the strange creatures. In my mind I am seeing mixtures of species, like the images of the Egyptian god – a combination of falcon and human. I do not know what this means.'

Neither do I, thought Ahn Jong-kyu.

Eu Mi remained silent.

'Your company is involved in genetic experiments though is it not? My generation know so little of these matters.' Chung Cha drained her cup of ginger tea, Eu Mi offered to get her another she declined.

The creeping, nervous sensation made his stomach tighten. The meal had been wonderful, but now he wondered if he could be able to keep it inside. Waves of nausea moved up and down his oesophagus. Rapid peristaltic movements, up and down.

Suddenly, he was not so sure about this dream job. He knew that the company did experiments in genetics, mixing different species. That was nothing new to anyone interested in the scientific community. He had no particular objections to their work. And ancient gods often depicted possessing human and animal characteristics, *take for instance Ganesh of the Hindu or the Egyptian gods like Anubis, half human and half jackal.* That was science fiction to him. Now though, her words made it seem as if there could be some danger in what he had presumed to be an otherwise wholesome practice. Not just her words though, the fact that she had seen his dreams. He could not explain that.

'What do you think about the clothes?' She questioned Ahn Jong-kyu.

'Clothes? Everyone wears them. They cover up our nakedness.'

She nodded as he spoke. 'Yes, you are right, clothes can often represent the persona or façade we present to others; one that may cover up the true intention of our motives. Eyes are symbols of sight, observation and discernment.' She leaned forward, her voice quiet. 'Perhaps wisdom or even enlightenment? I have never heard of clothes that can give wisdom.'

She leaned her head to one side. 'Clothing can have magical power, carrying the presence of the wearer. No, I have no clear understanding of what that means.' She closed her eyes, rolling her teeth over her bottom lip. 'The ladder, she opened her eyes, 'suggests moving from one situation to another, downwards seems to suggest going from a worse situation to an even more dangerous situation.' Chung Cha's jaw tightened, deep creases showing at the sides of her mouth, her voice barely a whisper.

He could feel Eu Mi trembling beside him. This was serious. By now the evening had grown dark, the sky taking on an inky colour. Time had slipped away. He coughed loudly, if only to break the silence, got up and closed the curtains; turning up the lights as he waved his hand in front of the dimmer switch.

Chung Cha had her eyes closed, her lips moving slightly, yet making no sound. *Was she meditating?* As she opened her eyes, a bluish glow seemed to emanate from them. He blinked and it was gone.

'Ahn Jong-kyu; you are being shown truth about your work. You have wanted to know if you are going in the right direction. This dream is to help you, to guide you. The application of this dream.' Her voice was suddenly stern. The humour had vanished. She had realised something. She breathed in, and then stood up, suddenly animated, 'You will have to make some very important choices in the days that lie ahead. There are hidden things taking place at your workplace, things that your people do not fully understand, but there will be grave consequences for their decisions.'

She paced as she spoke, moving in a small circle. Eu Mi sat on the edge of the couch staring at the older woman. Ahn Jong-kyu was shocked by the look on his wife's face, it was obvious that she had never seen her mother like this before.

Chung Cha stopped and smiled; her face was radiant, almost glowing. 'You will be given wisdom when the time comes. You will seek and you will find.'

His heart thumped in his chest, along with a tight sensation in his back. These were powerful words; he could feel them entering into his body, as sound waves that hit his bones and organs.

Living words.

She sat down, her face emanating light. 'In case you might not remember these words,' she reached for her handbag next to her chair. 'I have written for you.'

Chung Cha handed Ahn Jong-kyu a folded piece of white paper. 'It is all here, the dream, the meaning of the symbols from my perspective and the application. Perhaps the Lord will give me more information in the future?'

Her voice had returned to its usual timbre. She smiled at him again and extended her hand, offering the notes to him.

His hand trembled as he took them.

'Thank you Chung Cha. This has been… enlightening.' He hoped to continue the conversation in the morning before work.

She looked at her watch again. 'I must go to my room and spend some time with my Lord.' He nodded, not fully understanding her response. 'You can ask me any questions that you have tomorrow or afterwards. I will do my best to answer.'

Eu Mi spoke, 'Mother, do you need anything else?'

'No, my daughter.' She looked at Ahn Jong-kyu. 'You have work tomorrow and you need time to think. Tonight has been a very special time for all of us.' She stifled a yawn behind her hand.

'Chung Cha, thank you for sharing. You have given me a lot to consider I am grateful. I did not know that dreams could be shared in this way I have had the same dream many times.'

He watched her eyes grow wide, her mouth half open as if frozen in time. 'He has already shown you.' He nodded sheepishly, 'Then this is confirmation. It will surely come to pass.'

She had that faraway look in her eyes. *What does she mean?*

'What a wonderful evening. I will kiss my two sleeping beauties before I retire.'

Ahn Jong-kyu sighed deeply, as they left the living room, the feeling of panic raining down on him, filling him with cold fear. If Chung Cha was right then the work at IBC-Korea concealed more than could be seen with the eye. This dream was a warning – dark and sinister, perhaps even dangerous things were happening at IBC-Korea.

That night, Ahn Jong-kyu struggled to fall asleep. He remained awake, listening to Eu Mi's breathing. His mind raced. He was afraid, scared that, if he did sleep, the dream would come back. Hour after hour passed and he tossed and turned, gently tormented by the images so familiar to his night vision.

The alarm woke him up. He had fallen asleep but had not dreamt.

In fact, the dreams never returned.

THE RECRUITMENT DRIVE

MONDAY 28TH APRIL 2025

'Hello, Cornelius McDermott speaking.'

He actually wanted to say *Hello Professor McDermott speaking*. Today was not going well, his meeting with the Dean had reached stalemate – he was no closer to getting a pay rise or the professorship. Now he faced those unenthusiastic second year students this afternoon – why was he wasting his talent?

'Good afternoon, this is Phillippe Bernard, Head of Human Resources at IBC.'

IBC? Cornelius had heard of the company but remained at a loss as to why they were calling him. *Do they need some of my work, consultancy advice?*

'I would like you to consider taking a post with us in our Korean branch in Pohang.'

Cornelius would have dropped the phone, if it was not clamped between his neck and left ear. 'You want to offer me a job?' That seemed ridiculous, bordering on fantastical.

'Yes, we need a Head of department for our Cloning Division and you seemed like the ideal candidate. Perhaps I could explain our position?'

Now Cornelius was listening.

His undergraduate years at Edinburgh University had flown by and, on the whole, he enjoyed being part of the Roslin Institute. Closely following in the wake of Dolly the sheep; she had ended up being preserved in formaldehyde or something similar, he passed her corpse on a regular basis. He had won several prizes for his essays on cloning and his practical expertise in the laboratory, secretly the envy of the rest of his cohort.

Staying at Edinburgh for his MSc had made logical sense. Then the thrill of applying and being accepted on the doctorate programme at Cambridge, followed by the sense of fulfilment at the completion of the course after four years. Securing a teaching post at Imperial College immediately after the doctorate – well that was simply the icing on the academic cake.

Delivering his thesis had been one of the most nerve-wracking moments of his entire life. Then had come the writing... it had not only served as display, post-doctoral work, but had also brought his ideas into the public eye. He had published several books in quick succession.

The first considered a breakthrough in the link between cloning and human development, another beat on the drum for the developing school of transhumanism and the mantra, '*Progression towards Perfection*' became a major hit in the scientific community. Cornelius' style of writing had made his books accessible to non-scientists too, and his readership was wide. Television appearances and radio interviews followed.

Frequent teasing by other members of staff at Imperial centred on his newfound celebrity; on his importance to the wider, industrial, scientific community, despite the fact that he no longer had much time to spend either in laboratories or lecture theatres. There had been talk of a series of TV programmes aimed at making science more appealing to the wider population. This had fizzled into nothing. A great disappointment after so much excitement.

Of all his works, one had generated more controversy than he had expected. Titled '*The Future is for The Brave*', many of his critics accused him of revisiting the contentious field of eugenics, his public appeal seemed to wane. Hate mail followed, his brush with celebrity status seemed to be over. His controversial views also came to the attention of the authorities at the Imperial. A number of emergency meetings were held.

They had grilled him; thankfully he had not fallen to pieces, handling the issues that were voiced and proving beyond a shadow of doubt that he possessed sound ethical beliefs; and that he was still committed to his work at Imperial. However, it had opened the door for ongoing and uncomfortable discussions.

Well at least he had a job – though this would be his third year of at Imperial; his third year of feeling unappreciated.

Pushing for a professorship – in some ways it was similar to military warfare, requiring strategy and determination; battling against a very solid red brick wall. Memories of today's heated meeting were fresh in his mind.

Now IBC are offering me a job?

Phillippe presented a convincing case, they had read all of his works and were familiar with his CV and published papers. They had been following his profile on Sci-Link for some time – now he was glad he had forked out the exorbitant subscription. Of course, he would have to apply but they were sure he would be successful. Would he think about it?

The bleep marked the end the conversation.

Now his mind was spinning. A chance to be part of something so incredible with people who understood his way of thinking and the figures Phillippe had mentioned were astronomical. No professor earned that kind of salary at university level. His talent would be recognised.

Mum would be pleased too, and now he would have no excuse for not visiting. It was considerably easier to travel from South Korea to her native Australia.

Isn't it amazing how one call can change your day or your life.

Tuesday 27th May 2025

STAFF MEMORANDUM
TO ALL MEMBERS OF STAFF IN SCIENTIFIC DEPARTMENTS

Date: 27/05/25

Notification of Uniform Changes

As from 1st September 2025, all members of scientific departments will be required to wear the new regulation uniform whilst on duty. You will be hypermailed for your preferences regarding the colour and style of your uniform. Please indicate your size.

This new initiative will be of great benefit in your efforts to serve you and look after your health needs as they uniforms will benefit from the latest biosensors as well as the latest stain resistance coating.

The old uniform will be collected the day before, collection details will be sent to you.

All queries should be sent to Bernard@ibc-korea.com

IBC-Korea... building a family at work

Saturday 20th September 2025

Yet another request for a new cloning project. Cornelius was exasperated. Since joining IBC-Korea, his workload had more than doubled. Had he made the right decision in taking on the post?

At this particular moment in time he was having serious doubts.

Thursday 4th December 2025

The combination of adventure, an amazing salary and the thought of being part of such a pioneering organisation were too much for Chloe to pass up. Even during her brief time in South Korea, Chloe had convinced herself she could make a successful life in Pohang. Most of her debts could be paid off within two years as there were no accommodation costs and food was included.

This is incredible!

The cherry on the cake? Only being a research scientist at one of the most renowned biotech companies in the world. Can this really get any better?

Bethany could not stop crying when Chloe broke the devastating news, though she had been aware of her trip to South Korea, a permanent move had not been seriously considered.

Chloe decided to accept the position with IBC-Korea and her new life would begin on 3rd January 2026. That meant leaving before the end of the month – just after Christmas.

From Arizona to Massachusetts, now off to South Korea. Her baby had flown the nest, and then country, on oriental wings.

The thrill of adventure awaited her. Chloe found it hard to put into words. What more could she hope for?

PART IV

THE LIVING DOLL

PROJECT BEGINS

I B C - KOREA

Icilda Biotech Company – Korea
Inspiring future hope

CHRONOS

BUILDING THE DREAM TEAM

The revolutionary visual-audio news update lasted less than ninety seconds.

The brief announcement caused an upheaval in societal order and an earthquake in the scientific community; it allowed the legal modification of the human gene pool, forever transforming future generations. *Homo sapiens.* The term needed redefining. The genetic tweaking would produce progeny that needed to be classified, leading to fierce debate among the finest academic minds on the planet as they considered the potential evolutionary pathway of the new creations. Which species would be first to re-merge with their long lost relatives, the current rulers of the planet?

The Gaia International Institute had served as a shop front, propounding the central belief behind the intellectual and philosophical revolution; their funding supported by *the Light* and other influential groups who shared their ideals. A carefully planned, long term strategy, based on a sixty year plan, lay behind the shift in thinking; the initial architects including Alice Bailey and other significant prophetic voices, each heralding the new phase of enlightenment.

One hotly contested question: whose name would be associated with the new species? The silent starter's pistol opened an unofficial race to be the first to push through this sacred, invisible barrier; the privilege of having one's name immortalised, stirring curiosity and vanity amongst the scientific community.

The passing of the UN Treaty on Saturday January 10th 2026 signalled a moment of triumph for scientists chomping at the bit to carry out experiments based on incorporating the genes of other species into the human genome. The treaty on the uniqueness of all species recognised that all species had equal rights to exist, humans no longer held a unique position in the world, simply representing an expression of life.

Voting had been tense, the majority of the delegates on the Security Council were strongly in favour; others were vehement in their dissent. The majority vote resulted in an immediate decision. A number of delegates walked out, vowing never to return to what one irate representative said had amounted to a global dictatorship. Recent changes in voting procedure made it harder to veto any action sanctioned by the majority of members. History was strewn with too many examples wherein millions had lost their lives on account of a political delay at the UN.

With one ruling, the doors to cross-species investigation had been thrown open. Mixing other species with the human gene pool – no longer forbidden; the resulting entities would be named chimeras. Their place in the future, legally recognised and protected.

Supported by Amnesty International and a host of welfare agencies, The International Human Rights Committee fought long and hard to ensure that chimeras would not be treated as second class citizens; to set it in stone, that they would share all the legal rights of their human relatives. The right to freedom of speech, marriage, procreation, the vote, social benefits and access to housing – the list went on. The debates rolled on for months before the announcement. Finally, the persuasion and bickering translated into a framework for action.

Their hope was that other, future bio-technological developments would also be covered by the proposed bill. After all, nanotechnology was already widely accepted, robotic incorporation was now being discussed by leaders in all walks of society, adding artificial intelligence to organic processes was no longer seen as being anything other than normal.

The latter of these had been world changing in an immediate sense. Slavery was almost entirely seen as a thing of the past, robotic household auxiliaries made human labour unnecessary. They served in homes, hospitals, schools, state buildings, all types of industries; from agriculture to manufacture – the list of tasks was continually growing.

Those countries that accepted the resolution now set about incorporating the ruling into their national laws – more talks, more debates, more committees. A number of nations expressed their disgust and dismay, refusing to comply with its demands – they included the USA, parts of Europe (including the UK) and large sections of the Middle East. The world divided by the reassignment of order in *Kingdom Animalia*.

Viewing the announcement from the Internet portal in his office Karl Winwood, could not contain his joy. Instead, he cried out with delight. The forbidden things buried in the scientific subconscious could now emerge from their deep sleep, take form and become living matter – from subdued vision, flying into bright reality. He punched the air violently, several times, before letting out another delighted cheer.

The nervous knock on the door indicated that this was totally out of character. His PA, Ae Sook Chang, checked to make sure he was feeling alright, he watched her return to her work station through the viewing panel in his office door. Karl smiled to himself, swivelling several times on his leather chair. *At long last.*

Karl knew that the theoretical groundwork was already laid within the scientific community; the official race was now on. Rabbits and humans had already been combined genetically back in 2011. The embryos had been allowed to exist for up to the eleven days. That was then. Karl wondered just how many undercover experiments had gone on? How many foetuses were hidden away in secret places? Silently testifying to the fact that you did not have to wait until things are legally accepted in order to venture into virgin territory. Nobody would dare announce that his or her creations had gone to full term, never officially anyway.

If IBC were to be the first to have a breakthrough in the embryonic aspects of this unique technology... there could be opportunities well beyond Karl's wildest dreams.

Cyborgs – he thought: the combination of machine and human tissue, a synthesis and the organic with the manufactured machine. Elegantly portrayed in *Star Trek – First Contact* – a race of living machines.

What about other species being incorporated into the human gene pool? What abilities might be transferred?

His personal favourite, a fantasy of sorts, the idea of a combination of man and fish – aquatic and terrestrial. Was the city of Atlantis a myth or part of human history? He didn't know. But he did know, maybe new technologies could make it possible? He loved Patrick Duffy in the role of *The Man from Atlantis* – breathing with lungs and gills.

Cool – ultra cool.

Then what about human and alien species – the intergalactic cooperation modelled by the crew of *Starship Enterpise*. That was a little beyond him at present. He often thought that physics lagged behind biochemistry, robotics and computer science in recent years. *We can build new species so easily, but all we have to speak for space exploration is a fleet of unmanned rovers and satellites.* Nonetheless, he concluded, the possibilities were endless.

For the next hour he immersed himself in mapping out how his department's current projects could be redirected, adjusting to the new industrial climate while his people took hurried steps towards the creation of the first human chimeras. Other projects could be put on hold – *at least for a while.*

'Ae Sook, can you arrange a meeting with Esther as soon as possible? I am around till 18.00 this evening, Make it as soon as possible, top priority. I really mean that.'

The new portal face allowed digitally clear visual connection with the speaker as well as conscious group interfacing – technology never remained stationary. She looked nervous, the creases at the junction of her nose and forehead gave away her anxiety. 'Yes Karl. I will set this up immediately. Do you realise you have a meeting with Max at 14.00? He is flying back from London and should be in his office by—' she glanced at the clock face on her desk pad, '13.30. I'll let you know if there are any delays.'

'Thanks Ae Sook,' Karl responded politely.

With a touch of the sensor the display took on the IBC-Korea logo. Those last comments worried him – *Max is coming back from London!* The thought made his jaw muscle tighten clamping his teeth together, like a tetanus victim. This could be tricky. Max wanted an answer to the question that bugged Karl since that meeting in December. He toyed over the possible answers.

As much as he wanted to see things change he could not work alone. Just how much was he prepared to pay for the realisation of his vision of the future? Max was persuasive and direct, as the President and CEO of IBC he held a great deal of influence within the company and within the wider business world. Joining could mean everything. Powerful people with unlimited finances – the missing ingredients.

Was he ready to join them? Karl moved towards his office window that gave an extensive view of the pristine local bay.

He sighed deeply as he contemplated the possible consequences of his decision.

+++

Max did not tolerate lateness. Time and money merged; he had a reputation – dealing harshly with those who did not live by the same philosophy. Positions and promotions had been won and lost on this aspect of performance. Karl's knowledge of this prompted his early arrival outside Max's office at 13.45. He sat, feeling restless and disliking the growing tightness in the pit of his stomach. The question would come up at some point in the conversation, he wanted to be ready.

The oak door swung open. Max's frame silhouetted by the bright Korean sunlight. His silhouette emanating a glowing aura. Karl thought of familiar alien entry scenes from *Star Trek* episodes; the glare of the radiance forcing him to squint. For just a brief moment, he was mesmerised.

'Karl, good of you to come.' Max's voice broke the spell, Karl rose eagerly from his seat. *Like he had a choice.*

Max extended his right hand towards his potential protégé. The firm grip, displaying strength from both sides, suggesting equality and respect. Max let go of Karl's hand first before gesturing towards the low upholstered chair in front of his desk, smiling broadly during the action.

Karl accepted his place, hating it; being submissive unnerved him, leaving with a heightened sense of vulnerability. Having no power in a relationship; for him that amounted to no clear boundary, reality without definition. The scene felt dreamlike yet he knew his future rested on his ability to carry out his role with faultless execution. Karl kept his eyes on the floor on the floor as he walked to his seat. He hesitated, fighting the natural instinct to sit down, waiting for further instruction.

'Sit down Karl, we have much to discuss,' Max's tone seemed warm, his right hand pointing to the seat. Karl obeyed.

'How was your trip to London?' Karl asked, gazing at Max, inwardly hoping he would become his personal mentor. He wanted to make a good impression.

'Profitable, very profitable.' As far as Karl was concerned the answer was succinct, not giving anything away, no personal information. For a brief moment he felt wounded. Max continued to shuffle several sheets on his desk, picking up his Mont Blanc pen.

Like my dad, distracted, never paying attention to me. The thought flashed through Karl's mind and then was gone.

'I am sure you saw the announcements concerning the UN Resolution.' Max tapped his desk with his right index finger. Karl watched the manicured finger as it moved in perfect time, dancing to Max's words.

'I'm meeting with Esther first thing tomorrow morning,' Karl blurted out. 'We want all our research and preparation to put us in a very strong position. IBC could well be the world leader in this new field.' Karl hoped his initiative would impress Max. Then he spotted the signed photograph of Angelina and Brad, blatantly placed on the desk. *He obviously wants it to be seen.*

'Well done, already on the case.' The stare seemed to go right through his soul, Karl shivered. 'You may remember my offer to you last time we met.' He leaned forward, continuing, 'have you considered it?'

The combination of prickly underarm heat and sweaty palms, Karl recognised the symptoms, childhood had tutored him making him an expert on fear. *Calm down Karl, calm down*, he attempted to reassure himself with positive talk. *Everything is going to be all right.*

'I have thought very carefully. I am really honoured that you would consider m—'

'I simply need an answer.' Max held up his hand, the palm turned towards Karl.

'Then my answer is…' Karl's inner battle raged for a fraction of a second, his conscience standing in fierce opposition to his ambition. Conscience versus ambition – why did he have such strong doubts about *the Light*? The right answer could open the door for a new level of relationship with Max, the wrong one might strike a death blow to a promising future. 'Yes.' For the second time in their meeting, Max flashed Karl a full smile exposing teeth and gums.

'Well done Karl.' Once again Max stood, extending his hand. 'I will let you know the next time we meet. You will be in attendance.' The tone of his voice, switching from warmth to ice cold mingled with a strong hint of threat in microseconds.

Max turned away from Karl, moving a few steady paces. He stood in front of the large oil portrait on the wall to the right of his desk. Even from where he was sitting Karl could read the inscription on the gleaming brass plaque: *Lukas Octavius Augustine – Beloved Father*. The resemblance was striking, the same prominent forehead and nose. Max even stood in the same way, impersonating the figure. The two apparently united in purpose and intention.

A twinge of jealousy stabbed at Karl's gut. Something he would never know: paternal intimacy. It stabbed again. Karl folded his arms, considering the ways in which he had missed out. He knew nothing of the harmonious flow, of being together, sharing life, sharing truth, sharing wisdom. An inheritance of life, passing from one ancestor to the next – from father to son.

'I want IBC at the front of this race, not second or third. Do I make myself clear?' The hawk-stare was menacing. Karl felt as if he were shrinking. Being observed like a laboratory specimen under the microscope. Struggling to feel a sense of worth, of value – nothing came to mind.

Max's philosophy was no different to his own, yet hearing it said in that way made it sound foreign. The inner voice expressed its opinion, making him doubt his decision to join *the Light*.

'We recruited you because you were the best. Make sure you do not let me down.' Max spoke emphatically. 'Update me on every stage of the process. Weekly reports will be on my desk first thing on Monday mornings. I want to know everything: what moves, what breathes, who is pushing things forward. Everything.' Max's stern expression slide into a thin smile.

Reassurance, affirmation – Karl had been chosen because he was the best. That helped a lot. He unfolded his arms. *It's okay*. He had no plans to mess with Max Augustine.

'Yes, Max. I will see that you get those reports, starting from next week. We already have some embryos that are ready for transformation. In fact—'

'Thank you for the science briefing.' Still smiling Max continued, 'I want results and I want them—' The bleep of the Internet portal halted the conversation. 'Look, Karl, we will have to continue this conversation another time. I have an important call coming in from the States.' The internet portal continued to bleep. 'If you need anything – and I mean anything – send me an email. You may use my personal account. Thank you for your time.' Max sat down, lifting his right hand in Karl's direction.

Karl's feet bounced on the Aubusson carpet as he made his way towards the door; he was elated, joyous, buoyant, yet he also battled with a sense of failure. Karl, well aware that a wealth of other matters required Max's attention – he was an important person, after all, and wealthy too. Their appointment had reached its natural conclusion and now he was being sent away. He wished they could have talked further, he had so much he wanted to tell Max. So many ideas that bubbled away, ready to tumble out. He kept them in, kept his decorum.

Karl accepted the fact that he was not in control. That truth provoked an intense distaste, but there was nothing he could do about it. Max was bigger fish, older too. Karl admired him and, more to the point, aspired to his position. Feelings of inferiority skittered across his mind; he felt belittled, like he had been ignored and totally disrespected. He knew that it was not true, but that was how he felt. Max demanded a new level of subservience and he would have to put up with it. He would have to be Max's bitch. At least for the foreseeable future. The price of being connected, part of the inner circle. Karl closed the door carefully.

He remained totally unaware that some of the emotions he had just experienced were the daily burden of those who worked for him. He rarely ever did think about his staff's feelings towards him. He was an important man himself. *And busy.*

The door clicked shut. The younger man was gone. Max wondered if Karl could be trusted with… secrets; would he prove to be trustworthy, how would he cope with unquestioning obedience? Membership of *the Light* required absolute commitment, demonstrated by swearing oaths at different levels of accountability. No one could join without being recommended. Since he had introduced Karl, he took on the full responsibility for training and mentoring him.

Max titled his head to one side, allowing a half smile to emerge. Karl could be his pet project. He laughed dryly. So far, the man had shown promise, in great promise in fact. However, his need for affirmation and approval was so painfully obvious. That could have its uses. Max smiled to himself. *The boy really is a needy soul.*

Max's smile passed quickly. He tapped his pen on his desk three times, thoughtfully. Business relied on recognising market needs and being able to satisfy them, without exhausting their origin; it relied on pre-empting those needs. Manufacturing them, typically. Sustaining them, always. Karl's greatest needs would make him vulnerable. That would be an advantage; it would be a form of leverage that he could use to maximum effect.

Young Winwood was a scowling, smooth-faced man; handsome to a fault. Yet driven by ambition. Max nodded to himself – *naked ambition, the fuel of those who might go on to greatness*. It was a strength to be sure, but also, potentially, a blinding weakness. Being a member of *the Light* would help him. After all, its members were rewarded generously. Futures could be made or destroyed by association, and the group had the power to match-make anyone with anyone else amongst its ranks.

Somewhere outside of his head, Max registered the icon, flashing. Somebody was calling him.

He might turn out to be a useful asset, but Karl Winwood will need to be tested first. An active, evolving assessment would be needed; of his loyalty, his competence, his dedication. *And if he passes…* Only time would tell.

He stabbed the incoming call icon.

SUNDAY 11TH JANUARY 2026

When Cornelius started at IBC, Korea his team consisted of twenty-nine employees. The Cloning Team, TCT, made up of two Assistant Heads, three technical supervisors and twenty four technicians. The technicians divided between the three key areas of Natural Science: eight in the Plant Division, twelve in the Animal Division and four in the Human Technology Division.

The launch of the Living Doll Project, LDP, well that called for the reallocation of resources. The number of technicians in Human Technology increased from four to twelve. The plant Division acting the scapegoat, taking a hit for advancement – some of the projects would be passed onto other laboratories within the IBC family; IBC-Russia already fully operational while IBC-Israel was close to completion.

The steady stream of talent that flowed out of Pohang University of

Science and Technology provided a rich supply of skilled and hard-working students, hungry to make an impact on the genetic front. Meanwhile, the Human Resources Division scoured the world seeking out the very best academic minds using Sci-link – an online science job recruiting service housing thousands of regularly updated CVs – and IBC paid well. Backed by such a strong tools for recruitment, progress seemed inevitable. But difficult decisions still needed to be made and this was one of them. The ultimate decision decided by corroboration between the Financial department and the Executive Committee. Cornelius would be allowed to present his case but the final decision was not his. Possessing power yet being limited in its use. The price of being mortal and working for IBC.

The Cloning Division at IBC-Korea provided a key service, one essential to the success of many of the company's wider projects. Under the watchful eye of Cornelius McDermott the Division received requests on a daily basis, some for specimens already in existence, others for new species; ones that were about to be created. In line with the IBC policy on secrecy, much of the work was code named; many of the technicians worked according to their briefs, but with little to no knowledge of the pervious stages of processing that would have taken place on the cells before them. Nor did many of them know what would become of their projects. Questions were of course considered, but never voiced. The extensive use of CCTV surveillance, the digital recording of all meetings, the built in microphones on all computers and devices; all communications could be monitored. These steps were considered to be necessary precautions.

Although the introduction of built in biosensors in laboratory clothing might have been seen by some as an act of professional scrutiny by some, only the top echelons of management had full awareness of this new method of surveillance, along with a few people of the Human Resources Division. It was feared that this new level of integrative security would be perceived as particularly invasive.

With plans to introduce consciousness interfacing in the laboratory, it would only be a matter of time before staff members' patterns of thought would also be logged and checked. The workforce could see it coming, for the most part, but the generous rewards offered by IBC went a long way to compensate for the fact that every aspect of life within the company was available to be scrutinised by HR and Security alike. For most employees this was a price well worth paying; it represented part of an exchange, bringing the opportunity to be involved with cutting edge work, otherwise inaccessible resources and a considerably larger paycheque than anyone else was able to offer. Cornelius might have been dubious about this increasingly emergent culture of surveillance, but he had no complaints about his salary.

The cloning process could be completed at various stages of development from the start of the process, dealing with cloned gametes to natural and genetically modified embryos. With the latest DNA analysis scanner, every piece of genetic merchandise could be checked instantaneously for its genetic purity using MinION which could read the complete human genome in five minutes – this could then be compared with stored genomic records.

Any mutation in genetic composition could be repaired by nanobots. For this reason there was close corroboration between the Cloning Division, the Nanotechnology Division and the Cryogenics Division. Once cloning had completed its processing, samples were always stored for future use by the Cryogenics Division, while the remaining cells were sent back to their respective Divisions – Plant, Animal or Human Technology.

Meticulous recording keeping alongside digital labelling became key skills necessary to prevent chaos from reigning within the Cloning Division. The laboratory managers were carefully selected based on their strength in this area along with a first class academic background. Pressure became a daily part of the job, those who could not handle the workload quickly realised they were out of their depth. The Human Resources Division made fully use of personality profiling along with brain mapping data to ensure they provided scientific evidence that candidates would be able to cope with life in the very fast lane.

Cornelius ticked all the boxes; he was a perfect fit, the head of his department, with his extensive academic record, excellent laboratory practices and sound managerial skills. Nonetheless, he still had to await the outcome of the committee meetings – the long wait.

He had not smoked since he was a teenager however the stress of this new work had awakened the latent, nicotine hungry taste buds on his tongue and alerted the appropriate receptors in his brain. He was rediscovering the craving. The final outcome was due to be announced at 17.00. He checked his smartphone again; it was only 16.30. He had just finished his eighth cigarette of the day, two more left in the packet.

The thin stream of smoke swirled upwards, a white, faint stream of toxic chemicals. He knew it was a bad habit but he needed something – *immediate*

– to relieve the tension that had built behind his eyes. The bleep of his phone alerted him, he glanced at the screen. A text from Human Resources – "How to stop smoking in five easy steps" – along with a web link.

Then it hit him, he still had his uniform on. Were they really monitoring him that closely? It was hardly subtle. Perhaps they wanted it that way. He stubbed out the cigarette and made his way back into the air-conditioned building.

Eyes and ears everywhere – so it's more than a rumour.

MONDAY 12TH JANUARY 2026

Karl felt out of place amongst the select group. Global financiers, intelligence experts, oil barons, newspaper magnates, CEO in the military and industrial sectors, Vatican bankers, celebrities from film and television – the list went on.

He knew the familiar face of Max. *Isn't that Charles Ferrell, the founder of IBC-USA?* Karl recognised him from his pre-interview research. World renowned for the wealth created by his family's long involvement in mining and the diamond industry. The generous donations made by his charity foundation had given many homeless people and poorer families a second chance in life. Charles had openly committed 50% of his wealth to charitable work, something the media loved as did those who made a career out of attempts to secure donations from billionaires and above.

Charles's wealth had made Max's fortune look rather miniscule; the owner of a supermall beside a local shopkeeper. The former moved in the realm of trillions.

The role of Charles in helping birth IBC, well documented. Following the death of his only daughter due to SAD, he vowed to end this condition and investigate ways of eradicating other genetic diseases. Charles not only invested money in the project, he recruited mind's like Max as a way of spearheading many of the management structures and committees that were now in place.

The room, almost full. Karl scrutinised the key speaker. Judging from the conversations taking place around him most of the attendees were involved in business or had inherited wealth and sought to invest in ventures that promised high dividends. He did recognise several outspoken personalities from the film industry and a number of prominent academics. Max insisted that Karl attend. Now he felt totally isolated and well out of his comfort zone.

Max and Charles were key members of the committee who organised this meeting. The main speaker, a smartly dressed gentlemen of Asian origin. Standing at a little over six feet, with a neatly trimmed white beard, he carried about him an air of authority. Both Max and Charles seemed to have a great deal of respect for him, hanging on his every word, going out of their way to accommodate him. *Who is he?* Karl tried not to stare.

'Distinguished ladies and gentlemen. I think it is time that we start the proceedings. It is good to be in *the Light*.' Agreement was voiced from those in attendance. Charles continued, 'Tonight I present to you our guest speaker. Known for his wisdom, sought after for his insight and destined to be one of the greatest influences of the 21st century… Dr Karthik Kothaka.'

Dr Kothaka walked to the podium, openly acknowledging his audience. He graciously smiled at Charles. 'My fellow travellers, it is good to be in *the Light*.' Once again strong verbal agreement from the audience. Karl observed the solidarity in operation. One voice, one mind. In some ways it felt quite spooky. He shook off the precipitous shiver.

Dr Kothaka continued, 'We face many challenges as we continue along in our destinies. Tonight I want to share with you some of my insights and predictions concerning the future and how we should prepare ourselves for the trials that await us.'

A strange electrical energy permeated the room as the discourse unfolded. Karl tasted it, he recalled licking a 9V battery as a child, he was eight at the time. Mesmerising – empowering. He'd been feeling tired and anxious at the beginning of the meeting, but those sensations seemed to leave as he was captivated by Kothaka's words. An invisible power seemed to pulse in and out like a tide, moving back and forth throughout the room. *Like subtle static*, Karl thought, suddenly aware of the erect hairs on his arms.

For the next two hours, without a break, Dr Kothaka spoke of the growing world population and the need for science to step in and address key issues. He spoke of purifying those who would be the rulers in the future, to do everything possible prevent them from becoming contaminated by influences that threaten the existence of mankind. Whatever means necessary would be used to conserve the genetic superiority entrusted to the ruling authorities. Perhaps ways could be found to enhance this potential? He then went on to outline the events needing to happen in order to make this a reality.

In the final part of his speech he relayed the importance of fulfilling one's designated time on earth, making sure that life reached its natural conclusion and opening doors that held the mystery of the extended life span. He suggested that the science of cryogenics could provide the means of living beyond current limitations.

The audience erupted with thunderous applause, Karl applauded thought with less enthusiasm than his neighbours. Dr Kothaka received a standing ovation, not wanting to be the odd one out Karl stood too.

Dr Kothaka appeared modest and self-effacing, bowing before his audience. A respected member of the business community swiftly escorted Karthik from the stage; two security guards followed in close pursuit, whisking the two VIPS away. Charles and Max embraced each other warmly, basking in the electrified atmosphere. *This was major weird, some kind of special adult fraternity gathering.*

Karl's mind buzzed with excitement. A whole new set of images and thoughts summoned up by the man's oration. Much of what he had heard relied on the part of science; on its ability to shatter old paradigms and drive new advances. Karl recognised his own importance – without pioneering minds like his, Dr Kothaka would just be a dreamer. He did not agree with everything he had heard, but most of it fitted into his understanding of the future prospect of life on planet earth. And he wondered – *is this how they all feel? Each of these people?*

'You must be Karl, my name is Charles. Charles Ferrell.' He offered his hand.

Karl wondered if he looked shocked, even stunned by the realisation that someone as important as Charles was addressing and acknowledging him. All the same, the exchange was warm and open.

'Yes, my name is Karl… Dr Karl Winwood. I work at IBC-Korea.' He felt like a new employee desperately trying to impress his boss. His cheeks burned.

'Max tells me great things about you. How are things progressing? We are expecting great things from you.' Charles had clear brown eyes that had appeared soft at first glance. A deeper look revealed a sunken coldness. Chills went through Karl's body and, once again, he could feel goose bumps along the lengths of his arms.

'Yes sir, I will do my best.' Karl ignored the dryness in his mouth, hoping that he had expressed genuine desire.

'We expect nothing less.' Brief and to the point, Charles moved swiftly on, leaving Karl in a state of flux.

What's happening? Why do I feel so afraid? Why had joining the Light brought so much anxiety and concern to his mind?

Karl stood awkwardly, wondering which way to turn. He rubbed his left temple. These migraines seem to be a regular part of his life, starting on the same day that he had made his formal commitment to walk in the way of *the Light*.

TUESDAY 13TH JANUARY 2026

'You know that it is possible.'

Karl had no intention of listening to her and her arguments. Yes, she was an authority in her field, but he was the boss. If she did not know it now, she would by the end of their meeting.

Stubborn Esther, sticking to her traditional view on morality. Such a major limitation, preventing further exploration of the sort of unique and strange ideas that could lead to breakthroughs. Karl remained acutely aware that these were the sort of ideas that had always been the strength behind the pioneering arm of science. Now they needed to be cast aside to make way for progress.

'Yes, but "possible" does not mean that we actually need to go down that avenue,' Esther cocked her head. Karl thought she might be a step away from rolling her eyes in a play of exasperation. On that, at least, they were agreed: this conversation was certainly and phenomenally exasperating.

He sighed in mild annoyance, looking her in the face, one eyebrow raised. 'Are you trying to take some kind of moral stand? Aren't you the expert in cross species manipulation?'

'My work is based on plants! Crossing humans with other species is wrong. It is just wrong,' Esther's composure splintered.

I am winning. He fought to hold back the smirk that so wanted to emerge. 'Who says it is wrong? Why are you still clinging to the morals of the stone age man under the threat of a scary world, looking to something or someone to worship?' Karl smiled a little. *You'll run out of answers, Esther.* He shrugged, hoping that it would be taken as a comment on the futility of her position.

'Karl, there is nothing wrong about respecting life.' She sounded deadpan. Confident. But on the inside, Esther was furious. Who was he to question the foundations of ethical practice? 'Life is more than sequences of nucleotides and DNA. Just because we work in a lab does not mean we have to start thinking like lab rats. There is life beyond the walls of this compound.'

Esther leant back in her chair and waited for the inevitable tirade. *Any minute now,* she thought – *because he's like a spoilt child.*

Karl could almost see the fire in Esther's eyes. Suddenly, victory was not assured. He would not give her what she wanted, to see him to flounder and fall back on anger. He knew that too well. He fought the urge to yell at her and, instead, almost calmly, he continued, 'Put aside your moral crusade, Esther. Focus on the issues here. Are we are able to use the same techniques to transfer the DNA of other species into a human embryo?'

'In theory… yes.' Esther looked uncomfortable. Perhaps his pretence of patience had worked. 'Plant DNA is easier to manipulate than mammalian DNA. That much is basic.' She didn't bother hiding the insult.

'We firstly need to identify where we are going to insert the new material; there's no point in turning off key sequences that cannot be substituted. We have no guarantees that it will be accepted by the host DNA. Should we get past that stage, we cannot guarantee it will remain part of the genome, to be passed on during mitotic activity. Without that much, we'd have a one hit wonder – no future.'

He watched her pursing her lips, staring right at him. He held her gaze. 'Who has been able to do this so far?'

'Do you think anyone wants to be arrested? The resolution has only just been passed! No doubt there are some who are ahead of the game. I did hear of some work being done in the UK. Something to do with the generation of mixed embryos. This was only taken to the fourteenth day, as was allowed by legislation at the time. That would have been around… ,' she her racked her brain. 'Around 2011.'

Esther could no longer conceal her resentment, its heat burning in her throat. Even her tone had changed. She hated sacrificing even this much simple information.

Karl was not impressed, he already knew that. He sensed her strong dislike for him, coming off from her in mini waves. As if she was allowing it. Driving it even. He felt his patience give. 'Look it up.' Karl snapped. 'You're leaving the Plant Division. You're being transferred onto this project.'

She wasn't surprised – hadn't it all been leading to this anyway? – but neither was she happy with the announcement. Esther returned Karl's gaze. 'Has this been authorised by—'

Karl saw where the question was going and it irritated him. This was her last minute attempt to find a way out. 'You will be doing this or you had better start looking for a new post. Max says this is top priority, so it is.'

His eyes glowed with passion and a raw desire that she found unnerving – his tone bordered on menacing. He so wanted to win at this game, to satisfy his ferociously hungry ego. 'What about the team that I am managing? Who is taking over from me?' Esther offered this as a final, knowing it had little chance of success.

'You do have an assistant don't you? Promotion comes at the most inconvenient of times, doesn't it? Send them to Human Resources! We can get the paperwork sorted out another time. You are needed immediately.' Karl drew back. He had won but the insubordination had gotten to him. Work was stressful enough as it was at the moment. He didn't need this.

'Not so easy Karl,' Esther put up her hand, motioning for Karl to stop. 'Many things have to be tied up; we are in the middle of an important project to that is part of the contribution that IBC is making in the area of plant disease resistance. You'll recall that we won the Global Science Award last year, for the research my team spearheaded, remember?'

Karl did remember, Max had taken him to lunch over the project's success. As the Director, he had taken the glory. Even he could bring himself to admit, if only to himself, that Esther had done the better part of the hard work. He did respect her. He knew that he did. She was just so damned irritating. He looked at her, waiting for her to say something. His heart warming slightly.

'Okay. Okay, Esther. I understand. But it doesn't change matters much. As I said, you need to do this. You've got to the end of the day to sort things out.' Her expression did not change. 'You'll need to have moved your things by tomorrow afternoon. Talk to Human Resources about getting maintenance to arrange a moving team. I want you physically in place tomorrow morning. I will arrange for desk space to be made available for you, right next to my office in the Human Tech Division.'

He smiled. As far as he was concerned, he was doing her a favour. Esther knew it. He believed it. She was ultimately powerless. He was certain about one thing: what Max wanted, he got.

The matter was closed, it was just a case of sorting out the fine details. Esther was great at her work, the best in her field. That was why IBC employed her. Her expertise, earning her a place on the dream team.

Somewhat dejected, Esther made her way out of Karl's office wondering how she was going to break the news to her team. The truth was that they were like family, close knit, loyal – Esther loved each of them.

Her mind wandered back to the first time she had meet Karl as student back at MIT. His boldness had metamorphosed into arrogance, his confidence into superiority. The overwhelming sense of self-importance was repulsive; he had seemed like a brilliant young man. *Yes* – she thought – she actually hated Karl. He represented everything that she despised in science. The admission made her uncomfortable and sad in equal measure. She tried so hard to accept people. Now she faced the daily displeasure of working with him as her boss.

This was not going to be an easy afternoon.

SATURDAY 17TH JANUARY 2026

'In the light of our findings, we believe it is theoretically possible to create a chimera that will have an overall human physiology and anatomy provided that 1/3 of the human genome remains intact. The remaining 2/3 can be of other organisms. Initially we are thinking along the mammalian line but who is to say that in time other possibilities may open up.'

NATURE, MARCH 2020

Karl used the quote as part of his presentation to the assembled research team. The eleven scientists sat fascinated round the conference table. Apart from Esther. She didn't even attempt to conceal her resentment. Karl had assembled the best minds at IBC-Korea; this was *his* dream team.

'Through the work of Spiegal and Hinderson we know the essential genes and where they are located, if we are to have an overall human framework. This is now in the scientific domain.'

Karl lectured the group of eminent scientists, carefully selecting his words for maximum impact. 'Everybody knows this. If we are to get ahead, we need to decide on our choice species and then just get on with it. Today I announce to you that we are creating a new project. It will be code named the Living Doll Project. We are going to blend human genes,' Karl drew a deep breath, hesitating, '... with rabbit and chimpanzee genes.' He felt extremely proud of himself and his presentation as he watched invisible shock waves reverberate around the room, knocking into the minds of his colleagues.

They were totally stunned, wide open eyes stared back at him. Yes, he understood, this had never been done before and the idea of a human embryo with genetic information from two other species was a concept that would take some time to get used to.

Esther spoke. 'Why the combination of rabbit and chimpanzee?' She pulled her Armani designer frames down, peering at him.

'We already have extensive work on this combination. While you were absorbed in your botanical pursuits, our zoology sector have broken through to the point of producing viable embryos.' Karl glared at Esther, she always asked too many questions. Not about the work, it was about his authority.

'But no full term gestation.' She sounded triumphant.

Karl sighed. 'Yes, that has proved difficult.'

'Perhaps nature is fighting back by saying that it has no place for this work.' Esther scowled. Karl groaned inwardly; she really loved the sound of her own archaic rhetoric.

'It's nothing that we cannot get around. So back to your stations and let's get creating.' The meeting broke up generating a little muted laughter and a number of intense discussions.

Esther waited until the rest of the team had left before she vented her feelings on Karl. 'Where do you get these ideas from? I have never heard anything so ridiculous in my life. Rabbit and chimpanzee! Who came up with that?' She could feel the blood rushing through the veins in her neck.

'Esther, I am not about to enter into a discussion with you. This is the project, if you don't like it feel free to scan the latest edition of *Nature* – the recruitment section is towards the end of the project pages. There are plenty of botanical research positions at the moment. You can always vegetate elsewhere.'

Esther turned and walked away slowly. He had made a joke, so pleased with himself. Karl was ridiculous, yet the sense of heaviness descended upon her shoulders all the same. She had lost. The last few years had been such a great time for her career. IBC had given her an open door with no real limitations, budgeting to die for and the surrounding talent was incredible. However this new project seemed to have taken over, everything was being directed towards its success.

In her mind it was as if the company had been taken over by some invisible force which now controlled every available resource that was not tied up in existing projects. Top priority – the words kept being attached to every discussion about this annoying assignment. *Why is it so important? Why is the race to be first so crucial to IBC?* Changing the face of human evolution. She shivered. *Feels like the science train turned in the wrong direction.*

+++

Karl rubbed his right temple, feeling yet another migraine coming on. Ever since he had received the phone call from Max. Karl could only described it like being placed inside a strait jacket, watching it being fastened buckle by buckle, gradually restricting his movement until he became powerless.

He fought with unease. Not only did he have to attend another *Light* meeting, the species combinations in the Living Doll project had been dictated to him. Compounded by the fact that Esther had challenged them.

When Karl had attempted to ask Max about the edict, he had been referred to his oath of obedience. He could do no more than bully his staff into subservience. There was no oath between Karl and Esther. *What have I got myself into?* He was no longer in control of his own future. Rabbit, human and chimpanzee – he had no idea as to why.

What do I know about anything anymore?

The core group meeting was not going well. Cornelius sighed. His assistant heads and technical supervisors were assembled in the Cloning Division meeting room.

'I just seem to have become the marginalised part of this whole operation,' blurted out Akio. Cornelius tried to reassure him with kind words but he knew that the statement was partly true.

'Budgets are not unlimited. IBC is generous but not every wish and whim can be accommodated.' Cornelius, not convinced by his own rhetoric.

'I hardly think disease resistance in wheat is a whim.' Aiko drew breath before continuing, 'In the light of the potential global shortage I would have said it was paramount. This is vital research!'

Cornelius could see that Akio was losing control, the trembling lips and quivering hands spoke volumes. He didn't really know what to do about it. Unhindered, Akio continued, 'Things around here seem to have changed overnight yet no one seems to have told me a thing about it.'

Akio slammed his folders onto the table top, sending a desk-tidy into orbit. It came crashing down, showering pens in all directions. There was a moment of silence in which Cornelius despaired. He couldn't help but sympathise with his staff.

'Sorry.' Akio muttered as he gathered the stray pens. 'I feel really strongly about his and nobody seems to be listening.' He stared at Cornelius who nervously looked away.

Akio had served as a dedicated and committed member of the cloning team. Nonetheless, due to the executive changes in resource management priorities, Cornelius found himself forced to tell the man that his work was no longer important.

Cornelius assisted him. 'We still care about the wheat project – but others are ahead of us in this area.' He picked up three black biros and a pencil. 'So we are focusing on being pioneers rather than followers. This is part of the IBC philosophy. We are a frontrunner organisation, we thrive on breakthroughs not maintaining existing ideas.' Akio didn't like that, his sharp look revealing his anger.

To Cornelius it sounded like marketing spiel. *But it was true, wasn't it?*

Tears began to well in Akio's eyes, he fought hard to hold them back. 'So it looks like a case of move on to a new project or ship out. Cornelius, I have given the last five years of my life to this work. Where's the thanks? Where's the appreciation?'

No one attempted to answer the question. Plants research had suddenly dropped off the radar at IBC-Korea. Worst of all, no one knew why. There had been no obvious reason. Cornelius suspected that it wouldn't be long before people like Akio would begin to worry about the security of their positions with the company. The wind was changing.

'Your work is appreciated, you are one of the leading voices in the area,' Cornelius swallowed dryly. 'All we are doing is refocusing our energies and resources to keep IBC at front of the scientific community.'

The desk organiser was returned to its proper state. There was nothing to occupy his hands. Cornelius began wipe a sweating palm on his trousers then stopped himself. He was nervous, part of him wondered if the rest of the team realised.

Akio turned away, Cornelius watched as his body heaved accompanied by deep groans, his tears flowing down his face. It was painful to see him fumbling in his lab coat for a handkerchief.

The white handkerchief seemed to serve as a barrier between the two men. *A sign of surrender*, thought Cornelius, *or evidence of betrayal?*

Akio wailed. A neighbour attempted to put their arms around him and he violently resisted the act of compassion, refusing to be comforted. Some of the scientists finally turned away. Cornelius could sympathise with that too. Akio's tears were a sort of protest. They were testimony.

'Let's pick this up after lunch. Can we meet back at 1.30pm? It is now just after 12.30pm.' No one seemed to be listening to him. All eyes were still on Akio, but Cornelius continued, 'Bring in your new proposals Sarah. I also want to see up to date copies of the technical reports from the last week – we seem to have got off course.' He knew he could rely upon Sarah, as a technical assistant she personified efficiency.

'Akio, can you stay and speak to me?' Cornelius spoke tenderly.

A subdued group of scientists streamed out of the room and hushed silence hovered over their slow exit.

Cornelius glanced down at his watch; lunch would likely turn out to be a brief event. Firstly, he had to work out how to rebuild a crushed scientist. That or watch his whole team fall apart.

AN UNUSUAL FRIENDSHIP

Jukdo Market was the kind of place people dream about when they think of South Korea – colourful, noisy, the air saturated with exotic scents and bustling with energy. Alive.

Good noodles. Esther sipped the glass of red wine. She was enjoying a relaxing evening with Chloe. A rare moment – they were both off duty. Esther knew they respected each other; they wanted the same thing most of the time. Their approach seemed to be very different, yet their goals were shared.

Esther made it her duty to get to know the charges under her care, yes she was their boss but she cared for them as people. Each of them treated to free meal as her way of valuing and esteeming them as individuals. From her observations, fellowship over meals played a key part of life in the East – the shared table being a place of intimacy and openness. Tonight, Chloe's turn.

For a novice, she handled her chopsticks pretty well. Esther used the implements with skill. The mixture of spices exploded on her tongue, accompanied by their delicate aroma. *Delicious. Simply delicious.*

Bicycles would never be fully replaced – despite the wide availability of the hover board. Two or three occupants passed by in on a cycle; still a common sight on the streets of Pohang. Bells, shouts and more bells – lightening reflexes were needed before venturing on the streets and roads. The mixture of smells added another dimension to the evening – there were spices, newly picked herbs, corn oil, fresh fish and stir fried noodles. Such a contrast to the antiseptic, sterile smell and dehydrating air conditioning that made up their daily working environment in the lab. *Therapy for the olfactory receptors*, she smiled to herself.

Esther considered Chloe's progress with the chopsticks. 'Next time you are off, make sure you try the fish bar on the corner of the strip. Not to be missed.' She pointed in the right direction. Chloe continued to eat, buried in her plate of food.

'I'm so hungry. Sorry! I skipped lunch this afternoon because I'm a bit behind with the lab reports.' She didn't look up. Esther knew she had not been listening. Her recommendation had fallen on deaf ears.

'We're off duty now.' Esther's voice took on a stern tone. 'Let's leave work behind and enjoy the evening.' She took another sip of her wine. *Elderberries* – it reminded her of grandmother's garden in Israel.

'Sure, let's leave it behind.' Chloe finished the remaining noodles on her plate and finally looked up at Esther. 'Those prawns were delicious. Not too hot either,' she smiled brightly. 'Just right for a newcomer like me.'

+++

Two hours later, Chloe began retching violently in her bathroom. Half an hour after that she frantically called Esther. Hot and cold flushes ran through her body; she could not stop shivering. Despite all the layers of clothes she had hastily thrown on, she still felt as if she had been plunged into a bath of cold water.

Esther shut her phone. Chloe sounded really bad. She leapt out of bed grabbing items from her walk in wardrobe. Her DKNY jeans and an Armani white shirt and blue lambs wool jumper. Not very coordinated, but practical. *Poor Chloe*, she felt guilty. *Food poisoning? I hope not, I've never had a bad meal in Pohang*.

Black boots would have to do. She thrust her feet in, zipping them up as she perched on the edge of her bed. She grabbed her black leather jacket as she left her apartment, slamming the door shut.

Chloe's apartment was on the second floor within the staff complex on the IBC-Korea site.

One look at Chloe convinced Esther there was only option – a trip to the on-site hospital. She placed her hand on her damp forehead, it was burning up. Chloe trembled, as Esther tried to explain the decision. She retched twice before throwing up.

I suppose this is what friends are for. Esther wiped the foul smelling stuff off her designer jeans. *It's brown and yellow and disgusting.* And then – *these jeans were special edition.* A nearby towel served as a way of cleaning off most of the mess. Now to the hospital.

The IBC autocab sat silently outside Chloe's block. Esther's request text had been sent only three minutes before its arrival.

Eight minutes later they were in the hospital wing of the IBC-Korea site. Chloe worried Esther, she was delirious, totally incoherent. The medical staff responded efficiently and with genuine care. They looked after their own. A body scan revealed areas of inflammation in Chloe's digestive system, they immediately administered anti-inflammatory drugs using a Biomedi-pod.

Dr Zhang Wei insisted that she be kept in overnight. By then, Chloe had fallen asleep.

IBC company policy required line managers to contact the relatives of sick employees as a matter of course, in addition to the medical staff who dealt with patients. IBC wanted relatives to know that the company had a personal interest in each of its employees – the prided itself on being a family orientated organisation in which people mattered. Esther was now fully awake so she decided to contact the name listed under next of kin.

'Bethany Bartell. Okay, let's hope you are awake.'

After several rings, a tired voice answered, 'Hello'

'Good morning,' Esther remembered the time difference between the two zones. It was now 7.30am in Arizona. 'Is that Mrs Bartell?'

'Yes, Who am I speaking to?'

Esther licked her lower lip before replying, 'My name is Dr Esther Cohen, Head of Plant—' She placed her hand on her chest – *imagine getting my own title wrong !* 'Head of Human Technology at Icilda Biotech Company in Pohang.'

She could hear rustling in the background, 'Oh, okay… right.' The speaker sounded confused, unsure.

'I am ringing to talk to you about Chloe.' Esther wanted to sound professional without causing alarm.

'Chloe, what's the matter with Chloe?' Esther heard panic creeping into the speaker's voice, the words rushed, the tone raised by half an octave.

'Chloe has been admitted to our hospital at Pohang. She has a bad case of food poisoning.'

'Is she alright? Is she seriously ill?'

'No, she is fine, recovering well. IBC always contact immediate family when a member of staff is admitted into hospital. We just want you to be aware, but not to worry.'

The gasp, followed by the exhaled breath, told Esther that Bethany had understood the message. No doubt, she would probably have a million questions to ask, starting with whether she should get on a plane right away.

There was a pause, then the voice piped up.

'Can I speak to her?'

'Not right now, she is sleeping. However, I will arrange for her to make a call as soon as she is strong enough to do so. Your daughter is a very special person. I have grown to love her, it's almost like she is… my daughter too.' She wondered if that was too much information. But that was how she felt, even after a relatively short time. It was as if Chloe were part of her family.

Bethany remained silent. Esther continued, 'Chloe is kind hearted and generous, she works so hard. I am so glad she is on my team.'

'You said your name was Esther?'

'Yes, Dr Esther Cohen.'

'She has mentioned your name. I think you are quite new. You just joined the team.'

'That's right. I am the newcomer.' Esther laughed in a relaxed way. She felt comfortable; something about Bethany's voice and manner connected with her. 'I hear that she is great at baking.'

'Oh, she bakes! She never told me that. She used to watch me in the kitchen but she was never too keen on getting her hands dirty. I could tell you so many stories about Chloe.'

They were talking. According to Bethany the teenage years had been very tense. Esther was amazed that the girl's mother was be so happy to talk to a complete stranger about her only child. She obviously loved her dearly.

It transpired that Bethany had been both relieved and afraid at receiving the call. She was worried about the distance; she had a persistent fear that, one day, someone would ring her to tell her that Chloe was dead. Esther imagined that most long-distance parents felt something like that. Bethany said that it was something that she had learned to live with. This call was simply the closest she had ever come to the reality of her fears.

Although she had been feeling tired, the conversation invigorated Esther. They laughed like old friends, swapping stories about Chloe.

By the time they had finished, Esther talked her through the whole incident and explained in detail the findings of the scan and the medication that had been administered. Bethany seemed to feel reassured, the mood of the conversation lightened. She thanked Esther profusely, for her kindness and for spending so much time reassuring her. Esther reiterated her promise that Chloe would phone her mother.

It marked the first of many conversations that would take place between Esther and Bethany, by phone and even via F2FV, Face to Face Vision, a new development inspired by Skype. Despite their very different careers and the cultural rift between their educational backgrounds, they had Chloe in common. Neither of them mentioned the conversations to her of course – their little secret. If Esther had any worries about Chloe, she could always get in touch.

For Bethany, it became an important link between her home in Arizona and the strange world of South Korea. Esther appreciated the opportunity to voice her concerns about Chloe. Indeed, the many stories of her teenage days helped Esther gain a better understanding of Chloe's frequent moods.

Bethany's honesty gave Esther insight into Chloe's private world. Her strained relationship with her father – the beast had left for another woman. Of course that was in the past, and he had a new family now. Bethany still lived with the pain.

Esther found it all quite alien; having grown up in Tel Aviv, still speaking to her parents three or four times a week. At least one of those conversations would be with her father. Though retired, her parents continued to supervise their horticulture centre from a distance; it had been part of the family inheritance for several generations. It was where Esther had developed her love of plants. She could not imagine life without her beloved father, known in the neighbourhood as Papa Isaac. It seemed unlikely that Abigail and Joel would take over the land, they had their own careers and families; she had no plans to become a farmer.

Bethany's stories about Chloe that had them both in tears with laughter. She revealed her daughter's tender side, her reflective and insightful nature. Chloe had been journaling since she was ten. The time she spent on the task had changed as she grew up, but she still refused to go to bed until she had finished writing her memories of the day down in one form or another. Bethany said that she knew that they were her daughter's secrets, but that she could not resist the occasional peep into the hidden world of her brilliant child – she had discovered the 'hiding place' accidently. Anything she learned, she kept to herself. Chloe would have been incensed if she even suspected that her mother had been studying her inner world. Bethany discovered that the pain of losing her father had played on Chloe's mind long after she stopped talking about it. Deep down inside, she seemed to want to know him; and at the same time, struggled with resentment and abandonment.

It had taken her years to accept that as much as she tried to compensate for his absence she could not. In some ways she had been overindulgent with Chloe, feeling guilty for her failures as a mother, letting her have her way instead of being firm. That surprised Esther.

Bethany confided that she felt close to Esther, who agreed that there was a real bond between them. They were friends now. Bethany even told Esther about Chloe's fits of rage – the darker side of her nature.

Esther refused to judge people without sufficient evidence and that, at least, prevented her from limiting the potential of the people with whom she worked. Even though she knew so much about Chloe, she never once let on.

Chloe was allowed to be herself – hissy fits and all.

THE HUMAN FACTOR

'So, where are we going to get the human contribution to this process?' Esther and her curiosity. Always asking pertinent questions. Up until now, no mention had been made of the human component in the experiment.

'I have some contacts at an IVF clinic, they always have spare embryos. I've been promised an unlimited supply.' Karl had been confident of his answer. An informal deal. His heart sank at Esther's expression.

'Is that ethically sound? Aren't there laws governing this type of behaviour?' Esther seemed determined to make the most of her moment, 'What about parental authorisation? Don't they have the right to know that their little someone is about to become a new genetic experiment?'

'In Korea, things are a little easier. There's less red tape than in the USA and Europe. You know that yourself, Esther. It's why you're here. The local attitude is much more progressive.' A brief smirk passed across Karl's face, he replaced it with a more sombre expression.

'Are you sure you mean progressive? Maybe they are less well informed about the potential use of embryos. In my opinion—'

Esther's tirade was interrupted by a double knock on his office door. Before he could respond the door opened and in strode Chloe.

Esther nodded in acknowledgement; Chloe was certainly thriving as a research scientist; in Esther's opinion she remained an avid devotee of Karl.

'We've done it.' Chloe's voice trembled slightly. Esther recalled that tone in her own voice, some time ago. An underlying air of celebration along with an uncomfortable awe. Chloe's fragrance diffused into the office, floral tones mingled with vanilla highlights.

'Done what?' Karl's voice was eager.

'We managed to select the desirable rabbit genome features and completed the same process with the chimpanzee genome.' Chloe's face was dressed with a wide, beaming smile.

'So we won't end up with a chimera with long ears and a tail to match?' Esther had grown to hate that sarcasm in Karl.

'Basically… yes.' The girlish sound of her voice, she always spoke like that when she got excited. Childlike wonder, Esther felt she had lost that a long time ago. Especially since being part of the Human Technology Division.

Karl watched, observing Chloe's elation fade to something somewhere between fear and embarrassment. 'Check the data against the report produced by the team from Sweden. They did something similar a while back. If you agree with it, you have done well. You have looked at that release haven't you?' He was beginning to feel a strong confidence about some of the newer members of his team, that included Miss Bartell. Chloe was certainly attractive but this project was the focus of his attention. Brains and beauty, shame about her bank account. Two out of three on the LBL system.

'Yes I have… briefly.' He watched her holding her clipboard in one hand, the other hid behind her back.

'And that's all. Anything else?' As far as Karl was concerned the abrupt meeting was over. Yet Chloe stood there staring at him. 'What are you waiting for? Get moving!'

She left.

'Where were we? Ah yes… embryos. So, sourcing them will not be a problem. When will we be ready for them?' Karl rubbed the back of his neck, the heavy the weight of the project; three long months; the next progress report was due in a two days.

'That depends on how quickly the rabbit and chimpanzee genome selection takes. Once we have the key genes, we can work out where we are going to insert them into the human chromosomes.' Esther thought, *why do all days seem to run into one, long, bad day*; the late hours along with having to work closely with Karl were taking a toll on her self-esteem. It was getting harder to sleep at night as her mind was racing from the day's activities. Rest – a commodity that was becoming a rarity. *I really need a holiday.* She knew that with the way things were going Karl would not be receptive to such a notion.

'This whole thing is taking too long. By now we should be blending the species not working out which genes do what. Why am I surrounded by people who lack commitment and dedication?' Karl knew this was untrue; however he loved sparking a response in Esther. The Living Doll project highlighted major differences in their viewpoint and methodology. He relished every opportunity that increased the leverage he had. Every top dog needs an underdog in order to feel secure. In his mind, Esther served the purpose well.

'You are not the only one who is up half the night thinking about this project. If you don't like the team or if you can identify those who are not pulling their weight, you should be able to manage it.' Esther continued, 'that's what you are paid for.'

By now she had worked out that Karl's ambition fuelled his need for success. Science featured somewhere in the mix but it may as well have been a business plan or an art assignment. People like him needed to be the best – other people were there to be used. To prop up his ego whenever it started to deflate. People like Karl always ended up needing others, so his attitude – his "I am an island" way of thinking about himself – that would yield limited success in the world of science. Teamwork mattered. He could play at captain for a while, but she knew that he was no team player.

Karl felt the sudden acceleration; the dull throbbing of his neck arteries. He blurted, 'Are you implying—'

'It was just a suggestion Karl. I have assistants to check on; excuse me.' Esther decided to exit from the situation before things moved to the next level of confrontation. Another battle, another day.

She slammed the door behind her. Nothing was resolved.

MONDAY 20TH APRIL 2026

Chloe fidgeted as she sat waiting in Karl's office. He had been called away to deal with a major incident in the Cloning Division. Cornelius was about to get the sharp edge of the Karl's sword – a verbal reprimand. Surprisingly, he had left her alone in his personal space.

The meticulous state of the room. *He's a perfectionist,* she thought. Not a single sheet of paper out of place, even the paper clips were organised. The Sheafer pen right in the centre of the file, all that space behind the desk, the slightly elevated chair.

Karl in control.

The walls were covered with numerous certificates and newspaper clippings arranged on the walls, testimony to the brilliance of Dr Karl Winwood. A couple of pieces of art punctuated the professional look. *Was that a Banksy? Must be a copy. No way could he afford that kind of art.* She noted the Persian carpet.

Not only was he worshipped at IBC, he had a world-wide reputation for his dedication to human development. Requests for his advice were part of a normal day on the team; Chloe had landed the job of technical secretary – her reward for being the newbie on the team. Still, she enjoyed being wanted and it gave her a chance to get close to Karl. *Why was he so secretive about himself?*

Everyone knew that the job was demanding; surely though, being human was also part of the process? After all, this was Positive Mental Attitude week.

The honest truth? Her self-assessment? She was not feeling positive; at times verging on being mental; with enough attitude to go round the globe twice. Today was not a good day.

Is he actually human? She still felt guilty about the lie she had told about her investigation into other teams working on similar projects. Basic scientific process involved carrying out research. She had looked at a few reports but not the work of the Swedish team. Karl was not easily fooled; he knew his subject and his competitors. *Perhaps…*

'Sorry Chloe,' Karl mumbled as he returned, flustered. *Probably from his heated exchange with Cornelius.* Chloe knew McDermott by sight, but had no real connection with him. Esther spoke warmly of him.

'Thanks for sorting out the Berlin request. I may well have to visit on behalf of IBC. Actually, I want you to book an appointment with Hyun-jung, Max Augustine's PA. He wants to see you as soon as possible.'

Chloe looked up from the notes on her lap.

'Max wants to see *me?*' She pointed to herself. 'Why? Does he even know my name?' *How strange.*

'Can you do as you are told without asking questions? You sound just like Esther. It's tedious.' The tone of his voice changed, his words now coloured with irritation.

'I'm not like Esther.' Chloe was deeply offended at the suggestion that she was like Esther. She had her own mind and it was different from Esther. 'I always try to support you. You never give me a chance—'

'You're right you are not like Esther.' Karl closed in on Chloe with one of his piercing stares. 'Maybe you'll go further than she has in less time.' He paused and then continued, 'Look I have given you the message, make sure you make that appointment.'

Karl sat down heavily on his chair. Max had not told him why he wanted to see Chloe. He hated being outside the loop.

Chloe was fuming, compassion in short supply she asked, 'Did you want anything else?'

'No!' Karl answered sharply.

He watched her leave. Her long blonde braid swinging, a golden pendulum.

WEDNESDAY 22ND APRIL 2026

'Sit down Chloe.' Max smiled warmly and gestured towards one of the leather chairs in front of his teak panelled desk.

'Thank you so much.' Chloe smiled nervously, she calmed herself by thinking of one of the characters from her favourite comedy, *Blake's Seven*. Dayna Mellanby was a brave and loyal member of the team who could on occasion be reckless and naïve. *Just like me.* She eased herself down into the chair – it slid forward, almost knocking into Max's desk. Chloe blushed.

'How are things going at IBC?' enquired Max.

'I'm loving it, I feel so privileged. Everyone has been so helpful and welcoming,' a joyful tone flowed through her response.

'Yes, teamwork and being part of a family is part of what makes IBC special,' Max moved slowly and smoothly towards the massive portrait, looked like his dad or someone in his family line. 'You should do really well here.'

Chloe was still trying to work out why she was in this situation. No logical reason came to mind.

'You must be wondering why I wanted to see you. Karl keeps me updated on new talent and he has noticed your potential. How earnest are you about being a pioneer? Changing the face of science forever?' A sombre note crept into Max's voice, his eyes looked straight ahead, ignoring her.

'I love science. I've dedicated my life to my career,' Chloe answered sincerely.

'Science moves forward when radical people take unusual steps, even at a personal cost. Marie Curie paid for her work with her life. Such was her passion.' Max was standing directly beneath the painting now, looking at it. 'So how much are you willing to pay Chloe?'

He turned towards her, leaning forward to emphasise the gravity of the question. The fragrance of his cologne reached Chloe, the tones of cedar wood were soothing; almost hypnotic.

'I'm not sure what you mean?' The tightening of her stomach told her brain that something of gravity was about to disclosed.

'Would you be willing to personally pioneer a breakthrough in science? Would you like to leave your legacy behind for future generations to admire?' Max paused, allowing his words to hang in the atmosphere. 'Your courage, your dedication, your readiness to take risks?' Max breathed slowly before continuing. 'I would like you to consider donating some of your eggs to the Living Doll project.'

Chloe literally jumped in her seat. A gasp almost escaped from her mouth, she sucked it back in. Her cheeks started burning, the same sensation as staying too long on a poor quality sunbed.

'You seem shocked. This is a one off chance for you to change the world.' Max continued, seemingly unaffected by her response. 'For your willingness to take part in this project, you will be allowed to genetically modify any eggs that are not used with the latest range of nanotechnology techniques that we have available. For every egg that is used you will be paid $10,000. A gift for a gift, so to speak.' Max's benevolent tone made the request seem almost normal.

Chloe stared, hardly believing her ears. *Is he serious?*

'Yes, I am serious. This deal will be between you and me and no other person is to know the details of this agreement. Should this ever come to light it will mean a cardinal breach of my trust in you and that would not be good. I am giving you a chance to make history.'

Chloe's mouth would not work. No words came to her. Shock. She struggled against it, her lips moved – but she could make no sound.

'There will be no discussions with anyone over this conversation. If you decide to decline the offer, I will not be offended but I will not be quoted on this matter.' Max moved stealthily from behind his desk and stood in front of Chloe.

He's not a man to be messed with. The immediacy of his presence alarmed her – she drew a deep breath and another wave of his cologne brought memories of her father. For a moment, she reverted to the state of a two year old, a girl playing with her dad. Then she was back in Max's office.

The tonal threat seemed tangible and a chilling sensation moved up her legs. Yet something deep within her expressed excitement. *How strange, someone wants my eggs and I might even consider doing this.* The money was an added bonus of course. *Is this a moral dilemma or a scientific opportunity?*

'You have until the start of next week to come and see me. Make another appointment with Hyun-jung. Consider my offer carefully. I want you to do what you feel is best. And I want you to make the right decision for your work. I hope the two align.' He nodded to himself before moving away from her.

Chloe remained seated, waiting to be dismissed, sensing the meeting had reached its conclusion. Max began to read a report on his desk; seemingly oblivious to her sustained presence.

She crept out – tiptoeing, despite the plush carpet.

+ + +

As soon as Chloe left, Max stopped reading the report, placing it down on his desk; he activated the conference calling system on his Internet portal. Things had to be put in place immediately if the vision's timetable was to be met.

Dr Kothaka's assessment seemed to have been accurate enough. If he was right Chloe would be a suitable donor. Her ambition overcoming her moral objections to being part of this genetic revolution.

First call, the hospital wing of IBC-Korea. He spoke briefly to Dr Chun Hei Yoo who was responsible for the gynaecology ward; a tried and trusted employee who had been with IBC-Korea for a number of years. In the past she had proven her ability to remain silent when dealing with female surgical procedures.

Following this, he spoke to his personal financial manger arranging the protocol regarding the transfer of funds to Chloe's designated bank account should she go ahead with the venture. He could rely upon the wisdom and discretion of Richard Hayford. The man had served his family well over many years.

His final call, to Charles Ferrell. They spoke briefly and the conversation confirmed the successful completion of another stage of the latest IBC project. By the time Max had completed his last call, all of the necessary links in the chain were complete.

Eve was almost in position. Now to continue the search for a prospective Adam.

THURSDAY 23RD APRIL 2026

Karl seemed unnaturally keen to engage her in conversation that morning. And it was early! 'Hello Chloe,' he smiled warmly.

That's unusual, Karl being pleasant – super weird. His normal conversation starters were requests for information or orders regarding new assignments.

'Hello Karl – are you alright?' Chloe could not help but stare at him.

'How did your meeting with Max go?' Subtle as mallet, he made no attempt to conceal his interest. *He should mind his own business.*

'Oh, it was fine. He wanted to know how things were going over here. A sort introductory level view of things.' Of course he wanted more information however her reluctance to respond to the request seemed to annoy him. She watched as his complexion. *Like a chameleon.*

'Max is so friendly and caring. Imagine him showing a real interest in *my* career.' Chloe enjoyed the rare power of this moment.

'You are not *that* special. He interviews lots of people at IBC.' The resentful tone surfaced. Chloe suppressed a smile and adopted a naïve look. 'Make sure that you up-date the embryo log on the system. It's not been changed since Wednesday. Today is Thursday.' Karl spat out his response then left.

I seem to have ruffled his feathers. But he had ruffled hers too – earlier in the week. Perhaps this was simply payback.

Shaking her head, Chloe decided to let it go. She put a reminder on her smartphone – she would contact Hyun-jung. Her schedule gave her a couple of free hours next Tuesday afternoon.

Of course there were still a number of questions that needed answers – along with some guarantees. She wondered about Karl. Was it really the case that he could not cope with a diffusion of attention from Max? *If that's the case* – she thought – *he best beware. Time to let some new talent onto the scene.*

She chuckled to herself. It seemed as if today was going to be a good day. The offer continued to spin around in her head, eggs for sale, *my eggs*.

As much as she tried to push it away, it kept coming to the surface.

Chloe skipped as she made her way headed towards her desk, humming to herself – *Who will buy this wonderful morning*? She loved *Oliver – The Musical*.

FRIDAY 1ST MAY 2026

Dr Chun Hei Yoo glanced down briefly at the report in front of her. 'According to the health checks you are in good shape. The harvesting of your eggs should be no problem. I see from the uterus scan that there is one scar indicating a previous pregnancy.'

Dr Chun looked up, expecting an answer. Chloe's face turned ashen.

'I've had... an... abortion.' She stammered, 'I have no children.' Feelings of humiliation surfaced; her well-kept secret had been discovered, as she had knew it would.

The combination of shame and guilt gripped Chloe just around her throat, making it difficult for her to breathe. It was true to say her former years had been chaotic and frivolous. If she could turn back the clock she would do things very differently.

I was young and academic matters came first. Having children was not an option – my career and ambitions made the decisions more logical. The hold on Chloe's throat loosened. It was her choice, her body. No one had the right to judge her.

'That should not present any problems for future pregnancies. Your uterus looks in good shape. Your blood work was also fine. We can begin treatment in four days' time, that matches with day three of your oestrous cycle. This will involve some stimulation injections.' Dr Chun spoke with genuine empathy, her professional manner reassuring.

'On day six of your cycle you will need another injection. You will need to continue the injections for fourteen days, so by day twenty we can then harvest your eggs.' She nodded twice before continuing,' I have printed a calendar and I will show you how to do the injections at home, so you only need to come in just before harvesting. Do you have any questions?'

'What about side effects?' Chloe was more than a little anxious.

'Some women experience bloating and some discomfort in their abdomen. Nausea is not uncommon. You may find yourself very emotional, even unreasonably irritable,' Dr Chun did not want to misled her patient. 'We have seen some women suffer from insomnia. If you have any concerns, here's my smartphone number.'

Dr Chun held out her phone, sweeping it in close proximity to Chloe's.

Chloe touched the screen on her smartphone and tapped the exchange button. An immediate transfer of information took place.

'You can call me at any time. Mr Augustine tells me that you are a very special young lady and that I must take care of you.' She did not disclose the fact that some of the other young women whom she had treated at the request of Mr Augustine had not come for fertility treatment. On that, her lips were tightly sealed.

'Thank you Dr Chun. You've made things very clear.' Chloe rose from her seat, extending her hand towards the consultant. Dr Chun bowed forward in the traditional Korean manner. Respect and honour at all times – it was the Korean way. 'I will give you a call if I have any problems.'

The doubts started immediately but she dismissed them. Mom will be delighted with the extra money an any issues about keeping the house would be over. The mortgage sentence would be at and end.

No turning back now.

MONDAY 18TH MAY 2026

'Are you alright dear?' Esther looked puzzled.

For the last few days Chloe had not been herself. She failed to take the morning readings and forgot to notify Karl that she had contacted the team from Sweden working on a similar project. Chloe's efficiency had gained her the respect of the whole team; this new and strange behaviour was worrying.

'Time of the month. It's been really severe actually. I might go to the clinic just to make sure I haven't got an infection. Thanks for asking though.' Esther reminded Chloe of her mom.

'I need you back on form, we have so much riding on everyone pulling their weight. If you are not well – if you're not up to standard...' Esther hesitated. The weekly reports to Karl missed out nothing.

Every member of the team who was late or missed a deadline ended up in the document. Even Chloe. Karl insisted on detailed information and as much as Esther hated it, any failure to meet the Winwood standard meant a return of the report, along with a list of questions that needed to be answered. *I hate paperwork.* She hated having to run to Karl's beck and call.

'Don't worry, Esther. I will be fine.' The smartphone in her lab coat pocket vibrated, reminding her that another injection was due. Harvesting, now only four days away.

Chloe had worked out that she was owed three days annual leave. Day one would be for the harvesting procedure while the other two days – they would be for recovery. She hoped two days would be enough.

The recent directive from the Human Resources meant that after a designated number of lab hours and shifts you had to take time off. Karl hated it; everyone else loved it. She had carefully constructed a story about taking a couple of days off to go to Bukbu Beach to top up her sun tan; working in the lab did nothing to help her retain her tanned complexion. Everyone knew she loved her bronze look.

That was the cover story, in reality Chloe planned to say that she had ended up with a tummy bug or really bad period cramps instead, Esther would understand. Since they lived in different accommodation blocks, the chances of their accidental meeting were slim; besides Chloe knew Esther's weekly timetable. Knowing when to avoid any possible impromptu meetings.

She rubbed her abdomen, feeling the knots forming. Cramps again. 'Excuse me, Esther. I need to use the ladies.'

Esther watched Chloe rush off in the direction of the bathroom, obviously in pain. Not her normal self.

FRIDAY 22ND MAY 2026

The last few days of the procedure were extremely painful. Chloe struggled with the horrible side effects, including severe bloating and nausea. Dr Chun gave her some herbal medication to help the symptoms telling her she needed to be free of any chemical contamination.

The day of reaping arrived. Chloe decided to took an IBC autocab to the hospital wing even though it was only a short distance from her block. Walking was excruciating. Her distended abdomen pulsed.

As she entered the driverless car, the monitor scanned her ID badge and activated the facial recognition system. Once cleared, she leaned forward to allow the retinal scan to take place.

'Please identify yourself,' droned the female, android voice. They had still not quite managed to make the voice convincing. *So annoying*. It irked her.

'Chloe Bartell.' After two seconds the android responded 'Where would you like to go Chloe?' The vocal pattern recognition software required four milliseconds to scan and identify each voice.

'Hospital wing,' Chloe groaned as another wave of pain erupted from her abdomen.

The journey took eight minutes; she remembered riding in an almost identical cab with Esther. As she left the taxi, Chloe's focused on the idea of getting back to bed – after this ordeal was over.

+++

Dr Chun smiled triumphantly as she entered the private room on the northern wing of the clinic. 'Chloe, we managed to retrieve twelve eggs. Well done! No wonder you were in so much pain.'

'Is that good?' She blinked several times.

'Most women produce six to eight eggs. You have done really well. You'll need a couple of days to recover. I am going to prescribe you some pain relief and a dose of antibiotics to ensure that you don't end up with an infection.'

Dr Chun was delighted. Mr Augustine would be very happy. She would let him know before the afternoon shift changed.

'The storage of your eggs will take top priority. Mr Augustine has already explained the access protocol. If you need any more help from me then do give me a ring. The nurse will be in shortly, to take your vitals.' Dr Chun touched Chloe lightly on her shoulder. 'Once this has been done you are free to go. The reception desk will book an autocab for you if you need transportation. It has been a pleasure.'

Dr Chun bowed and, promptly, left the room.

Though sore, Chloe remained buoyant. *I've done it. Science will never be the same again. My eggs right at the start of the adventure?* It suddenly occurred to her that she was losing control of her future, her body, her cells. Someone else would be manipulating, altering even –

Chloe... stop it.

She wiped the side of her face, feeling weary. *I am doing this for me, and for science.* There wider implications... *Overwhelmingly positive implications.* This represented another shift in direction on the road to progress. And it was a personal success. *I'll be able to secure Mom's house, pay her back for all those years.*

The vibrations of her smartphone on the bedside table interrupted her thoughts. A text from Esther wishing her a good break and warning her not to get sunburned this time.

Not much chance of that *happening.* She began to chuckle, but the piercing pain in her abdomen killed all thoughts of mirth.

SATURDAY 23RD MAY 2026

Meetings with Max were normally brief. That one was one for the record books. Max had been charming and patience. Smooth as silk yet with a cobra-like undertone – a man with a mission that needed to be accomplished.

What an opportunity. Part of him doubted Max's words. They sounded too incredible, the stuff of fantasy.

No, he really meant it. Karl was being given the chance to become the father of this new technology. His DNA, his genetic material at the heart of the new project. He had been offered the opportunity of donating his sperm towards the Living Doll project. The thought of mini Karl's all over the planet thrilled him – *like a secret.* He laughed to himself. *Just as long as there are no custody cases or child maintenance issues!*

Not only would he be paid generously, he would have the honour of being a part of the new move in evolution. Leaving his mark on history, his mark on future generations. A place in science history.

Max had given him until Friday to make up his mind. He really didn't need that long.

Karl wondered if Chloe had been made a similar offer?

Yeah, that makes sense.

The timing, her closed lip secrecy about what happened during their meeting – a lot of coincidences. Yet he had no solid proof. Any number of people might be on Max's egg donor list. Karl wondered if he had a sperm donor list. *Is mine the only name on it? Are there others?*

He had no way of finding out, except by questioning Max, and that was not going to happen, or perhaps Chloe?

Bizarre – Chloe and I will be creating a child or children. True, she was pretty. No, she was beautiful. He hadn't quite thought of it in this context though.

His imagination shifted into top gear as he made his way back to the Human Technology Division.

TUESDAY 26TH MAY 2026

Charles was delighted by the news. Max had just updated him by phone. Adam and Eve had been selected, the process could move forward.

He had often wondered why those two. There were some obvious factors of course; in terms of their looks and intelligence, they were both outstanding. Karl made him look ordinary, while Chloe she had no idea how stunning she was. Their IQs were off the scale.

Was it their attitude towards life? Both had ambition in terms of scientific advancement, they were both committed, ready to sacrifice personal goals for the sake of moving human evolution forward. They were so in line with the project – on the same mental wavelength. Partners rather than employees. They seemed to understand the significance of the work.

Then the financial rewards, that was the payoff rather than the motivation. Max suggested that Karl had a real appetite for luxury, but he was not so sure about Chloe. He had grown up with money, he took it for granted. He supposed that it could become a real, consuming pursuit… to those who did not have it.

At the end of the day it was a mysterious selection process. Karthik had been very cagey about it, when Charles had asked him about Karl and Chloe. Either he knew more than he was saying or he was as much in the dark as he and Max.

Mysterious Dr Kothaka. He would be very pleased though; the vision was back on schedule.

He hated the training programme. So tedious, yet necessary. Another bunch of rookie students fresh from the academic factory. Cornelius smiled as they filed in and took their places in the lecture theatre.

They would be just like the rest – bright eyed, eager, sitting on the edges of their seats, writing down every word he uttered as if he was a living oracle. They would each possess a razor sharp intelligence and a deep sense of unreserved obedience. For them, this opportunity represented a stable future in a very uncertain world. The financial rewards would be immense, transforming their lives and those of their families. Loyalty to IBC resulted in huge financial rewards.

'The Living Doll Project presents a particular challenge to the Cloning Division. The germ line of the original gametes needs to be protected. Future living dolls will be cloned from the prototypic eggs and sperms. Twelve germ lines have been produced for the female contribution, two lines from each of the six eggs used in the investigation. The twelve germ lines are to be based on twelve sperms selected for the project.'

They wrote as he spoke, many looking up for a moment before scribbling furiously, as if they were trying to compete with each other.

His part of the programme – explaining the procedures. All the numbering systems and the terminology, reminding them of the need for meticulous lab practice. *But perhaps I could pass this particular job on to the technical advisors or technical managers?* On the other hand he still felt the need to have regular input into the students.

The same thing, repeated again and again. He even thought of recording the module, then he could let them sit and hear it for themselves. Or even getting a robot to do it. He wanted to be working, thinking, exploring; not explaining. But no, that wouldn't do. He still found it difficult to cope with the way that robotics had become integrated into ordinary life. It was not really his style – people needed the personal touch.

He listened to himself and realised that he had been talking, without really thinking.

This is so tedious.

'Cloned gametes are returned back to the Human Technology Division, who work in close association with the Animal Division, to decide the gene combinations and to incorporate the chosen species.'

They did not need to know the species that he was talking about. That would remain a trade secret.

'Once the chimeras have been created, their cellular activity is to be suspended, they are returned back to us for duplication. This will ensure that there are vast numbers of embryos available along with their respective genetic histories.' Still they wrote, an army of worker ants. Synchronised acidity. Robot-like. They would remain in the dark about the clumps of cells that would be passing before their very eyes. Obedient workers.

The Cryogenics Division was crucial to the success of the project; should things go wrong elsewhere, it would always be possible to return to an earlier stage or even to the original gametes, which were stored here. Genetic backing up.

Working in his sector required total focus and complete dedication. Life for workers, hour after hour of intense activity, day after day. He had already observed the range of emotions displayed by employees in the Cloning Division, ranging from pure excitement to utter panic and even stark fear.

'The ova in the Living doll Project are code named *germ line* α. Their identity numbers range from 234793 – 234805. Each ovum is given its code name and its number – such as germ line α 234793.' He stopped to take a sip of green tea. He continued. 'The sperm are identified by the code name *germ line* β along with their respective numbers ranging from 404376 – 404388.'

He wiped his forehead, and sighed. This really was quite tiring. 'Each of the gametes has been scanned for genetic defects, followed by nanobot-correction where necessary, ensuring their genetic perfection. The code name for the resulting embryos began with Darwin.'

Thankfully he had a slide show for the next part of the talk. The presentation rolled as the lights dimmed.

Detailed records enabled the history of the embryos to be traced from gametes to zygotes, through to embryos. Technicians became familiar with the nomenclature and numbering system allocated to the project; curiosity about the genetic sources of the embryos was often a topic of conversation that stepped beyond the walls of the IBC compound.

He had heard rumours of hushed discussions in the market place, or on the shores of Bukbu Beach, between employees from within the Divisions.

Cornelius simply accepted this eccentric aspect of Eastern culture. Some days it bugged him a lot. Secretly he hoped that one day they would rise up against the system and liberate themselves. He would support that.

Employees at IBC were amongst the highest paid workers in the whole of Pohang, enjoying perks and benefits that enabled them to live a lifestyle that their fellow inhabitants could only dream of. Foreign nationals enjoyed salaries which were often twice that which they could have earned in their respective homelands. The free healthcare, free accommodation on site, the use of IBC vehicles and the incredible recreational facilities; it made it hard to complain, even in the light of the demanding hours and relentless deadlines.

The presentation finished, he pressed the lighting button on his desk. The fluorescent glow returned to normal. Still they wrote.

'The first zygote inherited the number 666001. The number 666 represents the new pathway of human progression, while the 001 stands for the first of its kind. Each successive zygote has followed this system.' He coughed, all the eyes were focused on him. *What was the matter with them?* He was just the same as them, not some demi-god.

'After genetic modification, three digits are allocated in addition to the six from the zygote stage. So the name *Darwin 666001111221* would mean that two species have been incorporated.' He pointed to the image on the display.

I need some time off. Too much stress. They still had to cope with demands from other Divisions, thus the increasing workload and the need for more workers.

Esther's philosophy seemed to have rubbed off on him. Her people first stance was increasingly out of touch in a world that placed so much importance on technology. The IBC family model seemed to embody her values, seeking to encourage relationships. In truth, he was not the touchy feely type, yet found himself softening. The Korean authorities would not be happy with his pro-democratic stance, so he kept it to himself except when Esther was around.

He really needed another cigarette. The daily increase in pressure was starting to get to him. Smoking had become a regular part of his life. And those blinking texts on health. So annoying. Constantly prying into his private life, *so what if he wanted to kill himself slowly; what was that to do with IBC?* At times it felt like they had crossed the line.

He really did like Esther. She was not open to a relationship; refusing to mix business with pleasure. Pity. They would make a good team. He'd even started to write again, thanks to her encouragement. *Talent must not be wasted but utilised* – he could almost quote her word for word.

'Any questions?' No one responded. They never did. He dismissed them, watching them file out.

At least, it was over. He needed to give Esther a call, perhaps they could have another of her home cooked meals?

Cornelius was glad that they had met. She'd encouraged him to get back to his roots, to his inner itch. The loss of his drive had come soon after the rejection of the last book and the fallout of his sounding his most controversial musings. Writing, even the thought of it, left him feeling physically sick.

Esther did not agree with his ideals but thought that his voice added balance to the argument. She was all for free speech.

WEDNESDAY 10TH JUNE 2026

'"Chaos not order is the fate of all life if left to its own devices. External control ensures that life moves along smoothly."'

A quote from his school days did not seem the most appropriate way of dealing with the situation, but it was the first thing that came to mind. Cornelius could not believe it. Another quote floated through his mind, "Failure in effectively monitoring is often a precursor to disaster."

That was his job, that was why he was here. To maintain order. Hana Cha was about to feel the laser tip of his tongue.

'The embryo *Darwin 666003* is contaminated! The cells are riddled with bacterial and viral contamination! How has this happened?' Cornelius could feel the tiny spittle missiles, that accompanied his rantings, flying from his mouth. One landed on Hana's cheek. She did not move a muscle.

He had his back towards his desk, he stood towering over her about one arm's length from her. Face to face. He could see her lab coat trembling, her face deep red, eyes facing the floor. Not only was his job on the line, the whole Living Doll Project could be severely delayed. She was scared. The horrendous situation had occurred on her watch. She could not look at Cornelius, focusing on the label on his lab coat. 'I think—'

'Wrong answer,' interrupted Cornelius, 'I want to know in detail what happened. Have a report on my desk before you go home today. This is really terrible.'

Hana left Cornelius's office hastily while sweating profusely.

How could it have happened? When did it happen? All of her technicians were meticulous in their work – she would have it no other way. Contamination indicated that aseptic technique had not been followed. It could mean the daughter cells were infected or…

The thought made Hana want to be throw up. If the source cells were contaminated: total disaster. Providing lab protocol had been followed there was always a backup of original genetic material before any new procedures began. That way, the information could be saved and stored before the new cloning process was underway. This ensured that a technician could always revert to an earlier stage in the process. Contamination indicated that basic laboratory procedure had not been followed. *Had the backing up procedure taken place?* The lab report for that embryo would reveal the truth.

At her portal desk Hana activated her screen – an automatic retinal scan took place along with a visual check of her palm print. On her virtual keyboard she typed in the identification code, *Darwin 666003,* then tapped the virtual search button. Immediately the embryo report appeared.

'Review the history and give me a log update.' She rubbed her temple. Within a few minutes she knew the name of the technician, the date that the procedures had been carried out and the fact that a contamination check test had not been run. Someone was about to lose their job.

+++

'You wanted to see me?' Eun placed both of her arms behind her back and made a silent prayer to her ancestors.

'Close the door,' replied Hana, Eun obeyed. 'Sit down.'

Eun could sense intense heat behind on her left cheek, that only happened when she was terrified. She sat upright, looking at the sheets on Hana's desk.

'According to the data log you worked on *Darwin 666003* on 04/06/2026. Is that correct?' Hana paused briefly before going on, 'It has your digital signature on the report.' *You are guilty and you must pay for your mistake. That or you'll drag me with you, you idiot!*

'Yes, I think so. It was some time ago and I work on many different projects every day—'

'Are you aware of the laboratory protocol?' Hana cut across her technician's quiet voice, 'Did you run all of the required checks? Did you follow aseptic technique procedures?' Hana stood up, only the desk separating her from Eun. Her fingers pressed onto the surface of the desk, both thumbs gripping the edge.

Eun attempted to think back to the date in question. She was scared. Then, the bolt hit her, the work experience student – *Do Ho* – who had begged her to allow him to carry out a cloning procedure. Fear turned into horror, her hands claw-like, a sudden pain erupting in the centre of her chest.

Yes, Do Ho. She recalled her initial reservations – and the way that he had won her over. That persistent smile, those enchanting eyes and the fact that his father was an old school-friend of her father – that was to be respected. Korean culture required it to be so. How foolish she had been. Not only had she left him unsupervised, she had started a new project and it had run into difficulties. It was all coming back to her.

She had asked Hana to come and assist her, she knew she was out of her depths. The solution took so long, by the time that the matter had been resolved. She recalled completing the log report on the new project but… the thought made her shudder. She had shut down the file on 666003 without completing the technical report.

The following day she realised her error. She hastily retrieved the report, frantically finishing it, by then, the contamination must have already taken place. *How could she have been so stupid?* Eun knew she could not tell Hana what had actually transpired.

'I… must have,' her voice got quieter, phrases mumbled. 'I must—'
The words doomed her.

'You are incompetent. I repeat: incompetent!' Hana shrieked lapsing into Korean. 'Do you realise how serious this matter is? You could lose your job over this. You foolish, foolish person.'

Hana had some concern for the cowering technician. One of the responsibilities of the technical supervisor was to check the logs on all projects at the end of the day. Hana recognised that, in reality, the mistake was hers. However, she could not lose face in the presence of a junior team-member. 'Leave my office please. I will have to take action on this matter.'

Eun bowed slightly before rushing out of the office. She would have to bear the consequences of her actions; her misplaced act of kindness had backfired. It was almost impossible for her to concentrate on the assignments allocated to her that afternoon. Hardly a word passed from her lips during the rest of her shift.

As Hana typed the report for Cornelius, she began to cry. She had let herself down and now her family would suffer. Though she could and almost certainly would blame the technician, the truth of the matter was that it had been her duty to check the reports.

She had not. She had failed.

+++

By the end of the day, two people had been asked to leave their positions at IBC-Korea. Cornelius felt no remorse in contacting Human Resources, asking them to initiate dismissal proceedings. There were no second chances in South Korea and IBC had capitalised on that fact. It resulted in a high degree of efficiency but, in the process, human beings became a easily transferable commodity.

There would at least be the money owed up until the point of dismissal. There would be no severance pay. The employees would have twelve hours to clear their belongings from the laboratory and forty eight hours to move their property out of the accommodation block. Two new replacements would be sourced immediately. One would be an internal promotion from technician to Technical Supervisor – indeed, Chun Cha rejoiced at her sudden advance – and the other would be drawn from the long list of suitable applicants. There was nothing personal about the whole procedure. Relationships were simply second to performance.

Things moved swiftly at IBC. Cornelius dreaded writing the technical report that would soon be heading in Karl's direction. He would not be pleased at the latest set of developments. *Darwin 666003* had been backed up, the original genetic material had been stored before the contamination, however they were now four days behind schedule. This was a dreadful day for the Cloning Division.

As Karl stared down the eyepiece of the photon microscope, a rippling sensation raced down his back, accompanied by a sense of wonder. Reminding him of the time when he looked at views from the Hubble telescope. Awe and fascination.

The embryonic chimera divided before his very eyes. Now at the eight cell stage, this was nothing short of miraculous.

Karl had his own plans for a Genesis Project, just like the idea in *Star Trek – The Wrath of Khan*. Creating life from next to nothing. Very private investigations. 'So there has been no rejection of the additional DNA?'

Chloe shook her head and frowned. 'Not as far as we can detect. It is being held in the host DNA and is copied every time the cell undergoes mitosis.'

Being next to Karl in the lab, both exciting and frightening. His creative space. He was often entirely charming but she had seen – *more and more lately in fact* – that he could quickly switch, becoming a malicious individual. The precise moment of transition could not be predicted. A wrong answer, a hesitation presumed to be a withholding of information, an unsatisfactory lack of data – she could never tell when it was about to happen.

'Wow,' he said, 'Max will be ecstatic.'

'Max Augustine?' Chloe was surprised to hear his name in the lab.

'Oh, yes, he shows a real interest in all projects that are pushing into new areas of the industry.'

'Will he be visiting us on site?' She even dared to think of inviting Karl and some of the team around for a meal. She loved having people around, displaying her hospitality; it was a gift she enjoyed displaying. However life for her revolved around the lab, living quarter, gym and the occasional spree in Pohang. Entertaining people and making them happy, it made her day.

Having people around made her think of home, she missed close friends back home in the States. Still, being part of this project made her the envy of her former class mates at MIT. At times the excitement of being on the cutting edge of science gave way to deep feelings of sadness.

'How many embryos have been produced so far?' He continued, 'What stages of cell division are they at?'

'I'll check with—'

'You mean you don't' know? What are you being paid for?'

And there it was. He had snapped again. Chloe fought the urge to cry. Every time she thought she was getting somewhere with Karl. Every single time. This.

'Go and find out,' he looked up at her as if she had said something horrible, 'Now!'

Karl watched her leave, her golden braid tucked into the back her lab coat. He could not help smiling with satisfaction as he contemplated the dividing embryos under the microscope, his embryos. He tapped in a reminder on his smartphone to contact the Cloning Division. *These genetic profiles need to be preserved.*

He would personally check that the genotypes of the successful embryos had been kept up to date and that they could be mass produced at a future date. Cornelius had messed up once before, Karl would make sure if did not happen again, not now.

After all he might need them for the future – for his own little experiments.

Chloe headed down the corridor. Her body still felt weird after the fertility treatment; she found herself extremely emotional, the slightest of things would set her off. Even watching the embryos made her feel teary. Her eggs, her secret.

Karl, he was impossible. Having a meal with Karl, no chance, no way. She would invite other members of the team, but not him.

WEDNESDAY 24TH JUNE 2026

A tight fit. The whole team crammed into Esther's office. Bright sunlight warmed the room and helped create a jovial atmosphere in what might otherwise have been a very tense situation.

'We have now reached the fourteen cell stage. There are five embryos that responded well to the latest round of chemical stimulation. The remaining five did not progress beyond the eight cell stage.' Esther smiled wearily.

She was proud of the core group, made up of herself, Chloe, Ade and Hiroo. They supported her and she believed in them. She had no doubt that some of these people would go on to do great things – why, they were doing great things already. *It's like being a mother,* she thought. She loved it.

'Are we ready to try for implantation?' Chloe was fast on the uptake. As ever, she was a confident and hungry for progress. She relished the breaking of limitations. Esther knew this. But she also knew that in the midst of all her confidence, Chloe's insecurities could easily surface, exposing the vulnerable child. During those moments she needed reassurance and the occasional hug. Esther felt happy to oblige. Knowing her history helped a lot, Bethany's insights proved to be invaluable.

'The key things will be to select the surrogate mothers. Interviews are taking place as we speak. Human Resources will send the top twenty candidates to us. You'll be glad to know that the response to the advert was incredible.' Esther continued, 'Over two hundred women applied! Thankfully, the medical checks and all the other hard work will have been sorted out by the hospital staff.'

She smiled at Ade. He was Nigerian. His skin stood out in stark contrast with the brilliant white of his lab coat. 'Ade, could you get create a list of key questions that we need answers to?'

He nodded.

'Show it to me before you release it to the rest of the team. There should be some starter questions in the…' She thought for a moment, 'Sorry… in the surrogate mother folder. That's right.' She reassured herself, she had the occasional senior moment. More often since being on the Living Doll Project. 'Their psychological states are crucial. Check that we have the results of their personality profiles before we see them.'

Ade moved expeditiously, leaving the rest of the core team waiting for their respective assignments.

Esther was worried. Implantation carried risks. With no previous case studies to refer to, it was a step into the unknown. Her expertise in plant science provided little help on this project and she was forced to rely on the collective knowledge of her team – and, of course, Karl.

Volunteers would be compensated heavily but the personal impact could not be predicted. Any rejection of the embryo would precede a miscarriage, along with all the usual physiochemical and psychological repercussions. Any failure to conceive would also end their place on the programme and they would be denied the financial incentive that had brought them to IBC. Payment upon results. The longer you stayed on the programme, the heftier the reward.

Esther was aware of her own moral conscience, but she also knew that she was a scientist, not a social worker. Human Resources were paid to look after that side of things. All the same, she often wondered how – and secretly, *whether* – she could avoid emotional involvement. Her mind had wandered. She dispelled the ugly thoughts.

'Chloe, I want you to take the lead in the interviews – supported by Hiroo. Make an audio-visual record of the process. I want to be shown the top ten candidates. I will let you choose them and I will decide on the final five.'

Her confidence in Chloe had soared over the last few months. Despite her occasional emotional outbursts – which were, admittedly, increasingly difficult to deal with – the young woman was exceptional and the quality of her work was brilliantly unprecedented.

Chloe smiled and nodded. Esther had faith in her. Most importantly, she had shown it in front of the others. So often she felt like the new kid on the block – and in many ways she was. Her progress at IBC felt like a dream. Perhaps a little like fate; a little uncontrolled and, in that sense, a little scary. But here was Esther. Ready to acknowledge her; to support her in front of her colleagues.

She thought again of Karl – and of his rabid anger. But it was only fleeting. Admittedly, she thought, her new role would mean that her practical work would be placed on hold until the whole process was over. She would need to reorganise her daily activities and pass certain responsibilities on to one of the junior team members.

Who will I a—

'By the way, Karl requested that you contact him before you leave tonight.' Esther did not enjoy passing messages.

Chloe looked concerned, twisting her braid between her fingers. Her tick. 'Why does he want to see me?'

'You'll have to ask him yourself I suppose. Good luck!' Esther chose to avoid further involvement. It annoyed her that the young woman was still interested in him. *Even after his recent moods.* Whatever was happening between Chloe and Karl was only likely to annoy her more. She brushed it aside and continued, 'Okay, the rest of you, we need to get moving. It's going to be a long day.'

Visibly subdued, the remaining team members filed out of Esther's office. Their slow pace, low voices, the exchange of glances… speaking volumes. She felt for them.

'Paperwork, paperwork – the bane of my life,' Esther mumbled as she sat at her desk, 'I need a secretary.' She started preparing the latest update. It needed to be with Karl by the end of the day.

Things were progressing very well; even she was surprised at the recent rate of progress. The bleep of her smartphone reminded her that the Science Management Group were meeting later that afternoon. She knew that she was a good manager. A better scientist, but a good manager all the same. She really did hate the paperwork though. And she didn't like Karl. His attitude, mostly. It was all a little too much.

Esther carefully removed her glasses, wiping her brow slowly; she thought, *I am totally out of my depth.*

EARS THAT HEAR

The rep was back.

Ahn Jong-kyu wondered why they kept making changes to their clothing range. It seemed that clients would always demand the latest option. It was entirely typical of the fashion industry and he viewed the whole thing with cynicism. Admittedly, it was a clever business move. He was about to switch off from it all when the rep mentioned that the new range could be used to monitor not only the features picked up by the biosensor, but also communications. Speech patterns could be detected and, at a slight cost hike, micro-cameras could be incorporated into the IBC logo, enabling a detailed feed up to a range of three metres. Ahn Jong-kyu felt the mini tidal wave of shock just below his ribcage. The information could then be stored on the database computers and, should any issues arise, that data could be recalled and analysed.

Charles and Max made the immediate decision that this would be factored into IBC-Korea's general expenditure and accommodated by the central finance plan. There was no discussion with the rest of the committee, leaving their advisers to feeling redundant. All pretence of democracy vanishing from the room.

Clothing that could record conversations and enable colleagues to spy on each other – Ahn Jong-kyu shook his head several times in disbelief. The Head of the Human Resources Division, Phillippe Bernard, sat in on the meeting. He knew that when it came to confidentially and monitoring at work, local law was on the side of the employer. Ahn Jong-kyu looked across at Phillippe, who remained stony-faced and silent.

Suddenly Ahn Jong-kyu remembered the dream – clothes with eyes. *Clothes that could see!* Now he could interpret the symbol of the clothing. Ahn Jong-kyu's head seemed lighter, the room trembling ever so slightly. He breathed in deeply and regaining his composure.

The new lab coats would be issued in September 2026. Ahn Jong-kyu's eagerness to reopen his conversation with Chung Cha made him twitch; he wanted to leave the meeting and get on the phone to his mother in law. She was right.

All matters discussed by the Business and Financial committee remained confidential. He considered his own suit. He had purchased that himself, and from a very respectable tailors. It made him stand out in – he thought – the appropriate way. He used a good deal of his first or maybe second paycheque to buy that suit but he was suddenly very happy that it belonged to him in its entirety.

He was glad that he was not a scientist at IBC.

WEDNESDAY 15TH JULY 2026

Esther and Chloe stared at each other, struggling to believe the news they had just heard from Dr Chun. All of the pregnancy tests had come back negative, except for one.

Chloe appreciated Dr Chun's professionalism. The ways she acted as if this was the first time they had met.

'Karl will be livid, furious, perhaps even psychotic,' Chloe was trying to be funny. Esther certainly wasn't in the mood for merriment. 'Come on Esther, at least this is a trial run.'

'May I remind you that we have four women who have just lost out on a huge financial opportunity. How do you think that they'll explain this to their disappointed families?'

At times, Chloe seemed to lack the basic empathy that Esther thought it took to qualify as a human being. *If she had lost a baby, perhaps she would be more compassionate.*

Being ambitious was one thing, but not at the expense of humanity. Again, she asked herself, *what am I doing here?* A great many female scientists faced major threats to the basic instincts woven into the psychology of a woman. Care and nurture could be laid aside for the drive of industry and the pursuit of knowledge. *Ignored at what cost?* Esther knew that she didn't have an answer.

'Who's going to tell them?' Chloe looked worried. 'Is that down to the medical staff or do *we* have to get involved?'

'The medical staff will speak to the women involved, then Human Resources will take over. At least they'll have their expenses and transport costs met.' Esther sighed, feeling tightness just above her kidneys; early signs of stress overload. 'We are going to have to get back to the lab. This is not going to be an easy afternoon.'

Esther took off her Calvin Klein designer glasses, masaging her eyes through her eyelids. They felt exceptionally heavy today, living giant ball bearings – sleeping at night was becoming harder. 'By the way, you're right. Karl *is* going to be livid. I hope that the cloning section have done their job. We're going to need some more embryos.' Then the stomach churning feeling started again. She could feel it, revolving inside her, her inner emotional washing machine.

'So now we are pregnant. It begins,' said Chloe, twisting her braid pensively.

Esther's thoughts were deep, reflective; her fears whispering at her as an uncomfortable foreboding feeling swept through her body, leaving her cold. They had down all they could, it was up to nature to take its course.

For a moment, Chloe withdrew from the scene, looking out of the panoramic silver framed windows. The gorgeous view of the bay. A clear blue sky, fresh winds rolling waves towards the shore.

Her DNA had entered the cycle of life. It was a joy that she could not share with anyone else. A lonely secret, she bore the weight of it. Yet alongside that, deep sadness at the loss, the loss of the others.

Only she and a few other people would ever know that some of her children had passed from this world, inside the wombs of unknown women. Strangers she had selected during interviews. How ironic.

One of the embryos had survived. She was going to be a mother. While Esther looked pallid and tired, Chloe began to glow.

NATURE VERSUS THE PROJECT

Monday 20th July 2026

This was *not* good news.

Esther bit her lower lip The pregnancy, a failure. That came as no surprise. Nature selectively weeds out the weakest or the genetically abnormal – she knew that. It simply rips them out of its system. This represented a major road block.

She gazed at the framed photograph of her mother and father on the adjacent wall, hoping for inspiration. Sighing heavily, she refocused on the IBC-Korea logo, suspended on the flickering screen in front of her. The motto – *inspiring future hope* – seemed ironic.

With a blink of her left eye the screen came to life.

'Email,' she said. Though her voice was heavy, almost a shadow if itself, the machine responded. A blank proforma flashed onto the screen. Esther decided to dictate her thoughts to the rest of the team. They would need to meet that afternoon, immediately after lunch. Karl already knew. No doubt he would want to be present. She added his name to the list of recipients.

Where do we go now? Fresh ideas were desperately needed. The possible rejection of the host embryo would be the making or breaking of this whole enterprise.

She sighed again, another set of lab reports needed scrutiny before she could even think of having lunch. Cornelius, from the Cloning Division, had also requested a meeting. He wanted to iron out a few queries on the most recent samples that he had sent over.

Esther felt tired, even her bones were heavy – for the first time since she had joined IBC-Korea she sensed defeat. She removed her glasses, rubbing the bridge of her nose.

In some ways she would have been glad if the whole project was dropped and she could return to her world of botany. 'Life is not simple,' she spoke to herself, replacing her glasses.

The email programme responded by recording her words. 'Delete the last sentence. Add signature, check content, report to me before sending.'

Another difficult meeting was coming up.

TUESDAY 21ST JULY 2026

The Human Technology Division's group consisted of Hiroo, Chloe, Ade and Esther. Karl joined them. The meeting reached stalemate rapidly.

'So what *is* the next step?' Karl could not contain his irritation, 'We need to repeat the procedures.'

Esther scowled at Karl from across the conference table. 'We are taking about human pregnancies, not lab rats. We would need another set of women who are willing to act as surrogates.'

'Human Resources have long lists of willing subjects, Esther. So let's get moving. Chop chop.'

Esther leaned forward, 'Unless we can overcome the rejection issues, we have gone as far as we can go at this time. Nature has a way of saying 'no' in certain situations.'

'You're a scientist! Nature is not beyond *our* control! That is why we are where we are today. Let's try two embryos for each pregnancy. We'll need fewer surrogates, and we double our chances of success.' Karl looked tired.

Chloe wondered if he was sleeping. She wondered the same thing about Esther. 'Isn't that risky?' She raised an eyebrow questioningly.

Esther nodded in agreement, adding 'This whole venture is risky.'

Karl's expression made it blatantly clear that Esther had strayed beyond the line. 'If we don't take chances we are not going to make any progress.' Karl paused before continuing, 'The longest pregnancy lasted for three weeks. Why did that one go on for so long? Suggestions, people; now.'

Ade raised his hand and spoke, 'This mother already has two children, all of the other mothers had one child. Could it be related to the state of their immune systems?' All eyes were focused on him. 'Perhaps subsequent pregnancies face a less severe immune response?' He shrugged his shoulders, unsure of the validity of his comments.

'That is a very interesting thought.' Karl seemed pleased again. 'Why don't you check her blood work and compare it with the other subjects.

There may be some unique aspect that made all the difference. Good idea.' Karl smiled briefly.

Ade nodded vigorously while Esther wrote out his idea on the virtual screen projected onto the conference room wall.

Chloe added, 'Maybe the genes we have added from other species activate the immune response in the way a normal embryo does not. If we could change or dampen the response it may help.'

'Yet another good idea,' Karl nodded enthusiastically. 'I think I read a report a couple of years ago about the possibility of making changes to the immune response in cases where the blood type is different from that of the prospective mother. Who was it…?' Karl pondered for a moment, 'A team in… Where was it?' The memory came flooding back, 'Romania, that's it. Follow up that line, Chloe.'

The warm expression on Karl's face seemed strange. Chloe thought – *He's smiling at me. Wow!*

'Back to the mothers to be. How many should we use this time?' Esther tapped her pen on the table's surface, irritated.

'Choose six subjects this time. We want to leave our options open for the future.' Karl held up six fingers to emphasise his point. 'Ask Human Resources to run the ad campaign again, those who have already applied need not re-apply.' At the sound of the bleep, Karl looked at his phone resting on the table. A reminder – meeting with Max at 16.30. He so wanted to give him some good news.

'I'll get on to Cornelius to produce copies of our embryos. How are we going to select the ones we use this time?' Esther addressed Karl. 'I think the embryo used in the longest pregnancy should be used, that was *Darwin 666003114226.*'

'Yes Esther, that would be a good starting point.' Karl's response was positive. She hadn't really expected that. It took her a little off guard and Karl continued, 'I'll let you and the team decide on the other embryos you wish to include. At this stage we are playing a guessing game.'

The team appreciated his honesty.

'Right – I feel my work here is done. Excuse me I have a couple of other tasks to get to. Esther, send me the minutes from this meeting along with the reference numbers of the embryos that make the final cut.'

Esther nodded and Karl carried on with his instructions. 'We are going to need six in all. Doubling up on embryos could be an option; equal numbers of male and female at this stage.'

Karl collected his sheet, well aware that everyone was watching him. Still smiling again, he made a swift exit from the room leaving a somewhat bemused team with much to decide. He spun around, 'Oh by the way, tonight is Abba night, I expect to see everyone there.'

Esther shook her head.

<h2 style="text-align:center">WEDNESDAY 22ND JULY 2026</h2>

Dear Diary,

Yesterday night was a knockout! Everyone was stunned when I walked into the hall as Agnetha. Mouths dropped open. It was like stepping into a museum from the 1970s, the only occupants rigid pop star mannequins. Esther made an effort as an overweight Anni-Frid, those clothes were far too tight. Mutton comes to mind!! Still she made a fuss of me, calling me beautiful and stunning, asking me if I wanted to sing using the karaoke machine. I did not! Even Karl paid attention. He drinks too much for my liking. I saw him knocking back some very heavy liquor. Just cos it was free, courtesy of IBC! He talked a lot about Glenda. Nobody has met her yet, she seems to be his woman. The idiot tried to grope me, what did I ever see in him? I really liked him at the beginning; that is changing by the hour. I refused to dance with him.

We did this group dance thing, Esther and the rest of the team. That was fun, Esther is good fun to be around. She asked Karl to be involved. He refused, stood watching us, sulking because he got rebuffed. He is such a child.

I have a bit of a headache today. Not able to handle the liquor as I once did. That is a good thing I think. Have not done my science journal for a while, getting a bit slack, promise to sort that out…

HOW TO SOLVE A PROBLEM?

Here we are again, thought Karl as he sat in the same familiar chair in Max's office; he noted the new painting on wall, it looked like a Picasso.

Max adopting the same posture and position. *Is there something magnetic about that particular spot – or does he derive some cosmic energy from the portrait?*

'I do not derive *energy* from anything of which you are aware,' responded Max.

Karl jumped. For a blindly fearful moment he wondered if he'd spoken his thoughts aloud. His cheeks cooled rapidly, he could feel perspiration seeping through his shirt. *No, I did not! At least he th—*

Max seemed to glide into his chair before locking his eyes onto Karl's. 'The project seems to have lost momentum. Why?' Max drummed his French polished fingers on the teak desk. 'I expect so much from you, Karl.'

His words hit home. Karl found himself accepting personal responsibility for the slowed pace of the Living Doll project, his head dropped. The truth of the matter – the human body did not respond well to the introduction of foreign genetic matter, even when mingled with human genes.

'The rejection issue is delaying our progress. We are working on it.' Karl's tone was deeply apologetic, 'The next set of surrogate mothers are about to be impregnated.'

'I've read your report Karl; I know the facts.'

Max's face seemed to morph before Karl – a grotesque mask appeared on his face resembling a mixture of animals – a blend of a rabbit and a frog. A second pair of eyes superimposed over Max's natural ones; the shape of the pupil, reptilian. Karl tried not to stare but he felt repulsed at the sight.

Was it real or…? Like something from Star Trek.

The ellipse eyes blinked twice, the temporary mask vanished replaced by the dour face of Max which moved closer towards Karl's trembling frame.

'Why have we lost momentum? That was my original question.' Max stared coldly, then turned away from Karl.

'I think Esther may be part of it.' Karl continued, hurriedly, 'Her expertise is in plant genetics, she has to rely on the knowledge of those us who are trained in human and animal physiology and anatomy. She is admittedly brilliant in her field but—'

'Didn't you choose her for the project? Wasn't she the best for the job?'

Karl was unsure whether Max was being sarcastic. He didn't know how to respond. He paused for a second then forged ahead blindly, hoping that it would suffice.

'At the time she was, however we are now at the point where her knowledge is no longer an asset to the project. Her personal moral stance is a hindrance to the general atmosphere within the team.'

Somehow Max had opened up a vent in Karl, his thoughts came tumbling out. Almost as if he couldn't really help himself. The deep-seated resentment towards Esther, fuelled by being genuinely furious about her pushiness. All of those confrontations and arguments with Esther! She *was* a problem for the team. *She has to go.* The tinderbox spark became a flame fanned by Max's face contorted by disdain; Karl made his final decision. 'I feel that my initial suggestion was right, but she has become a liability.'

Max's response shook him. 'Then dispose of her.' Max turned away from Karl and looked at the portrait again.

Dispose of her. It sounded like he was talking about getting rid of an unwanted specimen from the lab. Karl glanced away for a second, unsure what to think.

'I put you in your position so that you could manage this project. If you cannot handle the job then step aside and let someone else take over. Momentum must be regained. I hope that I am making myself clear, *Karl*.'

Their eyes locked again, Karl looked down towards the floor.

'I expect to see change and soon. We have the next meeting of *the Light* group in two days – at the usual place and time. Charles will want to have a personal word with you about the project. Make sure you are ready to up-date him.' Max turned away from the portrait. 'We are finished.'

'Yes, Max. Thank you for your time.' Karl was reduced before him yet again. Inside he was furious. *You need me Max! My expertise, my leadership… and by the way my genetic material started this project.*

He suddenly stopped reasoning. Max seemed to know his very thoughts.

As if to confirm this, Max turned and giving him an extended arctic look of disdain. Karl rushed out, almost tripping on the deep pile carpet.

Once outside the office he leaned against the door, breathing heavily. Something weird was going down, and now he seemed to be caught up in the middle, enclosed.

Hyun-jung gave him a wry smile, before continuing her work. That was not the first time she had seen that particular look.

THURSDAY 20TH AUGUST 2026

Esther had sensed the change in Karl for some time, definitely over the last few weeks. He no longer held back his contempt, nor did he bother to disguise his disapproval of her ideas. It was as if he was trying to get her to reach the point of giving up. To throw in the towel and quit. However he had picked the *wrong* person.

Growing up in Tel Aviv, she learned to be prepared for any eventuality. The frequent air raid sirens, practices and the real thing, taught her to be flexible and mentally tough. A constant sense of grief and loss coloured her early years, culminating in the death of her brother.

The suicide bombing took place on Wednesday 22 November 2000 – at Hadera, the site of the attack – in the main street. A booby trapped car. Hamas claimed responsibility – two people died, one of them, her beloved brother, Samuel. His crime was being on patrol duty as part of his military service, when the bomb went off. She knew from bitter experience that not every death was reported on CNN. The silence of the media impacted the whole family, not to mention her neighbours back in Tel Aviv.

This woman is not for turning; just like the British Prime Minister Margaret Thatcher, one of her role models. Outspoken and fearless in the face of opposition, she transformed the face of the nation within a few years of her leadership. Hated by some, loved by others; people struggled to adopt a neutral stance. Esther wasn't dissimilar. People either loved her or hated her. It was obvious where Karl stood, He had side stepped into unbridled disgust.

The other team members had noticed as well. Chloe tried to stand up for Esther but was too conscious of the potential loss of favour from Karl, so she withdrew open support when sufficient pressure was applied. The other team members, Ade and Hiroo stayed out of the way whenever things got heated. Esther lived with the sense of increased isolation, well aware of the escalating tension.

The failure of the second round of pregnancies signalled the final straw. The longest pregnancy lasted only two weeks this time, a week less than the first attempt. The other implantations lasted a few days before being rejected. Six more women suffered the trauma of miscarriage and lost out on their money – double devastation. The project was most definitely on hold. Unless this issue of rejection could be overcome the Living Doll Project would remain a theoretical dream.

The day of the final miscarriage – the core team meeting could only be described as volcanic.

'Has anyone got any suggestions that have not been investigated?' Nobody responded to Karl's question. 'I still think this immune repression could be the way forward. Ade and Chloe put in some excellent work on investigating this but we seem to have come to dead end.' Karl nodded at them, making it so clear that they were his favourites.

Esther found him so predictable, his strategy – pitting one member against another. She raised her eyelids; knowing she had been the one who prompted this line of enquiry. She made contact with Louise Dalton, a specialist in immune system suppression in animal surrogate mothers. Esther could not be bothered to make a deal of the matter. *So what if the others got the credit?* It was hardly the point.

'Perhaps it is just not meant to be.' Esther made her voice sympathetic but stern.

'What did you say?' Karl slammed his fist on the table and glaring at Esther. 'We are trying to find a solution and all you can offer is your incessant defeatism! Do you even believe in this project?' He leaned in towards her, his body language close and threatening. 'Well?'

Esther sighed and took off her glasses. 'No, I don't believe in this project.' Carefully, she placed them on the table – a purposefully delicate antithesis to Karl's outburst, 'And if you recall, my area of expertise is in plants; not in playing God with human lives. You knew that when you brought me on board. And you knew that I didn't want to be involved. So no,' she locked eyes with Karl, 'I don't.'

There, she had finally voiced the thoughts that had been bugging her since that first meeting.

Come on Esther, you did wonder why the last Head of Human Technology left so quickly. She thought back to her initial trepidation. No doubt Karl had a part in that episode of the Division's life. *That's probably why they needed someone on the inside to fill the gap.*

Looking around at the other core team members, she noted that they all lacked the experience required should Karl wish for one of them to take on – *my position* – the role of Head of Human Technology. No chance of an internal appointment here. Suddenly everything became very clear. All this time… as if she had been holding her breath; now she could breathe again. It was finally out in the open.

Karl's turn. She watched the faint smile smeared on his face. It mutated into a menacing glare. 'So now we get to the bottom of this. You have been against this project from the outset. You're a Judas in the making.'

Karl's audience sat in stunned silence.

If Karl had intended to aggravate the situation he succeeded beyond his wildest dreams. The very mention of Judas was more than she could stand. Esther could feel the ripple of anger moving through her. Ascending.

She spoke, 'Karl Winwood, you are the nastiest and most deceptive person I have ever had the displeasure of meeting.' Her voice now sad, but furious. 'You manipulate and control everyone you come into contact.'

Esther picked up her glasses before continuing, leaning across the table, towards Karl. 'Frankly, I don't know how you sleep at night. Do you think I don't know about your Gestapo tactics. Does Max really need to be kept up to date so frequently – or are you simply scared? Do you need his authority? I think so. And I feel sorry for the rest of you,' she stood up then stepped back, gesturing around the room, 'because you have to work for this man too. At least I am in a position to stand up for myself.'

Esther put her glasses back on, sensing a note of triumph entering her voice. She continued, 'You should be ashamed of yourself, Karl.'

He licked his lips.

'To be honest Karl I have had enough of you and your accusations – those spoken and those unspoken. Until you came along I really enjoyed my work here, now I simply *hate it*.' She pushed her chair under the table then stood behind it. 'I will not be managed by a childish brute. If you want my resignation, you can have it.'

She had finished. The rest of the team were staring at her. Chloe looked sick. Ade's mouth acting as a fly-catcher.

'We're all pretty upset at the moment, let's not make any hasty decisions.' Karl attempted to calm the bomb blast. *But how dare she belittle me in front of the rest of the team? How dare she?*

If she resigned, a replacement would be needed. He would ensure the right type of person would replace her. Someone who could help them regain their lost momentum. Right now, the situation needed to be managed. Surely he could handle that. He hadn't got this far by losing his temper – at least he didn't think so. She had been right about one thing though. He was an excellent manipulator. And he would have to work this the right way for things to turn out in his favour. In a way, it was a challenge.

Karl continued to smile, licking his lips again. He turned his right palm up in a reassuring manner, 'Let's try calming dow—'

'Calm down?' Now Esther shouted, 'I have no intention of calming down, Karl! I am done here.' She felt herself crack as tears formed in the corners of her eyes.

Esther thought she heard Chloe stifle what might have been a sob from across the room. It seemed distant somehow. She began to gather her paperwork, looking at Karl sitting back in his chair, breathing heavily.

Without looking at the others, Esther turned and walked out of the meeting room.

Karl noted the reaction of the team members. Ade seemed to be listening to her footsteps as they faded, staring intently at the table before him. Chloe wiped her eyes, choking on something. Hiroo had no expression.

He waited a few seconds before speaking, 'Don't worry, people. Everyone is under pressure. Perhaps it's… early menopause.' The joke died in the air.

He glanced in Chloe's direction, hoping for some support. The incident switched on his migraine start button, the pain accelerating towards detonation point. The taste in his mouth, the sensitivity towards light. Esther's fault. Part of him envied her, she could leave. He remained trapped.

Chloe resembled a stiff necked swan, her head wobbling on the rigid support. The sullen expression unnerved him. She avoided eye contact, stood up and strode out, her shoes clicking out a fast rhythm.

I bet she's gone to comfort Esther.

Karl sensed his cheeks turning red. Waves of heat moved down from the top of his head to his lower jaw.

Why do I feel so stupid?

The remaining team members sat in silence.

'Let's break for now.' Karl realised that he was mumbling. He began to collect his own papers, 'We'll meet back later this afternoon,'

There was no meeting later that day. Karl hadn't even given them a time to return. Chloe and the others returned to their own tasks and eventually went back to their various accommodations at the end of the shift.

True to her word, Esther handed in her notice with immediate effect. A rushed meeting was held between Karl, Esther and the head of the Human Resources Division, Phillippe Bernard. Max took part via the Internet portal. Karl already had issues with Phillippe but decided to keep his feelings to himself on this occasion.

Phillippe attempted to calm the situation down, hoping to resolve the conflict. It became apparent that things had already escalated to the point of no return. Esther felt too deeply offended to consider returning to work in same team as Karl.

Max assured her of a good reference and told her that she would be allowed to stay at her IBC accommodation for a further two weeks; until she could find alternative living quarters. She was promised a generous severance package in light of her dedication during the time that she had been with the company – fifteen years of loyal service. He knew the silence clause in her contract prevented the disclosure of information about her clandestine activities at IBC.

However after the call Max gave instructions that Esther's server account was to be closed immediately, preventing her accessing any files related to her previous assignments. A temporary guest account was set up allowing her limited Internet access and the use of basic programmes.

Later that evening Max sent an email to Karl congratulating him on his problem solving skills. He smiled to himself as he typed it. *Karl will do just fine.*

As far as Esther was concerned, her time in South Korea had come to a bitter end and there was no doubt in her mind just who was responsible for this!

Chloe was devastated. Esther's departure opened her eyes to the reality of her management. Any feelings she had previously held for Karl transformed from hopeful affection to deep disdain. Karl stepped into Esther's previous position, taking on her responsibilities on top of his own. Chloe now had to work with him in a much closer relationship. She grew to see him as both cold and calculating. Esther had been right.

Very soon a familiar tightening sensation gripped her every time she was in his presence. Chloe moved from being nervous to feeling fear around him. As if a threat drew near the horizon.

With no one to confide in, Chloe returned to her daily journals. They gave her the opportunity to reflect of her innermost thoughts. Only Esther had known about their existence. The two had shared so much and it was only now that she realised that she had even told Esther about her crush on Karl. Esther had laughed it off at the time. Chloe had forgotten all about it, the memory came back to nipping at her. Now she reconsidered Esther's relationship with Karl. *How much did she think I was on his side?*

Alone and under pressure Chloe became resentful. Her dream job suddenly started to feel like a cold nightmare. The fact of her secret deal only added to the strain, on top of all that she began to suffer frequent headaches. Sleeping at night become increasingly difficult. Chloe visited the IBC pharmacist to seek chemical assistance, telling them that she could no longer rest properly. They issued her with a personalised Biomedi-pod which administered nightly sedatives. The impact and relief, immediate; her sleeping patter resumed normalcy. Chloe was appreciative but worried about her reliance on the drugs, her re-acqaintance with chemical stimulants or in this case depressants. She had been here before.

Rubbing at the bridge of her nose, Chloe sighed heavily. It was 23.30. She glanced again at the clock in her IBC accommodation's kitchen. Time for the Biomedi-pod. She closed her eyes.

Out of nowhere, she thought – *I've stopped dreaming.*

LOUISE SAVES THE DAY

SUNDAY 23RD AUGUST 2026

The job opportunity caught Louise totally off guard. She loved her work at Oxford. She knew her way around the place and the research project, that was extremely fulfilling. The cross species experiments had progressed from their initial conception, becoming a reality. Now she faced intimidation by the thought of leaving all of that behind. Yet at the same time she was a dedicated scientist in a progressive industry and the curiosity factor had always helped her push things forward. It was all too easy for inertia to set in.

Another rainy day in Oxford. Her laboratory space was disorganised, just like it always was. Tidiness had never been one of her strongest traits. Thankfully the lab technician, Alan, prevented chaos from taking over her allocated workspace. The view from her desk gave a panoramic sweep, providing her with a view of the grounds and the sleepy town that she called home.

Two years ago, an email request from IBC landed in her inbox. Answering the query had been relatively straight forward as it related to her own research area. Through that request she come across Dr Karl Winwood, the Director of Natural Sciences.

In December 2024, IBC-USA announced the breakthrough cure for muscular dystrophy. The project data now fully accepted by the medical community; the Reformed NHS managed to get the treatment at a knock down price. Louise had personally spoken to three patients who had received the treatment and were living normal lives. She was impressed.

More recently, Dr Esther Cohen, the Head of Human Technology had been in touch; she had wanted to discuss the role of immune system suppression in animal surrogate mothers. Again, Louise had been able to suggest possible techniques that might assist in the work of IBC. She had wondered how this could be relevant in the area of Human Technology. *Perhaps they were trying to spearhead the move towards transhumanism using animal hosts?* It seemed a little farfetched but one never knew with multi-corporate, independent science institutions. They seemed to have a very American brand of ambition.

She didn't really expect to see it in her lifetime, but she had often considered – even dreamed about – the use of genetic manipulation in transhumanism. There were so many possibilities – from disease prevention to age reduction and even the dramatic improvement of human functionality in future children. Esther had been pretty guarded during their face to face exchange over Intersky.

A recent UN Treaty had made it technically acceptable to change humans at the genetic level but the UK had refused vetoed the ruling and there was no way that Oxford would be going down that road. There had been too much public protest and the government had caved to the demands of the nation. The fact that the Church of England partially funded many UK universities, meant that their chosen pathways had to be acceptable to the religious establishment. Added to that the opposing voice of the House of Lords closed the door on transhumanism in the UK.

And now, soon after, there was the invitation. Karl's email had been more of a job description than anything else. He had underlined a great many sections of the text, where it applied to her experience, as if to show Louise how perfectly she fitted the proposed role. *Head of Human Technology at IBC-Korea.* This was the very job that Esther had been doing. *Does that mean she's left IBC?* Maybe she had been promoted. *Perhaps she can put in a good word for me?* However the management aspects of the job worried her.

Louise was curious but she didn't want to pry. Karl went to great length to highlight the fantastic opportunities that IBC had to offer and Louise noted that the proposed salary was far beyond anything she could have hoped to achieve in the research field of any of the UK academic institutions. Money had never really motivated Louise, except charity. But it truly was an amazing salary for a scientist.

At twenty six, planning for the future meant a lot more than it had at the start of her career. Oxford was an expensive place to rent a home. For the first time in her life she had been able to set aside money every month – but saving enough for a deposit would still take years on her current rate. The IBC job would allow her to generate enough to put down a deposit on a decent home in just three years. Free accommodation and meals too! That would release a huge amount of her salary for other purposes. Gaining a doctorate featured on Louise's list of things to do before she died. Cross species manipulation was another.

Marco, her wonderful Marco Broggani. He was due back from London later that afternoon. He had been selected to head a conference at Imperial College on the very topic that was consuming their shared time, day and night. They were hoping to publish their joint thesis in September 2026. Things were on track for this to be a strong possibility.

Spending time together had kindled genuine warmth between them. He respected her and she certainly respected him. That proved to be a solid foundation for a friendship. Louise could count her close relationships on one hand. Marco could be the one she had been looking for. Though he seemed very shy that made him even more appealing in Louise's eyes. A lot of her academic colleagues were incredibly arrogant and condescending. Marco was not like that at all.

Would they be able to survive such a massive geographic barrier? Did they actually have a proper relationship? She really cared for him, they were close. She wondered at times if they had a long term future. They had never spoken of the future, just the project and reaching its conclusion. Long term commitment – it made her so uneasy. What about life after the thesis? Why was love so confusing, was it love at all?

Now this.

The contract could be for three initial years with the possibility of extension. Louise would be stationed at IBC-Korea in Pohang.

Many of her vacations had been spent exploring China – she adored the people and the language. Mandarin had proved to be a major challenge, but being a student was good for her humility. Being fluent in Mandarin meant she now no longer needed to be escorted by a translator. That freedom allowed her to explore some of the villages off the beaten tourist tracks, giving her unique experiences of the culture, unknown to most foreigners.

During one of those treks, she had met Cheng and Da-Xia Li. They were a warm and generous couple who took her into their home, showing amazing hospitality while she visited the Shandong province. Louise had met their two gorgeous children, Bo and Chang. She loved being with them.

In their city, Qufu, she had seen so many street children, lost and abandoned. The look in their eyes had been eerie; as if they were close to giving up on life. She could not get their harrowing faces out of her mind.

When she asked about their welfare, Da-Xia explained about the one child rule and the impact on families that violated this edict. As a couple they were well off compared to many, but having a second child was not easy. The government funded orphanages were bursting at the seams, so street children was not uncommon. Da-Xia studied the floor the whole time; conscious she was disclosing confidential information.

As Louise listened, the words of Angelina Jolie fluttered back into her mind: "No matter how small, do something!"

These kids had no one to care for them, could I help in some way?

Louise interrogated Da-Xia about the situation. She confessed that they would love to help out, but their finances were stretched. Louise could see the way their empathy shaped their lives, so evident in the way they adored their own children. When Louise asked if having funds would help them to reach out to the children, Da-Xia became excited, saying they could do so much with regular foreign donations.

That was how the idea about an orphanage started. Louise talked this through with Sasha, who agreed to come on board. Together, they worked out how much they could afford and started to send money on a regular basis. Their support enabled the Li's to begin a small work in their home.

Since then, the Li family had rented a modest flat, moving their whole family. Three children had been taken off the streets. According to Cheng, the paperwork was horrendous; red tape upon red tape. However, they were committed and ploughed through.

The pictures and phone calls told their own story, they were ecstatic, tired but delighted. Louise admired them, selfless and genuine. She would have loved to do more.

If she took the job, would she be able to continue on her Chinese adventure; having enough to increase the funding on the orphanage, maybe even starting another one?

South Korea – she faced the prospect of learning a new language and adapting to a new culture. Dad would be pleased for her, whatever she decided to do; as long as she was happy. But what would Mum have to say about this? Louise had already planned to visit her parents the following week-end.

Marco had agreed to join the family. *When will I tell Mum and Dad? Over a meal or during a round of golf? I'm really not sure about this. This is totally out of the blue.*

Alan popped his head around the door, 'Louise, the dean needs to see you at 2pm. There's a faculty meltdown about to take place!'

'Not Renny again? What is the matter with that man?' Louise groaned.

'I'm not getting involved. Don't shoot the messenger.' As quickly as he had interrupted her thoughts, Alan disappeared.

She growled loudly. Professor Alfred Renny – a brilliant scientist, but such a pain in the neck. All of the evidence needed for a tribunal had been gathered. It would all depend on whether the dean was brave enough to tackle the issues at hand. Or maybe he hoped that Renny would find another post before he had to be ejected?

A useless supervisor – most of her work had been carried out without his assistance.

Marco, Renny, her parents and now IBC-Korea.

SUNDAY 30TH AUGUST 2026

'It's your shoot dear.' Patrick Dalton rested on his 9 iron, one arm behind his back. He knew he'd under clubbed that last shot. His troubles were just beginning. *I should have given it 85% instead of that feeble 60%.*

He'd already resigned himself to the fact that there was little chance of beating his daughter. *I taught her everything that she knows and now she's trumping me!*

It was a beautiful day in August, sunny and clear. Surprisingly, the course had very few players. August usually marked the peak of the holiday time.

'Oh, you're right.'

Louise seemed to be deep in thought. 'Are you okay? You seem a little distracted at the moment.' Patrick knew his daughter. Their relationship had only strengthened over time but her decision to move to Oxford meant that he did not see her as often as he would have liked. He worried that she took on too much, never one to say no.

'Dad, I'm thinking of moving.' Louise paused before blurting out her secret, 'Possibly to South Korea.' She winced, pulling her lips into two thin lines. Her pause calculated to allow time for the information to sink in before proceeding.

Still Louise after all these years.

'IBC have offered me a post as Head of Human Technology.'

He saw the way she looked at him, surveying his mood. Trying to work out what he thought, hoping to gauge his response.

The truth? It felt as if someone had punched him in the stomach. When he managed to speak, his voice was quiet, almost painful, 'Have you told your mum?'

'No, I thought I'd mention it to you first. Perhaps—'

'You want me to tell her?' He sighed, then chuckled. Louse had adopted this strategy on a number of occasions. Like the time that she had broken the patio window while playing with Adrian. It was clearly her who had taken the unsuccessful shoot. She immediately confessed to her Dad and sweetly asked him to tell her Mum. With Louise, persuasion came easily.

Patrick was deeply devoted to his daughter, obediently doing as she asked. The punishment would have been greater if Louise had taken charge of the situation. In the end her pocket money was stopped for three weeks. This raised enough money to purchase the putty to put the window back in place. The aim – to teach her a lesson. Even as an adult she was still using the same tactics.

'Would you mind?' Louise touched the back of her father's left hand gently. 'I will speak to her, Dad. But if you could soften her up first.'

'She'll throw at fit, Louise.' Patrick knew his wife too well. She would not take kindly to such shocking news. 'She'll start talking about you not caring for us, your lack of concern about our welfare. She will bring up marriage and grandchildren, and so on.'

'Oh, no – not the marriage talk,' she rolled her eyes. Louise had already had the hor d'oeuvres on this subject served when Marco had mentioned his sister's marriage in Tuscany. Anne, had started talking about how lovely Louise looked in white. Her mother was not a subtle woman. Louise had been mortified and Marco had blushed; almost choking on his fish cake.

'Dad, I want to… I want to eradicate genetic disease. To find ways of identifying and removing bad genes and replacing them with good ones.' The wind had just picked up, flapping her fringe which peeped out from under her baseball cap.

'Isn't that a little like playing God?' Patrick took a swing and watched the ball coursing down the course. *That was a good shot.*

'Well what's 'god' got to do with it? Where was 'god' when Adrian died?' Louise ground her foot as she spoke, exposing a patch of earth.

'Don't do that Louise. Your mother still believes in Him.'

'Well I don't.' She pulled her trolley along, her steps short and fast.

'Still, there are things we are meant to do and things that are beyond our control.' He called to her as she stomped her way towards the next hole.

She turned back to face him, 'Not beyond the control of science. Technology is changing all the time. It is just a matter of time before we can change too; we can change the human genome and remove disease, sickness and poverty. It's possible. We can stop the pain and suffering. Think of all the good that will come from our work. Making—'

'I have heard that that rhetoric before. Except the person speaking those words was on the cinema screen and on the way to becoming a scientific dictator.' He caught up with her, puffing slightly from the exertion. 'And I might add things ended up going very wrong. By the way, what is happening with you and Marco?'

'Why do you ask?' She hated the way she had just snapped at him.

'Well it would be nice to know if I will need my tuxedo at some point before I pack it away in the attic. You know I only wear it at weddings.' He remained calm, choosing to ignore her rude response.

He carefully lined up his next shot.

If I do this right, I could hit it right in the sweet spot. The shot sailed upwards before swerving to the left; her folded arms and sanctimonious look told him she had heard him swear.

'Oh Dad, you are just as bad as Mum. We are friends, good friends.' She unfolded her arms.

Louise and her ways. 'I am not saying you need to get married, Louise. I just asked what is happening? Are you in love with him?' He stood facing her.

'What do you mean by that?' She pushed her fringe away from her face, appearing to focus her attention on the choice of her next club.

'Scientists do still have a word for love in their lexicon, don't they?' He smiled as he said it. 'Your mum and I fell in love and that was why we got married. Life long commitment, forsaking all others; you know, all that vow stuff. Do you feel that way about him?'

'I'm not sure.' She took a swing and missed the shot.

Hope nibbled at the corner of his mind. 'Don't leave it too long dear, if you love tell him.' He checked his watch, before continuing, 'Marco should be here in the next hour… some men are a bit shy about their feelings, you know. Take me, for example.'

'You were shy with Mum?' She crouched down, both hands on the short club, her mouth half open.

'Yes, she made the first move. I was a bit embarrassed but thank goodness she did.' He paused for a moment in thought, surveying the course. 'You still think about Adrian, don't you? That eradicating genetic disease stuff is about him isn't it?' He nodded in defeat, accepting that there was no way he could win.

'Yes. He's my inspiration, Dad. He is always with me. Did you know that I still wear his signet ring?' She stood up, then opened the neck of her blue cotton shirt, proudly displaying her gold chain with the signet ring on. She watched his smile last a few seconds, then the sad expression took over.

'We still miss him. We will always love him. We will always love you. No matter what you do.'

'Thanks Dad,' she touched his arm, 'That means so much to me.'

'Are you really sure about this job? Is it what you want?' They walked side by side, pulling their trolleys. 'South Korea is not a bus ride from Beckenham.'

'There is no guarantee, I have to be interviewed. I'll probably we flying out to Pohang to have look and see if I like them and they like me.'

'Of course they will love you. Everyone does.'

'Dads always say things like that. It's in the father's manual.' They both laughed heartily.

'What do they have to offer?'

'They are the best in the field of genetic transformation, nanotechnology and… well, they're number one, Dad. I could make my dream come true.' She gazed into his eyes.

'You're doing that finger thing – you really are excited.' Louise immediately hid her hands behind her back, almost with a twinge of guilt. 'What can they offer you?'

'A chance to fulfil my dreams and earn a decent salary. I will be right on the cutting edge of science. With all the facilities, all the resources, the best talent from around the world.' She smiled. 'Dreams,' she looked into the distance, shielding her eyes from the glint of the burst of sunlight that illuminated the course, 'can come true at IBC.'

'You sound like their poster girl. You should listen to yourself.'

'Dad!'

'Just making an observation. So it looks as if you have already made your mind up. I guess I will be talking to your mother.' There was no way he was going to make the next shot. Defeat guaranteed.

The rest of the game passed by with very little progress made by either father or daughter. The news had knocked their concentration.

Patrick was right. Anne did throw a fit, and she did talk about the lack of concern Louise was showing for their welfare – but she did not mention either marriage or grandchildren. He wondered if Marco's presence somehow restrained his wife's sabre-sharp tongue.

SATURDAY 10TH OCTOBER 2026

The flight from Seoul to Pohang, so tedious. Louise sat nervously contemplating facing the final stage of the interview process, on her way to IBC-Korea.

She scanned through the latest edition of *Nature* on her generation II tablet, delighted to see that her joint thesis with Marco on cross-species manipulation techniques and cloning had finally made it to publication. She smiled contentedly as she reflected on the initial idea; when it seemed as if they were the craziest people in the world, the only ones who actually believed it could be done. They had managed to resolve almost all the critical elements of their work. Louise revelled in her moment of triumph

Another step forward, she sipped the tonic water, flavoured by a thin slice of lime. *I really want this post.*

Marco and Louise had decided to put things on hold. No major commitments. If either of them found someone else, there would be no guilt. Mum thought she was crazy to let him go. To be honest, if the friendship could not survive the time gap, it would hardly be the foundation of a marriage. He was moving to London, a lecturing post had opened up at Imperial College, he would be a fool not to take it. Part of her felt panicky, she had not taken her Dad's advice. Choosing to keep her feelings to herself.

The seat belt announcement cut through her train of thought. Glancing around at the other passengers she seemed very out of place. There was only one other non-Korean on the flight. A young lady with really long brown hair, seated two aisles in front of her.

Early on in the flight, just after the seat belt alert dimmed, she passed Louise's aisle seat, giving her the most dazzling smile

There was something about her elegant walk, full of poise and grace, like a ballet dancer; her beautiful, thick hair, loosely tied, reached halfway down her back. *Those blue eyes are so piercing.* Louise wondered why she was going to Pohang.

The circular thought came back, *am I ready for such a drastic change in culture – a completely different way of life?*

'Have you finished, Miss?' The flight attendant seemed tired but he clearly wanted to do a good job – the airline prided itself on its courtesy and commitment to care.

'Yes, thank you.' *So many things to think about.* She peered out of the window on her right, the bright autumn sun offered her no assistance. Huge decisions lay ahead. She sighed deeply. *I need some guidance.*

'Please fasten your seat belts.' There was the announcement again. All around her, obedient passengers responded to the request. Louise followed their lead.

WEDNESDAY 14TH OCTOBER 2026

'There is no way she is becoming the Head of Human Technology.' Phillippe slammed the file on his desk, emphasising his point. 'This does not make any sense.'

Karl curled his lower lip in annoyance.

Why does Phillippe think that he can determine what I want? What I need? He is Head of Human Resources, not Director of Natural Sciences. Surely my directorship trumps Phillippe's position? Yet, he conceded, his jurisdiction was not in the area of recruitment. 'She has the knowledge and expertise that we need to move this project forward.'

'Then make her a research scientist, not the leader of the whole section.' Phillippe's face turned various shades of pink; he wanted to shout, but he seemed to be exercising a great deal of self-control.

That man is so ugly, like a goblin. Karl could not help assessing his looks; a long thin nose, a sharp chin, and low height – *the size of a dwarf on steroids.*

'I could help her, Phillippe. Supervise her… give her a hand,' Karl offered his suggestion.

'She is not managerial material. This is a flagship research centre. This is a senior management position. Did you see her scores on the psychometric assessment, or her personality scores? Perhaps one day she might be managerial material but not now, Karl' He huffed as he massaged the edge of the table, rocking on his chair. Karl noted the height difference between Phillippe's chair and his. The man had a Napoleon complex.

'You heard her in the interview. She created an orphanage in China. Think about that – overcoming language barriers, overcoming bureaucracy, overcoming social barriers and—'

'We are not running a charity, Karl. I am in charge of recruitment. Not you. This is a senior post, she is, as you say "wet behind the ears" and she is yet to finish her doctorate. Not, I repeat, not managerial material. You are wrong on this one; very wrong.'

Something about the way Phillippe pointed made Karl want to get up and punch the toad right in his face.

'The team have just gone through a major crisis. They need maturity and strong leadership. Not some British, Oxford recruit who has just reached the very level that many of them left behind many years ago. She has no managerial expertise, none what so ever!' He grasped his face in his hands and groaned. 'The other members of the team would resent her from day one, especially when they find out about her level of qualification and lack of relevant experience. You would be… we would be opening ourselves up to a management nightmare.'

Karl rolled his pen in between his fingers, humming under his breathe. Phillippe's hands reached for the edge of his desk.

'Are you listening to me?'

His puffed out cheeks made him look like a hamster. *Momo had huge feeding pouches.* Karl smiled as the memory flitted through his mind.

'You are impossible Karl.' Phillippe shook his head, rolling his eyes. A great theatrical show, displaying his exasperation.

You're annoying me.

'Anyway there is nothing more for us to discuss. You may run the Science department but your powers do not extend to Human Resources.'

Karl detected a note of triumph in his tone, that so rattled him.

'There are other candidates with more experience of project management, higher qualifications and,' Phillippe wiped away the spittle gathering at the corners of his mouth, 'the decision does not lie in your hands. Thank you for your input, but you can leave it with me. If you would excuse me, I have a lot of paperwork to get on with.' He stood up, smiling, 'Nice of you to drop by though, Karl.'

Karl remained seated, smiling to himself. Poor Phillippe. He really thought he had power and authority. *It is not who you are, it is who you know.* All he needed to do was make one little phone call.

'I could supervise her work and see that she gets trained on the job. We can even give her a short term contract, say, six months. If that does not work out she can demoted and moved elsewhere.'

'Were you listening to me? This is not going to happen.' His left eyelid twitched uncontrollably, giving away his self-contained fury. Karl prided himself, nothing escaped his attention.

Oh yes it is. Karl stood up, placing his pen in his jacket pocket, 'Thanks for your time Phillippe. By the way, I want her to start as soon as possible.'

'Get out!' The polite façade slipped away. *A sweaty amphibian* – Phillippe looked like a frog in boiling water.

'Temper, temper' Karl waggled his finger. 'See you later.' No response from Phillippe, his eyelid still twitching.

Karl whistled loudly as walked down the corridor.

What Karl wants, Karl gets.

THURSDAY 15TH OCTOBER 2026

'Hello Karl,' the voice sounded low and listless.

'Oh Phillippe, how nice to hear from you.' Karl made no attempt to disguise his air of victory. 'How are things in Human Resources?' His smartphone resting on the table, in speaker mode. The display panel showed a crystal clear image of Phillippe seated on his little throne in his office.

'I don't know how you did it.'

'Did what?' Karl enjoyed the image of Phillippe squirming in his chair, having to make this call.

'You must have friends in high places.' The sneer on his face, unmistakeable.

Karl put on his best French accent, 'Moi?'

'I think this is a bad decision.'

'Is there something you want to tell me?' The canteen was virtually empty. Karl had opted for the early lunch shift, he had a meeting in the afternoon and looked forward to an amorous evening with Glenda.

There was a long pause, 'Louise is going to be the Head of Human Technology.'

He layered on the sarcasm and disdain, 'What a surprise!' *Why should I make this easy for Phillippe?*

'I still feel this is a bad choice, but Karl… you managed to undermine me.' He whispered the next part, 'I have a long memory.'

'Are you threatening me?' Karl's voice rose in volume and pitch; he found himself taken by a moment of rage.

'Calm down Karl. I am simply letting you know that you won this time. Paperwork will be sent your way, for your signature.'

Karl could feel his thighs trembling, the sudden rush of adrenaline pumping through his system. 'Don't mess with me Phillippe.' He nervously looked around at the other diners, staring at him. He lowered his voice, 'Don't you ever threaten me.'

'Karl, you are not reading this situation well. Perhaps we need to arrange for some… anger therapy training. I mean, we have read your personality profile.'

What was he insinuating? Karl breathed in deeply several times. Deciding not to respond to the bait.

'Speak to you soon. Please get the paperwork to me ASAP.'

Click.

Who does Phillippe think he is? The meal no longer looked inviting. *I have been given the job of running the project.*

One call to Max had put Phillippe back into his tiny box. Louise would be given on the job training and a short-term contract along with a supervised probationary period, under Karl's watchful eyes.

Who's the daddy now? Friends in high places. That made him smile like a Cheshire.

'Congratulations, Louise.' Louise looked up from her laboratory desk to see a radiant Professor Renny standing in front of her.

'Hello, Professor Renny. Sorry, what are you talking about?' Louise was utterly mystified.

'You never mentioned that you were leaving us for South Korea,' Professor Renny peered at Louise through his new bi-focal lenses.

Louise swallowed hard. He was absolutely right, she had not. But her references – she had to put him down as her referee! He could spoil everything if he had one of his weird moments. Her heart rate tripled.

'I've written you a glowing reference.' Professor Renny leaned towards her; close enough for her to feel his warm sour breath on her face. 'And in return, you will need to help my teaching assistant. There is this new module. I will give her the topics, you will do the research and lecture prep. That should keep you… busy.' He sounded so confident, as if a deal had been struck.

I feel sick. She didn't need the workload right now. However, Renny had the upper hand. That lazy sod was paid to lecture; her services came free of charge. She could report him but…

She heard herself agreeing to his terms. He shuffled off, thinking deep thoughts about the universe – she supposed – or perhaps about how little pedagogical work he would have to do this semester. As for her, well, now there was a massive amount of preparation. Louise grumbled to herself.

My workload is already excessive – I'm trying to earn a doctorate!

References were the last stage in the process. Professor Stanton loved her work so his reference would be outstanding at any rate. She looked around the familiar room.

All change. IBC-Korea here I come.

TUESDAY 8TH DECEMBER 2026

'I'm just not that good at coping with big changes.' Louise was multitasking, in conversation with Sasha while at the same time deciding which of her favourite books deserved to accompany her on the imminent journey to Pohang.

'Okay, anyway, I'll speak to you when you get back. Make sure you ring me.' The bleep of her smartphone indicated the end of the conversation. Louise smiled thankfully, Sasha had been a loyal friend for so many years; definitely worth her weight in gold.

Various titles paraded noisily before her, each declaring their right to be chosen. On the second row of her bookshelf, one book caught her attention. *The Tree of Life* combined visionary scientific thinking with a fantastic storyline. That book made a huge impact on Louise – influencing her life, strengthening her inner resolve to pursue a career in gene manipulation. She allowed her finger to slide down the gilded spine before she pulled it off the shelf.

As she opened it, a photograph fluttered slowly to the floor. Louise bent to retrieve it, a picture of Adrian. Memories flooded back. He looked about nine or ten, leaning against the swing that had been a familiar part of their early lives back in London.

That infectious smile etched on his face; he was always up to something. Louise felt tears stinging her eyes.

Sad. Then the old question – *why Adrian*? Louise gazed at the picture, almost expecting it to enter the conversation, perhaps to provide an explanation for her brother's death. He died so early in life.

'I'll never forget you Adrian.' She thought for a second, then continued, 'I'm going to work so hard, Adrian. To make sure that what you went through will become a thing of the past. I promise. I promise.'

Louise leaned against the bookcase, tracing her finger around the outline of his image. She kissed the photograph. 'I still wear your ring.'

Too many things needed doing. This was not the time to dwell on the past. She stood up and moved towards her half-packed case. *The Tree of Life* made the final cut. It joined the four other books that would be dispatched to South Korea.

A NEW MEMBER OF THE TEAM

SUNDAY 10TH JANUARY 2027

Nervous – that's an understatement. She wiped her damp palm on the leg of her brand new black trouser suit.

Louise sat in Karl's office while he gathered all the staff in the Human Technology Division. The strange, churning sensation in her abdomen testifying to the adrenaline surge.

She looked around the office, her apprehension tangible. A meticulously organised office; the walls covered with certificates and a couple of pieces of art as well. On the desk a framed photograph – looked like a younger version of Karl surrounded by his family. The Persian carpet seemed a bit OTT.

Louise spotted the Biomedi-pod tucked under a grey report on the desk. *I wonder what he is using that for?* Dr Winwood seemed like a picture of health.

Today marked the anniversary of the Treaty that created this opportunity. She heard rushed footsteps in the corridor, her thoughts returned to more pressing matters.

The door opened, Karl's voice filled the room, 'Louise, the team is ready for you now. Just relax and be yourself.'

His advice was sound, but Louise felt over-pressured. *Who on earth am I to feel that I can replace Dr Cohen – the Dr Esther Cohen?* Fluctuating patterns of self-doubt circulated through her mind, stopping now and then to accuse her of arrogance, or perhaps delusion. Somewhere though, the invisible voice of her confidence rose in defence.

Karl's frame blocked her initial view of the packed laboratory. As he stepped aside, she counted at least twenty-four people. A couple of scientists on her left made comments behind their hands. It was impossible to know what they were saying. Louise decided to let it pass – *if I start wondering what people are saying about me now, how can I ever hope to lead them?*

'Is everyone here?' Karl scanned and noted the faces of his team. Everybody had been summoned. He felt from the very start that Louise needed to establish herself. Chloe's petulant look told him that she was not happy with the appointment. He'd already had words with her. In her little mind she viewed herself more than capable of taking over from Esther.

As far as he was aware, she had not experienced enough of the key life-events required for the building of leadership skills. She was too sensitive, too emotionally volatile. Karl secretly wondered how the two ladies would get along. Claws out at dawn, meow!

'Good, then we had better get started. Sorry for taking you away from your tasks,' Karl talked, they listened. 'Can I introduce you to...' he hesitated.

What should I call her?

Part of her recruitment deal was she would be able to complete her doctorate while working for IBC. Long distance learning with a digital submission and an interlink viva voce. He needed to give the impression that she was more than he knew she was.

I might as well go for it.

'Dr Louise Dalton, who is taking over from Esther.' Karl emphasised the last statement, the old order was over; a new era had begun. 'Louise, would you like to say a few words?'

Karl smiled generously, gesturing in her direction. He stepped further to her right hand side, leaving her dangerously exposed. No doubts she would have something to say about *that* introduction. She seemed to have an opinion on most things.

'Hello!' Louise's voice cracked, she sounded like a teenage boy whose voice was breaking. *Not a good start Louise*, she chided herself. 'Sorry about that... nerves got the better of me.' Honesty seemed to be the best policy. A couple of the observers smiled. 'I am honoured to accept the position of Head of Human Technology. I am under no illusion that I am stepping into some very big shoes.'

The room erupted with laughter, Louise blushed.

Chloe looked at Ade, who looked back at her. He knew the history behind that joke...

Esther had large feet, always choosing to wear crocks. She had this habit of taking them off in her office, walking around in her bare feet, sometimes doing this during meetings and conferences. During one of those meetings, Chloe had been sitting next to her. On seeing her dark skinned feet she had whispered, 'What size are those?' Esther had blushed and whispered back, 'Size 14 USA/46.5 Europe. I find it so difficult to get designer shoes!'

Chloe could hardly keep herself quiet, eager to tell the rest of the team. The next day, while Esther was leading the team meeting, she mentioned innocently that big changes were happening. The whole room erupted, Chloe leading the explosion of mirth.

Louise was perplexed, 'What's so funny?'

'Private joke,' answered Chloe. From that time on, Esther had been known as *Dr Platypus* – unknown to her, of course. Louise's innocent comment took them all back to the old days. *Big shoes indeed...* Chloe sighed with regret.

'I'm not sure why that is funny, sorry if I have offended anyone.' Louise had read that managers need to be the peacemaker, leading the way, trying to resolve conflict.

The introduction lasted ten minutes. Louise laid out her personal philosophy and drew attention to the ways in which it aligned with the IBC outlook on life. Her manner was direct; she was not a person who minced words, making it clear that she would bring herself to the table; she had no plans to be a clone of Esther. Her emphasis on her ignorance and willingness to learn, the key part of her speech.

Her prep talk convinced some of them to give her a chance, instead of passing her off as a stuck up foreigner trying to take control.

The room emptied rapidly as the scientists returned to their pressing duties.

'That was really good Louise.' Karl was reluctant to over praise her, she had done well. Louise had excellent communication skills and a good dose of common sense. 'Great start.'

'Thank you Karl.' Louise took the compliment. 'I was so nervous,' she confessed. 'I hope I got the message across.' A jab of doubt pricked her; she massaged her forehead. So tight, like a mountain range had just emerged. Ridge after ridge.

'I'm sure you did. You were *really* good,' Karl offered reassurance. He reached out to touch Louise on her shoulder.

She immediately pulled away, looking at the startled expression on his face. 'I don't like being touched, if you don't mind,' an instructive tone entered into Louise voice.

'Sure, no problem,' he said, although, silently, he took offense. It had been an extension of care. *Who was she to pull away from him?* Still he would mould her into what he wanted. *Louise – brilliant but touchy.*

'So, will I be moving into the apartment block this afternoon?' Louise stared into Karl's face, sensing his discomfort at her rebuff.

'You—' He coughed and cleared his throat, taking a step back. 'You'll need to check with Human Resources.'

Karl walked away from her, sliding behind a vacant hot desk leaning on it. Anything to put a little distance between himself and this strange woman. *She's very weird. Really very weird.*

As far as Louise was concerned relying on first impressions was dangerous, they were seldom correct, the game of judging and being judged prevented clear heartfelt communication. *He comes across as really arrogant, and too touchy feely for me.*

She grimaced at she thought about his touch; the memory of Renny's breath on her face surfaced from her mind. Karl had better watch his hands or he would be in front of the HR panel for harassment at work. But it was only a passing thought. *It's easy to let that stuff stick,* she thought. *I hope it doesn't. I'm sure he's great.*

Esther's absence, her departure. *Why did she leave? This is an enormous responsibility I am taking on.*

Karl repeated his assurance, he would support her, but being a leader of so many people. Like standing on the top of a skyscraper, looking down. Wind rushing around you then suddenly you realise you might fall and go rushing to your death, sailing past floor after floor. That was how she felt at that moment.

Scared, petrified, bone trembling scared. *Are my knees knocking?*

Karl was smiling at her, gesturing for her to leave the room before him.

Oh, you can be a gentleman when you want to. She accepted his act of chivalry. He followed behind her.

SUNDAY 17TH JANUARY 2027

For the second time that morning Karl reminded Louise of the importance of completing "the log" on a daily basis. Email alerts would be sent to remind her if she happened to forget.

The log, a daily record of ideas, data, observations, techniques, failures, successes or anything else associated with the Living Doll Project. As the

Head of Human Technology, the overall responsibility rested upon her shoulders. Every team member could make a contribution to the log and the information would be collated to produce one overall report. It became affectionately known as *"The Bible'*.

Information contained in the log was automatically divided into two categories – public domain or trade secret. The computer software assessed information as it was added to the system. The material in the public domain could be shared with scientists beyond the walls of IBC who daily sought assistance or news requests from the media. The trade secrets were just that – confidential information that would not allowed to leave the walls of IBC, enabling them to retain their lead in this enterprising project.

The use of conscious interfacing in compiling the information represented a new breakthrough in collective collaboration. Developed by the IBC Computing Technology Division, the programme allowed writers to produce a brain map while they worked. This record would be stored along with written records. At a later stage, the brain map could be recalled, by using a word search facility it could be explored for any material that was not already mentioned in the record. When Louise first used the software in January 2027 she was initially sceptical – after two sessions, she became an avid fan.

The phase II version was introduced in December 2027. This added a new layer of interaction in the form of subconscious interfacing. The brain map could analyse activity in the subconscious while the information was being put into the programme. Key words could be used for searches, emotional colouring could also be taken into account – it could analyse the way in which temperament might affect the perception of information. Only IBC possessed this new technology, one of the reasons they were at the front of the race. Their Computing Division combed the Internet for top talent and paid handsomely to recruit the most innovative and fertile minds of technology. MIT was just one of their recruiting sites.

At the level of technicians, an individual was only allowed access to his or her own data. Supervisors could view the data recorded in the system by those under their authority. As Head of the Division Louise, could see the whole department's efforts and so retained control of the log.

Louise imagined senior members of staff and the top executives who shared the same level of security, could access all of the information.

Day by day *the Bible* grew, almost as if it possessed a life of its own.

Things rarely got to Louise; however, the situation with Chloe was becoming untenable. This young woman, of similar age to Louise, constantly managed to carry out instructions according to her own agenda. Not open rebellion, but just enough hesitation and alternative action to make the point that, in Chloe's eyes, the two were on equal terms. Things were being done, but they were being done in her way.

Louise wasn't sure if it was jealousy or something more complex, but she was struggling to cope with the intense feelings of irritation that accompanied her daily interactions with Chloe.

So far, her covert fact finding mission, to discover the reasons for Esther's departure, revealed only that she and Karl did not see eye to eye. Chloe remained tight-lipped about the whole situation. Ade had been more responsive; he seemed to be willing to give Louise a fair chance.

But Chloe's attitude… Louise had tried the compassionate approach, attempting to understand how she must be feeling after the departure of Esther. Louise remembered saying something along the lines of 'I'm sure Esther would have wanted you to stay focused.' The volcanic eruption that had accompanied Chloe's response shook her. With a seemingly uncontrollable rage, Chloe laid into Louise before returning to her task, stabbing at the keys on her computer.

Chloe knew she lost control of herself, it represented the venting of weeks of built up resentment, general rage and sadness. She knew she sounded bitter but didn't care. The tide of toxic emotions had polluted the air; the rest of the immediate team had all born witness and it generated a negative impact on the working day throughout the department. It had not been a pleasant experience and, of course, all of that would make its way onto the records, into the log.

Louise withdrew immediately. Despite her embarrassment she recognised that the issues on the table were nothing to do with her. However, as a manager, she needed to work out a strategy that allowed functional relationships in the team to continue and indeed develop; something that might provide a little resolution.

She spent the rest of the day hiding in her office, desperately reading about dealing with issues over replacing members of former management staff. It was a minefield. She gained a lot of knowledge and advice, realising she was not the first to go through this. She even thought of calling Karl. However, if she started running to him every time she had a problem he would lose faith in her and more importantly she would lose faith in herself. The six month probation period played on her mind, there was no future guarantee if she missed up. To top it all, she found herself biting her nails again.

Louise surveyed Chloe's CV, scanning down the screen before coming to rest abruptly on her educational background.

Chloe has been to Oxford!

In fact she had been there twice, once for a short term course, and then for a year of study as part of her doctorate programme. Louise continued reading, Chloe had spent time at Christ Church College on both occasions. Louise had been admitted to Jesus College, so knew the intense academic processes built into every course. She paused, trying to recall whether she had ever seen Chloe on campus – nothing came to mind.

Still, that meant that they had something in common. "Always find areas of common ground during conflict resolution", Louise recalled reading that phrase the previous evening while munching her way through a bowl of muesli. Now she realised that it could be used as a tool for reconciliation.

A quiet conversation with Chloe seemed in order. 'Shut down file,' Louise's instruction was obeyed. Maybe some girl time was in order.

THURSDAY 28TH JANUARY 2027

'What did you think of Oxford, Chloe?' Louise asked with genuine interest. It was late afternoon and the team meeting had just finished. Only Louise and Chloe remained in conference room.

'Why?'

Chloe's tone made it clear that the intrusion was not welcome. Louise continued, undeterred by the attempt to wall her out.

'I was just looking through all the CVs and I noticed that you spent some time at Oxford.' Louise continued, 'I just wanted to know what you thought.' She smiled sincerely, remembering to keep a safe distance; not wanting to intrude on Chloe's personal space.

'Well,' Chloe, hesitated before going on, 'it was a very special time.' Just thinking about Oxford brought a number of warmer feelings to the surface. Not only had she enjoyed the academic side of life, she remembered a long and recurring fling with Roger Grave. *Well,* she thought, *it was long by my standards*; they had lasted almost six months.

She thought before speaking, stopped herself a moment, then went on. 'I loved my time in the UK.' Suddenly she smiled.

On the inside, Louise cheered; she had touched a tender spot in Chloe.

+ + +

Louise sighed then asked him, 'What are you doing tonight?'

She had ten minutes before the results would be processed. Filling time was a necessity. Even Karl could manage some social interaction, it was better than the whirling of the DNA synthesiser.

'Tonight is film night.'

'What's that?' Louise was keen to engage in a conversation that was not about the Living Doll project.

'It used to be a ritual in the Kuhlman household.'

Karl had told her a few things about his upbringing. It was tragic, it helped her to begin to comprehend him as a person. He had a soft spot for the Kuhlmans, even now.

'Everyone got to choose a film which was watched by the whole family. Everyone had a night. Brenda loved girly movies, you know like *Miss Congeniality, Legally blonde.*'

He played the role of a girl really well, he wiggled as he mentioned the films. Louise laughed, a rare event in his company. A different side of Karl.

'Marvin, he was into Westerns, a great Clint Eastwood fan – "Make my day".' The pistol made with his finger emphasised his point. 'Jasper – it was *Toy Story* and those kind of living cartoon adventures. I got to love Woody.'

Louise could not help giggling. She loved those movies too.

'Darren was into adventure. *Indiana Jones, X-men, The Fantastic Four* and on and on.' He waved the air, almost becoming embarrassed at his disclosure.

'And what about *you* Karl? What did you choose?

'*Star Trek*, every time! There were so many episodes, so many films. By the time I got to the end of my list another one was being made. I think the whole family got to enjoy the series… eventually.'

Louise nodded, this was a rare moment of happiness in the company of Karl yet a feeling of sadness surfaced. Memories about Adrian, like a jack-in-the-box with a firmly pressed lid, just below the level of her consciousness mind. Ready to pop up at the slightest trigger, the jack liberated, bobbing and weaving from side to side bringing with it all the pain, sorrow and regret.

Adrian had loved *Star Trek*.

MONDAY 15TH FEBRUARY 2027

Louise had not expected them to become best friends over night... However, they were getting along without any personal arguments – a step in the right direction. That conversation back in January marked the beginning of a new phase. Louise could not discredit the significance of that expression of common ground.

Here she was in a noodle bar in Pohang, with Chloe, enjoying a meal; and at the very least, she thought, it proved that the two of them had managed to negotiate their way through the many issues that had threatened their professional relationship.

Louise recalled the moment that Chloe had invited her to the meal, the rueful look on her face had betrayed some inner conflict, she struggled to get the words out. In accepting the offer, Louise hoped that she had allowed Chloe some vital space; a place where she could to come to terms with whatever it was that was bothering her.

Chloe opened up, telling Louise frankly how much she had resented her for having replaced Esther. The two of them to discussing things as adults – Chloe promised to have a different attitude and outlook. She apologised for being so childish after all it was not as if Louise was responsible for Esther's departure; Chloe disclosed that Esther had been something of a mentor.

Louise could understand her feelings. A truce came into operation. The meal sealed that agreement.

The explosion of a whole chilli in Louise's mouth took her by surprise. In the midst of an intense moment of conversation, she had failed to notice the small green chilli mingled with the king prawns. A hidden assassin. The intensity of the heat activated every pain receptor on her tongue – she was in agony. Instinct took over and, frantically, she began fanning her burnt tongue, almost knocking over the water.

Water! She grabbed the glass and drained its contents. Relief was immediate if limited. Hot tears streamed down her face. Red faced and still in pain, she looked around to see if anyone had noticed the farce she had made out of her meal.

Chloe suppressed a chuckle. So Louise could not handle hot food. *A novice*, thought Chloe as she delicately picked up the last prawn on her plate, expertly popping it into her mouth with her chopsticks.

Louise had regained her composure, pouring herself another glass of water. She wiped her eyes and returned to the conversation. It was as if she hadn't missed a beat. It was impressive, even if the woman was struggling with her food.

Chloe smiled.

Louise is alright.

WEDNESDAY 17TH FEBRUARY 2027

'Chloe, told me about your voluntary work with children. That's wonderful.' Louise munched on her salad, 'Those anchovies were delicious.'

Karl's face flushed, she hoped her comments were not too inappropriate. This was part of her strategy, she wanted to make a good impression, to show interest in others. To let him know she was paying attention to what other people said; a sign of a good manager.

'Yes,' Karl mumbled, picking up his fork and twisting it into his plate of spaghetti.

'I have an orphanage in China.' Louise thought she would help him out. It seemed to do the trick.

'Where are the kids from?'

Louise finished her mouthful, 'Mainly abandoned children born to women who work in brothels; state owned ones.' She wondered if he would be shocked by her revelation. 'And also street people who cannot look after their children.'

He looked impressed, his eyes piercing and beautiful, 'How many children do you have?'

'Up to ten at any one time. I would love to expand but that's all I... I mean we... It's all we can afford. I run it with a friend of mine called Sasha. We set it up together. It's not huge but it's our own contribution to charity. It means we're at the reigns when it comes to spending money on it and so on. I would love to expand.'

'That really is great. Children are important, so is being loved and cared for... being wanted.' His eyes grew distant, his voice unusually quiet, reflective.

'I agree,' said Louise. She had twenty minutes before she needed to be back in the lab. Updating *the Bible* was at the top of her agenda. Karl had already reminded her about it. She sensed that they were in harmony.

THE SACRIFICE

Karthik vented his fury by releasing a stream of expletives – utterly out of character. The conversation with Charles had been awful.

He normally retained a peaceful composure, however frustration had gotten the better of him. All of the pregnancies lasted relatively short periods of time before failing. His power lay in his ability to present the visions; he could not do the work of the scientists in bringing it them to pass.

The unsleeping city lay before him. The double-glazing of his office in Delhi shielded him from the noise and the invasive odour that was a part of nightly life for most of the city's inhabitants. An idea came to him – *perhaps he needed to re-visit the vision?*

He reached for the third drawer down, pulling it open smoothly. Neatly categorised under IBC, he found the folder marked 'Fifty Year Plan.' He extracted the manila file, moving swiftly to his desk.

He slumped into his director's chair, then slowly opened the file. Karthik pushed his glasses up the bridge of his aquiline nose.

Twenty minutes passed. Karthik stopped reading. *This is the key part.* He studied the same portion three times. Of all the images on the page, the snake with its head seemed the most prominent. The next symbol in the sequence denoted a mighty harvest – a wheat field full of corn. Karthik needed instruction, enlightenment, even illumination.

Karthik adopted the lotus position in the centre of his office; his rhythmic breathing, an essential part of the process that led to the trance like state. Becoming one with his breathing, feeling the harmony, the unity of breath and heartbeat. Merging, slowing down the world, slowing down his heart; he became conscious of the pulsing of blood through his vessels, the rush of life. The river of purpose, the flow of being.

Stepping from the conscious to the subconscious. The state of entry, the doorway into transcendental meditation; the soothing background music enhancing the atmosphere, allowing him to recalibrate his thought waves. Here he could meet with the Teacher.

Within fifteen minutes he had gained the illumination that he sought. The Teacher had responded positively to his enquiry. The decapitated snake represented a sacrifice, one born in the year of the snake needed to be offered before the harvest.

A sacrifice would be needed, a human sacrifice. A chill passed through him, despite the external temperature. The Teacher sounded firm and adamant. At times, their communications disturbed Karthik. The Teacher could be ruthless and demanding, terrifying but, ultimately benevolent. They were engaged in good work. This would allow them to do even greater good.

Karthik's insatiable thirst for knowledge enabled him to navigate around the more frightening sentiments. At any rate, the requisite path to resolution demanded the shedding of human blood. This could not be avoided.

Just how much can the other two tolerate?

Karthik's concern stopped his thought process temporarily. Murder was obviously illegal and, more importantly to Karthik, it was morally repulsive. Yet without something of the sort, they might never enter into the realms of possibility that lay beyond the present horizon. Surely, the ends would justify the means; *would the act be redemptive? How could this be done?* He returned to his meditative realm, eager to find a resolution for the dilemma.

One born in the year of the snake will prove a suitable sacrifice.

SUNDAY 21ST FEBRUARY 2027

'I want all the biosensor information you have on the three subjects analysed and sent to me within the hour. Including their Bible feedback. Good day.' Max barked at Phillippe, not really caring what else he had to do that day, this was urgent.

Phillippe's face revealed his anxiety, the tepid smile not convincing him for even a microsecond. Max waved his hand at the image which blinked then disappeared, replaced by the IBC logo.

In the background the haunting melody of *Symphonie Fantastique*. Max was familiar with both the storyline and the music. The object of the artist's love was represented by violins and flutes, floating through the delightful melody; they were called the *"idée fixe"* – the object of fixation. The noise of the rest of the orchestra portrayed Berlioz's frustration and despair.

His last conversation with Charles still played on his mind, he had been so weak, sounding panicky. Karthik's conversation had unnerved Charles, scared him, even. Max saw the whole thing as a necessary evil. From the way he sounded though, even Karthik was baulking. The shedding of human blood was always tragic, but the vision demanded it. That was that. It was a necessary evil, needed to push things ahead.

He could imagine Charles having sleepless nights, worrying about it, that and the destiny of humanity. That man had too much heart. The world functioned on a dog eat dog mentality, the sooner he woke up to that the better. *Natural selection can be a cruel mistress – a ferocious bitch. Will Charles able to cope?* That was the pressing question.

Now the selection process would begin. Simon Cowell – childhood thoughts of the X factor came to mind. Mom loved the show so he had to sit through hours of the dross, Michelle also adored the show.

It seemed only he had the guts to do the dirty work. *Leave it to Max.* Karthik left the final choice to him.

Now he was playing the role of Simon. Three files, one unlucky candidate. The second movement started – an invitation to a ball. Two harps led the waltz as the music alternated between watching the dancers and spying on the Berlioz, desperately trying to gain the attention of his beloved.

Within the hour, Max knew their histories. Two seemed interesting but one stood out. From the biosensor feedback it appeared that the individual had had recent encounters with several drugs – mostly legal, one illegal. It seemed that the same subject was using perception medication on a regular basis. Traces of a mild sedative could be detected using the biosensors in the laboratory clothing. From the records, the employee had been using sedatives since 21st August 2026.

Why that date?

He checked his online diary. Amongst the items for that date, an electronic note – Dr Esther Cohen had handed in her notice on Thursday 20th August 2026.

'So someone is finding it difficult to sleep at night,' Max spoke aloud to himself, chuckling as if someone had told him an amusing joke. He continued to read the report.

There were also those traces of an illegal drug in their system – a small amount perhaps, but still significant. *Very foolish*, but then the staff did not know the real level of scrutiny they operated under. Investing in the surveillance clothing had been a smart move. He smiled to himself.

Max recognised the start of the fourth movement where Berlioz begins to reveal the truly sinister side of his imagination. He could quote from the programme notes, this is where Berlioz knows beyond all doubt that his love is not returned, poisons himself with opium. Causing him to plunge into sleep, accompanied by the most horrible visions.

The Internet portal hummed as he typed in all the candidates' names, along with their ascribed numerical IDs. He would have access to all available records: scientific folders, personal information, medical files, emails and Intersky face to face conversations. Nothing was hidden at IBC – all it took was the right level of authorisation. The medical file revealed everything, including any Biomedi-pod usage or any prescriptions drugs.

He wrote the information onto a notepad, preferring to keep something off the computer system. He never placed his full confidence in computing and technology.

Max stopped writing. In truth he could sympathise with Charles' worry. Even he could not disguise the fact that he felt very uncomfortable with the direction in which the project seemed to be heading. Nothing about *sacrifice* had been mentioned at the offset. At least, not outside of its metaphorical application to business. Now Dr Kothaka insisted that without it the project would be dead – that the other steps would never take place.

Selecting the final acts on the X factor. All had been weighed up and now one had to be chosen. He needed advice. *Who will be able to help without asking too many questions?*

Mr Henderson.

His business enterprise, not limited by geography. Max could only describe him as having an international outreach. Of course, he would demand first class travel and accommodation, and he would charge for the business advice. Assistance in carrying out the recommended action would cost extra. Even in South Korea, Max had contacts who were not so rigid in their moral parameters. Mr Henderson might need some local help.

'Hyun-jung, place a call to Mr Henderson, he is listed under consultants.'

'Right away Mr Augustine.' He waved at the portal, which went silent.

I know just the place for a rendezvous. A spot where there was little chance of their meeting causing suspicion. A quiet meeting between he and his advisor. The fifth movement finished – the satanic dream where Berlioz sees himself in the midst of witches and monster, all gathered for his funeral.

Bubku Beach would do nicely.

+++

They were the only ones in the staff room. Kitted out for comfort, including a relaxation zone complete with giant fluffy dice that served as seats, the latest computer games, endless types of sweets, drinks dispensers, and old fashioned newspapers. A place to chill out and forget about work. Louise hardly used it.

Karl, sometimes he talked about his childhood, other times he clammed up. Today was a closed day, he did not want to talk, as variable as British weather. He was such hard work.

'How did you get into the sciences then, Louise?' He cupped his mug with both hands.

'My brother loved science, it just crept up on me.' Her neck felt prickly, she scratched the annoying area.

'What's he's doing now?'

Louise sighed feeling slightly annoyed,' He died.'

She saw it in his eyes, genuine compassion, 'I am sorry, Louise. When did he die? You never mentioned him.'

'He died. He was…' She was tempted to go and get a newspaper, to do anything to get away from his interrogation.

Karl had a thoughtful look on his face, 'That must have been difficult. Losing a brother.' A sad countenance spread over his face, she could sense pain in his voice. Louise attempted to distract him; she did not want to talk about Adrian with him.

'And what about you, Karl?' She tried to sound enthusiastic.

'Bill Nye,' said Karl.

'I saw some of his videos at school, a bit OTT for me.' *Too American, all that drawling.*

'I loved him, his ideas, Brenda and Marvin—'

Louise interjected, 'Your adopted parents?'

Karl's forehead wrinkled, 'Yes, Brenda and Marvin Khulman.' He looked embarrassed at his confession, as if he had given away too much information. He rubbed his left eye, then tapped the edge of his mug.

'Of course, you were adopted. What happened to your real parents?' Now she was interested, realising there was more to Karl. Often his manners and abrupt nature put her off.

He played with his fingers, 'Dad, I have no idea, Momm—' He stopped abruptly, then continued, 'my mother died.'

Louise nodded her head, allowing a moment of silence. 'It's been tough stuff for both of us.'

Karl agreed,' Yes, it has.'

They finished their coffee break in silence.

MONDAY 22ND FEBRUARY 2027

Cold blooded murder. No disguising the ghastly reality.

Charles hated being tormented by the horrible thoughts. *Why such a high price tag for progress? What will happen if we refuse to comply? If we all stand up and said no! Is this some sort of sick test of our dedication to…*

He didn't know what to do next. Only Karthik did.

That's part of the damned problem. The moralist side of him could talk a great talk; this went against his nature.

Charles scratched his arm, his eczema kicking off again. Eleanor would have told him off. Yet there was no denying it, he still felt fuelled by an inner hunger, and it would not go away. This whole enterprise, all of his work, it could lead to the resurrection of Miranda. That kept him going, helped him make the hard decisions in life, even if it meant taking someone else's.

Is it justified? Of course not; there's no justification for this, Charles.

The simple fact was, he knew, that they were in too deep now. They had seen the proof, the successes, the breakthroughs, the potential; the extension of life was so close now.

He wondered how he would be able to live with himself if he did this, yet doubted he could live without Miranda; without the hope of her return. He wanted to reassure himself that he did everything possible to bring her back.

The bright lighting helped to make the place look alive, yet it housed an increasing number of candidates for cryogenic preservation, hoping for that chance at resurrection. The cold steel and huge wobbling pipes were accompanied by the whirl of maintenance robots on steel tracks, moving back and forth, supervising the sleeping.

She remained the same, unchanging. Her features were delicately preserved, liquid nitrogen replacing her blood, pumped around by a machine. It was an imitation of life, between slumber and death. The viewing panel ran parallel to her upper torso and face. You could even move the sliding panels to expose the patient up to their shoulders. He always did that when he came to visit. That way, he could see her face and talk to her. He lived with the hope that, one day, she would answer him back.

Charles touched the glass. Quietly, discreetly, he began to cry.

TUESDAY 23RD FEBRUARY 2027

'Would you like another drink sir?'

Max looked up briefly from the legal thriller, *The Partner* by John Grisham, one of his favourites. 'No, thanks,' he turned the page and, hastily, surveyed the growing number of tourists arriving on the beach.

Bukbu was located in Duho-dong, in the northern part of Pohang. Peppered with bars and restaurants, it remained a popular haunt for those who wanted to escape from the daily pressures that arose from the South Korean work ethic. Though relaxation had been factored into his presence there, Max had scheduled a business meeting. He glanced at the time on his smartphone while annoyance ran through him.

'He's late.' Max hated being kept waiting. Yet he had no choice. He and Mr Henderson went back a long way. He had called on his services many times since the incident with his wife. Not all of the jobs involved death. Most of them were used to scare the opposition, or to silence those whose mouths could get in the way of progress.

He finished his drink and tried to get back into the story. Patrick was just about to disclose yet another vital piece of information.

'Sorry Max, dreadful traffic.'

Mr Henderson was tall and well groomed, with impeccable manners. He had a strong, middle class, British accent. He did not fit Max's conception of a hit man.

He had once worked for MI6, or so he said, had completed a spell of work in the Middle East and had gone on to establish his own PR consultancy. He worked, for the most part, with politicians and business magnates, helping them to display a more genteel face to the rest of the world.

He was obviously stressed; punctuality being one of his company's guarantees, his voice smooth and velvety. Every word and syllable properly pronounced. 'The in house service on the flight was outstanding. I must recommend that airline.'

He sat down. Henderson was wearing tan, khaki chinos and crisp white shirt; designer shades tucked into his top pocket. A brown satchel briefcase rested in his lap.

'Would you like a drink?' Max closed his book, laying it on the Formica surface.

'Yes, that would be wonderful. How about a gin and tonic?' He placed the satchel next to his chair.

Max could never understand how he could be so down to earth and do what he did. The man reminded him of a character from a James Bond novel; he had that English suave, with a lethal, diamond sharp edge.

Max lifted three fingers gaining the attention of the waiter, who rushed over. A short conversation and the order was placed. Henderson looked happy.

'So what do you need doing?' Henderson's eyes were brown, deep set in his weathered face. He looked to be around fifty. Neat trimmed grey hair, with a neat moustache. He carried a sense of being organised.

Max pursued his lips, leaning back, 'Frankly, I need a victim. Someone whose death will be,' he moved closer whispering, 'seen as a tragic accident.'

'What do you mean? Maybe a suicide?'

'Maybe,' the return of the waiter halted Max's response. He nodded as the waiter left. 'Nothing that can be linked to IBC of course, well, at least not directly.'

He watched Henderson drink a full mouthful from the glass, then thump it down before wiping his mouth. 'Suicide... a bit tricky. There would have to be a history to prevent suspicion. You know what I mean; people realising that something is wrong; no one really being sure. Everyone too afraid to ask until it happens.'

This man knew his stuff. 'I need it done sooner rather than later.' Their spot was well away from prying ears. Max had chosen this location carefully. There was little CCTV in this area. It was known to be a place that the police did not frequent, where narcotics could be exchanged discreetly. Max supposed that there were bribes to that effect.

'Tell me about my parcel.'

A strange way of describing victims. Max reached into his jacket pocket and took out three photographs, he'd had them printed from the images on file.

'My, my. These are a varied lot. Still making up your mind?'

Max nodded, feeling as if he were back in school.

'Have you thought about afterwards?'

'Afterwards? What do you mean?' Max scratched his nose.

'Taking charge of the social network system. Controlling how things get out and what stays in the public arena. We live in a digital age, as you well know. You must take steps to get your message across, to establish certain assumptions. You need to manufacture things a little, you know. The way you want it to be.' His voice dropped in volume, as a young couple passed by, lost in their love talk. He smiled enviously, then continued, 'I can offer an extended PR strategy, indeed, I recommend it, and an excellent consultant from my firm; but of course that will cost you extra.'

Mr Henderson always offered extras and they always cost a lot. 'We have a strong PR team at IBC-Korea—'

'And an outstanding IT department! Or, as you call it, Computing Division. I hear great things about the IBC cloud. Tight as a miser's purse. Top of the range security. And,' he leaned forward so his face was close to Max's, 'I hear your surveillance techniques are… shall we say, in depth?' He winked.

Max felt his lower jaw drop, 'You know about…' He decided not to say any more.

Henderson sighed loudly, 'It is my job to know things, Max Augustine.' He looked into the distance and took another swig of his drink.

The waves were restless today; it was still pretty hot for February. Max wiped his forehead. Feeling uncomfortable, perhaps as a result of the heat and the growing sense of excitement and fear.

'Are any of them taking medication?'

'All of them.'

'That could be very useful. You've done good groundwork then.'

A question burned in Max's mind. 'Is this really your best rate,

Henderson? After all I am a repeat… customer.' He traced his finger over the cover of his book.

'Of course, you get a discount. I have looked after you before, and will look after you in the future. Just like my father looked after your father. We both know how this works, family matters. Business is business and family is family. But we both know that there's crossover.' He smiled again, making eye contact with Max before looking away, back out to sea.

That pleased Max. They would talk the finances over, striking the right deal for the right price. Henderson knew enough to put him away for a long time. He was thankful that client confidentiality was their speciality. That went back over generations. Even his grandfather had been a long term client with the company.

They had a lot to discuss.

WEDNESDAY 24TH FEBRUARY 2027

Why doesn't Charles confide in me?

This was the third night in a row – a reoccurring nightmare. Shaking and trembling in his sleep, both hands clutching his chest as he rolled from side to side. Moaning and muttering, the odd 'no' bursting from his lips. The sweat forming a chilled sheen on his face, tiny beads of perspiration peppering his upper lip.

Every time she woke him, the terror felt palpable; he seemed to appreciate her concerns but he would not divulge any of what he was seeing and feeling. Despite her best attempts to coax the information out of him, he remained silent, tight lipped and tormented.

She pulled up the top sheet, then plumped up the pillows. *Yes, that looks better. Perhaps new curtains and bedding will help to brighten up the bedroom?* It was 10.00 already, the morning rushing away. A busy day lay ahead.

Is it to do with his work? The pace seemed to have accelerated over the last couple of years. Charles was not getting any younger, he should be slowing down yet that inner drive compelled him to the streets. So many meetings with Max and Karthik. She felt like an outsider, the rest of them all had strong, common bonds. It was a men's club. Women strictly forbidden.

Charles was greying, his luscious locks thinning, and though he tried to keep it short, the signs of balding were peeking through the strands. It made no difference to her, but he was even thinking of having a hair transplant. Every so often he would bring it up, then it would drift into the background until the next time. A very late, mid-life crisis. Even his libido seemed to be on the wane. She smiled as she recalled those early days of passion and spontaneity. That was how they had managed to conceive Miranda.

He never talked about her, Miranda. Not even on her birthdays. Eleanor found herself being the one who brought Miranda into the conversation. As if he had been forgotten her; a lost memory discarded and filed away – sealed in a unmarked vault. *Why does he refuse to talk about her?*

She sat on the edge of the bed, gazing at the photos of Miranda on the walls, her short life in pictures.

Icilda was not like that, she kept her granddaughter's memory alive. They worked together on the disabled children's trust fund. Icilda tireless and driven. Despite her many problems.

Charles noticed it first. She forgot his birthday and wedding anniversary. When he skilfully challenged his mother she blamed her technology, the reminders had not come up.

Her mind used to be so sharp, she never forgot a date. That was until Alzheimer's started to erode sections of her brain. Forgetting dates was just the start of the turmoil. Eleanor had to mentally prepare for meetings with Icilda, repeating the same conversation three or four times. Even facing the fact that sometimes it took her a while to even acknowledge her presence, or the times when she would ask over and over again, who she was. Pictures helped, Eleanor always kept a few in her bag, just in case.

Looking back, she experienced a jolt of embarrassment; the early days of their relationship. The name-calling. As she became acquainted with Icilda, that view had changed; yes, she loved her Charles, but she also made room for Eleanor and Miranda. They were all welcome in her precise and ordered world.

Charles must be worried about his mother, but is that part of his current anxiety? Ralph had even talked of assisted suicide if things got that bad, not wanting to live without her; ready to share the same fate. Eleanor disagreed with the whole notion. Charles seemed to be open to persuasion. He even hoped the nanotechnology side of IBC's work might provide an answer. Parkinson's had virtually been eradicated. After all, Alzheimer's was not so different.

Life had been unfair to them. Miranda, now Icilda. Yet Eleanor's "lemonade out of lemons" philosophy had borne great fruit. The primary school in Tamil Naidu, South India, would be open in a few months; the secondary school thriving, offering education to many who would otherwise be denied even a basic school education. She enjoyed working with the motivated and committed local people who staffed the school, making such a fuss of her whenever she visited. The whole school came to welcome her when she could make the time – the heat, dust and flies made it hard for her to bear but, for the sake of her school, she endured those visits.

Karthik had been so helpful in establishing the school. Such a sweet man, sincere but lonely. Mysterious. You could see the loneliness in his eyes though. She wondered if he had ever really let anyone in. Charles and he were still friends after so many years, sharing such a long history. She had heard some of the stories from the past.

Of course, she never managed to live out her dream of being a headmistress, but she had been instrumental in educating others, giving them a bright future. Miranda made all that possible.

Charles had been so generous, funding the project and allowing her to manage the whole process, from architectural plans to interior design, choosing the furniture in the classrooms. It was so very satisfying. Africa was next on the list of places, her plans taking on an international perspective. Each school was named after her daughter – the Miranda Ferrell Secondary School, plus the name of the country. All children were welcome, those with and those without disability. it was simply key that they built a school community where every person mattered.

Her figure had matured; she turned to the side; the dressing mirror never lied. Yes, the flat stomach had long gone, but the voluptuous curves remained, plus the additional dress sizes that crept upwards never downwards. The Pilates classes and personalised step routine helped to maintain things most of the time. Charles had even offered to pay for an overhaul, plastic surgery combined with adipose sculpturing. She'd thought about it. In reality, her vanity did not stretch to that extreme. *Aging is part of life, why fight nature?*

Charles often talked about immortality; but who would want to live on and on? She worried sometimes… He and his group of elite friends and peers; some of their ideas were off the wall. She declined his invitation to know more, preferring to keep her feet firmly on the ground. Charles and the dreamers. It sounded like an awful aged rock band.

If he had another dream, or a nightmare, she would tell his father. *Maybe Ralph could speak some sense into him?* Yes, she was tired of his not sleeping; and it kept her awake as well.

She looked at her reflection, studying the rings under her eyes. Either he stopped having the dreams or he could cosy up to the duvet in one of the spare rooms – he could take his pick from any of the eight.

+++

The sleepless nights were taking their toll, frequent headaches were becoming a regular occurrence. Biomedi-pod administration was now a daily chore, alongside vitamin supplements; he had to have regular cholesterol stripping and blood purification treatments too.

Eleanor was nagging him, wanting to know what was wrong. He simply blamed it on his work, his schedule and his worries about Icilda.

If only she could be allowed to know…

FRIDAY 26TH FEBRUARY 2027

Max faced the prospect of having to find someone who would be happy to get their hands dirty with computer technology. His first choices were obvious: those who were part of the inner circle of *the Light* and worked within the Computer Technology Division of IBC-Korea.

Two candidates fitted the bill. Both of them active members within the group. Max knew full well that seniority within the group correlated with levels of allegiance. Only one of the two had ascended to the point of knowing some of the covert elements of the group's activities. Myles Beard seemed to be a likely candidate.

Max pondered the logistics of the operation, sketching out his plan. He bite the end of his pencil as he considered the options.

What about a reward? Perhaps Charles could recommend a suitable form of remuneration?

Besides he needed to be updated on the progress of the plan as did Karthik. He spoke Charles' name, the smartphone dialled it automatically.

+++

Max seemed to take it in his stride. Smiling and laughing as if nothing had happened; as if it was a perfectly normal deal. They had agreed to commit a crime, but, he had reasoned, it was not the first, nor the last indiscretion at IBC. It was something one simply had to do to favour progress.

Charles could not understand how the man managed to stay so detached. Panic hurled its way towards him whenever he even began to feel relaxed. The oppressive, accusing voice of conscience tormented him day in, day out. In the night, terror bled from every object – a window frame, from a door, even from a car seat. Everything came alive and spoke to him, calling him a murderer, a megalomaniac, a dictator, a criminal. He confided in Max but his friend's retort was too simple – 'Get some memory augmentation therapy, Charles. You're just stressing out.'

How did he do it? Anti-freeze, perhaps, circulating in his bloodstream. Max was a living cryogenic candidate. *How does he live with himself? How does anyone manage to live with him?* Then he thought of poor Michelle and her tragic death, *perhaps nobody could.*

Or maybe he deals with it like a disease, maybe he eradicates the guilt. Maybe he's just the truer visionary. His thoughts flitted back to Miranda, locked up in that cold chamber, waiting for his work to be complete.

Maybe MAT was not such a bad option. After all, he had vital work to do. Humane work. His real work. Charles sighed heavily. He'd book a session for the following week.

SATURDAY 27TH FEBRUARY 2027

Max closed the deal. The timeline was established. It was in motion.

They were all up to speed and appeared to be in full agreement. The three of them, Karthik, Max and Charles.

Karthik seemed okay but Max was worried about Charles. He said the right words but there was something in his eyes that revealed his true feelings. Sleepless nights and arguments with Eleanor, none of that boded well. *Was he about to crack up?*

A few select members of *the Light* were also aware of the arrangement, those in the higher echelons. One brave, up and coming leader, Aidan Johnson – his family had been loyal supporters for generations – voiced his displeasure and sense of unease. It was not at all unusual for acts of intimidation, even murder to be bought and sold within the business world, but a human sacrifice? He soon fell silent; they reminded him of his oath and the illegal loan that had taken his national business to the next level of success.

The deal would take place sooner rather than later.

The whole thing made Max nervous, yet he could not deny the sense of exaltation that partnered his anxiety.

MONDAY 1ST MARCH 2027

'You're late *again!*'

Karl could not believe the audacity, this was the third time in the last two weeks. Something had definitely changed in Chloe's behaviour since Esther's departure. Months had passed and she still seemed to be stuck in an emotional rut. Their relationship had become highly abrasive.

Chloe's tone often bordered on rudeness, openly and with an increasing level of venom. Karl noticed the physical changes too – her unkempt appearance, her hair out of place, failing to follow regulations; yet she was still a beauty.

'And…' Chloe was daring him, she knew it. *Come on – give it a try!* For now she decided to curb her feelings, leaving it at, 'I had a problem with my——'

'Just get the lab reports updated.' Karl was in no mood to deal with her today.

Louise overheard the conversation, then promptly buried her head in her report. She was not going to get in between those two. Some vicious bloodletting had clearly taken place at some point in their relationship.

She needed to build relationships; her strategy was to avoid the gossip and the internal politics as best she could.

Chloe had been very vocal, even candid, about her opinions on the matter of the *famous* Dr Karl Winwood. Once she got to know Chloe, Louise had been given the full account of Esther's sudden departure, on numerous occasions. It remained a sore issue.

If Louise had been an anxious woman, she might have been worried about her own position. As it was, she was managing quite well.

Panic attacks were rare these days.

TUESDAY 2ND MARCH 2027

Chloe was late again. Karl had taken all the abuse and open defiance he could. She was going to get the worst reprimand of her life, along with the start of disciplinary action.

His patience now wafer thin; she was taking liberties, still blaming him for Esther's departure. Karl planned the rebuke. It would be public, that way everyone else would see the folly of trying to cross him, Karl Winwood. *Yeah, just you wait.* Part of him eagerly anticipated her arrival.

He sensed the vibration of his quantum smartphone – hypermail alert. He checked the message – a request to ring Human Resources immediately on a matter of urgency.

'Sorry guys,' he was in the middle of talking to Ade, Hiroo and Louise, 'got to deal with an urgent situation. Can we meet in thirty minutes?' Karl excused himself.

Once in his office he uttered, 'Phone.' The voice activated Internet portal responded to his command, displaying the phone option. 'Human Resources – Phillippe Bernard.'

The news. It took his mind back to the scene…

The body of his mother. What he saw, what he felt came flooding back; the tidal wave behind a broken dam. The sobbing started from the base of his spine.

He called her name, no response – Mommy did not answer. He shook the body, whimpering, shouting, pleading. Promising – to be a good boy, to stop wetting the bed.

His legs buckled, bitterness on his lips, numbness along his shoulders. He stumbled forward, thumping against his desk, sending a framed photograph of the Kuhlmans crashing to the ground; he could feel his pulse thumping, getting louder and louder. The pace of his heart, double its normal speed, as if he were on the treadmill after building up to the peak of a workout. Breathing, suddenly difficult, as if he was choking.

Every thud of his heart vibrated in his chest cavity. Then came the gripping pain, vice like, squeezing across his ribs. A rubber band of intense pain. His heart squeezed cruelly by an invisible hand; an evil bully, twisting it, enjoying the pain, twisting it again.

Am I having a heart attack? But I'm only——

The tightness passed, the grip slackened. Broken glass lay strewn on the floor, his breathing became slow and laboured.

Blurry vision, ribs like rubber rods enclosing his enlarged heart, a sharp stabbing pain. Twisting upwards, a corkscrew of torment. Stilted breaths punctuated with long pauses.

Chloe would not be in today or in fact on any other day. She'd been found dead... in her apartment.

From what he could muster from Human Resources, she'd overdosed.

+++

The smell of incense hung heavily in the air and, through slightly parted lips, Karthik mumbled words totally incoherent to any would be observer. Lost in a trance.

The invisible conversation between pupil and teacher continued unabated.

Karthik felt the delight of his Teacher. The sacrifice offered on behalf of the project had proved acceptable. Favour was promised. Karthik sensed the delight of his master, relishing in his pleasure.

Chloe had been born in 2001. The breakthrough would come...

+++

Mr Henderson's consultant offered a clear strategy for dealing with the crisis. The first stage involved helping the staff before pathological patterns of thought and behaviour developed, swift intervention to stop them being established. The three A's were quoted – acknowledge the tragedy, apologise for the circumstances and act to stay ahead of the situation. Max immediately approved the initiation of the first step. Public, in your face news bulletins throughout the IBC networks, announcing the tragedy.

Then he instructed the PR department to adopt the suggested, stoic approach – this represented stage two – including close monitoring and regulation of all internal communication. He aimed to find out what people really thought and what they were saying on social media. Negative entries could be dealt with in a number of ways, one being to bombard the source of the negative report with messages offering an alternative prospective, from fictitious people. Max liked that one. Helplines were set up, allowing grief counselling twenty four hours a day for an indefinite time period. The consultant advised supporting staff through their grief.

The third stage involved dealing with speculation as to what occurred; rumours were likely to continue for some time. Social media sites should be bombarded with the message they wanted to get in the public area. That meant establishing a sophisticated digital cabinet war room to engage with the bloggers, social media and online communities that related to the staff at IBC-Korea. That was how the rumours about Chloe's drug use got out, they were also able to create a false memo trail that made her look like a long term abuser, detailing illegal exchanges with local drug dealers. An on-line smear campaign. Her death – a sad suicide attempt or misadventure.

The reputation of IBC had to be preserved at all costs.

After all, reputation is a frail rare flower.

Max was particularly concerned about the possible impact on equity and value of shares. He needed the lies, the accusations of drug abuse, if only to support his own innocence. But similarly, it couldn't be allowed to become quiet knowledge in the wider community that his vital employees were acting unprofessionally, taking illegal drugs. But he had nothing to worry about. Everything was being taken care of rather splendidly. In fact, all he had to do was check his phone occasionally to see how things were going.

That little consultancy package had added an extra $600,000 or WC1,080 000 (World Credits). He still preferred to think in dollars. In this case Max considered it money well spent.

+++

Karl thought Max's response had seemed weird. He'd simply said that he and the company were sorry to hear that a team member had died. That the company would move on, after a short period of mourning. The team would be responsible for great things to come and should not get caught up on the life, or death, of an employee. That these things happen.

Do they?

Karl had thought about it at the time.

Max wanted him to take centre stage in dealing with Chloe's mother and the press. IBC would spare no expense. Karl would be the coordinator for the funeral arrangements, he could rely on help from Human Resources.

And that was it!

The briefing lasting less than two minutes.

As he got into the lift, he sighed and straightened his suit jacket in its mirrored wall. *I hope they give me a better send off than that.*

+++

Awful. Just far too sad. A brilliant scientist was dead. Worse, a team member. Louise could not get her head around the situation. In some ways she was grateful that she had only just got to know Chloe, but she realised that this was selfish. The rest of the team were devastated.

A TIME TO REMEMBER

FRIDAY 5TH MARCH 2027

Seeing her daughter in the morgue shook Bethany to her core. Cold and motionless, displaying the gorgeous features that characterised her life, Chloe lay on the slab, shielded from public display.

She looked young – very young; like a teenager, rather than the twenty five year old woman. The adventure of her life, going to South Korea; a mother's nightmare, burying her child. This strange youthfulness seemed to better reflect her true age.

Touching her felt obscene, yet Bethany needed to have that moment of interaction with her daughter. Her blonde hair tied up in a professional plait while she was clothed in a simple white robe.

For Bethany her worst fear animated in 3D high definition with the digital sound channel on mute.

Even in death, Chloe was beautiful.

SATURDAY 6TH MARCH 2027

Bethany sat motionless as the eulogy continued. Her puffy eyes conveyed her deep and heartfelt grief, she refused to wear sunglasses – *why* should *I hide my sorrow?* Despite her best efforts, her mind kept flipping back to the moment at which she had heard the news.

Chloe's gone.

Receiving that phone call – the one she had dreaded, like a life size emotional vacuum pump sucking the life out of her soul. A violent vortex had swept through her existence, destroying everything that she had built, leaving her to deal with the devastation that lay in its wake.

They'd spared no expense; IBC provided a first class flight to South Korea. Dr Karl Winwood had even met her at the airport, they took a chauffeur driven car to the IBC-Korea site.

Hearing his voice and meeting Karl felt familiar, he'd been the one who had broken the devastating news to her in the first place. She thanked him for his kindness and expressed her desire to see Chloe's body.

Now it was about getting her home to Arizona. Karl seemed to understand, his sad eyes and gentle manner showed considerable compassion. Kind words, kind gestures. He was a real source of comfort in the midst of a living hideous daytime nightmare.

She dabbed her eyes again with her lace handkerchief. Stinging water from leaks that would not stop running.

+++

'In the world of science, sacrifice is always at the heart of progress,' Max hope he sounded genuine, his speech carefully crafted to present the company in the best possible light. 'Chloe inspired us all with her dedication and her no nonsense attitude. But she could also be extremely good fun. She was an incredible person. Her work will go on.'

Max shifted his body weight feeling awkward in the adopted pose, he cleared his throat before continuing. 'Let us spend a moment in silence, remembering Dr Chloe Bartell.'

Esther was surprised to find herself on the front row. It felt wrong, being back at IBC, next to Beth. Esther could see her hand trembling again, she took hold of it, caressing it gently. Dark glasses would have concealed those reddened eyes, but Bethany had no intention of hiding her emotions.

IBC had not informed her of Chloe's death directly, Beth had. Esther wanted to be there to support her friend. Arranging a special entry pass through the Human Resources Division had been very straight forward, indeed, her request for admission on compassionate grounds was readily accepted by Phillippe Bernard.

She glanced behind her. The current members of the "dream team" occupied the seats on the third row, supervisors and technicians sat side by side. She wondered how they were coping. Witnessing the death of a colleague in the midst of their research – it could either destroy or strengthen their resolve. *Will they be ready to fight on and finish what Chloe was once part of?*

What I was almost a part of.

Louise Dalton sat nearby; *her* replacement. She looked incredibly awkward. She must have hardly known Chloe. The woman – *girl* – could only have been on the team for a few months. Esther remembered her last day – Thursday 20th August 2026.

Ade filled her in on some of the inside story. They were all shocked. He confessed his own personal sense of remorse; why had they failed to notice the changes? The dimming of a star, so gradual. They had seen an angry Chloe, a moroseful Chloe. They had seen her crack fewer jokes and the baking had stopped. They had all noticed. He voiced the collective sense of guilt. They should have done more; they were part of a team. Then he made it personal, 'I should've done more, Esther.'

She hadn't known what to say. She had left, and Chloe was dead.

The official statement released by the company stated that 'Chloe died of a drug overdose.' This mystified many of the employees as it had already become common knowledge that Chloe used a Biomedi-pod. The things were 99.9% accurate in administering the correct dose; they were personalised and tailor made to match the individual's genetic information. Smart machines, that learned as the patient used them. Daily updates ensured that they functioned at their optimum level across the entirety of their lifespans.

How could an overdose have happened?

Many of the staff questioned this assessment of the situation and muted conversations were reported to have taken place all over the company's various sites.

The suicide theory also surfaced. Yet there was no suicide note. They had all been puzzled. The rumours abounded, about illegal drugs, but that was not the Chloe they knew. They did not match.

Word of Chloe's death had become widespread, the social media sites were electric. People said that the drugs, combined with the Biomedi-pod administered sedatives, had caused a heart failure. No one quite knew how they started; they simply seemed to circulate, possessing a life of their own and evolving amongst those employees at the IBC-Korea compound who had never really known Chloe.

Esther clapped politely as Max Augustine left the stage. It was a sign of his respect for the team that he was present. It was unusual for him to put in appearances of this sort. The subdued atmosphere was eerie and Esther determined it was not the kind of send-off that Chloe deserved. At least the place was full though. Some people had flown in from across the World. Chloe touched many lives.

Beth told her that IBC had asked her to choose the colour schemes for the event. She eventually chose to decorate the auditorium in Chloe's favourite colours – lavender and pale yellow. Esther couldn't imagine what that phone call must have been like. The realisation of Beth's deep seated fear. The distance. The loss.

Two large photographs of Chloe stood on either side of her coffin, her face appearing radiant and full of life. At the time she must have been in her early twenties. The stark contrast between the image and reality; she lay still in her elaborate wooden tomb.

Sleeping beauty.

Another brilliant life, cut off in its prime. Such a waste.

Tears trickled from her eyes awakening memories of Samuel. The dull pain of his loss surfaced now, here, mingling with the fresh wound left by Chloe's departure. She was here for Beth; that became her inner mantra as she contemplated the rest of the programme.

For some, the grief was genuine, for a few though, it was a mere duty, demanding pretence.

+++

'Esther, it is lovely to finally meet you, and of course to see you in person.'

Beth hugged Esther who relaxed in the embrace, feeling her heart going out to the grieving mother. She knew about the dark fear that had stalked Beth. Now it had its victim.

'I would have done anything to be here.' Esther looked intently at Beth, feeling the pain, sensing the depth of the woman's grief. She lived with her memory of Samuel, recalling the family-wide suffering that had accompanied his death. Yes, she could relate to Beth.

IBC had provided Beth with a private room to allow her personal space and a place to speak privately to those who wished to express their sentiments. Esther and Beth were alone.

'I've cleared up Chloe's things,' the pain of that statement resonated in Esther chest, it was like being elbowed in the sternum. 'There are some scientific journals that I would like you to have.'

Esther seemed shocked, Beth continued, 'You know how Chloe wrote down everything,' she leaned in, 'She kept several journals going, one personal, and one,' Beth looked unsure of herself, 'well, it's scientific. I would love you to have the science ones. They will probably meansomething to you but... not to me. And that was your time together.'

Beth turned away, feeling another wave of grief sweep over her. She gulped and waited – the wave passed.

'Oh Beth, thank you, thank you very much.' Esther reached out and took her hands, squeezing them firmly.

Genuine empathy, something about Esther touched Beth. *She really does understand what I am going through.* Beth received the comfort.

'I'll give them to you tomorrow, after we have breakfast. I am leaving in the afternoon,' she paused, 'with Chloe.'

S<small>UNDAY</small> 7<small>TH</small> M<small>ARCH</small> 2027

Esther sipped the freshly squeezed orange juice, watching Beth attempt to eat the croissant on her plate. *No appetite, I know that feeling.* She had hardly been able to eat for almost a whole week after Samuel's death.

Their conversation was light, funny stories about Chloe. A few colleagues stopped by the table to make a comment to Beth, expressing their sorrow and sympathy. Part of Esther wanted this to be a private occasion. Just the two of them.

Beth spoke of Chloe's kindness. Esther agreed, having seen some surprising acts of generosity in the lab, her attention to detail, remembering birthdays, anniversaries – personal stuff.

Beth explained Chloe's recent and important role in saving the house, after she had been made redundant by the supermarket. In a move to cut costs, the firm had fired all the managers then replaced them with outsiders who had been shipped in. Chloe's donation of her bonus helped to save the house. Now the mortgage had been paid off.

Bonus... Esther's ears pricked up. *Bonus? I have never had a bonus. What did she mean by that?*

Part of Esther wanted to probe deeper. Beth was talking about a large amount of money – something in the region of $60,000. She decided to ignore it, perhaps Chloe had some hidden savings? Money was not important at a time like, this, she decided to let the matter drop. It seemed that IBC were going to make a special financial gift to Beth as a mark of respect for Chloe. A scholarship fund would also be set up in her honour: she would be remembered.

Chloe's science journals. Esther certainly appreciated the gift. She tucked them into her handbag; they would go into her luggage when she finished packing. She promised herself that she would read them.

When though? She had no idea. Only if it felt right.

Both of them were leaving early that afternoon. She would return to Israel to pick up the pieces of her shattered career, Beth would go back to the States.

They were united as friends, through a common bond of bitter grief.

RESTORING TEAM SPIRIT

MONDAY 8TH MARCH 2027

"Tragedy unsettles us in our deepest places. Suddenly we realise that life is not as certain as we thought, our insecurities surface. We feel anxious for no reason."
Working Through Grief – Millicent Godfree
Psychology Today: February 2027

Louise studied the article on bereavement and readily identified with much of its content. What shocked her the most – according to the article, she had never gone through the grieving process over Adrian.

What a discovery. She remained trapped in anger and resentment never breaking free from the memory loop. She didn't even realise that she could. As a family they had never shared their emotions, soldiering on, keeping the stiff upper lip. They has sandpapered over the emotional fissures; they had simply kept going.

An anatomy of grief. She had lived with unprocessed anger, raw and catatonic. On the inside she had been raging at the universe, at god or something else equally vast and inexplicable. It had been suppressed, but it had flared up when she was probed. She recalled the time she had spent with her father at the golf course, before coming here; she'd had that outburst about god. Her emotions were like an internal generator, powering her.

You never went through the stages of grief. Stuck and stunted. How can I lead the team through grief if I can't even grieve properly for Adrian. I need to sort myself out first.

She had never seen it quite like this.

Her job was to steer the team back to the work at hand. Chloe was gone – that was the bitter truth. However, the Living Doll Project needed to go on. A sombre mood hung over the laboratory; people spoke in hushed tongues, as if normal conversations would be in some way offensive.

'She's gone, and we have got to go on.' It was an emphatic and strong statement.

RESTORING TEAM SPIRIT   503

The knock on her door made her jump. She gasped. The door was ajar. *Did they... Did they hear me?*

Ade stood there, on the threshold.

'Ah, Chloe... Oh, God. Sorry, I meant Louise.' He covered his lips, focusing his eyes on her desk. 'Sorry. We're ready for you in the meeting room, Louise. You said two thirty pm?'

Louise looked at the clock on her desk. It accused her – 14.40.

'Sorry Ade, I got lost in this article,' She lifted up the evidence trying to vindicate herself. The bottom line was that she had lost track of time.

Louise felt a twinge of guilt. She often got so caught up in her work that she would abandon all awareness of time. Pushing herself away from her desk, she followed Ade out of the office.

As they left, Ade turned to her, smiling wanly. A morbid thought skittered across her mind. *I would be late to my own funeral.*

TUESDAY 9TH MARCH 2027

Karl felt the moment when atmosphere in the laboratory shifted. It was just after 10am. Ade's raised his hand.

'I remember the incident with the chocolate muffins and... Esther.' He put on his best imitation of her voice, 'Thank you for those chocolate muffins. That was very sweet of you, but very naughty. 'He placed one hand on his hip, waggled the first finger of his other hand in front of an imaginary Chloe. 'What about my waist line?'

The room erupted in laughter as some relived that moment, others shared it for the first time. Even Ade beamed.

Karl watched, impressed. He had been concerned that Louise would be a little uptight about the whole situation, but she managed to make a difference to the way the employees were feeling and, somehow, she had helped them to regain their motivation. What surprised him was her level of self-disclosure. Her confession that she had failed to deal with the death of her brother, and her transparency about its long term consequences. That made him feel uncomfortable, but it was working. He placed his arms behind his back.

She was getting them to share their feelings with little stories, anecdotes; memories of Chloe that got them talking. It gave them permission to air those hidden, guilty feelings that could be acknowledged without shame, she walked them through the grieving process, explaining it step by step. Refocusing them, making the project about Chloe – about completing it *for* her.

Very smart. A true leader in the making. He had attended as an observer. The team were returning back to their stations, the session over.

He gave a thumbs up symbol to Louise, before heading out. They would catch up later, during their afternoon briefing session.

That went really well.

Louise gathered up her resources. She was surprised by how successful that had all been. She'd never had to do anything like that before. The memory of Chloe would live on and the project could now regain its former momentum.

There was still a vital hurdle to be overcome: the rejection of the embryos in the womb. Despite three trials, the longest pregnancy had lasted only three weeks. Until they resolved that issue there seemed little point in trying implantation again.

She sighed, resolving to put thoughts of Chloe's death out of her mind for now. She thought of the golf course. Her Dad. Home. Suddenly, mental lightning struck – *Dr Renny!*

There was a vague recollection of him mentioning some research he had been involved in recently; something about dealing with rejection, along the lines of antibody interruption. It had seemed to work, as far as she could remember. It had stopped the host cells from rejecting foreign material.

I wonder if this could be modified to stop the rejection of embryos?

Face to face with her 'irritating' supervisor, later that afternoon, on Intersky, Louise found out she had been wrong. It would not be effective in this situation. She felt deflated and her potentially brilliant solution turned out to be useless.

Dr Renny continued, suggesting that she try and contact a colleague of his from the famed Roslin Institute. The professor in question had experimentally manipulated the immune pathway, switching off the stages that led to rejection. Dr Renny recalled the use of a specific drug in this particular work, though he could not remember the name. He wished Louise well, then signed off.

Yet another rabbit hole, Louise chewed the end of her favourite pencil. Grateful for Renny's interest. When she checked the research faculty, she found out that he had been right. The technique did exist but there was a major problem – it had been used on bovine species rather than on humans. It would take weeks of trial testing to bring the drug around, and she would have to take it through an intensive range of external monitoring stages before it could be consumed by humans. It was too risky – too slow a process. The drug had an unknown safety status. Louise made that clear to Karl.

Karl did not agree. 'If it exists then why not try it?' He seemed to think he could win Louise over to his way of thinking. He tried every form of persuasion.

She stood up stiffly, looking down at him. She was having none of it. 'This is totally, I repeat, *totally* unethical.' *He actually wants to give this a trial.* She could not believe his audacity.

'I need to do some work on this. Leave it with me.' Karl dismissed Louise. She made her opinion known, slamming the door on departure.

+++

Karl did not want to talk; he hated the idea of voicing his emotions. Chloe's death, on top of all the others deaths he had to cope with. If felt like a pressure cooker on full heat, about to explode. The migraines were mountainous, earthquake like in their eruptions. The mediation level of Biomedi-pod had been increased, the updates registered that the old dosage was no longer effective. It was smart medicine, responding to the needs of the patient. Simply part of modern life.

Chloe. She had been afraid to show full support for Esther. He considered Louise… once Chloe got over her problems the two had seemed to get along. It used to be easy for him to pull Chloe onto his side, until things changed. He could pinpoint that to the period after Esther left. There had been a real change in her attitude and responsiveness, bordering on disrespect.

What did I do wrong?

He was snapping more than usual, his moods up and down, like the economies of third world countries that were non-integrated. Those still on the outside of the security of joining the World Unity movement – political, financial, social and for the religious crew that too.

Of course he knew that his behaviour impacted others. They were his vassals. He needed to feel their loyalty.

The way they looked at him – *is that fear or respect?*

Max seemed to be in a buoyant mood whenever they discussed the project. Their progress seemed to give him a deep thrill; he could hear it in the man's voice. It was almost as if he was singing down the line. His praise was more frequent, more open, and Karl couldn't help but feel that it was suggestive of a closer mentoring from Max.

Chloe.

He decided to put those thoughts to the back of his mind and keep them there, for now. At least they were making progress on the Living Doll Project… at last.

THURSDAY 11TH MARCH 2027

Karl hated being the bearer of bad news.

Max insisted that S-Tetrin v4 be administered to the surrogate mothers. The conversation only lasted a few minutes. Karl left Louise a message in her inbox informing her of the decision, taking the cowardly way out, he knew it was feeble.

Biostrips would be used throughout the "trial", ensuring there was constant monitoring of the bodily function of those who were willing to take part. They had signed a clause indemnifying IBC-Korea of any blame if procedures went wrong. *What more did Louise want?*

He spun around in his chair. Moving his head from side to side. Strict safety procedures would be in place. Very tight parameters would be set on the biostrips so that any changes from the acceptable norms of body function would be registered and alarms raised.

It was a good deal for all.

+++

Louise read the email and sat at her desk in silence, stunned.

It seemed as if the welfare of humans beings had dropped off the agenda. These innocent women would be used as human guinea pigs. How outrageous – once again, women's rights were being tossed aside for the sake of scientific progress and, indeed, the industry at large.

According to Karl, this directive had come from the highest level. There would be no further discussion.

Louise blamed herself. If she had kept quiet then none of this would be happening. Her fist made contact with her desk. Papers jumped, she wanted to scream.

Ade read through the instructions one more time, just to make sure he was clear before trying to explain the procedure to the rest of the technicians. Louise had given him the job of presenting. Esther had never allowed him to and he was glad to be given the opportunity, but he was worried at the same time.

Each of the subjects would receive 0.001mg of S-Tetrin v4 two days before the implantation process. This dosage would be continued until the placenta was fully established. Biomedi-pods would be used to administer the correct doses of S-Tetrin. Two embryos would be implanted – one male, one female. All the subjects would need to go into isolation for the whole period of their pregnancy.

He rehearsed the whole sequence six times before he felt happy.

+++

Ade's presentation was flawless.

Louise felt justified in having placed her trust in his abilities. He had such a charming way with people and she had seen that in his humility. On top of which, he could motivate others. An invaluable member of the team.

Louise smiled as she applauded his success.

One of the subjects, Hea Woo, produced a positive result on her second pregnancy test. The other two subjects did not.

Hea Woo's sentence was about to begin. The others were tearfully escorted away from the IBC-Korea compound. Their expenses would be covered but any dreams of earning a handsome reward were dashed. All that the team could do now was wait for nature to take its course – assisted by S-Tetrin v4 .

SECRETS

On her return to Tel Aviv, Esther packed Chloe's diaries away. She hadn't read them on the plane. She did not have the heart to. The girl had been her friend. In fact, Chloe had almost been like a daughter. She wasn't ready to go through it all again. The journals could wait.

A guilty feeling lingered with their possession – as if she had been handed stolen artefacts from a secret tomb. She could not work out why she felt this way.

The journals lay, in their original box, buried beneath the other boxes in the spare room of her apartment. They would stay undisturbed, their contents hidden.

SUNDAY 2ND MAY 2027

Hea Woo found the loneliness to be the hardest part of the pregnancy. The S-Tetrin treatment initiated the slow destruction of her immune system. Her body was left vulnerable to any and all potential infections. To help her cope with the demanding nature of her pregnancy, she remained in isolation, housed in a sterile environment.

Every aspect of life had to be checked for contamination. Food, clothing, books, entertainment and so on.

Anytime that Hea Woo came into contact with the world, the exchange had to be carefully scanned for microbial life. The same process also destroyed any and all bacterial and viral material.

Visitors had to undergo vigorous checks before being allowed into contact with her. The cleaning process took over an hour – the final stage required the visitor to put on surgical clothing that closely followed the contours of the body and formed a seal that went from the neck down to the feet. The hair was covered with a bacterial repellent, a material woven into caps and gloves, completing the sterile look. Finally, a mask covered the mouth and nose, made using a little treated silver, which filtered and purified the visitor's breath. Throughout each meeting, the room continued to be monitored for any microbial activity.

Louise decided to subject herself to this treatment regularly, visiting Hea Woo. It wasn't compulsory, but in her humanity, she wanted to reach out to this amazingly brave young woman. She was changing the face of human history. The scientists had completed their part of the process. All they could do was watch as the human body responded to the challenge.

She knew this was Hea Woo's third pregnancy. She had two other children. The rewards for completing the pregnancy were tremendous. Her family would be financially secure for many years to come. She was keen to take on the challenge.

Hea Woo eventually Louise that told her husband, Du-Ho, had felt very uncomfortable with the situation at first. However, when he was made redundant it seemed like a real opportunity. Taking on the challenge of childcare on his own had bruised his pride. It was not at all typical for South Korea. He changed his whole way of life to avoid meeting people and having to explain why he was taking on the childcare role.

Visits to see Hea Woo proved difficult. It became embarrassing for him to leave the children with neighbours when they knew he had a wife. Some questioned him as to her whereabouts – he told them she was in hospital, very ill.

Hea Woo often cried as she explained the situation to Louise, missing her husband and two children.

Some caring neighbours were touched by her misfortune, wanting to visit her and offer their sympathy. When he explained that this could not be done, some became very offended. He concealed any and all information about IBC-Korea, saying his wife had been sent overseas for the treatment. Neighbours viewed him with suspicion. How could he afford foreign treatment on his salary? Whispers and sniggers greeted him whenever he ventured. Many felt it shameful that he should be a home husband. Hea Woo felt that his shame was her shame, this whole situation made her so sad.

From Louise's perspective Hea Woo seemed to be adjusting to the rhythm of life at IBC-Korea. Her every need was fulfilled. Keeping her in perfect health became the top priority of the medical team. She had even decided to study for a MA, something she had not been able to do since marrying and starting a family. They had many warm conversations about English literature and American History, components of her course. Speaking English and understanding Western culture seen as a way of moving up the social ladder.

Information about her bodily changes were monitored and collected by biostrips which were changed once a week. Every feature of her health could be checked including hormone level, body temperature, water balance and blood sugar level.

Louise paid carefully attention to the data sharing it with rest of the team. Daily surveying this information and plotting Hea Woo's progress with great care. In her mind she toyed with the question, *what is it like to have life growing inside?*

She would be the first to undergo this treatment, but others would follow. In a reversal of roles, the guinea pig would become the teacher, while the scientists became the students.

Louise struggled to learn the Korean language due to the long hours spent in the laboratory. Her next option was to use a translator throat strap. This item would be placed around the throat, where it detected vibrations as the wearer spoke and translated the sound into the pre-programmed language. Although she missed the reality of fluency, the straps had made overseas work dramatically easier, rendering language learning relatively unnecessary for most of her contemporaries.

Her throat strap in place, Louise completed her sterile look by putting on the surgical mask. She was ready. The duty nurse allowed her into the sealed room. The door closed sucking out the air that had come in with her.

Hea Woo smiled. Louise recognised they were developing a close, warm friendship. Morning sickness caused Hea Woo a number of problems, her arm permanently attached to a drip. This was now the eighth week of pregnancy accompanied by soaring levels of progesterone circulating inside her body.

'Hea Woo,' Louise bowed, 'how are you?' A female, android voice repeated the question in Korean, the voice projection on the strap was excellent.

'I am feeling very sick today,' replied a female android voice in almost perfect English.

Louise was able to ask all the questions on her list and try to investigate the physiological aspects and their emotional counterparts. For all intents and purposes, things were progressing along the lines of a normal pregnancy.

Then they talked about life, Hea Woo's life. A contrast of lives.

The underlying guilt refused to go away. Louise committed to her acts of penance, still blaming herself yet in awe of the unfolding mystery.

THE ARRIVAL OF JACK AND JILL

Sunday 14th November 2027

The scans revealed that the downy hair on the bodies remained in place. Worrying.

By now the twins' hair should have begun to dissipate. Visions of hairy babies haunted the team. It would boil down to the selection of the genes, the hair genes from the chimpanzee should have been eliminated.

The waxy vernix caseosa that protected the twins from the lacerating effects of the amniotic fluid also remained in place. Close examination of the scans revealed that their eyelids were very thin. In normal babies the eyes would be sealed at this stage, covered by the eyelids. Even on the highest magnifications, the skin seemed almost transparent. From within the womb it was difficult to know they would act as screens or simply allow normal light through even when the eyes were closed. Only birth would reveal this. Seeing light all the time with no respite, not ideal

They might have problems with their eyesight – reasoned Louise. Their retinal output intensity would have to be monitored once they were born.

The due date was 12th December 2027. Hea Woo already looked like a beached whale. Her hormone levels were carefully controlled to prevent early contractions, her womb stretched to inhuman proportions. From their calculations the twins each weighed in at 4lb – underweight. They needed to reach full term if they were to have any chance of surviving outside the womb.

For Louise, Karl and the team living with anxiety became the norm. Dr Kothaka insisted on being regularly updated, Max took on that role.

Karthik planned to be in South Korea when the time came for the babies to enter the world.

Louise marked off the days on her calendar, in her apartment and in the office. Four weeks to go.

Sunday 28th November 2027

The alert indicated that Hea Woo had started bleeding. In the middle of the night she had complained of pains in her sides, shortly afterwards she fell unconscious and began to bleed from her cervix. The changes in her biorhythms indicated that she had a bacterial infection.

Panic swept through the isolation wing. How could any disease bypass all of the measures that were so carefully put in place?

Nanobots could be used but concern was raised over whether they could cross the placenta and become active in the unborn twins. The Head of Nanotechnology calmed the anxious doctors by explaining the nanobots could be programmed to become inactive when they came into contact with placental tissue. All it would take would be the proper programming. He would set about the task immediately.

Meanwhile Hea Woo regained consciousness and calmed the frayed nerves of the hospital team. The twins were not at risk.

The delivery of the nanobots resolved the crisis. It took nearly four hours for the robots to complete their job.

Louise did not sleep that night, choosing instead to keep up to date with every aspect of the treatment. Being pregnant was a traumatic experience for both Hea Woo and Louise.

Sunday 12th December 2027

Hea Woo was in labour, as if on cue, on the predicted delivery date. Only the medical staff were allowed in the delivery room.

In the IBC-Korea Human Technology Division, no one was doing any work. Karl allowed the lax atmosphere; he too felt the tension of the moment. They were almost there. No other scientist had declared that they had created a human chimera so far.

If IBC were first... Karl basked in the future glory of speaking to the world about their project.

Max and Karthik kept in close contact. Max found it hard to understand why Karthik possessed such a hungry for every detail, every contraction and cry; So far, Hea Woo had been in painful labour for twelve hours.

To the surprise of the hospital staff the female twin was born first. Naturally and without forceps, she came down the birth canal head first. Once born, she was handed to the midwife, who whisked her away for an immediate clean-up. After thirty seconds, the first cry rang out – the first cry of the human chimera released on the planet, blending with the billions of others sounds, a symphony of life.

Heard by only a few, the voice of transformation, the new beginning. An innocent and natural instinct, the sound of life, first breath.

The second birth was more complicated. The male child had not turned in the womb, now he facing a breech birth delivery. The experienced midwife took charge and decided to turn the child in the womb. The normally calm consultants and doctors were keen to go for the caesarean. They watched her skilled manoeuvring, ready with scalpels should there be any signs of distress.

Thirty minutes the second baby entered the world. He cried the minute he came out of the birth canal.

She weighed 5lb 4oz, he weighed 5lb 3oz.

Although it would remain a secret for some time, Hea Woo had made history – she had birthed the first pair of human chimeras. IBC-Korea had achieved the once-impossible. The first humans blended with rabbit and chimpanzee genes.

Champagne for all – that hypermail was most welcome among the team.

Louise sat at her desk, starting into the champagne flute as bubbles rose to its surface. When the news broke she found herself weeping uncontrollably. Perhaps it was the joy of knowing that the twins had arrived safely, or the knowledge that Hae Woo had survived the ordeal of her pregnancy? A partnership of ecstasy, relief and anxiety danced around in her thoughts, spinning in unison.

We did it.

Before she departed from the laboratory that evening she would write the statements that would close Phase I of the Bible – from conception to birth.

Karl sat alone in his office contemplating the news. *I now have two children and no childcare issues*, he smiled gleefully. A private thought known by only a few people in the world.

At the back of his mind, he wondered about their mother. It troubled him that a shroud of secrecy would have to remain in place about their origin. *What would be put on their birth certificates? Will they be issued with birth certificates?* He sipped his glass of champagne, continuing to mull over his thoughts.

The laboratory party went on for most of the evening.

UPBRINGING

Karl simply did as he was told. Max had given him the names. On hearing them, Karl thought of the nursery rhyme.

He made he made his way to the staff meeting in the Human Technology Division, walking with a confident stride.

There would be no official naming ceremony. Karl simply announced to the team that the twins would be called Jack and Jill. That was it, no explanation.

Louise was mystified by the whole process. *Perhaps this is just another idiosyncrasy at IBC-Korea?* Karl didn't even bother to respond when she asked him about it. He seemed a little miffed.

Then the pertinent matter was discussed – a genuine problem had been identified. Their eyelids were too thin. Instead of acting as light filters, their tiny eyes were exposed to continuous light. The skin resembling parchment, close to transparency, layered through with threadlike capillaries.

The issue had to be resolved and soon. The future sight of the twins could be in jeopardy. Light levels were dimmed in the nursery area to reduce the impact one their eyes. In the Human Technology laboratory, the team remained in deep discussion.

'We could use the stem cell gel,' offered Ade as he doodled on his notepad with his pencil. 'We could programme the cells so that we only activate the genes in connection with eyelid skin generation – slightly thinner than normal skin.'

The pencil snapped in his hand, he blushed. He was glad that no one would be able to tell. An advantage of his own skin. Vigorous, approving nods indicated that this was a great idea.

'How about we make use of nanobots too?' Rebecca Seles was proving to be a real asset on the team. Louise was impressed, Rebecca showed enthusiasm and determination. She had taken over Chloe's position on the team.

'They could carry out cell degeneration once the correct thickness of skin has been obtained. That would,' Rebecca looked around the group hoping for approval, 'prevent the skin becoming too thick.'

Louise pointed her pen directly at Rebecca, 'That is a brilliant idea!'

Rebecca breathed a sigh of relief, she had been accepted.

WEDNESDAY 15TH DECEMBER 2027

The medical staff at the IBC Hospital carried out the technique on the twin's third day of life. A cell growth accelerator applied regular doses of chemical that accelerated the reproduction rate of the eyelid skin cells. The eyes were bandaged follwed by an anxious four day wait began. Nobody knew if their sight would be permanently damaged; only time would reveal this hidden element of this new venture.

Back in the laboratory the daily routine was a good distraction from the concerns in the minds of the Human Technology Division. Lessons had to be learned from this error. Somebody had failed to identify the genes needed to produce the right thickness of skin in the eyelids. Such incompetency could hardly go unnoticed.

Since the pregnancy, new projects had been started. For the researchers it meant starting again with new species – projects did not stop just because the first phase of Living Doll Project had been completed.

The new combinations included further tri-genomic organism – fish combined with rabbit and human genes – just one of the items on the list of possibilities.

Life in the Human Technology Division was never static.

SUNDAY 19TH DECEMBER 2027

Beautiful skin, thought the nurse as she removed the bandages. The treatment had worked.

Later that morning during a visit, Louise expressed her delight. Calling it an early Christmas present for the team.

The new rhythm of the day suited Louise, she spent half of her day in the lab working on projects – the other half was spent in the secluded section of the hospital wing that housed the twins. The hospital time was spent monitoring, observing and monitoring the progress of the 'twinnes', her pet names for Jack and Jill. No one else called them by that name. She preferred to keep that to herself, only using it when alone with them.

A team of nurses and two registered nannies took care of all of their needs. That meant Louise had all the fun stuff but none of the nappies and baby sick, except if one of them deposited his or her stomach contents during observation time.

They were both sleeping and feeding well. The formula milk was specifically prepared for them. Their blood was monitored on a daily basis and the information used to make up the composition of the milk, ensuring maximum nutrient levels and ensuring all dietary requirements were always met at every feed.

In Louise's thinking this pattern would became normal throughout the world for those who could afford the technology. Of course, breast feeding was an option, however, various reports had concluded that the formula was best. The old method would drop out of fashion amongst those who could afford the new technology. Hopefully were that the price would drop making it become accessible for more and more of the population, not just for the 1%. Anyway it was a big step forward, the twinnes were benefitting from the treatment.

Each time she was with them, strong emotions seemed to overcome her. She felt tearful, even unsettled as she approached the ward and when she left. Maternal instinct, she supposed. Today they were both sound asleep.

Louise wondered whether the children's isolation would hinder their development. They stayed together but did not interact with anyone else apart from the nurses and the nannies. At this stage, it might not be a problem; it was probably a good thing that they did not come into contact with everyday germs. But thinking ahead… Louise decided to mention it to Karl during their next meeting.

They needed to be exposed to normal life if they were to have healthy immune systems, otherwise those systems would remain immature, leaving them open to future infections.

Six months, the twinnes were making fantastic progress. Their growth rate were almost three months ahead of that of normal children. Karl had initially been against mixing the children with others but changed his mind.

They spent three hours a day in the IBC-Korea crèche, supervised by their nannies. The other mums who attended knew that the twinnes were special, but none of them had been told the exact reasons why. Even the medical staff and the nannies were not privy to the truth about their origins.

Louise had listened to the occasional whispers at collection time, all they revealed was the fact that people thought that the two children were a little strange.

Crawling already. Both of them could sit up and pull themselves along with their well-developed arm muscles. What with their excellent balance; they could manage on all fours and still look cute.

Seeing how well they got on with each made Louise so happy, they seemed to understand and even pre-empt the others behaviour.

Playing with their many toys, they looked happy and contented. Louise concluded she was smitten by her adopted twinnes.

The select group completed their singing of 'happy birthday', before bursting into energetic applause. Jack and Jill clapped too, delighted to be the centre of attention.

As they sat in the middle of the sound mat, Louise thought that their squeals and shrieks were so joyful, truly wonderful.

Karl felt very irritated by the whole thing and made a weak excuse, having to do some urgent paperwork, just to get away from the scene.

There was no doubt about it, once Jack and Jill were on their feet, there was no stopping them. They could confidently squat and stand. Falling down did not seem to bother them at all, they would quickly regain their composure and go off running all over again. The whole experience – something very special. Louise felt a new zeal about life, her work at IBC and even hopeful about the future.

Everyone seemed to love them, talking to their nannies revealed they thought they had the best job in the world. They would have carried out the job without pay; Jack and Jill brought tremendous joy into the nursery wing of the IBC-Korea hospital.

After the party, Louise needed to update the records on coordination and reflex response. It had been two weeks since she had logged this aspect of their development. Grinning wildly, she congratulated herself on having landed such a cushy position.

MONDAY 4TH JUNE 2029

Another day. Louise rolled out of bed and made her way to the bathroom.

The shower always woke her up, tingling her skin and reminding her of the day that lay ahead. Today no different from the previous one. More test, more checks, another visit to the labs. The highlight of the day, Jack and Jill. She smiled, they made such a difference to her dull day.

The hair dryer seemed extra noisy today. She blasted at her hair till it was dry before giving it a quick brush. A dab of moisturiser, she smeared it all over her face. She checked the mirror just to make sure it had been absorbed.

Time to get dressed.

On final brush of her hair, she put on her gold chain with Adrian's ring attached, tucking it behind her blue satin top. It bulged slightly just under the top of her clavicle. Sometimes she wore it on top.

There she was ready for the day. She had fifteen minutes to get to the cafeteria for her breakfast. She fancied eggs and bacon today, a rare fry up. She decided to walk rather than take an IBC autocab.

I'll be piling on the pounds if I am not careful. She did not want to end up looking like a blimp. Easily done with all the delicious food served up by the IBC chefs.

The electronic door lock clinked behind her.

'Put that down, Jack!' Louise made the request for the second time.

Jack promptly threw the fluffy rabbit at Jill, hitting her in the face. She burst into tears, wailing uncontrollably. Louise rushed over, scooping her up. 'Sorry Jill, Jack is being naughty,' she glared at Jack, who responded by giggling and crawling towards the sound mat.

She needed a distraction. *What can I do? I know…* 'Let's play the string-along game!' exclaimed Louise.

Excited squeals came from Jack and Jill. This was one of their favourite games. Though funny, the game was designed to develop their coordination and motor skills.

Fun mattered to Louise; their lives were not normal. She knew that more than anyone. With two more Living Doll pregnancies on the way, life was becoming increasingly hectic. Moments like these helped to keep things in perspective.

It looked as if Jack was going to win yet again! He just kept going whereas Jill seemed to give up when facing a challenge.

Louise decided to find some strategies to build up Jill's confidence and prepare for the challenges of life. More pedagogic reading.

Whoever thought being a parent was easy had no kids of their own. Experience, an intense and thorough teacher.

Louise could imagine herself adopting a front row seat in evening classes – child psychology and development – but her schedule was already fully booked.

FRIDAY 14TH DECEMBER 2029

Louise and exhaustion were one.

The new surrogate mothers were struggling with the approved levels of S-Tetrin dosages. Another late night for her, gritty eyelids and grumpy mood, signs of her tiredness.

Bringing up children was not easy. Thankfully she only had to put up with this for three hours a day. She found a new respect surfacing for her parents – *what did Adrian and I put them through?*

From her data records the twins were growing at a rapid rate; far faster than any normal child. Reaching the age of two seemed to have increased the reproductive rate of their cells. They were the size of three year olds.

Jill was not going to let go. Her features, tight and distorted, as she concentrated on being determined. Jack assessed the situation, deciding that the swipe technique would work best. With one swift grab, he snatched the red fire engine.

'Mine,' he said, '… Mine!' Jack clung to his prize, holding it to his chest.

Jill had had enough. Tears fell down her cheeks, she turned to look at Louise, her eyes pleading for assistance.

Are these ones real, or simply crocodile tears? Louise scrutinised her expression. *Yes, they're for were real.*

Louise stood in front of Jack. 'Give it to me Jack!' In her mind it was not an option, Jack stood still for a moment, before deciding to crawl away with the fire engine in his right hand. Louise grabbed his right leg, promptly removing the prize from him. She saw the confused look move across his features, he stared at her, the look changed to naughty face.

They were openly testing each other's limits, not to mention her own. Even starting to argue. From her assessment, Louise concluded they had a vocabulary of 60 – 80 words; slightly above that expected in children of their age. She could not wait for this shift to be over.

'Here you are,' Louise placed the engine in Jill's eager hands. Her reward – a beaming, broad smile that exposed two missing front teeth.

SUNDAY 5TH MAY 2030

Frustration wanted to wrestle with her. Esther refused to give in yet feeling in no mood to take up the challenge.

The paper had to be somewhere! The infuriating question, where?

She was so annoyed with herself. Since getting back from South Korea restlessness had become an intimate friend of hers. It was a daily struggle, completed by the sense of being unsettled. The past year… so traumatic; so many things had gone wrong.

The start of May marked the official end of her recovery Sabbath. After leaving IBC she had felt totally exhausted, like a squeezed out tube of toothpaste, spent. Visiting friends in the USA helped her to reconnect with life. It was good to be back in Israel.

The offer of a job at Tel Aviv University had been amazing, almost miraculous. Perfect timing. Despite her reputation she still needed to gather all the relevant paperwork. Extracts from that missing research paper were a key part of her application.

She lifted the foremost plastic crate, spotting the white cardboard box – *Chloe's diaries.*

She paused, feel a tightening sensation in her lower stomach. Her initial impulse resurfaced – throw the diaries away without even looking at them. *Is it macabre to consider reading the memoirs of someone who has died?*

The voice of reason spoke; after all, memoirs and autobiographies contained the untold stories of those no longer around. Valuable lessons could be learned through the lives of others. Even so, Chloe's diaries seemed too close to home; that was what made it feel so wrong. They had shared noodles, heartaches, joys and even the occasional moment of tension when Esther had had to tell Chloe off over one or another misdemeanour.

Lifting the lid of the box, she gently removed the first diary then blew off the light layer of dust. She coughed, as the dust particles swirled in the air creating a fine mist.

The pages were chronologically organised, neatly presented. Chloe had beautiful spiralling handwriting, a point obscured by the use of computers and other work processing facilities. *Very scientific and technically accurate, almost devoid of feeling.* All aesthetic emotion seemed to have been edited out of the entries.

Perhaps she saved it for her personal diary?

Esther chided herself for becoming distracted by her find. The original matter still needed resolution.

I will read these, she decided, picking up the box and carrying it into the living room. *I'll look at them.*

First, she had to find that research paper.

MONDAY 6TH MAY 2030

Jill did not like the patented white shoes. Nothing that Louise said made any difference.

'I don't like them,' she stated emphatically.

'Jill…' Louise waited three seconds before she continued – the textbook had recommended this technique for dealing with pre-schoolers. It allowed time for the information to reach the relevant part of the brain. 'You need to put them on.' Louise spoke with a firm authoritative tone, also recommended by the book.

'I don't like them.' Louise sighed – stalemate. Theory and reality seemed to be completely when it came to handling children. Out of the corner of her eyes she spotted Jack, heading towards the chocolate milkshake on his table, still wearing his brand new white shirt.

She cringed in anticipation, knowing what was about to happen and not being able to do anything about it. 'Jack!' She hoped the tone of her voice would be enough to dissuade Jack from his set course. However, the milkshake attracted him like a homing beacon. He ignored her.

There was no way she could reach him before the collision. The milkshake seemingly statically attracted to his shirt which was bleeding, a pale brownish colour seeping across its surface.

In two days' time Jack and Jill were to be presented to the world. Louise had two objectives to fulfil on this occasion. Neither of them related to monitoring or observing the twins.

Today her roles were to check that their clothes fitted, and to say goodbye. They would remain in South Korea while she flew to Philadelphia, the location of the press announcement; the world would see them from the Miranda Ferrell auditorium. An image of them at least.

Wiping the chocolate milk from the shirt seemed pointless. She would have to get Lisa, the duty nanny, to have the shirt washed and pressed. All the same, she had to try something.

'Jill, come here please,' Louise dabbed at Jack's stained shirt. Jill obeyed, glaring at Jack as she stood next to him. Her tongue shoot out. He did the same back to her. 'Stop it you two.' Jill's sheepish look did not fool Louise.

'Jill, get your hair brush,' she produced it from behind her back. 'You knew, good girl.' As she brushed the luscious locks, she noticed the widow's peak. *Just like Karl's* she thought.

'JJ!' Louise used this term when she wanted to address both of them. 'I need both of you to listen.' She changed the tone of her voice, making it quiet, speaking slowly. Stern looks appeared on their faces, they knew she was serious. 'Louise, has something to tell you.'

When she finished, Jack started crying. The sobs started quietly then began to crescendo, the Jill joined in.

As far as they were concerned, a few days could well have been a lifetime. She knew they loved her deeply, to them she meant the world.

Louise wondered what they were feeling, what was going on in their minds? She imagined small cracks appearing over their hearts as they tried to cope with the news of her departure.

Living with a broken heart, she knew what that felt like. She had promised herself that she would not cry.

Her tears fell like tiny sphere, landing on their raven black hair as she hugged them tightly. If she felt so upset, then they must be devastated. The pain reminded her of losing Adrian. It seemed duller, less intense. She had started to work through her grief.

How long does it take to mend a broken heart?

+++

Sipping a mug of hot chocolate, Esther sat cross-legged on her green cloth settee. Almost a full hour had passed.

Absolutely fascinating, as if she were looking at the world through another pair of eyes. They had both shared the same experiences yet Chloe's perspective had been totally different. She believed passionately in what she was doing – the idea that her work made a contribution to the betterment of the human race drove her day after day. That sense of drive tangibly experienced through her writing. There was a definite absence of any emotional information – a professional appraisal of life in the laboratory. The very existence of the diaries violated the silence clause that all employees were forced to sign. If IBC knew about these diaries, their lawyers would be released like a pack of ferocious wolves. Apart from herself, only Beth knew of their existence.

Chloe's comments caused her to feel slightly put out, she winced inwardly. *Cheeky woman! Describing* me *as 'matron like'* – she felt insulted.

Chloe's descriptions of Karl dripped with hero worship; she even referred to him as the 'distinguished Dr Karl Winwood'. That must have been during her 'crush' phase, when she seemed to be infatuated with Karl *– thankfully it didn't last too long –* his personality had put an end to that. A slight emotional edge flavoured the words used to describe Karl. It made Esther smile as she recalled the hushed conversations she had shared with Chloe. Even her questions as to whether she stood any chance of dating him. Esther had advised her to avoid mixing business with pleasure. Chloe had been visibly disappointed.

Deeply enthralled in the potted history of the Living Doll Project, Esther continued to read late into the evening. From January 2026 until March 2026 – the first diary ended. Esther glanced up noting the time – 11.30pm! *Where have the hours gone?* She could read a little more or just go to bed… *maybe another half an hour.*

The second diary began on April 1st 2026. Twenty minutes later, Esther dropped the diary along with the fourth mug of hot chocolate. The rich brown liquid splattered all over the green couch and the diary. Esther's dressing gown did not escape the chocolate rain shower.

What she had just read made her bones shake, sent her mind into a crazy spin, an internal mental washing machine on the fastest setting – she felt numb and dizzy.

This cannot be true; this cannot be real – she tried to reassure herself.

The entry on 22nd April described Chloe's meeting with Max and his offer to *purchase* her *eggs*. *Chloe's eggs* were part of the Living Doll Project!

She's the mother of the chimeras.

Wet and tired, Esther could feel a growing sense of grief moving slowly through her body.

This was awful, really awful.

On returning from the kitchen with a dampened cloth, she began the salvaging operation, carefully blotting the pages of the diary, trying not to lose a single letter of the handwritten text. Then her dressing gown, the settee and finally the floor – her attempt achieved very little. The brown evidence only dimming slightly.

She read on.

The events of June 2026 described in immaculate detail. Emotion began to creep into the records as Chloe divulged her excitement at being asked to select her "surrogate" mothers. The overwhelming joy of knowing that one of the subjects had become pregnant, then the crushing devastation of miscarriage.

All of this had been bottled up on the inside – intense suffering in a secret world. Chloe's guilt had fuelled her detailed enquiries about the risks to subsequent pregnancies. She became much more reflective and compassionate towards the potential mothers.

Esther remembered her asking questions after the first failed set of pregnancies. Before that she had been rather jovial about the whole thing. Esther stopped – *it must have been… like losing a child. Oh Chloe!*

Her heart throbbed then pounded. *Has Beth read the other diaries*? She would also find out the truth behind the mortgage salvation that came through the bonus – *money for eggs*! A searing thought. What should she do with this information? *Will Beth want to know? What about IBC?* This put them in a whole new light. If they wanted to purchase eggs they could, but to use one of their own employees?

Fame, but at what price? Why did Chloe kept quiet about this? Esther grasped the sides of her face, her fingers raking the skin creating deep furrows, moving down towards her chin. This was truly shocking information.

Poor Chloe! Esther realised her departure must have been like a protective layer had been removed. All those childhood vulnerabilities must have all surfaced all at once. She must have felt alone, afraid, unsure even threatened? All the issues – the children her hidden secret – every time pregnancy is discussed. The torment disclosed entry after entry, Chloe living with her inner torment.

Chloe's' fragile state of mind started to impact on her writing. The entries became progressively less organised and more emotional. The professional tone disappeared while personal comments took their place – some out of pain, some full of accusation. Esther read that her departure seemed to mark a particularly significant point in Chloe's troubled mind. The venom she harboured for Karl expressed itself in profanity – horrible words underlined and in capital letters. Initial infatuation morphed into open hatred.

Esther's reading drew out more and more pain. She could have stopped, but the desire to know the sinister truth, however devastating, drove her on. It was now three in the morning.

Chloe made reference to her lack of sleep and the use of the Biomedi-pod. It seemed to have been effective. Chloe used it on a regular basis, keeping record of the times of administration and the dosage. A scientist to the end – *Chloe what happened to you? How did we lose you?*

The questions troubled Esther, going around and around in her head. The heating had gone off. She tightened the dressing gown around her body, shivering. It achieved little. The cold was on the inside.

There was no mention of experimental drugs. *Maybe she recorded those entries in her personal diaries?* Chloe kept meticulous records of every time she used the Biomedi-pod – the time of administration, the dosage and how effective the level was.

The entry on 28/02/2027 mentioned that there could be an issue with the dosage being administered by her Biomedi-pod. Chloe had been late to work on a few occasions. Waking up was difficult. She noted that the information transfer between the Biomedi-pod and the digital interface in the apartment might need seeing to.

Her final entry on 01/03/2027 stated that she had received a dose of 0.01 mg of the sedative at 11.35pm. Esther stopped reading, a faint memory surfaced. Beth had showed her the official autopsy; it plainly stated that a dose of approximately 0.1mg had been found in her body systems.

That was almost 10 times the dose that Chloe recorded. In truth that represented the difference between a deep sleep and organ failure. *How can there have been such a difference?* A voice in her mind told her something was wrong, this seemed very suspicious. *What about proof?* Only two people knew about Chloe's record of events.

The IBC hospital had taken care of all the medical matters relating to Chloe's death, including the autopsy. The death certificate stated that organ failure had been the cause of death. Chloe's body had responded badly to the sedative on this occasion. A case of chemical toxicity and body system over-reaction.

The coroner's conclusion was that the Biomedi-pod had administered an incorrect dosage. Computer technical error in a nutshell. The interactive devices worked to a high accuracy, 99.9%. They were smart devices, they could update themselves and monitor their patients recording their biological processes.

If she could get her hands on the data records...

Perhaps that is why IBC made such a generous *payment to Beth – to take her mind off the small details?* The sudden realisation was shocking. Esther's breathing rate became shallow, her pulse accelerated. Weakness engulfed her, something hit her in the stomach – dull like the butt of a shot gun.

She held her head in her hands, weeping uncontrollably. Sobs and groans erupting from the pit of her stomach. *This is too much to take in.* It was now 4.20am. Something was deeply wrong. Chloe's death now raised unanswered questions.

I have no idea what to do.

Dawn started to break, signalling a new day in Tel Aviv.

THURSDAY 9TH MAY 2030

Even the thought of talking to Beth about Chloe in the light of the new revelations – made Esther's stomach creep. As a mother, Beth had the right to know the truth about her daughter's murder. Using that word seemed to empower Esther... but the consequences of disclosure would be devastating.

It would mean the opening up of well mending wounds and would raise all kinds of questions about IBC… *about* my *work at IBC…* and *about their squeaky clean image. What other secrets are going on within theose well-protected walls?* Every day she delayed, the trail grew colder. The guilty feelings increased, day by day, in tiny increments; the easy thing was to simply do nothing. Just sit on the knowledge. Yet her inner voice would not be silenced or pacified.

Just when things were getting back to some kind of order!

Tel Aviv, such a prestigious university, and with it a very reasonable salary, though nothing like the exorbitant pay scale at IBC. Her parents had taught her: "If you have the love of family and friends, you are rich." Money was not everything, but it sure made opportunities accessible.

Even so, you could rise. You could be a dean. You could help people learn. That has to be better. But what would disclosure do to all that? Would you fall too, Esther?

Am I still bound to IBC?

The whole thing felt like an immense burden, and it was gaining mass. She did not want to add to her family's worries but it was getting to her. Her typically calm demeanour interrupted replaced by frequent moments of irritation. Her hearty appetite had been suppressed and, all of a sudden, she had found it hard to sleep. Even her shopping instinct had been affected. There was no other course of action but to tell Papa. His sagacity would be a guide; he would tell her the truth, plain and simple. What a shock this would be for him. None of her family knew the true nature of her work with the Living Doll Project. They all thought she was still on plant projects and had decided to leave IBC after a major disagreement with the management.

Papa would be disappointed with her deception, but if she knew anything, he knew how to forgive. How strange, it was not something that she had bought into. But they took their Judaism more seriously than she did. For her it was a thing in the background, neither a serious nor an active part of her identity. She enjoyed the feast days and most of the rituals –but, in her mind, it was all too much work for the already occupied women of the family. All of that cleaning and preparation. The men seemed to be exempt from that part of the process and she couldn't bring herself to condone it fully.

But yes, she would pop in and see him. A bottle of his favourite wine would help to sweeten what might turn out to be a bitter evening.

Esther approached the doorway, the bright luminescence of the security lamp revealing a dark cedar door. The glare reflected off of the surfaces of an ornate brass doorknocker and the mezuzah on the right lintel of the door frame, giving them the allure of blazing fiery gold.

Three well-spaced rhythmic knocks – her signature greeting. She listened to the shuffling, sedate footsteps making their way to the door, wondering if Papa's arthritis in his right hip was playing up, the slight drag every second step creating an unbalanced rhythm, suggesting a hobbling gait as if he were avoiding placing too much weight on the troubled leg.

'Esther, my darling. How lovely to see you. You know I always miss you when you are not here.'

'Papa, you are so full of charm,' she kissed him on both cheeks, 'Mama has had years of your silver tipped tongue.'

He laughed, tapping the nostril of his nose, then he saw the bottle. 'Ah, my favourite wine. You spoil me.' A twinkle danced in his eye. He still possessed his zest for life, even after such hard times.

'Come in and sit down, I am about to watch the news,' he gestured towards the living room. It had long been his area in the house.

'Thank you Papa, that would be good.' Time spent with Papa in his space had always been special, especially when she was a young girl. They were opportunities for bonding and heart to heart talking.

He sat down, then patted the cushion on his right. Esther took her place, feeling a dry sensation on her tongue. 'How is Mama? Still at Auntie Zelda's house?'

'You know how you women can talk. Three days! What is there to talk about that takes three days?' His exasperation was amplified by this wide-open, thick skinned hands.

'Papa,' she cleared her throat, 'I have something to tell you… it will be hard for you to hear.'

'Esther,' he tilted his head, took her hand, 'You know I believe in no secrets.'

She nodded, catching her next breath in her chest. She exhaled, 'We've spoken about this but I have more to tell you, Papa. You know that I had many reasons for leaving IBC. But you don't know that I have only made some of them known to you. There are others. Some that you will find hard to understand.' She studied his face, his eyes. 'I have been involved in something that crosses the boundaries that you hold sacred, and I am not comfortable with the things, the other things, that they asked me to do.'

His raised eyebrows meant that he was listening but not judging. 'I am all ears. The news can wait.'

Esther nodded in thanks, 'Papa, I don't really know how to say this. You will know the connotations. I was sworn to secrecy, but... Papa, IBC has been carrying out experiments on humans. To change humans.' His mouth was now as wide open as his eyes. He tilted his head to the other side. She could see him fighting the urge to speak, or to shake his head in disbelief. 'They...' She sighed, "I mean, we. We have been mixing humans with... other species.'

'Oy Vey!' He placed his right hand over his heart and looked upwards, his head swivelling from side to side.

She hoped his heart would be up to it.

+++

The journey back to her flat was hard. She decided to take a taxi. She wasn't sure she could walk very far like this. Papa had been horrified. He had cried and cried, both at the news and at the fact that Esther had concealed so much from him. She regretted telling him, but she knew that the burden of the past was too much for her to bear alone.

The news about Chloe – he had trembled as she'd told him the official story, and he seemed shaken when she told him about the diaries, giving him her version of the truth. His face was ashen and tense, at one point he put his hands to his ears as if to tell her to stop. Just before they reached his earlobes he pulled them away, shakily telling her to continue.

Shock upon shock. She had cried as the final details were shared. There was something disturbing about disclosing all of this to someone who wasn't – brainwashed and conditioned by working at IBC.

It was like an admission. It was as if she had been involved in something no ordinary person would dare touch. She couldn't help but think back to her family's history. To the history of her birthplace. To the lessons; the old family stories about Europe. No doubt her father had been thinking the same. He had not spoken for a long time, rocking gently as if he were praying. He wiped periodically at tears that leaked from his eyes.

'Science has entered into sacred ground. This is like the days of Noah.' Even her limited Torah knowledge recognised that he believed that this had been done before. "Nothing new under the sun," he often quoted.

His advice had been simple though, in the end: "Think carefully before you share this with Bethany. It will destroy her heart and fuel her bitterness. The money will no longer be a comfort, she will feel that she has been paid blood money."

Blood money.

IBC knew a lot about that. Money for eggs, and now compensation money for murder. The rain pattered on the windows, one drop joining another, making mini snake like rivulets. The questions repeated themselves in her head without relenting.

Karl Winwood. How much do you know? Augustine… why?

The rain kept falling. Alone, each drop was insignificant. But each joined another, like the beginnings of a flood. She wiped away a tear. A flood. Potentially revolutionary.

Decision time.

Papa had not made the choice for her, instead he allowed her to exercise her own will. He offered support, no matter what she chose to do. She told him he could tell Mama.

It reminded her of the story of David and Goliath. How could one man stand up against a giant and win? Taking on IBC! Beth and her together. Incredible, with the odds stacked against them. All of this, based on the diaries of a dead woman. Then she thought of the team and her replacement. All of them trapped in a web, unaware of the return of the spider that spun it.

Who would believe me?

And the fear!

It wouldn't leave her. She would have to pay for her actions too, if she went public. She had been complicit in their work, morally accountable, criminal perhaps. She kept reimagining that line, that line from the poem…

"I did not speak out… I did not speak out…"

The dread was creeping… all consuming.

You thought that you had flown that web, all the way to Israel? You never flew, Esther.

She didn't know how to feel. Emotional paralysis. *Do I have the courage to do this?*

She was not one for prayer but the words came out almost by mistake, there in the back of the taxi.

'Oh, JHVH.'

PART V

HARD LESSONS

I B C - KOREA

Icilda Biotech Company – Korea
Inspiring future hope

CHRONOS

SATURDAY 11TH MAY 2030

What went wrong?

Karl realised he had gone from feeling like Tiberius to wanting to run and hide, turning to Glenda and Jim Bream for company.

PR… Pathetic Retards! Their so called publicity stunt had turned into a world-wide farce, with him at the centre of the comedy. It was not fair. His face was unforgettable, and now it would be associated with this sham. Forever.

Max… what will he say? Will I lose my job?

Probably not. He was too important for that. *But there* will *be repercussions.* Karl raked his hand through his hair again. *Who could replace me in this particular role? No one I've ever met. There's that at least. Anyway I saved the day – I stopped the whole thing melting down. All thanks to me.*

That was a comfort.

The meeting would involve Max, Phillippe, the PR team and, of course, Karl. A post mortem meeting, masquerading as a conference.

Karl walked into the room, like a man sentenced to death. The slow paced strides of a condemned man on the way to the guillotine. Stomach churning, sweaty palms; he was genuinely scared.

Think positive, Karl. You are the man. Another voice spoke from inside… *that was true once.*

He quashed it. *No. I'm still the man.* He swept his hand through his locks, calming himself.

At least he still looked great.

+ + +

'I want to know how we get ourselves out of this pile of manure. Do you understand?'

Although he was not looking at Karl when he said it, it felt as if it were directed at him. The question was actually aimed Laura Ingram, Head of PR. He'd heard she was top of her class at University. *Didn't help her on this occasion.*

They were seated around the conference table. All six of them.

'We need to take back the—'

'I,' Max leaned over in her direction pointing in her face, 'fail to understand why we gave away the positon in the first place.'

Karl watched him slump back, turning away from her. His intention clear. She disgusted him. He could see the bitter hatred filling Max's blackened eyes – wells of cruelty. It was horrible. Karl had a sudden and uncomfortable feeling that Max had something powerful going on behind those eyes; perhaps in his life beyond the board room. He gulped, aware that his hands were still sweaty, making them slippery.

'You really lost it, didn't you Karl.' Max's head swerved, a slow rotation.

The sudden change in focus startled Karl. As if by magic, his right hand shook. He pushed it into his lap, holding it down.

'Well Laura, I hope your CV is up to date.' The eyeballing was over for now. Once again Laura, was the object of his interest. Karl, temporarily off the hook. His hand stopped trembling.

What could he say in his defence? How could he make up for the failure?

It wasn't my damned failure. It wasn't my team. But he doesn't want to hear that. What do I say? His mind was racing but all creativity seemed to be on hold.

He hoped that, by the time Max was finished with Laura, some of his venom would be vented. Perhaps it would leave less for Karl to endure when it came to his turn.

Death by snake bite, slow but certain.

+ + +

It was obvious, Louise agreed somewhat reluctantly. They would have to be tagged; chipped with the latest biochip. That way they could be traced anywhere on the planet, even into space. Their fame made this necessary. The level of security required in visiting them would need to be increased.

Facial and retinal scans were already in use. Finger print scans and voice analysis could be easily added to the list. Max typed them onto the screen.

Visiting them should be like getting into Fort Knox. The 21st century version.

MONDAY 13TH MAY 2030

Stella Apfelbaum had been such a help in the past. They shared similar views on feminism; she also wanted to hear the voice of women in science. Louise believed they had a bond, a real connection. Yet her write-up had been scathing. It had made Louise look like a sacred rabbit, caught in the glare of a jeep's headlights.

This interview would give Louise a chance to put things right. A second chance. This would be an interview with just the two of them, before a small audience. Stella had given her a list of questions in advance; then they would take questions from audience. Thankfully there would be a vetting process in place and a fifteen second time delay.

Louise hoped the answers would come out naturally. Karl was meant to do this interview but he had passed the buck, still seething from his public dressing down by Stella.

Let's hope that sisters will stick together.

The studio door opened, Stella came out with headphones round her neck. 'Are you ready, Louise?'

'As I ever will be.' Her skirt seemed to be stuck to the chair, making a slurping sound as she got up.

I really need to do something about these nerves. MAT was not off the option list.

SOLD TO THE HIGHEST BIDDER

The sense of anticipation exponentially spiked off the Richter scale. The Miranda Ferrell Auditorium at IBC-USA had been designed for an audience of around 120 people. It became clear that what had been posed as an intimate gathering would become a public window to the world. A nightmare for the PR department – one of the hardest decisions being who would not make the guest list for this bidding war.

Thankfully not his decision. Karl was so glad. Back on American soil, even if only for a few days.

Interest in the Living Doll Project spanned across the globe, something about the project had captured the imagination of all age ranges from small children to the elderly. The antics of Jack and Jill at the original press release won them a huge fan club, social media sites went crazy. The IBC website crashed twice, frantic IT workers had to plough through the night to cope with the demand for more information that overloaded the system causing the meltdown. The IBC phone lines were jammed with requests for interviews from news corporations and journalist, keen to pose the stream of questions being asked by curious viewers. Some members of the public hoped to speak to the twins in person, desperate fans creating elaborate stories even posing as heads of state and celebrities – one character pretended to be the King of England!

Not everyone rejoiced at their arrival. There were the hate campaigns, fierce and vocal; the Human Purity League demanded that they should be put down just like a sick animal, the more offensive sites offered horrific methods they considered suitable for the 'freak twins'. Phone polls showed that the public were divided over their existence. The topic became front line news, sales of articles on the twins broke recent records, beating even the previous figures secured by the announcement of the end of world hunger.

Karl, Louise and the PR department may have thought the whole thing was a disaster, and rightly so from their perspective; it had been a moment of personal and public torment. However, it became an Internet sensation, going viral within ten minutes of the meeting's end. The terrified faces of the twins had shocked some members of the public; the behaviour of the audience was also a topic of conversation. Jill's honest response to the proceedings ended up as a popular underground t-shirt slogan: "Maybe that's why they are so mean!" Their scared little faces underneath the IBC logo. An instant best seller.

Max felt that IBC had missed a trick by not capitalising on this, quickly publicising his legal threat to sue anyone who produced unauthorised merchandise. Certain things could not be stopped so easily, at least, not without an unnecessary fuss.

A number of the world's wealthiest people were prepared to be confined to a small space to be part of this historical auction event. The auditorium overloaded with hopeful bidders. A few members of the select audience were eager to be seen at the event; free publicity does not fall out of the sky, after all the eyes of the world were on IBC-USA.

The statistics scrolled across his quantum tablet – Karl could see there were at least three hundred people present in the auditorium, he had arranged for a camera feed link directly to his tablet. He could watch them; the eyes of the cameras allowing him to spy on the elite group he would have loved to be part of.

He sat alone in the side room that served as a waiting room reflecting on the event. The neat décor of little interest to him, he ignored the layout, mentally preparing for his moment in the limelight, yet again.

The secret bid had closed almost four days ago. The management board at IBC were ecstatic; the publicity had only intensified the bidders' desire to own a Living Doll. And with limited supplies available…

Only shareholders could take part in the process – amazingly, some new investors came on board after the press release fiasco. "All publicity is good" – at the time Karl had not been so sure, now he could see the cornucopia he was comforted. The last few weeks had been traumatic, now he was back in the driving seat.

Proceedings were due to start in fifteen minutes' time. Karl knew the plan – shareholders would be thanked for taking part in the event. Then the prize winner or highest bidders would be announced. End of the proceedings. Simple. He would introduce the event and then hand over to Max.

There had been some precursory checks to ensure that the prospective adopted parents could provide a stable home – personality profiles along with various asset checks, on top of the existing vetting processes for natural adoption. Human Resources had taken care of the whole process, going over things in meticulous detail.

The reference files thick and chunky, Karl had given up reading all the small print that went along with the event. After all he had no plans to bid for them, they were his kids anyway. The fruit of his loins, only no-one knew. His little secret.

He smiled innocuously to himself, *who's the daddy?*

Right now Karl should have been feeling confident and happy, instead he felt a deep sense of nervousness. *Why?* He was used to speaking at events, so it could not be that. *Was it the bidding?* No reason for that to make him nervous. He had gone through his checking ritual, three times. He looked fine.

Then it occurred to him – the children were going to live with strangers. This must be what it is like this for parents when their kids leave home, he reasoned.

For almost four years, the Living Dolls had consumed his thoughts and dreams. Now the work was about to pay off. His fingers formed a bridge, he tapped his forefingers together. A job well done.

Intermittent vibrations on the inside pocket of his grey designer jacket reminded him that it was time to get himself on stage. Time to get ready to rumble.

He took out his quantum smartphone and tapped the screen. After depositing his tablet into his attaché case, he left the waiting room, phone in hand.

The auto-alarm device activated as Karl stepped across the threshold.

Darkness descended upon the room.

+++

After clearing his throat, Max Augustine began, 'We at IBC are delighted that you have decided to own a part of our history. However, the winning bidders will also own a slice of history itself. The first human chimeras. The rules have been clear, so I will not keep you in suspense any longer.'

Karl handed Max the first sealed envelope, suddenly aware of the increasing rate of his heartbeat. Max looked sombre, sharing the immense weight of this moment.

Karl watched his manicured ringed hands tremble as Max peeled open the envelope. Throughout the room, he sensed the audience holding its breath; you could feel the tension.

'The first Living Doll will be going to… Lynette Valsteen.'

The Bauble lady. Finding out about her background and wealth excited Karl; still he would have to make do with Glenda.

Warm applause filled the room. Lynette owned a very successful Internet provider service based in Wyoming, USA. Waving vigorously from her seat on the second row Lynette looked ecstatic. Karl knew from her file that she had two other teenagers back at home.

'Will it be Jack or Jill?' queried Max.

'I'll take Jill, I've already got two boys at home.' She spoke loudly and with a strong Texan accent. Intense laughter erupted from the audience. She managed to make herself heard without a mike! *A woman with a big mouth and loads of cash,* thought Karl adopting his professional smile.

'That leaves Jack! May I have the second envelope Karl? Thank you.'

Shareholders sat on the edge of their seats, some almost squirming in their seats, looking worried. They knew it was their one final chance to be part of history, IBC history.

Karl could tell from the slow actions and hesitation that Max relished his moment of absolute control. He watched him breaking the seal, then withdrawing the gilt edged card. 'The second Living Doll is going to… Richard Harrison.'

Despite the rapid applause, many shareholders' beaming smiles had been replaced by a new mask. A subdued look. They were deeply disappointed. Karl watched a few who realised they were on display, weak applause accompanied by plastic happy expressions.

Karl had read that file too. Richard was married to Janice – despite the wealth of technology at their disposal, IVF remained unsuccessful. Six years of waiting for a child were about to end. Richard acknowledged his prize by standing and receiving the ovation offered by the envious nominees. Janice remained seated, overcome by emotion, weeping into her hands. They looked as if they had won the genetic lottery. *Give her your kerchief, man.*

Karl managed a half-hearted clap, then, when he realised he was on camera, he added more enthusiasm to the action, giving his broadest smile and most interested look. He still enjoyed the sight of his own face close up.

'Thank you for your time and interest. Others will have a chance in time. We will keep you informed about future opportunities. Have a good afternoon!'

Max brought proceedings to a close.

The buzz in the room filled the auditorium, Karl felt it had gone well now he had escorting duties to perform.

He whisked Richard, Janice and Lynnette off to a champagne reception where they signed the paper work that made them legal guardians of Jack and Jill, the adoption process completed by the twins gaining their respective surnames. He oversaw the whole process, posing for photographs with all the new parents.

Max assured him a share of the income from the bidding as a bonus for his part in the whole experience. *One percent of $800M or WC1440M.* Karl smiled to himself as the digital flashes popped. He had won big today.

Karl could already see how his newfound favour with Max's had raised his status within the company, he had survived the press release post mortem without too much permanent damage. He experienced a deep sense of satisfaction, like a warm towel draped on him after a massage, and with it pride.

Yet a tinge of sadness too. The Living Dolls were about to fly the nest. *Goodbye Jack and goodbye Jill.* No doubt they would face their own sorrow, being separated. The ten day orientation period, designed to help them negotiate this major break in their lives and routine and to get them used to their new parents. That still lay ahead for them.

This must be just like kids leaving home…

SATURDAY 15TH JUNE 2030

Despite all the problems, things had worked out. Karl reflected, he had done it. Projects were moving into new territories; the money was in the bank and there was now more opportunity for his ambition to flourish than ever before. He had survived Max's disappointment.

He swirled the golden, brown liquid in the glass and emptied it into his mouth in one go. All the things he had overcome and all the things that still lay ahead. Feet on the table, in his favourite place, Glenda's voice in the background, singing his chosen song selection.

Ambition. He did not see himself working at IBC forever; at least, not in the same position. Promotion, now a real possibility, but then he had plans of his own. If he stayed, what would he do next? It was the safe option. He was already near the top. Perhaps he could take one more promotion before the terrain became too treacherous? To rise any higher than that would mean executive responsibilities. That would mean being very close to Max. He knew that he could never risk anything stupid, so close to it, the real source of power… not so long as Augustine and Ferrell were behind IBC.

No, he had his own experiments, his own private projects. And now he had some finances to make that into a reality. Yes, things had turned out very well.

Should I go or should I stay?

What a glorious dilemma.

SUNDAY 16TH JUNE 2030

Karl signed the new contract. Two more years. With a new pay level and the possibility of promotion in three months. Yes, he would stay. But there was one small matter that needed his attention.

As he left the Human Resources Division, something troubled his mind. Someone else would have to move out of his way. A straight forward matter of incompetency. Disciplinary procedures would have to be initiated.

He would write his report tonight and send it to Phillippe. If he was staying then he needed to have a team that he could trust. People he could rely on, people who would not let him down.

MONDAY 17TH JUNE 2030

Two shocks. He had a job offer and he wanted to call it a day!

Louise felt like she was being pushed towards the edge of a high cliff face, against her will, a bulldozer in her back, always pressing forwards. She was dragging her heels in the hard, dry earth, trying to resist. The edge was growing dangerously close, inch by inch. She could see the raging sea in front of her, ready to accept her as an offering. Swallowing her up in its depths, stripping her of life and purpose.

Marco wanted a new life, one without her. The job offer would take him even further from her geographically. But in truth they were emotionally separated and had been for months. After all, had she not travelled all the way here, without him, without much care for his feelings? Without any expectations about them – they had agreed on that. Yet it still hurt, a dull deep inward pain that throbbed immediately above her kidneys.

Do I mean more to him than he means to me?

Her world was suddenly spinning out of control. Lost in the middle of a swirling, earth consuming tornado. He had done it by hypermail too.

What a coward! If only I could stop the day – halt! I've had enough.

She had a list of tasks the length of her leg. Add to that two meetings in one day. Karl was out on a trip, thankfully, so she could relax, as could the rest of the team.

She would have to tell Marco. If he still wanted to go, then she could not stop him. At least she had to try.

Louise, you have to fight for this. Being a coward is not the way out.

+++

What an awful day. Alone in her apartment, Louise reflected on the annulus horribilis that was unfolding before her eyes. Latin, often called the language of the dead, she could identify with that; feeling halfway to the grave herself.

Wrapped in her duvet, she could think. The comfy sofa and gentle, soothing voice of Nina Simone; equivalent to a big hug. She could do with a hug.

How ironic; Marco's job offer and now Dad being admitted to hospital! The verdict was still out as to whether he'd had a heart attack or stroke. It was not serious though, the doctors' verdict. It was a terrible reminder of his age, creeping towards sixty. Mum sounded calm, obviously trying to be brave. Telling Louise not to worry.

Add to that the news that Marco wants to call it a day! Go ahead and add it! Add that he's found some else!

She wanted to scream. A long loud shrill cry starting in her toes, moving up through her spine and exploding through her mouth, like a trumpet connected to a megaphone.

Marco – with someone else!

Three losses in one – losing the twinnes, losing Marco – *"he is a very good listener, wants a family, you can be open about yourself"* – and maybe Dad too! Someone had it in for her.

Was this payback? Revenge?

They are children, real children. They were a science project, now she was tormented by her own words.

How can I let them go?

She recalled the time after Adrian died, when she had raged to the universe, at the being that she held responsible for her pain and heartbreak. 'I hate you! What have I ever done to you!'

It was her cry to a god or a higher being or whatever it was that was out there. Or was it simply fate that this should have been? Purpose? Chance?

First Adrian, possibly Dad, at some point in the too near future. Two of the people she loved most in the world. So unfair, cruel, even sadistic. A childhood memory surfaced: she saw herself singing a song, with so much enthusiasm; her face beaming: *"Jesus loves me this I know, for the Bible tells me so."*

That was unlikely and untrue. *But the universe picked a fight with the wrong woman.*

We really are on our own. It is up to us to make our own future, carve out our own destiny... religious, not me.

Her visits to church as a youngster; why, they were social occasions, with Mum helping out at functions. Louise, still unsure as to whether Mum was a real believer or just a social climber.

Comforting perhaps, if you believe in that kind of thing. As she got older she saw it as a crutch, something for people to lean on.

When Sasha got religious... Louise had been so rude to her, angry that she had been sucked in. Sasha did retaliate, saying that she understood, that it was something you had to find out for yourself. Louise still felt guilty about her childish behaviour on that occasion. Never finding the courage to apologise. Sasha never brought it up.

That, bloody, Karl.

On top of everything else, the self-righteous parasite had gone and made a formal complaint against her, about her performance. Questioning her ability to lead, citing three managerial incidents. He must have collected them from the team, *traitors!* Technical failures, failure to update the Bible – she smiled bitterly at that: *religious, not me* – and failure to attend meetings.

What meetings was he even talking about? Did he hide them from me? Did he frame me?

A competency proceeding now underway. This was going to be the fight of her life.

It does not rain, it comes in bathtubs.

+ + +

The number just kept ringing. Her third attempt. She had already left two messages. Knowing him, he never checked his voicemails. The time difference complicated the whole thing. This would be the last chance she'd have before she went to bed.

Her heart boomed, she could feel the throb of the pulse in her right wrist, scared it might burst through her skin.

Making a confession. This was worse than any exam or lecture. To admit the feelings and emotions that were concealed beneath the façade of normalcy she erected each and every sorry day. Laying bare her soul, being naked before another person. It was new territory; a virgin landscape never yet explored, never even ventured into.

Admitting that she was in love.

The faint click made her hold her breathe. 'Hello,' he sounded sleepy. He should have been up by now.

'Hello Marco, it's me. Louise.'

'Oh hi Louise, how are you?'

'I'm fine. Look, there is something I need to tell you.' She paused, 'It is really important.' Her voice sounded strange to her, as if she were speaking through a wall of jelly. 'I need to tell you that,' she held her breathe, placing her hand on her chest. 'I love you Marco.'

He remained silent.

Her eyes blurred. This was her last attempt to undo the process she had set in motion a long time ago. If she failed he would be gone, lost forever. If she succeeded, a new phase of life would open before her.

Now the tears spurted out, choking her voice, muffling her words. 'Marco, did you hear me. I said that I love you.'

'Oh,' his silence added to the emotional pressure.

What's he thinking? Does he think that I'm crazy? Have I blown it?

'I thought you weren't really one for love. I thought you were married to you work, to science.' He swallowed, 'I've always loved you Louise. I've… I've just not had the guts to say it.'

Dad was right. Sometimes men need help. If he could have seen her smile, he would have been pushed into another room. It took up so much space. Feelings of giddiness, like jumping into an ocean of happiness, she wanted to shout and sing.

'I guess we have a lot to talk about,' Louise said, wiping her eyes.

'You know, I was ready to move on.' His confession sounded genuine.

'I know, I thought that I just had to try.' Her sniffs interspersed between her words.

'I am such a coward! Imagine how I would have felt if—'

'Let's talk about us. The way things could work out for us.'

'How long have you got?' She heard hope in his voice.

'Only a lifetime.'

TUESDAY 18TH JUNE 2030

The bear dream. Only this time it was different. It caught him! Shoving him to the ground, looming over its prey, globules of yellow saliva dripping onto him. Hot slimy drops of viscous liquid that soaked into his clothing, then into his skin. The bear moved closer, its yellow eyes blazing with madness.

Then it struck.

One swipe with its huge razor sharp claws. He felt the ripping sensation, like thick, sharp blades; white hot pain mingled with a dull, smouldering ache. He dared not look down.

The bear seemed dissatisfied with its attack. The look – thoughtful, as if it were reflecting its options.

The assault was repeated, with more force; he felt his ribcage splinter before it caved in. It was going for his heart…

The room was dark, still. He blinked several times, noticing his own erratic breathing and trembling body. He looked around for familiar objects, landmarks, as he made the transition from that zone into reality.

His chest hurt. He switched on the bedside lamp, then gingerly opened his pyjamas. It felt as if he'd been stabbed in the chest. There was no blood though. But he saw the three stripes, there on his skin.

He touched the burning, ridged surfaces. Each, the width of his thumb; running in length from his clavicle to the bottom of his sternum.

Is the Teacher is trying to kill me? Waves of intense paranoia followed. *What have I done wrong?*

All his attempts to appease his master; they'd seemed to have no impact – no evidence of mercy, no signs of clemency, leaving Karthik wrestling with his own sense of failure.

If only he could stem the panic rising in his stomach, like a living vine. After all this time, he began to conceive doubt, questioning the whole project. Thinking through a shimmering haze, moments of sharp clarity then the mist returned. As if, somewhere else, beyond conscious thought, he was realising the true nature of his work, and that of the Teacher.

Suddenly Karthik was afraid.

$$+++$$

Ade looked very sheepish as he stirred his cup of tea in the cafeteria, both of them on a well-earned break.

'I have just applied for a position at a new biotech company in the USA. If I get it, I will be leaving… once I work out my contract.' He looked up briefly, before returning his concentration to his favourite brew.

'That's great,' said Louise. She smiled, the muscles of her lips remaining in positon, but knowing the smile had left her eyes.

That is all I need. Yet another brick in the wall.

It could not get any worse.

$$+++$$

It did get worse. Two more pregnancies failed and, after three online interviews, Ade got the job.

He was relieved to be leaving.

Whoever came up with the concept of time in lieu deserved a medal, even a Nobel prize. A whole afternoon off and no one could question in. Not even Commandant Karl.

Louise booked three hours at the practice room in the recreation centre. Armed with her cello, this would be an afternoon of her favourite music. As she played, she would think; allowing her thoughts to flow. Call it music therapy.

What are my options?

She started with the *Swan* by Saint-Saens. Placing the music on the stand, Louise picked up her bow. With her cello in place, she played the first line, then closed her eyes.

I know this one off by heart. The wildest idea… Abduct the twinnes!

She could fly to China, disappear off the radar, get them new identities. *What about a boat trip – smuggling – a slow boat to China? Who do I know? The Li's… They could help.* Apart from them no one. Louise recognised that she was not acquainted with the shady side of life here, let alone anywhere else. It had never been her forte. An honest citizen to a fault, she paid her taxes, did her bit and more. *British values and all that.*

She had heard you could get a new one for a price. Things would need to be organised… *passports, flights*; security measures needed to be bypassed as well, they had already been chipped. She had written down this crazy idea. Yet she didn't like it. Forever being tracked by IBC… It would be her against the corporation, a life on the run. She called this the insanity option.

Me, a criminal – she could see her face on Newsnight or Crimewatch, BBC World. Along with the twines of course – *what would they call it? Child abduction; theft of research – intellectual property theft; smuggling human contraband – trafficking? It would fetch me life in prison, or a Chinese execution.* She imagined watching her mother crying, wondering where she had gone wrong; refusing to talk to anyone. Dad shielding the gate – no press allowed. Mum would never understand, Dad would be hurt, but underneath his cool exterior he would get it.

Teaching them Mandarin? They'd have no problems with that, actually. But would they be happy? Would I ever be happy, always looking over my shoulder? Watching for strangers. Losing contact with everyone, Dad, Mum, Sasha and even Marco?

No, Louise that is not even remotely possible. Let it go. She had already torn up the sheet into little pieces.

Next, *Badinerie* by Bach. It had been a while since she had played or heard this one. She decided to read the music.

All her life, she had spoken up for others; but never really spoken up for herself. Abandoning her needs and desires, success defined by virtue of her academic excellence, never as a result of her voice alone. Adrian's needs were always seen as more important, she was seen as secondary, she even understood that, *it was fair,* but she had always denied herself a certain way of life. She had been stuck in that mode all these years, denying herself happiness, a chance of a close relationship and even a family.

Her parents did not know the real truth about the twinnes, she had never told them. Besides, Mum still held onto her religious views.

Are we playing the roles of gods? They were certainly bursting through enough so-called divine boundaries, in the process of becoming creators. The sense of joyful wonder was exhilarating, even intoxicating.

What about their medical needs? Future issues? Changes? Sickness? Their special nutritional needs? An ordinary child might survive, but they were far from ordinary.

Another option – leaving IBC. The next piece was tricky, those rhythms needed full concentration. *Hungarian Dance No. 5,* by Brahms. Dad liked this one. She would play it for him.

She stopped. *What happened to my voice?* Saying what she wanted instead of living her life up just to please other people. It would be a tough battle.

She continued playing.

Leaving would allow her to work on her relationship with Marco. She could be with her family and let the twinnes to get on with their lives.

How can I let them go?

She could even think about settling down with her own family; perhaps her own, naturally produced children. A stable life, seeing her grandchildren; university research, maybe some part time work in the industrial sciences?

Would all that be dull compared to my current life?

Maybe she was dull, plain boring. Louise thought that, maybe, she could be dull, if she tried; highly intelligent but dull.

Next was *Prayer* – a movement from Bloch's Jewish Life, and the Faure Elegy. Though not religious, there was depth to this piece; you could really sense something unusual. Her former cello teacher, Lydia, had said that she managed to win a scholarship playing this piece. It became one of Louise's favourites after hearing it for the first time. Her hand was starting to ache, definitely out of practice. Losing her muscle tone.

Leaving IBC… after all they did not own *her*, even if the twinnes *were* their property. Could she face being without them – losing her sparkle? Life would be colder without the joy of the twinnes. She had buried the corpse of her own needs, but now it was up again, risen from the grave – stinking and decayed.

What do you do with a corpse?

Beastly, yet alive.

Hypocrites… She hated them, yet she was one of them too. Perhaps the biggest of all.

Or stay at IBC… With the competency procedures in operation she could lose her job or be demoted, possibly shifted to another IBC company. Israel was opening up.

She finally admitted it, faced it. She had allowed her dedication to science to override her personal, moral code. She had closed her eyes to numerous unethical practices, such as the use of S-Tetrin on human subjects. Knowing the truth, she had kept quiet; this would have to change. Maybe that was one of the reasons for which she was so unhappy, a vital clue about her mysterious, confused inner state. The twinnes had kept her busy and she had never faced the truth in full; rather, she had hidden from it. Now they were leaving… The pain resurfaced, mingling with a deep seated sense of dread and a woeful emptiness.

She and the truth, at least more of it. She could speak out or even confront them.

Then again she had just qualified for the eggs in storage programme. EiSP was a perk for female employees. It involved, to a literal degree, putting her eggs in the fridge, so she could use them later on, when she wanted to have children. She did want to be thirty or upwards, unmarried, with hard boiled eggs. It would be a tough battle. A lonely existence, hours of lab work, new Living Dolls being produced, more time with Karl and the team and being in South Korea.

Me against the corporation.

Karl… That would be a war all by itself. In reality, she was not sure she could stomach that man after this low, underhand swipe. He had issues, serious personality issues, maybe even mental issues. That could be part of her defence.

He needs psychiatric assessment, that one.

It boiled down to leaving or staying and fighting in her corner, she refused to keep quiet any longer. Stage one: to keep her job; stage two: the other issues that were on her mind.

She could not stop the adoption process – it was already set in stone. First she had to get through the orientation process. Ten days to make up her mind. Ten days to weigh up the options and make that a final decision.

Playing was getting extremely painful, her hand cramping around the bow.

Enough for now.

She gathered up her music and breathed in, slowly, deeply.

WEDNESDAY 19TH JUNE 2030

Louise did not usually remember her dreams. This one was exceptional, a little like the one in which Karl was about to slay her, the dream Louise called "the sacrifice". She hit the snooze button, resting on her pillows.

Five more minutes.

The whole thing… like watching a movie that gripped you, one you would never forget. That was how it felt. It was so real.

Adrian was full of health, striding and jumping around. He looked to be around sixteen. His body was like hers, fully functional, even physically fit. Louise sat on a bench while he whirled around the place, having fun. The beautiful meadow was full of life, sounds of nature turned up on full volume. Music somewhere in the background.

Suddenly he stopped, rushing towards Louise. He knelt down and asked, 'Can I have my ring back?' There was pure light in his eyes, intense like a white nova. 'Sorry, things were beyond my control. You couldn't stop me from dying. Glad about the exam, you did good Louise. You can let me go now. I am in a better place, with——'

Louise woke up. She looked around the room. It was typically messy. Normal. She rubbed at her eyes.

Where did that come from? The promise. This was about his promise, it made sense.

Things beyond my control.

He died, that was something he could not control. All her life she held him in bondage for this failure. This flaw. He could not keep his promise. A sense of relief washed over her. The ring, that was her connection with the past; her way of holding onto him. Tying him to his final words.

The guilt she had harboured, not being able to stop him from dying. All those years… not forgiving herself for her failure.

Was this why my voice taken away? Now she could trace it back to Adrian's death. She had never had a chance to say goodbye, her entrance exam had been the top priority.

He wanted her to let go. She gulped, thinking quickly. *I need to listen to that. He wants me to.*

Then another different voice – *Adrian wants you to, Louise.*

'Okay Adrian, I think I get it. I'll let you go,' she whispered the words and heard the background music from her dream, somewhere inside, deeply.

+++

Almost ready.

Louise looked at the gold chain laying on her dressing table, she touched Adrian's ring.

'Goodbye Adrian, I'm letting you go.' She smiled to herself. 'I will always love you but I can't carry you anymore. Your memory is in my heart. I have to live my life.'

The time for grief was over; it was time to move on. It took longer to get ready that day, she applied a spot of make-up and decided to tie her hair back. Liking the change, she looked herself over, in the mirror.

She faced another goodbye later on in the day. Not the final one but a medium sized one. The final goodbye would happen after the orientation process. She shivered at the thought.

+++

'If you bothered to manage this department, things might move forward,' he tapped his foot as he spoke, leaning against the bench.

'Do you know that one of IBC's Company values is respect.' She paused to allow her words to hit home, 'Karl, my friend, it's obvious that you have neither read nor understood the sentiments behind that part of the job.' She turned as if to walk away then changed her mind, she didn't pay his expression much attention but instead focused on her own voice, 'And by the way, if I want sarcasm, I will phone my mother.'

She was surprised at the sound of herself – confident, assured, commanding and authoritative. Out of the corner of her eyes, she spotted a couple of heads turning in her direction, obviously tuning into the conversation. The background noise made it hard to be heard, but she was used to speaking loudly.

Karl's mouth remained half closed, his eyes darting from side to side. Caught slightly off guard.

A thrill rolled around inside her stomach. She wanted to say, *the date on your birth certificate does not match your emotional age. Why don't you grow up?*

She opted for 'I will do what is expected. Just watch me.'

As she turned away, she could not help smiling. A cheesy, broad smile. If he had been in front of her, rather than gawping as she left him, he would have seen the small arm pump.

+++

Another one of those cryptic, self-destructive emails; anonymous and not easily traced. Once the timer reached its designated spot, the message disappeared forever, all evidence of its existence seemingly erased.

Who is sending them?

Each one seemed to build on the last: The first one was simple: "Do you want to know the truth about IBC?"

She had thought, *What truth? What are they going on about? Who is sending this? Why?*

An hour later, the second: "Do you want to know more?"

More what? She already had a ton of stuff to do without some mysterious individual sending her cryptic messages.

One hour after that the third one: "Whose DNA is at the centre of the Living Doll Project?"

Now *that* was a good question. Nobody knew, nor was anyone allowed to know that particular trade secret. *KFC eat your heart out.*

She certainly did not have access to that level of clearance, to the opportunity to find out such information.

Does Karl know? Who was to say it was from a person and not something artificially created?

She remembered reading *Frankenstein* back at school, as part of her iGCSE English course. The monster was made up of all kinds of odds and ends.

I wonder if Jack and Jill are like a modern version of Frankenstein, only created by IBC? The shiver seemed to emanate from her lower spine, rippling down her legs and then back up.

My Twinnes. To some, they would be viewed as freaks; growing up would be a challenge for them.

Just ask the monster... funny how the creator despised the creature in that story.

The world might not be ready for Jack and Jill; things might not turn out so great for them and the others when they hit their teenage years, when they reached adulthood.

Come on girl, no time to get philosophical.

If any more of those messages arrived she could notify the IT department. Then again, perhaps not. Someone, somewhere was asking some interesting questions.

What will be the next question?

If the sender was keeping to time, the answer would be known in forty five minutes time. Maybe they had set up an auto responder. She had just enough time to meet with Ade and to finish off the latest Bible entry.

I quite enjoy a good mystery.

+++

'Jack has a higher robot confidence score than Jill, which makes him more comfortable with artificial intelligence, he will be more ready to assimilate the technologies that are just around the corner.' Karl checked the readings again just to make sure.

'Okay, so how will this help?' Louise could not deny the data.

'Based on their reading, their artificial toys should be matched accordingly.' He shoved the catalogues in Louise's direction. 'His monitor will be incorporated into a teddy bear, Jill's into a doll.'

That made sense. Jack's teddy bear was threadbare. He loved it so much. Jill was building up a small community of dolls, male and female. One more would be a welcome addition.

'As the toys are living AIs they will grow and learn with the children. The nightly upload allowing their new knowledge to be incorporated into their artificial neurones, allowing processing and development.'

Karl knew that they would also serve as surveillance devices. They would listen to all their little secrets. He was glad that his old teddy was just a toy.

If it could talk... *those stories would have made Grimm's fairy tales look like Sesame Street.*

+++

'Twinnes, come over here I have something for you.'

They rushed over abandoning their game, eyes sparkling, smiles adorning their faces.

'Have you got a present?' Jack was looking up at Louise. Jill nodded, eager for her part in the action.

'Close your eyes,' Jack did.

'Jill, you are peeking!' Jill clamped her eyelids together, just to make a point.

'You can open them after I count to three.' Louise removed the AIs from the plastic sac, placing them on the floor, right in front of them. 'One... Two... Three!'

They both squealed, before clapping their hands and jumping up and down. If she hadn't been so used to them, Louise thought, their jumping might have seemed to be an almost eerie shadow of unison. She dispelled the idea, smiling proudly at their little display.

'Wow, a new teddy. Thank you,' Jack hugged it close to his chest, twisting from side to side.

'I will call her Cynthia.' Jill stroked her doll's hair, nodding.

'I hope you will enjoy playing with them. They are very special toys.'

'Hello Jack,' said the teddy. Jack dropped it, his little mouth open in shock.

'It can talk? Wow!' He started to jump again.

Jill looked jealous, her little mouth twisted into a knot. 'Mine does not talk, that is not fair.' She stamped her foot and folded her arms.

Something is wrong, thought Louise. It should have spoken. As if on cue the doll piped up, 'Don't be moody Jill. We are going to be great friends.'

If Louise could have taken a picture she would have. The look on Jill's face – entirely priceless.

Jill grabbed her new toy, clutching it just like Jack. Both of them cradling and loving the things.

Louise wiped her forehead. *Is this my peace offering.* Now came the really hard part.

'I need you to put down your toys and come to me,' Louise knelt down, 'Over here.' Opening both arms, she embraced them.

The twinnes snuggled close to her, filling her arms. She could feel their hearts thumping in their chests. She rested her head on both of them. Breathing in them. The lump in her stomach moved towards her throat, almost lodging there.

Inside, she knew that the clock was counting down.

They had one day left.

+++

'Karl, has a problem with strong women, that is why Glenda is such a perfect match for him,' she said loudly enough for him to overhear, since he often eavesdropped on her conversations. That could be something she would mention in her defence, his invasion into her privacy. Everyone had heard of Glenda, but no one had ever seen her. She never attended any of the social events.

Karl seemed to know things that she had said in private, so he must have been snooping. She hoped that he would hear her now. She was sick of him. A giggle emanated from her companion. Carol was a new technician in the department. Louise folded her arms and looked right in his direction.

Karl's face reddened. He got up and walked away, glaring at her. Carol furrowed her brow in mock confusion and more than a little genuine bemusement, 'Louise, what has got into you?'

Louise saw the look on her face. Carol's hand extended as she shook her head.

Louise smirked, 'I don't know… but I like it.'

+++

Fuming, Karl's head began to pound. He thought about Glenda.

The perfect match. After all, he had thought carefully about his criteria and the ideal personality traits that he required; she'd been created to fulfil his every whim. The progression from avatar to an interactive personality had been expensive. The use of 3D, interactive glasses with digital surround sound and an extra sensory skull-cap made it seem as if they were on a real date every time they met.

He thought about the next stage more often now than ever before; an android version. The perfect woman. That bonus could literally make his dreams come true.

At least he would not be alone. She would do, until another, real life Melissa came along. Another woman, loaded to the eyeballs.

+++

Ten messages in all. The final one an invitation to contact the sender. On very strict conditions, outside the walls of IBC. At an Internet café in Pohang. The sender obviously knew the local area.

They're afraid of IBC's surveillance.

They wanted to meet in a chat room, a public setting. That way they could talk in private, in a virtual room.

Louise felt torn, this was against IBC policy. She had no idea whether they could trace the interactions on her IQT tablet, or her desk computer. They probably could, but it was not something she could control. If she went to the café, that would be crossing into a whole new territory.

They, whoever they were, knew so much; much more than an outsider could know. They were on the inside, that much was clear.

I'm questioning the integrity of IBC… she had done that plenty. *And then that question about Chloe.*

"Did she jump or was she pushed?"

It was outrageous. *Or was it?*

Curiosity and that darn cat. Should she push into this or… if they knew something about Chloe, she had a duty as her last manager, as her friend, to know. It might all turn out to be a hoax.

But instinct told her that this was not the case.

The bait had worked. Hook, line and sinker.

+++

Karl stepped towards her in the way he normally did. She held out her hand preventing him moving any closer. 'Your name is not Private Space, as far as I know? So I would appreciate it if you could respect my boundaries.'

He stumbled backwards, lost for words, his eyes wide. She could see his brain whirling behind those wounded pupils, not quite connecting with his lips.

Strong women are a problem for him.

A defeat for Karl, a small victory for Louise. She had found herself. At last.

She smiled, not at Karl, but through him.

+++

'Hello Charles, how are you?'

Max looked tired, yet his voice sounded enthusiastic. 'I have seen better days, Max.' Weary, Charles felt his age. The eczema was giving him so much discomfort lately, despite his use of the very best lotion on the market. A member of the Nanotechnology Division had suggested they might be able to help.

'I have some news for you.'

Not another job, another mission. 'Not sure I want to hear it, Max.'

'Why not Charles? You always enjoy good news.'

'Cut the crap, what do you have to say?'

'There are some new demands being requested.'

Oh no... Charles sensed tingling in both hands. 'Demands? Whose demands?'

'The Teacher has new demands, Charles.'

'Since when did you become his oracle?' The tone of Max's voice annoyed Charles. Now Max wanted to displace Karthik, was that it?

Mystic Max! Long gone that sceptic, that night, that meal; long gone. Now converted Max, perhaps he was manoeuvring for power? Charles sighed wearily, 'What does Karthik have to say about this?'

'What Karthik does not know, K—'

Loyalty, Charles gave it and expected, especially from close friends. They had bonded for years now, they had walked close to the edge. But now, *he* wanted to cut Karthik out. Charles knew it. It was in the man's nature. He was cold. *Like a damned corpse.* Sliding up and out. Teeth bared. *Snake in the grass…* it seemed to be appropriate.

'And how is it that he does not know? What is going on?'

'Dear Charles, you sound so… so peeved?'

'I am. I don't know what you are playing at—'

'You should know me by now, I never play.'

'What if I choose not to meet these demands, what then?' Courage and guts, the stuff of heroes. Yet Charles did not see himself as either. Nowadays, getting through the day was hard enough. 'And what about Karthik? He is the voice!'

'*Was* the voice, past tense. Oh Charles, you will meet the demands, as you know you will, and I will tell you why.'

'What?' Charles snapped, this had gone far enough.

'Karthik is yesterday's news, Charles.'

'What is going on?'

'Revolution, Charles, Revolution.' Max's voice low and deliberate.

+ + +

Charles was shocked, Max amused.

He had finally realised the true nature of their relationship. Max congratulated himself, a master of deception.

I am so believable, so convincing.

The revelation about Miranda and his frequent visits had left him looking like a crumpled, Egyptian cotton sheet. Charles was riddled with guilt, yet blinded by his desire to see his beloved daughter brought back to life. Of course, Max had been lying about the Teacher.

He just wanted to know how far Charles would go.

Max's lieutenants in the cryogenic section had kept him updated on every visit, even placing the microdot microphones all over the tube. They had allowed him to hear Charles' loud breaths, rasping as he confessed and poured out his soul to his long dead daughter. The whole thing was, well, it was all so hilarious.

Teacher. Tool. One and the same, whatever it is. Yesterday's news. My future. Who's in control now, Charles? Karthik? No. Nor were you ever, either of you, you idiots. Max. Max Augustine.

Max smiled wryly. Everybody likes to talk to someone they trust. He reflected on the many conversations Charles had held with the corpse. All recorded for prosperity.

Max always covered the off camera stuff. Charles had taken on the public face of the venture. Max saw himself as the persuader, the manipulator, the controller of operations.

I am the practical problem solving type, cold but practical. Right and wrong is a choice, I just choose differently from others.

At least he was honest with himself not like Charles.

Every day he stared himself down in the mirror. He always asked himself the same question. *Are you a monster?* No, he saw himself as being ahead of the exponential curve. *There are no monsters.*

His heart rate increased ever so slightly, as it always did before a business deal, or the successful execution of a contract with Henderson.

He was committed. All the way to the end. Especially now that Karthik seemed to be losing his tarnish. Or did he think that Max had missed the fact that fresh revelation seemed to have dried up? The mystic's reign was fading. It was a ripe time for a change in leadership.

The Light might just benefit from my leadership. And now it is worth so much, much more.

He combed his fingers through his hair, only he needed to be connected to the source. That had not happened so far.

But oh, how he wanted it.

Another headache though?

Max rubbed his temple, the tender sport on the right side of his head. His Biomedi-pod usage seemed to have gone through the roof. *Why, it had become a regular part of his life?*

+++

After work she normally switched off. But, for some strange reason, Louise decided to check her hypermail account.

The memo was marked "confidential". She opened the digital document, curiosity panting quietly.

A vicious chest punch. Like her air supply had been kicked away, an immense pressure crushing her rib cage.

The adoption was more than bringing up the twinnes. It was part of the experiment. There it was, in black and white. IBC wanted to test the genome in the wider community. To check on their immune responses, their skills at social interaction, to troubleshoot the event of any and all integration issues.

Inside she was shaking, trembling through her skin. The sense of shock and betrayal felt like being plunged into a bath of scalding hot water.

She was mystified as to why the documents should have been passed in her direction. This was the first she had heard of this part of the work. Again that question. *Does Karl know? Who else is on the list?*

So, the smoke screen of welfare and social development. Widening the field of the experiment. She tasted the bile in her throat, bitterness biting into her.

And she was part of it. The internal volcano had boiled past the point of no return.

She was about to blow.

+ + +

The sound of Berlioz was unmistakable, haunting, in the background. A chorus of beings clothed in white, standing to attention. Max wondered if they were angels?

A powerful voice proclaimed, 'You are chosen. There is a shift in the axis of power. It is tipping in your favour.' The same words were repeated three times, each time the volume and force of the words increased.

A chorus in the background sang, 'Out with the old, in with the new.' The phrase repeated in sweet harmony.

The scene changed from the celestial act to that of dirty streets, in Paris. The style of the building, the lack of sanitation, the clothing of the people, the whole scene; it was reminiscent of The French Revolution. It was like a scene from Les Miserables.

Then he saw the scaffolding, the guillotine. Some poor victim had their head in place, ready for the chop. The crowds were excited, hungry for more blood. Revolution was rich in the air; the tide had turned.

A kind of unity, among those who wanted change, a despair and desolation amongst those who had lost their position. The end of their era.

Wooden Carts rolled along the filthy streets, bringing more of the condemned to their final destination.

The executioner was hooded, arms folded. Only his wretched eyes, nose and cruel mouth were visible. A horrible smile was etched across his face, peeking through his disguise.

Then he spotted Charles in the crowd, near the front. Dressed as a peasant, in rags and covered in filth. Bedraggled and sad, surrounded by others in a similar state. Did they want change too?

As if on cue, the crowd responded to the wave of hush that moved through them, a silent wave sweeping from the back to the front.

Silence.

The executioner sauntered towards the guillotine. The blade poised, glinting in the early morning sunrays. One pull of the lever and down it would come. Whoosh, then the dull tumbling sound as the head rolled off into the crowd.

The executioner pulled off his mask. Max gasped. That is me! The figure gave a knowing smile before pointing down to the quivering victim.

Time and space merged, Max stood on the platform, close enough to reach out.

The familiar head, it was Karthik. Max smiled.

The blade fell.

THURSDAY 20TH JUNE 2030

Hyun-jung grappled with feelings of injustice and rage. Her movements appeared jerky as she cleared her desk, her hands moistened by the tears that fell intermittently. One simple mistake, one small error – her job security gone, evaporated.

Yes she was going, but she knew so much. Her photographic memory had served her well throughout her life, she was confident that it would be an asset in the future. Mr Augustine had not been an easy man to work for, but she had managed.

Eagle eyed Karl Winwood had spotted the error, and he told Mr Augustine, who acted immediately. Telling her publically of her error and his grave disappointment in her. The whole building must have heard.

Her life at IBC over all because of a name; fired for putting a wrong name on a list. One small administrative error.

So many secrets in this place. They had already shut down her accounts, in case she thought of taking revenge by deleting files.

Despite her stoic appearance, Hyun-jung was furious. All the time and effort she had put into IBC and now this.

She would wait her time.

Things had changed. The attacks on his body increased in frequency, marks that were concealed by clothing; hand sized bruises, more slashes. Karthik often wondered whether he had done something wrong.

He cried out, receiving no answers. Even trying an extended fast, yet no response. The lines of communication seemed to have been severed. The vision stopped.

Why the violence? He had always been a willing student. *Why had the Teacher turned on him?* Confusion seethed inside his head. He searched for clues, something that marked the shift in the relationship. Nothing seemed to stand out.

The sense of heaviness and loss was immense.

Why the torture in the night? The manifestations on his body; acts of violence and abuse. He was like a battered husband who smiles and keeps up the pretence, bearing the wounds physically and emotionally. He was unable to get out of the relationship. Trapped.

Trapped. Without the meetings how could he lead *the Light*, how could he lead IBC? The flow of wisdom now dammed.

This would be his secret. No one could know that the oracle had been silenced. Business as usual. He hoped he could live off the sayings from the past, varying them enough to avoid arousing suspicion.

The vicious headaches were an unwelcome accompaniment to the abuse. At least his Biomedi-pod usage provided a little much needed relief.

+++

Last night…

Charles felt as if he was seeing Max for the first time, his true image coming into focus. He thought that they were friends. But no, Max was using him, watching him, even spying on him.

Max knew about Miranda, and judging by his subtle frequent comments he had been eavesdropping on Charles' intimate conversations with his daughter. The way he disclosed that information, just dropped in in casually, Charles knew that the man would not hesitate to use it against him if he ever needed leverage. It made his flesh ripple, as if ice cubes had been rubbed up and down his back. It was truly chilling. A complete lack of human warmth, no traces of compassion.

He had always dismissed that rhetoric, the idea that the upper echelons of society were stocked with psychopaths. He had always been able to look in the mirror and tell himself that it was not true. To look at Max, doing so much good for the world, side by side, changing it for the better.

I know how wrong I was. Taken in.

He felt like a complete fool, trusting someone who had no heart. Perhaps it had been replaced by a cold, reptilian, three-chambered pump? There was no humanity left. He preferred to imagine that it had been drained away over time. It was too hard to confront the possibility that he had been strung along from the beginning. He had to grieve for the loss of a compatriot, but he wanted to remember a friendship, not a scam. He clenched his fists, allowing them to vibrate as he tuned into to the rage that swirled in his chest.

He considered that once he might have seen himself as a wounded stag, desperately seeking a patch of ground in a dense forest, where he could lay down and contemplate the arrows piercing his flank. Now he just felt old. Old and stupid and only now seeing himself for what he had become. But still, he was so, so angry. The betrayals were instruments of torture, perhaps death.

All those times when he'd thought that they had been sharing from the heart. Max had been storing the information, like a computer, ready to download relevant sections and use them as weapons. How could he have been so blind? Max was an expert in intimidation and control. The man was a monster and a psychopath. He was more dangerous than Charles had ever imagined. He was no ally.

He rubbed his face, feeling drained and tired. Karthik had changed too. He was scared. They were all scared, except Max.

Karthik had told him about the three stripes that had appeared on his chest; they looked horrible, raised, deep and sore. A dream that crept into reality. *How could a creature from a dream inflict wounds on a living soul?*

Perhaps it's better that I can't sleep. Goosebumps rippled across his shoulders and down both arms. He felt the hairs pressing against his clothing.

Perhaps I can run?

He sighed and put the thought away. There was no escape from this now, none of them could escape. This was bigger than all of them put together, although he doubted that it was a sentiment shared by Max. Even so, it was clear to him. They were joined at the waist; trapped in a net; hostages in the web of an unseen spider.

Even MAT could not help erase the torment. He knew. He had tried.

+++

I wish that I had never made that promise.

It was the avalanche of emotions, their tears and hers all mingling together. No consolation in the room. She just felt that she had to say something, to try and appease the situation. The words just tumbled out.

'*I will not leave you.*'

It took a while for them to settle. The words were a sedative. Their distress diminished, their tears stopped. Why? Because they believed her. She had never intentionally lied to them, so they took her words for truth. They were comforted, soon returning to their playtime, all smiles and gurgling chuckles.

Something in her told her not to do it, but she did, against her better judgement. Now her own words were like a vibrant spectre.

It was the final day, before the orientation process. She was powerless to keep her own words, but she believed that a person should keep his or her word, no matter the cost.

The hypocritical side fought the sincere version of Louise.

She could not keep her words now and the realisation sent a chill through her chest.

Like Adrian, who did not keep his promise. Dying without waiting for her. Denying her the chance of saying goodbye. It all came tumbling out, she had resented him for that, for so long. She had held him as a hostage to his words, judging him by them, sentencing him to an immortal incarnation. Such was the silent transaction that had taken place within her heart, her childish heart.

Now it was so clear, emotions flooding her body; hidden, suppressed rage and disappointment. She felt weak, her knees almost giving way. This walk to their section, she had completed it so many times, yet now it seemed to be eternal. Her steps were deliberate and slow.

The underlying principle was that not keeping your promises was bad. It was an oddly simple supposition. Right now, she was guilty of the same offence, except it was towards them. Such things were magnified in the eyes and heart of a child. She knew it too well.

She had to fight her first response, to run away.

There was so much to do. The other pregnancies also needed her attention. If she could clone herself, she might just be able to keep up with her workload. Many things were possible at IBC. But not that. She was, herself, resigned to more work. She rubbed the back of her hand against her forehead.

Tiredness was part of life these days. There would be no get out clauses or rest periods coming up for a while.

+++

Louise knew that she had fifteen minutes left with twinnes before the final goodbye. The orientation programme started tomorrow.

A sense of heaviness sat in her stomach, exhaustion. Emotionally and physically drained, as if life had been vacuumed out of her soul. If she could put her finger on the source… impossible.

Was it the loss of the twinnes? Or the fact that they had been sold? Or IBC? The new pregnancies? The bigger experiment they were part of? The list of possibilities went on and on.

Too many things were bombarding her thoughts. She just wanted to wrap herself in a duvet, find the nearest bed and sleep. To just forget about everything.

Jack tugged on her sleeve, looking up into her face. His beautiful eyes were radiant with life – *he is so adorable.*

'Loo-is?'

His pronunciation is still not clear noted Louise. *He needs further speech therapy.*

'Yes, my darling Jack,' Louise swept him up in her arms, *he is getting so heavy!* She rested him on her hip, looking at his tense face.

'Who is A–drian?' Jack's question was innocently put.

'What do you mean, are you saying Adrian?' Louise was confused.

'Yes. A-drian,' he responded emphatically.

'I don't know,' Louise was mystified, 'Who is Adrian?' Jack played with her hair, 'He is *your* brother,' Jack said matter of fact. If she had not been holding him tightly, he would have dropped like a heavy stone.

'What are you talking about?' a creeping sensation tugged at the back of her neck.

Jack looked at her oddly. As if she of all people should know. 'Adrian had a funny car that he moved around in.' Jack looked around the room, still playing with her hair. 'He left you and your mummy and daddy. Are you leaving us Loo-is?' Jack stared straight into her eyes before turning away to focus on her playing with her hair again.

Louise could feel her body trembling. How did he know about Adrian? *I never mentioned him to Jack. Nor to anyone he would have talked to.* How could he have known about Adrian's wheelchair?

Jill spoke up, 'We know about Adrian.' She moved the truck around the track, gaining momentum all the time, then let go. The truck skidded off the surface and went crashing into the side of the toy box. She turned and looked in Louise's direction. 'He left you and your mummy.'

Louise put Jack down and moved towards Jill. This was becoming so uncomfortable. She considered her words carefully. 'Why have you two suddenly started talking about Adrian? How do you know about him? Has someone been telling you about where I grew up?'

Her right hand trembled, with increasing violence. That only happened when she was shaken. Like the time when she found out that Adrian would not get better despite her prayers. She gave up on God soon after that.

'No! We see him sometimes. He talks about you. He liked you.' Jill stood upright, looking straight at Louise.

How can she be saying such a thing, Adrian is dead!

'He can still see you even now.' Jack walked to Jill and took her hand, 'He misses you Loo-is,' continued Jack. 'You used to hold his hand like this.' Jack placed his right hand over the back of Jill's left hand and squeezed it twice.

Louise felt ill. *What was this?* And yes, that was the way she held Adrian's hand after he had lost sensation in his fingers. He still could detect her touch with the back of his hand. For a moment she wondered if she was actually going to be sick. This should not have been happening.

Someone – it was as if a hand touched her, but there was no one there. Suddenly she went very cold, her skin crawling, hairs rising on her forearms.

'We don't want you to go Louise,' Jill began to cry, her tears slowly tricked down her cheeks, silent streams that made a plopping sound as they hit the floor. 'We love you!'

She threw herself into Louise's' legs and hugged them tightly. 'Don't leave us,' she pleaded with passion. 'Don't let them take us away!'

The look on her face, it was more than Louise could bear. The tears gushed out, her chest heaved, the sobs coming from her belly button. Louise knelt down, warmly embracing Jill. She beckoned to Jack who toddled over to join in the group hug.

They cried together.

Her original plan on hold, she just wanted to explain the reason for their departure.

Jack and Jill were simply scared that Louise no longer loved them. Her image of cracked hearts was replaced by a clear image of two glass hearts, covered with tiny cracks that turned into crevices, fracturing the heart into minute, shattered pieces. For a moment, the strangeness of their words forgotten as waves of hot grief consumed the room.

The sound of breaking hearts, amplified by the natural sound system of the body. United in torment and sorrow.

FRIDAY 21ST JUNE 2030

Karthik woke up, gasping, desperate for the next breath. The new consciousness had entered the world.

The dream was still fresh in his mind. The Teacher had spoken. After a long period of silence, he had communicated something. There was an unfolding in motion; new stages of development that commenced with the fresh conscious evolution, expressed through the Living Dolls.

Oh, he was grateful, fearing that he had lost the connection – the intimate union. He wanted to express his devotion, his submission, by acting immediately.

+++

He accepted the homage of his student, breathing in the words like incense, fragrant; he adopted a Caesar like position, gratefully receiving Karthik's adulation.

Securing them had been difficult. After a promising start, his persuasive efforts were thwarted. Emotional maturity affecting his prime candidate, Karthik. Emotional puberty almost rendered him an unsuitable candidate. He had been lost to the cause for a time. Yet his thirst for knowledge remained; pasted over by intense activity, it remained. Pulsating under the surface until stirred, its rapid germination then growth, just like bamboo. Yes he was back on form, his mind diverted by ravenous desire.

Flesh, so frail.

+++

Karthik sensed this was a key moment in history. He set up an Intersky conference immediately, face to face with Max and Charles. They needed to know about this latest revelation.

+++

Now, seeing the three wiling subjects, it gave him such hope. They were all on board for the ride of their lives. Their unity, an act of worship and adoration.

+++

Neither Max nor Charles really understood what he was saying – that the children's eyes had been opened up to a new type of "seeing".

Both of them shared similar feelings of irritation. Karthik seemed to have failed to consider the time difference, waking them both out of their comfortable beds.

On second thoughts, it looks as if Charles had not slept for a decade. That haggard, weary look. Karthik knew the feeling too well.

+++

There would be a shift in the balance of power. History showed one empire rises at the expense of another. The Kothaka reign was coming to an end, the Augustine era rising again.

Like father, like son.

They had shown their commitment; human sacrifice no longer taboo to them. That represented a major breakthrough. They were willing to shed innocent blood. They served a vital purpose – Karthik, Charles, and Max.

He met their needs and provided a desirable service, they kept coming back for more.

+++

'They begin their ten day orientation period tomorrow. There is nothing we can do about that, Karthik.' Charles sounded adamant, Karthik and Max could hear him yawning loudly and he made no attempt to cover up his displeasure and tiredness.

Karthik noticed the glares Charles kept sending in Max's direction. Something had happened between them.

+++

They were often referred to as "flesh" or, as he preferred to call them, "meat".

The three of them… disposable commodities, mere puppets on his strings. Yet now, united in purpose, willing to do almost anything, drunk with their appearance of power and their hope for the future; they were so, very useful yet incredibly feeble.

It was just a case of keeping meat in service.

They had finally worked out how humans ticked.

+++

Max spoke up,' Papers have been signed and money has been exchanged. A deal had been struck. We cannot change our min—'

'We need to understand their power, and to monitor it,' Karthik's face seemed oddly tired, worn down. Max could swear that he saw fear in his eyes, that stifled look of sheer terror.

'How about using their biostrips?' Max continued, scratching his chin, 'We could add a voice analysis function and change the monitoring position, putting them just at the top of the collarbones,' he gestured as he spoke, indicating the specific location. 'That way, all of their conversations could be monitored. And don't forget their smart toys, their cuddly companions; the creatures interact with them, they record all their little secrets, all their and inner thoughts, exposed.'

Max failed to suppress the laughter that burst out, he covered his mouth still giggling. He was surprised by the sinister childishness of it. But it felt so good to laugh. Karthik looked stern, annoyed.

+ + +

He stepped back. Scrutinising the three.

Their technology was so primitive. They had been watching them for many years. Easily beguiled, hungry for immortality and knowledge. Their relentless pursuit of this; from experience he knew that it was not all they thought to be.
Their concept of time was so tedious.

Their desire for eternal life; it was so overrated. Those who had opted for the cryogenic pathway were little more than frozen meat. They had a pathetic, blind faith, trusting in those who operated and ran the system. Hoping for a better world.

What sort of low creature would put its trust in another piece of meat?

Meat. So much effort to prepare them for the ultimate harvest. Slow growing meat.

+ + +

Max had suffered through a long day of meetings the previous day. He was tired, irritable and in need of rest; now lethargy coloured his words, 'We can download the information when the system uploads at night. The contract states that they *must* wear the biostrips at all times so that we can monitor their functions. And of course, we can give them the latest models of their smart toys, ones that automatically connect with the Internet, whenever they are in range. And that will be almost all of the time, given their foster parents.' He yawned deeply, rubbing his swollen eyes.

Revolution happens in various ways. How exciting. How tiring.

'Great idea,' Charles nodded vigorously, rubbing his palms together. 'We'll keep an eye on them, Karthik. You don't need to worry.' A strong hint of hope and excitement entered into his voice.

Max felt sorry for the man, in an abstracted way. For him, it was just another step on the road to his bringing Miranda back from her rest. The way he was scratching his arm, you would think he was being attacked by an infestation of starving fleas.

+ + +

They were simply observers of the people. They could choose to intervene, or to remain aloof. But they were always seeking students. Rewarding the faithful with wisdom and knowledge. Devotees. Many, over the years. Name dropping was common amongst them, like collectors. Awful candidates peppered the list, as well as noble ones. Why, he had friends at the UN, in the European Parliament and the World Council of Churches, Heads of State… The list went on.

They were waiting for these creatures' technology to reach the point at which it might allow a new consciousness to come into being. And he was thrilled to be involved, at its helm in fact. It had arrived, by way of his meat. His flesh. His devotees. The creation of mixed of species was part of a much bigger plan. It would open the door for the introduction of a new type of spirituality.

Jack, Jill… It could have been any name, it served a purpose. Now he waited for them to become a portal, allowing new layers of consciousness to bloom. Others would follow. If they served their purpose, they would be rewarded.

A new age was dawning, accompanying the new consciousness.

+ + +

'It has begun,' Karthik's voice sounded different, as if someone else was speaking though him. Both Charles and Max felt the cold, otherness of his voice.

+ + +

The new consciousness, thin membranes around their view of life being ruptured, like the amniotic sacs around a baby allowing them to enter into a phase of life beyond that which they so idiotically called reality. One layer after another, torn open. Allowing new levels of infiltration. The ultimate goal was of course unity, oneness. They were pulled in by their desire to become one with the world, to rise to a state of godlike existence. They desired this for their reasons, he and his kind desired it for their own.

Two minds fusing yet the will of one would prevail over the other, the weaker succumbing to the stronger. Ruling over meat. That thought gave him a strange sense of satisfaction. The process was nearing its goal. Yes, it was deeply satisfying.

Their evolution processes intimately entwined. The symbiotic relationship changing over time, gradually becoming parasitic. The most successful parasites never kill the host, at least not right at the start. Ask any ichneumon fly. The progression glacier like, over hundreds of years, the gradual creep, call it succession.

Other trainees like Hitler, Mussolini, Genghis Khan. Yes, he could name drop if the occasion called for it. They were from a different age, with limited technology. Through them they had learned the ways of meat, its thought processes, its motivations, desires, greed, selfish ambition. He had learned their ways.

He understood their concept of fishing rather well. Bait was offered, then the wait. Until the prey tugged at the dainty morsel. That moment of connection, then the hook did its work. Caught in their flesh, then reeling them in, bit by bit. But that took time. Building trust and confidence, then moving onto reliance, like a virgin drug user looking for the high of the first hit but ignorant to the fact that the first moment will never return.

It was the vain pursuit of a fantasy, becoming more bound with every attempt. The addictive nature of meat, their brains wired for pleasure. Some sought that pleasure at the expense of others, even acting with cruelty to other pieces of meat. Still, it served their purposes, even if meat was lost in the process. There was plenty more, they bred like mice. Vermin. He disliked them intensely, but without them they had no legal grounds for the occupation of that earth covered realm. It was a pathway with a purpose.

Stupid, vain pieces of meat.

Charles – so hungry for immortality, and to be re-united with his daughter, filial ties

Max – so desperate for power

Karthik – such a thirst for knowledge

All meat was driven by its impulses. Such strange things, those organic, fleshy minds. Amazing that they had ever been allowed to grow in the first place. So erratic, so simple.

He had been well satisfied with the blood of the original broodmare, the bitch; motherhood so overrated. Those human ties.

He had a problem with nationalism though. It had blinded some of the best protégés he had raised, those from the past. A limited perspective, so common, yet clannish. Territorialism had a limited potential.

Global identity was the way forward, and had been for as long as he had been active. For developing world citizens, ready to accept a universal plan. Thinking on a much bigger scale. More aligned with their purposes.

+++

'Indeed, it has begun,' they found themselves being in total agreement, repeating in unison the same phrase. Robotic in sound, a note of unity in the sound. Oneness.

+++

The Teacher stepped forward, drinking their adoration.

ACKNOWLEDGEMENTS

To Lana, you gave me space and time to write, letting me off many of the household chores that needed attention. You dreamed about this project before it started. Thank you.

To Danielle, thank you for your artistic input, research, and helpful comments.

To my team of dedicated listeners who read and encouraged me in the embryonic stages of my ideas – Lynne, Sam and Grace and Lydia.

To Jocelyn, for your proofreading of the early stage of the project. Thanks for your excitement about the story. To Richard and Lee, your eagle eyes spotted so many typos. Amanda, you are an exceptional proofreader. Thank you.

To Kiran – you are a real gift. You believed in the story from the very first section you read. You have encouraged me, supported me, inspired me, and restored my love of reading. Your input and advice has helped turn this into an exciting piece of writing. You are so talented.

To John. When I told you that I was going to write a book, you accepted it and believed in me. Such confidence made the many hours of work tolerable.

To Diego, who turned my vague thoughts into beautiful illustrations. You painstakingly amended and corrected those images with patience and tolerance. Thank you.

To Joyce, you have advised, listened, suggested, and continually gave me ideas for the characters and their lives. You have encouraged me and believed that one day it would be printed.

To the many early readers – Kate, June, Cormac, Steve, Leah, Scott, Craig, and the Elance editors. Your honest feedback was immensely helpful.

To Robert and Mary, you two are amazing. You were more excited about this book than I was. You gave me so much encouragement and spiritual inspiration; you were the first to invest in this project. Thank you.

To Tony, you are a book guru. You know more about books than anyone else I know. You love books and inspire others to join you in this love affair. Your advice, insight, and daily chats have kept this project going.

To Quinlan, thank you for making Karthik's letter come to life.

A special thank you to Elance for allowing me access to a number of talent freelancers who added extra dimensions to the project.

To those who can see … you saw this project before it existed – you are the true seers.

To KGF, you brought me back from the brink. Thank you for your love.

To those who interceded – Dalia, Robert, Mama, Jennifer, Chandran, Savithri, Lynne, Caleb, John, Aaron, Jane, Christina, Luellen, and Lydia.

To Gerard, we only talked about animating this story. You are missed.

COMING 2017
THE STORY CONTINUES

THE LIVING DOLLS TRILOGY

The Living Dolls – Morphology
by
Christopher Labinjo

WWW.THELIVINGDOLLSBOOKS.CO.UK

WWW.THELIVINGDOLLSBOOKS.COM

For more information on the Living Dolls Trilogy including other books in the series, interviews with the characters, information about the development of the story, the graphic novel version of the books and lots more.

I would love to hear from you, join our mailing list and keep up to date with events.

Join us on Facebook! Search 'The Living Dolls – Origin'